midnight sun

STEPHENIE MEYER

ATOM

First published in Great Britain in 2020 by Atom
This paperback edition published in 2021

1 3 5 7 9 10 8 6 4 2

All characters and events in this publication, other than those clearly in the public domain, are fictitious and any resemblance to real persons, living or dead, is purely coincidental.

Cupid and Psyche, 1788, by Antonio Canova (1757–1822), marble sculpture.
Paris, Louvre Museum © NPL - DeA Picture Library

A CIP catalogue record for this book
is available from the British Library.

ISBN: 978-0-349-00364-1

Typeset by M Rules
Printed and bound in Great Britain by
Clays Ltd, Elcograf S.p.A.

Papers used by Atom are from well-managed forests
and other responsible sources.

Atom
An imprint of
Little, Brown Book Group
Carmelite House
50 Victoria Embankment
London EC4Y 0DZ

An Hachette UK Company
www.hachette.co.uk

www.atombooks.co.uk

This book is dedicated to all the readers who have been such a happy part of my life for the last fifteen years. When we first met, many of you were young teenagers with bright, beautiful eyes full of dreams for the future. I hope that in the years that have passed, you've all found your dreams and that the reality of them was even better than you'd hoped.

CONTENTS

1. FIRST SIGHT

THIS WAS THE TIME OF DAY WHEN I MOST WISHED I WERE able to sleep.

High school.

Or was *purgatory* the right word? If there *were* any way to atone for my sins, this ought to count toward the tally in some measure. The tedium was not something I grew used to; every day seemed more impossibly monotonous than the last.

Perhaps this could even be considered my form of sleep—if sleep was defined as the inert state between active periods.

I stared at the cracks running through the plaster in the far corner of the cafeteria, imagining patterns into them that were not there. It was one way to tune out the voices that babbled like the gush of a river inside my head.

Several hundred of these voices I ignored out of boredom.

When it came to the human mind, I'd heard it all before and then some. Today, all thoughts were consumed with the trivial drama of a new addition to the small student body. It took so little to work them up. I'd seen the new face repeated in thought after thought from every angle. Just an ordinary human girl. The excitement over her arrival was tiresomely predictable—it was the same reaction as one would get from flashing a shiny object at a group of toddlers. Half the sheep-like males were already imagining themselves infatuated with her, just because she was something new to look at. I tried harder to tune them out.

Only four voices did I block out of courtesy rather than distaste: my family, my two brothers and two sisters, who were so used to the lack of privacy in my presence that they rarely worried about it. I gave them what I could. I tried not to listen if I could help it.

Try as I may, still . . . I knew.

Rosalie was thinking, as usual, about herself—her mind was a stagnant pool with few surprises. She'd caught sight of her profile in the reflection off someone's glasses, and she was mulling over her own perfection. No one else's hair was closer to true gold, no one else's shape was quite so perfectly an hourglass, no one else's face was such a flawless, symmetrical oval. She didn't compare herself to the humans here; that juxtaposition would have been laughable, absurd. She thought of others like us, none of them her equal.

Emmett's usually carefree expression was crumpled with frustration. Even now, he ran one enormous hand through his ebony curls, twisting the hair into his fist. Still fuming over the wrestling match he'd lost to Jasper during the night. It would take all his limited patience to make it to the end of the school day to orchestrate a rematch. Hearing Emmett's thoughts never felt intrusive, because he never thought one thing that he would not say aloud or put into action. Perhaps I only felt guilty reading the others' minds because I knew there were things inside that they wouldn't want me to know. If Rosalie's mind was a stagnant pool, then Emmett's was a lake with no shadows, glass clear.

And Jasper was . . . suffering. I suppressed a sigh.

Edward. Alice called my name in her head and had my attention at once.

It was just the same as having my name called aloud. I was glad my given name had fallen out of style in the last few decades—it had been annoying in the past; anytime anyone thought of any Edward, my head would turn automatically.

My head didn't turn now. Alice and I were good at these private conversations. It was rare that anyone caught us. I kept my eyes on the lines in the plaster.

How is he holding up? she asked me.

I frowned, just a small change in the set of my mouth. Nothing that would tip the others off. I could easily be frowning out of boredom.

Jasper had been still for too long. He wasn't performing human ticks the way we all must, constantly in motion so as not to stand out, like Emmett pulling at his hair, Rosalie crossing her legs first one way then the next, Alice tapping her toes against the linoleum, or me, moving my head to stare at different patterns in the wall. Jasper looked paralyzed, his lean form ramrod straight, even his honey hair seeming not to react to the air wafting from the vents.

Alice's mental tone was alarmed now, and I saw in her mind that she was watching Jasper in her peripheral vision. *Is there any danger?* She searched ahead into the immediate future, skimming through visions of monotony for the source behind my frown. Even as she did so, she remembered to tuck one tiny fist under her sharp chin and blink regularly. She brushed a tuft of her short, jagged black hair out of her eyes.

I turned my head slowly to the left, as if looking at the bricks of the wall, sighed, and then turned to the right, back to the cracks in the ceiling. The others would assume I was playing human. Only Alice knew I was shaking my head.

She relaxed. *Let me know if it gets too bad.*

I moved only my eyes, up to the ceiling above, and back down.

Thanks for doing this.

I was glad I couldn't answer her aloud. What would I say? *My pleasure?* It was hardly that. I didn't enjoy tuning in to Jasper's struggles. Was it really necessary to experiment this way? Wouldn't the safer path be to just admit that he might never be able to handle his thirst as well as the rest of us could, and not push his limits? Why flirt with disaster?

It had been two weeks since our last hunting trip. That was not an immensely difficult time span for the rest of us. A little uncomfortable occasionally—if a human walked too close, if the wind blew the wrong way. But humans rarely walked too close. Their instincts told them what their conscious minds would never understand: We were a danger that must be avoided.

Jasper was very dangerous right now.

It did not happen often, but every now and then I would be struck by the obliviousness of the humans around us. We were all so accustomed to it, we always expected it, but occasionally it seemed more glaring than usual. None of them noticed us here, lounging at the battered cafeteria table, though an ambush of tigers sprawled in our places would be less lethal than we were. All they saw were five odd-looking people, close enough to human to pass. It was hard to imagine surviving with senses so incredibly dull.

At that moment, a small girl paused at the end of the closest table to ours, stopping to talk to a friend. She tossed her short, sandy hair, combing her fingers through it. The heaters blew her scent in our direction. I was used to the way that scent made me feel—the dry ache in my throat, the hollow yearn in my stomach, the automatic tightening of my muscles, the excess flow of venom in my mouth.

This was all quite normal, usually easy to ignore. It was harder just now, with the reactions stronger, doubled, as I monitored Jasper.

Jasper was letting his imagination get away from him. He was picturing it—picturing himself getting up from his seat next to Alice and going to stand beside the little girl. Thinking of leaning down and in, as if he were going to whisper in her ear, and letting his lips touch the arch of her throat. Imagining how the hot flow of her pulse beneath the weak barrier of her skin would feel under his mouth...

I kicked his chair.

He met my gaze, his black eyes resentful for a second, and then looked down. I could hear shame and rebellion war in his head.

"Sorry," Jasper muttered.

I shrugged.

"You weren't going to do anything," Alice murmured to him, soothing his mortification. "I could see that."

I fought back the frown that would give her lie away. We had to stick together, Alice and I. It wasn't easy, being the freaks among those who were already freaks. We protected each other's secrets.

"It helps a little if you think of them as people," Alice suggested, her high, musical voice racing too fast for human ears to understand, if any had been close enough to hear. "Her name is Whitney. She has a baby sister she adores. Her mother invited Esme to that garden party, do you remember?"

"I know who she is," Jasper said curtly. He turned away to stare out one of the small windows that were spaced just under the eaves around the long room. His tone ended the conversation.

He would have to hunt tonight. It was ridiculous to take risks like this, trying to test his strength, to build his endurance. Jasper should just accept his limitations and work within them.

Alice sighed silently and stood, taking her tray of food—her prop, as it were—with her and leaving him alone. She knew when he'd had enough of her encouragement. Though Rosalie and Emmett were more flagrant about their relationship, it was Alice and Jasper who knew each other's every need as well as their own. As if they could read minds, too—but only each other's.

Edward.

Reflex reaction. I turned to the sound of my name being called, though it wasn't being called, just thought.

My eyes locked for half a second with a pair of large, chocolate-brown human eyes set in a pale, heart-shaped face. I knew the face, though I'd never seen it myself before this moment. It had been foremost in every human head today. The new student, Isabella Swan. Daughter of the town's chief of police, brought to live here by some new custody situation. Bella. She'd corrected everyone who'd used her full name.

I looked away, bored. It took me a second to realize that she had not been the one to think my name.

Of course she's already crushing on the Cullens, I heard the first thought continue.

Now I recognized the "voice."

Jessica Stanley—it had been a while since she'd bothered me with her internal chatter. What a relief it had been when she'd gotten over her misplaced fixation. It used to be nearly impossible to escape her constant, ridiculous daydreams. I'd wished, at the time, that I could explain to her *exactly* what would have happened if my lips, and the teeth behind them, had gotten anywhere near her. That would have silenced those annoying fantasies. The thought of her reaction almost made me smile.

Fat lot of good it will do her, Jessica went on. *She's really not even pretty. I don't know why Eric is staring so much…or Mike.*

She flinched mentally on the latter name. Her new obsession, the generically popular Mike Newton, was completely oblivious to her. Apparently, he was not as oblivious to the new girl. Another child reaching for the shiny object. This put a mean edge to Jessica's thoughts, though she was outwardly cordial to the newcomer as she explained to her the commonly held knowledge about my family. The new student must have asked about us.

Everyone's looking at me today, too, Jessica thought smugly. *Isn't it lucky Bella has two classes with me? I'll bet Mike will want to ask me what she's—*

I tried to block the inane chatter out of my head before the petty and the trivial could drive me mad.

"Jessica Stanley is giving the new Swan girl all the dirty laundry on the Cullen clan," I murmured to Emmett as a distraction.

He chuckled under his breath. *I hope she's making it good*, he thought.

"Rather unimaginative, actually. Just the barest hint of scandal. Not an ounce of horror. I'm a little disappointed."

And the new girl? Is she disappointed in the gossip as well?

I listened to hear what this new girl, Bella, thought of Jessica's story. What did she see when she looked at the strange, chalky-skinned family that was universally avoided?

It was my responsibility to know her reaction. I acted as a lookout, for lack of a better word, for my family. To protect us. If anyone ever grew suspicious, I could give us early warning and an easy retreat. It happened occasionally—some human with an active imagination would see in us the characters of a book or a movie. Usually they got it wrong, but it was better to move on somewhere new than to risk scrutiny. Rarely, extremely rarely, someone would guess right. We didn't give them a chance to test their hypothesis. We simply disappeared, to become no more than a frightening memory.

That hadn't happened for decades.

I heard nothing, though I listened close beside where Jessica's frivolous internal monologue continued to gush. It was as if there were no one sitting beside her. How peculiar. Had the girl moved? That didn't seem likely, as Jessica was still babbling at her. I looked up, feeling off-balance. Checking on my extra "hearing"—it wasn't something I ever had to do.

Again, my gaze locked onto those wide brown eyes. She was sitting right where she had been before and looking at us—a natural thing to be doing, I supposed, as Jessica was still regaling her with the local gossip about the Cullens.

Thinking about us, too, would be natural.

But I couldn't hear a whisper.

Warm, inviting red stained her cheeks as she looked down, away from the embarrassing gaffe of getting caught staring at a stranger. It was good that Jasper was still gazing out the window. I didn't like to imagine what that easy pooling of blood would do to his control.

The emotions had been as clear on her face as if they were

spelled out in words: surprise, as she unknowingly absorbed the signs of the subtle differences between her kind and mine; curiosity, as she listened to Jessica's tale; and something more... Fascination? It wouldn't be the first time. We were beautiful to them, our intended prey. Then, finally, the embarrassment.

And yet, though her thoughts had been so clear in her odd eyes—odd because of the depth to them—I could hear only silence from the place she was sitting. Just... silence.

I felt a moment of unease.

This was nothing I'd ever encountered. Was there something wrong with me? I felt exactly the same as I always did. Worried, I listened harder.

All the voices I'd been blocking were suddenly shouting in my head.

...wonder what music she likes...maybe I could mention my new CD..., Mike Newton was thinking, two tables away—focused on Bella Swan.

Look at him staring at her. Isn't it enough that he has half the girls in school waiting for him to... Eric Yorkie's thoughts were caustic, and also revolving around the girl.

...so disgusting. You'd think she was famous or something.... Even Edward Cullen *staring....* Lauren Mallory was so jealous that her face, by all rights, should be dark jade in color. *And Jessica, flaunting her new best friend. What a joke...* Vitriol continued to spew from the girl's thoughts.

...I bet everyone has asked her that. But I'd like to talk to her. What's something more original? Ashley Dowling mused.

...maybe she'll be in my Spanish..., June Richardson hoped.

...tons left to do tonight! Trig, and the English test. I hope my mom... Angela Weber, a quiet girl whose thoughts were unusually kind, was the only one at the table who wasn't obsessed with this Bella.

I could hear them all, hear every insignificant thing they were thinking as it passed through their minds. But nothing at all from the new student with the deceptively communicative eyes.

And of course, I could hear what the girl said when she spoke to Jessica. I didn't have to read minds to be able to hear her low, clear voice on the far side of the long room.

"Which one is the boy with the reddish-brown hair?" I heard her ask, sneaking another look at me from the corner of her eye, only to glance quickly away when she saw that I was still staring.

If I'd had time to hope that hearing the sound of her voice would help me pinpoint the tone of her thoughts, I was instantly disappointed. Usually, people's thoughts came to them in a similar pitch to their physical voices. But this quiet, shy voice was unfamiliar, not one of the hundreds of thoughts bouncing around the room, I was sure of that. Entirely new.

Oh, good luck, idiot! Jessica thought before answering the girl's question. "That's Edward. He's gorgeous, of course, but don't waste your time. He doesn't date. Apparently none of the girls here are good-looking enough for him." She snorted quietly.

I turned my head away to hide my smile. Jessica and her classmates had no idea how lucky they were that none of them particularly appealed to me.

Beneath the transient humor, I felt a strange impulse, one I did not clearly understand. It had something to do with the vicious edge to Jessica's thoughts that the new girl was unaware of.... I felt the strangest urge to step in between them, to shield Bella Swan from the darker workings of Jessica's mind. What an odd thing to feel. Trying to ferret out the motivations behind the impulse, I examined the new girl one more time, through Jessica's eyes now. My staring had attracted too much attention.

Perhaps it was just some long-buried protective instinct—the strong for the weak. Somehow, this girl looked more fragile than her new classmates. Her skin was so translucent it was hard to believe it offered her much defense from the outside world. I could see the rhythmic pulse of blood through her veins under the clear, pale membrane.... But I should not concentrate on that. I was good at this life I'd chosen, but I was just as thirsty as Jasper and there was no point in inviting temptation.

There was a faint crease between her eyebrows that she seemed unaware of.

It was unbelievably frustrating! I could easily see that it was a strain for her to sit there, to make conversation with strangers, to be the center of attention. I could sense her shyness from the way she held her frail-looking shoulders, slightly hunched, as if she was expecting a rebuff at any moment. And yet I could only see, could only sense, could only imagine. There was nothing but silence from the very unexceptional human girl. I could hear nothing. Why?

"Shall we?" Rosalie murmured, interrupting my focus.

I turned my mind away from the girl with a sense of relief. I didn't want to continue to fail at this—failure was a rare thing for me, and even more irritating than it was uncommon. I didn't want to develop any interest in her hidden thoughts simply because they were hidden. No doubt when I did decipher them—and I *would* find a way to do so—they would be just as petty and trivial as any human's. Not worth the effort I would expend to reach them.

"So, is the new one afraid of us yet?" Emmett asked, still waiting for my response to his earlier question.

I shrugged. He wasn't interested enough to press for more information.

We got up from the table and walked out of the cafeteria.

Emmett, Rosalie, and Jasper were pretending to be seniors; they left for their classes. I was playing a younger role than they. I headed off for my junior-level Biology lesson, preparing my mind for the tedium. It was doubtful Mr. Banner, a man of no more than average intellect, would manage to pull out anything in his lecture that would surprise someone holding two medical degrees.

In the classroom, I settled into my chair and let my books—props, again; they held nothing I didn't already know—spill across the table. I was the only student who had a table to himself. The humans weren't smart enough to *know* that they feared me, but their innate survival instincts were enough to keep them away.

The room slowly filled as they trickled in from lunch. I leaned back in my chair and waited for the time to pass. Again, I wished I were able to sleep.

Because I'd been thinking about the new girl, when Angela Weber escorted her through the door, her name intruded on my attention.

Bella seems just as shy as me. I'll bet today is really hard for her. I wish I could say something…but it would probably just sound stupid.

Yes! Mike Newton thought, turning in his seat to watch the girls enter.

Still, from the place where Bella Swan stood, nothing. The empty space where her thoughts should be vexed and unnerved me.

What if it *all* went away? What if this was just the first symptom of some kind of mental decline?

I'd often wished that I could escape the cacophony. That I could be normal—as far as that was possible for me. But now I felt panicked at the thought. Who would I be without what I could do? I'd never heard of such a thing. I would see if Carlisle had.

The girl walked down the aisle beside me, headed to the teacher's desk. Poor girl; the seat next to me was the only one available. Automatically, I cleared what would be her side of the table, shoving my books into a pile. I doubted she would feel very comfortable there. She was in for a long semester—in this class, at least. Perhaps, though, sitting beside her, I'd be able to flush out her thoughts' hiding place…not that I'd ever needed close proximity before. Not that I would find anything worth listening to.

Bella Swan walked into the flow of heated air that blew toward me from the vent.

Her scent hit me like a battering ram, like an exploding grenade. There was no image violent enough to encompass the force of what happened to me in that moment.

Instantly, I was transformed. I was nothing close to the human I'd once been. No trace of the shreds of humanity I'd managed to cloak myself in over the years remained.

I was a predator. She was my prey. There was nothing else in the whole world but that truth.

There was no room full of witnesses—they were already collateral damage in my mind. The mystery of her thoughts was forgotten. Her thoughts meant nothing, for she would not go on thinking them much longer.

I was a vampire, and she had the sweetest blood I'd smelled in more than eighty years.

I hadn't imagined that such a scent could exist. If I'd known it did, I would have gone searching for it long ago. I would have scoured the planet for her. I could imagine the taste....

Thirst burned through my throat like fire. My mouth felt baked and desiccated, and the fresh flow of venom did nothing to dispel that sensation. My stomach twisted with the hunger that was an echo of the thirst. My muscles coiled to spring.

Not a full second had passed. She was still taking the same step that had put her downwind from me.

As her foot touched the ground, her eyes slid toward me, a movement she clearly meant to be stealthy. Her gaze met mine, and I saw myself reflected in the mirror of her eyes.

The shock of the face I saw there saved her life for a few thorny moments.

She didn't make it easier. When she processed the expression on my face, blood flooded her cheeks again, turning her skin the most delicious color I'd ever seen. The scent was a thick haze in my brain. I could barely think through it. My instincts raged, resisting control, incoherent.

She walked more quickly now, as if she understood the need to escape. Her haste made her clumsy—she tripped and stumbled forward, almost falling into the girl seated in front of me. Vulnerable, weak. Even more than usual for a human.

I tried to focus on the face I'd seen in her eyes, a face I

recognized with revulsion. The face of the monster inside me—the face I'd beaten back with decades of effort and uncompromising discipline. How easily it sprang to the surface now!

The scent swirled around me again, scattering my thoughts and nearly propelling me out of my seat.

No.

My hand gripped under the edge of the table as I tried to hold myself in my chair. The wood was not up to the task. My hand crushed through the strut and came away with a palmful of splintered pulp, leaving the shape of my fingers carved into the remaining wood.

Destroy evidence. That was a fundamental rule. I quickly pulverized the edges of the shape with my fingertips, leaving nothing but a ragged hole and a pile of shavings on the floor, which I scattered with my foot.

Destroy evidence. Collateral damage…

I knew what had to happen now. The girl would have to come sit beside me, and I would have to kill her.

The innocent bystanders in this classroom, eighteen other children and one man, could not be allowed to leave, having seen what they would soon see.

I flinched at the thought of what I must do. Even at my very worst, I had never committed this kind of atrocity. I had never killed innocents. And now I planned to slaughter twenty of them at once.

The face of the monster in my reflection mocked me.

Even as part of me shuddered away from him, another part was planning what would happen next.

If I killed the girl first, I would have only fifteen or twenty seconds with her before the humans in the room reacted. Maybe a little longer if at first they did not realize what I was doing. She would not have time to scream or feel pain; I would not kill her cruelly. That much I could give this stranger with her horribly desirable blood.

But then I would have to stop them from escaping. I wouldn't have to worry about the windows, too high up and small to provide an escape for anyone. Just the door—block that and they were trapped.

It would be slower and more difficult, trying to take them all down when they were panicked and scrambling, moving in chaos. Not impossible, but there would be much more noise. Time for lots of screaming. Someone would hear…and I'd be forced to kill even more innocents in this black hour.

And her blood would cool while I murdered the others.

The scent punished me, closing my throat with dry aching.…

So the witnesses first, then.

I mapped it out in my head. I was in the middle of the room, the row farthest from the front. I would take my right side first. I could snap four or five of their necks per second, I estimated. It would not be noisy. The right side would be the lucky side; they would not see me coming. Moving around the front and back down the left side, it would take me, at most, five seconds to end every life in this room.

Long enough for Bella Swan to see, briefly, what was coming for her. Long enough for her to feel fear. Long enough, maybe, if shock didn't freeze her in place, for her to work up a scream. One soft scream that would not bring anyone running.

I took a deep breath, and the scent was a fire that raced through my dry veins, burning out from my chest to consume every better impulse that I was capable of.

She was just turning now. In a few seconds, she would sit down inches away from me.

The monster in my head exulted.

Someone slammed shut a folder on my left. I didn't look up to see which of the doomed humans it was, but the motion sent a wave of ordinary, unscented air wafting across my face.

For one short second, I was able to think clearly. In that precious instant, I saw two faces in my head, side by side.

One was mine, or rather had been: the red-eyed monster that had killed so many people that I'd stopped counting.

Rationalized, justified murders. I had been a killer of killers, a killer of other, less powerful monsters. It was a god complex, I acknowledged that—deciding who deserved a death sentence. It was a compromise with myself. I had fed on human blood, but only by the loosest definition. My victims were, in their various dark pastimes, barely more human than I was.

The other face was Carlisle's.

There was no resemblance between the two faces. They were bright day and blackest night.

There was no reason for a resemblance to exist. Carlisle was not my father in the basic biological sense. We shared no common features. The similarity in our coloring was a product of what we were; every vampire was corpse-pale. The similarity in the color of our eyes was another matter—a reflection of a mutual choice.

And yet, though there was no basis for a resemblance, I'd imagined that my face had begun to reflect his, to an extent, in the last seventy-odd years that I had embraced his choice and followed in his steps. My features had not changed, but it seemed to me as though some of his wisdom had marked my expression, a little of his compassion could be traced in the set of my mouth, and hints of his patience were evident on my brow.

All those tiny improvements were lost in the monster's face. In a few moments, there would be nothing left in me that would reflect the years I'd spent with my creator, my mentor, my father in all the ways that counted. My eyes would glow red as a devil's; all likeness would be lost forever.

In my head, Carlisle's kind eyes did not judge me. I knew that he would forgive me for this horrible act. Because he loved me. Because he thought I was better than I was.

Bella Swan sat down in the chair next to me, her movements stiff and awkward—no doubt with fear—and the scent of her blood bloomed in an inescapable cloud around me.

I would prove my father wrong about me. The misery of this fact hurt almost as much as the fire in my throat.

I leaned away from her in revulsion—disgusted by the monster aching to take her.

Why did she have to come here? Why did she have to *exist*? Why did she have to ruin the little peace I had in this nonlife of mine? Why had this aggravating human ever been born? She would ruin me.

I turned my face away from her as a sudden fierce, irrational hatred washed through me.

I didn't want to be the monster! I didn't want to kill this roomful of harmless children! I didn't want to lose everything I'd gained in a lifetime of sacrifice and denial!

I wouldn't.

She couldn't make me.

The scent was the problem, the hideously appealing scent of her blood. If there was only some way to resist... if only another gust of fresh air could clear my head.

Bella Swan shook out her long, thick mahogany hair in my direction.

Was she insane?

No, there was no helpful breeze. But I didn't *have* to breathe.

I stopped the flow of air through my lungs. The relief was instantaneous, but incomplete. I still had the memory of the scent in my head, the taste of it on the back of my tongue. I wouldn't be able to resist even that for long.

Every life in this room was in danger while she and I were in it together. I should run. I *wanted* to run, to get away from the *heat* of her next to me, and the punishing pain of the burning, but I wasn't one hundred percent sure that if I unlocked my muscles to move, even just to stand, I wouldn't lash out and commit the slaughter I'd already planned.

But perhaps I could resist for an hour. Would one hour be enough time to gain control to move without striking? I doubted, then forced myself to commit. I would *make* it enough. Just enough time to get out of this room full of victims, victims that perhaps didn't have to *be* victims. If I could resist for one short hour.

It was an uncomfortable feeling, not breathing. My body did not need oxygen, but it went against my instincts. I relied on scent more than my other senses in times of stress. It led the way in the hunt; it was the first warning in case of danger. I did not often come across something as dangerous as I was, but self-preservation was just as strong in my kind as it was in the average human.

Uncomfortable, but manageable. More bearable than smelling *her* and not sinking my teeth through that fine, thin, see-through skin to the hot, wet, pulsing—

An hour! Just one hour. I must not think of the scent, the taste.

The silent girl kept her hair between us, leaning forward so that it spilled across her folder. I couldn't see her face to try to read the emotions in her clear, deep eyes. Was she trying to hide those eyes from me? Out of fear? Shyness? To keep her secrets?

My former irritation at being stymied by her soundless thoughts was weak and pale in comparison to the need—and the hate—that possessed me now. For I hated this frail girl beside me, hated her with all the fervor with which I clung to my former self, my love of my family, my dreams of being something better than what I was. Hating her, hating how she made me feel—it helped a little. Yes, the irritation I'd felt before was weak, but it, too, helped a little. I clung to any thought that distracted me from imagining what she would *taste* like....

Hate and irritation. Impatience. Would the hour never pass?

And when the hour ended...she would walk out of this room. And I would do what?

If I could control the monster, make him see that the delay would be worth it...I could introduce myself. *Hello, my name is Edward Cullen. May I walk you to your next class?*

She would say yes. It would be the polite thing to do. Even already fearing me, as I was sure she did, she would follow convention and walk beside me. It should be easy enough to lead her in the wrong direction. A spur of the forest reached out like a finger to touch the back corner of the parking lot. I could tell her I'd forgotten a book in my car....

Would anyone notice that I was the last person she'd been seen with? It was raining, as usual. Two dark raincoats heading in the wrong direction wouldn't pique too much interest or give me away.

Except that I was not the only student who was aware of her today—though no one was as blisteringly aware as I. Mike Newton, in particular, was conscious of every shift in her weight as she fidgeted in her chair—she was uncomfortable so close to me, just as anyone would be, just as I'd expected before her scent had destroyed all charitable concern. Mike Newton would notice if she left the classroom with me.

If I could last an hour, could I last two?

I flinched at the pain of the burning.

She would go home to an empty house. Police Chief Swan worked an eight-hour day. I knew his house, as I knew every house in the tiny town. His home was nestled right up against thick woods, with no close neighbors. Even had she time to scream, which she would not, there would be no one to hear.

That would be the responsible way to deal with this. I'd gone more than seven decades without human blood. If I held my breath, I could last two hours. And when I had her alone, there would be no chance of anyone else getting hurt. *And no reason to rush through the experience*, the monster in my head agreed.

It was sophistry to think that by saving the nineteen humans in this room with effort and patience, I would be less of a monster when I killed this innocent girl.

Though I hated her, I was absolutely aware that my hatred was unjust. I knew that what I really hated was myself. And I would hate us both so much more when she was dead.

I made it through the hour in this way—imagining the best ways to kill her. I tried to avoid imagining the actual *act*. That might be too much for me. So I planned strategy and nothing more.

Once, toward the very end, she peeked up at me through the fluid wall of her hair. I could feel the unjustified hatred burning out of me as I met her gaze—see the reflection of it in her frightened eyes. Blood painted her cheek before she could hide in her hair again, and I was nearly undone.

But the bell rang. And we—how cliché—were saved. She, from death. I, for just a short time, from being the nightmarish creature I feared and loathed.

Now I had to move.

Even focusing all my attention on the simplest of actions, I couldn't walk as slowly as I should; I darted from the room. If anyone had been looking, they might have suspected that there was something not right about my exit. No one was paying attention to me; all thoughts still swirled around the girl who was condemned to die in little more than an hour's time.

I hid in my car.

I didn't like to think of myself as having to hide. How cowardly that sounded. But I didn't have enough discipline left to be around humans now. Focusing so much of my efforts on not killing *one* of them left me no resources to resist the others. What a waste that would be. If I were to give in to the monster, I might as well make it worth the defeat.

I played a CD that usually calmed me, but it did little for me now. No, what helped most was the cool, wet air that drifted with the light rain through my open windows. Though I could remember the scent of Bella Swan's blood with perfect clarity, inhaling this clean air was like washing out the inside of my body from its infection.

I was sane again. I could think again. And I could fight again. I could fight what I didn't want to be.

I didn't have to go to her home. I didn't have to kill her. Obviously, I was a rational, thinking creature, and I had a choice. There was always a choice.

It hadn't felt that way in the classroom... but I was away from her now.

I didn't *have* to disappoint my father. I didn't have to cause my mother stress, worry...pain. Yes, it would hurt my adopted mother, too. And she was so gentle, so tender and loving. Causing someone like Esme pain was truly inexcusable.

Perhaps, if I avoided this girl very, very carefully, there was no need for my life to change. I had things ordered the way I liked them. Why should I let some aggravating and delicious nobody ruin that?

How ironic that I'd wanted to protect this human girl from the paltry, toothless threat of Jessica Stanley's snide thoughts. I was the last person who would ever stand as a protector for Isabella Swan. She would never need protection from anything more than she needed it from me.

Where was Alice? I suddenly wondered. Hadn't she seen me killing the Swan girl in a multitude of ways? Why hadn't she come to my aid—to stop me or help me clean up the evidence, whichever? Was she so absorbed with watching for trouble with Jasper that she'd missed this much more horrific possibility? Or was I stronger than I thought? Would I really not have done anything to the girl?

No. I knew that wasn't true. Alice must be concentrating very hard on Jasper.

I searched in the direction I knew my sister would be, in the small building used for English classes. It did not take me long to locate her familiar "voice." And I was right. Her every thought was turned to Jasper, watching his small choices with minute scrutiny.

I wished I could ask her advice, but at the same time, I was glad she didn't know what I was capable of. I felt a new burn through my body—the burn of shame. I didn't want any of them to know.

If I could avoid Bella Swan, if I could manage not to kill her—even as I thought that, the monster writhed and gnashed his teeth in frustration—then no one would have to know. If I could keep away from her scent...

There was no reason I shouldn't try, at least. Make a good choice. Try to be what Carlisle thought I was.

The last hour of school was almost over. I decided to put my new plan into action at once. Better than sitting here in the parking lot, where she might pass me and ruin my attempt. Again, I felt the unjust hatred for the girl.

I walked swiftly—a little too swiftly, but there were no witnesses—across the tiny campus to the office.

It was empty except for the receptionist, who didn't notice my silent entrance.

"Ms. Cope?"

The woman with the unnaturally red hair looked up and startled. It always caught them off guard, the little markers they didn't understand, no matter how many times they'd seen one of us before.

"Oh," she gasped, a little flustered. She smoothed her shirt. *Silly*, she thought to herself. *He's almost young enough to be my son.* "Hello, Edward. What can I do for you?" Her eyelashes fluttered behind her thick glasses.

Uncomfortable. But I knew how to be charming when I wanted to be. It was easy, since I was able to know instantly how any tone or gesture was taken.

I leaned forward, meeting her gaze as if I were staring deep into her flat brown eyes. Her thoughts were already in a flutter. This should be simple.

"I was wondering if you could help me with my schedule," I said in the soft voice I reserved for not scaring humans.

I heard the tempo of her heart increase.

"Of course, Edward. How can I help?" *Too young, too young*, she chanted to herself. Wrong, of course. I was older than her grandfather.

"I was wondering if I could move from my Biology class to a senior-level science. Physics, perhaps?"

"Is there a problem with Mr. Banner, Edward?"

"Not at all, it's just that I've already studied this material. . . ."

"In that accelerated school you all went to in Alaska. Right." Her thin lips pursed as she considered this. *They should all be in college. I've heard the teachers complain. Perfect 4.0s, never a hesitation with a response, never a wrong answer on a test—like they've found some way to cheat in every subject. Mr. Varner would rather believe that anyone was cheating in Trig than think a student was smarter than him. I'll bet their mother tutors them....* "Actually, Edward, Physics is pretty much full right now. Mr. Banner hates to have more than twenty-five students in a class—"

"I wouldn't be any trouble."

Of course not. Not a perfect Cullen. "I know that, Edward. But there just aren't enough seats as it is...."

"Could I drop the class, then? I could use the period for independent study."

"Drop Biology?" Her mouth fell open. *That's crazy. How hard is it to sit through a subject you already know? There* must *be a problem with Mr. Banner.* "You won't have enough credits to graduate."

"I'll catch up next year."

"Maybe you should talk to your parents about that."

The door opened behind me, but whoever it was did not think of me, so I ignored the arrival and concentrated on Ms. Cope. I leaned slightly closer and stared as if I was gazing more deeply into her eyes. This would work better if they were gold today instead of black. The blackness frightened people, as it should.

My miscalculation affected the woman. She flinched back, confused by her conflicting instincts.

"Please, Ms. Cope?" I murmured, my voice as smooth and compelling as it could be, and her momentary aversion eased. "Isn't there some other section I could switch to? I'm sure there has to be an open slot somewhere? Sixth-hour Biology can't be the only option...."

I smiled at her, careful not to flash my teeth so widely that it would scare her again, letting the expression soften my face.

Her heart drummed faster. *Too young*, she reminded herself frantically. "Well, maybe I could talk to Bob—I mean Mr. Banner. I could see if—"

A second was all it took to change everything: the atmosphere in the room, my mission here, the reason I leaned toward the red-haired woman. . . . What had been for one purpose was now for another.

A second was all it took for Samantha Wells to enter the room, place a signed tardy slip in the basket by the door, and hurry out again, in a rush to be away from school. A sudden gust of wind through the open door crashed into me, and I realized why that first person through the door had not interrupted me with her thoughts.

I turned, though I did not need to make sure.

Bella Swan stood with her back pressed to the wall beside the door, a piece of paper clutched in her hands. Her eyes were even larger than before as she took in my ferocious, inhuman glare.

The smell of her blood saturated every particle of air in the tiny, hot room. My throat burst into flames.

The monster glared back at me from the mirror of her eyes again, a mask of evil.

My hand hesitated in the air above the counter. I would not have to look back in order to reach across it and slam Ms. Cope's head into her desk with enough force to kill her. Two lives rather than twenty. A trade.

The monster waited anxiously, hungrily, for me to do it.

But there was always a choice—there *had* to be.

I cut off the motion of my lungs and fixed Carlisle's face in front of my eyes. I turned back to face Ms. Cope and heard her internal surprise at the change in my expression. She shrank away from me, but her fear did not form into coherent words.

Using all the control I'd mastered in my decades of self-denial, I made my voice even and smooth. There was just enough air left in my lungs to speak once more, rushing through the words.

"Never mind, then. I can see that it's impossible. Thank you so much for your help."

I spun and launched myself from the room, trying not to feel the warm-blooded heat of the girl's body as I passed within inches of it.

I didn't stop until I was in my car, moving too fast the entire way there. Most of the humans had cleared out already, so there weren't a lot of witnesses. I heard a sophomore, D. J. Garrett, notice and then disregard....

Where did Cullen come from? It was like he just came out of thin air.... There I go, with the imagination again. Mom always says...

When I slid into my Volvo, the others were already there. I tried to control my breathing, but I was gasping at the fresh air as if I'd been suffocated.

"Edward?" Alice asked, alarm in her voice.

I just shook my head at her.

"What the hell happened to you?" Emmett demanded, distracted for the moment from the fact that Jasper was not in the mood for his rematch.

Instead of answering, I threw the car into reverse. I had to get out of this lot before Bella Swan could follow me here, too. My own personal demon, tormenting me...I swung the car around and accelerated. I hit forty before I was out of the parking lot. On the road, I hit seventy before I made the corner.

Without looking, I knew that Emmett, Rosalie, and Jasper had all turned to stare at Alice. She shrugged. She couldn't see what had passed, only what was coming.

She looked ahead for me now. We both processed what she saw in her head, and we were both surprised.

"You're leaving?" she whispered.

The others stared at me now.

"Am I?" I snarled through my teeth.

She saw it then, as my resolve wavered and another choice spun my future in a darker direction.

"Oh."

Bella Swan, dead. My eyes, glowing crimson with fresh blood.

The search that would follow. The careful time we would wait before it was safe for us to pull out of Forks and start again…

"Oh," she said again. The picture grew more specific. I saw the inside of Chief Swan's house for the first time, saw Bella in a small kitchen with yellow cupboards, her back to me as I stalked her from the shadows, let the scent pull me toward her….

"Stop!" I groaned, not able to bear more.

"Sorry," she whispered.

The monster rejoiced.

And the vision in her head shifted again. An empty highway at night, the trees beside it coated in snow, flashing by at almost two hundred miles per hour.

"I'll miss you," she said. "No matter how short a time you're gone."

Emmett and Rosalie exchanged an apprehensive glance.

We were almost to the turnoff onto the long drive that led to our home.

"Drop us here," Alice instructed. "You should tell Carlisle yourself."

I nodded, and the car squealed to a sudden stop.

Emmett, Rosalie, and Jasper got out in silence; they would make Alice explain when I was gone. Alice touched my shoulder.

"You will do the right thing," she murmured. Not a vision this time—an order. "She's Charlie Swan's only family. It would kill him, too."

"Yes," I said, agreeing only with the last part.

She slid out to join the others, her eyebrows pulling together in anxiety. They melted into the woods, out of sight before I could turn the car around.

I knew the visions in Alice's head would be flashing from dark to bright like a strobe light as I sped back to Forks doing ninety. I wasn't sure where I was going. To say goodbye to my father? Or to embrace the monster inside me? The road flew away beneath my tires.

2. OPEN BOOK

I LEANED BACK AGAINST THE SOFT SNOWBANK, LETTING the dry powder reshape itself around my weight. My skin had cooled to match the air around me, and the tiny pieces of ice felt like velvet under my skin.

The sky above me was clear, brilliant with stars, glowing blue in some places, yellow in others. The stars created majestic, swirling shapes against the black backdrop of the empty universe—an awesome sight. Exquisitely beautiful. Or rather, it should have been exquisite. Would have been, if I'd been able to really see it.

It wasn't getting any better. Six days had passed, six days I'd hidden here in the empty Denali wilderness, but I was no closer to freedom than I had been since the first moment I'd caught her scent.

When I stared up at the jeweled sky, it was as if there were an obstruction between my eyes and its beauty. The obstruction was a face, just an unremarkable human face, but I couldn't quite seem to banish it from my mind.

I heard the approaching thoughts before I heard the footsteps that accompanied them. The sound of movement was only a faint whisper against the powder.

I was not surprised that Tanya had followed me here. I knew she'd been mulling over this coming conversation for the last few days, putting it off until she was sure of exactly what she wanted to say.

She sprang into sight about sixty yards away, leaping onto the tip of an outcropping of black rock and balancing there on the balls of her bare feet.

Tanya's skin was silver in the starlight, and her long blond curls shone pale, almost pink with their strawberry tint. Her amber eyes glinted as she spied me, half-buried in the snow, and her full lips stretched slowly into a smile.

Exquisite. *If* I'd really been able to see her. I sighed.

She hadn't dressed for human eyes; she wore only a thin cotton camisole and a pair of shorts. Crouching down on a promontory of stone, she touched the rock with her fingertips, and her body coiled.

Cannonball, she thought.

She launched herself into the air. Her shape became a dark, twisting shadow as she spun gracefully between the stars and me. She curled herself into a ball just as she struck the piled snowbank beside me.

A blizzard of snow flew up around me. The stars went black and I was buried deep in the feathery ice crystals.

I sighed again, breathing in the ice, but didn't move to unearth myself. The blackness under the snow neither hurt nor improved the view. I still saw the same face.

"Edward?"

Then snow was flying again as Tanya swiftly disinterred me. She brushed the powder from my skin, not quite meeting my gaze.

"Sorry," she murmured. "It was a joke."

"I know. It was funny."

Her mouth twisted down.

"Irina and Kate said I should leave you alone. They think I'm annoying you."

"Not at all," I assured her. "On the contrary, I'm the one who's being rude—abominably rude. I'm very sorry."

You're going home, aren't you? she thought.

"I haven't...entirely...decided that yet."

But you're not staying here. Her thought was wistful now.

"No. It doesn't seem to be...helping."

Her lips pushed out into a pout. "That's my fault, isn't it?"

"Of course not." She hadn't made anything easier, for certain, but the face that haunted me was the only true impediment.

Don't be a gentleman.

I smiled.

I make you uncomfortable, she accused.

"No."

She raised one eyebrow, her expression so disbelieving that I had to laugh. One short laugh, followed by another sigh.

"All right," I admitted. "A little bit."

She sighed, too, and put her chin in her hands.

"You're a thousand times lovelier than the stars, Tanya. Of course, you're already well aware of that. Don't let my stubbornness undermine your confidence." I chuckled at the unlikeliness of *that*.

"I'm not used to rejection," she grumbled, her lower lip pushing out into an attractive pout.

"Certainly not," I agreed, trying with little success to block out her thoughts as she fleetingly sifted through memories of her thousands of successful conquests. Mostly, Tanya preferred human men—they were much more populous for one thing, with the added advantage of being soft and warm. And always eager, definitely.

"Succubus," I teased, hoping to interrupt the images flickering in her head.

She grinned, flashing her teeth. "The original."

Unlike Carlisle, Tanya and her sisters had discovered their consciences slowly. In the end, it was their fondness for human men that turned them against the slaughter. Now the men they loved...lived.

"When you showed up here," Tanya said slowly, "I thought that..."

I'd known what she'd thought. And I should have guessed that she would feel that way. But I'd not been at my best for analytical thinking in that moment.

"You thought that I'd changed my mind."

"Yes." She scowled.

"I feel horrible for toying with your expectations, Tanya. I didn't mean to—I wasn't thinking. It's just that I left in...quite a hurry."

"I don't suppose you'd tell me why?"

I sat up and folded my arms across my chest, my shoulders rigid. "I'd prefer not to talk about it. Please forgive my reserve."

She was quiet again, still speculating. I ignored her, trying in vain to appreciate the stars.

She gave up after a silent moment, and her thoughts pursued a new direction.

Where will you go, Edward, if you leave? Back to Carlisle?

"I don't think so," I whispered.

Where would I go? I could not think of one place on the entire planet that held any interest for me. There was nothing I wanted to see or do. Because no matter where I went, I would not be going *to* anywhere—I would only be running *from*.

I hated that. When had I become such a coward?

Tanya threw her slender arm around my shoulders. I stiffened but did not flinch from her touch. She meant it as nothing more than friendly comfort. Mostly.

"I think that you *will* go back," she said, her voice taking on just a hint of her long-lost Russian accent. "No matter what it is...or who it is...that haunts you. You'll face it head-on. You're the type."

Her thoughts were as certain as her words. I tried to embrace the vision of myself that she saw. The one who faced things head-on. It was pleasant to think of myself that way again. I'd never doubted my courage, my ability to face difficulty, before that horrible hour in a high school Biology class such a short time ago.

I kissed her cheek, pulling back swiftly when she twisted her face toward mine. She smiled ruefully at my quickness.

"Thank you, Tanya. I needed to hear that."

Her thoughts turned petulant. "You're welcome, I guess. I wish you would be more reasonable about things, Edward."

"I'm sorry, Tanya. You know you're far too good for me. I just...haven't found what I'm looking for yet."

"Well, if you leave before I see you again...goodbye, Edward."

"Goodbye, Tanya." As I said the words, I could see it. I could see myself leaving. Being strong enough to go back to the one place I wanted to be. "Again, thank you."

She was on her feet in one nimble move, and then she was running away, ghosting across the snow so quickly that her feet had no time to sink in. She left no prints behind her. She didn't look back. My rejection bothered her more than she'd let on before, even in her thoughts. She wouldn't want to see me again before I left.

My mouth twisted downward. I didn't like hurting Tanya, though her feelings were not deep, hardly pure, and, in any case, not something I could return. It still made me feel less than a gentleman.

I put my chin on my knees and stared up at the stars again, though I was suddenly anxious to be on my way. I knew that Alice would see me coming home, that she would tell the others. This would make them happy—Carlisle and Esme especially. But I gazed at the stars for one more moment, trying to see past the face in my head. Between me and the brilliant lights in the sky, a pair of bewildered chocolate-brown eyes wondered at my motives, seeming to ask what this decision would mean for *her*. Of course, I couldn't be sure that was really the information her curious eyes sought. Even in my imagination, I couldn't hear her thoughts. Bella Swan's eyes continued to question, and an unobstructed view of the stars continued to elude me. With a heavy sigh, I gave up and got to my feet. If I ran, I would be back to Carlisle's car in less than an hour.

In a hurry to see my family—and wanting very much to be the Edward who faced things head-on—I raced across the starlit snowfield, leaving no footprints.

"It's going to be okay," Alice breathed. Her eyes were unfocused, and Jasper had one hand lightly under her elbow, guiding her forward as we walked into the run-down cafeteria in a close-huddled group. Rosalie and Emmett led the way, Emmett looking ridiculously like a bodyguard in the middle of hostile territory. Rose looked wary, too, but much more irritated than protective.

"Of course it is," I grumbled. Their behavior was ludicrous. If I weren't positive that I could handle this moment, I would have stayed home.

The sudden shift from our normal, even playful morning—it had snowed in the night, and Emmett and Jasper were not above taking advantage of my distraction to bombard me with slushballs; when they got bored with my lack of response, they'd turned on each other—to this overdone vigilance would have been comical if it weren't so irritating.

"She's not here yet, but the way she's going to come in... she won't be downwind if we sit in our regular spot."

"*Of course* we'll sit in our regular spot. Stop it, Alice. You're getting on my nerves. I'll be absolutely fine."

She blinked once as Jasper helped her into her seat, and her eyes finally focused on my face.

"Hmm," she said, sounding surprised. "I think you're right."

"*Of course* I am," I muttered.

I hated being the focus of their concern. I felt a sudden sympathy for Jasper, remembering all the times we'd hovered protectively over him. He met my glance briefly, and grinned.

Annoying, isn't it?

I glowered at him.

Was it just last week that this long, drab room had seemed so killingly dull to me? That it had seemed almost like sleep, like a coma, to be here?

Today my nerves were stretched tight—piano wires, tensed to sing at the lightest pressure. My senses were hyperalert; I scanned every sound, every sight, every movement of the air that touched my skin, every thought. Especially the thoughts. There was only one sense that I kept locked down, refused to use. Smell, of course. I didn't breathe.

I was expecting to hear more about the Cullens in the thoughts that I sifted through. All day I'd been waiting, searching for whichever new acquaintance Bella Swan might have confided in, trying to see the direction the new gossip would take. But there was nothing. No one particularly noticed the five vampires in the cafeteria, just as before the girl had come. Several of the humans here were still thinking of her, still thinking the same thoughts from last week. Instead of finding this unutterably boring, I was now fascinated.

Had she said nothing to anyone about me?

There was no way that she had not noticed my black, murderous glare. I had seen her react to it. Surely, I'd traumatized her. I was convinced that she would have mentioned it to someone, maybe even have exaggerated the story a bit to make it better. Given me a few menacing lines.

And then she'd also heard me trying to get out of our shared Biology class. She must have wondered, after seeing my expression, whether she was the cause. A normal girl would have asked around, compared her experience to others', looked for common ground that would explain my behavior so she didn't feel singled out. Humans were constantly desperate to feel normal, to fit in. To blend in with everyone else around them, like a featureless flock of sheep. The need was particularly strong during the insecure adolescent years. This girl would be no exception to that rule.

But no one at all took notice of us sitting here, at our usual table. Bella must be exceptionally shy if she'd hadn't confided in anyone. Perhaps she had spoken to her father; maybe that was the strongest relationship…though that seemed unlikely, given that she had spent so little time with him throughout her life. She would be closer to her mother. Still, I would have to pass by Chief Swan sometime soon and listen to what he was thinking.

"Anything new?" Jasper asked.

I concentrated, allowing all the swarms of thoughts to invade my mind again. There wasn't anything that stood out; no one was thinking of us. Despite my earlier worries, it didn't seem that there was anything wrong with my abilities, aside from the silent girl. I'd shared my concerns with Carlisle upon my return, but he'd only ever heard of talents growing stronger with practice. Never did they atrophy.

Jasper waited impatiently.

"Nothing. She…must not have said anything."

All of them raised eyebrows at this news.

"Maybe you're not as scary as you think you are," Emmett said, chuckling. "I bet I could have frightened her better than *that*."

I rolled my eyes at him.

"Wonder why…?" He puzzled again over my revelation about the girl's unique silence.

"We've been over that. I don't *know*."

"She's coming in," Alice murmured then. My body froze. "Try to look human."

"Human, you say?" Emmett asked.

He held up his right fist, twisting his fingers to reveal the snowball he'd saved in his palm. It had not melted there; he'd squeezed it into a lumpy block of ice. He had his eyes on Jasper, but I saw the direction of his thoughts. So did Alice, of course. When he abruptly hurled the ice chunk at her, she flicked it away with a casual flutter of her fingers. The ice ricocheted across the length of the cafeteria, too fast to be visible to human eyes, and shattered with a sharp crack against the brick wall. The brick cracked, too.

The heads in that corner of the room all turned to stare at

the pile of broken ice on the floor, and then swiveled to find the culprit. They didn't look farther than a few tables away. No one looked at us.

"Very human, Emmett," Rosalie said scathingly. "Why don't you punch through the wall while you're at it?"

"It would look more impressive if you did it, gorgeous."

I tried to pay attention to them, keeping a grin fixed on my face as though I were part of their banter. I did not allow myself to look toward the line where I knew she was standing. But that was all I was listening to.

I could hear Jessica's impatience with the new girl, who seemed to be distracted, too, standing motionless in the moving line. I saw, in Jessica's thoughts, that Bella Swan's cheeks were once more colored bright pink with blood.

I pulled in a few short, shallow breaths, ready to quit breathing if any hint of her scent touched the air near me.

Mike Newton was with the two girls. I heard both his voices, mental and verbal, when he asked Jessica what was wrong with the Swan girl. It was distasteful the way his thoughts wrapped around her, the flicker of already established fantasies that clouded his mind while he watched her start and look up from her reverie as though she'd forgotten he was there.

"Nothing," I heard Bella say in that quiet, clear voice. It seemed to ring like a struck bell over the babble in the cafeteria, but I knew that was just because I was listening for it so intently.

"I'll just get a soda today," she continued as she moved to catch up with the line.

I couldn't help flickering one glance in her direction. She was staring at the floor, the blood slowly fading from her face. I looked away quickly, to Emmett, who laughed at the now pained-looking smile on my face.

You look sick, brother mine.

I rearranged my features so the expression would seem casual and effortless.

Jessica was wondering aloud about the girl's lack of appetite. "Aren't you hungry?"

"Actually, I feel a little sick." Her voice was lower, but still very clear.

Why did it bother me, the protective concern that suddenly emanated from Mike Newton's thoughts? What did it matter that there was a possessive edge to them? It wasn't my business if Mike Newton felt unnecessarily anxious for her. Perhaps this was the way everyone responded to her. Hadn't I wanted, instinctively, to protect her, too? Before I'd wanted to kill her, that is...

But *was* the girl ill?

It was hard to judge—she looked so delicate with her translucent skin.... Then I realized that I was worrying, just like that dimwitted boy, and I forced myself not to think about her health.

Regardless, I didn't like monitoring her through Mike's thoughts. I switched to Jessica's, watching carefully as the three of them chose which table to sit at. Fortunately, they sat with Jessica's usual companions, at one of the first tables in the room. Not downwind, just as Alice had promised.

Alice elbowed me. *She's going to look soon. Act human.*

I clenched my teeth behind my grin.

"Ease up, Edward," Emmett said. "Honestly. So you kill one human. That's hardly the end of the world."

"You would know," I murmured.

Emmett laughed. "You've got to learn to get over things. Like I do. Eternity is a long time to wallow in guilt."

Just then, Alice tossed a smaller handful of ice that she'd been hiding into Emmett's unsuspecting face.

He blinked, surprised, and then grinned in anticipation.

"You asked for it," he said as he leaned across the table and shook his ice-encrusted hair in her direction. The snow, melting in the warm room, flew out from his hair in a thick shower of half liquid, half ice.

"Ew!" Rose complained as she and Alice recoiled from the deluge.

Alice laughed, and we all joined in. I could see in Alice's head how she'd orchestrated this perfect moment, and I knew that the girl—I should stop thinking of her that way, as if she were the only girl in the world—that *Bella* would be watching us laugh and play, looking as happy and human and unrealistically ideal as a Norman Rockwell painting.

Alice kept laughing and held her tray up as a shield. The girl—Bella—must still be staring at us.

...staring at the Cullens again, someone thought, catching my attention.

I looked automatically toward the unintentional call, easily recognizing the voice as my eyes found their destination—I'd been listening to it so much today.

But my eyes slid right past Jessica and focused on the girl's penetrating gaze.

She looked down quickly, hiding behind her thick hair again.

What was she thinking? The frustration seemed to be getting more acute as time went on, rather than dulling. I tried—uncertain, for I'd never done this before—to probe with my mind at the silence around her. My extra hearing had always come to me naturally, without asking; I'd never had to work at it. But I concentrated now, trying to break through whatever armor surrounded her.

Nothing but silence.

What is *it about her?* Jessica thought, echoing my own irritation.

"Edward Cullen is staring at you," she whispered in the Swan girl's ear, adding a giggle. There was no hint of her jealous annoyance in her tone. Jessica seemed to be skilled at feigning friendship.

I listened, too engrossed, to the girl's response.

"He doesn't look angry, does he?" she whispered back.

So she *had* noticed my wild reaction last week. Of course she had.

The question confused Jessica. I saw my own face in her thoughts as she checked my expression, but I did not meet her glance. I was still concentrating on the girl, trying to hear *something*. Intent focus didn't seem to help at all.

"No," Jess told her, and I knew that she wished she could say yes—how it rankled her, my staring—though there was no trace of that in her voice. "Should he be?"

"I don't think he likes me," the girl whispered back, laying her head down on her arm as if she were suddenly tired. I tried to understand the motion, but I could only make guesses. Maybe she *was* tired.

"The Cullens don't like anybody," Jess reassured her. "Well, they don't notice anybody enough to like them." *They never used to.* Her thought was a grumble of complaint. "But he's still staring at you."

"Stop looking at him," the girl said anxiously, lifting her head from her arm to make sure Jessica obeyed the order.

Jessica giggled, but did as she was asked.

The girl did not look away from her table for the rest of the hour. I thought—though, of course, I could not be sure—that this was deliberate. It seemed as though she wanted to look at me. Her body would shift slightly in my direction, her chin would begin to turn, and then she would catch herself, take a deep breath, and stare fixedly at whoever was speaking.

I ignored the other thoughts around the girl for the most part, as they were not, momentarily, about her. Mike Newton was planning a snowball fight in the parking lot after school, not seeming to realize that the snow had already shifted to rain. The flutter of soft flakes against the roof had become the more common patter of raindrops. Could he really not hear the change? It seemed loud to me.

When the lunch period ended, I stayed in my seat. The humans filed out, and I caught myself trying to distinguish the sound of her footsteps from the rest, as if there were something important or unusual about them. How stupid.

My family made no move to leave, either. They waited to see what I would do.

Would I go to class, sit beside the girl, where I could smell the absurdly potent scent of her blood and feel the warmth of her pulse in the air on my skin? Was I strong enough for that? Or had I had enough for one day?

As a family, we'd already discussed this moment from every possible angle. Carlisle disapproved of the risk, but he wouldn't impose his will on mine. Jasper disapproved nearly as much, but from fear of exposure rather than any concern for humankind. Rosalie only worried about how it would affect her life. Alice saw so many obscure, conflicting futures that her visions were atypically unhelpful. Esme thought I could do no wrong. And Emmett just wanted to compare stories about his own experiences with particularly appealing scents. He pulled Jasper into his reminiscing, though Jasper's history with self-control was so short and so uneven that he was unable to be sure he'd ever had an analogous struggle. Emmett, on the other hand, remembered two such incidents. His memories of them were not encouraging. But he'd been younger then, not as adept at self-control. Surely, I was stronger than that.

"I... *think* it's okay," Alice said, hesitant. "Your mind is set. I *think* you'll make it through the hour."

But Alice knew well how quickly a mind could change.

"Why push it, Edward?" Jasper asked. Though he didn't want to feel smug that I was the weak one now, I could hear that he did, just a little. "Go home. Take it slow."

"What's the big deal?" Emmett disagreed. "Either he will or he won't kill her. Might as well get it over with, either way."

"I don't want to move yet," Rosalie complained. "I don't want to start over. We're almost out of high school, Emmett. *Finally*."

I was evenly torn on the decision. I wanted, wanted badly, to face this head-on rather than running away again. But I didn't want to push myself too far, either. It had been a mistake last week for Jasper to go so long without hunting; was this just as pointless a mistake?

I didn't want to uproot my family. None of them would thank me for that.

But I wanted to go to my Biology class. I realized that I wanted to see her face again.

That's what decided it for me. That curiosity. I was angry with myself for feeling it. Hadn't I promised myself that I wouldn't let the silence of the girl's mind make me unduly interested in her? And yet, here I was, most unduly interested.

I wanted to know what she was thinking. Her mind was closed, but her eyes were very open. Perhaps I could read them instead.

"No, Rose, I think it really will be okay," Alice said. "It's... firming up. I'm ninety-three percent sure that nothing bad will happen if he goes to class." She looked at me, inquisitive, wondering what had changed in my thoughts that made her vision of the future more secure.

Would curiosity be enough to keep Bella Swan alive?

Emmett was right, though—why not get it over with, either way? I would face the temptation head-on.

"Go to class," I ordered, pushing away from the table. I turned and strode away from them without looking back. I could hear Alice's worry, Jasper's censure, Emmett's approval, and Rosalie's irritation trailing after me.

I took one last deep breath at the door of the classroom, and then held it in my lungs as I walked into the small, warm space.

I was not late. Mr. Banner was still setting up for today's lab. The girl sat at my—at *our* table, her face down again, staring at the folder she was doodling on. I examined the sketch as I approached, interested in even this trivial creation of her mind, but it was meaningless. Just a random scribbling of loops within loops. Perhaps she was not concentrating on the pattern, but thinking of something else?

I pulled my chair back with unnecessary roughness, letting it scrape across the linoleum—humans always felt more comfortable when noise announced someone's approach.

I knew she heard the sound; she did not look up, but her hand missed a loop in the design she was drawing, making it unbalanced.

Why didn't she look up? Probably she was frightened. I must be sure to leave her with a different impression this time. Make her think she'd been imagining things before.

"Hello," I said in the quiet voice I used when I wanted to make humans more comfortable, forming a polite smile with my lips that would not show any teeth.

She looked up then, her wide brown eyes startled and full of silent questions. It was the same expression that had been obstructing my vision for the past week.

As I stared into those oddly deep brown eyes—the color was like milk chocolate, but the clarity was more comparable to strong tea, there was a depth and transparency; near her pupils, there were tiny flecks of agate green and golden caramel—I realized that my hate, the hate I'd imagined this girl somehow deserved for simply existing, had evaporated. Not breathing now, not tasting her scent, I found it hard to believe that anyone so vulnerable could ever be deserving of hatred.

Her cheeks began to flush, and she said nothing.

I kept my eyes on hers, focusing only on their questioning depths, and tried to ignore the appetizing color of her skin. I had enough breath to speak for a while longer without inhaling.

"My name is Edward Cullen," I said, though she already knew it. It was the polite way to begin. "I didn't have a chance to introduce myself last week. You must be Bella Swan."

She seemed confused—there was that little pucker between her eyes again. It took her half a second longer than it should have to respond.

"How do you know my name?" she demanded, and her voice shook just a little.

I must have truly terrified her, and this made me feel guilty. I laughed gently—it was a sound that I knew made humans more at ease.

"Oh, I think everyone knows your name." Surely, she must have realized that she'd become the center of attention in this monotonous place. "The whole town's been waiting for you to arrive."

She frowned as if this information was unpleasant. I supposed, being shy as she appeared to be, attention would seem like a bad thing to her. Most humans felt the opposite. Though they didn't want to stand out from the herd, at the same time they craved a spotlight for their individual uniformity.

"No," she said. "I meant, why did you call me Bella?"

"Do you prefer Isabella?" I asked, perplexed that I couldn't see where this question was leading. I didn't understand. She'd made her preference clear many times that first day. Were all humans this incomprehensible without the mental context as a guide? How much I must rely on that extra sense. Would I be completely blind without it?

"No, I like Bella," she answered, leaning her head slightly to one side. Her expression—if I was reading it correctly—was torn between embarrassment and confusion. "But I think Charlie—I mean my dad—must call me Isabella behind my back. That's what everyone here seems to know me as." Her skin darkened one shade pinker.

"Oh," I said, and quickly looked away from her face.

I'd just realized what her questions meant: I had slipped up—made an error. If I hadn't been eavesdropping on all the others that first day, then I would have addressed her initially by her full name. She'd noticed the difference.

I felt a pang of unease. It was very quick of her to pick up on my slip. Quite astute, especially for someone who was supposed to be terrified by my proximity.

But I had bigger problems than whatever suspicions about me she might be keeping locked inside her head.

I was out of air. If I were going to speak to her again, I would have to inhale.

It would be hard to avoid speaking. Unfortunately for her, sharing this table made her my lab partner, and we would have to work together today. It would seem odd—and incomprehensibly rude—for me to ignore her while we did the lab. It would make her more suspicious, more afraid.

I leaned as far away from her as I could without moving my seat, twisting my head out into the aisle. I braced myself, locking my muscles in place, and then sucked in one quick chestful of air, breathing through my mouth alone.

Ahh!

It was intensely painful, like swallowing burning coals. Even without smelling her, I could taste her on my tongue. The craving was every bit as strong as that first moment I'd caught her scent last week.

I gritted my teeth and tried to compose myself.

"Get started," Mr. Banner commanded.

It took every single ounce of self-control I'd achieved in seventy-four years of hard work to turn back to the girl, who was staring down at the table, and smile.

"Ladies first, partner?" I offered.

She looked up at my expression and her face went blank. Was there something off? In her eyes, I saw the reflection of my usual human-friendly composition of features. The facade looked perfect. Was she frightened again? She didn't speak.

"Or, I could start, if you wish," I said quietly.

"No," she said, and her face went from white to red again. "I'll go ahead."

I stared at the equipment on the table—the battered microscope, the box of slides—rather than watch the blood wax and wane under her clear skin. I took another quick breath, through my teeth, and winced as the taste scorched the inside of my throat.

"Prophase," she said after a quick examination. She started to remove the slide, though she'd barely examined it.

"Do you mind if I look?" Instinctively—stupidly, as if I were one of her kind—I reached out to stop her hand from removing the slide. For one second, the heat of her skin burned into mine. It was like an electric pulse—the heat shot through my fingers and up my arm. She yanked her hand out from under mine.

"I'm sorry," I muttered. Needing somewhere to look, I grasped the microscope and stared briefly into the eyepiece. She was right.

"Prophase," I agreed.

I was still too unsettled to look at her. Breathing as quietly as I could through my gritted teeth and trying to ignore the fiery thirst, I concentrated on the simple assignment, writing the word on the appropriate line on the lab sheet and then switching out the first slide for the next.

What was she thinking now? What had it felt like to her when I had touched her hand? My skin must have been ice-cold—repulsive. No wonder she was so quiet.

I glanced at the slide.

"Anaphase," I said to myself as I wrote it on the second line.

"May I?" she asked.

I looked up, surprised to see that she was waiting expectantly, one hand half-stretched toward the microscope. She didn't *look* afraid. Did she really think I'd gotten the answer wrong?

I couldn't help but smile at the hopeful expression on her face as I slid the microscope toward her.

She stared into the eyepiece with an eagerness that quickly faded. The corners of her mouth turned down.

"Slide three?" she asked, not looking up from the microscope, but holding out her hand. I dropped the next slide into her palm, keeping my skin far from hers this time. Sitting beside her was like sitting next to a heat lamp. I could feel myself warming slightly to the higher temperature.

She did not look at the slide for long. "Interphase," she said nonchalantly—perhaps trying a little too hard to sound that way—and pushed the microscope toward me. She did not touch the paper, but waited for me to write the answer. I checked—she was correct again.

We finished this way, speaking one word at a time and never meeting each other's eyes. We were the only ones done—the others in the class were having a harder time with the lab. Mike Newton seemed to be having trouble concentrating; he was trying to watch Bella and me.

Wish he'd stayed wherever he went, Mike thought, eyeing me sulfurously. Interesting. I hadn't realized the boy harbored any specific ill will toward me. This was a new development, about as recent as the girl's arrival, it seemed. Even more interestingly, I found—to my surprise—that the feeling was mutual.

I looked down at the girl again, bemused by the vast range of havoc and upheaval that, despite her ordinary, unthreatening appearance, she was wreaking on my life.

It wasn't that I couldn't see what Mike was going on about. She was actually sort of pretty for a human, in an unusual way. Better than being beautiful, her face was...unexpected. Not quite symmetrical—her narrow chin out of balance with her wide cheekbones; extreme in the coloring—the contrast of her light skin and dark hair; and then there were the eyes, too big for her face, brimming over with silent secrets....

Eyes that were suddenly boring into mine.

I stared back at her, trying to guess even one of those secrets.

"Did you get contacts?" she asked abruptly.

What a strange question. "No." I almost smiled at the idea of improving *my* eyesight.

"Oh," she mumbled. "I thought there was something different about your eyes."

I felt suddenly colder again as I realized that I was not the only one attempting to ferret out secrets today.

I shrugged, my shoulders stiff, and glared straight ahead to where the teacher was making his rounds.

Of course there was something different about my eyes since

the last time she'd stared into them. To prepare myself for today's ordeal, today's temptation, I'd spent the entire weekend hunting, satiating my thirst as much as possible, overdoing it, really. I'd glutted myself on the blood of animals, not that it made much difference in the face of the outrageous flavor floating on the air around her. When I'd glared at her last, my eyes had been black with thirst. Now, my body swimming with blood, my eyes were a warm gold—light amber.

Another slip. If I'd seen what she meant with her question, I could have just told her yes.

I'd sat beside humans for two years now at this school, and she was the first to examine me closely enough to note the change in my eye color. The others, while admiring the beauty of my family, tended to look down quickly when we returned their stares. They shied away, blocking the details of our appearances in an instinctive endeavor to keep themselves from understanding. Ignorance was bliss to the human mind.

Why did it have to be *this* girl who would see too much?

Mr. Banner approached our table. I gratefully inhaled the gush of clean air he brought with him before it could mix with her scent.

"So, Edward," he said, looking over our answers, "didn't you think Isabella should get a chance with the microscope?"

"Bella," I corrected him reflexively. "Actually, she identified three of the five."

Mr. Banner's thoughts were skeptical as he turned to look at the girl. "Have you done this lab before?"

I watched, engrossed, as she smiled, looking slightly embarrassed.

"Not with onion root."

"Whitefish blastula?" Mr. Banner probed.

"Yeah."

This surprised him. Today's lab was something he'd pulled from a senior-class course. He nodded thoughtfully at the girl. "Were you in an advanced placement program in Phoenix?"

"Yes."

She was advanced, then, intelligent for a human. This did not surprise me.

"Well," Mr. Banner said, pursing his lips, "I guess it's good you two are lab partners." He turned and walked away, mumbling "So the other kids can get a chance to learn something for themselves" under his breath. I doubted the girl could hear that. She began scrawling loops across her folder again.

Two slips so far in one half hour. An extremely poor showing on my part. Though I had no idea at all what the girl thought of me—how much did she fear, how much did she suspect?—I knew I needed to put forth a better effort to leave her with a new impression. Something to quell her memories of our ferocious last encounter.

"It's too bad about the snow, isn't it?" I said, repeating the small talk that I'd heard a dozen students discuss already. A boring, standard topic of conversation. The weather—always safe.

She stared at me with obvious doubt in her eyes—an abnormal reaction to my very normal words. "Not really."

I tried to steer the conversation back to trite paths. She was from a much brighter, warmer place—her skin seemed to reflect that somehow, despite its fairness—and the cold must make her uncomfortable. My icy touch certainly had.

"You don't like the cold," I guessed.

"Or the wet," she agreed.

"Forks must be a difficult place for you to live." *Perhaps you should not have come here*, I wanted to add. *Perhaps you should go back where you belong.*

I wasn't sure I wanted that, though. I would always remember the scent of her blood—was there any guarantee that I wouldn't eventually follow her? Besides, if she left, her mind would forever remain a mystery, a constant, nagging puzzle.

"You have no idea," she said in a low voice, glowering past me for a moment.

Her answers were never what I expected. They made me want to ask more questions.

"Why did you come here, then?" I demanded, realizing instantly that my tone was too accusatory, not casual enough for the conversation. The question sounded rude, prying.

"It's . . . complicated."

She blinked, leaving it at that, and I nearly imploded out of curiosity—in that second, it burned almost as hot as the thirst in my throat. Actually, I found that it was getting slightly easier to breathe; the agony was becoming a tiny bit more bearable through familiarity.

"I think I can keep up," I insisted. Perhaps common courtesy would compel her to answer my questions as long as I was impolite enough to ask them.

She stared down silently at her hands. This made me impatient. I wanted to put my hand under her chin and tilt her head up so that I could read her eyes. But of course I could never touch her skin again.

She looked up suddenly. It was a relief to be able to see the emotions in her eyes. She spoke in a rush, hurrying through the words.

"My mother got remarried."

Ah, this was human enough, easy to understand. Sorrow flitted across her face, bringing the small pucker back between her brows.

"That doesn't sound so complex," I said, my voice gentle without my working to make it that way. Her dejection left me oddly helpless, wishing there was something I could do to make her feel better. A strange impulse. "When did that happen?"

"Last September." She exhaled heavily—not quite a sigh. I froze for a moment as her warm breath brushed my face.

"And you don't like him," I guessed after that short pause, still fishing for more information.

"No, Phil is fine," she said, correcting my assumption. There was a hint of a smile now around the corners of her full lips. "Too young, maybe, but nice enough."

This didn't fit with the scenario I'd been constructing in my head.

"Why didn't you stay with them?" My voice was too eager; it sounded like I was being nosy. Which I was, admittedly.

"Phil travels a lot. He plays ball for a living." The little smile grew more pronounced; this career choice amused her.

I smiled, too, without choosing the expression. I wasn't trying to make her feel at ease. Her smile just made me want to smile in response—to be in on the secret.

"Have I heard of him?" I ran through the rosters of professional ballplayers in my head, wondering which Phil was hers.

"Probably not. He doesn't play *well*." Another smile. "Strictly minor league. He moves around a lot."

The rosters in my head shifted instantly, and I'd tabulated a list of possibilities in less than a second. At the same time, I was imagining the new scenario.

"And your mother sent you here so that she could travel with him," I said. Making assumptions seemed to get more information out of her than questions did. It worked again. Her chin jutted out, and her expression was suddenly stubborn.

"No, she did not send me here," she said, and her voice had a new, hard edge to it. My assumption had upset her, though I couldn't quite see how. "I sent myself."

I could not guess at her meaning, or the source behind her pique. I was entirely lost.

There was just no making sense of the girl. She wasn't like other humans. Maybe the silence of her thoughts and the perfume of her scent were not the only unusual things about her.

"I don't understand," I admitted, hating to concede.

She sighed and stared into my eyes for longer than most normal humans were able to stand.

"She stayed with me at first, but she missed him," Bella explained slowly, her tone growing more forlorn with each word. "It made her unhappy . . . so I decided it was time to spend some quality time with Charlie."

The tiny pucker between her eyes deepened.

"But now you're unhappy," I murmured. I kept speaking my hypotheses aloud, hoping to learn from her refutations. This one, however, did not seem as far off the mark.

"And?" she said, as if this was not even an aspect to be considered.

I continued to stare into her eyes, feeling that I'd finally gotten my first real glimpse into her soul. I saw in that one word where she ranked herself among her own priorities. Unlike most humans, her own needs were far down the list.

She was selfless.

As I saw this, the mystery of the person hiding inside this quiet mind began to clear a little.

"That doesn't seem fair," I said. I shrugged, trying to seem casual.

She laughed, but there was no amusement in the sound. "Hasn't anyone ever told you? Life isn't fair."

I wanted to laugh at her words, though I, too, felt no real amusement. I knew a little something about the unfairness of life. "I believe I *have* heard that somewhere before."

She stared back at me, seeming confused again. Her eyes flickered away, and then came back to mine.

"So that's all," she told me.

I was not ready to let this conversation end. The little *v* between her eyes, a remnant of her sorrow, bothered me.

"You put on a good show." I spoke slowly, still considering this next hypothesis. "But I'd be willing to bet that you're suffering more than you let anyone see."

She made a face, her eyes narrowing and her mouth twisting into a lopsided frown, and she looked back toward the front of the class. She didn't like it when I guessed right. She wasn't the average martyr—she didn't want an audience for her pain.

"Am I wrong?"

She flinched slightly, but otherwise pretended not to hear me.

That made me smile. "I didn't think so."

"Why does it matter to you?" she demanded, still staring away.

"That's a very good question," I admitted, more to myself than to her.

Her discernment was better than mine—she saw right to the core of things while I floundered around the edges, sifting blindly through clues. The details of her very human life should *not* matter to me. It was wrong for me to care what she thought. Beyond protecting my family from suspicion, human thoughts were not significant.

I was not used to being the less intuitive of any pairing. I relied on my extra hearing too much—I clearly was not as perceptive as I gave myself credit for.

The girl sighed and glowered toward the front of the classroom. Something about her frustrated expression was humorous. The whole situation, the whole conversation, was humorous. No one had ever been in more danger from me than this small human girl—at any moment I might, distracted by my ridiculous absorption in the conversation, inhale through my nose and attack her before I could stop myself—and *she* was irritated because I hadn't answered her question.

"Am I annoying you?" I asked, smiling at the absurdity of it all.

She glanced at me quickly, and then her eyes seemed to get trapped by my gaze.

"Not exactly," she told me. "I'm more annoyed at myself. My face is so easy to read—my mother always calls me her open book."

She frowned, disgruntled.

I stared at her in amazement. She was upset because she thought I saw through her *too easily*. How bizarre. I'd never expended so much effort to understand someone in all my life—or rather existence, as *life* was hardly the right word. I did not truly have a *life*.

"On the contrary," I disagreed, feeling strangely…wary, as

if there were some hidden danger here that I was failing to see. Beyond the very obvious danger, something more...I was suddenly on edge, the premonition making me anxious. "I find you very difficult to read."

"You must be a good reader, then," she guessed, making her own assumption, which was, again, right on target.

"Usually," I agreed.

I smiled at her widely then, letting my lips pull back to expose the rows of gleaming, steel-strong teeth behind them.

It was a stupid thing to do, but I was abruptly, unexpectedly desperate to get some kind of warning through to the girl. Her body was closer to me than before, having shifted unconsciously in the course of our conversation. All the little markers and signs that were sufficient to scare off the rest of humanity did not seem to be working on her. Why did she not cringe away from me in terror? Surely she had seen enough of my darker side to realize the danger.

I didn't get to see if my warning had the intended effect. Mr. Banner called for the class's attention just then, and she turned away from me at once. She seemed a little relieved for the interruption, so maybe she understood unconsciously.

I hoped she did.

I recognized the fascination growing inside me, even as I tried to root it out. I could not afford to find Bella Swan interesting. Or rather, *she* could not afford that. Already, I was anxious for another chance to talk to her. I wanted to know more about her mother, her life before she came here, her relationship with her father. All the meaningless details that would flesh out her character further. But every second I spent with her was a mistake, a risk she shouldn't have to take.

Absentmindedly, she tossed her thick hair just at the moment that I allowed myself another breath. A particularly concentrated wave of her scent hit the back of my throat.

It was like the first day—like the grenade. The pain of the burning dryness made me dizzy. I had to grasp the table again to keep myself in my seat. This time I had slightly more control. I didn't break anything, at least. The monster growled inside me but took no pleasure in my pain. He was too tightly bound. For the moment.

I stopped breathing altogether and leaned as far from the girl as I could.

No, I could not afford to find her fascinating. The more interesting I found her, the more likely it was that I would kill her. I'd already made two minor slips today. Would I make a third, one that was *not* minor?

As soon as the bell sounded, I fled from the classroom—probably destroying whatever impression of politeness I'd halfway constructed in the course of the hour. Again, I gasped at the clean, wet air outside as though it was a healing attar. I hurried to put as much distance as possible between myself and the girl.

Emmett waited for me outside the door of our Spanish class. He read my wild expression for a moment.

How did it go? he wondered warily.

"Nobody died," I mumbled.

I guess that's something. When I saw Alice ditching there at the end, I thought...

As we walked into the classroom, I saw his memory from just a few moments earlier, seen through the open door of his last class: Alice walking briskly and blank-faced across the grounds toward the science building. I felt his remembered urge to get up and join her, and then his decision to stay. If Alice needed his help, she would ask.

I closed my eyes in horror and disgust as I slumped into my seat. "I hadn't realized it was that close. I didn't think I was going to... I didn't see that it was that bad," I whispered.

It wasn't, he reassured me. *Nobody died, right?*

"Right," I said through my teeth. "Not this time."

Maybe it will get easier.

"Sure."

Or maybe you kill her. He shrugged. *You wouldn't be the first one to mess up. No one would judge you too harshly. Sometimes a person just smells too good. I'm impressed you've lasted this long.*

"Not helping, Emmett."

I was revolted by his acceptance of the idea that I would kill the girl, that this was somehow inevitable. Was it her fault that she smelled so good?

I know when it happened to me..., he reminisced, taking me back with him half a century, to a country lane at dusk, where a middle-aged woman was pulling her dried sheets down from a line strung between apple trees. I'd seen this before, the strongest of his two encounters, but the memory seemed particularly vivid now—perhaps because my throat still ached from the last hour's scorching. Emmett remembered the smell of apples hanging heavy in the air—the harvest was over and the rejected fruits were scattered on the ground, the bruises in their skin leaking their fragrance out in thick clouds. A freshly mowed field of hay was a background to that scent, a harmony. He walked up the lane, all but oblivious to the woman, on an errand for Rosalie. The sky was purple overhead, orange over the mountains to the west. He would have continued up the meandering cart path and there would have been no reason to remember the evening, except that a sudden night breeze blew the white sheets out like sails and fanned the woman's scent across Emmett's face.

"Ah," I groaned quietly. As if my own remembered thirst was not enough.

I know. I didn't last half a second. I didn't even think about resisting.

His memory became far too explicit for me to stand.

I jumped to my feet, my teeth locked hard.

"*Estás bien*, Edward?" Mrs. Goff asked, startled by my sudden movement. I could see my face in her mind, and I knew that I looked far from well.

"*Perdóname*," I muttered as I darted for the door.

"Emmett, *por favor, puedes ayudar a tu hermano?*" she asked, gesturing helplessly toward me as I rushed out of the room.

"Sure," I heard him say. And then he was right behind me.

He followed me to the far side of the building, where he caught up to me and put his hand on my shoulder.

I shoved his hand away with unnecessary force. It would have shattered the bones in a human hand, and the bones in the arm attached to it.

"Sorry, Edward."

"I know." I drew in deep gasps of air, trying to clear my head and lungs.

"Is it as bad as that?" he asked, trying not to think of the scent and the flavor of his memory as he asked, and not quite succeeding.

"Worse, Emmett, worse."

He was quiet for a moment.

Maybe...

"No, it would not be better if I got it over with. Go back to class, Emmett. I want to be alone."

He turned without another word or thought and walked quickly away. He would tell the Spanish teacher that I was sick, or ditching, or a dangerously out of control vampire. Did his excuse really matter? Maybe I wasn't coming back. Maybe I had to leave.

I returned to my car to wait for school to end. To hide. Again.

I should have spent the time making decisions or trying to bolster my resolve, but, like an addict, I found myself searching through the babble of thoughts emanating from the school buildings. The familiar voices stood out, but I wasn't interested in listening to Alice's visions or Rosalie's complaints right now. I found Jessica easily, but the girl was not with her, so I continued searching. Mike Newton's thoughts caught my attention, and I located her at last, in Gym with him. He was unhappy because I'd spoken to her today in Biology. He was running over her response when he'd brought the subject up.

I've never seen him actually say more than a word here or there to anyone. Of course he would decide to talk to Bella. I don't like the way he looks at her. But she didn't seem too excited about him. What did she say to me earlier? "Wonder what was with him last Monday." Something like that. Didn't sound like she cared. It couldn't have been much of a conversation....

He cheered himself with the idea that Bella had not been interested in her exchange with me. This annoyed me quite a bit, so I stopped listening to him.

I put in a CD of violent music, and then turned it up until it drowned out other voices. I had to concentrate on the music very hard to keep myself from drifting back to Mike Newton's thoughts to spy on the unsuspecting girl.

I cheated a few times as the hour drew to a close. Not spying, I tried to convince myself. I was just preparing. I wanted to know exactly when she would leave the gym, when she would be in the parking lot. I didn't want her to take me by surprise.

As the students started to file out the gym doors, I got out of my car, not sure why I did it. The rain was light—I ignored it as it slowly saturated my hair.

Did I want her to see me here? Did I hope she would come to speak to me? What was I doing?

I didn't move, though I tried to convince myself to get back in the car, knowing my behavior was reprehensible. I kept my arms folded across my chest and breathed very shallowly as I watched her walk slowly toward me, her mouth turning down at the corners. She didn't look at me. A few times she glanced up at the clouds with a scowl, as if they had offended her.

I was disappointed when she reached her car before she had to pass me. Would she have spoken to me? Would I have spoken to her?

She got into a faded red Chevy truck, a rusted behemoth that was older than her father. I watched her start the truck—the old engine roared louder than any other vehicle in the lot—and then hold her hands out toward the heating vents. The cold was uncomfortable to her—she didn't like it. She combed her fingers through her thick hair, pulling locks through the stream of hot air as though she was trying to dry them. I imagined what the cab of that truck would smell like, and then quickly drove out the thought.

She glanced around as she prepared to back out, and finally looked in my direction. She stared back at me for only half a second, and all I could read in her eyes was surprise before she tore them away and jerked the truck into reverse. And then squealed to a stop again, the back end of the truck missing a collision with Nicole Casey's compact by mere inches.

She stared into her rearview mirror, her mouth hanging open, horrified at her near miss. When the other car had pulled past her, she checked all her blind spots twice and then inched out of the parking space so cautiously that it made me grin. It was as though she thought she was *dangerous* in her decrepit truck.

The thought of Bella Swan being dangerous to anyone, no matter what she was driving, had me laughing while the girl drove past me, staring straight ahead.

3. RISK

TRULY, I WAS NOT THIRSTY, BUT I DECIDED TO HUNT again that night. A small ounce of prevention, inadequate though I knew it to be.

Carlisle came with me. We hadn't been alone together since I'd returned from Denali. As we ran through the black forest, I heard him thinking about that hasty goodbye last week.

In his memory, I saw the way my features had been twisted in fierce despair. I felt again his surprise and sudden worry.

"Edward?"

"I have to go, Carlisle. I have to go now.*"*

"What's happened?"

"Nothing. Yet. But it will if I stay."

He'd reached for my arm. I'd seen how it had hurt him when I'd cringed away from his hand.

"I don't understand."

"Have you ever...has there ever been a time...?"

I watched myself take a deep breath, saw the wild light in my eyes through the filter of his deep concern.

"Has any one person ever smelled better to you than the rest of them? Much *better?"*

"Oh."

When I'd known that he understood, my face had fallen with

shame. He'd reached out to touch me, ignoring it when I'd recoiled again, and left his hand on my shoulder.

"Do what you must to resist, Son. I will miss you. Here, take my car. The tank is full."

He was wondering now if he'd done the right thing then, sending me away. Wondering if he had hurt me with his lack of trust.

"No," I whispered as I ran. "That was what I needed. I might so easily have betrayed that trust if you'd told me to stay."

"I'm sorry you're suffering, Edward. But you should do what you can to keep the Swan child alive. Even if it means that you must leave us again."

"I know, I know."

"Why *did* you come back? You know how happy I am to have you here, but if this is too difficult..."

"I didn't like feeling a coward," I admitted.

We'd slowed—we were barely jogging through the darkness now.

"Better that than to put her in danger. She'll be gone in a year or two."

"You're right, I know that." Contrarily, his words only made me more anxious to stay. The girl would be gone in a year or two....

Carlisle stopped running and I stopped with him. He turned to examine my expression.

But you're not going to run, are you?

I hung my head.

Is it pride, Edward? There's no shame in—

"No, it isn't pride that keeps me here. Not now."

Nowhere to go?

I laughed shortly. "No. That wouldn't stop me if I could make myself leave."

"We'll come with you, of course, if that's what you need. You only have to ask. You've moved on without complaint for the rest of them. They won't begrudge you this."

I raised one eyebrow.

He laughed. "Yes, Rosalie might, but she owes you. Anyway, it's much better for us to leave now, no damage done, than for us to leave later, after a life has been ended." All humor was gone by the end.

I flinched at his words.

"Yes," I agreed. My voice sounded hoarse.

But you're not leaving?

I sighed. "I should."

"What holds you here, Edward? I'm failing to see...."

"I don't know if I can explain." Even to myself, it made no sense.

He measured my expression for a long moment.

No, I do not see. But I will respect your privacy, if you prefer.

"Thank you. It's generous of you, seeing as how I give privacy to no one." With one exception. And I was doing what I could to deprive her of that, wasn't I?

We all have our quirks. He laughed again. *Shall we?*

He'd just caught the scent of a small herd of deer. It was hard to rally much enthusiasm for what was, even under the best of circumstances, a less than mouthwatering aroma. Right now, with the memory of the girl's blood fresh in my mind, the smell actually turned my stomach.

I sighed. "Let's," I agreed, though I knew that forcing more blood down my throat would help so little.

We both shifted into a hunting crouch and let the unappealing scent pull us silently forward.

It was colder when we returned home. The melted snow had refrozen; it was as if a thin sheet of glass covered everything—each pine needle, each fern frond, each blade of grass was iced over.

While Carlisle went to dress for his early shift at the hospital, I stayed by the river, waiting for the sun to rise. I felt almost... *swollen* from the amount of blood I'd consumed, but I knew the lack of actual thirst would mean little when I sat beside the girl again.

Cool and motionless as the stone I sat on, I stared at the dark water running beside the icy bank, stared right through it.

Carlisle was right. I should leave Forks. They could spread some story to explain my absence. Boarding school in Europe. Visiting distant relatives. Teenage runaway. The story didn't matter. No one would question too intensely.

It was just a year or two, and then the girl would disappear. She would go on with her life—she would *have* a life to go on with. She'd go to college somewhere, start a career, perhaps marry someone. I could picture that—I could see the girl dressed all in white and walking at a measured pace, her arm through her father's.

It was odd, the pain that image caused me. I couldn't understand it. Was I begrudging of her future because it was something I could never have? That made no sense. Every one of the humans around me had that same potential ahead of them—a life—and I rarely stopped to envy them.

I should leave her to her future. Stop risking her life. That was the right thing to do. Carlisle always chose the right way. I should listen to him now. I would.

The sun rose behind the clouds, and the faint light glistened off all the frozen glass.

One more day, I decided. I would see her one more time. I could handle that. Perhaps I would mention my pending disappearance, set the story up.

This was going to be difficult. I could feel that in the heavy reluctance that was already making me think of excuses to stay—to extend the deadline to two days, three, four.... But I would do the right thing. I knew I could trust Carlisle's advice. And I also knew that I was too conflicted to make the right decision alone.

Much too conflicted. How much of this reluctance came from my obsessive curiosity, and how much came from my unsatisfied appetite?

I went inside to change into fresh clothes for school.

Alice was waiting for me, sitting on the top step at the edge of the third floor.

You're leaving again, she accused me.

I sighed and nodded.

I can't see where you're going this time.

"I don't know where I'm going yet," I whispered.

I want you to stay.

I shook my head.

Maybe Jazz and I could come with you?

"They'll need you all the more if I'm not here to watch out for them. And think of Esme. Would you take half her family away in one blow?"

You're going to make her so unhappy.

"I know. That's why you have to stay."

That's not the same as having you here, and you know it.

"Yes. But I have to do what's right."

There are many right ways, and many wrong ways, though, aren't there?

For a brief moment, she was swept away into one of her strange visions; I watched along with her as the indistinct images flickered and whirled. I saw myself mixed in with strange shadows that I couldn't make out—hazy, imprecise forms. And then, suddenly, my skin was glittering in the bright sunlight of a small open meadow. This was a place I knew. There was a figure in the meadow with me, but again, it was indistinct, not *there* enough to recognize. The images shivered and disappeared as a million tiny choices rearranged the future again.

"I didn't catch much of that," I told her when the vision went dark.

Me either. Your future is shifting around so much I can't keep up with any of it. I think, *though…*

She stopped, and she flipped through a vast collection of other recent visions for me. They were all the same—blurry and vague.

"I *think* something is changing," she said out loud. "Your life seems to be at a crossroads."

I laughed grimly. "You do realize that you sound like a carnival fortune-teller, right?"

She stuck out her tiny tongue at me.

"Today is all right, though, isn't it?" I asked, my voice abruptly apprehensive.

"I don't see you killing anyone today," she assured me.

"Thanks, Alice."

"Go get dressed. I won't say anything—I'll let you tell the others when you're ready."

She stood and darted back down the stairs, her shoulders hunched slightly. *Miss you. Really.*

Yes, I would really miss her, too.

It was a quiet ride to school. Jasper could feel that Alice was upset about something, but he knew that if she wanted to talk about it, she would have done so already. Emmett and Rosalie were oblivious, having another of their moments, gazing into each other's eyes with wonder—it was rather disgusting to watch from the outside. We were all quite aware how desperately in love they were. Or maybe I was just being bitter because I was the only one alone. Some days it was harder than others to live with three sets of perfectly matched lovers. This was one of them.

Maybe they would all be happier without me hanging around, ill-tempered and belligerent as the old man I should be by now.

Of course, the first thing I did when we reached the school was to look for the girl. Just preparing myself again.

Right.

It was embarrassing how my world suddenly seemed to be empty of everything but her.

It was easy enough to understand, though, really. After eighty years of the same thing every day and every night, any change became a point of absorption.

She had not yet arrived, but I could hear the thunderous chugging of her truck's engine in the distance. I leaned against the side of the car to wait. Alice stayed with me while the others went straight to class. They were already bored with my fixation—it was incomprehensible to them how any human could hold my interest for so long, no matter how appealing she smelled.

The girl drove slowly into view, her eyes intent on the road and her hands tight on the wheel. She seemed anxious about something. It took me a second to figure out what that something was, to realize that every human wore the same expression today. Ah, the road was slick with ice, and they were all trying to drive more carefully. I could see she was taking the added risk seriously.

That seemed in line with what little I had learned of her character. I added this to my small list: She was a serious person, a responsible person.

She parked not too far from me, but she hadn't noticed me standing here yet, staring at her. I wondered what she would do when she saw me? Blush and walk away? That was my first guess. But maybe she would stare back. Maybe she would come to talk to me.

I took a deep breath, filling my lungs hopefully, just in case.

She got out of the truck with care, testing the slick ground before she put her weight on it. She didn't look up, and that frustrated me. Maybe I would go talk to her....

No, that would be wrong.

Instead of turning toward the school, she made her way to the rear of her truck, clinging to the side of the truck bed in a droll way, not trusting her footing. It made me smile, and I felt Alice's eyes on my face. I didn't listen to whatever this made her think—I was having too much fun watching the girl check her snow chains. She actually looked in some danger of falling, the way her feet were sliding around. No one else was having trouble—had she parked in the worst of the ice?

She paused there, staring down with a strange expression on her face. It was...tender. As if something about the tire was making her...*emotional*?

Again, the curiosity ached like a thirst. It was as if I *had* to know what she was thinking—as if nothing else mattered.

I would go talk to her. She looked like she could use a hand anyway, at least until she was off the slick pavement. Of course, I couldn't offer her that, could I? I hesitated, torn. As averse as she seemed to be to snow, she would hardly welcome the touch of my cold white hand. I should have worn gloves—

"NO!" Alice gasped aloud.

Instantly, I scanned her thoughts, guessing at first that I had made a poor choice and she saw me doing something inexcusable. But it had nothing to do with me at all.

Tyler Crowley had chosen to take the turn into the parking lot at an injudicious speed. This choice would send him skidding across a patch of ice.

The vision came just half a second before the reality. Tyler's van rounded the corner as I was still watching what had pulled the horrified gasp from Alice's lips.

No, this vision had nothing to do with me, and yet it had *everything* to do with me, because Tyler's van—the tires right now hitting the ice at the worst possible angle—was going to spin across the lot and crush the girl who had become the uninvited focal point of my world.

Even without Alice's foresight it would have been simple enough to read the trajectory of the vehicle, flying out of Tyler's control.

The girl, standing in the exactly wrong place at the back of her truck, looked up, confused by the sound of the screeching tires. She looked straight into my horror-struck eyes, and then turned to watch her approaching death.

Not her! The words shouted in my head as if they belonged to someone else.

Still locked into Alice's thoughts, I saw the vision suddenly shift, but I had no time to see what the outcome would be.

I launched myself across the lot, throwing myself between the skidding van and the frozen girl. I moved so fast that everything was a streaky blur except for the object of my focus. She didn't see me—no human eyes could have followed my flight—still staring at the hulking shape that was about to grind her body into the metal frame of her truck.

I caught her around the waist, moving with too much urgency to be as gentle as she would need me to be. In the hundredth of a second between yanking her slight form out of the path of death and crashing to the ground with her in my arms, I was vividly aware of her fragile, breakable body.

When I heard her head thump against the ice, it felt as though I had turned to ice, too.

But I didn't even have a full second to ascertain her condition. I heard the van behind us, grating and squealing as it twisted around the sturdy iron body of the girl's truck. It was changing course, arcing, coming for her again—as though she were a magnet, pulling it toward us.

A word I'd never said before in the presence of a lady slid between my clenched teeth.

I had already done too much. As I'd nearly flown through the air to push her out of the way, I'd been fully aware of the mistake I was making. Knowing that it was a mistake did not stop me, but I was not oblivious to the risk I was taking—not just for myself, but for my entire family.

Exposure.

And *this* certainly wouldn't help, but there was no way I was going to allow the van to succeed in its second attempt to take her life.

I dropped her and threw my hands out, catching the van before it could touch the girl. The force of it hurled me back into the car parked beside her truck, and I could feel its frame buckle behind my shoulders. The van shuddered and shivered against the unyielding obstacle of my arms, and then swayed, balancing unstably on its two far tires.

If I moved my hands, the back tire of the van was going to fall onto her legs.

Oh, for the *love* of *all* that was *holy*, would the catastrophes never end? Was there anything else that could go wrong? I could hardly sit here, holding the van up, and wait for rescue. Nor could I throw the van away—there was the driver to consider, his thoughts incoherent with panic.

With an internal groan, I shoved the van so that it rocked away from us for an instant. As it fell back toward me, I caught it under the frame with my right hand while I wrapped my left arm around the girl's waist again and dragged her out from under the threatening tire, pulling her tight against my side. Her body moved limply as I swung her around so that her legs would be in the clear—was she conscious? How much damage had I done to her in my impromptu rescue attempt?

I let the van drop, now that it could not hurt her. It crashed to the pavement, all the windows shattering in unison.

I knew that I was in the middle of a crisis. How much had she seen? Had any other witnesses watched me materialize at her side and then juggle the van while I tried to keep her out from under it? These questions *should* be my biggest concern.

But I was too anxious to really care about the threat of exposure as much as I should. Too panic-stricken that I might have injured her in my effort to save her life. Too frightened to have her this close to me, knowing what I would smell if I allowed myself to inhale. Too aware of the heat of her soft body, pressed against mine—even through the double obstacle of our jackets, I could feel that heat.

The first fear was the greatest fear. As the screaming of the witnesses erupted around us, I leaned down to examine her face, to see if she was conscious—hoping fiercely that she was not bleeding anywhere.

Her eyes were open, staring in shock.

"Bella?" I asked urgently. "Are you all right?"

"I'm fine." She said the words automatically in a dazed voice.

Relief, so exquisite it was nearly pain, washed through me at the sound of her voice. I sucked in a breath through my teeth and for once did not mind the agony of the accompanying burn in my throat. In a strange way, I almost welcomed it.

She struggled to sit up, but I was not ready to release her. It felt somehow…safer? Better, at least, having her tucked into my side.

"Be careful," I warned her. "I think you hit your head pretty hard."

There had been no smell of fresh blood—a great mercy, that—but this did not rule out internal damage. I was abruptly anxious to get her to Carlisle and a full complement of radiology equipment.

"Ow," she said, her tone comically shocked as she realized I was right about her head.

"That's what I thought." Relief made it funny to me, made me almost *giddy.*

"How in the…?" Her voice trailed off, and her eyelids fluttered. "How did you get over here so fast?"

The relief turned sour, the humor vanished. She *had* noticed too much.

Now that it appeared the girl was in decent shape, the anxiety for my family became severe.

"I was standing right next to you, Bella." I knew from experience that if I was very confident as I lied, it made any questioner less sure of the truth.

She struggled to move again, and this time I allowed it. I needed to breathe so that I could play my role correctly. I needed space from her warm-blooded heat so that it would not combine with her scent to overwhelm me. I slid away from her, as far as was possible in the small space between the wrecked vehicles.

She stared up at me, and I stared back. To look away first was a mistake only an incompetent liar would make, and I was not an incompetent liar. My expression was smooth, benign. It seemed to confuse her. That was good.

The accident scene was surrounded now. Mostly students, children, peering and pushing through the cracks to see if any mangled bodies were visible. There was a babble of shouting and a gush of shocked thought. I scanned the thoughts once to make sure there were no suspicions yet, and then tuned them out and concentrated only on the girl.

She was distracted by the bedlam. She glanced around, her expression still stunned, and tried to get to her feet.

I put my hand lightly on her shoulder to hold her down.

"Just stay put for now." She *seemed* all right, but should she really be moving her neck? Again, I wished for Carlisle. My years of theoretical medical study were no match for his centuries of hands-on medical practice.

"But it's cold," she objected.

She had almost been crushed to death two distinct times, and it was the cold that worried her. A chuckle slid through my teeth before I could remember that the situation was not funny.

Bella blinked, and then her eyes focused on my face. "You were over there."

That sobered me again.

She glanced toward the south, though there was nothing to see now but the crumpled side of the van. "You were by your car."

"No, I wasn't."

"I saw you," she insisted. Her voice was childlike in her stubbornness. Her chin jutted out.

"Bella, I was standing with you, and I pulled you out of the way."

I stared deeply into her eyes, trying to will her into accepting my version—the only rational version on the table.

Her jaw set. "No."

I tried to stay calm, to not panic. If only I could keep her quiet for a few moments to give me a chance to destroy the evidence... and undermine her story by disclosing her head injury.

Shouldn't it be easy to keep this silent, secretive girl quiet? If only she would follow my lead, just for a few moments...

"Please, Bella," I said, and my voice was too intense, because I suddenly *wanted* her trust. Wanted it badly, and not just in regard to this accident. A stupid desire. What sense would it make for her to trust *me*?

"Why?" she asked, still defensive.

"Trust me," I pleaded.

"Will you promise to explain everything to me later?"

It made me angry to have to lie to her again, when I so wished that I could somehow deserve her confidence. When I answered her, it was a retort.

"Fine."

"Fine," she echoed in the same tone.

While the rescue attempt began around us—adults arriving, authorities called, sirens in the distance—I tried to ignore the girl and get my priorities in the right order. I searched through every mind in the lot, the witnesses and the latecomers both, but I could find nothing dangerous. Many were surprised to see me here beside Bella, but all assumed—as there was no other possible conclusion—that they had just not noticed me standing by the girl before the accident.

She was the only one who didn't accept the easy explanation, but she would be considered the least reliable witness. She had been frightened, traumatized, not to mention sustaining a blow to her head. Possibly in shock. It would be acceptable for her story to be confused, wouldn't it? No one would give it much credence above so many other spectators'.

I winced when I caught the thoughts of Rosalie, Jasper, and Emmett, just arriving on the scene. There would be hell to pay for this tonight.

I wanted to iron out the indentation my shoulders had made in the tan car, but the girl was too close. I'd have to wait until she was distracted.

It was frustrating to wait—so many eyes on me—as the humans struggled with the van, trying to pull it away from us. I might have helped them, just to speed the process, but I was already in enough trouble and the girl had sharp eyes. Finally, they were able to shift it far enough away for the EMTs to get to us with their stretchers.

A familiar grizzled face appraised me.

"Hey, Edward," Brett Warner said. He was also a registered nurse, and I knew him well from the hospital. It was a stroke of luck—the only luck today—that he was the first through to us. In his thoughts, he was noting that I looked alert and calm. "You okay, kid?"

"Perfect, Brett. Nothing touched me. But I'm afraid Bella here might have a concussion. She really hit her head when I yanked her out of the way."

Brett turned his attention to the girl, who shot me a fierce look of betrayal. Oh, that was right. She was the quiet martyr—she'd prefer to suffer in silence.

She did not contradict my story immediately, though, and this made me feel easier.

The next EMT tried to insist that I allow myself to be treated, but it wasn't too difficult to dissuade him. I promised I would have my father examine me, and he let it go. With most humans, speaking with cool assurance was all that was needed. Most humans, just not the girl, of course. Did she fit into *any* of the normal patterns?

As they put a neck brace on her—and her face flushed scarlet with embarrassment—I used the moment of distraction to quietly rearrange the shape of the dent in the tan car with the back of my foot. Only my siblings noticed what I was doing, and I heard Emmett's mental promise to catch anything I missed.

Grateful for his help—and more grateful that Emmett, at least, had already forgiven my dangerous choice—I was more relaxed as I climbed into the front seat of the ambulance next to Brett.

The chief of police arrived before they had gotten Bella into the back of the ambulance.

Though Bella's father's thoughts were past words, the panic and concern emanating from the man's mind drowned out just about every other thought in the vicinity. Wordless anxiety and guilt, a great swell of them, washed out of him as he saw his only daughter on the gurney.

When Alice had warned me that killing Charlie Swan's daughter would kill him, too, she had not been exaggerating.

My head bowed with that guilt as I listened to his panicked voice.

"Bella!" he shouted.

"I'm completely fine, Char—Dad." She sighed. "There's nothing wrong with me."

Her assurance barely soothed his dread. He turned at once to the closest EMT and demanded more information.

It wasn't until I heard him speaking, forming perfectly coherent sentences despite his panic, that I realized that his anxiety and concern were *not* wordless. I just...could not hear the exact words.

Hmm. Charlie Swan was not as silent as his daughter, but I could see where she got it from. Interesting.

I'd never spent much time around the town's police chief. I'd always taken him for a man of slow thought—now I realized that *I* was the one who was slow. His thoughts were partially concealed, not absent. I could only make out the tenor, the tone of them.

I wanted to listen harder, to see if I could find in this new, lesser puzzle the key to the girl's secrets. But Bella had been loaded into the back by then, and the ambulance was on its way.

It was hard to tear myself away from this possible solution to the mystery that had come to obsess me. But I had to think now—to look at what had been done today from every angle. I had to listen, to make sure that I had not put us all in so much danger that we would have to leave immediately. I had to concentrate.

There was nothing in the thoughts of the EMTs to worry me. As far as they could tell, there wasn't anything seriously wrong with the girl. And Bella was sticking to the story I'd provided, for now.

The first priority, when we reached the hospital, was to see Carlisle. I hurried through the automatic doors, but I was unable to totally forgo watching after Bella. I figuratively kept one eye on her through the paramedics' thoughts.

It was easy to find my father's familiar mind. He was in his small office, all alone—the second stroke of luck in this luckless day.

"Carlisle."

He'd heard my approach and was alarmed as soon as he saw my face. He jumped to his feet and leaned forward across the neatly organized walnut desk.

Edward—you didn't—?

"No, no, it's not that."

He took a deep breath. *Of course not. I'm sorry I entertained the thought. Your eyes, of course, I should have known.* He noted my still-golden eyes with relief.

"She's hurt, though, Carlisle, probably not seriously, but—"

"What happened?"

"A ridiculous car accident. She was in the wrong place at the wrong time. But I couldn't just stand there—let it crush her...."

Start over, I don't understand. How were you involved?

"A van skidded across the ice," I whispered. I stared at the wall behind him while I spoke. Instead of a throng of framed diplomas, he had one simple oil painting—a favorite of his, an undiscovered Hassam. "She was in the way. Alice saw it coming, but there wasn't time to do anything but really *run* across the lot and shove her out of the way. No one noticed...except for her. I had to stop the van, too, but again, nobody saw that...besides her. I'm...I'm sorry, Carlisle. I didn't mean to put us in danger."

He circled the desk and embraced me for a short moment before stepping back.

You did the right thing. And it couldn't have been easy for you. I'm proud of you, Edward.

I could look him in the eye then. "She knows there's something...wrong with me."

"That doesn't matter. If we have to leave, we leave. What has she said?"

I shook my head, a little frustrated. "Nothing yet."

Yet?

"She agreed to my version of events—but she's expecting an explanation."

He frowned, pondering this.

"She hit her head—well, I did that," I continued quickly. "I knocked her to the ground fairly hard. She seems fine, but...I don't think it will take much to discredit her account."

I felt like a cad just saying the words.

Carlisle heard the distaste in my voice. *Perhaps that won't be necessary. Let's see what happens, shall we? It sounds like I have a patient to check on.*

"Please," I said. "I'm so afraid that I hurt her."

Carlisle's expression brightened. He smoothed his fair hair—just a few shades lighter than his golden eyes—and laughed.

It's been an interesting day for you, hasn't it? In his mind, I could see the irony, and it was humorous, at least to him. Quite the reversal of roles. Somewhere during that short, thoughtless second when I'd sprinted across the icy lot, I had transformed from killer to protector.

I laughed with him, remembering how sure I'd been that Bella would never need protecting from anything more than from me. There was an edge to my laugh because, van notwithstanding, that was still entirely true.

I waited alone in Carlisle's office—one of the longest hours I had ever lived—listening to the hospital full of thoughts.

Tyler Crowley, the van's driver, looked to be hurt worse than Bella, and the attention shifted to him while she waited her turn to be x-rayed. Carlisle kept in the background, trusting the PA's diagnosis that the girl was only slightly injured. This made me anxious, but I knew he was right. One glance at his face and she would be immediately reminded of me, of the fact that there was something not right about my family, and that might set her talking.

She certainly had a willing enough partner to converse with. Tyler, consumed with guilt over the fact that he had almost killed her, couldn't seem to shut up about it. I could see her expression through his eyes, and it was clear that she wished he would stop. How did he not see that?

There was a tense moment for me when Tyler asked her how she'd gotten out of the way.

I waited, frozen, as she hesitated.

"*Um...*," he heard her say. Then she paused for so long that Tyler wondered if his question had confused her. Finally, she went on. *"Edward pulled me out of the way."*

I exhaled. And then my breathing accelerated. I'd never heard her speak my name before. I liked the way it sounded—even just hearing it through Tyler's thoughts. I wanted to hear it for myself....

"*Edward Cullen*," she said, when Tyler didn't realize whom she meant. I found myself at the door, my hand on the knob. The desire to see her was growing stronger. I had to remind myself of the need for caution.

"He was standing next to me."

"Cullen?" Huh. That's weird. "I didn't see him." I could have sworn... "Wow, it was all so fast, I guess. Is he okay?"

"I think so. He's here somewhere, but they didn't make him use a stretcher."

I saw the thoughtful look on her face, the suspicious tightening of her eyes, but these little changes in her expression were lost on Tyler.

She's pretty, he was thinking, almost in surprise. *Even all messed up. Not my usual type. Still... I should take her out. Make up for today.*

I was out in the hall then, halfway to the emergency room, without thinking for one second about what I was doing. Luckily, the nurse entered the room before I could—it was Bella's turn for X-rays. I leaned against the wall in a dark nook just around the corner and tried to get a grip on myself while she was wheeled away.

It didn't matter that Tyler thought she was pretty. Anyone

would notice that. There was no reason for me to feel . . . how *did* I feel? Annoyed? Or was *angry* closer to the truth? That made no sense at all.

I stayed where I was for as long as I could, but impatience got the best of me and I took a roundabout way to the radiology room. She'd already been moved back to the ER, but I was able to peek at her X-rays while the nurse's attention was elsewhere.

I felt calmer when I had. Her head was fine. I hadn't hurt her, not really.

Carlisle caught me there.

You look better, he commented.

I just looked straight ahead. We weren't alone, the halls full of orderlies and visitors.

Ah, yes. He stuck her X-rays to the lightboard, but I didn't need a second look. *I see. She's absolutely fine. Well done, Edward.*

The sound of my father's approval created a mixed reaction in me. I would have been pleased, except that I knew he would not approve of what I was going to do now. At least, he would not approve if he knew my real motivations.

"I think I'm going to go talk to her—before she sees you," I murmured under my breath. "Act natural, like nothing happened. Smooth it over." All acceptable reasons.

Carlisle nodded absently, still looking over the X-rays. "Good idea. Hmm."

I looked to see what had his interest.

Look at all the healed contusions! How many times did her mother drop her? Carlisle laughed to himself at his joke.

"I'm beginning to think the girl just has really bad luck. Always in the wrong place at the wrong time."

Forks is certainly the wrong place for her, with you here.

I flinched.

Go ahead. Smooth things over. I'll join you momentarily.

I walked away quickly, feeling guilty. Perhaps I was too good a liar if I could fool Carlisle.

When I got to the ER, Tyler was mumbling under his breath, still apologizing. The girl was trying to escape his remorse by pretending to sleep. Her eyes were closed, but her breathing was not even, and now and then her fingers would twitch impatiently.

I stared at her face for a long moment. This was the last time I would see her. The fact triggered an acute aching in my chest. Was it because I hated to leave any puzzle unsolved? That did not seem enough of an explanation.

Finally, I took a deep breath and moved into view.

When Tyler saw me, he started to speak, but I put one finger to my lips.

"Is she sleeping?" I murmured.

Bella's eyes snapped open and focused on my face. They widened momentarily, and then narrowed in anger or suspicion. I remembered that I had a role to play, so I smiled at her as if nothing unusual had happened this morning—besides a blow to her head and a bit of imagination run wild.

"Hey, Edward," Tyler said. "I'm really sorry—"

I raised one hand to halt his apology. "No blood, no foul," I said wryly. Without thinking, I smiled too widely at my private joke.

Tyler shivered and looked away.

It was amazingly easy to ignore Tyler, lying no more than four feet from me, his deeper wounds still oozing blood. I'd never understood how Carlisle was able to do that—ignore the blood of his patients in order to treat them. Wouldn't the constant temptation be so distracting, so dangerous? But now...I could see how, if you were focusing on something else *hard* enough, the temptation would be nothing at all.

Even fresh and exposed, Tyler's blood had nothing on Bella's.

I kept my distance from her, seating myself on the foot of Tyler's mattress.

"So, what's the verdict?" I asked her.

Her lower lip pushed out a little. "There's nothing wrong with me at all, but they won't let me go. How come you aren't strapped to a gurney like the rest of us?"

Her impatience made me smile again.

I could hear Carlisle in the hall now.

"It's all about who you know," I said lightly. "But don't worry, I came to spring you."

I watched her reaction carefully as my father entered the room. Her eyes went round and her mouth actually fell open in surprise. I groaned internally. Yes, she'd certainly noticed the resemblance.

"So, Miss Swan, how are you feeling?" Carlisle asked. He had a wonderfully soothing bedside manner that put most patients at ease within moments. I couldn't tell how it affected Bella.

"I'm fine," she said quietly.

Carlisle clipped her X-rays to the lightboard by the bed. "Your X-rays look good. Does your head hurt? Edward said you hit it pretty hard."

She sighed and said "It's fine" again, but this time impatience leaked into her voice. She glowered once in my direction.

Carlisle stepped closer to her and ran his fingers gently over her scalp until he found the bump under her hair.

I was caught off guard by the wave of emotion that crashed upon me.

I had seen Carlisle work with humans a thousand times. Years ago, I had even assisted him informally—though only in situations where blood was not involved. So it wasn't a new thing to me, to watch him interact with the girl as if he were as human as she was. I'd envied his control many times, but that was not the same as this emotion. I envied him more than his control. I ached for the difference between Carlisle and me—that he could touch her so gently, without fear, knowing he would never harm her.

She winced, and I twitched in my seat. I had to concentrate for a moment to regain my relaxed posture.

"Tender?" Carlisle asked.

Her chin jerked up a fraction. "Not really," she said.

Another small piece of her character fell into place: She was brave. She didn't like to show weakness.

Possibly the most vulnerable creature I'd ever seen, and she didn't want to seem weak. A chuckle slid through my lips.

She shot another glare at me.

"Well," Carlisle said, "your father is in the waiting room—you can go home with him now. But come back if you feel dizzy or have trouble with your eyesight at all."

Her father was here? I swept through the thoughts in the crowded waiting room, but I couldn't pick his subtle mental voice out of the group before she was speaking again, her face anxious.

"Can't I go back to school?"

"Maybe you should take it easy today," Carlisle suggested.

Her eyes flickered back to me. "Does *he* get to go to school?"

Act normal, smooth things over...ignore the way it feels when she looks me in the eye....

"Someone has to spread the good news that we survived," I said.

"Actually," Carlisle corrected, "most of the school seems to be in the waiting room."

I anticipated her reaction this time—her aversion to attention. She didn't disappoint.

"Oh no," she moaned, and put her hands over her face.

I liked that I'd finally guessed right. That I was beginning to understand her.

"Do you want to stay?" Carlisle asked.

"No, no!" she said quickly, swinging her legs over the side of the mattress and sliding down until her feet were on the floor. She stumbled forward, off-balance, into Carlisle's arms. He caught and steadied her.

Again, the envy flooded through me.

"I'm fine," she said before he could comment, faint pink in her cheeks.

Of course, that wouldn't bother Carlisle. He made sure she was balanced, and then dropped his hands.

"Take some Tylenol for the pain," he instructed.

"It doesn't hurt that bad."

Carlisle smiled as he signed her chart. "It sounds like you were extremely lucky."

She turned her face slightly, to stare at me with hard eyes. "Lucky Edward happened to be standing next to me."

"Oh, well, yes," Carlisle agreed quickly, hearing the same thing in her voice that I heard. She hadn't written her suspicions off as imagination. Not yet.

All yours, Carlisle thought. *Handle it as you think best*.

"Thanks so much," I whispered, quick and quiet. Neither human heard me. Carlisle's lips turned up a tiny bit at my sarcasm as he turned to Tyler. "I'm afraid that *you'll* have to stay with us just a little bit longer," he said as he began examining the superficial lacerations left by the shattered windshield.

Well, I'd made the mess, so it was only fair that I had to deal with it.

Bella walked deliberately toward me, not stopping until she was uncomfortably close. I remembered how I had hoped, before all the chaos, that she would approach me. This was like a mockery of that wish.

"Can I talk to you for a minute?" she hissed at me.

Her warm breath swept across my face and I had to stagger back a step. Her appeal had not abated one bit. Every time she was near me, it triggered all my worst, most urgent instincts. Venom flowed in my mouth, and my body yearned to strike—to wrench her into my arms and crush her throat to my teeth.

My mind was stronger than my body, but only just.

"Your father is waiting for you," I reminded her, my jaw clenched tight.

She glanced toward Carlisle and Tyler. Tyler was paying us no attention at all, but Carlisle was monitoring my every breath.

Carefully, Edward.

"I'd like to speak to you alone, if you don't mind," she insisted in a low voice.

I wanted to tell her that I did mind very much, but I knew I would have to do this eventually. I might as well get on with it.

I was full of so many conflicting emotions as I stalked out of the room, listening to her stumbling footsteps behind me, trying to keep up.

I had a show to put on now. I knew the role I would play—I had the character down: I would be the villain. I would lie and ridicule and be cruel.

It went against all my better impulses—the human impulses that I'd clung to through so many years. I'd never wanted to deserve trust more than in this moment, when I had to destroy all possibility of it.

It made it worse to know that this would be the last memory she would have of me. This was my farewell scene.

I turned on her.

"What do you want?" I asked coldly.

She cringed back slightly from my hostility. Her eyes turned bewildered, her face shifting into the very expression that had haunted me.

"You owe me an explanation," she said in a small voice. What little color she had drained from her ivory skin.

It was very hard to keep my voice harsh. "I saved your life—I don't owe you anything."

She flinched—it stung like acid to watch my words hurt her.

"You promised," she whispered.

"Bella, you hit your head, you don't know what you're talking about."

Her chin came up then. "There's nothing wrong with my head."

She was angry now, and that made it easier for me. I met her glare, arranging my face so it was colder, harder.

"What do you want from me, Bella?"

"I want to know the truth. I want to know why I'm lying for you."

What she wanted was only fair—it frustrated me to have to deny her.

"What do you *think* happened?" I nearly growled.

Her words poured out in a torrent. "All I know is that you weren't anywhere near me—Tyler didn't see you, either, so don't tell me I hit my head too hard. That van was going to crush us both—and it didn't, and your hands left dents in the side of it—and you left a dent in the other car, and you're not hurt at all—and the van should have smashed my legs, but you were holding it up. . . ." Suddenly, she clenched her teeth together and her eyes were glistening with unshed tears.

I stared at her, my expression thoroughly derisive, though what I really felt was awe; she had seen everything.

"You think I lifted a van off you?" I asked, elevating the level of sarcasm in my tone.

She answered with one stiff nod.

My voice grew more mocking. "Nobody will believe that, you know."

She made an effort to control her emotions—her anger, it looked like. When she answered me, she spoke each word with slow deliberation. "I'm not going to tell anybody."

She meant it—I could see that in her eyes. Even furious and betrayed, she would keep my secret.

Why?

The shock of it ruined my carefully designed expression for half a second, and then I pulled myself together.

"Then why does it matter?" I asked, working to keep my voice severe.

"It matters to me," she said intensely. "I don't like to lie—so there'd better be a good reason why I'm doing it."

She was asking me to trust her. Just as I wanted her to trust me. But this was a line I could not cross.

My voice stayed callous. "Can't you just thank me and get it over with?"

"Thank you," she said, and then she fumed in silence, waiting.

"You're not going to let it go, are you?"

"No."

"In that case..." I couldn't tell her the truth if I wanted to... and I *didn't* want to. I'd rather she made up her own story than know what I was, because nothing could be worse than the truth—I was an undead nightmare, straight from the pages of a horror novel. "I hope you enjoy disappointment."

We scowled at each other.

She flushed pink and ground her teeth again. "Why did you even bother?"

Her question wasn't one that I was expecting or prepared to answer. I lost my hold on the role I was playing. I felt the mask slip from my face, and I told her—this one time—the truth.

"I don't know."

I memorized her face one last time—it was still set in lines of anger, the blood not yet faded from her cheeks—and then I turned and walked away from her.

4. VISIONS

I WENT BACK TO SCHOOL. THIS WAS THE RIGHT THING TO do, the most inconspicuous way to behave.

By the end of the day, almost all the other students had returned to class, too. Just Tyler and Bella and a few others—who were probably using the accident as a chance to ditch—remained absent.

It shouldn't have been so hard for me to do the right thing. But all afternoon, I was gritting my teeth against the urge that had me yearning to ditch, too—in order to go find the girl again.

Like a stalker. An obsessed stalker. An obsessed vampire stalker.

School today was—somehow, impossibly—even more boring than it had seemed just a week ago. Coma-like. It was as if the color had drained from the bricks, the trees, the sky, the faces around me.... I stared at the cracks in the walls.

There was another right thing I should be doing... that I was not. Of course, it was also a wrong thing. It all depended on one's perspective.

From the perspective of a Cullen—not just a vampire, but a *Cullen*, someone who belonged to a family, such a rare state in our world—the right thing would have gone something like this:

"I'm surprised to see you in class, Edward. I heard you were involved in that awful accident this morning."

"Yes, I was, Mr. Banner, but I was the lucky one." A friendly smile. "I didn't get hurt at all. I wish I could say the same for Tyler and Bella."

"How are they?"

"I think Tyler is fine... just some superficial scrapes from the windshield glass. I'm not sure about Bella, though." A worried frown. "She might have a concussion. I heard she was pretty incoherent for a while—seeing things, even. I know the doctors were worried...."

That's how it should have gone. That's what I owed my family.

"I'm surprised to see you in class, Edward. I heard you were involved in that awful accident this morning."

No smile. "I wasn't hurt."

Mr. Banner shifted his weight from foot to foot, uncomfortable.

"Do you have any idea how Tyler Crowley and Bella Swan are? I heard there were some injuries...."

I shrugged. "I wouldn't know."

Mr. Banner cleared his throat. "Er, right...," he said, my cold stare making his voice sound a bit strained.

He walked quickly back to the front of the classroom and began his lecture.

It was the wrong thing to do. Unless you looked at it from a more obscure point of view.

It just seemed so... so *unchivalrous* to slander the girl behind her back, especially when she was proving more trustworthy than I could have dreamed. She hadn't said anything to betray me, despite having good reason to do so. Would I betray her when she had done nothing but keep my secret?

I had a nearly identical conversation with Mrs. Goff—just in Spanish rather than in English—and Emmett gave me a long look.

I hope you have a good explanation for what happened today. Rose is on the warpath.

I rolled my eyes without looking at him.

I actually had come up with a perfectly sound explanation. Just suppose I *hadn't* done anything to stop the van from crushing the girl. I recoiled from that thought. But if she *had* been hit, if she'd been mangled and bleeding, the red fluid spilling, wasting on the blacktop, the scent of the fresh blood pulsing through the air…

I shuddered again, but not just in horror. Part of me shivered in desire. No, I would not have been able to watch her bleed without exposing us all in a much more flagrant and shocking way.

It was a perfectly sound excuse…but I wouldn't use it. It was too shameful.

And I hadn't thought of it until long after the fact, regardless.

Look out for Jasper, Emmett went on, oblivious to my reverie. *He's not as angry…but he's more resolved.*

I saw what he meant, and for a moment the room swam around me. The flash of rage was so all-consuming that a red haze clouded my vision. I thought I would choke on it.

EDWARD! GET A GRIP! Emmett shouted at me in his head. His hand came down on my shoulder, holding me in my seat before I could jump to my feet. He rarely used his full strength—there was almost never a need, for he was so much stronger than any vampire we'd ever encountered—but he used it now. He gripped my arm, rather than pushing me down. If he'd been pushing, the chair under me would have collapsed.

EASY! he ordered.

I tried to calm myself, but it was hard. The rage burned in my head.

Jasper's not going to do anything until we all talk. I just thought you should know the direction he's headed.

I concentrated on relaxing and felt Emmett's hand loosen.

Try not to make more *of a spectacle of yourself. You're in enough trouble as it is.*

I took a deep breath and Emmett released me.

I searched around the room routinely, but our confrontation had been so short and silent that only a few people sitting behind Emmett had even noticed. None of them knew what to make of it, and they shrugged it off. The Cullens were freaks—everyone knew that already.

Damn, kid, you're a mess, Emmett added, sympathy in his tone.

"Bite me," I muttered under my breath, and I heard his low chuckle.

Emmett didn't hold grudges, and I probably ought to have been more grateful for his easygoing acceptance. But I could see that Jasper's intentions made sense to him, that he was considering how it might be the best course of action.

The rage simmered, barely under control. Yes, Emmett was stronger than I was, but he'd yet to beat me in a wrestling match. He claimed that this was because I cheated, but hearing thoughts was just as much a part of who I was as his immense strength was a part of him. We were evenly matched in a fight.

A fight? Was that where this was headed? Was I going to fight with my *family* over a human I barely knew?

I thought about that for a moment, thought about the fragile feel of the girl's body in my arms in juxtaposition with Jasper, Rose, and Emmett—supernaturally strong and fast, killing machines by nature.

Yes, I would fight for her. Against my family. I shuddered.

But it wasn't fair to leave her undefended when I was the one who'd put her in danger!

I couldn't win alone, though, not against the three of them, and I wondered who my allies would be.

Carlisle, certainly. He would not fight anyone, but he would be wholly against Rose's and Jasper's designs. That might be all I needed.

Esme, doubtful. She would not side *against* me, either, and she would hate to disagree with Carlisle, but she would be for any plan that kept her family intact. Her first priority would not be what was right, but *me*. If Carlisle was the soul of our family, then Esme was the heart. He gave us a leader who deserved following; she made that following into an act of love. We all loved each other—even under the fury I felt toward Jasper and Rose right now, even planning to fight them to save the girl, I knew that I loved them.

Alice...I had no idea. It would probably depend on what she saw coming. She would side with the winner, I imagined.

So I would have to do this without help. I wasn't a match for them alone, but I wasn't going to let the girl be hurt because of me. That might mean evasive action.

My rage dulled a bit with the sudden black humor. I tried to imagine how the girl would react to my kidnapping her. Of course, I rarely guessed her reactions right—but what other response could she have besides terror?

I wasn't sure how to manage that, though—kidnapping her. I wouldn't be able to stand being close to her for very long. Perhaps I would just deliver her back to her mother. Even that much would be fraught with danger. For her.

And also for me, I realized suddenly. If I were to kill her by accident...I wasn't certain exactly how much pain that would cause me, but I knew it would be multifaceted and intense.

The time passed quickly while I mulled over all the complications ahead of me: the argument waiting for me at home, the conflict with my family, the lengths I might be forced to go to afterward.

Well, I couldn't complain that life *outside* this school was monotonous. The girl had changed that much.

Emmett and I walked silently to the car when the bell rang. He was worrying about me and worrying about Rosalie. He knew he would have no choice when it came time to pick sides, and it bothered him.

The others were waiting for us in the car, also silent. We were a very quiet group. Only I could hear the shouting.

Idiot! Lunatic! Moron! Jackass! Selfish, irresponsible fool! Rosalie kept up a constant stream of insults at the top of her mental lungs. It made it hard to hear the others, but I ignored her as best I could.

Emmett was right about Jasper. He was sure of his course.

Alice was troubled, worrying about Jasper, flipping through images of the future. No matter which direction Jasper came at the girl, Alice always saw me there, blocking him. Interesting... neither Rosalie nor Emmett was with him in these visions. So Jasper planned to work alone. That would even things up.

Jasper was the best, certainly the most experienced fighter among us. My one advantage lay in that I could hear his moves before he made them.

I had never fought more than playfully with my brothers—just horsing around. I felt sick at the thought of really trying to hurt Jasper.

No, not that. Just to block him. That was all.

I concentrated on Alice, memorizing Jasper's different avenues of attack.

As I did that, her visions shifted, moving farther and farther away from the Swans' house. I was cutting him off earlier.

Stop that, Edward! she snapped. *It can't happen this way. I won't let it.*

I didn't answer her, I just kept watching.

She began searching further ahead, into the misty, unsure realm of distant possibilities. Everything was shadowy and vague.

The entire way home, the charged silence did not lift. I parked in the big garage off the house. Carlisle's Mercedes was there, next to Emmett's big Jeep, Rose's M3, and my Vanquish. I was glad Carlisle was already home—this silence could end explosively, and I wanted him there when that happened.

We went straight to the dining room.

The room was, of course, never used for its intended purpose. But it was furnished with a long, oval mahogany table surrounded by chairs—we were scrupulous about having all the correct props in place. Carlisle liked to use it as a conference room. In a group with such strong and disparate personalities, sometimes it was necessary to discuss things in a calm, seated manner.

I had a feeling that the setting was not going to help much today.

Carlisle sat in his usual spot at the eastern head of the room. Esme was beside him—they held hands on top of the table.

Esme's eyes were on me, their golden depths full of concern.

Stay. It was her only thought. She had no idea of what was about to start; she was just worried about me.

I wished I could smile at the woman who was truly a mother to me, but I had no reassurances for her now.

I sat on Carlisle's other side.

Carlisle had a better sense of what was coming. His lips were pressed tightly together and his forehead was creased. The expression looked too old for his young face.

As everyone else sat, I could see the lines being drawn.

Rosalie sat directly across from Carlisle, at the other end of the long table. She glared at me, never looking away.

Emmett sat beside her, his face and thoughts both wry.

Jasper hesitated, and then went to stand against the wall behind Rosalie. He was decided, regardless of the outcome of this discussion. My teeth locked together.

Alice was the last to come in, and her eyes were focused on something far away—the future, still too indistinct for her to make use of it. Without seeming to think about it, she sat next to Esme. She rubbed her forehead as if she had a headache. Jasper twitched uneasily and considered joining her, but he kept his place.

I took a deep breath. I had started this—I should speak first.

"I'm sorry," I said, looking first at Rose, then Jasper, and then Emmett. "I didn't mean to put any of you at risk. It was thoughtless, and I take full responsibility for my hasty action."

Rosalie glared at me balefully. "What do you mean, 'take full responsibility'? Are you going to fix it?"

"Not the way you mean," I said, working to keep my voice even and quiet. "I was already planning to leave before this happened. I'll go now . . ." *If I believe that the girl will be safe*, I amended in my head. *If I believe that none of you will touch her.* "The situation will resolve itself."

"No," Esme murmured. "No, Edward."

I patted her hand. "It's just a few years."

"Esme's right, though," Emmett said. "You can't go anywhere. That would be the *opposite* of helpful. We have to know what people are thinking, now more than ever."

"Alice will catch anything major," I disagreed.

Carlisle shook his head. "I think Emmett is right, Edward. The girl will be more likely to talk if you disappear. It's all of us leave, or none of us."

"She won't say anything," I insisted quickly. Rose was building up to the explosion, and I wanted this fact out there first.

"You don't know her mind," Carlisle reminded me.

"I know this much. Alice, back me up."

Alice stared up at me wearily. "I can't see what will happen if we just ignore this." She glanced at Rose and Jasper.

No, she couldn't see that future—not when Rosalie and Jasper were so decided against ignoring the incident.

Rosalie's palm smacked down on the table with a loud bang. "We can't allow the human a chance to say anything. Carlisle, you *must* see that. Even if we decided to all disappear, it's not safe to leave stories behind us. We live so differently from the rest of our kind—you know there are those who would love an excuse to point fingers. We have to be more careful than anyone else!"

"We've left rumors behind us before," I reminded her.

"Just rumors and suspicions, Edward. Not eyewitnesses and evidence!"

"Evidence!" I scoffed.

But Jasper was nodding, his eyes hard.

"Rose—" Carlisle began.

"Let me finish, Carlisle. It doesn't have to be any big production. The girl hit her head today. So maybe that injury turns out to be more serious than it looked." Rosalie shrugged. "Every mortal goes to sleep with the chance of never waking up. The others would expect us to clean up after ourselves. Technically, that would make it Edward's job, but this is obviously beyond him. You know I'm capable of control. I would leave no evidence behind me."

"Yes, Rosalie, we all know how proficient an assassin you are," I snarled.

She hissed at me, momentarily beyond words. If only that could last.

"Edward, please," Carlisle said. Then he turned to Rosalie. "Rosalie, I looked the other way in Rochester because I felt that you were owed your justice. The men you killed had wronged you monstrously. This is not the same situation. The Swan girl is entirely innocent."

"It's not personal, Carlisle," Rosalie said through her teeth. "It's to protect us all."

There was a brief moment of silence while Carlisle thought through his answer. When he nodded, Rosalie's eyes lit up. She should have known better. Even if I hadn't been able to read his thoughts, I could have anticipated his next words. Carlisle never compromised.

"I know you mean well, Rosalie, but...I'd like very much for our family to be *worth* protecting. The occasional...accident or lapse in control is a regrettable part of what we are." It was very like him to include himself in the plural, though he had never had such a lapse himself. "To murder a blameless child in cold blood is another thing entirely. I believe the risk she presents, whether she speaks her suspicions or not, is nothing to the greater risk. If we make exceptions to protect ourselves, we risk something much more important. We risk losing the essence of who we are."

I controlled my expression very carefully. It wouldn't do at all to grin. Or to applaud, as I wished I could.

Rosalie scowled. "It's just being responsible."

"It's being callous," Carlisle corrected gently. "Every life is precious."

Rosalie sighed heavily and her lower lip pouted out. Emmett patted her shoulder. "It'll be fine, Rose," he encouraged in a low voice.

"The question," Carlisle continued, "is whether we should move on."

"No," Rosalie moaned. "We just got settled. I don't want to start on my sophomore year in high school again!"

"You could keep your present age, of course," Carlisle said.

"And have to move again that much sooner?" she countered.

Carlisle shrugged.

"I *like* it here! There's so little sun, we get to be almost *normal*."

"Well, we certainly don't have to decide now. We can wait and see if it becomes necessary. Edward seems certain of the Swan girl's silence."

Rosalie snorted.

But I was no longer worried about Rose. I could see that she would go along with Carlisle's decision, no matter how infuriated she was with me. Their conversation had moved on to unimportant details.

Jasper remained unmoved.

I understood why. Before he and Alice had met, he'd lived in a combat zone, a relentless theater of war. He knew the consequences of flouting the rules—he'd seen the grisly aftermath with his own eyes.

It said much that he had not tried to calm Rosalie down with his extra faculties, nor did he now try to rile her up. He was holding himself aloof from this discussion—above it.

"Jasper," I said.

He met my gaze, his face expressionless.

"She won't pay for my mistake. I won't allow that."

"She benefits from it, then? She should have died today, Edward. I would only set that right."

I repeated myself, emphasizing each word. *"I will not allow it."*

His eyebrows shot up. He wasn't expecting this—he hadn't imagined that I would act to stop him.

He shook his head once. "And I will not let Alice live in danger, even a slight danger. You don't feel about anyone the way I feel about her, Edward, and you haven't lived through what I've lived through, whether you've seen my memories or not. You don't understand."

"I'm not disputing that, Jasper. But I'm telling you now, I won't allow you to hurt Isabella Swan."

We stared at each other—not glaring, but measuring the opposition. I felt him sample the mood around me, testing my determination.

"Jazz," Alice said, interrupting us.

He held my gaze for a moment more, and then looked at her. "Don't bother telling me you can protect yourself, Alice. I already know that. It doesn't change—"

"That's not what I'm going say," Alice interrupted. "I was going to ask you for a favor."

I saw what was on her mind, and my mouth fell open with an audible gasp. I stared at her, shocked, only vaguely aware that everyone besides Alice and Jasper was now eyeing me warily.

"I know you love me. Thanks. But I would really appreciate it if you didn't try to kill Bella. First of all, Edward's quite serious and I don't want you two fighting. Secondly, she's my friend. At least, she's *going* to be."

It was clear as glass in her head: Alice, smiling, with her icy white arm around the girl's warm, fragile shoulders. And Bella was smiling, too, her arm around Alice's waist.

The vision was rock solid; only the timing of it was unsure.

"But... Alice...," Jasper gasped. I couldn't manage to turn my head to see his expression. I couldn't tear myself away from the image in Alice's vision in order to hear his thoughts.

"I'm going to love her someday, Jazz. I'll be very put out with you if you don't let her be."

I was still locked into Alice's thoughts. I saw the future shimmer as Jasper's resolve floundered in the face of her unexpected request.

"Ah," she sighed—his indecision had cleared a new future. "See? Bella's not going to say anything. There's nothing to worry about."

The way she said the girl's name... like they were already close confidants.

"Alice," I choked. "What... does this...?"

"I told you there was a change coming. I don't know, Edward." But she locked her jaw, and I could see that there was more. She was trying not to think about it. She was focusing very hard on Jasper suddenly, though he was too stunned to have progressed much in his decision-making.

She did this sometimes when she was trying to keep something from me.

"What, Alice? What are you hiding?"

I heard Emmett grumble. He always got frustrated when Alice and I had these kinds of conversations.

She shook her head, trying not to let me in.

"Is it about the girl?" I demanded. "Is it about Bella?"

She had her teeth gritted in concentration, but when I spoke Bella's name, she slipped. Her slip only lasted the tiniest portion of a second, but that was long enough.

"NO!" I shouted. I heard my chair hit the floor, and only then realized I was on my feet.

"Edward!" Carlisle was on his feet, too, gripping my shoulder. I was barely aware of him.

"It's solidifying," Alice whispered. "Every minute you're more decided. There are really only two ways left for her. It's one or the other, Edward."

I could see what she saw... but I could not accept it.

"No," I said again. There was no volume to my denial. My legs felt hollow, and I had to brace myself against the table. Carlisle's hand fell away.

"That is *so* annoying," Emmett complained.

"I have to leave," I whispered to Alice, ignoring him.

"Edward, we've already been over that," Emmett said loudly. "That's the best way to start the girl talking. Besides, if you take off, we won't know for sure if she's talking or not. You have to stay and deal with this."

"I don't see you going anywhere, Edward," Alice told me. "I don't know if you *can* leave anymore." *Think about it*, she added silently. *Think about leaving.*

I understood what she meant. Yes, the idea of never seeing the girl again was...painful. I'd already felt that in the hospital hallway where I'd given her such a harsh farewell. But now leaving was even more necessary. I couldn't sanction either future I'd apparently condemned her to.

I'm not entirely sure of Jasper, Edward, Alice went on. *If you leave, if he thinks she's a danger to us...*

"I don't hear that," I contradicted her, still only halfway aware of our audience. Jasper was wavering. He would not do something that would hurt Alice.

Not right this moment. Will you risk her life, leave her undefended?

"Why are you doing this to me?" I groaned. My head fell into my hands.

I was not Bella's protector. I could not be that. Wasn't Alice's divided future enough proof of that?

I love her, too. Or I will. It's not the same, but I want her around for that.

"Love her, *too*?" I whispered, incredulous.

She sighed. *You are* so *blind, Edward. Can't you see where you're headed? Can't you see where you already are? It's more inevitable than the sun rising tomorrow morning. See what I see....*

I shook my head, horrified. "No." I tried to shut out the visions she revealed to me. "I don't have to follow that course. I'll leave. I *will* change the future."

"You can try," she said, her voice skeptical.

"Oh, *come on*!" Emmett bellowed.

"Pay attention," Rose hissed at him. "Alice sees him falling for a *human*! How classically Edward!" She made a gagging sound.

I scarcely heard her.

"What?" Emmett said, startled. Then his booming laugh echoed through the room. "Is that what's been going on?" He laughed again. "Tough break, Edward."

I felt his hand touch my arm, but I shook it off absently. I couldn't pay attention to him.

"*Fall* for a human?" Esme repeated in a stunned voice. "For the girl he saved today? Fall in *love* with her?"

"What do you see, Alice? Exactly," Jasper demanded.

She turned toward him. I continued to stare numbly at the side of her face.

"It all depends on whether he is strong enough. Either he'll kill her himself"—she turned to meet my gaze again, glaring—"which would *really* irritate me, Edward, not to mention what it would do to *you*—" She faced Jasper again. "Or she'll be one of us someday."

Someone gasped; I didn't look to see who.

"That's not going to happen!" I was shouting again. "Either one!"

Alice spoke as if she hadn't heard me. "It all depends," she repeated. "He may be *just* strong enough not to kill her—but it will be close. It will take an amazing amount of control," she mused. "More, even, than Carlisle has. The only thing he's not strong enough to do is stay away from her. That's a lost cause."

I couldn't find my voice. No one else seemed to be able to, either. The room was still.

I stared at Alice, and everyone else stared at me. I could see my own horrified expression from five different viewpoints.

After a long moment, Carlisle sighed. "Well, this... complicates things."

"I'll say," Emmett agreed. His voice was still close to laughter. Trust Emmett to find the joke in the destruction of my life.

"I suppose the plans remain the same, though," Carlisle said thoughtfully. "We'll stay, and watch. Obviously, no one will... hurt the girl."

I stiffened.

"No," Jasper said quietly. "I can agree to that. If Alice sees only two ways—"

"No!" My voice was not a shout or a growl or a cry of despair, but some combination of the three. "No!"

I had to leave, to be away from the noise of their thoughts—Rosalie's self-righteous disgust, Emmett's humor, Carlisle's never-ending patience....

Worse: Alice's confidence. Jasper's confidence in that confidence.

Worst of all: Esme's... *joy*.

I stalked out of the room. Esme reached for my hand as I passed, but I didn't acknowledge the gesture.

I was running before I was out of the house. I cleared the lawn and river in one bound and raced into the forest. The rain was back again, falling so heavily that I was drenched in a few seconds. I liked the thick sheet of water—it made a wall between me and the rest of the world. It closed me in, let me be alone.

I ran due east, over and through the mountains without breaking my straight course, until I could see a hazy hint of Seattle lights on the other side of the sound. I stopped before I touched the borders of human civilization.

Shut in by the rain, all alone, I finally made myself look at what I had done—at the way I had mutilated the future.

First, the vision of Alice and the girl with their arms around each other, walking together in the forest near the high school—the trust and friendship was so obvious it sang out from the image. Bella's wide chocolate eyes were not confused in this vision, but still full of secrets—in this moment, they seemed to be happy secrets. She did not flinch away from Alice's cold arm.

What did it mean? How much did she know? In that still-life moment from the future, what did she think of *me*?

Then the other image, so much the same, yet now colored by horror. Alice and Bella on the front porch of my house, their arms still wrapped around each other in trusting friendship. But now there was no difference between those arms—both were white, smooth as marble, hard as steel. Bella's eyes were no longer the color of chocolate. The irises were a shocking, vivid crimson. The secrets in them were unfathomable—acceptance or desolation? It was impossible to tell. Her face was cold and immortal.

I shuddered. I could not suppress the questions, similar, but different: What did it mean—how had this come about? And what did she think of me now?

I could answer that last one. If I forced her into this empty half life through my weakness and selfishness, surely she would hate me.

But there was one even more horrifying image—worse than any I'd ever held inside my head.

My own eyes, deep crimson with human blood, the eyes of the monster. Bella's broken body in my arms, ashy white, drained, lifeless. It was so concrete, so clear.

I couldn't stand to see this. Could not bear it. I tried to banish it from my mind, tried to see something, anything else. Tried to see again the expression on her living face that had obstructed my view for the last chapter of my existence. All to no avail.

Alice's bleak vision filled my head, and I writhed internally with the agony it caused. Meanwhile, the monster in me was overflowing with glee, jubilant at the likelihood of his success. It sickened me.

This could not be allowed. There had to be a way to circumvent the future. I would not let Alice's visions direct me. I could choose a different path. There was always a choice.

There had to be.

5. INVITATIONS

HIGH SCHOOL. PURGATORY NO LONGER, IT WAS NOW PURELY hell. Torment and fire... yes, I had both.

I was doing everything correctly now. Every *i* dotted, every *t* crossed. No one could complain that I was shirking my responsibilities.

To please Esme and protect the others, I stayed in Forks. I returned to my old schedule. I hunted no more than the rest of them. Every day, I attended high school and played human. Every day, I listened carefully for anything new about the Cullens—there was never anything new. The girl did not speak one word of her suspicions. She just repeated the same story—I'd been standing with her and then pulled her out of the way—till her eager listeners got bored and stopped looking for more details. There was no danger. My hasty action had hurt no one.

No one but myself.

I was determined to change the future. Not the easiest task to set for oneself, but there was no other choice I could live with.

Alice said that I would not be strong enough to stay away from the girl. I would prove her wrong.

I'd thought the first day would be the hardest. By the end of it, I'd been *sure* that was the case. I'd been wrong, though.

It had rankled, knowing that I would hurt the girl. I'd

comforted myself with the fact that her pain would be nothing more than a pinprick—just a tiny sting of rejection—compared to mine. Bella was human, and she knew that I was something else, something wrong, something frightening. She would probably be more relieved than wounded when I turned my face away from her and pretended that she didn't exist.

"Hello, Edward," she'd greeted me that first day back in Biology. Her voice had been pleasant, friendly, one hundred eighty degrees from the last time I'd spoken with her.

Why? What did the change mean? Had she forgotten? Decided she had imagined the whole episode? Could she possibly have forgiven me for not following through on my promise?

The questions had stabbed and twisted like the thirst that attacked me every time I breathed.

Just one moment to look in her eyes. Just to see if I could read the answers there....

No. I could not allow myself even that. Not if I was going to change the future.

I'd moved my chin an inch in her direction without looking away from the front of the room. I'd nodded once, then turned my face straight forward.

She did not speak to me again.

That afternoon, as soon as school was finished, my role played, I ran halfway to Seattle, as I had the day before. It seemed that I could handle the aching just slightly better when I was flying over the ground, turning everything around me into a green blur.

This run became my daily habit.

Did I love her? I did not think so. Not yet. Alice's glimpses of that future had stayed with me, though, and I could see how easy it would be to fall into loving Bella. It would be exactly like falling: effortless. Not letting myself love her was the opposite of falling—it was pulling myself up a cliff face, hand over hand, the task as grueling as if I had no more than mortal strength.

More than a month passed, and every day it got harder. That made no sense to me—I kept waiting to get over it, to have the struggle become easier or at least level off. This must be what Alice had meant when she'd predicted that I would not be able to stay away from the girl. She had seen the escalation of the pain.

But I could handle pain.

I would not destroy Bella's future. If I was destined to love her, then wasn't avoiding her the very least I could do?

Avoiding her was about the limit of what I could bear, though. I could pretend to ignore her and never look her way. I could pretend that she was of no interest to me. But I still hung on every breath she took, every word she spoke.

I couldn't watch her with my eyes, so I watched her through the eyes of others. The vast majority of my thoughts revolved around her as though she was the center of my mind's gravity.

As this hell ground on, I lumped my torments into four categories.

The first two were familiar. Her scent and her silence. Or rather—to take the responsibility on myself, where it belonged—my thirst and my curiosity.

The thirst was the most primal of my torments. It was my habit now to simply not breathe at all in Biology. Of course, there were always the exceptions—when I had to answer a question, and I would need my breath to speak. Each time I tasted the air around the girl, it was the same as the first day—fire and need and brutal violence desperate to break free. It was hard to cling even slightly to reason or restraint in those moments. And, just like that first day, the monster in me would roar, so close to the surface.

The curiosity was the most constant of my torments. The question was never out of my mind: *What is she thinking* now? When I heard her quiet sigh. When she twisted a lock of hair absently around her finger. When she threw her books down with more force than usual. When she rushed into class late. When she tapped her foot impatiently against the floor. Each movement caught in my peripheral vision was a maddening mystery. When she spoke to the other human students, I analyzed her every word and tone. Was she speaking her thoughts, or what she thought she should say? It often sounded to me as though she was trying to say what her audience expected, and this reminded me of my family and our daily life of illusion—we were better at it than she was. But why would she have to play a role? She was one of them—a human teenager.

Only...she occasionally didn't behave like one. For example, when Mr. Banner assigned a group project in Biology. It was his practice to let the students choose their partners. As always happened with group projects, the bravest of the ambitious students—Beth Daws and Nicholas Laghari—quickly asked if I would join them. I shrugged my acceptance. They knew I would complete my portion perfectly, and theirs, too, if they left it undone.

It was unsurprising that Mike allied himself with Bella. What was unexpected was Bella's insistence on the third member of their group, Tara Galvaz.

Mr. Banner usually had to assign Tara to a group. She looked more surprised than pleased when Bella tapped her on the shoulder and awkwardly asked if she wanted to work with her and Mike.

"Whatever," Tara responded.

When she was back at her seat, Mike hissed at her, "She's a total stoner. She won't do any work. I think she's failing Biology."

Bella shook her head and whispered back, "Don't worry about it. I'll catch whatever she misses."

Mike wasn't appeased. "Why did you *do* that?"

It was the same question I was dying to ask her, though not in the same tone.

Tara was, in fact, failing Biology. Mr. Banner was thinking about her now, both surprised and touched by Bella's choice.

No one ever gives that kid a chance. Nice of Bella—she's kinder than most of these cannibals.

Had Bella noticed how Tara was usually ostracized by the rest of the class? I could imagine no reason besides kindness for reaching out to her, especially with Bella's shyness in the way. I wondered how much discomfort it had caused her and decided it was probably more than any other human here would have been willing to go through for a stranger.

Given Bella's grasp of Biology, I wondered if the grade from this project would even save Tara from failure, in this class at least. And that was exactly what happened.

Then there was the time at lunch when Jessica and Lauren were talking about the number-one dream destinations on their bucket lists. Jessica chose Jamaica, only to feel immediately one-upped when Lauren countered with the French Riviera. Tyler chimed in with Amsterdam, thinking of the famous red-light district, and the others began sounding off. I waited anxiously for Bella's answer to the question, but before Mike (who liked the idea of Rio) could ask for her take, Eric enthusiastically named Comic Con, and the table erupted in laughter.

"What a dork," Lauren hissed.

Jessica snickered. "I know, right?"

Tyler rolled his eyes.

"You're never going to get a girlfriend," Mike told Eric.

Bella's voice, louder than her usual timid volume, cut into the melee.

"No, that's cool," Bella insisted. "That's where I'd want to go, too."

Mike was immediately backpedaling. "I mean, I guess some of the costumes are cool. Slave Leia." *Should have kept my mouth shut.*

Jessica and Lauren exchanged a glance, frowning.

Ugh, please, Lauren thought.

"We should totally go," Eric enthused at Bella. "I mean, after we save up enough." *Comic Con with Bella! Even better than Comic Con alone…*

Bella was thrown for a second, but after a quick glance at Lauren's expression, she doubled down. "Yeah, I wish. It's probably way too expensive though, right?"

Eric started breaking down ticket prices and hotels versus sleeping in a car. Jessica and Lauren returned to their earlier conversation while Mike listened unhappily to Eric and Bella.

"Do you think it's a two-day drive or three?" Eric was asking.

"No idea," Bella said.

"Well, how long a drive is it from here to Phoenix?"

"You can do it in two days," she said with confidence. "If you're willing to drive fifteen hours a day."

"San Diego should be a little closer than that, right?"

I seemed to be the only one who noticed the light bulb going on over Bella's head.

"Oh yeah, San Diego definitely is closer. Still two days for sure, though."

It was clear she hadn't even known the location of Comic Con. She'd only chimed in to save Eric from teasing. It was revealing of her character—I was always compiling my list—but now I would never know where she would have chosen for herself. Mike was nearly as dissatisfied, but he seemed oblivious to her real motivations.

It was often like this with her: never stepping out of her quiet comfort zone except for someone else's perceived need; changing the subject whenever her circle of human friends grew too cruel to one another; thanking a teacher for their lesson if that teacher seemed down; giving up her locker for a more inconvenient location so two best friends could be neighbors; smiling a certain smile that never surfaced for her contented friends, only revealing itself to someone who was hurting. Little things that none of her acquaintances or admirers ever seemed to see.

Through all these little things, I was able to add the most important quality to my list, the most revealing of them all, as simple as it was rare. Bella was *good*. All the other things added up to that whole: Kind and self-effacing and unselfish and brave—she was good through and through. And no one seemed aware of that besides me. Though Mike was certainly observing her nearly as often.

And right there was the most surprising of my torments: Mike Newton. Who would have ever dreamed that such a generic, boring mortal could be so infuriating? To be fair, I should have felt some gratitude to him; more than the others, he kept the girl talking. I learned so much about her through these conversations, but Mike's assistance with this project only aggravated me. I didn't want him to be the one who unlocked her secrets.

It helped that he never noticed her small revelations, her little slips. He knew nothing about her. He'd created a Bella in his head who didn't exist—a girl just as generic as he was. He hadn't observed the unselfishness and bravery that set her apart from other humans, didn't hear the abnormal maturity of her spoken thoughts. He didn't perceive that when she spoke of her mother, she sounded like a parent speaking of a child rather than the other way around—loving, indulgent, slightly amused, and fiercely protective. He didn't hear the patience in her voice when she feigned interest in his rambling stories, and didn't guess at the compassion behind that patience.

These helpful discoveries did not warm me to the boy, however. The possessive way he viewed Bella—as if she were an acquisition to be made—provoked me almost as much as his crude fantasies about her. He was becoming more confident of her, too, as time passed, for she seemed to prefer him over those he considered his rivals—Tyler Crowley, Eric Yorkie, and even, sporadically, myself. He would routinely sit on her side of our table before Biology began, chattering at her, encouraged by her smiles. Just polite smiles, I told myself. All the same, I frequently amused myself by imagining backhanding him across the room and into the far wall. It probably wouldn't injure him fatally....

Mike didn't often think of me as a rival. After the accident, he'd worried that Bella and I would bond from the shared experience, but obviously the opposite had resulted. Back then, he had still been bothered that I'd singled Bella out over her peers for attention. But now I ignored her just as thoroughly as the others, and he grew complacent.

What was she thinking now? Did she welcome his attention?

And finally, the last of my torments, the most painful: Bella's indifference. As I ignored her, she ignored me. She never tried to speak to me again. For all I knew, she never thought about me at all.

This might have driven me mad—or worse, broken my resolution—except that she sometimes stared at me as she had before. I didn't see it for myself, as I could not allow myself to look at her, but Alice always warned us; the others were still wary of the girl's problematic knowledge.

It eased some of the pain that she gazed at me from a distance every now and then. Of course, she was probably just wondering exactly what kind of an aberration I was.

"Bella's going to stare at Edward in a minute. Look normal," Alice said one Tuesday in March, and the others were careful to fidget and shift their weight.

I paid attention to how often she looked in my direction. It pleased me, though it should not have, that the frequency did not decline as time passed. I didn't know what it meant, but it made me feel better.

Alice sighed. *I wish…*

"Stay out of it, Alice," I said under my breath. "It's not going to happen."

She pouted. Alice was anxious to form her envisioned friendship with Bella. In a strange way, she missed the girl she didn't know.

I'll admit, you're better than I thought. You've got the future all snarled up and senseless again. I hope you're happy.

"It makes plenty of sense to me."

She snorted delicately.

I tried to shut her out, too impatient for conversation. I wasn't in a very good mood—tenser than I let any of them see. Only Jasper was aware of how tightly wound I was, feeling the stress emanate out of me with his unique ability to both sense and influence the moods of others. He didn't understand the reasons behind the moods, though, and—since I was constantly in a foul temper these days—he disregarded it.

Today would be a hard one. Harder than the day before, as was the pattern.

Mike Newton was going to ask Bella on a date.

A girls' choice dance was on the near horizon, and he'd been hoping very much that Bella would ask him. That she had not done so had rattled his confidence. Now he was in an uncomfortable bind—I enjoyed his discomfort more than I should have—because Jessica Stanley had just invited him. He didn't want to say yes, still hopeful that Bella would choose him (and prove him the victor over her other would-be suitors), but he didn't want to say no and end up missing the dance altogether. Jessica, hurt by his hesitation and guessing the reason behind it, was thinking daggers at Bella. Again, I had the instinct to place myself between her and Jessica's angry thoughts. I understood the instinct better now, but that only made it more frustrating when I could not act on it.

To think it had come to this! I was utterly fixated on the petty high school dramas that I'd once held so in contempt.

Mike was working up his nerve as he walked Bella to Biology. I listened to his struggles as I waited for them to arrive. The boy was weak. He had waited for this dance purposely, afraid to let his infatuation be known before she had shown a marked preference for him. He didn't want to make himself vulnerable to rejection, preferring that she take that leap first.

Coward.

He sat down on our table again, comfortable through long familiarity, and I imagined the sound it would make if his body hit the opposite wall with enough force to break most of his bones.

"So," he said to the girl, his eyes on the floor. "Jessica asked me to the spring dance."

"That's great," Bella answered immediately and with enthusiasm. It was hard not to smile as Mike processed her tone. He'd been hoping for dismay. "You'll have a lot of fun with Jessica."

He scrambled for the right response. "Well…" He hesitated and almost turned tail. Then he rallied. "I told her I had to think about it."

"Why would you do that?" she demanded. Her tone was disapproving, but there was the faintest hint of relief there as well.

What did *that* mean? An unexpected, intense fury made my hands clench into fists.

Mike did not hear the relief. His face flushed red—fierce as I suddenly felt, this seemed like an open invitation—and he looked at the floor again as he spoke.

"I was wondering if…well, if you might be planning to ask me."

Bella hesitated.

In that moment, I saw the future more clearly than Alice ever had.

The girl might say yes to Mike's unspoken question now, or she might not, but either way, someday soon, she would say yes to someone. She was lovely and intriguing, and human males were not oblivious to this fact. Whether she would settle for someone in this lackluster crowd, or wait until she was free from Forks, the day would come that she *would* say yes.

I saw her life as I had before—college, career…love, marriage. I saw her on her father's arm again, dressed in gauzy white, her face flushed with happiness as she moved to the sound of Wagner's "Bridal Chorus."

The pain I felt while I imagined this future reminded me of the agony of transformation. It consumed me.

And not just pain, but outright *rage*.

The fury ached for some kind of physical outlet. Though this insignificant, undeserving boy might not be the one Bella would say yes to, I yearned to pulverize his skull with my fist, to let him stand as a proxy for whoever it would be.

I didn't understand this emotion—it was such a tangle of pain and fury and desire and despair. I had never felt it before; I couldn't put a name to it.

"Mike, I think you should tell her yes," Bella said in a gentle voice.

Mike's hopes plummeted. I would have enjoyed that under other circumstances, but I was lost in the aftershock and the remorse for what the pain and fury had done to me.

Alice was right. I was *not* strong enough.

Right now, she would be watching the future spin and twist, become mangled again. Would this please her?

"Did you already ask someone?" Mike asked sullenly. He glanced at me, suspicious for the first time in many weeks. I realized I had betrayed my interest; my head was inclined in Bella's direction.

The wild envy in his thoughts—envy for whomever this girl preferred to him—suddenly put a name to my emotion.

I was jealous.

"No," the girl said with a trace of humor in her voice. "I'm not going to the dance at all."

Through all the remorse and anger, I felt relief at her words. It was wrong, dangerous even, to consider Mike and the other mortals interested in Bella as rivals, but I had to concede that they had become just that.

"Why not?" Mike asked harshly. It offended me that he used this tone with her. I bit back a growl.

"I'm going to Seattle that Saturday," she answered.

The curiosity was not as vicious as it would have been before—now that I was fully intending to find out the answers to everything. I would know the reasons behind this new revelation soon enough.

Mike's voice turned unpleasantly wheedling. "Can't you go some other weekend?"

"Sorry, no." Bella was brusquer now. "So you shouldn't make Jess wait any longer—it's rude."

Her concern for Jessica's feelings fanned the flames of my jealousy. This Seattle trip was clearly an excuse to say no—did she refuse purely out of loyalty to her friend? She was more than selfless enough for that. Did she actually wish she could say yes? Or were both guesses wrong? Was she interested in someone else?

"Yeah, you're right," Mike mumbled, so demoralized that I almost felt pity for him. Almost.

He dropped his eyes from the girl, cutting off my view of her face in his thoughts.

I wasn't going to tolerate that.

I turned to read her face myself, for the first time in more than a month. It was a sharp relief to allow myself this. I imagined it would feel the same to press ice to an aching burn. An abrupt cessation of pain.

Her eyes were closed, and her hands pressed against the sides of her face. Her shoulders curved inward defensively. She shook her head ever so slightly, as if she were trying to push some thought from her mind.

Frustrating. Fascinating.

Mr. Banner's voice pulled her from her reverie, and her eyes slowly opened. She looked at me immediately, perhaps sensing my gaze. She stared up into my eyes with the same perplexed expression that had haunted me for so long.

I didn't feel remorse or guilt or rage in that second. I knew they would come again, and soon, but for this one moment I rode a strange, jittery high. As if I had triumphed rather than lost.

She didn't look away, though I stared with inappropriate intensity, trying vainly to read her thoughts through her liquid brown eyes. They were full of questions, rather than answers.

I could see the reflection of my own eyes, black with thirst. It had been nearly two weeks since my last hunting trip; this was not the safest day for my will to crumble. But the blackness did not seem to frighten her. She still did not look away, and a soft, devastatingly appealing pink began to color her skin.

What are you thinking now?

I almost asked the question aloud, but at that moment, Mr. Banner called my name. I picked the correct answer out of his head and glanced briefly in his direction, sucking in a quick breath.

"The Krebs Cycle."

Thirst scorched my throat—tightening my muscles and filling my mouth with venom—and I closed my eyes, trying to concentrate through the desire for her blood that raged inside me.

The monster was stronger than before, rejoicing. He embraced this dual future that gave him a fifty-fifty chance at what he craved so viciously. The third, shaky future I'd tried to construct through willpower alone had collapsed—destroyed by common jealousy, of all things—and he was so much closer to his goal.

The remorse and guilt now burned with the thirst, and if I'd had the ability to produce tears, they would have filled my eyes now.

What had I done?

Knowing the battle was already lost, there seemed to be no reason to resist what I wanted. I turned to stare at the girl again.

She had hidden in her hair, but I could see that her cheek was deep crimson now.

The monster liked that.

She did not meet my gaze again but twisted a strand of her dark hair nervously between her fingers. Her delicate fingers, her fragile wrist—they were so breakable, looking for all the world as though just my breath could snap them.

No, no, no. I could not do this. She was too breakable, too good, too precious to deserve this. I couldn't allow my life to collide with hers, to destroy it.

But I couldn't stay away from her, either. Alice was right about that.

The monster inside me hissed with annoyance as I struggled.

My brief hour with her passed all too quickly, while I vacillated between the rock and the hard place. The bell rang, and she started collecting her things without looking at me. This disappointed me, but I could hardly expect otherwise. The way I had treated her since the accident was inexcusable.

"Bella?" I said, unable to stop myself. My willpower lay in shreds.

She hesitated before looking at me. When she turned, her expression was guarded, suspicious.

I reminded myself that she had every right to distrust me. That she should.

She waited for me to continue, but I just stared at her, reading her face. I pulled in shallow mouthfuls of air at regular intervals, fighting my thirst.

"What?" she finally said, a hard edge to her voice. "Are you speaking to me again?"

I wasn't sure how to answer her question. *Was* I speaking to her again, in the sense that she meant?

Not if I could help it. I would try to help it.

"No, not really," I told her.

She closed her eyes, which only made things more difficult. It cut off my best avenue of access to her feelings. She took a long, slow breath without opening her eyes, and spoke. "Then what do you want, Edward?"

Surely this was not a normal human way to converse. Why did she do it?

But how to answer her?

With the truth, I decided. I would be as truthful as I could with her from now on. I didn't want to deserve her distrust, even if earning her trust was impossible.

"I'm sorry," I told her. That was truer than she would ever know. Unfortunately, I could only safely apologize for the trivial. "I'm being very rude, I know. But it's better this way, really."

Her eyes opened, their expression still wary. "I don't know what you mean."

I tried to get as much of a warning through to her as was allowed. "It's better if we're not friends." Surely, she could sense that much. She was a bright girl. "Trust me."

Her eyes tightened, and I remembered that I had said those words to her before—just before breaking a promise. I winced when her teeth clenched together with a sharp *click*—she clearly remembered, too.

"It's too bad you didn't figure that out earlier," she said angrily. "You could have saved yourself all this regret."

I stared at her in shock. What did she know of my regrets?

"Regret? Regret for what?" I demanded.

"For not just letting that stupid van squish me!" she snapped.

I froze, stunned.

How could she be thinking *that*? Saving her life was the one acceptable thing I'd done since I met her. The only thing I was not ashamed of, that made me glad I existed at all. I'd been fighting to keep her alive since the first moment I'd caught her scent. How could she doubt my one good deed in all this mess?

"You think I regret saving your life?"

"I *know* you do," she retorted.

Her estimation of my intentions left me seething. "You don't know anything."

How confusing and incomprehensible the workings of her mind were! She must not think in the same way as other humans at all. That must be the explanation behind her mental silence. She was entirely other.

She jerked her face away, gritting her teeth again. Her cheeks were flushed, with anger this time. Slamming her books together in a pile, she yanked them up into her arms, and marched toward the door without meeting my stare.

Even as vexed as I felt, something about her anger softened my annoyance. I wasn't sure exactly what it was that made her exasperation somehow . . . endearing.

She walked stiffly, without looking where she was going, and her foot caught on the lip of the doorway. Her things all crashed to the ground. Instead of bending to get them, she stood rigidly straight, not even looking down, as if she was not sure the books were worth retrieving.

No one was here to watch me. I flitted to her side and had her books in order before she had even examined the mess.

She bent halfway, saw me, and then froze. I handed her books back to her, making sure my icy skin never touched hers.

"Thank you," she said in a sharp voice.

"You're welcome." My voice was still rough with my former irritation, but before I could clear my throat and try again, she'd wrenched herself upright and stomped away toward her next class.

I watched until I could no longer see her angry figure.

Spanish passed in a blur. Mrs. Goff never questioned my abstraction—she knew my Spanish was superior to hers and gave me a great deal of latitude—leaving me free to think.

So I couldn't ignore the girl. That much was obvious. But did it mean I had no choice but to destroy her? That could *not* be the only available future. There had to be some other choice, some delicate balance. I tried to think of a way.

I didn't pay much attention to Emmett until the hour was nearly up. He was curious—Emmett was not overly intuitive about the shades in others' moods, but he could see the obvious change in me. He wondered what had happened to remove the unrelenting glower from my face. He struggled to define the change, and finally decided that I looked *hopeful.*

Hopeful? Was that how I seemed from the outside?

I pondered the idea as we walked to the Volvo, wondering what exactly I should be hoping *for.*

But I didn't have long to ponder. Sensitive as I always was to thoughts about the girl, the sound of Bella's name in the heads of those humans I really should not think of as rivals caught my attention. Eric and Tyler, having heard—with much satisfaction—of Mike's failure, were preparing to make their moves.

Eric was already in place, positioned against her truck where she could not avoid him. Tyler's class was being held late to receive an assignment, and he was in a desperate hurry to catch her before she escaped.

This I had to see.

"Wait for the others here, all right?" I murmured to Emmett.

He eyed me suspiciously, but then shrugged and nodded.

Kid's lost his damn mind, he thought, amused.

Bella was on her way out of the gym, and I waited where she would not see me. As she got closer to Eric's ambush, I strode forward, setting my pace so that I would walk by at the right moment.

I watched her body stiffen when she caught sight of the boy waiting for her. She froze for a moment, then relaxed and moved forward.

"Hey, Eric," I heard her call in a friendly voice.

I was abruptly and unexpectedly anxious. What if this gangly teen with his unhealthy skin was somehow pleasing to her? Perhaps her earlier kindness to him had not been entirely selfless?

Eric swallowed loudly, his Adam's apple bobbing. "Hi, Bella."

She seemed unconscious of his nervousness.

"What's up?" she asked, unlocking her truck without looking at his frightened expression.

"Uh, I was just wondering…if you would go to the spring dance with me?" His voice broke.

She finally looked up. Was she taken aback, or pleased? Eric couldn't meet her gaze, so I couldn't see her face in his mind.

"I thought it was girls' choice," she said, sounding flustered.

"Well, yeah," he agreed wretchedly.

This pitiable boy did not irritate me as much as Mike Newton did, but I couldn't find it in myself to feel sympathy for his angst until after Bella had answered him in a gentle voice.

"Thank you for asking me, but I'm going to be in Seattle that day."

He'd already heard this; still, it was a disappointment.

"Oh," he mumbled, barely daring to raise his eyes to the level of her nose. "Well, maybe next time."

"Sure," she agreed. Then she bit down on her lip, as if she regretted leaving him a loophole. That pleased me.

Eric slumped forward and walked away, headed in the wrong direction from his car, his only thought escape.

I passed her in that moment and heard her sigh of relief. I laughed before I could catch myself.

She whirled at the sound, but I stared straight ahead, trying to keep my lips from twitching in amusement.

Tyler was behind me, almost running in his hurry to catch her before she could drive away. He was bolder and more confident than the other two. He'd only waited to approach Bella this long because he'd respected Mike's prior claim.

I wanted him to succeed in catching her for two reasons. If—as I was beginning to suspect—all this attention was annoying to Bella, I wanted to enjoy watching her reaction. But if it was not—if Tyler's invitation was the one she'd been hoping for—then I wanted to know that, too.

I measured Tyler Crowley as competition, knowing it was reprehensible to do so. He seemed tediously average and unremarkable to me, but what did I know of Bella's preferences? Maybe she liked average boys.

I winced at that thought. I could never be an average boy. How foolish it was to set myself up as a candidate for her affections. How could she ever care for someone who was, by default, the villain of the story?

She was too good for a villain.

Though I ought to have let her escape, my inexcusable curiosity kept me from doing what was right. Again. But what if Tyler missed his chance now, only to contact her later when I would have no way of knowing the outcome? I pulled my Volvo out into the narrow lane, blocking her exit.

Emmett and the others were on their way, but he'd described my strange behavior to them, and they were walking slowly, staring at me, trying to decipher what I was doing.

I watched the girl in my rearview mirror. She glowered toward the back of my car without meeting my gaze, looking as if she wished she were driving a tank rather than a rusted Chevy.

Tyler hurried to his car and got in line behind her, grateful for my inexplicable conduct. He waved at her, trying to catch her attention, but she didn't notice. He waited a moment, and then left his car, forcing his gait into a saunter as he sidled up to her passenger-side window. He tapped on the glass.

She jumped, and then stared at him in confusion. After a second, she rolled the window down manually, seeming to have some trouble with it.

"I'm sorry, Tyler," she said, her voice irritated. "I'm stuck behind Cullen."

She said my surname in a hard voice.

"Oh, I know," Tyler said, undeterred by her mood. "I just wanted to ask you something while we're trapped here."

His grin was cocky.

I was gratified by the way she blanched at his obvious intent.

"Will you ask me to the spring dance?" he said, no thought of defeat in his mind.

"I'm not going to be in town, Tyler," she told him, irritation still plain in her voice.

"Yeah, Mike said that."

"Then why—?" she started to ask.

He shrugged. "I was hoping you were just letting him down easy."

Her eyes flashed, then cooled. "Sorry, Tyler," she said, not sounding sorry at all. "I really am going out of town."

Given her usual practice of putting the needs of others above her own, I was a little surprised at her steely resolve when it came to this dance. Where did it spring from?

Tyler accepted her excuse, his self-assurance untouched. "That's cool. We still have prom."

He strutted back to his car.

I was right to have waited for this.

The horrified expression on her face was priceless. It told me what I should not so desperately have needed to know—that she had no feelings for any of these human males who wished to court her.

Also, her expression was possibly the funniest thing I'd ever seen.

My family arrived then, confused that I was, for a change, rocking with laughter rather than scowling murderously at everything in sight.

What's so funny? Emmett wanted to know.

I just shook my head as Bella revved her noisy engine angrily. She looked like she was wishing for a tank again.

"Let's go!" Rosalie hissed impatiently. "Stop being an idiot. If you *can*."

Her words didn't annoy me—I was too entertained. But I did as she asked.

No one spoke to me on the way home. I continued to chuckle every now and again, thinking of Bella's face.

As I turned onto the drive—speeding up now that there were no witnesses—Alice ruined my mood.

"So do I get to talk to Bella now?" she asked suddenly.

"No," I snapped.

"Not fair! What am I waiting for?"

"I haven't decided anything, Alice."

"Whatever, Edward."

In her head, Bella's two destinies were clear again.

"What's the point in getting to know her?" I mumbled, suddenly morose. "If I'm just going to kill her?"

Alice hesitated for a second. "You have a point," she admitted.

I took the final hairpin turn at ninety miles an hour, and then screeched to a stop an inch from the rear garage wall.

"Enjoy your run," Rosalie said smugly as I threw myself out of the car.

But I didn't go running today. Instead, I went hunting.

The others were scheduled to hunt tomorrow, but I couldn't afford to be thirsty now. I overdid it, drinking more than necessary, glutting myself again—a small grouping of elk and one black bear I was lucky to stumble across this early in the year. I was so full it was uncomfortable. Why couldn't that be enough?

Why did her scent have to be so much stronger than anything else?

And not just her scent—whatever it was about her that marked her for disaster. She'd been in Forks for mere weeks and already she'd twice come within inches of a violent end. For all I knew, right at this very moment she could have wandered into the path of another death sentence. What would it be this time? A meteorite smashing through her roof and crushing her in her bed?

I could hunt no more and the sun was still hours and hours from rising. Now that it had occurred to me, the idea of the meteorite and all its possible allies was hard to dismiss. I tried to be rational, to consider the odds against all the disasters I could imagine, but that didn't help. What were the odds, after all, that the girl would come to live in a town with a decent percentage of vampires as permanent residents? What were the odds that she would appeal to one so perfectly?

What if something happened to her in the night? What if I went to school tomorrow, every sense and feeling focused onto the space where she should be, and her seat was empty?

Abruptly, the risk felt unacceptable.

The only way I could be *positive* she was safe was if there was someone in place to catch the meteorite before it could touch her. The jittery high swept through me again when I realized that I was going to go find the girl.

It was past midnight, and Bella's house was dark and quiet. Her truck was parked against the curb, her father's police cruiser in the driveway. There were no conscious thoughts anywhere in the neighborhood. I watched the house from the blackness of the forest that bordered it on the east.

There was no evidence of any kind of danger…aside from myself.

I listened and picked out the sound of two people breathing inside the house, two even heartbeats. So all must be well. I leaned against the trunk of a young hemlock and settled in to wait for stray meteorites.

The problem with waiting was that it freed up the mind for all kinds of speculation. Obviously the meteorite was just a metaphor for all the unlikely things that could go wrong. But not every danger would streak across the sky with a brilliant splash of fire. I could think of many that would give no warning, hazards that could slink into the dark house silently, that might already be there.

These were ridiculous worries. This street didn't have a natural gas line, so a carbon monoxide leak was improbable. I doubted they used coal frequently. The Olympic Peninsula had very little in the way of dangerous wildlife. Anything large I would be able to hear now. There were no venomous snakes, scorpions, or centipedes, and just a few spiders, none of them deadly to a healthy adult, and unlikely to be found indoors regardless. Ridiculous. I *knew* that. I *knew* I was being irrational.

But I felt anxious, unsettled. I couldn't push the dark imaginings from my mind. If I could just *see* her...

I would take a closer look.

In only half a second, I had crossed the yard and scaled the side of the house. This upstairs window would be a bedroom, probably the master. Maybe I should have started in the back. Less conspicuous that way. Dangling from the eave above the window by one hand, I looked through the glass, and my breath stopped.

It was her room. I could see her in the one small bed, her covers on the floor and her sheets twisted around her legs. She was perfectly fine, of course, as the rational part of me had already known. Safe...but not at ease. As I watched, she twitched restlessly and threw one arm over her head. She did not sleep soundly, at least not this night. Did she sense the danger near her?

I was repulsed by myself as I watched her toss again. How was I any better than some sick peeping tom? I *wasn't* any better. I was much, much worse.

I relaxed my fingertips, about to let myself drop. But first I allowed myself one long look at her face.

Still not peaceful. The little furrow was there between her eyebrows, the corners of her mouth turned down. Her lips trembled, and then parted.

"Okay, Mom," she muttered.

Bella talked in her sleep.

Curiosity flared, overpowering self-disgust. So long I'd tried to hear her and failed. The lure of those unprotected, unconsciously spoken thoughts was impossibly tempting.

What were human rules to me, after all? How many did I ignore on a daily basis?

I thought of the multitude of illegal documents my family needed to live as we liked. False names and false histories, driver's licenses that let us enroll in school and medical credentials that allowed Carlisle to work as a doctor. Papers that made our strange grouping of nearly identically aged adults comprehensible as a family. None of it would be necessary if we didn't try to have brief periods of permanence, if we didn't prefer to have a *home*.

Then, of course, there was the way we funded our lives. Insider trading laws didn't apply to psychics, but it certainly wasn't honest, what we did. And the transfer of inheritances from one fabricated name to another wasn't legal, either.

And then there were all the *murders*.

We didn't take them lightly, but obviously none of us had ever been punished by human courts for our crimes. We covered them up—also a crime.

Then why should I feel so guilty over one little misdemeanor? Human laws had never applied to me. And this was hardly my first adventure with breaking and entering.

I knew I could do this safely. The monster was restless but well fettered.

I would keep a careful distance. I would not harm her. She would never know I'd been here. I only wanted to be certain that she was safe.

It was all rationalization, evil arguments from the devil on my left shoulder. I knew that, but I had no angel on the right. I would behave as the nightmarish creature that I was.

I tried the window, and it was not locked, though it stuck due to long disuse. I took a deep breath—my last for however long I was near her—and slid the glass slowly aside, cringing at each faint groan of the metal frame. Finally it was open wide enough for me to ease through.

"Mom, wait...," she muttered. "Scottsdale Road is faster...."

Her room was small—disorganized and cluttered, but not unclean. There were books piled on the floor beside her bed, their spines facing away from me, and CDs scattered by her inexpensive CD player—the one on top was just a clear jewel case. Stacks of papers surrounded a computer that looked like it belonged in a museum dedicated to obsolete technologies. Shoes dotted the wooden floor.

I wanted very much to go read the titles of her books and CDs, but I was determined to take no more risks. Instead, I went to sit in an old rocking chair in the far corner of the room. My anxiety eased, the dark thoughts receded, and my mind was clear.

Had I really once believed her average-looking? I thought of that first day, and my disgust for the human boys who were so fascinated by her. But when I remembered her face in their minds then, I could not understand why I had not immediately found her beautiful. It seemed an obvious thing.

Right now—with her dark hair tangled and wild around her pale face, wearing a threadbare t-shirt full of holes with tatty sweatpants, her features relaxed in unconsciousness, her full lips slightly parted—she took my breath away. Or would have, I thought wryly, if I were breathing.

She did not speak. Perhaps her dream had ended.

I stared at her face and tried to think of some way to make the future bearable.

Hurting her was not bearable. Did that mean my only choice was to try to leave again?

The others could not argue with me now. My absence would

not put anyone in danger. There would be no suspicion, nothing to link anyone's thoughts back to the accident.

I wavered as I had this afternoon, and nothing seemed possible.

A small brown spider crawled out from the edge of the closet door. My arrival must have disturbed it. *Eratigena agrestis*—a hobo spider, from its size a juvenile male. Once considered dangerous, more recent scientific study had proven its venom inconsequential to humans. However, its bite was still painful.... I reached out with one finger and crushed it silently.

Perhaps I should have let the creature be, but the thought of anything hurting her was intolerable.

And then suddenly, all my thoughts were intolerable, too.

Because I could kill every spider in her home, cut the thorns off every rosebush she might one day touch, block every speeding car that got within a mile of her, but there was no task I could perform that would make *me* something other than what I was. I stared at my white, stone-like hand—so grotesquely inhuman—and despaired.

I could not hope to compete against the human boys, whether these specific boys appealed to her or not. I was the villain, the nightmare. How could she see me as anything else? If she knew the truth about me, it would frighten and repulse her. Like the intended victim in a horror movie, she would run away, shrieking in terror.

I remembered her first day in Biology... and knew that this was exactly the right reaction for her to have.

It was foolishness to imagine that if I had been the one to ask her to the silly dance, she would have canceled her hastily made plans and agreed to go with me.

I was not the one she was destined to say yes to. It was someone else, someone human and warm. And I could not even let myself—someday, when that yes was said—hunt him down and kill him, because she deserved him, whoever he was. She deserved happiness and love with whomever she chose.

I owed it to her to do the right thing now. I could no longer pretend that I was only *in danger* of loving this girl.

After all, it really didn't matter if I left, because Bella could never see me the way I wished she would. Never see me as someone worthy of love.

Could a dead, frozen heart break? It felt as though mine would.

"Edward," Bella said.

I froze, staring at her unopened eyes.

Had she awakened, caught me here? She *looked* asleep, yet her voice had been so clear.

She sighed a quiet sigh, and then moved restlessly again, rolling to her side—still fast asleep and dreaming.

"Edward," she mumbled softly.

She was dreaming of me.

Could a dead, frozen heart beat again? It felt as though mine was about to.

"Stay," she sighed. "Don't go. Please... don't go."

She was dreaming of me, and it wasn't even a nightmare. She wanted me to stay with her, there in her dream.

I struggled to find words to name the feelings that flooded through me, but I had no words strong enough to hold them. For a long moment, I drowned in them.

When I surfaced, I was not the same man I had been.

My life was an unending, unchanging midnight. It must, by necessity, always be midnight for me. So how was it possible that the sun was rising now, in the middle of my midnight?

At the time I became a vampire, trading my soul and mortality for immortality in the searing pain of transformation, I had truly been frozen. My body had turned into something more like stone than flesh, enduring and unchanging. My *self*, also, had frozen as it was—my personality, my likes and dislikes, my moods and desires; all were fixed in place.

It was the same for the rest of them. We were all frozen. Living stone.

When change came for one of us, it was a rare and permanent thing. I had seen it happen with Carlisle, and then a decade later with Rosalie. Love had changed them in an eternal way, a way that would never fade. More than eighty years had passed since Carlisle found Esme, and yet he still looked at her with the incredulous eyes of first love. It would always be so for them.

It would always be so for me, too. I would always love this fragile human girl, for the rest of my limitless existence.

I gazed at her unconscious face, feeling that love for her settle into every portion of my stone body.

She slept more peacefully now, a slight smile on her lips.

I began to plot.

I loved her, and so I would try to be strong enough to leave her. I knew I wasn't that strong now. I would work on that one. But perhaps I was strong enough to circumvent the future in another way.

Alice had seen only two futures for Bella, and now I understood them both.

Loving her would not keep me from killing her if I let myself make mistakes.

Yet I could not feel the monster now, could not find him anywhere in me. Perhaps love had silenced him forever. If I killed her now, it would not be intentional, only a horrible accident.

I would have to be inordinately careful. I would never, ever be able to let my guard down. I would have to control my every breath. I would have to keep an always cautious distance.

I would not make mistakes.

I finally understood that second future. I'd been baffled by that vision—what could possibly happen to result in Bella becoming a prisoner to this immortal half life? Now—devastated by longing for the girl—I could understand how I might, in unforgivable selfishness, ask my father for that favor. Ask him to take away her life and her soul so that I could keep her forever.

She deserved better.

But I saw one more future, one thin wire that I might be able to walk, if I could keep my balance.

Could I do it? Be with her and leave her human?

Deliberately, I locked my body into perfect stillness, froze it in place, then took a deep breath. Another, then another, letting her scent rip through me like wildfire. The room was thick with her perfume; her fragrance was layered on every surface. My head swam from the pain, but I fought the spinning. I would have to get used to this if I were going to attempt any kind of regular proximity to her. Another deep, burning breath.

I watched her sleeping until the sun rose behind the eastern clouds, plotting and breathing.

I got home just after the others had left for school. I changed quickly, avoiding Esme's questioning eyes. She saw the feverish light in my face and felt both worry and relief. My long melancholy had pained her greatly, and she was glad that it seemed to be over.

I ran to school, arriving a few seconds after my siblings did. They did not turn, though Alice at least must have known that I stood here in the thick woods that bordered the pavement. I waited until no one was looking and then strolled casually from between the trees into the lot full of parked cars.

I heard Bella's truck rumbling around the corner, and I paused behind a Suburban, where I could watch without being seen.

She drove into the lot, glaring at my Volvo for a long moment before she parked in one of the most distant spaces, a frown on her face.

It was strange to remember that she was probably still angry with me, and with good reason.

I wanted to laugh at myself—or kick myself. All my plotting and planning was entirely moot if she didn't care for me, too, wasn't it? Her dream could have been about something completely random. I was such an arrogant fool.

Well, it was so much the better for her if she didn't care for me. That wouldn't stop me from pursuing her, from trying. But I would listen for her *no*. I owed her that. I owed her more. I owed her the truth I was not allowed to give her. So I would give her as much truth as I could. I would try to warn her. And when she confirmed that I would never be the one she would say *yes* to, I would leave.

I walked silently forward, wondering how best to approach her.

She made it easy. Her truck key slipped through her fingers as she got out of the cab, and fell into a deep puddle.

She reached down, but I got to it first, retrieving it before she had to put her fingers in the cold water.

I leaned back against her truck as she started and then straightened up.

"How do you *do* that?" she demanded.

Yes, she was still angry.

I offered her the key. "Do what?"

She held her hand out, and I dropped it into her palm. I took a deep breath, pulling in her scent.

"Appear out of thin air," she clarified.

"Bella, it's not my fault if you are exceptionally unobservant." The words were wry, almost a joke. Was there anything she didn't see?

Did she hear how my voice wrapped around her name like a caress?

She glared at me, not appreciating my humor. Her heartbeat sped—from anger? From fear? After a moment, she looked down.

"Why the traffic jam last night?" she asked without meeting my eyes. "I thought you were supposed to be pretending I don't exist, not irritating me to death."

Still very angry. It was going to take some effort to make things right with her. I remembered my resolve to be truthful.

"That was for Tyler's sake, not mine. I had to give him his chance." And then I laughed. I couldn't help it, thinking of her expression yesterday. Concentrating so hard on keeping her safe, on controlling my physical response to her, left me fewer resources to manage my emotions.

"You—" she gasped, and then broke off, appearing to be too furious to finish. There it was—that same expression. I choked back another laugh. She was mad enough already.

"And I'm not pretending you don't exist," I finished. It felt right to make my tone casual, teasing. I didn't want to frighten her more. I had to hide the depth of my feelings, keep things light.

"So you *are* trying to irritate me to death? Since Tyler's van didn't do the job?"

A quick flash of anger pulsed through me. How could she honestly believe that?

It was irrational for me to be so affronted—she didn't know all the effort I'd expended to keep her alive, she didn't know that I'd fought with my family for her, she didn't know of the transformation that had happened in the night. But I was angry all the same. Emotion unmanaged.

"Bella, you are utterly absurd," I snapped.

Her face flushed, and she turned her back on me. She began to walk away.

Remorse. My anger was unfair.

"Wait," I pleaded.

She did not stop, so I followed her.

"I'm sorry, that was rude. I'm not saying it isn't true"—it *was* absurd to imagine that I wanted her harmed in any way—"but it was rude to say it, anyway."

"Why won't you leave me alone?"

Was this my *no*? Was that what she wanted? Was my name in her dream truly meaningless?

I remembered perfectly the tone of her voice, the expression on her face as she had asked me to stay.

But if she now said no . . . well, then that would be that. I knew what I would have to do.

Keep it light, I reminded myself. This could be the last time I would see her. If that was the case, I needed to leave her with the right memory. So I would play the normal human boy. Most importantly, I would give her a choice, and then accept her answer.

"I wanted to ask you something, but you sidetracked me." A course of action had just occurred to me, and I laughed.

"Do you have a multiple personality disorder?" she asked.

It must seem that way. My mood was wildly erratic, so many new emotions coursing through me.

"You're doing it again," I pointed out.

She sighed. "Fine then. What do you want to ask?"

"I was wondering if, a week from Saturday..." I watched the shock cross her face, and fought back another laugh. "You know, the day of the spring dance—"

She cut me off, finally returning her eyes to mine. "Are you trying to be *funny*?"

"Will you please allow me to finish?"

She waited in silence, her teeth pressing into her soft lower lip.

That sight distracted me for a second. Strange, unfamiliar reactions stirred deep in my forgotten human core. I tried to shake them off so I could play my role.

"I heard you say you were going to Seattle that day, and I was wondering if you wanted a ride?" I offered. I'd realized that, better than just learning about her plans, I might *share* them. If she said yes.

She stared at me blankly. "What?"

"Do you want a ride to Seattle?" Alone in a car with her—my throat burned at the thought. I took a deep breath. *Get used to it.*

"With who?" she asked, confused.

"Myself, obviously," I said slowly.

"Why?"

Was it really such a shock that I would want her company? She must have applied the worst possible meaning to my past behavior.

"Well," I said as casually as possible, "I was planning to go to Seattle in the next few weeks, and to be honest, I'm not sure if your truck can make it." It felt safer to tease her than to allow myself to be too serious.

"My truck works just fine, thank you very much for your concern," she said in the same surprised voice. She started walking again. I kept pace with her.

Not an explicit rejection, but close. Was she being polite?

"But can your truck make it there on one tank of gas?"

"I don't see how that is any of your business," she grumbled.

Her heart was beating faster again, her breath coming more quickly. I thought the teasing should put her at ease, but maybe I was frightening her again.

"The wasting of finite resources is everyone's business." My response sounded normal and casual to me, but I couldn't tell if it she heard it the same way. Her silent mind left me always foundering.

"Honestly, Edward, I can't keep up with you. I thought you didn't want to be my friend."

A thrill shot through me when she spoke my name, and I was back in her room, hearing her call out to me, wanting me to stay. I wished I could live in that moment forever.

But on this point, only honesty was acceptable.

"I said it would be better if we weren't friends, not that I didn't want to be."

"Oh, thanks, now that's *all* cleared up," she said sarcastically.

She paused, under the edge of the cafeteria's roof, and met my gaze again. Her heartbeats stuttered. In fear or anger?

I chose my words carefully. She needed to *see*. To understand that it was in her best interest to tell me to go.

"It would be more...*prudent* for you not to be my friend." Staring into the melted chocolate depths of her eyes, I entirely lost my hold on *light*. "But I'm tired of trying to stay away from you, Bella." The words felt like they'd burned their way out of my mouth.

Her breathing stopped, and in the second it took for it to restart, I panicked. I'd truly terrified her, hadn't I?

All the better. I would collect my *no* and attempt to bear it.

"Will you go to Seattle with me?" I demanded, point-blank.

She nodded, her heart drumming loudly.

Yes. She'd said yes to *me*.

And then my conscience smote me. What would this cost her?

"You really should stay away from me," I warned her. Did she hear me? Would she escape the future I was threatening her with? Couldn't I do anything to save her from *me*?

Keep it light, I shouted at myself. "I'll see you in class."

And instantly remembered that I would not see her in class. She scattered my thoughts so thoroughly.

I had to concentrate to stop myself from running as I fled.

6. BLOOD TYPE

I FOLLOWED HER ALL DAY THROUGH OTHER PEOPLE'S eyes, barely aware of my own surroundings.

Not Mike Newton's eyes, because I couldn't stand any more of his offensive fantasies, and not Jessica Stanley's, because her resentment toward Bella was irritating. Angela Weber was a good choice when her eyes were available. She was kind—her head was an easy place to be. And then sometimes it was the teachers who provided the best view.

I was surprised, watching Bella stumble through the day—tripping over cracks in the sidewalk, stray books, and, most often, her own feet—that the people I eavesdropped on thought of her as *clumsy*.

I considered that. It was true that she often had trouble staying upright. I remembered her stumbling into the desk that first day, sliding around on the ice before the accident, staggering against the low lip of the doorframe yesterday. How odd—they were right. She *was* clumsy.

I didn't know why this was so funny to me, but I laughed out loud as I walked from American History to English and several people shot me wary glances, then looked away quickly from my exposed teeth. How had I never noticed this before? Perhaps because there was something very graceful about her in stillness, the way she held her head, the arch of her neck…

There was nothing graceful about her now. Mr. Varner watched as she caught the toe of her boot on the carpet and literally fell into her chair.

I laughed again.

The time moved with incredible sluggishness while I waited for my chance to see her with my own eyes. Finally, the bell rang. I strode quickly to the cafeteria to secure my spot. I was one of the first in the room. I chose a table that was usually empty, and was sure to remain that way with me seated here.

When my family entered and saw me sitting alone in a new place, they were not surprised. Alice must have warned them.

Rosalie stalked past me without a glance.

Idiot.

Rosalie and I had never had an easy relationship—I'd offended her the very first time she'd heard me speak, and it was downhill from that point on—but it seemed as though she was even more ill-tempered than usual the last few days. I sighed. Rosalie made everything about herself.

Jasper gave me half a smile as he walked by.

Good luck, he thought doubtfully.

Emmett rolled his eyes and shook his head.

Lost his mind, poor kid.

Alice was beaming, her teeth shining too brightly.

Can I talk to Bella now*??*

"Keep out of it," I said under my breath.

Her face fell, and then brightened again.

Fine. Be stubborn. It's only a matter of time.

I sighed again.

Don't forget about today's Biology lab, she reminded me.

I nodded. It irked me that Mr. Banner had made these plans. I'd wasted so many hours in Biology, sitting next to her while pretending to ignore her; it was painfully ironic to me that I would miss that hour with her today.

While I waited for Bella to arrive, I followed her in the eyes of the freshman who was walking behind Jessica on his way to the cafeteria. Jessica was babbling about the upcoming dance, but Bella said nothing in response. Not that Jessica gave her much of a chance.

The moment Bella walked through the door, her eyes flashed to the table where my siblings sat. She stared for a moment, and then her forehead crumpled and her eyes dropped to the floor. She hadn't noticed me here.

She looked so... *sad*. I felt a powerful urge to get up and go to her side, to comfort her somehow, only I didn't know what she would find comforting. Jessica continued to jabber about the dance. Was Bella upset that she was going to miss it? That didn't seem likely.

But if that were true... I wished I could offer her that option. Impossible. The physical proximity required by a dance would be too dangerous.

She bought a drink for her lunch and nothing else. Was that right? Didn't she need more nutrition? I'd never paid much attention to a human's diet before.

Humans were quite exasperatingly fragile! There were a million different things to worry about.

"Edward Cullen is staring at you again," I heard Jessica say. "I wonder why he's sitting alone today."

I was grateful to Jessica—though she was even more resentful now—because Bella's head snapped up and her eyes searched until they met mine.

There was no trace of sadness in her face now. I let myself hope that she'd felt unhappy because she'd thought I'd left school early, and that hope made me smile.

I motioned with my finger for her to join me. She looked so startled by this that I wanted to tease her again. So I winked, and her mouth fell open.

"Does he mean *you*?" Jessica asked rudely.

"Maybe he needs help with his Biology homework," she said in a low, uncertain voice. "Um, I'd better go see what he wants."

This was almost another yes.

She stumbled twice on her way to my table, though there was nothing in her way but perfectly even linoleum. Seriously, how *had* I missed this? I'd been paying more attention to her silent thoughts, I supposed. What else had I not seen?

She was almost to my new table. I tried to prepare myself. *Keep it honest, keep it light*, I chanted silently.

She stopped behind the chair across from me, hesitating. I inhaled deeply, through my nose this time rather than my mouth.

Feel the burn, I thought dryly.

"Won't you sit with me today?" I asked her.

She pulled the chair out and sat, staring at me the whole while. She seemed nervous. I waited for her to speak.

It took a moment, but finally she said, "This is different."

"Well..." I hesitated. "I decided as long as I was going to hell, I might as well do it thoroughly."

What had made me say that? I supposed it was honest, at least. And perhaps she'd hear the unsubtle warning my words implied. Maybe she would realize that she should get up and walk away as quickly as possible.

She didn't get up. She stared at me, waiting, as if I'd left my sentence unfinished.

"You know I don't have any idea what you mean," she said when I didn't continue.

That was a relief. I smiled. "I know."

It was hard to ignore the thoughts screaming at me from behind her back—and I wanted to change the subject anyway.

"I think your friends are angry at me for stealing you."

This did not appear to concern her. "They'll survive."

"I may not give you back, though." I didn't even know if I was trying to tease her again, or just being honest now. Being near her jumbled all my thoughts.

Bella swallowed loudly.

I laughed at her expression. "You look worried." It really *shouldn't* be funny. She should worry.

"No." I knew this must be a lie; her voice broke, betraying her fraud. "Surprised, actually.... What brought all this on?"

"I told you," I reminded her. "I got tired of trying to stay away from you. So I'm giving up." I held my smile in place with a bit of effort. This wasn't working at all—trying to be honest and casual at the same time.

"Giving up?" she repeated, baffled.

"Yes—giving up trying to be good." And, apparently, giving up trying to be casual. "I'm just going to do what I want now, and let the chips fall where they may." That was honest enough. Let her see my selfishness. Let that warn her, too.

"You lost me again."

I was selfish enough to be glad that this was the case. "I always say too much when I'm talking to you—that's one of the problems." A rather insignificant problem, compared to the rest.

"Don't worry," she reassured me. "I don't understand any of it."

Good. Then she'd stay. "I'm counting on that."

"So, in plain English, are we friends now?"

I pondered that for a second. "Friends...," I repeated. I didn't like the sound of that. It wasn't...enough.

"Or not," she mumbled, looking embarrassed.

Did she think I didn't like her that much?

I smiled. "Well, we can try, I suppose. But I'm warning you now that I'm not a good friend for you."

I waited for her response, torn in two—wishing she would finally hear and understand, thinking I might die if she did. How melodramatic.

Her heart beat faster. "You say that a lot."

"Yes, because you're not *listening* to me," I said, too intense again. "I'm still waiting for you to believe it. If you're smart, you'll avoid me."

I could only guess at the pain I would feel when she understood enough to make the right choice.

Her eyes tightened. "I think you've made your opinion on the subject of my intellect clear, too."

I wasn't exactly sure what she meant, but I smiled in apology, guessing that I must have accidentally offended her.

"So," she said slowly. "As long as I'm being…not smart, we'll try to be friends?"

"That sounds about right."

She looked down, staring intently at the lemonade bottle in her hands.

The old curiosity tormented me.

"What are you thinking?" I asked. It was an immense relief to say the words out loud at last. I couldn't remember how it felt to need oxygen in my lungs, but I wondered if the relief of inhaling had been a little like this.

She met my gaze, and her breathing sped while her cheeks flushed faint pink. I inhaled, tasting that in the air.

"I'm trying to figure out what you are."

I held the smile on my face, locking my features, while panic twisted through my body.

Of course she was wondering that. She had a bright mind. I couldn't hope for her to be oblivious to something so obvious.

"Are you having any luck with that?" I asked as nonchalantly as I could manage.

"Not too much," she admitted.

I chuckled with sudden relief. "What are your theories?"

They couldn't be worse than the truth, no matter what she'd come up with.

Her cheeks turned brighter red, and she said nothing. I could feel the warmth of her blush.

I would try my persuasive tone. It worked well on normal humans.

I smiled encouragingly. "Won't you tell me?"

She shook her head. "Too embarrassing."

Ugh. Not knowing was worse than anything else. Why would her speculations embarrass her?

"That's *really* frustrating, you know."

My complaint sparked something in her. Her eyes flashed and her words flowed more swiftly than usual.

"No, I can't *imagine* why that would be frustrating at all—just because someone refuses to tell you what they're thinking, even if all the while they're making cryptic little remarks specifically designed to keep you up at night wondering what they could possibly mean... now, why would that be frustrating?"

I frowned at her, upset to realize that she was right. I wasn't being fair. She couldn't know the loyalties and limitations that tied my tongue, but that didn't change the disparity as she saw it.

She went on. "Or better, say that person also did a wide range of bizarre things—from saving your life under impossible circumstances one day to treating you like a pariah the next, and he never explained any of that, either, even after he promised. That, also, would be *very* non-frustrating."

It was the longest speech I'd ever heard her make, and it gave me a new quality for my list.

"You've got a bit of a temper, don't you?"

"I don't like double standards."

She was completely justified in her irritation, of course.

I stared at Bella, wondering how I could possibly do anything right by her, until the silent shouting in Mike Newton's head distracted me. He was so irate, so immaturely vulgar, that it made me chuckle again.

"What?" she demanded.

"Your boyfriend seems to think I'm being unpleasant to you—he's debating whether or not to come break up our fight." I would love to see him try. I laughed again.

"I don't know who you're talking about," she said in an icy voice. "But I'm sure you're wrong, anyway."

I very much enjoyed the way she disowned him with one indifferent sentence.

"I'm not. I told you, most people are easy to read."

"Except me, of course."

"Yes. Except for you." Did she have to be the exception to everything? "I wonder why that is?"

I stared into her eyes, trying again.

She looked away, then opened her lemonade and took a quick drink, her eyes on the table.

"Aren't you hungry?" I asked.

"No." She eyed the empty space between us. "You?"

"No, I'm not hungry," I said. I was definitely not that.

She stared down, her lips pursed. I waited.

"Can you do me a favor?" she asked, suddenly meeting my gaze again.

What would she want from me? Would she ask for the truth that I wasn't allowed to tell her—the truth I didn't want her to ever, ever know?

"That depends on what you want."

"It's not much," she promised.

I waited, curiosity flaring excruciatingly, as usual.

"I just wondered...," she said slowly, staring at the lemonade bottle, tracing its lip with her littlest finger, "if you could warn me beforehand the next time you decide to ignore me for my own good? Just so I'm prepared."

She wanted a warning? Then being ignored by me must be a bad thing. I smiled.

"That sounds fair," I agreed.

"Thanks," she said, looking up. Her face was so relieved that I wanted to laugh with my own relief.

"Then can I have one in return?" I asked hopefully.

"One," she allowed.

"Tell me *one* theory."

She flushed. "Not that one."

"You didn't qualify, you just promised one answer," I argued.

"And you've broken promises yourself," she argued back.

She had me there.

"Just one theory—I won't laugh."

"Yes, you will." She seemed very sure of that, though I couldn't imagine anything that would be funny about it.

I gave persuasion another try. I stared deep into her eyes—an easy thing to do with eyes so deep—and whispered, "Please?"

She blinked, and her face went totally blank.

Well, that wasn't exactly the reaction I'd been going for.

"Er, what?" she asked a second later. She looked disoriented. Was something wrong with her?

I tried again.

"Please tell me just one little theory," I pleaded in my soft, non-scary voice, holding her gaze in mine.

To my surprise and satisfaction, it finally worked.

"Um, well, bitten by a radioactive spider?"

Comic books? No wonder she thought I would laugh.

"That's not very creative," I chided her, trying to hide my fresh relief.

"I'm sorry, that's all I've got," she said, offended.

This relieved me even more. I was able to tease her again.

"You're not even close."

"No spiders?"

"Nope."

"And no radioactivity?"

"None."

"Dang," she sighed.

"Kryptonite doesn't bother me, either," I said quickly—before she could ask about *bites*—and then I had to chuckle, because she thought I was a superhero.

"You're not supposed to laugh, remember?"

I pressed my lips together.

"I'll figure it out eventually," she promised.

And when she did, she would run.

"I wish you wouldn't try," I said, all teasing gone.

"Because...?"

I owed her honesty. Still, I tried to smile, to make my words sound less threatening. "What if I'm not a superhero? What if I'm the bad guy?"

Her eyes widened by a fraction and her lips fell slightly apart. "Oh," she said. And then, after another second, "I see."

She'd finally heard me.

"Do you?" I asked, working to conceal my agony.

"You're dangerous?" she guessed. Her breathing hiked, and her heart raced.

I couldn't answer her. Was this my last moment with her? Would she run now? Could I be allowed to tell her that I loved her before she left? Or would that frighten her more?

"But not bad," she whispered, shaking her head, no fear evident in her clear eyes. "No, I don't believe that you're bad."

"You're wrong," I breathed.

Of course I was bad. Wasn't I rejoicing now, finding she thought better of me than I deserved? If I were a good person, I would have stayed away from her.

I stretched my hand across the table, reaching for the lid to her lemonade bottle as an excuse. She did not flinch away from my suddenly closer hand. She really was not afraid of me. Not yet.

I spun the lid like a top, watching it instead of her. My thoughts were in a snarl.

Run, Bella, run. I couldn't make myself say the words out loud.

She jumped to her feet. Just as I started to worry that she'd somehow heard my silent warning, she said, "We're going to be late."

"I'm not going to class today."

"Why not?"

Because I don't want to kill you. "It's healthy to ditch class now and then."

To be precise, it was healthier for the humans if the vampires ditched on days when human blood would be spilled. Mr. Banner was blood typing today. Alice had already ditched her morning class.

"Well, I'm going," she said. This didn't surprise me. She was responsible—she always did the right thing.

She was my opposite.

"I'll see you later, then," I said, trying for casual again, staring down at the whirling lid. *Please save yourself. Please never leave me.*

She hesitated, and I hoped for a moment that she would stay with me after all. But the bell rang and she hurried away.

I waited until she was gone, and then I put the lid in my pocket—a souvenir of this most consequential conversation—and walked through the rain to my car.

I put on my favorite calming CD—the same one I'd listened to that first day—but I wasn't hearing Debussy's notes for long. Other notes were running through my head, a fragment of a tune that pleased and intrigued me. I turned down the stereo and listened to the music in my head, playing with the fragment until it evolved into a fuller harmony. Automatically, my fingers moved in the air over imaginary piano keys.

The new composition was really coming along when my attention was caught by a wave of mental anguish.

Is she going to pass out? What do I do? Mike panicked.

A hundred yards away, Mike Newton was lowering Bella's limp body to the sidewalk. She slumped unresponsively against the wet concrete, her eyes closed, her skin chalky as a corpse.

I nearly took the door off the car.

"Bella?" I shouted.

There was no change in her lifeless face when I yelled her name.

My whole body went colder than ice. This was like a confirmation of every ludicrous scenario I'd imagined. The very moment she was out of my sight...

I was aware of Mike's aggravated surprise as I sifted furiously through his thoughts. He was only thinking of his anger toward me, so I didn't know what was wrong with Bella. If he'd done something to harm her, I would annihilate him. Not even the tiniest fragment of his body would ever be recovered.

"What's wrong—is she hurt?" I demanded, trying to focus his thoughts. It was maddening to have to walk at a human pace. I should not have called attention to my approach.

Then I could hear her heart beating and her even breath. As I watched, she squeezed her eyes more tightly shut. That eased some of my panic.

I saw a flicker of memories in Mike's head, a splash of images from the Biology room. Bella's head on our table, her fair skin turning green. Drops of red against the white cards.

Blood typing.

I stopped where I was, holding my breath. Her scent was one thing, her flowing blood was another altogether.

"I think she's fainted," Mike said, anxious and resentful at the same time. "I don't know what happened. She didn't even stick her finger."

Relief washed through me, and I breathed again, tasting the air. Ah, I could smell the tiny bleed of Mike Newton's puncture wound. Once, that might have appealed to me.

I knelt beside her while Mike hovered next to me, furious at my intervention.

"Bella. Can you hear me?"

"No," she moaned. "Go away."

The relief was so exquisite that I laughed. She wasn't in danger.

"I was taking her to the nurse," Mike said. "But she wouldn't go any farther."

"I'll take her. You can go back to class," I said dismissively.

Mike's teeth clenched together. "No. I'm supposed to do it."

I wasn't going to stand around arguing with the moron.

Thrilled and terrified, half-grateful to and half-aggrieved by the predicament that made touching her a necessity, I gently lifted Bella from the sidewalk and held her in my arms, touching only her rain jacket and jeans, keeping as much distance between our bodies as possible. I was striding forward in the same movement, in a hurry to have her safe—farther away from me, in other words.

Her eyes popped open, astonished.

"Put me down," she ordered in a weak voice—embarrassed again, I guessed from her expression. She didn't like to show weakness. But her body was so limp I doubted she would be able to stand on her own, let alone walk.

I ignored Mike's shouted protest behind us.

"You look awful," I told her, unable to stop grinning, because there was nothing wrong with her but a light head and a weak stomach.

"Put me back on the sidewalk," she said. Her lips were white.

"So you faint at the sight of blood?" A twisted kind of irony.

She closed her eyes and pressed her lips together.

"And not even your own blood," I added, my grin widening.

We arrived at the front office. The door was propped open an inch, and I kicked it out of my way.

Ms. Cope jumped, startled. "Oh my," she gasped as she examined the ashen girl in my arms.

"She fainted in Biology," I explained, before her imagination could get too out of hand.

Ms. Cope hurried to get the door to the nurse's office. Bella's eyes were open again, watching her. I heard the elderly nurse's internal astonishment as I laid the girl carefully on the one shabby bed. As soon as Bella was out of my arms, I put the width of the room between us. My body was too excited, too eager, my muscles tense and the venom flowing. She was so warm and fragrant.

"She's just a little faint," I reassured Mrs. Hammond. "They're blood typing in Biology."

She nodded, understanding now. "There's always one."

I stifled a laugh. Trust Bella to be that one.

"Just lie down for a minute, honey," Mrs. Hammond said. "It'll pass."

"I know," Bella said.

"Does this happen a lot?" the nurse asked.

"Sometimes," Bella admitted.

I tried to disguise my laughter as coughing.

This brought me to the nurse's attention. "You can go back to class now," she said.

I looked her straight in the eye and lied with perfect confidence. "I'm supposed to stay with her."

Hmm. I wonder. . . . Oh well. Mrs. Hammond nodded.

It worked just fine on the nurse. Why did Bella have to be so difficult?

"I'll go get you some ice for your forehead, dear," the nurse said, slightly uncomfortable from looking into my eyes—the way a human *should* be—and left the room.

"You were right," Bella moaned, closing her eyes.

What did she mean? I jumped to the worst conclusion: She'd accepted my warnings.

"I usually am," I said, trying to keep the amusement in my voice; it sounded sour now. "But about what in particular this time?"

"Ditching is healthy," she sighed.

Ah, relief again.

She was silent then. She just breathed slowly in and out. Her lips were beginning to turn pink. Her mouth was slightly out of balance, her upper lip just a little too full to match the lower. Staring at her mouth made me feel strange. Made me want to move closer to her, which was not a good idea.

"You scared me for a minute there," I said, trying to restart the conversation. The quiet was painful in an odd way, leaving me alone without her voice. "I thought Newton was dragging your dead body off to bury it in the woods."

"Ha ha," she responded.

"Honestly—I've seen corpses with better color." This was actually true. "I was concerned that I might have to avenge your murder." And I would have.

"Poor Mike," she sighed. "I'll bet he's mad."

Fury pulsed through me, but I contained it quickly. Her concern was surely just pity. She was kind. That was all.

"He absolutely loathes me," I told her, cheered by that idea.

"You can't know that."

"I saw his face—I could tell." It was probably true that reading his face would have given me enough information to make that particular deduction. All this practice with Bella was sharpening my skill.

"How did you see me? I thought you were ditching." Her face looked better—the green undertone had vanished from her translucent skin.

"I was in my car, listening to a CD."

Her mouth twitched, like my very ordinary answer had surprised her somehow.

She opened her eyes again when Mrs. Hammond returned with an ice pack.

"Here you go, dear," the nurse said as she laid it across Bella's forehead. "You're looking better."

"I think I'm fine," Bella said, and she sat up while pulling the ice pack away. Of course. She didn't like to be taken care of.

Mrs. Hammond's wrinkled hands fluttered toward the girl, as if she were going to push her back down, but just then Ms. Cope opened the door to the office and leaned in. With her appearance came the smell of fresh blood, just a whiff.

Invisible in the office behind her, Mike Newton was still very angry, wishing the heavy boy he dragged now was the girl who was in here with me.

"We've got another one," Ms. Cope said.

Bella quickly jumped down from the cot, eager to be out of the spotlight.

"Here," she said, handing the compress back to Mrs. Hammond. "I don't need this."

Mike grunted as he half-shoved Lee Stephens through the door. Blood was still dripping down the hand Lee held to his face, trickling toward his wrist.

"Oh no." This was my cue to leave—and Bella's, too, it seemed. "Go out to the office, Bella."

She stared up at me, surprised.

"Trust me—go."

She whirled and caught the door before it swung shut, rushing through to the office. I followed a few inches behind her. Her swinging hair brushed my hand.

She turned to look at me, still unsure.

"You actually listened to me." That was a first.

Her small nose wrinkled. "I smelled the blood."

I stared at her in blank surprise. "People can't smell blood."

"Well, I can—that's what makes me sick. It smells like rust... and salt."

My face froze, still staring.

Was she really even human? She *looked* human. She felt soft as a human. She smelled human—well, better actually. She acted human...sort of. But she didn't think like a human, or respond like one.

What other option was there, though?

"What?" she demanded.

"It's nothing."

Mike Newton interrupted us then, entering the room with resentful, violent thoughts.

"*You* look better," he said to her rudely.

My hand twitched, wanting to teach him some manners. I would have to watch myself, or I would end up actually killing this obnoxious boy.

"Just keep your hand in your pocket," she said. For one wild second, I thought she was talking to me.

"It's not bleeding anymore," he answered sullenly. "Are you going back to class?"

"Are you kidding? I'd just have to turn around and come back."

That was very good. I'd thought I was going to have to miss this whole hour with her, and now I got extra time instead. A gift I obviously did not deserve.

"Yeah, I guess...," Mike mumbled. "So are you going this weekend? To the beach?"

What was this? They had plans. Anger froze me in place. It was a group trip, though. Mike was sorting through the other invitees in his head, counting places. It wasn't just the two of them. That didn't help my fury. I leaned motionlessly against the counter, controlling my response.

"Sure, I said I was in," she promised him.

So she'd said yes to him, too. The jealousy burned, more painful than thirst.

"We're meeting at my dad's store, at ten." *And Cullen's NOT invited.*

"I'll be there," she said.

"I'll see you in Gym, then."

"See you," she replied.

He shuffled off to his class, his thoughts full of ire. *What does she see in that freak? Sure, he's rich, I guess. Girls think he's hot, but I don't see that. Too...too perfect. I bet his dad experiments with plastic surgery on all of them. That's why they're all so white and pretty. It's not natural. And he's sort of... scary-looking. Sometimes, when he stares at me, I'd swear he's thinking about killing me. Freak.*

Mike wasn't entirely unperceptive.

"Gym," Bella repeated quietly. A groan.

I looked at her and saw that she was unhappy about something again. I wasn't sure why, but it was clear that she didn't want to go to her next class with Mike, and I was all for that plan.

I went to her side and bent close to her face, feeling the warmth of her skin radiating out to my lips. I didn't dare breathe.

"I can take care of that," I murmured. "Go sit down and look pale."

She did as I asked, sitting in one of the folding chairs and leaning her head back against the wall, while behind me, Ms. Cope came out of the back room and went to her desk. With her eyes closed, Bella looked as if she'd passed out again. Her full color hadn't come back yet.

I turned to the receptionist. Hopefully, Bella was paying

attention to this, I thought sardonically. This was how a human was *supposed* to respond.

"Ms. Cope?" I asked, using my persuasive voice again.

Her eyelashes fluttered, and her heart sped up. *Get ahold of yourself!* "Yes?"

That was interesting. When Shelly Cope's pulse quickened, it was because she found me physically attractive, not because she was frightened. I was used to that around human females, those who'd grown somewhat acclimatized to my kind through continued exposure...yet I hadn't considered that explanation for Bella's racing heart.

I liked that thought, perhaps too much. I smiled my careful, human-soothing smile, and Ms. Cope's breathing got louder.

"Bella has Gym next hour, and I don't think she feels well enough. Actually, I was thinking I should take her home now. Do you think you could excuse her from class?" I stared into her depthless eyes, enjoying the havoc that this wreaked on her thought processes. Was it possible that Bella...?

Ms. Cope had to swallow loudly before she answered. "Do you need to be excused, too, Edward?"

"No, I have Mrs. Goff. She won't mind."

I wasn't paying much attention to her now. I was exploring this new possibility.

Hmm. I would have liked to believe that Bella found me attractive like other humans did, but when did Bella ever have the same reactions as other humans? I shouldn't get my hopes up.

"Okay, it's all taken care of. You feel better, Bella."

Bella nodded weakly—overacting a bit.

"Can you walk, or do you want me to carry you again?" I asked, amused by her poor theatrics. I knew she would want to walk—she wouldn't want to be weak.

"I'll walk," she said.

Right again.

She got up, hesitating for a moment as if to check her balance. I held the door for her, and we walked out into the rain.

I watched her as she lifted her face to the light rain with her eyes closed, a slight smile on her lips. What was she thinking? Something about this action seemed off, and I quickly realized why the posture looked unfamiliar to me. Normal human girls wouldn't raise their faces to the drizzle that way; normal human girls usually wore makeup, even here in this wet place.

Bella never wore makeup, nor should she. The cosmetics industry made billions of dollars a year from women who were trying to attain skin like hers.

"Thanks," she said, smiling at me now. "It's almost worth getting sick to miss Gym."

I stared across the campus, wondering how to prolong my time with her. "Anytime," I said.

"So are you going? This Saturday, I mean?" She sounded hopeful.

Ah, her hope eased the sting of my jealousy. She wanted me with her, not Mike Newton. And I wanted to say yes. But there were many things to consider. For one, the sun would be shining this Saturday.

"Where are you all going, exactly?" I tried to keep my voice nonchalant, as if the answer didn't matter much. Mike had said *beach*, though. Not much chance of avoiding sunlight there. Emmett would be irritated if I canceled our plans, but that wouldn't stop me if there was any way to spend the time with her.

"Down to La Push, to First Beach."

It was impossible, then.

I managed my disappointment, then glanced down at her, smiling wryly. "I really don't think I was invited."

She sighed, already resigned. "I just invited you."

"Let's you and I not push poor Mike any further this week. We don't want him to snap." I thought about snapping *poor Mike* myself, and enjoyed the mental picture intensely.

"Mike-schmike," she said, dismissive again. I smiled.

And then she started to walk away from me.

Without thinking about my action, I automatically reached out and caught her by the back of her rain jacket. She jerked to a stop.

"Where do you think you're going?" I was upset—almost angry that she was leaving. I hadn't had enough time with her.

"I'm going home," she said, clearly baffled as to why this should upset me.

"Didn't you hear me promise to take you safely home? Do you think I'm going to let you drive in your condition?" I knew she wouldn't like *that*—my implication of weakness on her part. But I needed to practice for the Seattle trip—to see if I could handle her proximity in an enclosed space. This was a much shorter journey.

"What condition?" she demanded. "And what about my truck?"

"I'll have Alice drop it off after school." I pulled her back toward my car carefully. Apparently, walking *forward* was challenging enough for her.

"Let go!" she said, twisting sideways and nearly tripping. I held one hand out to catch her, but she righted herself before it was necessary. I shouldn't be looking for excuses to touch her. That started me thinking again about Ms. Cope's reaction to me, but I filed it away for later. There was much to be considered on that front.

I let her go as she asked, and then regretted it—she immediately tripped and stumbled into the passenger door of my car. I would have to be even more careful, to take into account her poor balance.

"You are so *pushy*!"

She was right. My behavior was odd, and that was the kindest description. Would she tell me *no* now?

"It's open."

I got in on my side and started the car. She held her body rigidly, still outside, though the rain had picked up and I knew she didn't like the cold and wet. Water was soaking through her thick hair, darkening it to near-black.

"I am perfectly capable of driving myself home!"

Of course she was. But I craved her time in a way that I'd never really wanted anything else before. Not immediate and demanding like thirst, this was something different, a different kind of want, and different kind of pain.

She shivered.

I rolled the passenger-side window down and leaned toward her. "Please get in, Bella."

Her eyes narrowed, and I guessed that she was debating whether or not to make a run for it.

"I could drag you back...," I joked, wondering if my guess was correct. The consternation on her face told me it was.

Her chin held stiffly in the air, she opened her door and climbed in. Her hair dripped on the leather, and her boots squeaked against each other.

"This is completely unnecessary," she said.

I thought she looked more embarrassed than really angry. Was my behavior entirely offside? I *thought* I was teasing, that I was acting like the average besotted teenage boy, but what if I'd gotten it wrong? Did she feel coerced? I realized she had every reason to.

I didn't know how to do this. How to court her as a normal, human, modern man in the year two thousand and five. As a human, I'd only learned the customs of my time. Thanks to my strange gift, I knew quite well how people thought now, what they did, how they acted, but when I tried to act casual and modern it seemed all wrong. Probably because I wasn't normal or modern or human. And it wasn't as if I'd learned anything usable from my family. None of them had had anything near a normal courtship, even excepting the two other qualifications.

Rosalie and Emmett had been the cliché, the classic love-at-first-sight story. There had never been a moment when either one had questioned what they were to each other. In the first second

Rosalie saw Emmett, she'd been drawn to the innocence and honesty that had evaded her in life, and she wanted him. In the first second that Emmett saw Rosalie, he saw a goddess whom he had worshiped without cease ever since. There had never been an awkward first conversation full of doubt, never a fingernail-biting moment of waiting for a yes or no.

Alice and Jasper's union had been even less normal. For all the twenty-eight years up to their first meeting, Alice had known she would love Jasper. She'd seen years, decades, centuries, of their future lives together. And Jasper, feeling all her emotions in that long-awaited moment, the purity and certainty and depth of her love, couldn't help but be overwhelmed. It must have felt like a tsunami to him.

Carlisle and Esme had been slightly more typical than the others, I supposed. Esme had already been in love with Carlisle—much to his shock—but not through any mystical, magical means. She'd met Carlisle as a girl and, drawn to his gentleness, wit, and otherworldly beauty, formed an attachment that had haunted her for the rest of her human years. Life had not been kind to Esme, and so it was not surprising that this golden memory of a good man had never been supplanted in her heart. After the burning torment of transformation, when she'd awakened to the face of her long-cherished dream, her affections were entirely his.

I'd been on hand to caution Carlisle about her unforeseen reaction. He'd expected that she would be shocked by her transformation, traumatized by the pain, horrified by what she'd become, much as I had been. He'd expected to have to explain and apologize, to soothe and to atone. He knew there was a good chance that she would have preferred death, that she would despise him for the choice made without her knowledge or consent. So the fact that she had been immediately prepared to join this life—not really the life, but to join *him*—was not something he was ready for.

He'd never seen himself as a possible object of romantic love before that moment. It seemed contrary to what he was—a vampire, a monster. The knowledge I gave him changed the way he looked at Esme, the way he looked at himself.

More than that, it was very a powerful thing, *choosing* to save someone. It was not a decision any sane individual made lightly. When Carlisle chose me, he'd already felt a dozen binding emotions toward me before I'd even awakened to what was happening. Responsibility, anxiety, tenderness, pity, hope, compassion...there was a natural ownership to the act that I'd never experienced, only heard about through his thoughts and Rosalie's. He already felt like my father before I knew his name. For me, it was effortless and instinctive to fall into my role as son. Love came easily—though I'd always attributed that more to who he was as a person than to his initiating my conversion.

So whether for these reasons, or whether it was because Carlisle and Esme were simply meant to be...even with my gift to hear it all as it happened, I would never know. She loved him, and he quickly found he could return that love. It was a very short period of time before his surprise changed to wonder, to discovery, and to romance. So much happiness.

Just a few moments of easily overcome awkwardness, all smoothed out with the help of a little mind reading. Nothing so awkward as this. None of them had been clueless and floundering like me.

Not a full second had passed while these less complicated pairings passed through my mind; Bella was just closing her door. I quickly turned up the heater so she wouldn't be uncomfortable, and lowered the music to a background volume. I drove toward the exit, watching her from the corner of my eye. Her lower lip was jutting out stubbornly.

Suddenly she looked at the stereo with interest, her sulky expression disappearing. "Clair de Lune?" she asked.

A fan of the classics? "You know Debussy?"

"Not well," she said. "My mother plays a lot of classical music around the house—I only know my favorites."

"It's one of my favorites, too." I stared at the rain, considering that. I actually had something in common with the girl. I'd begun to think that we were opposites in every way.

She seemed more relaxed now, staring at the rain like me, with unseeing eyes. I used her momentary distraction to experiment with breathing.

I inhaled carefully through my nose.

Potent.

I clutched the steering wheel tightly. The rain made her smell better. I wouldn't have thought that was possible. My tongue tingled in anticipation of the taste.

The monster wasn't dead, I realized with disgust. Just biding his time.

I tried to swallow against the burn in my throat. It didn't help. This made me angry. I had so little time with the girl. Look at the lengths I'd already had to go to in order to secure an extra fifteen minutes. I took another breath and fought with my reaction. I *had* to be stronger than this.

What would I be doing if I weren't the villain of this story? I asked myself. How would I be using this valuable time?

I would be learning more about her.

"What is your mother like?" I asked.

Bella smiled. "She looks a lot like me, but she's prettier."

I eyed her skeptically.

"I have too much Charlie in me," she went on. "She's more outgoing than I am, and braver."

Outgoing, I believed. Braver? I wasn't sure.

"She's irresponsible and slightly eccentric, and she's a very unpredictable cook. She's my best friend." Her voice had turned melancholy. Her forehead creased.

As I had noticed before, her tone sounded more like parent than child.

I stopped in front of her house, wondering too late if I was supposed to know where she lived. No, this wouldn't be suspicious in such a small town, with her father a public figure.

"How old are you, Bella?" She must be older than her peers. Perhaps she'd been late to start school, or been held back. That didn't seem likely, though, bright as she was.

"I'm seventeen," she answered.

"You don't seem seventeen."

She laughed.

"What?"

"My mom always says I was born thirty-five years old and that I get more middle-aged every year." She laughed again, and then sighed. "Well, someone has to be the adult."

This clarified things for me. It was easy to understand how the irresponsibility of the mother would result in the maturity of the daughter. She'd had to grow up early, to become the caretaker. That's why she didn't like being cared for—she felt it was her job.

"You don't seem much like a junior in high school yourself," she said, pulling me from my reverie.

I frowned. For everything I perceived about her, she perceived too much in return. I changed the subject.

"So why did your mother marry Phil?"

She hesitated a minute before answering. "My mother... she's very young for her age. I think Phil makes her feel even younger. At any rate, she's crazy about him." She shook her head indulgently.

"Do you approve?" I wondered.

"Does it matter?" she asked. "I want her to be happy... and he is who she wants."

The unselfishness of her comment would have shocked me except that it fit in all too well with what I'd learned of her character.

"That's very generous.... I wonder."

"What?"

"Would she extend the same courtesy to you, do you think? No matter who your choice was?"

It was a foolish question, and I could not keep my voice casual while I asked it. How stupid to even consider someone approving of *me* for her daughter. How stupid to even think of Bella choosing me.

"I—I think so," she stuttered, reacting in some way to my gaze. Was it fear? I thought of Ms. Cope again. What were the other tells? Wide eyes could designate both emotions. The fluttering lashes, though, seemed to point away from fright. Bella's lips were parted....

She recovered. "But she's the parent, after all. It's a little bit different."

I smiled wryly. "No one too scary, then."

"What do you mean by scary? Multiple facial piercings and extensive tattoos?" She grinned at me.

"That's one definition, I suppose." A very nonthreatening definition, to my mind.

"What's your definition?"

She always asked the wrong questions. Or exactly the right ones, maybe. The ones I didn't want to answer, at any rate.

"Do you think that *I* could be scary?" I asked her, trying to smile a little.

She thought it through before answering me in a serious voice. "Hmm...I think you *could* be, if you wanted to."

I was serious, too. "Are you frightened of me now?"

She answered at once, not thinking this one through. "No."

I smiled more easily. I did not think she was entirely telling the truth, but neither was she truly lying. She wasn't frightened enough to want to leave, at least. I wondered how she would feel if I told her she was having this discussion with a vampire, and then cringed internally at her imagined reaction.

"So, now are you going to tell me about your family? It's got to be a much more interesting story than mine."

A more frightening one, at least.

"What do you want to know?" I asked cautiously.

"The Cullens adopted you?"

"Yes."

She hesitated, then spoke in a small voice. "What happened to your parents?"

This wasn't so hard. I wasn't even having to lie to her. "They died a very long time ago."

"I'm sorry," she mumbled, clearly worried about having hurt me.

She was worried about *me*. Such a strange feeling, to see her care, even in this common way.

"I don't really remember them that clearly," I assured her. "Carlisle and Esme have been my parents for a long time now."

"And you love them," she deduced.

I smiled. "Yes. I couldn't imagine two better people."

"You're very lucky."

"I know I am." In that one circumstance, the matter of parents, my luck could not be denied.

"And your brother and sister?"

If I let her push for too many details, I would have to lie. I glanced at the clock, disheartened that my time with her was up, but also relieved. The pain was severe, and I worried that the burn in my throat might suddenly flare up hot enough to control me.

"My brother and sister, and Jasper and Rosalie for that matter, are going to be quite upset if they have to stand in the rain waiting for me."

"Oh, sorry, I guess you have to go."

She didn't move. She didn't want our time to be up, either.

The pain was not so bad, really, I thought. But I should be responsible.

"And you probably want your truck back before Chief Swan gets home, so you don't have to tell him about the Biology incident." I grinned at the memory of her embarrassment in my arms.

"I'm sure he's already heard. There are no secrets in Forks." She said the name of the town with distinct distaste.

I laughed at her words. No secrets, indeed. "Have fun at

the beach." I glanced at the pouring rain, knowing it would not last, and wishing more strongly than usual that it could. "Good weather for sunbathing." Well, it would be by Saturday. She would enjoy that. And her happiness had become the most important thing. More important than my own.

"Won't I see you tomorrow?"

The worry in her tone pleased me, but also made me yearn to not have to disappoint her.

"No. Emmett and I are starting the weekend early." I was angry at myself now for having made the plans. I could break them... but there was no such thing as too much hunting at this point, and my family was going to be concerned enough about my behavior without me revealing how obsessive I was turning. I still wasn't sure exactly what madness had possessed me last night. I really needed to find a way to control my impulses. Perhaps a little distance would help with that.

"What are you going to do?" she asked, sounding not at all happy with my revelation.

More pleasure, more pain.

"We're going to be hiking in the Goat Rocks Wilderness, just south of Rainier." Emmett was eager for bear season.

"Oh, well, have fun," she said halfheartedly. Her lack of enthusiasm pleased me again.

As I stared at her, I began to feel almost agonized at the thought of saying even a temporary goodbye. She was so soft, so vulnerable. It seemed foolhardy to let her out of my sight, where anything could happen to her. And yet, the worst things that could happen to her would result from being with me.

"Will you do something for me this weekend?" I asked seriously.

She nodded, though clearly mystified by my intensity.

Keep it light.

"Don't be offended, but you seem to be one of those people who just attract accidents like a magnet. So... try not to fall into the ocean or get run over or anything, all right?"

I smiled ruefully at her, hoping she couldn't see the real sorrow in my eyes. How much I wished that she wasn't so much better off away from me, no matter what might happen to her there.

Run, Bella, run. I love you too much, for your good or mine.

She was offended by my teasing; I must have done it wrong again. She glared at me. "I'll see what I can do," she snapped, jumping out into the rain and slamming the door as hard as she could behind her.

I curled my hand around the key I'd just picked from her jacket pocket and inhaled her scent deeply as I drove away.

7. MELODY

I HAD TO WAIT WHEN I GOT BACK TO SCHOOL. THE FINAL hour wasn't out yet. That was good, because I had things to think about and I needed the alone time.

Her scent lingered in the car. I kept the windows up, letting it assault me, trying to get used to the feel of intentionally torching my throat.

Attraction.

It was a problematic thing to contemplate. So many sides to it, so many different meanings and levels. Not the same thing as love, but tied up in it inextricably.

I had no idea if Bella was attracted to me. (Would her mental silence somehow continue to get more and more frustrating until I went mad? Or was there a limit that I would eventually reach?)

I tried to compare her physical responses to others', like the receptionist and Jessica Stanley, but the comparison was inconclusive. The same markers—changes in heart rate and breathing patterns—could just as easily mean fear or shock or anxiety as they did interest. Certainly other women, and men, too, had reacted to my face with instinctive apprehension. Many more had that response than the alternative. It seemed unlikely that Bella could be entertaining the same kinds of thoughts that Jessica Stanley used to have. After all, Bella knew very well that there was something wrong with me, even if she didn't know exactly what it was. She had touched my icy skin, and then yanked her hand away from the chill.

And yet... I remembered those fantasies that used to repulse me, but remembered them with Bella in Jessica's place.

I was breathing more quickly, the fire clawing up and down my throat.

What if it had been *Bella* imagining me with my arms wrapped around her fragile body? Feeling me pull her tightly against my chest and then cupping my hand under her chin? Brushing the heavy curtain of her hair back from her blushing face? Tracing the shape of her full lips with my fingertips? Leaning my face closer to hers, where I could feel the heat of her breath on my mouth? Moving closer still...

But then I flinched away from the daydream, knowing, as I had known when Jessica had imagined these things, what would happen if I got that close to her.

Attraction was an impossible dilemma, because I was already too attracted to Bella in the worst way.

Did I want Bella to be attracted to me, a woman to a man?

That was the wrong question. The right question was *should* I want Bella to be attracted to me that way, and the answer was no. Because I was not a human man, and that wasn't fair to her.

With every fiber of my being, I ached to be a normal man, so that I could hold her in my arms without risking her life. So that I could be free to spin my own fantasies, fantasies that didn't end with her blood on my hands, her blood glowing in my eyes.

My pursuit of her was indefensible. What kind of relationship could I offer her, when I couldn't risk touching her?

I hung my head in my hands.

It was all the more confusing because I had never felt so human in my whole life—not even when I *was* human, as far as I could recall. In those days, my thoughts had all been turned to a soldier's glory. The Great War had raged through most of my adolescence, and I'd been only nine months away from my eighteenth birthday when the influenza had struck. I had just vague impressions of those human years, murky memories that became less real with every passing decade. I remembered my mother most clearly and felt an ancient ache when I thought of her face. I recalled dimly how much she had hated the future I'd raced eagerly toward, praying every night when she said grace at dinner that the "horrid war" would end. I had no memories of another kind of yearning. Besides my mother's love, there was no other love that had made me wish to stay.

This was entirely new to me. I had no parallels to draw, no comparisons to make.

The love I felt for Bella had come purely, but now the waters were muddied. I wanted very much to be able to touch her. Did she feel the same way?

That didn't matter, I tried to convince myself.

I stared at my white hands, hating their hardness, their coldness, their inhuman strength....

I jumped when the passenger door opened.

Ha. Caught you by surprise. There's a first, Emmett thought as he slid into the seat. "I'll bet Mrs. Goff thinks you're on drugs, you've been so erratic lately. Where were you today?"

"I was...doing good deeds."

Huh?

I chuckled. "Caring for the sick, that kind of thing."

That confused him more, but then he inhaled and caught the scent in the car.

"Oh. The girl again?"

I scowled.

This is getting weird.

"Tell me about it," I mumbled.

He inhaled again. "Hmm, she does have a quite a flavor, doesn't she?"

The snarl broke through my lips before his words had even registered all the way, an automatic response.

"Easy, kid, I'm just sayin'."

The others arrived then. Rosalie noticed the scent at once and glowered at me, still not over her irritation. I wondered what her real problem was, but all I could hear from her were insults.

I didn't like Jasper's reaction, either. Like Emmett, he noticed Bella's appeal. Not that the scent had, for either of them, a thousandth portion of the draw it had for me, but it still upset me that her blood was sweet to them. Jasper had poor control.

Alice skipped to my side of the car and held her hand out for Bella's truck key.

"I only saw that I was," she said—as was her habit—obscurely. "You'll have to tell me the whys."

"This doesn't mean—"

"I know, I know. I'll wait. It won't be long."

I sighed and gave her the key.

I followed her to Bella's house. The rain was pounding down like a million tiny hammers, so loud that Bella's human ears might not hear the thunder of the truck's engine. I watched her window, but she didn't come to look out. Maybe she wasn't there. There were no thoughts to hear.

It made me sad that I couldn't hear enough of her thoughts even to check on her—to make sure she was happy, or safe, at the very least.

Alice climbed into the back and we sped home. The roads were empty, and so it only took a few minutes. We trooped into the house, and then went to our various pastimes.

Emmett and Jasper were in the middle of an elaborate game of chess, utilizing eight joined boards spread out along the glass back wall, and their own complicated set of rules. They wouldn't let me play; only Alice would play games with me anymore.

Alice went to her computer just around the corner from them and I could hear her monitors sing to life. She was working on a fashion design project for Rosalie's wardrobe, but Rosalie did not join her today, to stand behind her and direct cut and color as Alice's hand traced over the touch-sensitive screens. Instead, today Rosalie sprawled sullenly on the sofa and started flipping through twenty channels a second on the flat screen, never pausing. I could hear her trying to decide whether or not to go out to the garage and tune her BMW again.

Esme was upstairs, humming over a set of blueprints. She was always designing something new. Perhaps she would build this one for our next home, or the one after that.

Alice leaned her head around the wall after a moment and started mouthing Emmett's next moves—Emmett sat on the floor with his back to her—to Jasper, who kept his expression very smooth as he cut off Emmett's favorite knight.

And, for the first time in so long that I felt ashamed, I went to sit at the exquisite grand piano stationed just off the entryway.

I ran my hand gently up the scales, testing the pitch. The tuning was still perfect.

Upstairs, Esme's pencil paused and she cocked her head to the side.

I began the first line of the tune that had suggested itself to me in the car today, pleased that it sounded even better than I'd imagined.

Edward is playing again, Esme thought joyously, a smile breaking across her face. She got up from her drafting desk and flitted silently to the head of the stairs.

I added a harmonizing line, letting the central melody weave through it.

Esme sighed with contentment, sat down on the top step, and leaned her head against a baluster. *A new song. It's been so long. What a lovely tune.*

I let the melody lead in a new direction, following it with the bass line.

Edward is composing again? Rosalie thought, and her teeth clenched together in fierce resentment.

In that moment, she slipped, and I could read all her underlying outrage. I saw why she was in such a poor temper with me. Why killing Isabella Swan had not bothered her conscience at all.

With Rosalie, it was always about vanity.

The music came to an abrupt halt, and I laughed before I could help myself, a sharp bark of amusement that broke off quickly as I threw my hand over my mouth.

Rosalie turned to glare at me, her eyes sparking with mortified fury.

Emmett and Jasper turned to stare, too, and I heard Esme's confusion. She was downstairs in a flash, pausing to glance between Rosalie and me.

"Don't stop, Edward," Esme encouraged after a strained moment.

I started playing again, turning my back on Rosalie while trying very hard to control the grin stretching across my face. She got to her feet and stalked out of the room, more angry than embarrassed. But certainly quite embarrassed.

If you say one word, I will put you down like a dog.

I smothered another laugh.

"What's wrong, Rose?" Emmett called after her. Rosalie didn't turn. Back ramrod straight, she continued to the garage and then squirmed under her car as if she could bury herself there.

"What's that about?" Emmett asked me.

"I don't have the faintest idea," I lied.

Emmett grumbled, frustrated.

"Keep playing," Esme urged. My fingers had paused again.

I did as she asked, and she came to stand behind me, putting her hands on my shoulders.

The song was compelling, but incomplete. I toyed with a bridge, but it didn't seem right somehow.

"It's charming. Does it have a name?" Esme asked.

"Not yet."

"Is there a story to it?" she asked, a smile in her voice. This gave her very great pleasure, and I felt guilty for having neglected my music for so long. It had been selfish.

"It's... a lullaby, I suppose." I got the bridge right then. It led easily to the next movement, taking on a life of its own.

"A lullaby," she repeated to herself.

There *was* a story to this melody, and once I saw that, the pieces fell into place effortlessly. The story was a sleeping girl in a narrow bed, dark hair thick and wild and twisted like seaweed across the pillow....

Alice left Jasper to his own skill and came to sit next to me on the bench. In her trilling, wind-chime voice, she sketched out a wordless descant two octaves above the melody.

"I like it," I murmured. "But how about this?"

I added her line to the harmony—my hands flying across the keys to work all the pieces together—modifying it a bit, taking it in a new direction.

She caught the mood and sang along.

"Yes. Perfect," I said.

Esme squeezed my shoulder.

But I could see the conclusion now, with Alice's voice rising above the tune and taking it to another place. I could see how the song must end, because the sleeping girl was perfect just the way she was, and any change at all would be wrong, a sadness. The song drifted toward that realization, slower and lower. Alice's voice lowered, too, and became solemn, a tone that belonged under the echoing arches of a candlelit cathedral.

I played the last note, and then bowed my head over the keys.

Esme stroked my hair. *It's going to be fine, Edward. This is going to work out for the best. You* deserve *happiness, my son. Fate owes you that.*

"Thank you," I whispered, wishing I could believe it. And that my happiness was the one that mattered.

Love doesn't always come in convenient packages.

I laughed once without humor.

You, out of everyone on this planet, are perhaps best equipped to deal with such a difficult quandary. You are the best and the brightest of us all.

I sighed. Every mother thought the same of her son.

Esme was still full of joy that my heart had finally been touched after all this time, no matter the potential for tragedy. She'd thought I would always be alone.

She'll have to love you back, she thought suddenly, catching me by surprise with the direction of her thoughts. *If she's a bright girl.* She smiled. *But I can't imagine anyone being so slow they wouldn't see the catch* you *are.*

"Stop it, Mom, you're making me blush," I teased. Her words, though improbable, did cheer me.

Alice laughed and picked out the top hand of "Heart and Soul." I grinned and completed the simple harmony with her. Then I favored her with a performance of "Chopsticks."

She giggled, then sighed. "So I wish you'd tell me what you were laughing at Rose about," Alice said. "But I can see that you won't."

"No."

She flicked my ear with her finger.

"Be nice, Alice," Esme chided. "Edward is being a gentleman."

"But I want to *know.*"

I laughed at the whining tone she put on. Then I said, "Here, Esme," and began playing her favorite song, an unnamed tribute to the love I'd watched between her and Carlisle for so many years.

"Thank you, dear." She squeezed my shoulder again.

I didn't have to concentrate to play the familiar piece. Instead I thought of Rosalie, still figuratively writhing in humiliation in the garage, and grinned to myself.

Having just discovered the potency of jealousy for myself, I had a small amount of pity for her. It was a wretched way to feel. Of course, her jealously was a thousand times more petty than mine. Quite the dog in the manger scenario.

I wondered how Rosalie's life and personality would have been different if she had not always been the most beautiful. Would she have been a happier person—less egocentric? More compassionate?—if beauty hadn't at all times been her strongest selling point? Well, I supposed it was useless to wonder, because the past was done, and she always *had* been the most beautiful. Even when human, she had ever lived in the spotlight of her own loveliness. Not that she'd minded. The opposite—she'd loved admiration above all else. That hadn't changed with the loss of her mortality.

It was no surprise, then, taking this need as a given, that she'd been offended when I had not, from the beginning, worshiped her beauty the way she expected all males to worship. Not that she'd wanted *me* in any way—far from it. But it had aggravated her that I did not want her, despite that.

It was different with Jasper and Carlisle—they were already both in love. I was completely unattached, and yet still remained obstinately unmoved.

I'd thought that old resentment buried, that she was long past it. And she had been...until the day I finally found someone whose beauty touched me the way hers had not. Of course. I should have realized how that would annoy her. I probably would have, had I not been so preoccupied.

Rosalie had relied on the belief that if I did not find *her* beauty worth worshiping, then certainly there was no beauty on earth that would reach me. She'd been furious since the moment I'd saved Bella's life, guessing, with her shrewd, competitive intuition, the interest that I was all but unconscious of myself.

Rosalie was mortally offended that I found some insignificant human girl more appealing than her.

I suppressed the urge to laugh again.

It bothered me some, though, the way she saw Bella. Rosalie actually thought the girl *plain*. How could she believe that? It seemed incomprehensible to me. A product of the jealousy, no doubt.

"Oh!" Alice said abruptly. "Jasper, guess what?"

I saw what she'd just seen, and my hands froze on the keys.

"What, Alice?" Jasper asked.

"Peter and Charlotte are coming to visit next week! They're going to be in the neighborhood. Isn't that nice?"

"What's wrong, Edward?" Esme asked, feeling the tension in my shoulders.

"Peter and Charlotte are coming to *Forks*?" I hissed at Alice.

She rolled her eyes at me. "Calm down, Edward. It's not their first visit."

My teeth clenched. It *was* their first visit since Bella had arrived, and her sweet blood didn't appeal just to me.

Alice frowned at my expression. "They never hunt here. You know that."

But Jasper's brother of sorts and the little vampire he loved were not like us; they hunted the usual way. They could not be trusted around Bella.

"When?" I demanded.

She pursed her lips unhappily but told me what I needed to know. *Monday morning. No one is going to hurt Bella.*

"No," I agreed, and then turned away from her. "You ready, Emmett?"

"I thought we were leaving in the morning?"

"We're coming back by midnight Sunday. I guess it's up to you when you want to leave."

"Okay, fine. Let me say goodbye to Rose first."

"Sure." With the mood Rosalie was in, it would be a short goodbye.

You really have lost it, Edward, he thought as he headed toward the back door.

"I suppose I have."

"Play the new song for me, one more time," Esme asked.

"If you'd like that," I agreed, though I was a little hesitant to follow the tune to its unavoidable end—the end that had set me aching in unfamiliar ways. I thought for a moment, and then pulled the bottle cap from my pocket and set it on the empty music rack. That helped a bit—my little memento of her *yes*.

I nodded to myself, and started playing.

Esme and Alice exchanged a glance, but neither one asked.

"Hasn't anyone ever told you not to play with your food?" I called to Emmett.

"Oh, hey, Edward!" he shouted back, grinning and waving at me. The bear took advantage of his distraction to rake its heavy paw across Emmett's chest. The sharp claws shredded through his shirt and squealed across his skin like knives across steel.

The bear bellowed at the high-pitched noise.

Aw hell, Rose gave me this shirt!

Emmett roared back at the enraged animal.

I sighed and sat down on a convenient boulder. This might take a while.

But Emmett was almost done. He let the bear try to take his head off with another swipe of the paw, laughing as the blow bounced off and sent the beast staggering back. The bear roared and Emmett roared again through his laughter. Then he launched himself at the animal, which stood a head taller than him on its hind legs, and their bodies fell to the ground tangled up together, taking a mature spruce tree down with them. The bear's growls cut off with a gurgle.

A few minutes later, Emmett jogged over to where I was waiting for him. His shirt was destroyed, torn and bloodied, sticky with sap and covered in fur. His dark curly hair wasn't in much better shape. He had a huge grin on his face.

"That was a strong one. I could almost feel it when he clawed me."

"You're such a child, Emmett."

He eyed my smooth, clean white button-down. "Weren't you able to track down that mountain lion, then?"

"Of course I was. I just don't eat like a savage."

Emmett laughed his booming laugh. "I wish they were stronger. It would be more fun."

"No one said you had to fight your food."

"Yeah, but who else am I going to fight with? You and Alice cheat, Rose never wants to mess up her hair, and Esme gets mad if Jasper and I *really* go at it."

"Life is hard all around, isn't it?"

Emmett grinned at me, shifting his weight a bit so that he was suddenly poised to take a charge.

"C'mon Edward. Just turn it off for one minute and fight fair."

"It doesn't turn off," I reminded him.

"Wonder what that human girl does to keep you out," Emmett mused. "Maybe she could give me some pointers."

My good humor vanished. "Stay away from her," I growled through my teeth.

"Touchy, touchy."

I sighed. Emmett came to sit beside me on the rock.

"Sorry. I know you're going through a tough spot. I really am trying to not be *too* much of an insensitive jerk, but since that's sort of my natural state..."

He waited for me to laugh at his joke, and then made a face.

So serious all the time. What's bugging you now?

"Thinking about her. Well, worrying, really."

"What's there to worry about? *You* are *here*." He laughed loudly.

I ignored his joke again, but answered his question. "Have you ever thought about how fragile they all are? How many bad things can happen to a mortal?"

"Not really. I guess I see what you mean, though. I wasn't much match for a bear that first time around, was I?"

"Bears," I muttered, adding a new fear to the already large pile. "That would be just her luck, wouldn't it? Stray bear in town. Of course it would head straight for Bella."

Emmett chuckled. "You sound like a crazy person. You can hear that, right?"

"Just imagine for one minute that Rosalie was human, Emmett. And she could run into a bear...or get hit by a car...or *lightning*...or fall down stairs...or get sick—get a *disease*!" The words burst from me stormily. It was a relief to let them out—they'd been festering inside me all weekend. "Fires and earthquakes and tornadoes! Ugh! When's the last time you watched the news? Have you *seen* the kinds of things that happen to them? Burglaries and homicides..." My teeth clenched together, and I was abruptly so infuriated by the idea of another *human* hurting her that I couldn't breathe.

"Whoa, whoa! Hold up, there, kid. She lives in Forks, remember? So she gets rained on." He shrugged.

"I think she has some serious bad luck, Emmett, I really do. Look at the evidence. Of all the places in the world she could go, she ends up in a town where *vampires* make up a significant portion of the population."

"Yeah, but we're vegetarians. So isn't that good luck, not bad?"

"With the way she smells? Definitely bad. And then, more bad luck, the way she smells to *me*." I glowered at my hands, hating them again.

"Except that you have more self-control than just about anyone but Carlisle. Good luck again."

"The van?"

"That was just an accident."

"You should have seen it coming for her, Em, again and again. I swear, it was like she had some kind of magnetic pull."

"But you were there. That was good luck."

"Was it? Isn't this the worst luck any human could ever possibly have—to have a *vampire* fall in *love* with them?"

Emmett considered that quietly for a moment. He pictured the girl in his head, and found the image uninteresting. *Honestly, I can't really see the draw.*

"Well, I can't really see Rosalie's allure, either," I said rudely. "*Honestly*, she seems like more work than any pretty face is worth."

Emmett chuckled. "I don't suppose you'd tell me..."

"I don't know what her problem is, Emmett," I lied with a sudden, wide grin.

I saw his intent in time to brace myself. He tried to shove me off the rock, and there was a loud cracking sound as a fissure opened in the stone between us.

"Cheater," he muttered.

I waited for him to try another time, but his thoughts took a different direction. He was picturing Bella's face again, but imagining it whiter, imagining her eyes bright red.

"No," I said, my voice strangled.

"It solves your worries about mortality, doesn't it? And then you wouldn't want to kill her, either. Isn't that the best way?"

"For me? Or for her?"

"For you," he answered easily. His tone added the *of course.*

I laughed humorlessly. "Wrong answer."

"I didn't mind so much," he reminded me.

"Rosalie did."

He sighed. We both knew that Rosalie would do anything, give up anything, if it meant she could be human again. Anything. Even Emmett.

"Yeah, Rose did," he acquiesced quietly.

"I can't...I shouldn't...I'm *not* going to ruin Bella's life. Wouldn't you feel the same if it were Rosalie?"

Emmett thought about that for a moment. *You really...love her?*

"I can't even describe it, Em. All of a sudden, this girl's the whole world to me. I don't see the *point* of the rest of the world without her anymore."

But you won't change her? She won't last forever, Edward.

"I know that," I groaned.

And, as you've pointed out, she's sort of breakable.

"Trust me—that I know, too."

Emmett was not a tactful person, and delicate discussions were not his forte. He struggled now, wanting very much not to be offensive.

Can you even touch her? I mean, if you love *her... wouldn't you want to, well,* touch *her?*

Emmett and Rosalie shared an intensely physical love. He had a hard time understanding how one *could* love without that aspect.

I sighed. "I can't even think of that, Emmett."

Wow. So what are your options, then?

"I don't know," I whispered. "I'm trying to figure out a way to... to leave her. I just can't fathom how to make myself stay away."

With a deep sense of gratification, I suddenly realized that it was *right* for me to stay—at least for now, with Peter and Charlotte on their way. She was safer with me here, temporarily, than she would be if I were gone. For the moment, I could be her unlikely protector.

The thought made me anxious. I itched to be back so that I could fill that role for as long as possible.

Emmett noticed the change in my expression. *What are you thinking about?*

"Right now," I admitted a bit sheepishly, "I'm dying to run back to Forks and check on her. I don't know if I'll make it to Sunday night."

"Uh-uh! You are *not* going home early. Let Rosalie cool down a little bit. Please! For my sake."

"I'll try to stay," I said doubtfully.

Emmett tapped the phone in my pocket. "Alice would call if there were any basis for your panic attack. She's as weird about this girl as you are."

I couldn't argue with that. "Fine. But I'm not staying past Sunday."

"There's no point in hurrying back—it's going to be sunny, anyway. Alice said we were free from school until Wednesday."

I shook my head rigidly.

"Peter and Charlotte know how to behave themselves."

"I really don't care, Emmett. With Bella's luck, she'll go

wandering off into the woods at exactly the wrong moment and—" I flinched. "I'm going back Sunday."

Emmett sighed. *Exactly like a crazy person.*

Bella was sleeping peacefully when I climbed up to her bedroom window early Monday morning. I'd brought oil to grease the mechanism—entirely surrendering to that particular devil—and the window now moved silently out of my way.

I could tell by the way her hair lay smooth across the pillow that she'd had a less restless night than the last time I was here. She had her hands folded under her cheek like a small child, and her mouth was slightly open. I could hear her breath moving slowly in and out between her lips.

It was an amazing relief to be here, to be able to see her again. I realized that I wasn't truly at ease unless that was the case. Nothing was right when I was away from her.

Not that all was right when I was with her, either. I sighed and then inhaled, letting the thirst-fire rake down my throat. I'd been away from it too long. The time spent without pain and temptation made it all the more forceful now. It was bad enough that I was afraid to go kneel beside her bed so that I could read the titles of her books. I wanted to know the stories in her head, but I was afraid of more than my thirst, afraid that if I let myself get that close to her, I would want to be closer still.

Her lips looked very soft and warm. I could imagine touching them with the tip of my finger. Just lightly...

That was exactly the kind of mistake I had to avoid.

My eyes ran over her face again and again, examining it for changes. Mortals changed all the time—I was anxious at the thought of missing anything.

I thought she looked...tired. As though she hadn't gotten enough sleep this weekend. Had she gone out?

I laughed silently and wryly at how much that upset me. So what if she had? I didn't own her. She wasn't mine.

No, she wasn't mine—and I was sad again.

"Mom," she murmured quietly. "No... let me. Please..."

The stress mark between her brows, shaped like a small *v*, was etched deep. Whatever Bella's mother was doing in her dream, it clearly worried her. She rolled suddenly to her other side, but her eyelids never flickered.

"Yes, yes," she muttered, and then sighed. "*Ugh*. It's too green."

One of her hands twitched, and I noticed that there were shallow, barely healed scrapes across the heel of her palm. She'd been hurt? Even though it was obviously not a serious injury, it still disturbed me. I considered the location and decided she must have tripped. That seemed a reasonable explanation, all things considered.

She pleaded with her mother a few more times, mumbled something about the sun, then slipped into a quieter sleep and did not move again.

It was comforting to think that I wouldn't have to puzzle over any of these small mysteries forever. We were *friends* now—or, at least, trying to be friends. I could ask her about her weekend—about the beach, and whatever late-night activity had made her look so weary. I could ask what had happened to her hands. And I could laugh a little when she confirmed my theory about them.

I smiled gently as I wondered whether she *had* fallen in the ocean. I wondered if she'd had a pleasant time on the outing. I wondered if she'd thought about me at all. If she'd missed me even the tiniest portion of the amount that I'd missed her.

I tried to picture her in the sun on the beach. The picture was incomplete, though, because I'd never been to First Beach myself. I only knew how it looked from pictures.

I felt a tiny qualm of unease as I thought about the reason I'd never once been to the pretty beach located just a short run from my home. Bella had spent the day at La Push—a place where I was forbidden, by treaty, to go. A place where a few old men still remembered the stories about the Cullens, remembered and believed them. A place where our secret was known.

I shook my head. I had nothing to worry about there. The Quileutes were bound by treaty, too. Even had Bella run into one of those aging sages, they could reveal nothing. And why would the subject ever be broached? No—the Quileutes were perhaps the *one* thing I did not have to worry about.

I was angry with the sun when it began to rise. It reminded me that I could not satisfy my curiosity for days to come. Why did it choose to shine now?

With a sigh, I ducked out her window before it was light enough for anyone to see me here. I meant to stay in the thick forest by her house and see her off to school, but when I got into the trees, I was surprised to find the trace of her scent lingering on the narrow pathway there.

I followed it quickly, curiously, becoming more and more worried as it led deeper into the darkness. What had Bella been doing out *here*?

The trail she'd left stopped abruptly, in the middle of nowhere in particular. She'd gone just a few steps off the path, into the ferns, where she'd touched the trunk of a fallen tree. Perhaps sat there…

I sat where she had and looked around. All she would have been able to see was ferns and forest. It had probably been raining—the scent was washed out, having never set deeply into the tree.

Why would Bella have come to sit here alone—and she had been alone, no doubt about that—in the middle of the wet, murky forest?

It made no sense, and unlike those other points of curiosity, I could hardly bring this up in casual conversation.

So, Bella, I was following your scent through the woods after I left your room—just some minor breaking and entering, no need for worry, I was…exterminating spiders…. Yes, that would be quite the icebreaker.

I would never know what she'd been thinking and doing here, and that had my teeth grinding in frustration. Worse, this was far too much like the scenario I'd imagined for Emmett—Bella wandering alone in the woods, where her scent would call to anyone who had the senses to track it.

I groaned. She didn't just have bad luck, she *courted* it.

Well, for this moment she had a protector. I would watch over her, keep her from harm, for as long as I could justify it.

I suddenly found myself wishing that Peter and Charlotte would make an extended stay.

8. GHOST

I DID NOT SEE MUCH OF JASPER'S GUESTS FOR THE TWO sunny days that they were in Forks. I only went home at all so that Esme wouldn't worry. Otherwise, my existence seemed like that of a specter rather than a vampire. I hovered, invisible in the shadows, where I could follow the object of my love and obsession—where I could see her and hear her in the minds of the lucky humans who could walk through the sunlight beside her, sometimes accidentally brushing the back of her hand with their own. She never reacted to such contact; their hands were just as warm as hers.

The enforced absence from school had never been a trial like this before. But the sun seemed to make her happy, so I could not resent it too much.

Monday morning, I eavesdropped on a conversation that had the potential to destroy my confidence and make the time spent away from her truly torturous. As it ended up, though, it rather made my day.

I had to feel some little respect for Mike Newton. He had more courage than I'd given him credit for. He had not simply given up and slunk away to nurse his wounds—he was going to try again.

Bella got to school quite early and, seeming intent on enjoying the sun while it lasted, sat at one of the seldom-used picnic benches while she waited for the first bell to ring. Her hair caught the sun in unexpected ways, giving off a reddish shine that I had not anticipated.

Mike found her there, doodling again, and was thrilled at his good luck.

It was agonizing only to be able to watch, powerless, bound to the forest's shadows by the bright sunlight.

She greeted him with enough enthusiasm to make him ecstatic, and me the opposite.

See, she likes me. She wouldn't smile like that if she didn't. I bet she wanted to go to the dance with me. Wonder what's so important in Seattle....

He perceived the change in her hair. "I never noticed before—your hair has red in it."

I accidentally uprooted the young spruce tree my hand was resting on when he pinched a strand of her hair between his fingers.

"Only in the sun," she said. To my deep satisfaction, she cringed away from him slightly when he tucked the strand behind her ear.

It took Mike a minute to build up his courage, wasting some time on small talk.

She reminded him of the essay we all had due on Wednesday. From the faintly smug expression on her face, hers was already done. He'd forgotten altogether, and that severely diminished his free time.

Finally he got to the point—my teeth were clenched so hard they could have pulverized granite—and even then, he couldn't make himself ask the question outright.

"I was going to ask if you wanted to go out."

"Oh," she said.

There was a brief silence.

"Oh"? What does that mean? Is she going to say yes? Wait—I guess I didn't really ask.

He swallowed hard.

"Well, we could go to dinner or something...and I could work on it later."

Stupid—that wasn't a question either.

"Mike..."

The agony and fury of my jealousy was every whit as powerful as it had been last week. I wanted so badly to race across the campus, too fast for human eyes, and snatch her up—to steal her away from the boy I hated so much in this moment I could have killed him for no reason but to enjoy it.

Would she say yes to him?

"I don't think that would be the best idea."

I breathed again. My rigid body relaxed.

Seattle was just an excuse, after all. Shouldn't have asked. What was I thinking? Bet it's that freak, Cullen.

"Why?" he asked sullenly.

"I think..." She hesitated. "And if you ever repeat what I'm saying right now, I will cheerfully beat you to death—"

I laughed out loud at the sound of a death threat coming through her lips. A jay shrieked, startled, and launched itself away from me.

"But I think that would hurt Jessica's feelings."

"Jessica?" *What? But...oh. Okay. I guess...huh.*

His thoughts were no longer coherent.

"Really, Mike, are you *blind*?"

I echoed her sentiment. She shouldn't expect everyone to be as perceptive as she was, but really this instance was beyond obvious. With as much trouble as Mike had had working himself up to ask Bella out, did he imagine it wasn't just as difficult for Jessica? It must be selfishness that made him blind to others. And Bella was so unselfish, she saw everything.

Jessica. Huh. Wow. Huh. "Oh," he managed to say.

Bella used his confusion to make her exit.

"It's time for class, and I can't be late again."

Mike became an unreliable viewpoint from then on. He found, as he turned the idea of Jessica around in his head, that he rather liked the thought of her finding him attractive. It was second place, not as good as if Bella had felt that way.

She's cute, though, I guess. Decent body—bigger boobs than Bella's. A bird in the hand…

He was off then, on to new fantasies that were just as vulgar as the ones about Bella, but now they only irritated rather than infuriated. How little he deserved either girl; they were almost interchangeable to him. I stayed clear of his head after that.

When Bella was out of sight, I curled up against the cool trunk of an enormous madrone tree and danced from mind to mind, keeping her in view, always glad when Angela Weber was available to look through. I wished there were some way to thank the Weber girl for simply being a nice person. It made me feel better to think that Bella had one friend worth having.

I watched Bella's face from whichever angle I was given, and I could see that she was upset about something. This surprised me—I thought the sun would be enough to keep her smiling. At lunch, I saw her glance time and time again toward the empty Cullen table, and that thrilled me. Perhaps she missed me, too.

After school, she had plans to go out with the other girls—I automatically planned my own surveillance—but these were postponed when Mike invited Jessica out on the date he'd designed for Bella.

So I went straight to her home instead, doing a quick sweep of the woods to make sure no one dangerous had wandered too close. I knew Jasper had warned his one-time brother to avoid the town—citing my insanity as both explanation and danger—but I wasn't taking any chances. Peter and Charlotte had no intention of causing animosity with my family, but intentions were changeable things.

All right, I was overdoing it. I knew that.

As if she was aware I was watching, as if she took pity on the agony I felt when I couldn't see her, Bella came out to the backyard after a long hour indoors. She had a book in her hand and a blanket under her arm.

Silently, I climbed into the higher branches of the closest tree overlooking the yard.

She spread the blanket on the damp grass and then lay on her stomach and started flipping through the worn, obviously often-read book, trying to find her place. I read over her shoulder.

Ah—more classics. *Sense and Sensibility.* She was an Austen fan.

I tasted the way the sunshine and open air affected her scent. The heat seemed to sweeten the smell. My throat flamed with desire, the pain fresh and fierce again because I had been away from her for so long. I spent a moment controlling that, forcing myself to breathe through my nose.

She read quickly, crossing and recrossing her ankles in the air. I knew the book, so I did not read along with her. Instead, I was watching the sunlight and wind playing in her hair when her body suddenly stiffened, and her hand froze on the page. She'd reached the last page of chapter two. The page began midsentence: "perhaps, in spite of every consideration of politeness or maternal affection on the side of the former, the two ladies might have found it impossible to have lived together so long—"

She grabbed a thick section of the book and shoved it roughly over, almost as if something on the page had angered her. But what? It was early in the story, just setting up the first conflict between mother-in-law and daughter-in-law. The main hero, Edward Ferrars, was introduced. Elinor Dashwood's merits were extolled. I thought through the previous chapter, searching for something potentially offensive in Austen's overly polite prose. What could have upset her?

She stopped on the title page for *Mansfield Park*. Beginning a new story—the book was a compilation of novels.

But she'd only made it to page seven—I was following along this time; Mrs. Norris was detailing the danger of Tom and Edmund Bertram not encountering their cousin Fanny Price until they were all adults—when Bella's teeth ground together and she slammed the book shut.

Taking a deep breath as if to calm herself, she tossed the book aside and rolled onto her back. She pushed her sleeves up her forearms, exposing more of her skin to the sun.

Why would she have reacted thus to what was obviously a familiar story? Another mystery. I sighed.

She lay very still now, moving just once to yank her hair away from her face. It fanned out over her head, a river of chestnut. And then she was motionless again.

She made a very serene picture, there in the sunlight. Whatever peace had evaded her before seemed to find her now. Her breathing slowed. After several long minutes her lips began to tremble. Mumbling in her sleep.

I felt an uncomfortable spasm of guilt. Because what I was doing now was not precisely *good*, but it wasn't anywhere near as bad as my nightly pursuits. I wasn't technically even trespassing now—the base of this tree grew from the next lot over—let alone doing something more felonious. But I knew that when night came, I would continue to do wrong.

Even now, part of me *wanted* to trespass. To jump to the ground, landing silently on my toes, and ease into her circle of sunshine. Just to be closer to her. To hear her murmured words as though she was whispering them to me.

It wasn't my unreliable morality that held me back—it was the thought of myself in the sun's glare. Bad enough that my skin was stone and inhuman in shadow; I didn't want to look at Bella and myself side by side in the sunlight. The difference between us was already insurmountable, painful enough without that image also in my head. Could I be any more grotesque? I imagined her terror if she opened her eyes and saw me there beside her.

"Mmm...," she moaned.

I leaned back against the tree trunk, deeper into shadow.

She sighed. "Mmm."

I did not fear that she had woken. Her voice was just a low, wistful murmur.

"Edmund. Ahh."

Edmund? I thought again of where she'd quit reading. Just as Edmund Bertram had been named for the first time.

Ha! She wasn't dreaming of me at all, I realized blackly. The self-loathing returned in force. She was dreaming of fictional characters. Perhaps that had always been the case, and all along her dreams had been filled with Hugh Grant in a cravat. So much for my conceit.

She said nothing more that was intelligible. The afternoon passed and I watched, feeling helpless again, as the sun slowly sank in the sky and the shadows crawled across the lawn toward her. I wanted to push them back, but of course the darkness was inevitable; the shadows took her. When the light was gone, her skin looked too pale—ghostly. Her hair was dark again, almost black against her face.

It was a frightening thing to watch—like witnessing Alice's visions come to fruition. Bella's steady, strong heartbeat was the only reassurance, the sound that kept this moment from feeling like a nightmare.

I was relieved when her father arrived home.

I could hear little from him as he drove down the street toward the house. Some vague annoyance...in the past, something from his day at work. Expectation mixed with hunger—I guessed that he was looking forward to dinner. But his thoughts were so quiet and contained that I could not be sure I was right. I only got the gist of them.

I wondered what her mother sounded like—what the genetic combination had been that had formed her so uniquely.

Bella started awake, jerking up to a sitting position when the tires of her father's car hit the brick driveway. She stared around herself, seeming confused by the unexpected darkness. For one brief moment, her eyes touched the shadows where I hid, but then flickered quickly away.

"Charlie?" she asked in a low voice, still peering into the trees surrounding the small yard.

The door of his car slammed shut, and she looked to the

sound. She got to her feet quickly and gathered her things, casting one more look back toward the woods.

I moved into a tree closer to the back window near the small kitchen, and listened to their evening. It was interesting to compare Charlie's words to his muffled thoughts. His love and concern for his only child were nearly overwhelming, and yet his words were always terse and casual. Most of the time, they sat in companionable silence.

I heard her discuss her plans to go shopping the following evening in Port Angeles with Jessica and Angela, and I refined my own plans as I listened. Jasper had not warned Peter and Charlotte to stay clear of Port Angeles. Though I knew that they had fed recently and had no intention of hunting anywhere in the vicinity of our home, I would watch her, just in case. After all, there were always others of my kind out there. And, of course, all those human dangers that I had never much considered before now.

I heard her worry aloud about leaving her father to prepare dinner alone, and smiled at this proof to my theory—yes, she was the caretaker here, too.

And then I left, knowing I would return while she was asleep, ignoring every ethical and moral argument against my behavior.

But I certainly would not trespass on her privacy the way the peeping tom would have. I was here for her protection, not to leer at her in the way Mike Newton no doubt would, were he agile enough to move through the treetops. I would not treat her so crassly.

My house was empty when I returned, which was fine by me. I didn't miss the confused or disparaging thoughts, questioning my sanity. Emmett had left a note stuck to the newel post.

Football at the Rainier field—c'mon! Please?

I found a pen and scrawled the word *sorry* beneath his plea. The teams were even without me, in any case.

I went for the shortest of hunting trips, contenting myself with the smaller, gentler creatures that did not taste as good as the other predators, and then changed into fresh clothes before I ran back to Forks.

Bella did not sleep as well tonight. She thrashed in her blankets, her face sometimes worried, sometimes forlorn. I wondered what nightmare haunted her...and then realized that perhaps I didn't really want to know.

When she spoke, she mostly muttered derogatory things about Forks in a glum voice. Only once, when she sighed out the words "Come back" and her hand twitched open—a wordless plea—did I have a chance to hope she might be dreaming of me.

The next day of school, the *last* day the sun would hold me prisoner, was much the same as the day before. Bella seemed even gloomier than yesterday, and I wondered if she would bow out of her plans—she didn't seem in the mood. But, being Bella, she would probably put her friends' enjoyment above her own.

She wore a deep blue blouse today, and the color set her skin off perfectly, making it look like fresh cream.

School ended, and Jessica agreed to pick the other girls up.

I went home to get my car. When I found that Peter and Charlotte were there, I decided I could afford to give the girls an hour or so as a head start. It would have been a struggle to follow them, driving at the speed limit—hideous thought.

Everyone was gathered in the bright great room. Peter and Charlotte both noticed my abstraction as I belatedly welcomed them, apologizing halfheartedly for my absence, kissing her cheek and shaking his hand. I was unable to concentrate enough to join the group conversation. As soon I as could politely extricate myself, I drifted to the piano and began playing quietly.

What a strange creature, the Alice-sized, white-blond Charlotte was thinking. *And he was so normal and pleasant the last time we met.*

Peter's thoughts were in sync with hers, as was usually the case.

It must be the animals. The lack of human blood drives them mad eventually, he was concluding. His hair was just as fair as hers, and almost as long. They were very similar—except for size, as he was nearly as tall as Emmett. A well-matched pair, I'd always thought.

Why even bother coming home? Rosalie sneered.

Ah, Edward. I hate to see him suffering so. Esme's joy was becoming corrupted by her concern. She *should* be concerned. This love story she envisioned for me was careening toward tragedy more perceptibly every moment.

Have fun in Port Angeles tonight, Alice thought cheerfully. *Let me know when I'm allowed to talk to Bella.*

You're pathetic. I can't believe you missed the game last night just to watch somebody sleep, Emmett grumbled.

Everyone but Esme stopped thinking about me after a moment, and I kept my playing subdued so that I would not attract notice.

I did not pay attention to them for a long while, just letting the music distract me from my unease. It was never not distressing to have the girl out of sight. I only returned my focus to their conversation when the goodbyes grew more final.

"If you see Maria again," Jasper was saying, a little warily, "tell her I wish her well."

Maria was the vampire who had created both Jasper and Peter—Jasper in the latter half of the nineteenth century, Peter more recently, in the nineteen forties. She'd looked Jasper up once when we were in Calgary. It had been an eventful visit—we'd had to move immediately. Jasper had politely asked her to keep her distance in the future.

"I don't imagine we'll cross paths soon," Peter said with a laugh—Maria was undeniably dangerous and there was not much love lost between her and Peter. Peter had, after all, been instrumental in Jasper's defection. Jasper had always been Maria's favorite; she considered it a minor detail that she had once planned to kill him. "But, should it happen, I certainly will."

They were shaking hands then, preparing to depart. I let the song I was playing trail off to an unsatisfying end and got hastily to my feet.

"Charlotte, Peter," I said, nodding.

"It was nice to see you again, Edward," Charlotte said doubtfully. Peter just nodded in return.

Madman, Emmett threw after me.

Idiot, Rosalie thought at the same time.

Poor boy. Esme.

And Alice, in a chiding tone. *They're going straight east, to Seattle. Nowhere near Port Angeles*. She showed me the proof in her visions.

I pretended I hadn't heard that. My excuses were already flimsy enough.

Once in my car, I felt more relaxed. The robust purr of the engine Rosalie had boosted for me—last year, when she was in a better mood—was soothing. It was a relief to be in motion, to know that I was getting closer to Bella with every mile that flew away under my tires.

9. PORT ANGELES

IT WAS TOO BRIGHT FOR ME TO DRIVE INTO TOWN WHEN I got to Port Angeles. The sun was still high overhead, and though my windows were tinted dark enough to provide some protection, there was no reason to take unnecessary risks. *More* unnecessary risks, I should say.

How condescendingly I'd once judged Emmett for his thoughtless ways and Jasper for his lack of discipline—and now I was consciously flouting all the rules with a wild abandon that made their lapses look like nothing at all. I used to be the responsible one.

I sighed.

I was certain I would be able to find Jessica's thoughts from a distance—hers were louder than Angela's, but once I found the first, I'd be able to hear the second. Then, when the shadows lengthened, I could get closer. Just outside the town, I pulled off the road onto an overgrown driveway that appeared to be infrequently used.

I knew the general direction to search in—there were not many places to shop for dresses in Port Angeles. It wasn't long before I found Jessica, spinning in front of a three-way mirror, and I could see Bella in her peripheral vision, appraising the long black dress she wore.

Bella still looks pissed. Ha ha. Angela was right—Tyler was full of it. I can't believe she's so upset about it, though. At least she knows she has a backup date for the prom. What if Mike doesn't have fun at the dance and doesn't ask me out again? What if he asks Bella to the prom? Does he think she's prettier than me? Does she *think she's prettier than me?*

"I think I like the blue one better. It really brings out your eyes."

Jessica smiled at Bella with false warmth while eyeing her suspiciously.

Does she really think that? Or does she want me to look like a cow on Saturday?

I was already tired of listening to Jessica. I searched close by for Angela—ah, but Angela was in the process of changing dresses, and I skipped quickly out of her head to give her some privacy.

Well, there wasn't much trouble Bella could get into in a department store. I'd let them shop and then catch up with them when they were done. It wouldn't be long until dark—the clouds were beginning to return, drifting in from the west. I could only catch glimpses of them through the thick trees, but I could see how they would hurry the sunset. I welcomed them, craved them more than I had ever yearned for their shadows before. Tomorrow I could sit beside Bella in school again, monopolize her attention at lunch. I could ask her all the questions I'd been saving up.

So she was furious about Tyler's presumption. I'd seen that in his head—that he'd meant it literally when he'd spoken of the prom, that he was staking a claim. I pictured her expression from that other afternoon—the outraged disbelief—and laughed. I wondered what she would say to him about this. Or perhaps she was more likely to pretend ignorance, to bluff and hope it would put him off? It would be interesting to see.

The time went slowly while I waited for the shadows to lengthen. I checked in periodically with Jessica; her mental voice was the easiest to find, but I didn't like to linger there long. I saw the place they were planning to eat. It would be dark by dinnertime . . . maybe I would coincidentally choose the same restaurant. I touched the phone in my pocket, thinking of inviting Alice out to join me. She would love that, but she would also want to talk to Bella. I wasn't sure if I was ready to have Bella *more* involved with my world. Wasn't one vampire trouble enough?

I checked in routinely with Jessica again. She was thinking about her jewelry, asking Angela's opinion.

"Maybe I should take the necklace back. I've got one at home that would probably work, and I spent more than I was supposed to." My mom is going to freak out. What was I thinking?

"I don't mind going back to the store. Do you think Bella will be looking for us, though?"

What was this? Bella wasn't with them? I stared through Jessica's eyes first, then switched to Angela's. They were on the sidewalk in front of a line of shops, just turning back the other way. Bella was nowhere in sight.

Oh, who cares about Bella? Jess thought impatiently, before answering Angela's question. *"She's fine. We'll get to the restaurant in plenty of time, even if we go back. Anyway, I think she wanted to be alone."* I got a brief glimpse of the bookshop Jessica thought Bella had gone to.

"*Let's hurry, then*," Angela said. *I hope Bella doesn't think we ditched her. She was so nice to me in the car before. But she's seemed kind of blue all day. I wonder if it's because of Edward Cullen? I'll bet that was why she was asking about his family.*

I should have been paying better attention. What had I missed here? Bella was off wandering by herself, and she'd been asking about me? Angela was paying attention to Jessica now—Jessica was babbling about that imbecile Mike—and I could get nothing more from her.

I judged the shadows. The sun would be behind the clouds

soon enough. If I stayed on the west side of the road, where the buildings would shade the street from the fading light…

I started to feel anxious as I drove through the sparse traffic into the center of town. This wasn't something I had considered—Bella setting off on her own—and I had no idea how to find her. I *should* have considered it.

I knew Port Angeles well. I drove straight to the bookstore in Jessica's head, hoping my search would be short, but doubting it would be so easy. When did Bella ever make it easy?

Sure enough, the little shop was empty except for the anachronistically dressed woman behind the counter. This didn't look like the kind of place Bella would find interesting—too new age for a practical person. I wondered if she'd even bothered to go inside.

There was a patch of shade I could park in. It made a dark pathway right up to the awning of the shop. I really shouldn't. Wandering around in the sunlit hours was not safe. What if a passing car threw the sun's reflection on me at just the wrong moment?

But I didn't know how else to look for Bella!

I parked and got out, keeping to the side of deepest shadow. I strode quickly into the store, noting the faint trace of Bella's scent in the air. She had been here, on the sidewalk, but there was no hint of her fragrance inside the shop.

"Welcome! Can I help—?" the saleswoman began to say, but I was already out the door.

I followed Bella's scent as far as the shade would allow, stopping when I got to the edge of the sunlight.

How powerless it made me feel—fenced in by the line between dark and light that stretched across the sidewalk in front of me.

I could only guess that she'd continued across the street, heading south. There wasn't really much in that direction. Was she lost? Well, that possibility didn't sound entirely out of character.

I got back in the car and drove slowly through the streets, looking for her. I stepped out into a few other patches of shadow, but only caught her scent once more, and the direction of it confused me. Where was she trying to go?

I drove back and forth between the bookstore and the restaurant a few times, hoping to see her on her way. Jessica and Angela were already there, trying to decide whether to order or to wait for Bella. Jessica was pushing for ordering immediately.

I began flitting through the minds of strangers, looking through their eyes. Surely, someone must have seen her somewhere.

I got more and more anxious the longer she remained missing. I'd not considered before how difficult she might prove to find once, like now, she was out of my sight and off her normal paths.

The clouds were massing on the horizon, and in a few more minutes, I would be free to track her on foot. It wouldn't take me long then. It was only the sun that made me so helpless now. Just a few more minutes, and then the advantage would be mine again and it would be the human world that was powerless.

Another mind, and another. So many trivial thoughts.

...think the baby has another ear infection...

Was it six-four-oh or six-oh-four...?

Late again. I ought to tell him....

Aha! Here she comes!

There, at last, was her face. Finally, someone had noticed her!

The relief lasted for only a fraction of a second, and then I read more fully the thoughts of the man who was gloating over her face where she hesitated in the shadows.

His mind was a stranger to me, and yet, not totally unfamiliar. I had once hunted exactly such minds.

"NO!" I roared, and a volley of snarls erupted from my throat. My foot shoved the gas pedal to the floor, but where was I going?

I knew the general direction his thoughts came from, but the location was not specific enough. Something, there had to be something—a street sign, a storefront, something in his sightline that would give him away. But Bella was deep in shadow, and his eyes were focused only on her frightened expression—enjoying the fear there.

Her face was blurred in his mind by the memory of other faces. Bella was not his first victim.

The sound of my growls shook the frame of the car but did not distract me.

There were no windows in the wall behind her. Somewhere industrial, away from the more populated shopping district. My car squealed around a corner, swerving past another vehicle, heading in what I hoped was the right direction. By the time the other driver honked, the sound was far behind me.

Look at her shaking! The man chuckled in anticipation. The fear was the draw for him—the part he enjoyed.

"Stay away from me." Her voice was low and steady, not a scream.

"Don't be like that, sugar."

He watched her flinch at a rowdy laugh that came from another direction. He was irritated with the noise—*Shut up, Jeff!* he thought—but he enjoyed the way she cringed. It excited him. He began to imagine her pleas, the way she would beg....

I hadn't realized that there were others with him until I'd heard the loud laughter. I scanned out from him, desperate for something that I could use. He was taking the first step in her direction, flexing his hands.

The minds around him were not the cesspool that his was. They were all slightly intoxicated, not one of them realizing how far the man they called Lanny planned to go with this. They were blindly following Lanny's lead. He'd promised them a little fun....

One of them glanced down the street, nervous—he didn't want to get caught harassing the girl—and gave me what I needed. I recognized the cross street he stared toward.

I flew under a red light, sliding through a space just wide enough between two cars in the moving traffic. Horns blared behind me.

My phone vibrated in my pocket. I ignored it.

Lanny moved slowly toward the girl, drawing out the suspense—the moment of terror that aroused him. He waited for her scream, preparing to savor it.

But Bella locked her jaw and braced herself. He was surprised—he'd expected her to try to run. Surprised and slightly disappointed. He liked to chase his prey down, feel the adrenaline of the hunt.

Brave, this one. Maybe better, I guess—more fight in her.

I was a block away. The fiend could hear the roar of my engine now, but he paid it no attention, too intent on his victim.

I would see how he enjoyed the hunt when *he* was the prey. I would see what he thought of *my* style of hunting.

In another compartment of my head, I was already sorting through the horrors I'd borne witness to in my vigilante days, searching for the most painful of them. I had never tortured my prey, no matter how much they had deserved it, but this man was different. He would suffer for this. He would writhe in agony. The others would merely die for their part, but this creature named *Lanny* would beg for death long before I would give him that gift.

He was in the road, crossing toward her.

I spun sharply around the corner, my headlights washing across the scene and freezing the rest of them in place. I could have run down the leader, who leaped out of the way, but that was too easy a death for him.

I let the car spin out, swinging all the way around so that I was facing back the way I'd come and the passenger door was closest to Bella. I threw that open, and she was already running toward the car.

"Get in," I snarled.

What the hell?

Knew this was a bad idea! She's not alone.

Should I run?

Think I'm going to throw up....

Bella jumped through the open door without hesitating, pulling it shut behind her.

And then she looked up at me with the most trusting expression I had ever seen on a human face, and all my violent plans crumbled.

It took much, much less than a second for me to see that I could not leave her in the car in order to deal with the four men in the street. What would I tell her, not to watch? Ha! When did she ever do what I asked?

Would I drag them away, out of her sight, and leave her alone here? It was a long shot that another psychopath would be prowling the streets of Port Angeles tonight, but it was a long shot that there was even a first! Here was proof positive that I was not insane—like a magnet, she drew all things dangerous toward herself. If I were not close enough to provide it, some other evil would take my place.

It would feel like part of the same motion to her as I accelerated, taking her away from her pursuers so quickly that they gaped after my car with uncomprehending expressions. She would not recognize my instant of hesitation.

I couldn't even hit him with my car. That would frighten her.

I wanted his death so savagely that the need for it rang in my ears, clouded my sight, and was a bitter flavor on my tongue, stronger than the burn of my thirst. My muscles were coiled with the urgency, the craving, the necessity of it. I *had* to kill him. I would peel him slowly apart, piece by piece, skin from muscle, muscle from bone. . . .

Except that the girl—the only girl in the world—was clinging to her seat with both hands, staring at me, her eyes strangely calm and unquestioning. Vengeance would have to wait.

"Put on your seat belt," I ordered. My voice was rough with the hate and bloodlust. Not the usual bloodlust. I had long been committed to abstaining from human blood, and I would not let this creature change that. This would be retribution only.

She locked the seat belt into place, jumping slightly at the sound it made. That little noise made her jump, yet she did not flinch as I tore through the town, ignoring all traffic guides. I could feel her eyes on me. She seemed oddly relaxed. It didn't make sense—not with what had just happened to her.

"Are you okay?" she asked, her voice rough with stress and fear.

She wanted to know if *I* was okay?

Was I okay?

"No," I realized, and my tone seethed with rage.

I took her to the same unused drive where I'd spent the afternoon engaged in the poorest surveillance ever kept. It was black now under the trees.

I was so furious that my body froze in place there, utterly motionless. My ice-locked hands ached to crush her attacker, to grind him into pieces so mangled that his body could never be identified.

But that would entail leaving her here alone, unprotected in the dark night.

My mind was replaying scenes from my hunting days, images I wished I could forget. Especially now, with the urge to kill so much stronger than any hunting compulsion I'd ever felt before.

This man, this abomination, was not the worst of his kind, though it was difficult to sort the depths of evil into a merit-based order. Still, I remembered the very worst. There had never been any question that he deserved that title.

Most of the men I'd hunted back in my days of acting as judge, jury, and executioner had felt some level of remorse, or at least fear of being caught. Many of them turned to alcohol or drugs to silence their worries. Others compartmentalized, created fractures in their personalities and lived as two men, one for the light and one for the dark.

But for the worst, the vilest aberration I'd ever encountered, remorse was not an issue.

I'd never found anyone who embraced his own evil so thoroughly—who *enjoyed* it. He was utterly delighted by the world he'd created, a world of helpless victims and their tortured screams. Pain was the object of all his pursuits, and he'd gotten very good at creating it, at prolonging it.

I was committed to my rules, to my justification for all the blood I claimed. But in this instance, I wavered. To let this particular man die swiftly seemed far too easy an escape for him.

It was the closest I ever came to crossing that line. Still, I killed him as quickly and efficiently as I killed all the rest.

It might have gone differently if two of his victims had not been in that basement of horrors when I discovered him. Two young women, already badly injured. Though I carried them both to a hospital at the greatest speed I was capable of, only one survived.

I hadn't had time to drink his blood. That didn't matter. There were so many others who deserved to die.

Like this Lanny. He was an atrocity, too, but surely not worse than the one I'd remembered. Why did it feel right then, imperative, that he suffer so much more?

But first—

"Bella?" I asked through my teeth.

"Yes?" she responded huskily. She cleared her throat.

"Are *you* all right?" That was really the most important thing, the first priority. Retribution was secondary. I *knew* that, but my body was so filled with rage that it was hard to think.

"Yes." Her voice was still thick—with fear, no doubt.

And so I could not leave her.

Even if she wasn't at constant risk for some infuriating reason—some joke the universe was playing on me—even if I could be *sure* that she would be perfectly safe in my absence, I could not leave her alone in the dark.

She must be so frightened.

Yet I was in no condition to comfort her—even if I knew exactly how that was to be accomplished, which I did not. Surely she could feel the brutality radiating out of me, surely that much was obvious. I would frighten her even more if I could not calm the lust for slaughter boiling inside me.

I needed to think about something else.

"Distract me, please," I pleaded.

"I'm sorry, what?"

I barely had enough control to try to explain what I needed.

"Just..." I couldn't think of how to express it. I picked the closest word I could think of. "Prattle about something unimportant until I calm down." It was a poor word choice, I realized as soon as it was out, but I couldn't find much room to care. Only the fact that she needed me held me inside the car. I could hear the man's thoughts, his disappointment and anger. I knew where to find him. I closed my eyes, wishing that I couldn't see anyway.

"Um..." She hesitated—trying to make sense of my request, I imagined, or perhaps offended?—then she continued. "I'm going to run over Tyler Crowley tomorrow before school?" She said this like it was a question.

Yes—this was what I needed. Of course Bella would come up with something unexpected. As it had been before, the threat of violence coming through her lips was jarring, comical. If I had not been burning with the urge to kill, I would have laughed.

"Why?" I barked out, to force her to speak again.

"He's telling everyone that he's taking me to prom," she said, her voice filled with outrage. "Either he's insane or he's still trying to make up for almost killing me last... well you remember it," she inserted dryly. "And he thinks *prom* is somehow the correct way to do this. So I figure if I endanger his life, then we're even, and he can't keep trying to make amends. I don't need enemies and maybe Lauren would back off if he left me alone. I might have to total his Sentra, though," she went on, thoughtful now. "If he doesn't have a ride, he can't take anyone to prom...."

It was encouraging to see that she sometimes got things wrong. Tyler's persistence had nothing to do with the accident. She didn't seem to understand the appeal she held for the human boys at the high school. Did she not see the appeal she had for me, either?

Ah, it was working. The baffling processes of her mind were

always engrossing. I was beginning to gain control of myself, to see something beyond vengeance and slaughter.

"I heard about that," I told her. She had stopped talking, and I needed her to continue.

"*You* did?" she asked incredulously. And then her voice was angrier than before. "If he's paralyzed from the neck down, he can't go to the prom, either."

I wished there was some way I could ask her to continue with the threats of death and bodily harm without sounding insane. She couldn't have picked a better way to calm me. And her words—just sarcasm in her case, hyperbole—were a reminder I dearly needed in this moment.

I sighed, and opened my eyes.

"Better?" she asked timidly.

"Not really."

No, I was calmer, but not better. Because I'd just realized that I could not kill the fiend named Lanny. The only thing in this moment that I wanted more than to commit a highly justifiable murder was this girl. And though I couldn't have her, just the dream of having her made it impossible for me to go on a killing spree tonight.

Bella deserved better than a killer.

I'd spent more than seven decades trying to be something—anything—other than a killer. Those years of effort could never make me worthy of the girl sitting beside me. And yet, I felt that if I returned to that life for even one night, I would surely put her out of my reach forever. Even if I didn't drink their blood—even if I didn't have that evidence blazing red in my eyes—wouldn't she sense the difference?

I was trying to be good enough for her. It was an impossible goal. But I couldn't bear the thought of giving up.

"What's wrong?" she whispered.

Her scent filled my nose, and I was reminded why I could not deserve her. After all this, even as much as I loved her . . . she still made my mouth water.

I would give her as much honesty as I could. I owed her that.

"Sometimes I have a problem with my temper, Bella." I stared out into the black night, wishing both that she would hear the horror inherent in my words and that she would not. Mostly that she would not. *Run, Bella, run. Stay, Bella, stay.* "But it *wouldn't* be helpful for me to turn around and hunt down those..." Just thinking about it almost pulled me from the car. I took a deep breath, letting her scent scorch down my throat. "At least, that's what I'm trying to convince myself."

"Oh."

She said nothing else. How much had she understood? I glanced at her furtively, but her face was unreadable. Blank with shock, perhaps. Well, she wasn't screaming in horror. Not yet.

"Jessica and Angela will be worried," she said quietly. Her voice was very calm, and I was not sure how that could be. *Was* she in shock? Maybe tonight's events hadn't sunk in for her yet. "I was supposed to meet them."

Did she want to be away from me? Or was she just concerned about her friends' worry?

I didn't answer her but started the car and took her back. The nearer I got to the town, the harder it was to hold on to my purpose. I was just so *close* to him....

If it was impossible—if I could never belong to nor deserve this girl—then where was the sense in letting the man go unpunished? Surely I could allow myself that much.

No. I wasn't giving up. Not yet. I wanted her too much to surrender.

We were at the restaurant where she was supposed to meet her friends before I'd even begun to make sense of my thoughts. Jessica and Angela were finished eating, and both now truly worried about Bella. They were on their way to search for her, heading off along the dark street.

It was not a good night for them to be wandering.

"How did you know where...?" Bella's unfinished question interrupted me, and I realized that I had made yet another gaffe.

I'd been too distracted to remember to ask her where she was supposed to meet her friends.

But instead of finishing the inquiry and pressing the point, Bella just shook her head and half smiled.

What did *that* mean?

Well, I didn't have time to puzzle over her strange acceptance of my stranger knowledge. I opened my door.

"What are you doing?" she asked, sounding startled.

Not letting you out of my sight. Not allowing myself to be alone tonight. In that order. "I'm taking you to dinner."

Well, this should be interesting. It seemed like another night entirely when I'd imagined bringing Alice along and pretending to choose the same restaurant as Bella and her friends by accident. And now here I was, practically on a date with the girl. Only it didn't count, because I wasn't giving her a chance to say no.

She already had her door half-open before I'd walked around the car—it wasn't usually so frustrating to have to move at an inconspicuous speed—instead of allowing me to get it for her.

I waited for her to join me, getting more anxious as her girlfriends continued toward the dark corner.

"Go stop Jessica and Angela before I have to track them down, too," I ordered quickly. "I don't think I could restrain myself if I ran into your other friends again." No, I would not be strong enough for that.

She shuddered, and then quickly collected herself. She took half a step after them, calling, "Jess! Angela!" in a loud voice. They turned, and she waved her arm over her head to catch their attention.

Bella! Oh, she's safe! Angela thought with relief.

Late much? Jessica grumbled to herself, but she, too, was thankful that Bella wasn't lost or hurt. This made me like her a little more than I had.

They hurried back, and then stopped, shocked, when they saw me beside her.

Uh-uh! Jess thought, stunned. *No freaking way!*

Edward Cullen? *Did she go away by herself to find him? But why would she ask about them being out of town if she knew he was here . . . ?* I got a brief flash of Bella's mortified expression when she'd asked Angela if my family was often absent from school. *No, she couldn't have known*, Angela decided.

Jessica's thoughts were moving past the surprise and on to suspicion. *Bella's been holding out on me.*

"Where have you been?" she demanded, staring at Bella, but peeking at me from the corner of her eye.

"I got lost. And then I ran into Edward," Bella said, waving one hand toward me. Her tone was remarkably normal. As though that were truly all that had happened.

She must be in shock. That was the only explanation for her calm.

"Would it be all right if I joined you?" I asked—to be polite. I knew that they'd already eaten.

Holy crap *but he's hot!* Jessica thought, her head suddenly slightly incoherent.

Angela wasn't much more composed. *Wish we hadn't eaten. Wow. Just. Wow.*

Now why couldn't I do that to Bella?

"Er . . . sure," Jessica agreed.

Angela frowned. "Um, actually, Bella, we already ate while we were waiting," she admitted. "Sorry."

Shut up! Jessica complained internally.

Bella shrugged casually. So at ease. Definitely in shock. "That's fine—I'm not hungry."

"I think you should eat something," I disagreed. She needed sugar in her bloodstream—though it smelled sweet enough as it was, I thought wryly. The horror was going to come crashing down on her momentarily, and an empty stomach wouldn't help. She was an easy fainter, as I knew from experience.

These girls wouldn't be in any danger if they went straight home. Danger didn't stalk *their* every step.

And I'd rather be alone with Bella—as long as she was willing to be alone with me.

"Do you mind if I drive Bella home tonight?" I said to Jessica before Bella could respond. "That way you won't have to wait while she eats."

"Uh, no problem, I guess. . . ." Jessica stared intently at Bella, looking for some sign that this was what she wanted.

She probably wants him to herself. Who wouldn't? Jess thought. At the same time, she watched Bella wink.

Bella *winked*?

"Okay," Angela said quickly, in a hurry to be out of the way if that was what Bella wanted. And it seemed that she did want that. "See you tomorrow, Bella . . . Edward." She struggled to say my name in a casual tone. Then she grabbed Jessica's hand and began towing her away.

I would find some way to thank Angela for this.

Jessica's car was close by in a bright circle of light cast by a streetlamp. Bella watched them carefully, a little crease of concern between her eyes, until they were in the car, so she must be somewhat aware of the danger she'd been in. Jessica waved as she drove away, and Bella waved back. It wasn't until the car disappeared that she took a deep breath and turned to look up at me.

"Honestly, I'm not hungry," she said.

Why had she waited for them to be gone before speaking? Did she truly want to be alone with me—even now, after witnessing my literal homicidal rage?

Whether or not that was the case, she was going to eat something.

"Humor me," I said.

I held the restaurant door open for her and waited.

She sighed and walked through.

I walked beside her to the podium where the hostess waited. Bella still seemed entirely self-possessed. I wanted to touch her hand, her forehead, to check her temperature. But my cold hand would repulse her, as it had before.

Oh my. The hostess's rather loud mental voice intruded into my consciousness. *My, oh my.*

It seemed to be my night to turn heads. Or was I only noticing it more because I wished so much that Bella would see me this way? We were always attractive to our prey, but I'd never thought so much about it before. Usually—unless, as with people like Shelly Cope and Jessica Stanley, there was constant repetition to dull the horror—the fear kicked in fairly quickly after the initial attraction.

"A table for two?" I prompted when the hostess didn't speak.

Mmm! What a voice! "Oh, er, yes. Welcome to La Bella Italia. Please follow me." Her thoughts were preoccupied—calculating.

Maybe she's his cousin. She couldn't be his sister, they don't look anything alike. But family, definitely. He *can't be with* her.

Human eyes were clouded; they saw nothing clearly. How could this small-minded woman find my physical lures—snares for prey—so attractive and yet be unable to see the soft perfection of the girl beside me?

Well, no need to help her out, just in case, the hostess thought as she led us to a family-sized table in the middle of the most crowded part of the restaurant. *Can I give him my number while she's there?* she mused.

I pulled a bill from my back pocket. People were invariably cooperative when money was involved.

Bella was already taking the seat the hostess indicated without objection. I shook my head at her, and she hesitated, cocking her head to one side with curiosity. Yes, she would be very curious tonight. A crowd was not the ideal place for this conversation.

"Perhaps something more private?" I requested of the hostess, handing her the money. She started, surprised, and then her hand curled around the tip.

"Sure."

She peeked at the bill while she led us around a dividing wall. *Fifty dollars for a better table? Rich, too. That makes sense—I bet his jacket cost more than my last paycheck. Damn. Why does he want privacy with* her?

She offered us a booth in a quiet corner of the restaurant where no one would be able to see us—to see Bella's reactions to whatever I would tell her. I had no clue as to what she would want from me tonight. Or what I would give her.

How much had she guessed? What explanation of tonight's events had she invented to make sense of it all?

"How's this?" the hostess asked.

"Perfect," I told her and, feeling slightly annoyed by her resentful attitude toward Bella, smiled widely at her, baring my teeth. Let her see me clearly.

Whoa. "Um...your server will be right out." *He can't be real. Maybe she'll disappear...maybe I'll write my number on his plate with marinara.* She wandered away, listing slightly to the side.

Odd. She still wasn't frightened. I suddenly remembered Emmett teasing me in the cafeteria, so many weeks ago. *I'll bet I could have frightened her better than that.*

Was I losing my edge?

"You really shouldn't do that to people." Bella interrupted my thoughts in a disapproving tone. "It's hardly fair."

I stared at her critical expression. What did she mean? I hadn't frightened the hostess at all, despite my intentions. "Do what?"

"Dazzle them like that—she's probably hyperventilating in the kitchen right now."

Hmm. Bella was very nearly right. The hostess was only semi-coherent at the moment, describing her incorrect assessment of me to her friend on the waitstaff.

"Oh, come on," Bella chided me when I didn't answer immediately. "You *have* to know the effect you have on people."

"I dazzle people?" That was an interesting way of phrasing it. Accurate enough for tonight. I wondered why the difference....

"You haven't noticed?" she asked, still critical. "Do you think everybody gets their way so easily?"

"Do I dazzle *you*?" I voiced my curiosity impulsively, and then the words were out, and it was too late to recall them.

But before I had time to regret too deeply speaking the words aloud, she answered, "Frequently." And her cheeks took on a faint pink glow.

I dazzled her.

My silent heart swelled with a hope more intense than I could ever remember having felt before.

"Hello," someone said—the waitress, introducing herself. Her thoughts were loud, and more explicit than the hostess's, but I tuned her out. I stared at Bella instead, watching the blood spreading across her cheekbones, noticing not how that made my throat flame, but rather how it brightened her fair face, how it set off the cream of her skin.

The waitress was waiting for something from me. Ah, she'd asked for our drink order. I continued to gaze at Bella, and the waitress grudgingly turned to look at her, too.

"I'll have a Coke?" Bella said, as if asking for approval.

"Two Cokes," I amended. Thirst—normal, human thirst—was a sign of shock. I would make sure she had the extra sugar from the soda in her system.

She looked healthy, though. More than healthy. She looked radiant.

"What?" she demanded—wondering why I was staring, I guessed. I was vaguely aware that the waitress had left.

"How are you feeling?" I asked.

She blinked, surprised by the question. "I'm fine."

"You don't feel dizzy, sick, cold?"

She was even more confused now. "Should I?"

"Well, I'm actually waiting for you to go into shock." I half smiled, expecting her denial. She would not want to be taken care of.

It took her a moment to answer me. Her eyes were slightly unfocused. She looked that way sometimes when I smiled at her. Was she... dazzled?

I would have loved to believe that.

"I don't think that will happen. I've always been very good at repressing unpleasant things," she answered, a little breathless.

Did she have a lot of practice with unpleasant things, then? Was her life always this hazardous?

"Just the same," I told her, "I'll feel better when you have some sugar and food in you."

The waitress returned with the Cokes and a basket of bread. She put them in front of me and asked for my order, trying to catch my eye in the process. I indicated that she should attend to Bella, and then went back to tuning her out. She had a vulgar mind.

"Um..." Bella glanced quickly at the menu. "I'll have the mushroom ravioli."

The waitress turned back to me eagerly. "And you?"

"Nothing for me."

Bella made a slight face. Hmm. She must have noticed that I never ate food. She noticed everything. And I always forgot to be careful around her.

I waited till we were alone again.

"Drink," I insisted.

I was surprised when she complied immediately and without objection. She drank until the glass was entirely empty, so I pushed the second Coke toward her, frowning a little. Thirst, or shock?

She drank a little more, and then shuddered once.

"Are you cold?"

"It's just the Coke," she said, but she shivered again, her lips trembling slightly as if her teeth were about to chatter.

The pretty blouse she wore looked too thin to protect her adequately. It clung to her like a second skin, almost as fragile as the first. "Don't you have a jacket?"

"Yes." She looked around herself, a little perplexed. "Oh—I left it in Jessica's car."

I pulled off my jacket, wishing that the gesture was not marred by my body temperature. It would have been nice to offer her a warm coat. She stared at me, her cheeks flushing again. What was she thinking now?

I handed her the jacket across the table, and she put it on at once, and then shuddered again.

Yes, it would be very nice to be warm.

"Thanks," she said. She took a deep breath, and then pushed the too-long sleeves back to free her hands. She took another deep breath.

Was the evening finally settling in? Her color was still good. Her skin was cream and roses against the deep blue of her shirt.

"That color blue looks lovely with your skin," I complimented her. Just being honest.

She looked well, but there was no point in taking chances. I pushed the basket of bread toward her.

"Really," she objected, guessing my motives. "I'm not going into shock."

"You should be—a *normal* person would be. You don't even look shaken." I stared at her, disapproving, wondering why she couldn't be normal and then wondering whether I really wanted her to be that way.

"I feel very safe with you," she explained, her eyes again filled with trust. Trust I didn't deserve.

Her instincts were all wrong—backward. That must be the problem. She didn't recognize danger the way a human being should be able to. She had the opposite reaction. Instead of running, she lingered, drawn to what should frighten her.

How could I protect her from myself when *neither* of us wanted that?

"This is more complicated than I'd planned," I murmured.

I could see her turning my words over in her head, and I wondered what she made of them. She took a breadstick and began to eat without seeming aware of the action. She chewed for a moment, and then leaned her head to one side thoughtfully.

"Usually you're in a better mood when your eyes are so light," she said in a casual tone.

Her observation, stated so matter-of-factly, left me reeling. "What?"

"You're always crabbier when your eyes are black—I expect it then. I have a theory about that," she added lightly.

So she had come up with her own explanation. Of course she had. I felt a deep sense of dread as I wondered how close she'd come to the truth.

"More theories?"

"Mm-hm." She chewed on another bite, entirely nonchalant. As if she weren't discussing the aspects of a demon with the demon himself.

"I hope you were more creative this time," I lied when she didn't continue. What I really hoped was that she was *wrong*—miles wide of the mark. "Or are you still stealing from comic books?"

"Well, no, I didn't get it from a comic book," she said, a little embarrassed. "But I didn't come up with it on my own, either."

"And?" I asked between my teeth.

Surely she would not speak so calmly if she were about to scream.

As she hesitated, biting her lip, the waitress reappeared with Bella's food. I paid the server little attention as she set the plate in front of Bella and then asked if I wanted anything.

I declined, but asked for more Coke. The waitress hadn't noticed the empty glasses.

"You were saying?" I prompted anxiously as soon as Bella and I were alone again.

"I'll tell you about it in the car," she said in a low voice. Ah, this would be bad. She wasn't willing to speak her guesses around others. "If…," she tacked on suddenly.

"There are conditions?" I was so tense I almost growled the words.

"I do have a few questions, of course."

"Of course," I agreed, my voice hard.

Her questions would probably be enough to tell me where her thoughts were heading. But how would I answer them? With responsible lies? Or would I drive her away with truth? Or would I say nothing, unable to decide?

We sat in silence while the waitress replenished her supply of soda.

"Well, go ahead," I said, jaw locked, when she was gone.

"Why are you in Port Angeles?"

That was too easy a question—for her. It gave away nothing, while my answer, if truthful, would give away much too much. Let her reveal something first.

"Next," I said.

"But that's the easiest one!'

"Next," I said again.

She was frustrated by my refusal. She looked away from me, down at her food. Slowly, thinking hard, she took a bite and chewed with deliberation.

Suddenly, as she ate, a strange comparison entered my head. For just a second, I saw Persephone, pomegranate in hand. Dooming herself to the underworld.

Is that who I was? Hades himself, coveting springtime, stealing it, condemning it to endless night. I tried unsuccessfully to shake the impression.

She washed her bite down with more Coke, and then finally looked up at me. Her eyes were narrow with suspicion.

"Okay then," she said. "Let's say, hypothetically, of course, that…someone…could know what people are thinking, read minds, you know—with a few exceptions."

It could be worse.

This explained that little half smile in the car. She was quick—no one else had ever guessed this about me. Except for Carlisle, and it had been rather obvious then, in the beginning, when I'd answered all his thoughts as if he'd spoken them to me. He'd understood before I had.

This question wasn't so bad. While it was clear that she knew there was something wrong with me, it was not as serious as it could have been. Mind reading was, after all, not a facet of vampire canon. I went along with her hypothesis.

"Just *one* exception," I corrected. "Hypothetically."

She fought a smile—my vague honesty pleased her. "All right, with one exception, then. How does that work? What are the limitations? How would...that someone...find someone else at exactly the right time? How would he know that she was in trouble?"

"Hypothetically?"

"Sure." Her lips twitched, and her liquid brown eyes were eager.

"Well..." I hesitated. "If...that someone—"

"Let's call him 'Joe,'" she suggested.

I had to smile at her enthusiasm. Did she really think the truth would be a good thing? If my secrets were pleasant, why would I keep them from her?

"Joe, then," I agreed. "If Joe had been paying attention, the timing wouldn't have needed to be quite so exact." I shook my head and repressed a shudder at the thought of how close I had been to being too late today. "Only you could get into trouble in a town this small. You would have devastated their crime rate statistics for a decade, you know."

Her lips turned down at the corners and pouted out. "We were speaking of a hypothetical case."

I laughed at her irritation.

Her lips, her skin...they looked so soft. I wanted to see if they were as velvety as they appeared. Impossible. My touch would be repellent to her.

"Yes, we were," I said, returning to the conversation before I could depress myself too thoroughly. "Shall we call you 'Jane'?"

She leaned across the table toward me, all humor and irritation gone from her expression.

"How did you know?" she asked, her voice low and intense.

Should I tell her the truth? And if so, what portion?

I wanted to tell her. I wanted to deserve the trust I could still see on her face.

As if she could hear my thoughts, she whispered, "You can trust me, you know." She reached one hand forward as if to touch my hands where they rested on top of the empty table before me.

I pulled them back—hating the thought of her reaction to my frigid stone skin—and she dropped her hand.

I knew that I could trust her with protecting my secrets. She was entirely honorable, good to the core. But I couldn't trust her not to be horrified by them. She *should* be horrified. The truth *was* horror.

"I don't know if I have a choice anymore," I murmured. I remembered that I'd once teased her by calling her *exceptionally unobservant*. Offended her, if I'd been judging her expressions correctly. Well, I could right that one injustice, at least. "I was wrong—you're much more observant than I gave you credit for." And though she might not realize it, I'd given her plenty of credit already.

"I thought you were always right," she said, smiling as she teased me.

"I used to be." I used to know what I was doing. I used to be always sure of my course. And now everything was chaos and tumult. Yet I wouldn't trade it. Not if the chaos meant that I could be near Bella.

"I was wrong about you on one other thing as well," I went on, setting the record straight on a second point. "You're not a magnet for accidents—that's not a broad enough classification. You are a magnet for *trouble*. If there is anything dangerous within a ten-mile radius, it will invariably find you." Why her? What had she done to deserve any of this?

Bella's face turned serious again. "And you put yourself into that category?"

Honesty was more important in regard to this question than any other. "Unequivocally."

Her eyes narrowed slightly—not suspicious now, but oddly concerned. Her lips curved into that one specific smile that I had only seen on her face when she was confronted with someone else's pain. She reached her hand across the table again, slowly and deliberately. I pulled my hands an inch away from her, but she ignored that, determined to touch me. I held my breath—not because of her scent now, but because of the sudden, overwhelming tension. Fear. My skin would disgust her. She would run away.

She brushed her fingertips lightly across the back of my hand. The heat of her gentle, willing touch was like nothing I'd ever felt before. It was almost pure pleasure. Would have been, except for my fear. I watched her face as she felt the cold stone of my skin, still unable to breathe.

Her smile of concern shifted into something wider, something warmer.

"Thank you," she said, meeting my stare with an intense gaze of her own. "That's twice now."

Her soft fingers lingered against my skin as if they found it pleasant to be there.

I answered her as casually as I was able. "Let's not try for three, agreed?"

She scowled a little at that, but nodded.

I pulled my hands out from under hers. As exquisite as her touch felt, I wasn't going to wait for the magic of her tolerance to pass, to turn to revulsion. I hid my hands under the table.

I read her eyes; though her mind was silent, I could perceive both trust and wonder there. I realized in that moment that I *wanted* to answer her questions. Not because I owed it to her. Not because I wanted her to trust me.

I wanted her to *know* me.

"I followed you to Port Angeles," I told her, the words spilling out too quickly for me to edit them. I knew the danger of the truth, the risk I was taking. At any moment, her unnatural calm could shatter into hysterics. Contrarily, knowing this only had me talking faster. "I've never tried to keep a specific person alive before and it's much more troublesome than I would have believed. But that's probably just because it's you. Ordinary people seem to make it through the day without so many catastrophes."

I watched her, waiting.

She smiled wider again. Her clear, dark eyes seemed deeper than ever.

I'd just admitted to stalking her, and she was smiling.

"Did you ever think that maybe my number was up that first time, with the van, and that you've been interfering with fate?" she asked.

"That wasn't the first time," I said, staring down at the dark maroon tablecloth, my shoulders bowed in shame. Barriers down, the truth still spilling free recklessly. "Your number was up the first time I met you."

It was true, and it angered me. I had been positioned over her life like the blade of a guillotine—as though it was ordained by fate, just as she said. As if she had been marked for death by that cruel, unjust fate, and—since I'd proved an unwilling tool—it continued to try to execute her. I imagined the fate personified, a grisly, jealous hag, a vengeful harpy.

I wanted something, someone, to be responsible for this, so that I would have something concrete to fight against. Something, anything to destroy, so that Bella could be safe.

Bella was very quiet. Her breathing had accelerated.

I looked up at her, knowing I would finally see the fear I was waiting for. Had I not just admitted how close I'd been to killing her? Closer than the van that had come within slim inches of crushing the life from her body. And yet, her face was still calm, her eyes still tightened only with concern.

"You remember?"

"Yes," she said, her voice level and grave. Her deep eyes were full of awareness.

She knew. She knew that I had wanted to murder her. Where were her screams?

"And yet here you sit," I said, pointing out the inherent contradiction.

"Yes, here I sit...because of you." Her expression altered, turned curious, as she unsubtly changed the subject. "Because somehow you knew how to find me today...?"

Hopelessly, I pushed one more time at the barrier that protected her thoughts, desperate to understand. It made no logical sense to me. How could she even care about the rest with that glaring truth on the table?

She waited, only curious. Her skin was pale, which was natural for her, but it still concerned me. Her dinner sat nearly untouched in front of her. If I continued to tell her too much, she was going to need a buffer when the shock set in at last.

I named my terms. "You eat, I'll talk."

She processed that for half a second, and then threw a bite into her mouth with a speed that belied her calm. She was more anxious for my answer than her eyes let on.

"It's harder than it should be—keeping track of you," I told her. "Usually I can find someone very easily, once I've heard their mind before."

I watched her face carefully as I said this. Guessing right was one thing, having it confirmed was another.

She was motionless, her eyes blank. I felt my teeth clench together as I waited for her panic.

But she just blinked once, swallowed loudly, and then quickly scooped another bite into her mouth. Eager for me to continue.

"I was keeping tabs on Jessica," I went on, watching each word as it sank in. "Not carefully—like I said, only you could find trouble in Port Angeles." I couldn't resist adding that. Was she aware that other human lives were not so plagued with near-death experiences, or did she think the things that happened to her were normal? "And at first I didn't notice when you took off on your own. Then, when I realized that you weren't with her anymore, I went looking for you at the bookstore I saw in her head. I could tell that you hadn't gone in, and that you'd gone south . . . and I knew you would have to turn around soon. So I was just waiting for you, randomly searching through the thoughts of people on the street—to see if anyone had noticed you so I would know where you were. I had no reason to be worried . . . but I was strangely anxious. . . .” My breath came faster as I remembered that feeling of panic. Her scent blazed in my throat and I was glad. It was a pain that meant she was alive.

As long as I burned, she was safe.

“I started to drive in circles, still . . . listening.” I hoped the word made sense to her. This had to be confusing. “The sun was finally setting, and I was about to get out and follow you on foot. And then—”

As the memory took me—perfectly clear and as vivid as if I was in the moment again—I felt the same murderous fury wash through my body, locking it into ice.

I wanted him dead. He *should* be dead. My jaw clenched tight as I concentrated on holding myself here at the table. Bella still needed me. That was what mattered.

“Then what?” she whispered, her dark eyes huge.

“I heard what they were thinking,” I said through my teeth, unable to keep the words from coming out in a growl. “I saw your face in his mind.”

I still knew precisely where to find him. His black thoughts sucked at the night sky, pulling me toward them.

I covered my face, knowing my expression was that of a hunter, a killer. I fixed her image behind my closed eyes to control myself. The delicate framework of her bones, the thin sheath of her pale skin—like silk stretched over glass, incredibly soft and easy to shatter. She was too vulnerable for this world. She *needed* a protector. And through some twisted mismanagement of destiny, I was the closest thing available.

I tried to explain my violent reaction so that she would understand.

“It was very . . . hard—you can’t imagine how hard—for me to simply take you away, and leave them . . . alive,” I whispered. “I could have let you go with Jessica and Angela, but I was afraid if you left me alone, I would go looking for them."

For the second time tonight, I confessed to an intended murder. At least this one was defensible.

She was quiet as I struggled to control myself. I listened to her heartbeat. The rhythm was irregular, but it slowed as the time passed until it was steady again. Her breathing, too, was low and even.

I was too close to the edge. I needed to get her home before…

Would I kill him, then? Would I become a murderer again when she trusted me? Was there any way to stop myself?

She'd promised to tell me her latest theory when we were alone. Did I want to hear it? I was anxious for it, but would the reward for my curiosity be worse than not knowing?

At any rate, she must have had enough truth for one night.

I looked at her again, and her face was paler than before, but composed.

"Are you ready to go home?" I asked.

"I'm ready to leave," she said, choosing her words carefully, as if a simple *yes* did not fully express what she wanted to say.

Frustrating.

The waitress returned. She'd heard Bella's last statement as she'd dithered on the other side of the partition, wondering what more she could offer me. I wanted to roll my eyes at some of the offerings she'd had in mind.

"How are we doing?" she asked me.

"We're ready for the check, thank you," I told her, my eyes on Bella.

The waitress's breathing spiked and she was momentarily—to use Bella's phrasing—dazzled by my voice.

In a sudden moment of perception, hearing the way my voice sounded in this inconsequential human's head, I realized why I seemed to be attracting so much admiration tonight—unmarred by the usual fear.

It was because of Bella. Trying so hard to be safe for her, to be less frightening, to be *human*, I truly had lost my edge. The other humans saw only beauty now, with my innate horror so carefully under control.

I looked up at the waitress, waiting for her to recover herself. It was sort of humorous, now that I understood the reason.

"S-sure. Here you go." She handed me the folder with the bill, thinking of the card she'd slid in behind the receipt. A card with her name and telephone number on it.

Yes, it was rather funny.

I had money ready again. I gave the folder back at once, so she wouldn't waste any time waiting for a call that would never come.

"No change," I told her, hoping the size of the tip would assuage her disappointment.

I stood, and Bella quickly followed suit. I wanted to offer her my hand, but I thought that might be pushing my luck a little too far for one night. I thanked the waitress, my eyes never leaving Bella's face. Bella seemed to be finding something amusing, too.

I walked as close beside her as I dared. Close enough that the warmth coming off her was like a physical touch against the left side of my body. As I held the door for her, she sighed quietly, and I wondered what regret weighed on her. I stared into her eyes, about to ask, when she suddenly looked at the ground, seeming embarrassed. It made me more curious, even as it made me reluctant to ask. The silence between us continued while I opened her door for her and then got into the car.

I turned the heater on—the warmer weather had come to an abrupt end; the cold car would be uncomfortable for her. She huddled in my jacket, a small smile on her lips.

I waited, postponing the conversation until the lights of the boardwalk faded. It made me feel more alone with her.

Was that the right thing? The car seemed very small. Her scent swirled through it with the current of the heater, building and strengthening. It grew into its own force, like a third entity in the car. A presence that demanded recognition.

It had that; I burned. The burning was acceptable, though. It seemed strangely appropriate to me. I had been given so much tonight—more than I'd expected. And here she was, still willingly at my side. I owed something in return for that. A sacrifice. A burnt offering.

Now if I could just keep it to that—just burn, and nothing more. But the venom filled my mouth, and my muscles tensed in anticipation, as if I were hunting.

I had to keep such thoughts from my mind. And I knew what would distract me.

"Now," I said to her, fear of her response taking the edge off the burn. "It's your turn."

10. THEORY

"CAN I ASK JUST ONE MORE?" SHE ENTREATED INSTEAD of answering my demand.

I was on edge, anxious for the worst. And yet, how tempting it was to prolong this moment. To have her with me, willingly, for just a few seconds longer. I sighed at the dilemma, and then said, "One."

"Well..." She hesitated for a moment, as if deciding which question to voice. "You said you knew I hadn't gone into the bookstore, and that I had gone south. I was just wondering how you knew that."

I glared out the windshield. Here was another question that revealed nothing on her part, and too much on mine.

"I thought we were past all the evasiveness," she said, her tone critical and disappointed.

How ironic. She was relentlessly evasive, without even trying.

Well, she wanted me to be direct. And this conversation wasn't going anywhere good, regardless.

"Fine, then," I said. "I followed your scent."

I wanted to watch her face, but I was afraid of what I would see. Instead, I listened to her breath accelerate and then stabilize. She spoke again after a moment, and her voice was steadier than I would have expected.

"And then you didn't answer one of my first questions...," she said.

I looked down at her, frowning. She was stalling, too.

"Which one?"

"How does it work—the mind-reading thing?" she asked, reiterating her question from the restaurant. "Can you read anybody's mind, anywhere? How do you do it? Can the rest of your family...?" She trailed off, flushing again.

"That's more than one," I said.

She just looked at me, waiting for her answers.

And why not tell her? She'd already guessed most of this, and it was an easier subject than the one that loomed.

"No, it's just me. And I can't hear anyone, anywhere. I have to be fairly close. The more familiar someone's...'voice' is, the farther away I can hear them. But still, no more than a few miles." I tried to think of a way to describe it so that she would understand. An analogy that she could relate to. "It's a little like being in a huge hall filled with people, everyone talking at once. It's just a hum—a buzzing of voices in the background. Until I focus on one voice, and then what they're thinking is clear. Most of the time I tune it all out—it can be very distracting. And then it's easier to seem *normal*"—I scowled—"when I'm not accidentally answering someone's thoughts rather than their words."

"Why do you think you can't hear me?" she wondered.

I gave her another truth and another analogy.

"I don't know," I admitted. "The only guess I have is that maybe your mind doesn't work the same way the rest of theirs do. Like your thoughts are on the AM frequency and I'm only getting FM."

I realized as soon as the words were out that she would not like this analogy. The anticipation of her reaction had me smiling. She didn't disappoint.

"My mind doesn't work right?" she asked, her voice rising. "I'm a freak?"

Ah, the irony again.

"I hear voices in my mind and you're worried that *you're* the freak." I laughed. She understood all the small things, and yet the big ones she got backward. Always the wrong instincts.

Bella was gnawing on her lip, and the crease between her eyes was etched deep.

"Don't worry," I reassured her. "It's just a theory...." And there was a more important theory to be discussed. I was anxious to get it over with. Each passing second was beginning to feel more and more like borrowed time. "Which brings us back to you."

She sighed, still chewing her lip—I worried that she would hurt herself. She stared into my eyes, her face troubled.

"Aren't we past all the evasions now?" I asked quietly.

She looked down, struggling with some internal dilemma. Suddenly, she stiffened and her eyes flew wide open. Fear flashed across her face for the first time.

"Holy crow!" she gasped.

I panicked. What had she seen? How had I frightened her?

Then she shouted, "Slow down!"

"What's wrong?" I didn't understand where her terror was coming from.

"You're going a hundred miles an hour!" she yelled at me. She flashed a look out the window, and recoiled from the dark trees racing past us.

This little thing, just a bit of speed, had her shouting in fear?

I rolled my eyes. "Relax, Bella."

"Are you trying to kill us?" she demanded, her voice high and tight.

"We're not going to crash," I promised her.

She sucked in a sharp breath, and then spoke in a slightly more level tone. "Why are you in such a hurry?"

"I always drive like this."

I met her gaze, amused by her shocked expression.

"Keep your eyes on the road!" she shouted.

"I've never been in an accident, Bella. I've never even gotten a ticket." I grinned at her and touched my forehead. It made it even more comical—the absurdity of being able to joke with her about something so secret and strange. "Built-in radar detector."

"Very funny," she said sarcastically, her voice still more frightened than angry. "Charlie's a cop, remember? I was raised to abide by traffic laws. Besides, if you turn us into a Volvo pretzel around a tree trunk, you can probably just walk away."

"Probably," I repeated, and then laughed without humor. Yes, we would fare quite differently in a car accident. She was right to be afraid, despite my driving abilities. "But you can't."

With a sigh, I let the car drift to a crawl. "Happy?"

She eyed the speedometer. "Almost."

Was this still too fast for her? "I hate driving slow," I muttered, but let the needle slide down another notch.

"This is slow?" she asked.

"Enough commentary on my driving," I said impatiently. How many times had she dodged my question now? Three times? Four? Were her speculations that horrific? I had to know—immediately. "I'm still waiting for your latest theory."

She bit her lip again, and her expression became upset, almost pained.

I reined in my impatience and softened my voice. I didn't want her to be distressed.

"I won't laugh," I promised, wishing that it were only embarrassment that made her unwilling to talk.

"I'm more afraid that you'll be angry with me," she whispered.

I forced my voice to stay even. "Is it that bad?"

"Pretty much, yeah."

She looked down, refusing to meet my eyes. The seconds passed.

"Go ahead," I encouraged.

Her voice was small. "I don't know how to start."

"Why don't you start at the beginning?" I remembered her words before dinner. "You said you didn't come up with this on your own."

"No," she agreed, and then was silent again.

I thought about things that might have inspired her. "What got you started—a book? A movie?"

I should have looked through her collections when she was out of the house. I had no idea if Bram Stoker or Anne Rice was there in her stack of worn paperbacks.

"No," she said again. "It was Saturday, at the beach."

I hadn't expected that. The local gossip about us had never strayed into anything too bizarre—or too precise. Was there a new rumor I'd missed? Bella peeked up from her hands and saw the surprise on my face.

"I ran into an old family friend—Jacob Black," she went on. "His dad and Charlie have been friends since I was a baby."

Jacob Black—the name was not familiar, and yet it reminded me of something...some *time*, long ago....I stared out the windshield, flipping through memories to find the connection.

"His dad is one of the Quileute elders," she said.

Jacob Black. *Ephraim Black*. A descendant, no doubt.

It was as bad as it could get.

She knew the truth.

My mind was flying through the ramifications as the car flew around the dark curves in the road, my body rigid with anguish—motionless except for the small, automatic actions it took to steer.

She knew the truth.

But...if she'd learned the truth Saturday...then she'd known it all evening long, and yet...

"We went for a walk," she went on. "And he was telling me about some old legends—trying to scare me, I think. He told me one..."

She stopped short, but there was no need for her qualms now. I knew what she was going to say. The only mystery left was why she was here with me now.

"Go on," I said.

"About vampires," she breathed, the words less than a whisper.

Somehow, it was even worse than knowing that she knew, hearing her speak the word aloud. I flinched at the sound of it, and then controlled myself again.

"And you immediately thought of me?" I asked.

"No. He...mentioned your family."

How ironic that it would be Ephraim's own progeny that would violate the treaty he'd vowed to uphold. A grandson, or great-grandson perhaps. How many years had it been? Seventy?

I should have realized that it was not the old men who *believed* in the legends that would be the danger. Of course, the younger generation—those who had been warned but would think the ancient superstitions laughable—that was where the danger of exposure lay.

I supposed this meant I was now free to slaughter the small, defenseless tribe on the coastline, were I so inclined. Ephraim and his pack of protectors were long dead.

"He just thought it was a silly superstition," Bella said suddenly, her voice edged with a new anxiety, almost as if she could read *my* thoughts. "He didn't expect me to think anything of it."

Out of the corner of my eye, I saw her hands twist uneasily.

"It was my fault," she said after a brief pause, and then she hung her head as if she was ashamed. "I forced him to tell me."

"Why?" It wasn't so hard to keep my voice level now. The worst was already done. As long as we spoke of the details of the revelation, we didn't have to move on to the consequences of it.

"Lauren said something about you—she was trying to provoke me." She made a little face at the memory. I was slightly distracted, wondering how Bella would be provoked by someone talking about me. "And an older boy from the tribe said your family didn't come to the reservation, only it sounded like he meant something different. So I got Jacob alone and I tricked it out of him."

Her head dropped even lower as she admitted this, and her expression looked...guilty.

I looked away from her and laughed out loud; it was a

hard-edged sound. *She* felt guilty? What could she possibly have done to deserve censure of any kind?

"Tricked him how?" I asked.

"I tried to flirt—it worked better than I thought it would," she explained, and her voice turned incredulous at the memory of that success.

I could just imagine—considering the attraction she seemed to hold for all things male, totally unconscious on her part—how overwhelming she would be when she *tried* to be attractive. I was suddenly full of pity for the unsuspecting boy she'd unleashed such a potent force on.

"I'd like to have seen that," I said, and then I laughed again with dark humor. I wished I could have heard the boy's reaction, witnessed the devastation for myself. "And you accused me of dazzling people—poor Jacob Black."

I wasn't as angry with the source of my exposure as I would have expected to feel. He didn't know better. And how could I expect anyone to deny this girl what she wanted? No, I only felt sympathy for the damage she would have done to his peace of mind.

I felt her blush heat the air between us. I glanced at her, and she was staring out her window. She didn't speak again.

"What did you do then?" I prompted. Time to get back to the horror story.

"I did some research on the internet."

Ever practical. "And did that convince you?"

"No," she said. "Nothing fit. Most of it was kind of silly. And then—"

She broke off again, and I heard her teeth lock together.

"What?" I demanded. What had she found? What had made sense of the nightmare for her?

There was a short pause, and then she whispered, "I decided it didn't matter."

Shock froze my thoughts for a half second, and then it all fit together. Why she'd sent her friends away tonight rather than escape with them. Why she had gotten into my car with me again instead of running, screaming for the police.

Her reactions were always wrong—always completely wrong. She pulled danger toward herself. She invited it.

"It didn't *matter*?" I said through my teeth, anger filling me. How was I supposed to protect someone so…so…so determined to be unprotected?

"No," she said in a low voice that was inexplicably tender. "It doesn't matter to me what you are."

She was impossible.

"You don't care if I'm a monster? If I'm not *human*?"

"No."

I started to wonder if she was entirely stable.

I supposed that I could arrange for her to receive the best care available.…Carlisle would have the connections to find her the most skilled doctors, the most talented therapists. Perhaps something could be done to fix whatever it was that was wrong with her, whatever it was that made her content to sit beside a vampire with her heart beating calmly and steadily. I would watch over the facility, naturally, and visit as often as she allowed.

"You're angry," she sighed. "I shouldn't have said anything."

As if her hiding these disturbing tendencies would help either of us.

"No. I'd rather know what you're thinking—even if what you're thinking is insane."

"So I'm wrong again?" she asked, a bit belligerent now.

"That's not what I was referring to!" My teeth clenched together again. "'*It doesn't matter*'!" I repeated in a scathing tone.

She gasped. "I'm right?"

"Does it *matter*?" I countered.

She took a deep breath. I waited angrily for her answer.

"Not really," she said, her voice composed again. "But I *am* curious."

Not really. It didn't really matter. She didn't care. She knew I was inhuman, a horror, and this didn't really matter to her.

Aside from my worries about her sanity, I began to feel a swelling of hope. I tried to quash it.

"What are you curious about?" I asked her. There were no secrets left, only minor details.

"How old are you?" she asked.

My answer was automatic and ingrained. "Seventeen."

"And how long have you been seventeen?"

I tried not to smile at her patronizing tone. "A while," I admitted.

"Okay," she said, abruptly enthusiastic. She smiled up at me. When I stared back, anxious again about her mental health, she smiled wider. I frowned.

"Don't laugh," she warned. "But how can you come out during the daytime?"

I laughed despite her request. Her research had not netted her anything unusual, it seemed. "Myth," I told her.

"Burned by the sun?"

"Myth."

"Sleeping in coffins?"

"Myth."

Sleep had not been a part of my life for so long—not until these last few nights, as I'd watched Bella dreaming.

"I can't sleep," I murmured, answering her question more fully.

She was silent for a moment.

"At all?" she asked.

"Never," I breathed.

As I met her penetrating gaze, read the surprise and the sympathy there, I abruptly yearned for sleep. Not for oblivion, as I had before, not to escape boredom, but because I wanted to *dream.* Maybe if I could be unconscious, if I could dream, I could live for a few hours in a world where she and I could be together. She dreamed of me. I wanted to dream of her.

She stared back at me, her expression full of wonder. I had to look away.

I could not dream of her. She should not dream of me.

"You haven't asked me the most important question yet," I said. The stone heart in my silent chest felt colder and harder than before. She had to be forced to understand. At some point, she must be made to see that this all *did* matter—more than any other consideration. Considerations like the fact that I loved her.

"Which one is that?" she asked, surprised and unaware.

This only made my voice harder. "You aren't concerned about my diet?"

"Oh. That." She spoke in a quiet tone that I couldn't interpret.

"Yes, that. Don't you want to know if I drink blood?"

She cringed away from my question. Finally.

"Well, Jacob said something about that," she said.

"What did Jacob say?"

"He said you didn't...hunt people. He said your family wasn't supposed to be dangerous because you only hunted animals."

"He said we weren't dangerous?" I repeated cynically.

"Not exactly," she clarified. "He said you weren't *supposed* to be dangerous. But the Quileutes still didn't want you on their land, just in case."

I stared at the road, my thoughts in a hopeless snarl, my throat aching with the familiar fire.

"So, was he right?" she asked, as calmly as if she were confirming a weather report. "About not hunting people?"

"The Quileutes have a long memory."

She nodded to herself, thinking hard.

"Don't let that make you complacent, though," I said quickly. "They're right to keep their distance from us. We are still dangerous."

"I don't understand."

No she didn't. How to make her see?

"We...*try*," I told her. "We're usually very good at what we do. Sometimes we make mistakes. Me, for example, allowing myself to be alone with you."

Her scent was still a force in the car. I was growing used to it,

I could almost ignore it, but there was no denying that my body still yearned toward her for the worst possible reason. My mouth was swimming with venom. I swallowed.

"This is a mistake?" she asked, and there was heartbreak in her voice. The sound of it disarmed me. She wanted to be with me—despite everything, she wanted to be with me.

Hope swelled again, and I beat it back.

"A very dangerous one," I told her truthfully, wishing the truth could really somehow cease to matter.

She didn't respond for a moment. I heard her breathing change—it hitched in strange ways that did not sound like fear.

"Tell me more," she said suddenly, her voice distorted by anguish.

I examined her carefully.

She appeared to be in some kind of pain. How had I allowed *this*?

"What more do you want to know?" I asked, trying to think of a way to keep her from hurting. She should not hurt. I couldn't let her be hurt.

"Tell me why you hunt animals instead of people," she said, still anguished.

Wasn't it obvious? Or maybe this didn't matter to her, either.

"I don't *want* to be a monster," I muttered.

"But animals aren't enough?"

I searched for another comparison, a way that she could understand. "I can't be sure, of course, but I'd compare it to living on tofu and soy milk; we call ourselves vegetarians, our little inside joke. It doesn't completely satiate the hunger—or rather thirst. But it keeps us strong enough to resist. Most of the time." My voice got lower. I was ashamed of the danger I had allowed her to be in. Danger I continued to allow. "Sometimes it's more difficult than others."

"Is it very difficult for you now?"

I sighed. Of course she would ask the question I didn't want to answer. "Yes," I admitted.

I expected her physical response correctly this time: Her breathing held steady, her heart kept its even pattern. I expected it, but I did not understand it. How could she not be afraid?

"But you're not hungry now," she declared, perfectly sure of herself.

"Why do you think that?"

"Your eyes," she said, her tone offhand. "I told you I had a theory. I've noticed that people—men in particular—are crabbier when they're hungry."

I chuckled at her description: *crabby*. There was an understatement. But she was dead right, as usual. "You are observant, aren't you?" I laughed again.

She smiled a little, the crease returning between her eyes as if she were concentrating on something.

"Were you hunting this weekend, with Emmett?" she asked after my laugh had faded. The casual way she spoke was as fascinating as it was frustrating. Could she really accept so much in stride? I was closer to shock than she seemed to be.

"Yes," I told her, and then, as I was about to leave it at that, I felt the same urge I'd had in the restaurant: I wanted her to know me. "I didn't want to leave," I went on slowly, "but it was necessary. It's a bit easier to be around you when I'm not thirsty."

"Why didn't you want to leave?"

I took a deep breath, and then turned to meet her gaze. This kind of honesty was difficult in a very different way.

"It makes me . . . anxious"—I supposed that word would suffice, though it wasn't strong enough—"to be away from you. I wasn't joking when I asked you to try not to fall in the ocean or get run over last Thursday. I was distracted all weekend, worrying about you. And after what happened tonight, I'm surprised that you did make it through a whole weekend unscathed." Then I remembered the scrapes on her palms. "Well, not totally unscathed," I amended.

"What?"

"Your hands," I reminded her.

She sighed and her lips turned down. "I fell."

"That's what I thought," I said, unable to contain my smile. "I suppose, being you, it could have been much worse—and that possibility tormented me the entire time I was away. It was a very long three days. I really got on Emmett's nerves." Honestly, that didn't belong in the past tense. I was probably still irritating Emmett, and all the rest of my family, too. Except Alice.

"Three days?" she asked, her voice suddenly sharp. "Didn't you just get back today?"

I didn't understand the edge in her voice. "No, we got back Sunday."

"Then why weren't any of you in school?" she demanded. Her irritation confused me. She didn't seem to realize that this question was one that related to mythology again.

"Well, you asked if the sun hurt me, and it doesn't," I said. "But I can't go out in the sunlight—at least, not where anyone can see."

That distracted her from her mysterious annoyance. "Why?" she asked, leaning her head to one side.

I doubted I could come up with the appropriate analogy to explain this one. So I just told her, "I'll show you sometime," and then immediately wondered if this was a promise I would end up breaking—I'd said the words so casually, but I could not imagine actually following through.

It wasn't something to worry about now. I didn't know if I could be allowed see her again, after tonight. Did I love her enough yet to be able to bear leaving her?

"You might have called me," she said.

What an odd conclusion. "But I knew you were safe."

"But *I* didn't know where *you* were. I—" She came to an abrupt stop, and looked at her hands.

"What?"

"I didn't like it," she said shyly, the skin over her cheekbones warming. "Not seeing you. It makes me anxious, too."

Are you happy *now?* I demanded of myself. Well, here was my reward for hoping.

I was bewildered, elated, horrified—mostly horrified—to realize that all my wildest fantasies were not so far off the mark. This was why it didn't matter to her that I was a monster. It was exactly the same reason that the rules no longer mattered to me. Why right and wrong were no longer compelling influences. Why all my priorities had shifted one rung down to make room for this girl at the very top.

Bella cared for me, too.

I knew it could be nothing in comparison to how I loved her—she was mortal, changeable. She wasn't locked in with no hope of recovery. But still, she cared enough to risk her life to sit here with me. To do so gladly.

Enough that it would cause her pain if I did the right thing and left her.

Was there anything I could do now that would *not* hurt her? Anything at all?

Every word we spoke here—each one of them was another pomegranate seed. That strange vision in the restaurant had been more on point than I'd realized.

I should have stayed away. I should never have come back to Forks. I would cause her nothing but pain.

Would that stop me from staying now? From making it worse?

The way I felt at this moment, feeling her warmth against my skin…

No. Nothing would stop me.

"Ah," I groaned to myself. "This is wrong."

"What did I say?" she asked, quick to take the blame on herself.

"Don't you see, Bella? It's one thing for me to make myself miserable, but a wholly other thing for you to be so involved. I don't want to hear that you feel that way." It was the truth, it was a lie. The most selfish part of me was flying with the knowledge that she wanted me as I wanted her. "It's wrong. It's not safe. I'm dangerous, Bella—please, grasp that."

"No." Her lips pouted out stubbornly.

"I'm serious." I was battling with myself so strongly—half-desperate for her to accept my warnings, half-desperate to keep the warnings from escaping—that the words came through my teeth as a growl.

"So am I," she insisted. "I told you, it doesn't matter what you are. It's too late."

Too late? The world was bleakly black and white for one endless second as I watched the shadows crawl across the sunny lawn toward Bella's sleeping form in my memory. Inevitable, unstoppable. They stole the color from her skin, and plunged her into darkness, into the underworld.

Too late? Alice's vision swirled in my head, Bella's bloodred eyes staring back at me impassively, expressionless. But there was no way that she could *not* hate me for that future. Hate me for stealing everything from her.

It could not be too late.

"Never say that," I hissed.

She stared out her window, and her teeth bit into her lip again. Her hands were balled into tight fists in her lap. Her breathing hitched.

"What are you thinking?" I had to know.

She shook her head without looking at me. I saw something glisten, like a crystal, on her cheek.

Agony. "Are you crying?" I'd made her *cry*. I'd hurt her that much.

She scrubbed the tear away with the back of her hand.

"No," she lied, her voice breaking.

Some long-buried instinct had me reaching out toward her—in that one second I felt more human than I ever had. And then I remembered that I was . . . not. And I lowered my hand.

"I'm sorry," I said, my jaw locked. How could I ever tell her how sorry I was? Sorry for all the stupid mistakes I'd made. Sorry for my never-ending selfishness. Sorry that she was so unfortunate as to have inspired this first, and last, tragic love of mine. Sorry also for the things beyond my control—that I'd been the executioner chosen by fate to end her life in the first place.

I took a deep breath—ignoring my wretched reaction to the flavor in the car—and tried to collect myself.

I wanted to change the subject, to think of something else. Lucky for me, my curiosity about the girl was insatiable.

"Tell me something," I said.

"Yes?" she asked huskily, tears still in her voice.

"What were you thinking tonight, just before I came around the corner? I couldn't understand your expression—you didn't look that scared, you looked like you were concentrating very hard on something." I remembered her face—forcing myself to forget whose eyes I was looking through—the look of determination there.

"I was trying to remember how to incapacitate an attacker," she said, her voice more composed. "You know, self-defense. I was going to smash his nose into his brain." Her composure did not last to the end of her explanation. Her tone twisted until it seethed with hate. This was no hyperbole, and her fury was not humorous now. I could see her frail figure—just silk over glass—overshadowed by the meaty, heavy-fisted human monsters who would have hurt her. The fury boiled in the back of my head.

"You were going to fight them?" I wanted to groan. Her instincts were deadly—to herself. "Didn't you think about running?"

"I fall down a lot when I run," she said sheepishly.

"What about screaming for help?"

"I was getting to that part."

I shook my head in disbelief. "You were right," I told her, a sour edge to my voice. "I'm definitely fighting fate trying to keep you alive."

She sighed, and glanced out the window. Then she looked back at me.

"Will I see you tomorrow?" she demanded abruptly.

As long as were on our way down to hell—why not enjoy the journey?

"Yes—I have a paper due, too." I smiled at her, and it felt good to do this. Clearly, hers were not the only instincts that were backwards. "I'll save you a seat at lunch."

Her heart fluttered; my dead heart felt warmer.

I stopped the car in front of her father's house. She made no move to leave me.

"Do you *promise* to be there tomorrow?" she insisted.

"I promise."

How could doing the wrong thing give me so much happiness? Surely there was something amiss in that.

She nodded to herself, satisfied, and started to remove my jacket.

"You can keep it," I assured her quickly. I rather wanted to leave her with something of myself. A token, like the bottle cap that was in my pocket now. "You don't have a jacket for tomorrow."

She handed it back to me, smiling ruefully. "I don't want to have to explain to Charlie," she told me.

I would imagine not. I smiled at her. "Oh, right."

She put her hand on the door handle, and then stopped. Unwilling to leave, just as I was unwilling for her to go.

To have her unprotected, even for a few moments...

Peter and Charlotte were well on their way by now, long past Seattle, no doubt. But there were always others.

"Bella?" I asked, amazed at the pleasure there was in simply speaking her name.

"Yes?"

"Will you promise me something?"

"Yes," she agreed easily, and then her eyes tightened as if she'd thought of a reason to object.

"Don't go into the woods alone," I warned her, wondering if this request would trigger the objection in her eyes.

She blinked, startled. "Why?"

I glowered into the untrustworthy darkness. The lack of light was no problem for *my* eyes, but neither would it trouble another hunter.

"I'm not always the most dangerous thing out there," I told her. "Let's leave it at that."

She shivered, but recovered quickly and was even smiling when she told me, "Whatever you say."

Her breath touched my face, so sweet.

I could stay here all night like this, but she needed her sleep. The two desires seemed equally strong as they continually warred inside me: wanting her versus wanting her to be well.

I sighed at the impossibilities. "I'll see you tomorrow," I said, knowing that I would see her much sooner than that. She wouldn't see *me* until tomorrow, though.

"Tomorrow, then," she agreed as she opened her door.

Agony again, watching her leave.

I leaned after her, wanting to hold her here. "Bella?"

She turned, and then froze, surprised to find our faces so close together.

I, too, was overwhelmed by the proximity. The heat rolled off her in waves, caressing my face. I could all but feel the silk of her skin.

Her heartbeat stuttered, and her lips fell open.

"Sleep well," I whispered, and leaned away before the urgency in my body—either the familiar thirst or the very new and strange hunger I suddenly felt—could make me do something that might hurt her.

She sat there motionless for a moment, her eyes wide and stunned. Dazzled, I guessed.

As was I.

She recovered—though her face was still a bit bemused—and half fell out of the car, tripping over her feet and having to catch the frame of the car to right herself.

I chuckled—hopefully it was too quiet for her to hear.

I watched her stumble her way up to the pool of light that surrounded the front door. Safe for the moment. And I would be back soon to make sure.

I could feel her eyes follow me as I drove down the dark street. Such a different sensation than I was accustomed to. Usually, I could simply *watch* myself through someone's following eyes, were I of a mind to. This was strangely exciting—this intangible sensation of watching eyes. I knew it was just because they were *her* eyes.

A million thoughts chased each other through my head as I drove aimlessly into the night.

For a long time I circled through the streets, going nowhere, thinking of Bella and the incredible release of having the truth known. No longer did I have to dread that she would find out what I was. She knew. It didn't matter to her. Even though this was obviously a bad thing for her, it was amazingly liberating for me.

More than that, I thought of Bella and requited love. She couldn't love me the way I loved her—such an overpowering, all-consuming, crushing love would probably break her fragile body. But she felt strongly enough. Strongly enough to subdue the instinctive fear. Strongly enough to want to be with me. And being with her was the greatest happiness I had ever known.

For a while—as I was all alone and hurting no one else for a change—I allowed myself to feel that happiness without dwelling on the tragedy. Just to be thrilled that she cared for me. Just to exult in the triumph of winning her affection. Just to imagine sitting close to her tomorrow, hearing her voice and earning her smiles.

I replayed that smile in my head, seeing her full lips pull up at the corners, the hint of a dimple that touched her pointed chin, the way her eyes warmed and melted. Her fingers had felt so warm and soft on my hand tonight. I imagined how it would feel to touch the delicate skin that stretched over her cheekbones—silky, warm . . . so fragile. Silk over glass . . . frighteningly breakable.

I didn't see where my thoughts were leading until it was too late. As I dwelt on that devastating vulnerability, other images of her face intruded on my fantasies.

Lost in the shadows, pale with fear—yet her jaw tight and determined, her eyes full of concentration, her slim body braced to strike at the hulking forms that gathered around her, nightmares in the gloom.

"Ah," I groaned as the simmering hate that I'd all but forgotten in the joy of loving her burst again into an inferno of rage.

I was alone. Bella was, I trusted, safe inside her home; for a moment I was fiercely glad that Charlie Swan—head of the local law enforcement, trained and armed—was her father. That ought to mean something, provide some shelter for her.

She was safe. It would not take me so very long to destroy the mortal who would have harmed her.

No. She deserved better. I could not allow her to care for a murderer.

But...what about the others?

Bella was safe, yes. Angela and Jessica were also, surely, safe in their beds.

Yet a predator was loose on the streets of Port Angeles. A human monster—did that make him the humans' problem? We did not often involve ourselves with human problems, aside from Carlisle and his constant work to heal and save. For the rest of us, our weakness for human blood was a serious impediment to becoming closely entangled with them. And of course there were our distant wardens, the de facto vampire police force, the Volturi. We Cullens lived too differently. Drawing their attention with any poorly considered superhero-esque performances would be extremely dangerous to our family.

This was definitely a mortal concern, not of our world. To commit the murder I ached to commit was wrong. I knew that. But leaving him free to attack again could not be the right thing, either.

The blond hostess from the restaurant. The waitress I'd never really looked at. Both had irritated me in a trivial way, but that did not mean they deserved to be in danger.

I turned the car north, accelerating now that I had a purpose. Whenever I had a dilemma that was beyond me—something tangible like this—I knew where to go for help.

Alice was sitting on the porch, waiting for me. I pulled to a stop in front of the house rather than going around to the garage.

"Carlisle's in his study," she told me before I could ask.

"Thank you," I said, tousling her hair as I passed.

Thank you *for returning my call*, she thought sarcastically.

"Oh." I paused by the door, pulling out my phone and flipping it open. "Sorry. I didn't even check to see who it was. I was… busy."

"Yeah, I know. I'm sorry, too. By the time I saw what was going to happen, you were on your way."

"It was close," I murmured.

Sorry, she repeated, ashamed of herself.

It was easy to be generous, knowing that Bella was fine. "Don't be. I know you can't catch everything. No one expects you to be omniscient, Alice."

"Thanks."

"I almost asked you out to dinner tonight—did you catch that before I changed my mind?"

She grinned. "No, I missed that one, too. Wish I'd known. I would have come."

"What were you concentrating on that you missed so much?"

Jasper's thinking about our anniversary. She laughed. *He's trying not to make a decision on my gift, but I think I have a pretty good idea….*

"You're shameless."

"Yep."

She pursed her lips and stared up at me, a hint of accusation in her expression. *I paid better attention afterward. Are you going to tell them that she knows?*

I sighed. "Yes. Later."

I won't say anything. Do me a favor and tell Rosalie when I'm not around, okay?

I flinched. "Sure."

Bella took it pretty well.

"Too well."

Alice grinned at me. *Don't underestimate Bella.*

I tried to block the image I didn't want to see—Bella and Alice, best of friends.

Impatient now, I sighed heavily. I wanted to be through with the next part of the evening; I wanted it over with. But I was a little worried to leave Forks.

"Alice...," I began. She saw what I was planning to ask.

She'll be fine tonight. I'm keeping a better watch now. She sort of needs twenty-four-hour supervision, doesn't she?

"At least."

"Anyway, you'll be with her soon enough."

I took a deep breath. The words were beautiful to me.

"Go on—get this done so you can be where you want to be," she told me.

I nodded and hurried up to Carlisle's room.

He was waiting for me, his eyes on the door rather than the thick book on his desk.

"I heard Alice tell you where to find me," he said, and smiled.

It was a relief to be with him, to see the empathy and deep intelligence in his eyes. Carlisle would know what to do.

"I need help."

"Anything, Edward," he promised.

"Did Alice tell you what happened to Bella tonight?"

Almost happened, he amended.

"Yes, almost. I've a dilemma, Carlisle. You see, I want...very much...to kill him." The words started to flow, fast and passionate. "So much. But I know that would be wrong, because it would be vengeance, not justice. All anger, no impartiality. Still, it can't be right to leave a serial rapist and murderer wandering Port Angeles! I don't know the humans there, but I can't let someone else take Bella's place as his victim. Those other women—it's not right—"

His wide, unexpected smile stopped the rush of my words cold.

She's very good for you, isn't she? So much compassion, so much control. I'm impressed.

"I'm not looking for compliments, Carlisle."

"Of course not. But I can't help my thoughts, can I?" He smiled again. *I'll take care of it. You can rest easy. No one else will be harmed in Bella's place.*

I saw the plan in his head. It wasn't exactly what I wanted—it did not satisfy my craving for brutality—but I could see that it was the right thing.

"I'll show you where to find him," I said.

"Let's go."

He grabbed his black bag on the way. I would have preferred a more aggressive form of sedation—like a cracked skull—but I would let Carlisle do this his way.

We took my car. Alice was still on the steps. She grinned and waved as we drove away. I saw that she had looked ahead for me. We would have no difficulties.

The trip was very short on the dark, empty road. I left off my headlights to keep from attracting attention. It made me smile to think how Bella would have reacted to *this* pace. I'd already been driving slower than usual—to prolong my time with her—when she'd objected.

Carlisle was thinking of Bella, too.

I didn't foresee that she would be so good for him. That's unexpected. Perhaps this was somehow meant to be. Perhaps it serves a higher purpose. Only...

He pictured Bella with snow-cold skin and bloodred eyes, and then flinched away from the image.

Yes. Indeed. *Only.* Because how could there be any good in destroying something so pure and lovely?

I glowered into the night, all the joy of the evening destroyed.

Edward deserves happiness. He's owed *it.* The fierceness of Carlisle's thoughts surprised me. *There must be a way.*

I wished I could believe either of his hopes. But there was no higher purpose to what was happening to Bella. Just a vicious harpy, an ugly, bitter fate who could not bear for her to have the life she deserved.

I did not linger in Port Angeles. I took Carlisle to the dive bar where the twisted thing named Lanny was drowning his disappointment with his friends—two of whom had already passed out. Carlisle could see how hard it was for me to be so close—to hear the fiend's thoughts and see his memories, memories of Bella mixed in with those of less fortunate girls whom no one could save now.

My breathing sped. My hands clenched the steering wheel.

Go, Edward, he told me gently. *I'll make the rest of them safe. You go back to Bella.*

It was exactly the right thing to say. Her name was the only distraction that meant anything to me.

I left Carlisle in the car, and ran back to Forks in a straight line through the sleeping forest. It took less time than the first journey in the speeding car. It was just minutes later that I scaled the side of her house and slid her window out of my way.

I sighed silently with relief. Everything was just as it should be. Bella was safe in her bed, dreaming, her wet hair tangled across the pillow.

But unlike most nights, she was curled into a small ball with the covers stretched taut around her shoulders. Cold, I guessed. Before I could settle into my usual seat, she shivered in her sleep, and her lips trembled.

I thought for a brief moment, and then eased out into the hallway, exploring another part of her house for the first time.

Charlie's snores were loud and even. I could almost catch the edge of his dream. Something with the rush of water and patient expectation…fishing, maybe?

There, at the top of the stairs, was a promising-looking

cupboard. I opened it hopefully and found what I was looking for. I selected the thickest blanket from the tiny linen closet and took it back into her room. I would return it before she woke, and no one would be the wiser.

Holding my breath, I cautiously spread the blanket over her. She didn't react to the added weight. I returned to the rocking chair.

While I waited anxiously for her to warm up, I thought of Carlisle, wondering where he was now. I knew his plan would go smoothly—Alice had seen that.

Thinking of my father made me sigh—Carlisle gave me too much credit. I wished I were the person he thought me to be. That person, the one who deserved happiness, might hope to be worthy of this sleeping girl. How different things would be if I could be that Edward.

Or, if I could not be what I should, at least there should be some balance in the universe to cancel out my darkness. Should there not be an equal and opposite good? I'd envisioned the hag-faced fate as some explanation for the terrifying and improbable nightmares that kept coming for Bella—first myself, then the van, and then the noxious beast tonight. But if that fate had so much power, shouldn't there be a force in place to thwart it?

Someone like Bella ought to have a protector, a guardian angel. She deserved that. And yet, clearly, she'd been left defenseless. I would love to believe an angel or anything else was watching over her, anything that would give her a measure of protection, but when I tried to imagine that champion, it was obvious such a thing was impossible. What guardian angel would have allowed Bella to come *here*? To cross my path, formed, as she was, in such a fashion that there was no way I could possibly overlook her? A ridiculously potent scent to demand my attention, a silent mind to enflame my curiosity, a quiet beauty to hold my eyes, a selfless soul to earn my awe. Factor in the total lack of self-preservation so she was not repelled by me, and then of course add the wide streak of appallingly bad luck that put her always in the wrong place at the wrong time.

There could be no stronger evidence that guardian angels were a fantasy. No one needed or deserved one more than Bella. Yet any angel that could have allowed us to meet must be so irresponsible, so reckless, so...*harebrained*, that it could not possibly be on the side of good. I'd rather the loathsome harpy were real than any celestial being so ineffectual. At least I could fight against the ugly fate.

And I would fight, I would keep fighting. Whatever force it was that wanted to hurt Bella would have to go through me. No, she had no guardian angel. But I would do my best to make up for the lack.

A guardian vampire—there was a stretch.

After about a half hour, Bella relaxed out of the tight ball. Her breathing got deeper and she started to murmur. I smiled, satisfied. It was a small thing, but at least she was sleeping more comfortably tonight because I was here.

"Edward," she sighed, and she smiled, too.

I shoved tragedy aside for the moment and let myself be happy again.

11. INTERROGATIONS

CNN BROKE THE STORY FIRST.

I was glad it hit the news before I had to leave for school. I was anxious to hear how the humans would phrase the account, and what amount of attention it would garner. Luckily, it was a heavy news day. There was an earthquake in South America and a political kidnapping in the Middle East. So it ended up only earning a few seconds, a few sentences, and one grainy picture.

"Orlando Calderas Wallace, suspected murderer wanted in the states of Texas and Oklahoma, was apprehended last night in Portland, Oregon, thanks to an anonymous tip. Wallace was found unconscious in an alley early this morning, just a few yards from a police station. Officials are unable to tell us at this time whether he will be extradited to Houston or Oklahoma City to stand trial."

The picture was unclear, a mug shot, and he'd had a thick beard at the time of the photograph. Even if Bella saw it, she would probably not recognize him. I hoped she wouldn't; it would only frighten her needlessly.

"The coverage here in town will be light. It's too far away to be considered of local interest," Alice told me. "It was a good call to have Carlisle take him out of state."

I nodded. Bella didn't watch much TV regardless, and I'd never seen her father watching anything besides sports channels.

I'd done what I could. This repugnant creature no longer hunted, and I was not a murderer. Not recently, anyway. I'd been right to trust Carlisle, as much as I still wished the wretch had not gotten off quite so easily. I caught myself hoping he would be extradited to Texas, where the death penalty was so popular.

No. That didn't matter. I would put this behind me and concentrate on what was most important.

I'd left Bella's room less than an hour ago. I was already aching to see her again.

"Alice, do you mind—"

She cut me off. "Rosalie will drive. She'll act pissed, but you know she'll enjoy the excuse to show off her car." Alice trilled a laugh.

I grinned at her. "See you at school."

Alice sighed, and my grin became a glare.

I know, I know, she thought. *Not yet. I'll wait until you're ready for Bella to know me. You should know, though, this isn't just me being selfish. Bella's going to like me, too.*

I didn't answer her as I hurried out the door. That was a different way of viewing the situation. Would Bella *want* to know Alice? To have a vampire for a girlfriend?

Knowing Bella, that idea probably wouldn't bother her in the slightest.

I frowned to myself. What Bella wanted and what was best for Bella were two very separate things.

I started to feel uneasy as I parked my car in Bella's driveway. The human adage said that things looked different in the morning—that things changed when you slept on them. Would I look different to Bella in the weak light of a foggy day? More or less sinister than I had in the blackness of night? Had the truth sunk in while she slept? Would she finally be afraid?

Her dreams had been peaceful, though, last night. When she'd spoken my name, time and time again, she'd smiled. More than once she'd murmured a plea for me to stay. Would that mean nothing today?

I waited nervously, listening to the sounds of her inside the house—the fast, stumbling footsteps on the stairs, the sharp rip of a foil wrapper, the contents of the refrigerator crashing against each other when the door slammed. It sounded as though she was in a hurry. Anxious to get to school? The thought made me smile, hopeful again.

I glanced at the clock. I supposed that—taking into account the velocity her decrepit truck must limit her to—she *was* running a little late.

Bella rushed out of the house, her book bag sliding off her shoulder, her hair coiled into a messy twist that was already coming apart on the nape of her neck. The thick green sweater she wore was not enough to keep her thin shoulders from hunching against the cold fog.

The long sweater was too big for her, unflattering. It masked her slender figure, turning all her delicate curves and soft lines into a shapeless jumble. I appreciated this almost as much as I wished that she had worn something more like the soft blue blouse she had on last night. The fabric had clung to her skin in such an appealing way, cut low enough to reveal the mesmerizing shape of her collarbones, curling out from the hollow of her throat. The blue had flowed like water along the subtle shape of her body.

It was better—essential—that I kept my thoughts far, far away from that shape, so I was grateful for the unbecoming sweater. I couldn't afford to make mistakes, and it would be a monumental mistake to dwell on the strange hungers that thoughts of her lips...her skin...her body...were shaking loose inside me. Hungers that had evaded me for a hundred years. But I could not allow myself to think of touching her, because that was impossible.

I would break her.

Bella turned away from the door in such a hurry that she nearly ran right by my car without noticing it.

Then she skidded to a stop, her knees locking like a startled colt's. Her bag slid farther down her arm, and her eyes flew wide as they focused on the car.

I got out, taking no care to move at human speed, and opened the passenger door for her. I would not try to deceive her anymore—when we were alone, at least, I would be myself.

She looked up at me, startled again as I seemingly materialized out of the fog. And then the surprise in her eyes changed to something else, and I was no longer afraid—or hopeful—that her feelings for me had changed in the course of the night. Warmth, wonder, fascination, all swam in the translucent depths of her eyes.

"Do you want to ride with me today?" I asked. Unlike dinner last night, I would let her choose. From now on, it must always be her choice.

"Yes, thank you," she murmured, climbing into my car without hesitation.

Would it ever cease to thrill me that I was the one she was saying yes to?

I flashed around the car, eager to join her. She showed no sign of being shocked by my sudden reappearance.

The happiness I felt when she sat beside me this way had no precedent. As much as I enjoyed the love and companionship of my family, despite the various entertainments and distractions my world had to offer, I had never been happy like this. Even knowing that it was wrong, that this couldn't possibly end well, could not keep the smile from my face for long when we were together.

My jacket was folded over the headrest of her seat. I saw her eyeing it.

"I brought the jacket for you," I told her. This was my excuse, had I needed to provide one, for showing up uninvited this morning. It was cold. She had no jacket. Surely this was an acceptable form of chivalry. "I didn't want you to get sick or something."

"I'm not quite that delicate," she said, staring at my chest rather than my face, as if she were hesitant to meet my eyes. But she put the coat on before I could resort to coaxing or begging.

"Aren't you?" I muttered to myself.

She looked out at the road as I accelerated toward the school. I could only stand the silence for a few seconds. I had to know what her thoughts were this morning. So much had changed between us since the last time the sun was up.

"What, no twenty questions today?" I asked, keeping it light again.

She smiled, seeming glad that I'd broached the subject. "Do my questions bother you?"

"Not as much as your reactions do," I told her honestly, smiling in response to hers.

Her mouth turned down. "Do I react badly?"

"No, that's the problem. You take everything so coolly—it's unnatural." Not one scream so far. How could that be? "It makes me wonder what you're really thinking." Of course, everything she did or didn't do made me wonder that.

"I always tell you what I'm really thinking."

"You edit."

Her teeth pressed into her lip again. She didn't seem to notice when she did this—it was an unconscious response to tension. "Not very much."

Just those words were enough to have my curiosity raging. What did she purposely keep from me?

"Enough to drive me insane," I said.

She hesitated, and then whispered, "You don't want to hear it."

I had to think for a moment, run through our entire conversation last night, word for word, before I made the connection. Perhaps it took so much concentration because I couldn't imagine anything that I wouldn't want her to share with me.

And then—because the tone of her voice was the same as last night; there was suddenly pain there again—I remembered. Once, I had asked her not to speak her thoughts. *Never say that*, I'd all but snarled at her. I had made her cry....

Was this what she kept from me? The depth of her feelings about me? That my being a monster didn't matter to her, and that she thought it was too late for her to change her mind?

I was unable to speak, because the joy and pain were too strong for words, the conflict between them too wild to allow for a coherent response. It was silent in the car except for the steady rhythms of her heart and lungs.

"Where's the rest of your family?" she asked suddenly.

I took a deep breath—registering the scent in the car with true pain for the first time; I was getting used to this, I realized with satisfaction—and forced myself to be casual again.

"They took Rosalie's car." I parked in the open spot next to the car in question. I hid my smile as I watched her eyes grow round. "Ostentatious, isn't it?"

"Um, wow. If she has *that*, why does she ride with you?"

Rosalie would have enjoyed Bella's reaction...if she were being objective about Bella, which probably wouldn't happen.

"Like I said, it's ostentatious. We *try* to blend in."

Of course, Bella was totally oblivious to the inherent contradiction of my own car. It was no accident we were most often seen in the Volvo—a car celebrated above all for its safety. Safety, the one thing vampires would never need from a vehicle. Few would recognize the less common racing edition, not to mention the aftermarket work we'd done.

"You don't succeed," she told me, and then she laughed a carefree laugh.

The blithe, wholly untroubled sound of her laughter warmed my hollow chest.

"So why did Rosalie drive today if it's more conspicuous?" she wondered.

"Hadn't you noticed? I'm breaking *all* the rules now."

My answer should have been mildly frightening—so of course, Bella smiled at it.

Once out of the car, I walked as close to her as I dared, watching carefully for any sign that my proximity upset her. Twice her hand twitched toward me and she snatched it back. It *looked* like she wanted to touch me.... My breath sped.

"Why do you have cars like that at all? If you're looking for privacy?" she asked as we walked.

"An indulgence," I admitted. "We all like to drive fast."

"Figures," she mumbled, her tone sour.

She didn't look up to see my answering grin.

Nuh-uh! I don't believe *this! How the hell did Bella pull this off?*

Jessica's mental boggling interrupted my thoughts. She was waiting for Bella, taking refuge from the rain under the edge of the cafeteria's roof, with Bella's winter jacket over her arm. Her eyes were wide with disbelief.

Bella noticed her, too, in the next moment. A faint pink touched her cheek when Bella registered Jessica's expression.

"Hey, Jessica. Thanks for remembering," Bella greeted her. Jessica handed her the jacket wordlessly.

I would be polite to Bella's friends, whether or not they were good friends. "Good morning, Jessica."

Whoa...

Jessica's eyes popped even wider, but she did not flinch or take a step back as I expected. Though she'd often found me alluring in the past, she'd always kept a safe distance before, the way all our admirers unconsciously did. It was strange and amusing...and, honestly, a bit embarrassing...to realize how much being near Bella had softened me. It seemed as though no one was afraid of me anymore. If Emmett found out about this, he would be laughing for the next century.

"Er...hi," Jessica mumbled, and her eyes flashed to Bella's face, full of significance. "I guess I'll see you in Trig."

You are so going to spill. Details. I have to have details! Edward freaking CULLEN!!

Bella's mouth twitched. "Yeah, I'll see you then."

Jessica's thoughts ran wild as she hurried to her first class, peeking back at us now and then.

The whole story. I'm not accepting anything less. Did they plan to meet up last night? Are they dating? How long? How could she keep this a secret? Why would she want *to? It can't be a casual thing—she has to be seriously into him. I* will *find out. I wonder if she's made out with him? Oh, swoon....* Jessica's thoughts were suddenly disjointed, and she let wordless fantasies swirl through her head. I winced at her speculations, and not just because she'd replaced Bella with herself in the mental pictures.

It couldn't be like that. And yet I...I wanted...

I resisted making the admission, even to myself. In how many wrong ways would I want Bella? Which one would end up killing her?

I shook my head and tried to lighten up.

"What are you going to tell her?" I asked Bella.

"Hey!" she whispered fiercely. "I thought you couldn't read my mind!"

"I can't." I stared at her, surprised, trying to make sense of her words. Ah—we must have been thinking the same thing at the same time. "However," I told her, "I can read hers—she'll be waiting to ambush you in class."

Bella groaned, and then let the jacket slide off her shoulders. I didn't realize that she was giving it back at first—I wouldn't have asked for it; I would rather she kept it...a token—so I was too slow to offer her my help. She handed me the jacket and put her arms through her own.

"So, what are you going to tell her?" I pressed.

"A little help? What does she want to know?"

I smiled, and shook my head. I wanted to hear what she was thinking without a prompt. "That's not fair."

Her eyes tightened. "No, you not sharing what you know—now that's not fair."

Right—she didn't like double standards.

"She wants to know if we're secretly dating," I said slowly. "And she wants to know how you feel about me."

Her eyebrows shot up—not startled, but ingenuous now. Playing innocent.

"Yikes," she murmured. "What should I say?"

"Hmmm." She always tried to make me give away more than she did. I pondered how to respond.

A wayward lock of her hair, slightly damp from the fog, draped across her shoulder and curled around the place where her collarbone was hidden by the ridiculous sweater. It drew my eyes, pulled them across the other hidden lines....

I reached for it carefully, not touching her skin—the morning was chill enough without my touch—and twisted it back into place in her untidy bun so that it wouldn't distract me again. I remembered when Mike Newton had touched her hair, and my jaw flexed at the memory. She had flinched away from him then. Her reaction now was nothing the same; instead, there was a rush of blood under her skin, and a sudden, uneven thumping of her heart.

I tried to hide my smile as I answered her question.

"I suppose you could say yes to the first...if you don't mind." Her choice, always her choice. "It's easier than any other explanation."

"I don't mind," she whispered. Her heart had not found its normal rhythm yet.

"And as for her other question..." I couldn't hide my smile now. "Well, I'll be listening to hear the answer to that one myself."

Let Bella consider *that*. I held back my laugh as shock crossed her face.

I turned quickly, before she could ask any more questions. I had a difficult time not giving her whatever she asked for. And I wanted to hear *her* thoughts, not mine.

"I'll see you at lunch," I called back to her over my shoulder, an excuse to check that she was still staring after me. Her mouth was hanging open. I turned again and laughed.

As I paced away, I was vaguely aware of the shocked and speculative thoughts that swirled around me—eyes bouncing back and forth between Bella's face and my retreating figure. I paid them little attention. I couldn't concentrate. It was hard enough to keep my feet moving at an acceptable speed as I crossed the soggy grass to my first class. I wanted to run—really run, so fast that I would disappear, so fast that it would feel like flying. Part of me was flying already.

I put the jacket on when I got to class, letting her fragrance swim thick around me. I would burn now—let the scent desensitize me—and it would be easier to ignore it later, when I was with her again at lunch.

It was a good thing that my teachers no longer bothered to call on me. Today might have been the day they caught me out, unprepared and answerless. My mind was in so many places this morning; only my body was in the classroom.

Of course I was watching Bella. That was becoming natural—as automatic as breathing, something I barely thought about consciously. I heard her conversation with a demoralized Mike Newton. She quickly directed the conversation to Jessica, and I grinned so wide that Rob Sawyer, who sat at the desk to my right, flinched visibly and slid deeper into his seat, away from me.

Ugh. Creepy.

Well, I hadn't lost it entirely.

I was also loosely monitoring Jessica, watching her refine her questions for Bella. I could barely wait for fourth period, ten times as eager and anxious as the curious human girl who wanted fresh gossip.

And I was listening to Angela Weber.

I had not forgotten the gratitude I felt to her—for thinking nothing but kind things toward Bella in the first place, and then for her help last night. So I waited through the morning, looking for something she wanted. I assumed it would be easy; like any other human, she must desire some bauble or toy. Several, probably. I would deliver something anonymously and call us even.

But Angela proved almost as unaccommodating as Bella with her thoughts. She was oddly content for a teenager. Happy. Perhaps this was the reason for her unusual kindness—she was one of those rare people who had what she wanted and wanted what she had. If she wasn't paying attention to her teachers and her notes, she was thinking of the twin little brothers she was taking to the beach this weekend—anticipating their excitement with almost maternal pleasure. She cared for them often, but was not resentful of this fact. It was very sweet.

But not really helpful to me.

There had to be something she wanted. I would just have to keep looking. But later. It was time for Bella's Trigonometry class with Jessica.

I wasn't watching where I was going as I made my way to English. Jessica was already in her seat, both her feet tapping impatiently as she waited for Bella to arrive.

Conversely, once I settled into my assigned seat in the classroom, I became utterly still. I had to remind myself to fidget now and then to keep up the charade. It was difficult; my thoughts were so focused on Jessica's. I hoped she would pay attention, really try to read Bella's face for me.

Jessica's tapping intensified when Bella walked into the room.

She looks...glum. Why? Maybe there's nothing going on with Edward Cullen. That would be a disappointment. Except...then he's still available....If he's suddenly interested in dating, I don't mind helping out with that.

Bella's face didn't look glum, it looked reluctant. She was worried—she knew I would hear all of this.

"*Tell me everything!*" Jess demanded while Bella was still removing her jacket to hang it on the back of her seat. She was moving with deliberation, unwillingly.

Ugh, she's so slow. Let's get to the juicy stuff!

"*What do you want to know?*" Bella stalled as she took her seat.

"*What happened last night?*"

"*He bought me dinner, and then he drove me home.*"

And then? C'mon, there has to be more than that! She's lying anyway, I know that. I'm going to call her on it.

"*How did you get home so fast?*"

I watched Bella roll her eyes at the suspicious Jessica.

"*He drives like a maniac. It was terrifying.*"

She smiled a tiny smile, and I laughed out loud, interrupting Mr. Mason's announcements. I tried to turn the laugh into a cough, but no one was fooled. Mr. Mason shot me an irritated look, but I didn't even bother to listen to the thought behind it. I was hearing Jessica.

Huh. She sounds like she's telling the truth. Why is she making me pull this out of her, word by word? I would be bragging at the top of my lungs.

"*Was it like a date—did you tell him to meet you there?*"

Jessica watched confusion cross Bella's expression, and was disappointed at how genuine it seemed.

"*No—I was* very *surprised to see him there,*" Bella told her.

What is going on? "But he picked you up for school today?" There has to be more to the story.

"*Yes—that was a surprise, too. He noticed I didn't have a jacket last night.*"

That's not very much fun, Jessica thought, disappointed again.

I was tired of her line of questioning—I wanted to hear something I didn't already know. I hoped she wasn't so dissatisfied that she would skip the questions I was waiting for.

"*So are you going out again?*" Jessica demanded.

"*He offered to drive me to Seattle Saturday because he thinks my truck isn't up to it—does that count?*"

Hmm. He sure is going out of his way to... well, take care of her, sort of. There must be something there on his side if not on hers. How could THAT be? Bella's crazy.

"*Yes.*" Jessica answered Bella's question.

"*Well, then, yes,*" Bella concluded.

"*Wow... Edward Cullen.*" *Whether she likes him or not, this is major.*

"*I know,*" Bella sighed.

The tone of her voice encouraged Jessica. *Finally—she sounds like she gets it!*

I wondered if Jessica was reading Bella's tone correctly. I wished she would ask Bella to explain what she meant, instead of assuming.

"*Wait!*" Jessica said, suddenly remembering her most vital question. "*Has he kissed you?*" *Please say yes. And then describe every second!*

"*No,*" Bella mumbled, and then she looked down at her hands, her face falling. "*It's not like that.*"

Damn. I wish... ha. Looks like she does, too.

I frowned. Bella did look upset about something, but it couldn't be disappointment, as Jessica assumed. She couldn't want that. Not knowing what she knew. She couldn't want to be that close to my *teeth*. For all she knew, I had fangs.

I shuddered.

"*Do you think Saturday...?*" Jessica prodded.

Bella looked even more frustrated as she said, "*I really doubt it.*"

Yeah, she does wish. That sucks for her.

Was it because I was watching all this through the filter of Jessica's perceptions that it seemed as though she was right?

For a half second I was distracted by the idea, the impossibility, of what it would be like to try to kiss Bella. My lips to her lips, cold stone to warm, yielding silk....

And then she dies.

I shook my head, wincing, and refocused.

"*What did you talk about?*" *Did you talk to him, or did you make him drag every ounce of information out of you, like this?*

I smiled ruefully. Jessica wasn't far off.

"I don't know, Jess, lots of stuff. We talked about the English essay a little."

A very little. I smiled wider.

Oh, c'MON. "Please, Bella! Give me some details."

Bella deliberated for a moment.

"Well...okay, I've got one. You should have seen the waitress flirting with him—it was over the top. But he didn't pay any attention to her at all."

What a strange detail to share. I was surprised Bella had even noticed. It seemed an inconsequential thing.

Interesting.... "That's a good sign. Was she pretty?"

Hmm. Jessica thought more of it than I did.

"*Very*," Bella told her. *"And probably nineteen or twenty."*

Jessica was momentarily distracted by a memory of Mike on their date Monday night—Mike being a little too friendly with a waitress whom Jessica did not consider pretty at all. She shoved the memory away and, stifling her irritation, returned to her quest for details.

"Even better. He must like you."

"*I* think *so*," Bella said slowly, and I was on the edge of my seat, my body rigidly still. *"But it's hard to tell. He's always so cryptic."*

I must not have been as transparently obvious and out of control as I'd thought. Still, observant as she was...how could she not realize that I was in love with her? I sifted through our conversation, almost surprised that I hadn't said the words out loud. It had felt as though that knowledge was the subtext of every communication between us.

Wow. How do you sit there across from a male model and make conversation? "I don't know how you're brave enough to be alone with him," Jessica said.

Shock flashed across Bella's face. "*Why?*"

Weird reaction. What does she think I meant? "He's so..."

What's the right word? "Intimidating. I wouldn't know what to say to him." I couldn't even speak English to him today, and all he said was good morning. I must have sounded like such an idiot.

Bella smiled. *"I do have some trouble with incoherency when I'm around him."*

She must be trying to make Jessica feel better. She was almost unnaturally self-possessed when we were together.

"*Oh well,*" Jessica sighed. *"He* is *unbelievably gorgeous."*

Bella's face was suddenly colder. Her eyes flashed the same way they did when she resented some injustice. Jessica didn't process the change in her expression.

"*There's a lot more to him than that,*" Bella snapped.

Oooh. Now we're getting somewhere. "Really? Like what?"

Bella gnawed her lip for a moment. *"I can't explain it right,"* she finally said. *"But he's even more unbelievable* behind *the face."* She looked away from Jessica, her eyes slightly unfocused, as if she was staring at something very far away.

I was reminded of how it felt when Carlisle or Esme praised me beyond what I deserved. This emotion was similar, but more intense, more consuming.

Sell stupid somewhere else—there's nothing *better than that face! Unless it's his body. Swoon. "Is that possible?"* Jessica giggled.

Bella didn't turn. She continued to stare into the distance, ignoring Jessica.

A normal person would be gloating. Maybe if I keep the questions simple. Ha ha. Like I'm talking to a kindergartener. "So you like him, then?"

I was rigid again.

Bella didn't look at Jessica. *"Yes."*

"I mean, do you really *like him?"*

"Yes."

Look at that blush!

"How much *do you like him?"* Jessica demanded.

The English room could have gone up in flames and I wouldn't have noticed.

Bella's face was bright red now—I could almost feel the heat from the mental picture.

"*Too much*," she whispered. "*More than he likes me. But I don't see how I can help that.*"

Shoot! What did Mr. Varner just ask? "Um—which number, Mr. Varner?"

It was good that Jessica could no longer quiz Bella. I needed a minute.

What on earth was the girl thinking *now*? "More than he likes me"? How did she come up with *that*? "But I don't see how I can help that"? What was that supposed to mean? I couldn't fit a rational explanation to the words. They were practically senseless.

It seemed I couldn't take anything for granted. Obvious things, things that made perfect sense, somehow got twisted up and turned backward in that bizarre brain of hers.

I glared at the clock, gritting my teeth. How could mere minutes feel so impossibly long to an immortal? Where was my perspective?

My jaw was tight throughout Mr. Varner's entire Trigonometry lesson. I heard more of that than the lecture in my own class. Bella and Jessica didn't speak again, but Jessica peeked at Bella several times, and once noticed that her face was brilliant scarlet again for no apparent reason.

Lunch couldn't come fast enough.

I wasn't sure whether Jessica would get some of the answers I was waiting for when the class was over, but Bella was quicker than she was.

As soon as the bell sounded, Bella turned to Jessica.

"*In English, Mike asked me if you said anything about Monday night*," Bella said, a smile pulling at the corners of her lips. I understood this for what is was—offense as the best defense.

Mike asked about me? Joy made Jessica's mind suddenly unguarded, softer, without its usual snide edge. *"You're kidding! What did you say?"*

That was all I was going to get from Jessica today, clearly. Bella was smiling as though she was thinking the same thing. As though she'd won the round.

Well, lunch would be another story.

I moved apathetically through Gym class with Alice, the way we always moved when it came to physical activity with humans. She was my teammate, naturally. No one human would ever choose to partner with one of us. It was the first day of badminton. I sighed with boredom, swinging the racket in slow motion to tap the birdie back to the other side. Lauren Mallory was on the other team; she missed. Alice was twirling her racket like a baton, staring at the ceiling. She took a step closer to the net, and Lauren flinched two steps back.

We all hated Gym, Emmett especially. Throwing games was an affront to his personal philosophy. Gym seemed worse today than usual—I felt just as irritated as Emmett always did. Before my head could explode with impatience, Coach Clapp called the games and sent us out early. I was ridiculously grateful that he'd skipped breakfast—a fresh attempt to diet—and the consequent hunger had him in a hurry to leave campus to find a greasy lunch somewhere. He promised himself he would start over tomorrow....

This gave me enough time to get to the math building before Bella's class ended.

Enjoy yourself, Alice thought as she headed off to meet Jasper. *Just a few days more to be patient. I suppose you won't say hi to Bella for me, will you?*

I shook my head, exasperated. Were all psychics so smug?

FYI, it's going to be sunny on both sides of the sound this weekend. You might want to rearrange your plans.

I sighed as I continued in the opposite direction. Smug, but definitely useful.

I leaned against the wall by the door, waiting. I was close enough that I could hear Jessica's voice through the bricks as well as her thoughts.

"You're not sitting with us today, are you?" *She looks all... lit up. I bet there's* tons *she didn't tell me.*

"I don't *think* so," Bella answered, oddly unsure.

Hadn't I promised to spend lunch with her? What was she *thinking*?

They came out of the classroom together, and both girls' eyes widened when they saw me. But I could only hear Jessica.

Nice. Wow. Oh yeah, there's more going on here than she's telling me.

"See you later, Bella."

Bella walked toward me, pausing a step away, still unsure. Her skin was pink across her cheekbones.

I knew her well enough now to be sure that there was no fear behind her hesitation. Apparently, this was about some gulf she imagined between her feelings and mine. *More than he likes me.* Absurd!

"Hello," I said, my voice a tad curt.

Her face got brighter pink. "Hi."

She didn't seem inclined to say anything else, so I led the way to the cafeteria and she walked silently beside me.

The jacket had worked—her scent was not the blow it usually was. It was just an intensification of the pain I already felt. I could ignore it more easily than I once would have believed possible.

Bella was restless as we waited in line, toying absently with the zipper on her jacket and shifting nervously from foot to foot. She glanced at me often, but whenever she met my gaze, she looked down as if embarrassed. Was this because so many people were staring at us? Maybe she could hear the loud whispers—the gossip was verbal as well as mental today.

Or maybe she realized from my expression that I was going to want some explanations.

She didn't say anything until I was assembling her lunch. I didn't know what she liked—not yet—so I grabbed one of everything.

"What are you doing?" she hissed in a low voice. "You're not getting all that for me?"

I shook my head, and shoved the tray up to the register. "Half is for me, of course."

She raised one eyebrow skeptically, but said nothing more as I paid for the food and escorted her to the table we'd sat at last week. It seemed like much more than a few days ago. Everything was different now.

She sat across from me again. I pushed the tray toward her.

"Take whatever you want," I encouraged.

She picked up an apple and twisted it in her hands, a speculative look on her face.

"I'm curious."

What a surprise.

"What would you do if someone dared you to eat food?" she continued in a low voice that wouldn't carry to human ears. Immortal ears were another matter, if those ears were paying attention. I frowned.

"You're always curious," I complained. Oh well. It wasn't as though I hadn't had to eat before. It was part of the charade. An unpleasant part.

I reached for the closest thing, and held her eyes while I bit off a small piece of whatever it was. Without looking, I couldn't tell. It was as slimy and chunky and repulsive as any other human food. I chewed swiftly and swallowed, trying to keep the grimace off my face. The gob of food moved slowly and uncomfortably down my throat. I sighed as I thought of how I would have to choke it back up later. Disgusting.

Bella's expression was shocked. Impressed.

I wanted to roll my eyes. Of course we would have perfected such deceptions. "If someone dared you to eat dirt, you could, couldn't you?"

Her nose wrinkled and she smiled. "I did once...on a dare. It wasn't so bad."

I laughed. "I suppose I'm not surprised."

How could he? That selfish jackass! How could he do this to us? Rosalie's piercing mental shriek broke through my humor.

"Easy, Rose," I heard Emmett whisper from across the cafeteria. His arm was around her shoulders, holding her tight into his side—restraining her.

Sorry, Edward, Alice thought guiltily. *She could tell Bella knew too much from your conversation...and, well, it would have been worse if I hadn't told her the truth right away. Trust me on that.*

I winced at the mental picture that followed, at what would have happened if I'd admitted to Rosalie that Bella knew I was a vampire when we were at home, where Rosalie didn't have a façade to keep up. I'd have to hide my Aston Martin somewhere out of state if she didn't calm down by the time school was over. The sight of my favorite car, mangled and burning, was upsetting—though I knew I'd earned the retribution.

Jasper was not much happier.

I'd deal with the others later. I only had so much time allotted to be with Bella, and I wasn't going to waste it.

Edward and Bella look cozy, don't they? As I tried to ignore Rosalie, Jessica's thoughts intruded. This time I didn't mind the interruption. *Good body language. I'll give Bella my take later. He's leaning toward her just the way he should if he's interested. He looks interested. He looks...perfect.* Jessica sighed. *Yum.*

I met Jessica's curious eyes, and she looked away nervously, cringing back into her seat. *Hmmm. Probably better to stick to Mike. Reality, not fantasy....*

Little time had passed, but Bella had noticed my abstraction.

"Jessica's analyzing everything I do," I said, using the lesser distraction as my excuse. "She'll break it down for you later."

Rosalie's outrage continued, a caustic inner monologue that

barely paused for a second or two as she searched her memory for fresh insults to hurl my way. I forced the sound into the background, determined to be present with Bella.

I pushed the plate of food back toward Bella—pizza, I realized—wondering how best to begin. My former frustration flared as her words repeated in my head: *More than he likes me. But I don't see how I can help that.*

She took a bite from the same slice of pizza. It amazed me how trusting she was. Of course, she didn't know I was venomous—not that sharing food would hurt her. Still, I expected her to treat me differently. As something other. She never did.

I would start off gently.

"So the waitress was pretty, was she?"

She raised the eyebrow again. "You really didn't notice?"

As if any woman could hope to capture my attention from Bella. Absurd, again.

"No. I wasn't paying attention. I had a lot on my mind."

"Poor girl," Bella said, smiling.

She liked that I hadn't found the waitress interesting in any way. I could understand that. How many times had I imagined crippling Mike Newton in the Biology room?

But she couldn't honestly believe that her human feelings, the fruition of seventeen short mortal years, could be stronger than this demolition ball of emotion that had wrecked me after a century of emptiness?

"Something you said to Jessica..." I couldn't keep my voice casual. "Well, it bothers me."

She was immediately on the defensive. "I'm not surprised you heard something you didn't like. You know what they say about eavesdroppers."

Eavesdroppers never hear any good of themselves, that was the saying.

"I warned you I would be listening," I reminded her.

"And I warned you that you didn't want to know everything I was thinking."

Ah, she was thinking of when I'd made her cry. Remorse made my voice thicker. "You did. You aren't precisely right, though. I do want to know what you're thinking—everything. I just wish . . . that you wouldn't be thinking some things."

More half lies. I knew I *shouldn't* want her to care about me. But I did. Of course I did.

"That's quite a distinction," she grumbled, scowling at me.

"But that's not really the point at the moment."

"Then what is?"

She leaned toward me, her hand cupped lightly around her throat. It drew my eye—distracted me. How soft that skin must feel . . .

Focus, I commanded myself.

"Do you truly believe that you care more for me than I do for you?" I asked. The question sounded ridiculous to me, as though the words were scrambled.

She froze for a moment; even her breathing stopped. Then she looked away, blinking quickly. Her breath came in a low gasp.

"You're doing it again," she murmured.

"What?"

"Dazzling me," she admitted, meeting my eyes warily.

"Oh." I wasn't quite sure what to do about that. I was still thrilled that I *could* dazzle her. But it wasn't helping the progress of the conversation.

"It's not your fault." She sighed. "You can't help it."

"Are you going to answer the question?" I demanded.

She stared at the table. "Yes."

That was all she said.

"Yes, you are going to answer, or yes, you really think that?" I asked impatiently.

"Yes, I really think that," she said without looking up. There was a faint undertone of gloom in her voice. She blushed again, and her teeth moved unconsciously to worry her lip.

Abruptly, I realized that this was very hard for her to admit, because she truly believed it. And I was no better than that coward, Mike, asking her to confirm her feelings before I'd confirmed my own. It didn't matter that I felt I'd made my side abundantly clear. It hadn't gotten through to her, and so I had no excuse.

"You're wrong," I promised. She must hear the tenderness in my voice.

Bella looked up to me, her eyes opaque, giving nothing away. "You can't know that," she whispered.

"What makes you think so?" I wondered. I inferred that she thought I was underestimating her feelings because I couldn't hear her thoughts. But, in truth, the problem was that she was grossly underestimating *mine.*

She stared back at me, furrowing her brows, teeth against her lip. For the millionth time, I wished desperately that I could just *hear* her.

As I was about to start begging, she held up a finger to keep me from speaking.

"Let me think," she requested.

As long as she was simply organizing her thoughts, I could be patient.

Or I could pretend to be.

She pressed her hands together, twining and untwining her slender fingers. She watched her hands as if they belonged to someone else while she spoke.

"Well, aside from the obvious," she murmured. "Sometimes… I can't be sure—*I* don't know how to read minds—but sometimes it seems like you're trying to say goodbye when you're saying something else." She didn't look up.

She'd caught that, had she? Did she realize that it was only weakness and selfishness that kept me here? Did she think less of me for that?

"Perceptive," I breathed, and then watched in horror as pain twisted her expression. I hurried to contradict her assumption. "That's exactly why you're wrong, though—" I began, and then paused, remembering the first words of her explanation. They bothered me, though I didn't understand them. "What do you mean, 'the obvious'?"

"Well, look at me," she said.

I *was* looking. All I ever did was look at her.

"I'm absolutely ordinary," she explained. "Well, except for the bad things like all the near-death experiences and being so clumsy that I'm almost disabled. And look at you." She fanned the air toward me, like she was making some point so obvious it wasn't worth spelling out.

She thought she was ordinary? She thought that I was somehow preferable to her? In whose estimation? Silly, narrow-minded, blind humans like Jessica or Ms. Cope? How could she not realize that she was the most beautiful...the most exquisite...? Those words weren't even enough.

And she had no idea.

"You don't see yourself very clearly, you know," I told her. "I'll admit you're dead-on about the bad things...." I laughed humorlessly. I did not find the evil fate who hunted her comical. The clumsiness, however, was sort of funny. Sweet. Would she believe me if I told her she was beautiful, inside and out? Perhaps she would find corroboration more persuasive. "But you didn't hear what every human male in this school was thinking on your first day."

Ah, the hope, the thrill, the eagerness of those thoughts. The speed with which they'd turned to impossible fantasies. Impossible, because she wanted none of them.

I was the one she said yes to.

My smile must have been smug.

Her face was blank with surprise. "I don't believe it," she mumbled.

"Trust me just this once—you are the opposite of ordinary."

She wasn't used to compliments, I could see that. She flushed, and changed the subject. "But I'm not saying goodbye."

"Don't you see? That's what proves me right. I care the most, because if I can do it..." Would I ever be unselfish enough to do the right thing? I shook my head in despair. I would have to find the strength. She deserved a life. Not what Alice had seen coming for her. "If leaving is the right thing to do..." And it had to be the right thing, didn't it? Bella didn't belong with me. She'd done nothing to deserve my underworld. "Then I'll hurt myself to keep from hurting you, to keep you safe."

As I said the words, I willed them to be true.

She glared at me. Somehow, my words had angered her. "And you don't think I would do the same?" she demanded furiously.

So furious—so soft and fragile. How could she ever hurt anyone? "You'd never have to make the choice," I told her, depressed anew by the vast difference between us.

She stared at me, concern replacing the anger in her eyes and bringing out the little pucker between them.

There was something truly wrong with the order of the universe if someone so good and so breakable did not merit a guardian angel to keep her out of trouble.

Well, I thought with dark humor, *at least she has a guardian vampire*.

I smiled. How I loved my excuse to stay. "Of course, keeping you safe is beginning to feel like a full-time occupation that requires my constant presence."

She smiled, too. "No one has tried to do away with me today," she said lightly, and then her face turned speculative for half a second before her eyes went opaque again.

"Yet," I added dryly.

"Yet," she agreed—to my surprise. I'd expected her to deny any need for protection.

Across the cafeteria, Rosalie's complaints were gaining in volume rather than dwindling.

Sorry, Alice thought again. She must have seen me wince.

But hearing her reminded me that I had some business to attend to.

"I have another question for you," I said.

"Shoot," Bella said, smiling.

"Do you really need to go to Seattle this Saturday, or was that just an excuse to get out of saying no to all your admirers?"

She scowled at me. "You know, I haven't forgiven you for the Tyler thing yet. It's your fault that he's deluded himself into thinking I'm going to prom with him."

"Oh, he would have found a chance to ask you without me—I just really wanted to watch your face."

I laughed now, remembering her aghast expression. Nothing I'd told her about my own dark story had ever made her look so horrified.

"If I'd asked you, would you have turned *me* down?"

"Probably not," she said. "But I would have canceled later—faked an illness or a sprained ankle."

How strange. "Why would you do that?"

She shook her head, as if she was disappointed that I did not understand at once. "You've never seen me in Gym, I guess, but I would have thought that you would understand."

Ah. "Are you referring to the fact that you can't walk across a flat, stable surface without finding something to trip over?"

"Obviously."

"That wouldn't be a problem. It's all in the leading."

For a brief fraction of a second, I was overwhelmed by the idea of holding her in my arms at a dance—where she would surely wear something pretty and delicate rather than this hideous sweater.

With perfect clarity, I remembered how her body had felt under mine after I'd thrown her out of the way of the oncoming van. Stronger than the panic or the desperation, I could remember that sensation. She'd been so warm and so soft, fitting easily into my own stone shape...

I wrenched myself back from the memory.

"But you never told me—" I said quickly, preventing her from arguing with me, as she clearly intended to do. "Are you resolved on going to Seattle, or do you mind if we do something different?"

Devious—giving her a choice without giving her the option of getting away from me for the day. Hardly fair. But I had made her a promise last night. Too casually, too thoughtlessly, but still... if I was ever going to earn the trust she'd given me despite my unworthiness, I would have to keep every promise I could. Even if the idea terrified me.

The sun would be shining Saturday. I could show her the real me, if I was brave enough to endure her horror and disgust. I knew just the place to take such a risk.

"I'm open to alternatives," Bella said. "But I do have a favor to ask."

A qualified yes. What would she want from me?

"What?"

"Can I drive?"

Was this her idea of humor? "Why?"

"Well, mostly because when I told Charlie I was going to Seattle, he specifically asked if I was going alone and, at the time, I was. If he asked again, I probably wouldn't lie, but I don't think he *will* ask again, and leaving my truck at home would just bring up the subject unnecessarily. And also, because your driving frightens me."

I rolled my eyes at her. "Of all the things about me that could frighten you, you worry about my driving." Truly, her brain worked backward. I shook my head, disgusted. Why couldn't she fear the right things? Why couldn't I want her to?

I wasn't able to keep up the playful tone of our banter. "Won't you want to tell your father that you're spending the day with me?" I asked, darkness seeping into my voice as I thought of all the reasons that was important, already guessing what her answer would be.

"With Charlie, less is always more," Bella said, certain of this fact. "Where are we going, anyway?"

"The weather will be nice," I told her slowly, fighting the panic and indecision. How much would I regret this choice? "So I'll be staying out of the public eye... and you can stay with me, if you'd like to."

Bella caught the significance at once. Her eyes were bright and eager. "And you'll show me what you meant, about the sun?"

Maybe, like so many times before, her reaction would be the opposite of what I expected. I smiled at that possibility, struggling to return to the lighter moment. "Yes. But"—she hadn't said yes—"if you don't want to be...alone with me, I'd still rather you didn't go to Seattle by yourself. I shudder to think of the trouble you could find in a city that size."

Her lips pressed together; she was offended.

"Phoenix is three times bigger than Seattle—just in population. In physical size—"

"But apparently your number wasn't up in Phoenix," I said, cutting off her justifications. "So I'd rather you stayed near me."

She could stay forever and it would not be long enough.

I shouldn't think that way. We didn't have forever. The passing seconds counted more than they ever had before; each second changed her while I remained untouched. Physically, at least.

"As it happens, I don't mind being alone with you," she said.

No—because her instincts were backward.

"I know." I sighed. "You should tell Charlie, though."

"Why in the world would I do that?" she asked, appalled by the idea.

I glared at her, though the anger was, as usual, directed at myself. How I wished I had a different answer for her.

"To give me some small incentive to bring you back," I hissed. She should give me that much—one witness to compel me to be cautious.

Bella swallowed loudly and stared at me for a long moment. What did she see?

"I think I'll take my chances," she said.

Ugh! Did she get some thrill out of risking her life? Some shot of adrenaline she craved?

Will you shut up! Rosalie's mental scream peaked, breaking into my absorption. I saw what she thought of this conversation, of exactly how much Bella already knew. I glanced back automatically to see Rosalie glowering furiously, but I realized I simply did not care. Let her destroy the car. It was just a toy.

"Let's talk about something else," Bella suggested suddenly.

I looked back at her, wondering how she could be so oblivious to what really counted. Why wouldn't she see me for the monster I was? Rosalie certainly did.

"What do you want to talk about?"

Her eyes darted left and then right, as if checking to make sure there were no eavesdroppers. She must be planning to introduce another myth-related topic. Her gaze froze for a second and her body stiffened, and then she looked back to me.

"Why did you go to that Goat Rocks place last weekend... to hunt? Charlie said it wasn't a good place to hike, because of bears."

So oblivious. I stared at her, raising one eyebrow.

"Bears?" she gasped.

I smiled wryly, watching that sink in. Would this make her take me seriously? Would anything?

Just tell her everything. It's not like we have rules, Rosalie's thoughts hissed at me. I struggled to not hear her.

Bella pulled her expression together. "You know, bears are not in season," she said severely, narrowing her eyes.

"If you read carefully, the laws only cover hunting with weapons."

She lost control over her face again for a moment. Her lips fell open.

"Bears?" she said again, a tentative question this time rather than a gasp of shock.

"Grizzly is Emmett's favorite."

I watched her eyes as she worked through the astonishment and recovered.

"Hmm," she murmured. She took a bite of the pizza, looking down. She chewed thoughtfully, and then took a drink.

"So," she said, finally looking up. "What's your favorite?"

I supposed I should have expected something like that, but I hadn't.

"Mountain lion," I answered brusquely.

"Ah," she said in a neutral tone. Her heartbeat continued steady and even, as if we were discussing a favorite restaurant.

Fine, then. If she wanted to act like this was nothing unusual...

"Of course, we have to be careful not to impact the environment with injudicious hunting," I told her, my voice detached and clinical. "We try to focus on areas with an overpopulation of predators—ranging as far away as we need. There's always plenty of deer and elk here, and they'll do, but where's the fun in that?"

She listened with a politely interested expression, as if I were a guide in a museum describing a painting. I had to smile.

"Where indeed," she murmured calmly, taking another bite of pizza.

"Early spring is Emmett's favorite bear season," I continued in the same tone. "They're just coming out of hibernation, so they're more irritable."

Seventy years later, and he still hadn't gotten over losing that first match.

"Nothing more fun than an irritated grizzly bear," Bella agreed, nodding solemnly.

I couldn't hold back a chuckle as I shook my head at her illogical calm. It had to be put on. "Tell me what you're really thinking, please."

"I'm trying to picture it—but I can't," she said, the crease appearing between her eyes. "How do you hunt a bear without weapons?"

"Oh, we have weapons," I told her, and then flashed her a wide smile. I expected her to recoil, but she was very still, watching me. "Just not the kind they consider when writing hunting laws. If you've ever seen a bear attack on television, you should be able to visualize Emmett hunting."

She glanced toward the table where the others sat, and shuddered.

Finally. And then I laughed at myself, because I knew part of me was wishing she would stay oblivious.

Her dark eyes were wide and deep as she stared at me now. "Are you like a bear, too?" she asked in an almost-whisper.

"More like the lion, or so they tell me," I told her, striving to sound detached again. "Perhaps our preferences are indicative."

Her lips pulled up a tiny bit at the corners. "Perhaps," she repeated. And then her head leaned to the side, and curiosity was easy to read in her eyes. "Is that something I might get to see?"

For a moment, it was so clear in my head—Bella's crumpled, bloodless body in my arms—as though I were the one who had seen the vision, rather than just watching it in Alice's mind. But I didn't need foresight to illustrate this horror; the conclusion was obvious.

"Absolutely not," I snarled at her.

She jerked away from me, shocked and frightened by my sudden rage.

I leaned back, too, wanting to put space between us. She was never going to see, was she? She wouldn't do one thing to help me keep her alive.

"Too scary for me?" she asked, even-voiced. Her heart, however, was still moving in double time.

"If that were it, I would take you out tonight," I retorted through my teeth. "You *need* a healthy dose of fear. Nothing could be more beneficial for you."

"Then why?" she demanded, undeterred.

I glared at her blackly, waiting for her to be afraid. *I* was afraid.

Her eyes remained curious, impatient, nothing more. She waited for her answer, not giving in.

But our hour was up.

"Later," I snapped, and I rose to my feet. "We're going to be late."

She looked around, disoriented, as though she'd forgotten we were at lunch. As though she'd forgotten we were even at school and was surprised that we were not alone in some private place. I understood that feeling exactly. It was hard to remember the rest of the world when I was with her.

She got up quickly, bobbling once, and threw her bag over her shoulder.

"Later, then," she said, and I could see the determination in the set of her mouth. She would hold me to that.

12. COMPLICATIONS

BELLA AND I WALKED SILENTLY TO BIOLOGY. WE PASSED Angela Weber, lingering on the sidewalk, discussing an assignment with a boy from her Trigonometry class. I scanned her thoughts perfunctorily, expecting more disappointment, only to be surprised by their wistful tenor.

Ah, so there *was* something Angela wanted. Unfortunately, it wasn't something that could be easily gift wrapped.

I felt strangely comforted for a moment, hearing Angela's hopeless yearning. A sense of kinship passed through me, and I was, in that second, at one with the kind human girl.

It was oddly consoling to know that I wasn't the only one living out a tragic love story. Heartbreak was everywhere.

In the next second, I was abruptly and thoroughly irritated. Because Angela's story didn't *have* to be tragic. She was human and he was human and the difference that seemed so insurmountable in her head was truly ridiculous compared to my own situation. There was no *reason* for her broken heart. What a wasteful sorrow. Why shouldn't this one story have a happy ending?

I wanted to give her a gift.... Well, I would give her what she wanted. Knowing what I did of human nature, it probably wouldn't even be very difficult. I sifted through the consciousness of the boy beside her, the object of her affections, and he did not seem unwilling, he was just stymied by the same difficulty she was.

All I would have to do was plant the suggestion.

The plan formed easily; the script wrote itself without effort on my part. I would need Emmett's help—getting him to go along with this was the only real difficulty. Human nature was so much easier to manipulate than immortal nature.

I was pleased with my solution, with my gift for Angela. It was a nice diversion from my own problems. Would that mine were as easily fixed.

My mood was slightly improved as Bella and I took our seats. Maybe I should be more positive. Maybe there was some solution out there for us that was escaping me, the way Angela's obvious solution was so invisible to her. Not likely.... But why waste time with hopelessness? I didn't have time to waste when it came to Bella. Each second mattered.

Mr. Banner entered pulling an ancient TV and VCR. He was skipping through a section he wasn't particularly interested in—genetic disorders—by showing a movie for the next three days. *Lorenzo's Oil* was not a cheerful piece, but that didn't stop the excitement in the room. No notes, no testable material. The humans exulted.

It didn't matter to me, either way. I hadn't been planning on paying attention to anything but Bella.

I did not pull my chair away from hers today to give myself space to breathe. Instead, I sat close beside her like any normal human would. Closer than we sat inside my car, close enough that the left side of my body felt submerged in the heat from her skin.

It was a strange experience, both enjoyable and nerve-racking, but I preferred this to sitting across the table from her. It was more than I was used to, and yet I quickly realized that it was not enough. I was not satisfied. Being this close to her only made me want to be closer still.

I had accused her of being a magnet for danger. Right now, it felt as though that was the literal truth. I *was* danger, and with every inch I allowed myself nearer to her, her attraction grew in force.

And then Mr. Banner turned the lights out.

It was odd how much of a difference this made, considering that the lack of light meant little to my eyes. I could still see just as perfectly as before. Every detail of the room was clear.

So why the sudden shock of electricity in the air? Was it because I knew that I was the only one who could see clearly? That both Bella and I were invisible to the others? As though we were alone, just the two of us, hidden in the dark room, sitting so close beside each other.

My hand moved toward her without my permission. Just to touch her hand, to hold it in the darkness. Would that be such a horrific mistake? If my skin bothered her, she only had to pull away.

I yanked my hand back, folded my arms tightly across my chest, and clenched my hands closed. No mistakes, I'd promised myself. If I held her hand, I would only want more—another insignificant touch, another move closer to her. I could feel that. A new kind of desire was growing in me, working to override my self-control.

No mistakes.

Bella folded her arms securely across her own chest, and her hands balled up into fists, identical to mine.

What are you thinking? I was dying to whisper the words to her, but the room was too quiet to get away with even a whispered conversation.

The movie began, lightening the darkness just a bit. Bella glanced up at me. She noted the rigid way I held my body—just like hers—and smiled. Her lips parted slightly, and her eyes seemed full of warm invitations.

Or perhaps I was seeing what I wanted to see.

I smiled back. Her breathing caught with a low gasp and she looked quickly away.

That made it worse. I didn't know her thoughts, but I was suddenly positive that I had been right before, and that she *wanted* me to touch her. She felt this dangerous desire just as I did.

Between her body and mine, the electricity hummed.

She didn't move all through the hour, holding her stiff, controlled pose as I held mine. Occasionally she would peek at me again, and the humming current would jolt through me with a sudden shock.

The hour passed—slowly, and yet not slowly enough. This was so new, I could have sat like this with her for days, just to experience the feeling fully.

I had a dozen different arguments with myself while the minutes passed, rationality struggling with desire.

Finally, Mr. Banner turned the lights on again.

Under the bright fluorescents, the atmosphere of the room returned to normal. Bella sighed and stretched, flexing her fingers in front of her. It must have been uncomfortable for her to hold that position for so long. It was easier for me—stillness came naturally.

I chuckled at the relieved expression on her face. "Well, that was interesting."

"Umm," she murmured, clearly understanding what I referred to, but making no comment. What I wouldn't give to hear what she was thinking *right now.*

I sighed. No amount of wishing was going to help with that.

"Shall we?" I asked, standing.

She made a face and got unsteadily to her feet, her hands splayed out as if she was afraid she was going to fall.

I could offer her my hand. Or I could place that hand underneath her elbow—just lightly—and steady her. Surely that wouldn't be such a horrible infraction.

No mistakes.

She was very quiet as we walked toward the gym. The crease was in evidence between her eyes, a sign that she was deep in thought. I, too, was thinking deeply.

One touch of my skin wouldn't hurt her, my selfish side contended.

I could easily moderate the pressure of my hand. It wasn't exactly difficult. My tactile sense was better developed than a human's: I could juggle a dozen crystal goblets without breaking any of them; I could stroke a soap bubble without popping it. As long as I was firmly in control of myself.

Bella was like a soap bubble—fragile and ephemeral. *Temporary.*

How long would I be able to justify my presence in her life? How much time did I have? Would I have another chance like this chance, like this moment, like this second? She would not always be within my arm's reach.

Bella turned to face me at the gym door, and her eyes widened at the expression on my face. She didn't speak. I looked at myself in the reflection of her eyes and saw the conflict raging in my own. I watched my face change as my better side lost the argument.

My hand lifted without a conscious command for it to do so. As gently as if she were made of the thinnest glass, as if she were fragile as the bubble I'd imagined, my fingers stroked the warm skin that covered her cheekbone. It heated under my touch, and I could feel the pulse of blood speed beneath her transparent skin.

Enough, I ordered, though my hand was aching to shape itself to the side of her face. *Enough.*

It was difficult to pull my hand back, to stop myself from moving closer to her than I already was. A thousand different possibilities ran through my mind in an instant—a thousand different ways to touch her. The tip of my finger tracing the shape of her lips. My palm cupping her chin. Pulling the clip from her hair and letting it spill out across my hand. My arms winding around her waist, holding her against the length of my body.

Enough.

I forced myself to turn, to step away from her. My body moved stiffly—unwilling.

I let my mind linger behind to watch her as I walked swiftly away, almost running from the temptation. I caught Mike Newton's thoughts—they were the loudest—while he watched Bella walk past him in oblivion, her eyes unfocused and her cheeks red. He glowered and suddenly my name was mingled with curses in his head. I couldn't help grinning slightly in response.

My hand was tingling. I flexed it and then curled it into a fist, but it continued to sting painlessly.

No, I hadn't hurt her—but touching her had still been a mistake.

It felt like simmering coals, as though a dull version of my thirsting burn had spread throughout my entire body.

The next time I was close to her, would I be able to stop myself from touching her again? And if I touched her a second time, would I be able to stop at that?

No more mistakes. That was it. *Savor the memory, Edward,* I told myself grimly, *and keep your hands to yourself.* That, or I would have to force myself to leave…somehow. Because I couldn't allow myself near her if I insisted on making errors.

I took a deep breath and tried to steady my thoughts.

Emmett caught up to me outside the English building.

"Hey, Edward." *He's looking better. Weird, but better. Happy.*

"Hey, Em." Did I look happy? I supposed, despite the chaos in my head, I felt something close to it.

Way to keep your mouth shut, kid. Rosalie's going to rip your tongue out.

I sighed. "Sorry I left you to deal with that. Are you angry with me?"

"Naw. Rose'll get over it. It was bound to happen anyway." *With what Alice sees coming…*

Alice's visions were not what I wanted to think about right now. I stared forward, my teeth locking together.

As I searched for a distraction, I caught sight of Ben Cheney entering the Spanish room ahead of us. Ah—here was my chance to give Angela Weber her gift.

I stopped walking and caught Emmett's arm. "Hold on a second."

What's up?

"I know I don't deserve it, but would you do me a favor anyway?"

"What favor?" he asked, curious.

Under my breath—and at a speed that would have made the words incomprehensible to a human—I explained to him what I wanted.

He stared at me when I was done, his thoughts as blank as his face.

"So?" I prompted. "Will you help me do it?"

It took him a minute to respond. "But, *why*?"

"C'mon, Emmett. Why *not*?"

Who are you and what have you done with my brother?

"Aren't you the one who complains that school is always the same? This is something a little different, isn't it? Consider it an experiment—an experiment in human nature."

He stared at me for another moment before he caved. "Well, it *is* different, I'll give you that. Okay, fine." Emmett snorted and then shrugged. "I'll help you."

I grinned at him, feeling more enthusiastic about my plan now that he was on board. Rosalie was a pain, but I would always owe her one for choosing Emmett; no one had a better brother than mine.

Emmett didn't need to practice. I whispered his lines to him once under my breath as we walked into the classroom.

Ben was already in his seat behind mine, assembling his homework to hand in. Emmett and I both sat and did the same thing. The classroom was not quiet yet; the murmur of subdued conversation would continue until Mrs. Goff called for attention. She was in no hurry, appraising the quizzes from the last class.

"So," Emmett said, his voice louder than necessary. "Did you ask Angela Weber out yet?"

The sound of papers rustling behind me came to an abrupt stop as Ben froze, his attention suddenly riveted on our conversation.

Angela? They're talking about Angela?

Good. I had his interest.

"No," I said, shaking my head slowly to appear regretful.

"Why not?" Emmett improvised. "Are we lacking in courage?"

I frowned at him. "No. I heard that she was interested in someone else."

Edward Cullen was going to ask Angela *out? But...no. I don't like that. I don't want him near her. He's...not right for her. Not...safe.*

I hadn't anticipated the chivalry, the protective instinct. I'd been aiming for jealousy. But whatever worked.

"You're going to let that stop you?" Emmett asked scornfully, improvising again. "Not up for the competition?"

I glared at him, but made use of what he gave me. "Look, I guess she really likes this Ben person. I'm not going to try to convince her otherwise. There are other girls."

The reaction in the chair behind me was electric.

"Who?" Emmett asked, back to the script.

"My lab partner said it was some kid named Cheney. I'm not sure I know who he is."

I bit back my smile. Only the haughty Cullens could get away with pretending not to know every student at this tiny school.

Ben's head was whirling with shock. *Me? Over Edward Cullen? But why would she like* me*?*

"Edward," Emmett muttered in a lower tone, rolling his eyes toward the boy. "He's right behind you," he mouthed, so obviously that the human could easily read the words.

"Oh," I muttered back.

I turned in my seat and glanced once at the boy behind me. For a second, the black eyes behind the glasses were frightened, but then he stiffened and squared his shoulders, affronted by my clearly disparaging evaluation. His chin shot out and an angry flush darkened his golden-brown skin.

"Huh," I said arrogantly as I turned back to Emmett.

He thinks he's better than me. But Angela doesn't. I'll show him....

Perfect.

"Didn't you say she was taking Yorkie to the dance, though?" Emmett asked, snorting as he said the name of the boy whom many scorned for his awkwardness.

"That was a group decision, apparently." I wanted to be sure that Ben was clear on this. "Angela's shy. If B—well, if a guy doesn't have the nerve to ask her out, she'd never ask him."

"You like shy girls," Emmett said, back to improvisation. *Quiet girls. Girls like...hmm, I don't know. Maybe Bella Swan?*

I grinned at him. "Exactly." Then I returned to the performance. "Maybe Angela will get tired of waiting. Maybe I'll ask her to the prom."

No, you won't, Ben thought, straightening up in his chair. *So what if she's taller than me? If she doesn't care, then neither do I. She's the nicest, smartest, prettiest girl in this school...and she wants* me.

I liked this Ben. He seemed bright and well-meaning. Maybe even worthy of a girl like Angela.

I gave Emmett a thumbs up under the desk as Mrs. Goff stood and greeted the class.

Okay, I'll admit it—that was sort of fun, Emmett thought.

I smiled to myself, pleased that I'd been able to shape one love story's forward progress. I was positive that Ben would follow through, and Angela would receive my anonymous gift. My debt was repaid.

How silly humans were, to let a six-inch height difference confound their happiness.

My success put me in a good mood. I smiled again as I settled into my chair and prepared to be entertained. After all, as Bella had pointed out at lunch, I'd never seen her in action in Gym class before.

Mike's thoughts were the easiest to pinpoint in the babble of voices that swarmed through the gym. His mind had gotten far too familiar over the last few weeks. With a sigh, I resigned myself to listening through him. At least I could be sure that he would be paying attention to Bella.

I was just in time to hear him offer to be her badminton partner; as he made the suggestion, other partnerings with Bella ran through his mind. My smile faded, my teeth clenched together, and I had to remind myself that murdering Mike Newton was still not permitted.

"Thanks, Mike—you don't have to do this, you know."

"Don't worry, I'll keep out of your way."

She grinned at him, and flashes of numerous accidents—always in some way connected to Bella—flashed through Mike's head.

Mike played alone at first, while Bella hesitated on the back half of the court, holding her racket gingerly, as though it might explode if moved too roughly. Then Coach Clapp ambled by and ordered Mike to let Bella play.

Uh oh, Mike thought as Bella moved forward with a sigh, holding her racket at an awkward angle.

Jennifer Ford served the birdie directly toward Bella with a smug twist to her thoughts. Mike saw Bella lurch toward it, swinging the racket yards wide of her target, and he rushed in to try to save the volley.

I watched the path of Bella's racket with alarm. Sure enough, it hit the taut net and sprung back at her, clipping her forehead before it spun out to strike Mike's arm with a resounding *thwack*.

Ow. Ow. Ungh. That's going to leave a bruise.

Bella was kneading her forehead. It was hard to stay in my seat where I belonged, knowing she was hurt. But what could I do, even if I were there? And it didn't seem to be serious. I hesitated, watching.

The coach laughed. *"Sorry, Newton." That girl's the worst jinx I've ever seen. Shouldn't inflict her on the others.*

He turned his back deliberately and moved to watch another game so that Bella could return to her former spectator's role.

Ow, Mike thought again, massaging his arm. He turned to Bella. *"Are you okay?"*

"Yeah, are you?" she asked sheepishly.

"I think I'll make it." Don't want to sound like a crybaby. But, man, that hurts!

Mike swung his arm in a circle, wincing.

"*I'll just stay back here*," Bella said, embarrassment rather than pain on her face. Maybe Mike had gotten the worst of it. I certainly *hoped* that was the case. At least she wasn't playing anymore. She held her racket so carefully behind her back, her expression full of remorse.…I had to disguise my laugh as coughing.

What's funny? Emmett wanted to know.

"Tell you later," I muttered.

Bella didn't venture into the game again. The coach ignored her and let Mike play alone.

I breezed through the quiz at the end of the hour, and Mrs. Goff let me go early. I was listening intently to Mike as I walked across the campus. He'd decided to confront Bella about me.

Jessica swears they're dating. Why? Why did he have to pick her?

He didn't recognize the real phenomenon—that she'd picked *me*.

"So."

"So what?" she wondered.

"You and Cullen, huh?" You and the freak. I guess, if a rich guy is that important to you…

I gritted my teeth at his degrading assumption.

"That's none of your business, Mike."

Defensive. So it's true. Crap. "I don't like it."

"*You don't have to*," she snapped.

Why can't she see what a circus sideshow he is? Like they all are. The way he stares at her. It gives me chills to watch. "He looks at you like . . . like you're something to eat."

I cringed, waiting for her response.

Her face turned bright red, and her lips pressed together as though she was holding her breath. Then, suddenly, a giggle burst through her lips.

Now she's laughing at me. Great.

Mike turned, thoughts sullen, and wandered off to change.

I leaned against the gym wall and tried to compose myself.

How could she have laughed at Mike's accusation—so entirely on target that I began to worry that Forks was becoming too *aware.* Why would she laugh at the suggestion that I could kill her, when she knew that it was entirely true?

What was *wrong* with her?

Did she have a morbid sense of humor? That didn't fit with my idea of her character, but how could I be sure? Or maybe my notion of the foolish angel was true in one respect: She had no sense of fear at all. Brave—that was one word for it. Others might say stupid, but I knew how bright she was. No matter what the reason, was it this strange lack of fear that put her in danger so constantly? Maybe she would always need me here.

Just like that, my mood was soaring.

If I could discipline myself, make myself safe, then perhaps it would be right for me to stay close to her.

When she walked through the gym doors, her shoulders were stiff and her lower lip was between her teeth again—a sure sign of anxiety. But as soon as her eyes met mine, her posture relaxed and a wide smile spread across her face. It was an oddly peaceful expression. She walked right to my side without hesitation, only stopping when she was so close that her body heat crashed over me like a breaking wave.

"Hi," she whispered.

The happiness I felt in this moment was, again, without precedent.

“Hello,” I said, and then—because with my mood suddenly so light, I couldn’t resist teasing her—I added, “How was Gym?”

Her smile wavered. “Fine.”

She was a poor liar.

“Really?” I asked, about to press the issue—I was still concerned about her head; was she in pain?—but then Mike Newton’s thoughts were so loud, they broke my concentration.

I hate him. I wish he would die. I hope he drives that shiny car right off a cliff. Why couldn’t he just leave her alone? Stick to his own kind—to the freaks.

“What?” Bella demanded.

My eyes refocused on her face. She looked at Mike’s retreating back, and then at me again.

“Newton’s getting on my nerves,” I admitted.

Her mouth fell open, and her smile disappeared. She must have forgotten that I’d had the power to watch through her calamitous last hour, or hoped that I hadn’t used it. “You weren’t listening again?”

“How’s your head?”

“You’re unbelievable!” she said through her teeth, and then she turned away from me and stalked furiously toward the parking lot. Her skin flushed dark red—she was embarrassed.

I kept pace with her, hoping that her anger would pass soon. She was usually quick to forgive me.

“You were the one who mentioned how I’d never seen you in Gym,” I explained. “It made me curious.”

She didn’t answer. Her eyebrows pulled together.

She came to a sudden halt in the parking lot when she realized that the way to my car was blocked by a crowd of mostly male students.

I wonder how fast they’ve gone in this thing.

Look at the SMG shift paddles. I’ve never seen those outside of a magazine.

Nice side grilles!

Sure wish I had sixty thousand dollars lying around. . . .

This was exactly why it was better for Rosalie to only use her car out of town.

I wound through the throng of lustful boys to my own car. After a second of hesitation, Bella followed suit.

"Ostentatious," I muttered as she climbed in.

"What kind of car is that?" she wondered.

"An M3."

She frowned. "I don't speak *Car and Driver.*"

"It's a BMW." I rolled my eyes and then focused on backing out without running anyone down. I had to lock eyes with a few boys who didn't seem willing to move out of my way. A half second meeting my gaze seemed to be enough to convince them.

"Are you still angry?" I asked her. Her frown had relaxed.

"Definitely," she answered curtly.

I sighed. Maybe I shouldn't have brought it up. Oh well. I could try to make amends, I supposed. "Will you forgive me if I apologize?"

She thought about that for a moment. "Maybe... if you mean it," she decided. "*And* if you promise not to do it again."

I wasn't going to lie to her, and there was no way I was agreeing to *that*. Perhaps if I offered her a different exchange.

"How about if I mean it, *and* I agree to let you drive this Saturday?" I shuddered internally at the thought.

The furrow popped into existence between her eyes as she considered the new bargain. "Deal," she said after a moment of thought.

Now for my apology.... I'd never *tried* to dazzle Bella on purpose before, but this seemed like a good moment. I stared deep into her eyes as I drove away from the school, wondering whether I was doing it right. I used my most persuasive tone.

"Then I'm very sorry I upset you."

Her heartbeat thudded louder than before, and the rhythm was abruptly staccato. Her eyes were huge. She looked stunned.

I half smiled. It seemed as though I'd succeeded. Of course, I was having a bit of difficulty looking away from her eyes, too.

Equally dazzled. It was a good thing I had this road memorized.

"And I'll be on your doorstep bright and early Saturday morning," I added, finishing the agreement.

She blinked swiftly, shaking her head as if to clear it. "Um," she said, "it doesn't help with the Charlie situation if an unexplained Volvo is left in the driveway."

Ah, how little she still knew about me. "I wasn't intending to bring a car."

"How—?" she started to ask.

I interrupted her. The answer would only bring on another round of questions. "Don't worry about it. I'll be there, no car."

She put her head to one side, and looked for a second as though she was going to press for more, but then seemed to change her mind.

"Is it later yet?" she asked, reminding me of our unfinished conversation in the cafeteria today.

I should have just answered her other question. This one was much more unappealing. "I suppose it is later," I agreed unwillingly.

I parked in front of her house, tensing as I tried to think of how to explain... without making my monstrous nature too evident, without frightening her again. Or was it wrong to minimize my darkness?

She waited with the same politely interested mask she'd worn at lunch. If I'd been less anxious, her preposterous calm would have made me laugh.

"And you still want to know why you can't see me hunt?" I asked.

"Well, mostly I was wondering about your reaction," she said.

"Did I frighten you?" I asked, positive that she would deny it.

"No." It was such an obvious lie.

I tried not to smile, and failed. "I apologize for scaring you." And then my smile vanished with the momentary humor. "It was just the very thought of you being there... while we hunted."

"That would be bad?"

The mental picture was too much—Bella, so vulnerable in the empty darkness; myself, out of control.... I tried to banish it from my head. "Extremely."

"Because...?"

I took a deep breath, concentrating for one moment on the burning thirst. Feeling it, managing it, proving my dominion over it. It would never control me again—I willed that to be true. I *would* be safe for her. I stared toward the welcome clouds without really seeing them, wishing I could believe that my determination would make any difference if I were hunting when I crossed her scent.

"When we hunt... we give ourselves over to our senses," I told her, thinking through each word before I spoke it. "Govern less with our minds. Especially our sense of smell. If you were anywhere near me when I lost control that way..."

I shook my head in agony at the thought of what would—not what *might*, but what *would*—surely happen then.

I listened to the spike in her heartbeat, and then turned, restless, to read her eyes.

Bella's face was composed, her eyes grave. Her mouth was pursed just slightly in what I guessed was concern. But concern for what? Her own safety? Was there any hope that I'd finally made the realities clear? I continued to stare at her, trying to translate her ambiguous expression into sure fact.

She gazed back. Her eyes grew round after a moment, and her pupils dilated, though the light had not changed.

My breathing accelerated, and suddenly the quiet in the car seemed to be humming, just as in the darkened Biology room this afternoon. The electric current raced between us again, and my desire to touch her was, briefly, stronger even than the demands of my thirst.

The throbbing electricity made it feel as if I had a pulse again. My body sang with it. As though I were human. More than anything in the world, I wanted to feel the heat of her lips against mine. For one second, I struggled desperately to find the strength, the control, to be able to put my mouth so close to her skin.

She sucked in a ragged breath, and only then did I realize that when I had started breathing faster, she had stopped breathing altogether.

I closed my eyes, trying to break the connection between us.

No more mistakes.

Bella's existence was tied to a thousand delicately balanced chemical processes, all so easily disrupted: The rhythmic expansion of her lungs, that flow of oxygen was life or death to her. The fluttering cadence of her fragile heart could be stopped by so many stupid accidents or illnesses or . . . by me.

I did not believe that any member of my family—except possibly Emmett—would hesitate if he or she were offered a chance back, if he or she could trade immortality for mortality again. Rosalie and I, Carlisle, too, would stand in fire for it. Burn for as many days or centuries as were necessary.

Most of our kind prized immortality above all else. There were even humans who craved this, who searched in dark places for those who could give them the blackest of gifts.

Not us. Not my family. We would trade anything to be human.

But none of us, not even Rosalie, had ever been as desperate for a way back as I was now.

I opened my eyes and stared at the microscopic pits and flaws in the windshield, as though there was some solution hidden in the imperfect glass. The electricity had not faded, and I had to concentrate to keep my hands on the wheel.

My right hand began to sting without pain again, from when I'd touched her before.

"Bella, I think you should go inside now."

She obeyed at once, without comment, getting out of the car and shutting the door behind herself. Did she feel the potential for disaster as clearly as I did?

Did it hurt her to leave, as it hurt me to see her go? The only solace was that I would see her soon. Sooner than she would see me. I smiled at that, then rolled the window down and leaned across to speak to her one more time. It was safer now, with the heat of her body outside the car.

She turned to see what I wanted, curious.

Always so curious, though I'd answered almost all of her many questions. My own curiosity was entirely unsatisfied. That wasn't fair.

"Oh, Bella?"

"Yes?"

"Tomorrow it's my turn."

Her forehead puckered. "Your turn to what?"

"Ask the questions." Tomorrow, when we were in a safer place, surrounded by witnesses, I would get my own answers. I grinned at the thought, and then turned away because she made no move to leave. Even with her outside the car, the echo of the electricity zinged in the air. I wanted to get out, too, to walk her to her door as an excuse to stay beside her.

No more mistakes. I hit the gas, and then sighed as she disappeared behind me. It seemed as though I was always running toward Bella or away from her, never staying in place. I would have to find some way to hold my ground if we were ever going to have any peace.

My house appeared calm and silent from the outside as I drove past, heading for the garage. But I could hear the turmoil—both spoken aloud and silently thought—inside. I threw one wistful glance in the direction of my favorite car—still pristine, for now—before I headed out to face the beautiful ogre under the bridge. I couldn't even make the short walk from the garage to the house before being accosted.

Rosalie shot out the front door as soon as my footsteps were audible. She planted herself at the base of the stairs, her lips pulled back over her teeth.

I stopped twenty yards away, and there was no aggression in my stance. I knew I deserved this.

"I'm so sorry, Rose," I told her before she had even gathered her thoughts to attack. I probably wouldn't get to say much more.

Her shoulders squared, her chin jerked up.

How could you have been so stupid?

Emmett came slowly down the stairs behind her. I knew that if Rosalie attacked me, Emmett would come between us. Not to protect me. To keep her from provoking me enough that I would fight back.

"I'm sorry," I told her again.

I could see that she was surprised by the lack of sarcasm in my voice, my quick capitulation. But she was too angry to accept apologies yet.

Are you happy now?

"No," I said, the ache in my voice giving proof to the denial.

Why did you do it, then? Why would you tell her? Just because she asked? The words themselves weren't so harsh—it was her mental tone that was edged with needle-sharp points. Also in her mind was Bella's face—just a caricature of the face I loved. As much as Rosalie hated me in this moment, it was nothing to the hate she felt for Bella. She wanted to believe this hate was justified, founded solely on my bad behavior—that Bella was only a problem because she was now a danger to us. A broken rule. Bella knew too much.

But I could see how much her judgment was clouded by her jealousy of the girl. It was more now than the fact that I found Bella so much more compelling than I had Rosalie. Her jealousy had twisted and shifted focus. Bella had everything Rosalie wanted. She was human. She had choices. Rose was outraged that Bella would put this in jeopardy, that she would flirt with the darkness when she had other options.

Rose thought she might even trade faces with the girl she thought of as homely, if she could have her humanity in the bargain.

Though Rosalie was trying not to think all these things while she waited for my answer, she couldn't keep them entirely out of her head.

"Why?" she demanded out loud when I still said nothing. She didn't want me to keep reading. "Why did you tell her?"

"I'm actually surprised you were able to," Emmett said before I could respond. "You rarely say the word, even with us. It's not your favorite."

He was thinking how much Rose and I were alike in this, how we both avoided the title to the nonlife we hated. Emmett had no such reservations.

What would it be like to feel the way Emmett did? To be so practical, so free from regret? To be able to so easily accept and move forward?

Rose and I would both be happier people if we could follow his example.

Seeing this—our similarities—so clearly made it even easier to excuse the venom-tipped needles that Rose was still thinking my way.

"You're not wrong," I said to Emmett. "I doubt I would ever have been able to say it myself."

Emmett cocked his head to the side. Behind him, inside the house, I could feel the shock from the rest of our audience. Only Alice was unsurprised.

"Then *how*?" Rosalie hissed.

"Don't overreact," I said, without much hope. Her eyebrows shot up. "It wasn't an intentional breach. It's probably something we should have foreseen."

"What are you talking about?" she demanded.

"Bella is friends with the great-grandson of Ephraim Black."

Rosalie froze with surprise. Emmett, too, was taken off guard. They were no more prepared for this direction than I had been.

Carlisle appeared in the doorway. This was more than just a fight between Rosalie and me now.

"Edward?" he asked.

"We should have known, Carlisle. Of course the elders would

warn the next generation when we came back. And of course the next generation wouldn't credit any of it. It's just a silly story to them. The boy who answered Bella's questions didn't believe anything he was telling her."

I wasn't anxious about Carlisle's reaction. I knew how he would respond. But I was listening very intently to Alice's room now, to hear what Jasper would think.

"You're right," Carlisle said. "Naturally, it would play out that way." He sighed. "It's bad luck Ephraim's progeny had such a knowledgeable audience."

Jasper listened to Carlisle's response, and he was concerned. But his thoughts were more about leaving with Alice than silencing the Quileutes. Alice was already watching his ideas for the future, and preparing to refute them. She had no intention of going anywhere.

"Hardly bad luck," Rosalie said through her teeth. "It's Edward's fault that the girl knows anything."

"True," I agreed quickly. "This is my fault. I *am* sorry."

Please, Rosalie thought directly at me. *Enough with the roll-over routine. Stop playing so penitent.*

"I'm not playing," I said to her. "I know I'm to blame for all of this. I've made an enormous mess of everything."

"Alice told you I was thinking of burning your car, didn't she?"

I smiled—sort of. "She did. But I deserve that. If it makes you feel better, have at it."

She looked at me for a long moment, thinking about going ahead with the destruction. Testing me, to see if I was bluffing.

I shrugged at her. "It's just a toy, Rose."

"You've changed," she said from between her teeth again.

I nodded. "I know."

She whirled and stalked off toward the garage. But she was the one bluffing. If it wouldn't hurt me, there was no point to the exercise. Of all my family, she was the only one who loved cars the way I did. Mine was too beautiful to vandalize for no reason.

Emmett looked after her. "I don't suppose you'd give me the full story now."

"I don't know what you're talking about," I said innocently. He rolled his eyes, then followed Rosalie.

I looked at Carlisle and mouthed Jasper's name.

He nodded. *Yes, I can imagine. I'll speak with him.*

Alice appeared in the doorway. "He's waiting for you," she said to Carlisle. Carlisle smiled at her—a little wryly. Though we were as used to Alice as it was possible to be, she was often uncanny. Carlisle patted her short black hair as he passed her.

I sat at the top of the stairs and Alice sat beside me, both of us listening to the conversation upstairs. There was no tension in Alice—she knew how it would end. She showed me, and my tension vanished as well. The conflict was over before it started. Jasper admired Carlisle as much as any of us did, and he was happy to follow his lead...until he thought Alice might be in danger. I found that I understood Jasper's perspective more easily now. It was strange how much I hadn't understood before Bella. She had changed me more than I'd known it was possible for me to change and still remain myself.

13. ANOTHER COMPLICATION

I DID NOT FEEL THE USUAL GUILT WHEN I RETURNED TO Bella's room that night, though I knew I should. But it felt like the correct course of action—the only right thing to be doing. I was there to burn my throat as much as possible. I would train myself to ignore her scent. It could be accomplished. I would not allow this to be a difficulty between us.

Easier said than done. But I knew this helped. Practice. Embrace the pain, let that be the strongest reaction. Beat the element of desire entirely out of myself.

There was no peace in Bella's dreams. And no peace for me, watching her twitch restlessly and hearing her whisper my name over and over. The physical pull, that overwhelming chemistry from the darkened classroom, was even stronger here in her night-black bedroom. Though she was not aware of my presence, she seemed to feel it, too.

She woke herself more than once. The first time she did not open her eyes; she merely buried her head under her pillow and groaned. That was good luck for me—a second chance I didn't deserve, since I didn't put it to good use and leave as I should have. Instead, I sat on the floor in the farthest dark-shadowed corner of the room, and trusted that her human eyes would not spot me here.

She didn't catch me, even the time that she got up and stalked to the bathroom for a glass of water. She moved angrily, perhaps frustrated that sleep still evaded her.

I wished there was some action I could take, as before with the warm blanket from the cupboard. But I could only watch as I burned, useless to her. It was a relief when she finally sank into a dreamless unconsciousness.

I was in the trees when the sky lightened from black to gray. I held my breath—this time to keep the scent of her from escaping. I refused to let the pure morning air erase the ache in my throat.

I listened to breakfast with Charlie, struggling again to find the words in his thoughts. It was fascinating—I could guess at the reasons behind the words he said aloud, almost *feel* his intentions, but they never resolved into full sentences the way everyone else's thoughts did. I found myself wishing that his parents were still alive. It would be interesting to trace this genetic trait further back.

The combination of his inarticulate thoughts and his spoken words were enough for me to piece together his general mindset this morning. He was worried about Bella, physically and emotionally. He felt similarly concerned about the idea of Bella roaming Seattle alone as I would—only not quite so maniacally. Then again, his information was not as up-to-date as mine; he had no idea about the number of close calls she'd lived through recently.

She worded her reply to him very carefully, but it was only technically not a lie. She was obviously not planning to tell him about her change of plans. Or about me.

Charlie was also worried about the fact that she wasn't going to the dance on Saturday. Was she disappointed about this? Was she feeling rejected? Were the boys at school cruel to her? He felt helpless. She didn't *look* depressed, but he suspected that she would hide anything negative from him. He resolved to call her mother during the day and ask for advice.

At least, that was what I *thought* he was thinking. I might have misconstrued parts.

I retrieved my car while Charlie loaded his. As soon as he had driven around the corner, I pulled into the driveway to wait. I saw the curtain twitch in her window, then heard her stumbling footsteps race down the stairs.

I stayed in my seat, rather than get out to hold the door for her as I perhaps should have. But I thought it was more important to watch. She never acted the way I expected, and I needed to be able to anticipate correctly; I needed to study her, to learn the ways she moved when left to her own devices, to try to anticipate her motivations. She hesitated a moment outside the car, then let herself in with a small smile—a little shy, I thought.

She wore a dark, coffee-colored turtleneck today. It was not tight, but still fitted closely to her shape, and I missed the ugly sweater. It was safer.

This was supposed to be about her reactions, but I was abruptly overwhelmed with my own. I didn't know how I could feel so peaceful with everything that was hanging over both our heads, but being with her was an antidote to pain and anxiety.

I took a deep breath through my nose—not *every* kind of pain—and smiled.

"Good morning. How are you today?"

The evidence of her restless night was obvious in her face. Her translucent skin hid nothing. But I knew she wouldn't complain.

"Good, thank you," she said with another smile.

"You look tired."

She ducked, shaking her hair around her face in a move that seemed habitual. It obscured part of her left cheek. "I couldn't sleep."

I grinned at her. "Neither could I."

She laughed, and I absorbed the sound of her happiness.

"I guess that's right," she said. "I suppose I slept just a little bit more than you did."

"I'd wager you did."

She peered at me around her hair, eyes lit up in a way I recognized. Curious. "So what did you do last night?"

I laughed quietly, glad I had an excuse not to lie to her. "Not a chance. It's my day to ask questions."

The little frown mark appeared between her eyebrows. "Oh, that's right. What do you want to know?" Her tone was slightly skeptical, as though she couldn't believe I had any real interest. She seemed to have no idea how curious I was.

There were so many things I didn't know. I decided to start slow.

"What's your favorite color?"

She rolled her eyes—still doubting my interest level. "It changes from day to day."

"What's your favorite color today?"

She thought for just a second. "Probably brown."

I assumed she was mocking me, and my tone shifted to match her sarcasm. "Brown?"

"Sure," she said, and then she was unexpectedly on the defensive. Perhaps I should have expected this. She never liked judgments. "Brown is warm. I miss brown. Everything that's supposed to be brown—tree trunks, rocks, dirt—is all covered up with squashy green stuff here!"

Her tone brought back the sound of her sleeping complaint the other night. *Too green*—was this what she had meant? I stared at her, thinking how right she was. Honestly, looking into her eyes now, I realized that brown was my favorite, too. I couldn't imagine any shade more beautiful.

"You're right," I told her. "Brown is warm."

She started to blush a little and unconsciously retreated deeper into her hair. Carefully, bracing myself for any unexpected reaction, I swept her hair behind her shoulder so that I could have full access to her face again. The only reaction was a sudden increase in her heart rate.

I turned into the school lot and parked in the spot next to my usual place; Rosalie had taken that.

"What music is in your CD player right now?" I asked as I twisted the keys from the ignition. I'd never trusted myself that close to her while she'd slept, and the unknown teased me.

Her head cocked to the side, and it seemed as though she was trying to remember. "Oh, right," she said. "It's Linkin Park. *Hybrid Theory*."

Not what I was expecting.

As I pulled the identical CD from my car's music cache, I tried to imagine what this album meant to her. It didn't seem to match any of her moods that I'd seen, but then, there was so much I didn't know.

"Debussy to this?" I wondered.

She stared at the cover, and I could not understand her expression.

"Which is your favorite song?"

"Mmm," she murmured, still looking at the cover art. " 'With You,' I think."

I thought through all the lyrics quickly. "Why that one?"

She smiled a little and shrugged. "I'm not sure."

Well, that didn't help much.

"Your favorite movie?"

She thought about her answer for a brief moment.

"I'm not sure I can pick just one."

"Favorite movies, then?"

She nodded as she climbed out of the car. "Hmm. Definitely *Pride and Prejudice*, the six-hour one with Colin Firth. *Vertigo*. And... *Monty Python and the Holy Grail*. There are more... but I'm blanking...."

"Tell me when you think of them," I suggested as we walked toward her English class. "While you consider that, tell me what your favorite scent is."

"Lavender. Or... maybe clean laundry." She'd been looking straight ahead, but suddenly her eyes cut over to me for a second, and a faint pink colored her cheek.

"Was there more?" I prompted, wondering what that look meant.

"No. Just those."

I wasn't sure why she would omit part of her answer to such a simple query, but I rather thought she had.

"What candy do you like best?"

On this she was very decided. "Black licorice and Sour Patch Kids."

I smiled at her enthusiasm.

We were at her classroom now, but she hesitated at the door. I, too, was in no hurry to separate from her.

"Where would you like to travel to most?" I asked—I assumed she was not going to tell me Comic Con.

She leaned her head to one side, her eyes narrowing in thought. Inside the classroom, Mr. Mason was clearing his throat to get the class's attention. She was about to be late.

"Think about it and give me your answer at lunch," I suggested.

She grinned and reached for the door, then turned back to look at me. Her smile faded, and the *v* appeared between her eyes.

I could have asked her what she was thinking, but that would have delayed her, possibly gotten her in trouble. And I thought I knew. At least, I knew how I felt, letting that door close between us.

I forced myself to smile encouragingly. She darted inside as Mr. Mason started to lecture.

I walked quickly to my own class, knowing I would spend the day ignoring everything around me again. I was disappointed, though, because no one spoke to her in any of her morning classes, so there was nothing new to learn. Just glimpses of her staring into space, her expression abstracted. The time dragged while I waited to see her again with my own eyes.

When she left her Trigonometry class, I was already in place, waiting for her. The other students stared and speculated, but Bella just hurried toward me with a smile.

"*Beauty and the Beast*," she announced. "And *The Empire Strikes Back*. I know that's everyone's favorite, but..." She shrugged.

"For good reason," I assured her.

We fell into step. Already it felt natural to shorten my stride, to lower my head so it was closer to hers.

"Did you think about my travel question?"

"Yes...I think Prince Edward Island. *Anne of Green Gables*, you know. But I'd also like to see New York. I've never been to a big city that was mostly vertical. Just sprawl places like LA and Phoenix. I'd like to try hailing a cab." She laughed. "And then, if I can go anywhere, I'd want to go to England. See all the stuff I've been reading about."

This led toward my next avenue of inquiry, but I wanted to be thorough before I moved on.

"Tell me your favorite places that you've already been."

"Hmm. I liked the Santa Monica Pier. My mom said Monterey was better, but we never did get that far up the coast. We mostly stayed in Arizona; we didn't have a lot of time for travel and she didn't want to waste all of it in the car. She liked to visit places that were supposed to be haunted—Jerome, the Domes, pretty much any ghost town. We never saw any ghosts, but she said that was my fault. I was too skeptical, I scared them all away." She laughed again. "She loves the Ren Faire, we go to the one in Gold Canyon every year.... Well, I missed it this year, I guess. Once we saw the wild horses at the Salt River. That was cool."

"Where's the farthest place from home you've ever been?" I asked, starting to become a little concerned.

"Here, I guess," she said. "Farthest north from Phoenix, anyway. Farthest east—Albuquerque, but I was so young then, I don't remember. Farthest west would probably be the beach in La Push."

She went suddenly quiet. I wondered if she was thinking of her last visit to La Push, and all that she had discovered there. We were in the cafeteria line at this point, and she quickly picked out what she wanted rather than waiting for me to buy one of everything. She was also swift to pay for herself.

"You've never left the country?" I persisted once we reached our empty table. Part of me wondered if my sitting here had made it off-limits forever.

"Not yet," she said cheerfully.

Though she'd only had seventeen years to explore, I still felt surprised. And...guilty. She'd seen so little, experienced such a meager amount of what life had to offer. It was impossible that she could truly know what she wanted now.

"*Gattaca*," she said, chewing a bite of apple with a thoughtful expression. She hadn't noticed my sudden mood shift. "That was a good one. Have you seen it?"

"Yes. I liked it, too."

"What's *your* favorite movie?"

I shook my head and smiled. "It's not your turn."

"Seriously, I'm so boring. You must be out of questions."

"It's my day," I reminded her. "And I'm not at all bored."

She pursed her lips, as though she wanted to argue some more about my interest level, but then she smiled. I guessed she didn't really believe me, but had decided she would be fair about it. This *was* my day to ask questions.

"Tell me about books."

"You can't make me choose a favorite," she insisted almost fiercely.

"I won't. Tell me everything you like."

"Where do I start? Um, *Little Women*. That was the first big book I read. I still read it pretty much every year. Everything Austen, though I'm not a huge fan of *Emma*—"

Austen I already knew, having seen her battered anthology the day she read outside, but I wondered at the exclusion.

"Why not?"

"Ugh, she's so full of herself."

I grinned and she continued without prompting.

"*Jane Eyre*. I read that one pretty often, too. That's my idea of a heroine. Everything by any Brontë. *To Kill a Mockingbird*, obviously. *Fahrenheit 451*. All of the Chronicles of Narnia, but especially *The Voyage of the Dawn Treader. Gone with the Wind*. Douglas Adams and David Eddings and Orson Scott Card and Robin McKinley. Did I already say L. M. Montgomery?"

"I assumed as much from your travel hopes."

She nodded, then looked conflicted. "Did you want more? I'm going on too much."

"Yes," I assured her. "I want more."

"These aren't in any kind of order," she cautioned me. "My mom had a bunch of Zane Grey paperbacks. Some of them were pretty good. Shakespeare, mostly the comedies." She grinned. "See, out of order. Um, everything by Agatha Christie. Anne McCaffrey's dragon books... and speaking of great dragons, Jo Walton's *Tooth and Claw. The Princess Bride*, much better than the movie..." She tapped her finger against her lips. "There are a million more, but I'm blanking again."

She looked a little stressed.

"That's enough for now." She'd done more exploring in fiction than in reality, and I was surprised she'd listed a book I'd not yet read—I would have to find a copy of *Tooth and Claw*.

I could see elements of the stories in her makeup—characters that had shaped the context of her world. There was a bit of Jane Eyre in her, a portion of Scout Finch and Jo March, a measure of Elinor Dashwood, and Lucy Pevensie. I was sure I would find more connections as I learned more about her.

It was like putting together a puzzle, one with hundreds of thousands of pieces, and no depiction of the complete image to serve as a guide. Time-consuming, with many false leads, but ultimately I would be able to see the whole picture.

She interrupted my thoughts. "*Somewhere in Time*. I love that movie. I can't believe I didn't think of it right away."

It wasn't one of my favorites. The idea that the two lovers could only be together in heaven after their deaths rubbed me the wrong way. I changed the subject.

"Tell me about the music you like."

She paused to swallow again. And then, unexpectedly, she blushed.

"What's wrong?" I asked.

"Well, I'm...not super musical, I guess. The Linkin Park CD was a gift from Phil. He's trying to update my tastes."

"What were you into, pre-Phil?"

She sighed, lifting her hands helplessly. "I just listened to what my mom had."

"Classical music?"

"Sometimes."

"And other times?"

"Simon and Garfunkel. Neil Diamond. Joni Mitchell. John Denver. That kind of thing. She's like me—she listens to what her mother listened to. She liked to do sing-alongs on our road trips." Suddenly the asymmetrical dimple appeared with her wide grin. "Remember those definitions of scary we talked about before?" She laughed. "Until you've heard my mom and me trying to hit the high notes in the *Phantom of the Opera* soundtrack, you've never known true fear."

I laughed with her, but wished I could see and hear that. I imagined her on a bright road, winding through the desert with the windows down, the sun bringing out the red shine in her hair. I wished I knew what her mother looked like, and even what kind of car it was, so my picture could be more precise. I wanted to be there with her, to listen to her sing badly, to watch her smile in the sun.

"Favorite TV show?"

"I don't watch a lot of TV."

I wondered if she was afraid to go into detail, worried again about me being bored. Maybe a few softball questions would relax her.

"Coke or Pepsi?"

"Dr Pepper."

"Favorite ice cream?"

"Cookie dough."

"Pizza?"

"Cheese. Boring but true."

"Football team?

"Um, pass?"

"Basketball?"

She shrugged. "I'm not really a sports person."

"Ballet or opera?"

"Ballet, I guess. I've never been to the opera."

I was not unaware that this list I was compiling had a use besides just learning to understand as much as I could of her. I was also learning things that might please her. Gifts I might give her. Places I could take her. Little things and bigger things. It was presumptuous in the extreme to imagine that I could ever have that kind of standing in her life. But how I wished....

"What's your favorite gemstone?"

"Topaz." She said this in a decided way, but then her eyes suddenly tightened and red flushed across her cheekbones.

She'd done this before when I asked about scents. I'd let it go then, but not this time. I was sure the other unmet curiosity would torment me enough.

"Why does that make you...embarrassed?" I wasn't sure I had the emotion right.

She shook her head quickly, staring down at her hands. "It's nothing."

"I'd like to understand."

She shook her head again, still refusing to look at me.

"Please, Bella?"

"Next question."

Now I was desperate to know. Frustrated.

"Tell me," I insisted. Rudely. I felt ashamed at once.

She didn't look up. She twisted a strand of her hair back and forth between her fingertips.

But she finally answered.

"It's the color of your eyes today," she admitted. "I suppose if you asked me in two weeks, I'd say onyx."

Just as my favorite color was now a deep chocolate brown.

Her shoulders had slumped, and suddenly I recognized her posture. It was just the same as yesterday, when she'd hesitated to answer my question about whether she believed she cared more for me than I did for her. I'd put her in the same position again, of confirming her interest in me without receiving an assurance in return.

Cursing my curiosity, I returned to my questions. Perhaps my obvious fascination with every detail of her personality would convince her of the obsessive level of my interest.

"What kinds of flowers do you prefer?"

"Um, dahlias. For looks. Lavender and lilac for fragrance."

"You don't like to watch sports, but did you ever play on a team?"

"Just in school, when they made me."

"Your mother never put you on a soccer team?"

She shrugged. "My mom liked to keep the weekends open for adventures. I did Girl Scouts for a while, and once she put me in a dance class, but that was a *mistake*." She raised her eyebrows as if daring me to doubt her. "She thought it would be convenient because it was close enough for me to walk there after school, but no convenience was worth the mayhem."

"Mayhem, really?" I asked skeptically.

"If I had Ms. Kamenev's number, she would corroborate my story."

She looked up suddenly. All around us, the other students were gathering their things. How had the time passed so quickly?

She stood in response to the commotion, and I rose with her, gathering her trash onto the tray while she slung on her backpack. She reached as if to take the tray from me.

"I've got it," I said.

She huffed quietly, a little exasperated. She still didn't like being taken care of.

I couldn't focus on my still-unanswered questions as we walked to Biology. I was remembering yesterday, wondering if that same tension, with the yearning and the electricity, would be present today. And sure enough, as soon as the lights went off, all the same overwhelming cravings returned. I had positioned my chair farther from hers today, but it didn't help.

There was still that selfish part of me arguing that holding her hand would not be so wrong, even suggesting that this might be a good way to test her reactions, to prepare myself for being alone together. I tried to ignore the selfish voice and the temptation as best I could.

Bella was trying, too, I could tell. She leaned forward, chin propped against her arms, and I could see her fingers gripping under the edge of the desk so tightly that her knuckles were white. It made me wonder what precise temptation she was struggling against. Today she didn't look at me. Not once.

There was so much I didn't understand about her. So much I couldn't ask.

My body was ever so slightly leaning toward her now. I pulled myself back.

When the lights came back on, Bella sighed, and if I'd had to guess, I would have named her expression *relief*. But relief from what?

I walked beside her to her next class, fighting the same internal battle as the day before.

She stopped at the door and looked up at me with her clear, deep eyes. Was that expectation, or confusion? An invitation or a warning? What did *she* want?

This is just a question, I told myself as my hand reached out to her of its own volition. *Another kind of question.*

Braced, not breathing, I let just the back of my hand graze the side of her face, from her temple to her narrow jaw. Like yesterday, her skin warmed to my touch, her heart beat faster. Her head tilted just a fraction of a centimeter as she leaned into my caress.

It was another kind of answer.

I walked away from her quickly again, knowing that this one aspect of my self-control was compromised, my hand smarting in the same painless way.

Emmett was already seated when I arrived at the Spanish classroom. So was Ben Cheney. They were not the only two to note my entrance. I could hear the other students' curiosity, Bella's name thought alongside mine, the speculation. . . .

Ben was the only human not thinking of Bella. My presence made him bristle a little, but he wasn't antagonistic. He'd already spoken to Angela and made a date for this weekend. Her reception of his invitation had been warm, and he was still riding the high. Though he was wary of my intentions, he was cognizant that I had acted as catalyst for his current happiness. As long as I stayed away from Angela, he had no problem with me. There was even a hint of gratitude, though he had no idea this was exactly the outcome I'd desired, too. He seemed a clever boy—he rose in my estimation.

Bella was in Gym, but as in the second half of yesterday's class, she did not participate. Her eyes were far away whenever Mike Newton turned to look at her. She was obviously elsewhere in her head. Mike guessed that anything he had to say to her would be unwelcome.

Guess I never really had a chance, he thought, half-resigned, half-sullen. *How did it even happen? It was, like, overnight. Guess when Cullen wants something, it doesn't take him long to get it.* The images that followed, his ideas of what I'd *gotten,* were offensive. I stopped listening.

I didn't like his perspective. As though Bella had no will of her own. Surely, she'd been the one to choose, hadn't she? If she had ever asked me to leave her alone, I would have turned around and walked the other way. But she'd wanted me to stay, then and now.

My thoughts drifted back to check in on the Spanish classroom, and they naturally tuned in to the most familiar voice, but my mind was tangled around Bella as usual, so for a moment I didn't realize what I was hearing.

And then my teeth clamped together so hard that even the humans near me heard. One boy looked around for the source of the cracking sound.

Oops, Emmett thought.

I curled my hands into fists and concentrated on staying in my seat.

Sorry, I was trying not to think about that.

I glanced at the clock. Fifteen minutes before I could punch him in the face.

I didn't mean any harm. Hey, I took your side, right? Honestly, Jasper and Rose are just being silly, betting against Alice. It's the easiest wager I'll ever win.

A wager about this weekend, whether Bella would live or die.

Fourteen and a half minutes.

Emmett squirmed in his seat, well aware what my total motionlessness indicated.

C'mon, Ed. You know it wasn't serious. Anyway, it's not even about the girl. You know better than I do whatever's going on with Rose. Something between you two, I guess. She's still mad, and she wouldn't admit for all the world that she's actually rooting for you.

He always gave Rosalie the benefit of the doubt, and though I knew that I was just the opposite—I *never* gave her the benefit of the doubt—I didn't think he was right this time. Rosalie would be pleased to see me fail in this. She would be happy to see Bella's poor choices receive what she considered their just reward. And then she'd still be jealous as Bella's soul escaped to whatever waited beyond.

And Jazz—well, you know. He's tired of being the weakest link. You're kind of too perfect with the self-control, and it gets annoying. Carlisle's different. Admit it, you're a little... smug.

Thirteen minutes.

For Emmett and Jasper, this was just some sticky pit of

quicksand I'd created for myself. Fail or succeed—to them, in the end it was nothing more than another anecdote about me. Bella wasn't part of the equation. Her life was only a marker in the bet they'd made.

Don't take it personally.

There was another way? Twelve and a half minutes.

You want me to back out of it? I will.

I sighed, and let the rigidity of my pose relax.

What was the point of stoking my anger? Should I blame them for their inability to understand? How could they?

How meaningless it all was. Infuriating, yes, but…would I have been any different if it hadn't been my life that had changed? If it hadn't been about Bella?

Regardless, I didn't have time to fight with Emmett now. I would be waiting for Bella when she was done with Gym. So many more pieces to the puzzle I needed to discover.

I heard Emmett's relief as I darted out the door at the first sound of the bell, ignoring him.

When Bella walked through the gymnasium door and saw me, a smile spread across her face. I felt the same relief I had in the car this morning. All my doubts and torments seemed to lift from my shoulders. I knew that they were still very real, but the weight was so much easier to carry when I could see her.

"Tell me about your home," I said as we walked to the car. "What do you miss?"

"Um…my house? Or Phoenix? Or do you mean here?"

"All of those."

She looked at me questioningly—was I serious?

"Please?" I asked as I held her door for her.

She raised one eyebrow as she climbed in, still doubting.

But when I was inside and we were alone again, she seemed to relax.

"Have you never been to Phoenix?"

I smiled. "No."

"Right," she said. "Of course. The sun." She speculated about that silently for a moment. "It creates some kind of a problem for you...?"

"Indeed." I wasn't about to try to explain that answer. It was really something that had to be seen to be understood. Also, Phoenix was a little too close for comfort to the lands the aggressive Southern clans claimed, but that wasn't a story I wanted to get into, either.

She waited, wondering if I would elaborate.

"So tell me about this place I've never seen," I prompted.

She considered for a moment. "The city is mostly very flat, not much taller than one or two stories. There are a few baby skyscrapers downtown, but that was pretty far away from where I lived. Phoenix is huge. You can drive through suburbs all day. Lots of stucco and tile and gravel. It's not all soft and squishy like it is here—everything is hard and most things have thorns."

"But you like it."

She nodded with a grin. "It's so...open. Just all sky. The things we call mountains are really just hills—hard, thorny hills. But most of the valley is a big, shallow bowl and it feels like it's filled with sunlight all the time." She illustrated the shape with her hands. "The plants are like modern art compared to the stuff here—lots of angles and edges. Mostly spiky." Another grin. "But they're all open, too. Even if there are leaves, they're just feathery, sparse things. Nothing can really hide there. Nothing keeps the sun out."

I stopped the car in front of her house. My usual spot.

"Well, it does rain occasionally," she amended. "But it's different there. More exciting. Lots of thunder and lightning and flash floods—not just the nonstop drizzle thing. And it smells better there. That's the creosote."

I knew the evergreen desert shrubs she referred to. I'd seen them through a car window in Southern California—only at night. They weren't much to look at.

"I've never smelled the scent of creosote," I admitted.

"They only smell in the rain."

"What is it like?"

She thought about that for a moment. "Sweet and bitter at the same time. A little like resin, a little like medicine. But that sounds bad. It smells *fresh*. Like clean desert." She chuckled. "That's not helpful, is it?"

"On the contrary. What else have I missed, not visiting Arizona?"

"Saguaros, but I'm sure you've seen pictures."

I nodded.

"They're bigger than you'd expect, when you see them in person. It takes all the newbies by surprise. Have you ever lived anywhere with cicadas?"

"Yes," I laughed. "We were in New Orleans for a while."

"Then you know," she said. "I had a job last summer at a plant nursery. The screaming—it's like nails on a chalkboard. It drove me crazy."

"What else?"

"Hmm. The colors are different. The mountains—hills or whatever—are mostly volcanic. Lots of purple rock. It's dark enough that it holds a lot of heat from the sun. So does the blacktop. In the summer, it never cools off—frying an egg on the sidewalk is not an urban myth. But there's lots of green from the golf courses. Some people keep lawns, too, though I think that's crazy. Anyway, the contrast in the colors is cool."

"What's your favorite place to spend time?"

"The library." She grinned. "If I hadn't already outed myself as a huge nerd, I guess that makes it obvious. I feel like I've read every fiction book in the little branch near me. The first place I went when I got my license was the central library downtown. I could live there."

"Where else?"

"In the summer, we'd go to the pool at Cactus Park. My mom had me in swimming lessons there before I could walk. There was always some story in the news about a toddler drowning, and it freaked her out. In the winter, we'd go to Roadrunner Park. It's not huge, but it had a little lake. We'd sail paper boats when I was a kid. Nothing very exciting, like I've been trying to tell you...."

"I think it sounds lovely. I don't remember much about my childhood."

Her teasing smile faded, and her eyebrows pulled together. "That must be difficult. And strange."

It was my turn to shrug. "It's all I know. Certainly nothing to worry about."

She was quiet for a long time, turning this over in her head.

I waited out her silence for as long I as could stand it before I finally asked, "What are you thinking?"

Her smile was more subdued now. "I have a lot of questions. But I know—"

We spoke the words simultaneously.

"Today is my day."

"Today is your day."

Our laughs were synchronized now, too, and I thought how strangely easy it was to be with her this way. Just close enough. The danger felt far away. I was so entertained I was nearly oblivious to the pain in my throat, though it was not dull. It just wasn't as interesting to think about as she was.

"Have I sold you on Phoenix yet?" she asked after another quiet moment.

"Perhaps I need a bit more persuasion."

She considered. "There's this one kind of acacia tree—I don't know what it's called. It looks like all the others, thorny, half-dead." Her expression was suddenly full of longing. "But in the springtime, it has these yellow fuzzy blossoms that look like pom-poms." She demonstrated the size, pretending to hold a blossom between her thumb and index finger. "They smell... amazing. Like nothing else. Really faint, delicate—you'll get a sudden hint of them in the breeze and then it's gone. I should have included them with my favorite scents. I wish someone would make a candle or something.

"And then the sunsets are incredible," she continued, switching subjects abruptly. "Seriously, you'll never see anything close here." She thought for another moment. "Even in the middle of the day, though, the *sky*—that's the main thing. It's not blue like the sky here—when you can even see it here. It's brighter, paler. Sometimes it's almost white. And it's everywhere." She emphasized her words with her hand, tracing an arc over her head. "There's so much more sky there. If you get away from the lights of the city a little bit, you can see a million stars." She smiled a wistful smile. "You really ought to check it out some night."

"It's beautiful to you."

She nodded. "It's not for everybody, I guess." She paused, thoughtful, but I could see that there was more, so I let her think.

"I like the . . . minimalism," she decided. "It's an honest sort of place. It doesn't hide anything."

I thought of everything that was hidden from her here, and I wondered if her words meant that she was aware of this, of the invisible darkness gathered around her. But she stared at me with no judgment in her eyes.

She didn't add anything more, and I thought by the way she was tucking her chin just slightly she might again be feeling like she was talking too much.

"You must miss it a great deal," I prompted.

Her expression didn't cloud over the way I half expected. "I did at first."

"But now?"

"I guess I'm used to it here." She smiled as though she was more than simply resigned to the forest and the rain.

"Tell me about your home there."

She shrugged. "It's nothing unusual. Stucco and tile, like I said. One story, three bedrooms, two baths. I miss my little bathroom most. Sharing with Charlie is stressful. Gravel and cactus outside. Everything inside is vintage seventies—wood paneling, linoleum, shag carpet, mustard Formica counters, the works. My mom's not big on renovations. She claims the dated stuff has character."

"What is your bedroom like?"

Her expression made me wonder if there was a joke I wasn't getting. "Now or when I lived there?"

"Now?"

"I think it's a yoga studio or something. My stuff is in the garage."

I stared, surprised. "What will you do when you go back?"

She didn't seem concerned. "We'll shove the bed back in somehow."

"Wasn't there a third bedroom?"

"That's her craft room. It would take an act of God to make space for a bed in there." She laughed blithely. I would have thought she'd be planning to spend more time with her mother, but she spoke as though her time in Phoenix was past rather than future. I recognized the feeling of relief this engendered but tried to keep it off my face.

"What was your room like when you lived there?"

A minor blush. "Um, messy. I'm not the most organized."

"Tell me about it."

Again she gave me the *you must be kidding* look, but when I didn't retract, she complied, miming the shapes with her hands.

"It's a narrow room. Twin bed on the south wall and dresser on the north under the window, with a pretty tight aisle in between. I did have a little walk-in closet, which would have been cool, if I could have kept it tidy enough to be able to actually walk into it. My room here is bigger and less of a disaster, but that's because I haven't been here long enough make a serious mess."

I made my face smooth, hiding the fact that I knew very well what her room was like here, and also my surprise that her room in Phoenix had been *more* cluttered.

"Um..." She looked to see if I wanted more, and I nodded to encourage her. "The ceiling fan is broken, just the light works, so I had a big noisy fan on top of the dresser. It sounds like a wind tunnel in the summer. But it's a lot better for sleep than the rain here. The sound of the rain isn't *consistent* enough."

The thought of rain had me glancing at the sky, and then being shocked by the dimness of the light. I couldn't understand the way time bent and compressed when I was with her. How was our allotment up already?

She misunderstood my preoccupation.

"Are you finished?" she asked, sounding relieved.

"Not even close," I told her. "But your father will be home soon."

"Charlie!" she gasped, as though she'd forgotten that he existed. "How late is it?" She looked at the dashboard clock as she asked.

I stared at the clouds—though they were thick, it was obvious where the sun must be behind them.

"It's twilight," I said. The time when vampires came out to play—when we never had to fear that a shifting cloud might cause us trouble—when we could enjoy the last remnants of light in the sky without worrying that we would be exposed.

I looked down to find her staring curiously at me, hearing more in my tone than just the words I'd spoken.

"It's the safest time of day for us," I explained. "The easiest time. But also the saddest, in a way...the end of another day, the return of the night." So many years of night. I tried to shake off the heaviness in my voice. "Darkness is so predictable, don't you think?"

"I like the night," she said, contrary as usual. "Without the dark, we'd never see the stars." A frown rearranged her features. "Not that you see them here much."

I laughed at her expression. So, still not entirely reconciled to Forks. I thought of the stars she'd described in Phoenix and wondered if they were like the stars in Alaska—so bright and clear and *close*. I wished that I could take her there tonight so we could make the comparison. But she had a normal life to lead.

"Charlie will be here in a few minutes," I told her. I could just hear a hint of his mind, perhaps a mile out, driving slowly this way. His mind was on her. "So, unless you want to tell him that you'll be with me Saturday..."

I understood that there were many reasons Bella wouldn't want to her father to know about our involvement. But I wished... not just because I needed that extra encouragement to keep her safe, not just because I thought the threat to my family would help control my monster. I wished she would... *want* her father to know me. Want me to be part of the normal life she led.

"Thanks, but no thanks," she said quickly.

Of course it was an impossible wish. Like so many others.

She started to organize her things as she prepared to leave. "So is it my turn tomorrow, then?" she asked. She glanced up at me with bright, curious eyes.

"Certainly not! I told you I wasn't done, didn't I?"

She frowned, confused. "What more is there?"

Everything. "You'll find out tomorrow."

Charlie was getting closer. I reached across her to open her door, and heard her heart start thumping loudly and unevenly. Our eyes met, and it *seemed* like an invitation again. Could I be allowed to touch her face, just one more time?

And then I froze, my hand on her door handle.

Another car was headed to the corner. It was not Charlie's; he was still two streets up, so I'd paid little attention to these unfamiliar thoughts heading, I assumed, to one of the other houses on the street.

But one word caught my attention now.

Vampires.

Ought to be safe enough for the boy. No reason to run into any vampires here, the mind thought, *even if this is neutral territory. I hope I was right to bring him into town.*

What were the odds?

"Not good," I breathed.

"What is it?" she asked, anxious as she processed the change in my face.

There was nothing I could do now. What rotten luck.

"Another complication," I admitted.

The car turned onto the short street, heading directly for Charlie's house. As the headlights lit up my car, I heard a young, enthusiastic reaction from the other mind inside the old Ford Tempo.

Wow. Is that an S60 R*? I've never seen one in real life before. Cool. Wonder who drives one of those around here? Custom-painted aftermarket front splitter... semi-slicks... That thing must tear the road up. I need to get a look at the exhaust....*

I didn't concentrate on the boy, though I'm sure I would have enjoyed the knowledgeable interest another day. I opened her door, throwing it wider than necessary, then I jerked away, leaning forward toward the oncoming lights, waiting.

"Charlie's around the corner," I warned her.

She jumped quickly out into the rain, but there wasn't any time for her to get inside before they saw us together. She slammed the door, but then hesitated there, staring at the oncoming vehicle.

The car parked facing mine, its headlights shining directly into my car.

And suddenly the older man's thoughts were screaming with shock and fear.

Cold one! Vampire! Cullen!

I stared out the windshield, meeting his gaze.

There was no way I would find any resemblance to his grandfather; I'd never seen Ephraim in his human form. But this would be Billy Black, no doubt, with his son Jacob.

As if to confirm my assumption, the boy leaned forward with a smile.

Oh, it's Bella!

A small part of me noted that, yes, she had definitely done some damage during her snooping in La Push.

But I was mostly focused on the father, the one who knew.

He was correct before—this was neutral territory. I had as much right to be here as he did, and he knew that. I could see it in the tightening of his frightened, angry face, the clenching of his jaw.

What is it doing here? What should I do?

We'd been in Forks for two years; no one had been harmed. But his horror couldn't have been stronger if we'd been slaughtering a new victim every day.

I glared at him, my lips pulling back just slightly from my teeth in an automatic response to his hostility.

It would not be helpful to antagonize him, though. Carlisle would be displeased if I did something to worry the old man. I could only hope that he adhered to our treaty better than his son had.

I peeled out, the boy appreciating the sound of my tires—only street legal by the smallest degree—as they squealed against the wet pavement. He turned to analyze the car's exhaust as I drove away.

I passed Charlie as I went around the next corner, slowing automatically as he noted my speed with a businesslike frown. He continued home, and I could hear the muffled surprise in his thoughts, wordless but clear, as he took in the car waiting in front of his house. He forgot all about the silver Volvo that had been speeding.

I stopped two streets up and left my car parked unobtrusively beside the forest between two wide-spaced lots. In seconds I was soaking wet, hidden in the thick branches of the spruce that overlooked her backyard, the same place I'd hidden on that first sunny day.

It was hard to follow Charlie. I didn't hear anything worrisome in his vague thoughts. Just enthusiasm—he must have been happy to see his visitors. Nothing had been said to upset him . . . yet.

Billy's head was a seething mass of questions as Charlie greeted him and ushered him inside. As far as I could tell, Billy hadn't made any decisions. I was glad to hear thoughts of the treaty mixed in with his agitation. Hopefully that would tie his tongue.

The boy followed Bella as she escaped to the kitchen—ah, his infatuation was clear in his every thought. But it was not hard to listen to his mind, the way it was with Mike Newton or her other admirers. There was something very…engaging about Jacob Black's mind. Pure and open. It reminded me a bit of Angela's, only not so demure. I felt suddenly sorry that this particular boy was born my enemy. His was the rare kind of mind that was easy to be inside. Restful, almost.

In the front room, Charlie had noticed Billy's abstraction, but did not ask. There was some strain between them—an old disagreement from long ago.

Jacob was asking Bella about me. Once he heard my name, he laughed.

"Guess that explains it, then," he said. "I wondered why my dad was acting so strange."

"That's right," Bella responded with overdone innocence. "He doesn't like the Cullens."

"Superstitious old man," the boy muttered.

Yes, we should have foreseen that it would be this way. Of course the young members of the tribe would see their history as myth—embarrassing, humorous, even more so because the elder members took it so seriously.

They rejoined their fathers in the front room. Bella's eyes were always on Billy while he and Charlie watched television. It looked as if, like me, she was waiting for a breach.

None came. The Blacks left before it was very late. It was a school night, after all. I followed them on foot back to the boundary line between our territories, just to be sure that Billy didn't ask his son to turn around. But his thoughts were still confused. There were names I didn't know, people he would consult with tonight. Even as he continued to panic, he knew what the other elders would say. Seeing a vampire face-to-face had unsettled him, but it changed nothing.

As they drove past the point where I could hear them, I felt fairly sure that there was no new danger. Billy would follow the rules. What choice did he have? If we broke the treaty, there was nothing the old men could actually do about it. They'd lost their teeth. If *they* broke the treaty...well, we were even stronger than before. Seven instead of five. Surely that would make them careful.

Though Carlisle would never allow us to enforce the treaty that way. Instead of heading directly back to Bella's house, I decided to make a detour to the hospital. My father had a late shift tonight.

I could hear his thoughts in the emergency ward. He was examining a delivery truck driver from Olympia with a deep puncture wound in his hand. I walked into the lobby, recognizing Jenny Austin at the desk. She was preoccupied with a call from her teenage daughter and barely acknowledged my wave as I passed her.

I didn't want to interrupt, so I just walked past the curtain Carlisle was hidden behind and then continued on to his office. He would recognize the sound of my footsteps—unaccompanied by a heartbeat—and then my scent. He would know I wanted to see him, and that it wasn't an emergency.

He joined me in his office only moments later.

"Edward? Is everything all right?"

"Yes. I just wanted you to know right away—Billy Black saw me at Bella's house tonight. He said nothing to Charlie, but..."

"Hmm," Carlisle said. *We've been here so long, it would be unfortunate if tensions arose again.*

"It's probably nothing. He just wasn't prepared to be two yards away from a *cold one*. The others will talk him down. After all, what can they do about it?"

Carlisle frowned. *You shouldn't think of it that way.* "Though they've lost their protectors, they are in no danger from us."

"No. Of course not."

He shook his head slowly, puzzling about the best course of action. There didn't seem to be one, other than ignoring this unlucky encounter. I'd already come to the same conclusion.

"Will you...be coming home soon?" Carlisle asked suddenly.

I felt ashamed as soon as he voiced his question. "Is Esme very upset with me?"

"Not upset *with* you…*about* you, yes." *She worries. She misses you.*

I sighed and nodded. Bella would be safe enough inside her house for a few hours. Probably. "I'll go home now."

"Thank you, Son."

I spent the evening with my mother, letting her fuss over me a bit. She made me change into dry clothes—more to protect the floors she'd spent so much time finishing than anything else. The others had cleared out, and I saw that this was her request; Carlisle had called ahead. I appreciated the quiet. We sat at the piano together and I played as we talked.

"How *are* you, Edward?" was her first question. It wasn't a casual query. She was anxious about my answer.

"I'm…not entirely sure," I told her honestly. "It's up and down."

She listened to the notes for a moment, occasionally touching a key that would harmonize with the tune.

She causes you pain.

I shook my head. "I cause my own pain. It's not her fault."

It's not your fault, either.

"I am what I am."

And that's not your fault.

I smiled humorlessly. "You blame Carlisle?"

No. Do you?

"No."

Then why blame yourself?

I didn't have a ready answer. Truly, I did not resent Carlisle for what he had done, and yet…didn't someone have to be to blame? Wasn't that person me?

I hate to see you suffer.

"It's not all suffering." Not yet.

This girl…she makes you happy?

I sighed. "Yes…when I'm not getting in my own way. She does indeed."

"Then that's all right." She seemed relieved.

My mouth twisted. "Is it?"

She was silent, her thoughts analyzing my answers, picturing Alice's face, thinking of her visions. She was aware of the wager and also that I knew about it. She was upset with Jasper and Rose.

What will it mean for him, if she dies?

I cringed, yanking my fingers off the keys.

"I'm sorry," she said swiftly. "I didn't mean to—"

I shook my head, and she fell silent. I stared at my hands, cold and sharp-angled, inhuman.

"I don't know how…," I whispered. "How I move past that. I can't see anything…nothing past that."

She put her arms around my shoulders, lacing her fingers together into a tight knot. "That's not going to happen. I know it won't."

"I wish I could be as sure."

I stared at her hands, so much like mine, but not. I couldn't hate them the same way. They were stone, too, but not…not a monster's hands. They were a mother's hands, kind and gentle.

I am sure. You won't hurt her.

"So you've placed your money with Alice and Emmett, I see."

She unlaced her fingers to smack me lightly on the shoulder. "This is not a joking matter."

"No, it isn't."

But when Jasper and Rosalie lose, I won't be angry if Emmett rubs it in a bit.

"I doubt he'll disappoint you there."

Nor will you disappoint me, Edward. Oh, my son, how I do love you. When the hard part is over…I'm going to be very happy, you know. I think I will love this girl.

I looked at her with raised eyebrows.

You wouldn't be so cruel as to keep her from me, would you?

"Now you sound just like Alice."

"I don't know why you fight her on anything. Easier to embrace the inevitable."

I frowned but started playing again. "You're right," I said after a moment. "I won't hurt her."

Of course you won't.

She kept her arms around me, and after a few moments I laid my head against the top of hers. She sighed, and hugged me tighter. It made me feel vaguely childlike. As I had told Bella, I didn't have memories of being a child, nothing concrete. But there was a kind of sense memory in the feeling of her arms around me. My first mother must have held me, too; it must have comforted me in the same way.

When the song was finished, I sighed and straightened up.

You'll go to her now?

"Yes."

She frowned, confused. *What do you do all night?*

I smiled. "Think . . . and burn. And listen."

She touched my throat. "I don't like that this causes you pain."

"That's the easiest part. It's nothing, really."

And the hardest part?

I thought about that for a minute. There were lots of answers that could be true, but one felt the *most* true.

"I think . . . that I can't be human with her. That the best version is the one that is impossible."

Her eyebrows pulled together.

"Everything will be all right, Esme." It was so easy for me to lie to her. I was the only one who could ever lie in this house.

Yes, it will be. She couldn't be in better hands.

I laughed, again without humor. But I would try to prove my mother right.

14. CLOSER

It was peaceful in Bella's room tonight. Even the fitful rain, which usually made her uneasy, did not disturb her. Despite the pain, I was peaceful, too—calmer than I'd been in my own home with my mother's arms around me. Bella mumbled my name in her sleep, as she often did, and smiled as she said it.

In the morning, Charlie mentioned her cheerful mood over breakfast, and it was my turn to smile. At least, if nothing else, I made her happy, too.

She climbed into my car quickly today, with a wide, eager smile, seeming just as hungry to be together as I was.

"How did you sleep?" I asked her.

"Fine. How was your night?"

I smiled. "Pleasant."

She pursed her lips. "Can I ask what you did?" I could imagine what my level of interest would be if I had to spend eight hours unconscious, totally unaware of her. But I wasn't ready to answer that question now...or maybe ever.

"No. Today is still mine."

She sighed and rolled her eyes. "I don't think there's anything I haven't told you."

"Tell me more about your mother."

It was one of my favorite subjects, because it was obviously one of hers.

"Okay. Um, my mom is kind of... wild, I guess? Not like a tiger is wild, like a sparrow, like a deer. She just, doesn't do well in cages? My gran—who was totally normal, by the way, and had no idea where my mom came from—used to call her a will-o'-the-wisp. I got the feeling that raising my mom through her teenage years was no cakewalk. Anyway, it's pretty hard for her to stay in one place very long. Getting to wander off with Phil with no sure end destination in mind... well, I think it's the happiest I've ever seen her. She tried really hard for me, though. Made do with weekend adventures and constantly switching jobs. I did what I could to free her from all the mundane stuff. I imagine Phil will do the same. I feel like... kind of a bad daughter. Because I'm a little relieved, you know?" She made an apologetic face, turning her palms up. "She doesn't have to stay in place for me anymore. That's a weight off. And then Charlie... I never thought about him needing me, but he really does. That house is too empty for him."

I nodded thoughtfully, sifting through this mine of information. I wished I could meet this woman who had shaped so much of Bella's character. Part of me would have preferred that Bella had an easier, more traditional childhood—that she could have gotten to be the child. But she wouldn't have been the same person, and truly, she didn't seem resentful in any way. She liked to be the caretaker, liked to be needed.

Perhaps this was the real secret as to why she was drawn to me. Had anyone ever needed her more?

I left her at her classroom door, and the morning passed much as the day before. Alice and I sleepwalked our way through Gym. I watched Bella's face through Jessica Stanley's eyes again, noting, as the human girl did, how very little of Bella seemed to be in the classroom at all.

I wonder why Bella doesn't want to talk about it? Jessica wondered. *Keeping him to herself, I guess. Unless she was telling the truth before, and there's nothing actually happening.* Her mind ran over Bella's denials on Wednesday morning—*It's not like that*, when Jessica had asked about kissing—and her inference that Bella had looked disappointed.

That would be like torture, Jessica thought now. *Look but don't touch.*

The word startled me.

Like *torture*? Obviously an exaggeration, but...would such a thing actually cause Bella pain—no matter how minor? Surely not, knowing as she did the realities of the situation. I frowned and caught Alice's questioning glance. I shook my head at her.

She looks happy enough, Jessica was thinking, watching Bella as she stared through the clerestory windows with unfocused eyes. *She must have been lying to me. Or there have been new developments.*

Oh! Alice's sudden stillness alerted me at the same time as her mental exclamation. The picture in her mind was of the cafeteria at some near future date and...

Well, it's about time! she thought, breaking into a huge grin.

The pictures developed—Alice standing behind my shoulder in the cafeteria today, across the table from Bella. The very brief introduction. How it began was not yet fixed. It wavered, dependent on some other factor. But it would be soon, if not today.

I sighed, absently swatting the birdie back across the net. It flew better than it would have had my attention been focused; I scored a point as the coach blew his whistle to end class. Alice was already moving toward the door.

Don't be such a baby. It's not much. And I can already see that you won't stop me.

I closed my eyes and shook my head. "No, it *won't* be very much," I agreed quietly as we walked together.

"I can be patient. Baby steps."

I rolled my eyes.

It was always a relief when I could leave the secondary vantage points behind and just see Bella for myself, but I was still thinking about Jessica's assumptions when Bella came through the classroom door. She smiled a wide, warm smile, and it looked to me, too, like she was very happy. I shouldn't worry about impossibilities when they weren't bothering her.

There was one line of questions that I had been reluctant to open thus far. But with Jessica's thoughts still in my head, I was suddenly more curious than I was averse.

We sat at what was now our usual table, and she picked at the food I'd gotten for her—I'd been quicker than her today.

"Tell me about your first date," I said.

Her eyes got bigger, and her cheeks flushed. She hesitated.

"You're not going to tell me?"

"I'm just not sure... what actually counts."

"Put the qualifications at their lowest setting," I suggested.

She stared toward the ceiling, thinking with her lips pursed. "Well, then I guess that would be Mike—a different Mike," she said quickly when my expression changed. "He was my square-dancing partner in the sixth grade. I was invited to his birthday party—it was a movie." She smiled. "The second *Mighty Ducks*. I was the only one who showed up. Later, people said it was a date. I don't know who started that rumor."

I'd seen the school pictures in her father's house, so I had a mental reference for eleven-year-old Bella. It sounded like things weren't so different for her then. "That's perhaps setting the bar a little too low."

She grinned. "You said the lowest setting."

"Continue, then."

Her lips twisted to the side as she considered. "A few friends were going to the ice rink with some boys. They needed me to even up the numbers. I wouldn't have gone if I'd realized that it meant I was matched up with Reed Merchant." She shuddered delicately. "And of course, I figured out pretty quickly that ice skating was a bad idea. My injuries were minor, but the plus side was that I got to sit by the snack bar and read for the rest of the night." She smiled, almost... triumphantly.

"Shall we skip to an actual date?"

"You mean like, someone asked me out in advance and then we went someplace alone together?"

"That sounds like a workable definition."

She smiled the same triumphant smile. "Sorry, then, I've got nothing."

I frowned. "No one ever asked you out on a date before you came here? Really?"

"I'm not totally sure. Is it a date? Is it just friends hanging out?" She shrugged. "Not that it mattered much. I never had time for either. After a while the word gets around, and no one asks again."

"Were you actually busy? Or making excuses like you do here?"

"Actually busy," she insisted, a little offended. "Running a house is time-consuming, and I usually had a part-time job, too, not to mention school. If I'm going to get to college, I'm going to need a full-ride scholarship, and—"

"Hold that thought," I interrupted. "Before we move on to the next subject, I'd like to finish this one. If you hadn't been so busy, were any of these invitations ones you would have liked to accept?"

She tilted her head to the side. "Not really. I mean, other than just to have a night out. They weren't particularly interesting boys."

"And other boys? Who didn't ask?"

She shook her head, her clear eyes appearing to hide nothing. "I wasn't paying that much attention."

My eyes narrowed. "So you never met anyone you wanted?"

She sighed again. "Not in Phoenix."

We stared at each other for a moment while I processed the fact that, just as she was my first love, according to this I was also her first...infatuation at the very least. This alignment pleased me in some strange way, but also troubled me. Surely this was a warped, unhealthy way for her to begin her romantic life. And then there was the knowledge that she would be both first and last for me. It would not be the same for a human heart.

"I know it's not my day, but—"

"No, it's not."

"C'mon," she insisted. "I just spilled my entire embarrassing lack-of-dating history."

I smiled. "Mine is quite similar, actually—minus the ice-skating and trick birthday parties. I haven't been paying much attention, either."

She looked like she didn't quite believe me, but it was true. I'd also had a few offers I'd turned down. Not quite the same kind of offers, I admitted to myself, picturing Tanya's pouting face.

"Which college would you like to go to?" I asked.

"Um..." She shook her head just slightly, as if to adjust to the new subject. "Well, I used to think ASU was the most practical, because I could live at home. But with Mom moving around now, I guess my field is more open. It will have to be a state school—something reasonable—even with a scholarship. When I first came here...well, I was glad that Charlie doesn't live close enough to Washington State to make *that* practical."

"Are you disparaging our fine state's Cougars?"

"Nothing against the institution—just the weather."

"And if you could go anywhere—if the cost were no object—where would you go?"

While she considered my question about this hypothetical future, I tried to picture a future that *I* could live with. Bella at twenty, at twenty-two, twenty-four...how long before she outgrew me, unchanging as I was? I would accept that time limit if it meant that she could be healthy and human and happy. If only I could make myself safe for her, right for her, make myself fit into that happy picture for every second of the time that she allowed me.

I wondered again how I could make this happen—be with her without negatively impacting her life. Stay in Persephone's spring, keep her safe from my underworld.

It was easy to see that she wouldn't be happy in my usual haunts. Obviously. But as long as she wanted me, I would follow her. It would mean many slow days indoors, but that was such a negligible price, it was barely worth noting.

"I'd have to do some research. Most of the fancy schools are in the snow zone." She grinned. "I wonder what colleges in Hawaii are like?"

"Lovely, I'm sure. And after school? What then?" I realized how important it was for me to know *her* plans for the future. So I didn't derail them. So I could shape this unlikely future into the best version to suit her.

"Something with books. I always thought I would teach like—well, not *exactly* like my mom. If I could... I'd like to teach on a college level somewhere—probably a community college. Elective English classes—so that everyone who's signed up is there because they want to be."

"Is that what you've always wanted?"

She shrugged. "Mostly. I once thought of working for a publisher—as an editor or something." Her nose wrinkled. "I did some research. It's a lot easier to get a job as a teacher. Much more practical."

Her dreams all had clipped wings—not like those of the usual teenager off to conquer the world. Obviously a product of facing realities long before she should have had to.

She took a bite of her bagel, chewing thoughtfully. I wondered if she was still thinking of the future, or something else. I wondered whether she saw any glimpse of me in that future.

My mind strayed to tomorrow. It should have thrilled me—the idea of a whole day with her. So much time. But I could only think of the moment when she would see what I really was. When I could no longer hide behind my human façade. I tried to imagine her response, and though I was so often wrong when trying to predict her feelings, I knew it could only go two ways. The only valid reaction besides revulsion would be terror.

I wanted to believe that there was a third possibility. That she would forgive what I was as she had done so often in the past. That she would accept me despite everything. But I couldn't picture it.

Would I have the nerve to keep my promise? Could I live with myself if I hid this from her?

I thought of the first time I'd seen Carlisle in the sun. I was very young then, still obsessed with blood over anything else, but that sight had caught my attention the way little else had. Though I trusted Carlisle utterly, though I'd already begun to love him, I felt fear. It was all too impossible, too alien. The instinct to defend myself was triggered, and it was several long moments before his calm and reassuring thoughts could have any effect on me. Eventually he talked me into stepping forward myself, to see that the phenomenon did no harm.

And I remembered seeing myself in the brilliant morning light and realizing—more profoundly than I ever had thus far—that I had no relationship at all to my former self. That I was not human.

But it wasn't fair to hide myself from her. It was a lie of omission.

I tried to see her with me in the meadow, what the picture would look like if I weren't a monster. It was such a beautiful, peaceful place. How I wished she could enjoy it with me still there.

Edward, Alice thought urgently, a hint of panic in her tone that froze me in place.

Suddenly, I was caught up in one of Alice's visions, staring into a bright circle of sunlight. Disorienting, because I'd just been imagining myself and Bella there—the little meadow where no one ever went besides me—so I wasn't sure at first that I was seeing inside Alice's mind and not my own.

But it was different from my own picture—future, not past. Bella stared at me, rainbows dancing across her face, her eyes fathomless. So I *was* brave enough.

It's the same place, Alice thought, her mind full of a horror that did not match the vision. Tension, perhaps, but horror? What did she mean, *the same place*?

And then I saw it.

Edward! Alice protested shrilly. *I love her, Edward!*

But she didn't love Bella the way I did. Her vision was preposterous. Wrong. She was blinded somehow, seeing impossibilities. Lies.

Not even a half a second had passed. Bella was still chewing, thinking about some mystery I would never know. She wouldn't have seen the quick flash of dread across my face.

It was just an old vision. No longer valid. Everything had changed since then.

Edward, we have *to talk.*

There was nothing for Alice and me to talk about. I shook my head ever so slightly, just once. Bella didn't see.

Alice's thoughts were a command now. She shoved the picture I couldn't bear back into the forefront of my mind.

I love her, Edward. I won't let you just ignore this. We're leaving, and we're going to work this through. I'll give you till the end of the period. Make your excuses—oh!

Her totally benign vision from this morning in Gym interrupted her string of orders. The brief introduction. I saw exactly how it would happen now, down to the second. So this offensive, invalid, outdated vision was the catalyst missing before? My teeth clenched together.

Fine. We would talk. I would sacrifice my time with Bella this afternoon to show Alice how wrong she was. In truth, I knew I wouldn't be able to rest until I'd made her see that, made her admit she was off this time.

She saw the future shift as my mind changed. *Thank you.*

Odd, given the sudden life and death turn to my afternoon, how crushing it was to lose the time I'd counted on. It should be such a small thing—just a few minutes, really.

I tried to shake off the horror that Alice had inflicted on me so that I wouldn't ruin the minutes I had left.

"I should have let you drive yourself today," I said, working hard to keep the desperation out of my voice.

Her eyes snapped up to mine. She swallowed. "Why?"

"I'm leaving with Alice after lunch."

"Oh." Her face fell. "That's okay, it's not that far of a walk."

I frowned. "I'm not going to make you walk home." Did she really think I would leave her stranded? "We'll go get your truck and leave it here for you."

"I don't have my key with me," she said, and sighed. This was some huge, insurmountable obstacle to her. "I really don't mind walking."

"Your truck will be here, and the key will be in the ignition," I told her. "Unless you're afraid someone might steal it." The sound of her engine was as good as a car alarm. Possibly louder. I forced a laugh at the mental image, but the sound was off.

Bella pursed her lips and her eyes went opaque. "All right," she said. Was she doubting my abilities?

I tried to smile confidently—I *was* confident that I could not fail in such a simple task—but my muscles were too tight to manage it correctly. She didn't seem to notice. It looked like she was dealing with her own disappointment.

"So," she said. "Where are you going?"

Alice showed me the answer to Bella's question.

"Hunting." I could hear that my voice was suddenly darker. It was something I would have found time for, regardless. The necessity of this excursion was as frustrating as it was shameful. But I wouldn't lie to her about it.

"If I'm going to be alone with you tomorrow, I'm going to take whatever precautions I can." I stared into her eyes, wondering if she could see the fear in my own. Alice's vision was overpowering my composure. "You can always cancel, you know." *Please, walk away. Don't turn back.*

She looked down, her face blanching paler than before. Would she finally listen? Alice's vision would mean nothing if Bella told me now to leave her alone. I knew I could do it, if it was what Bella asked for. My heart felt poised to rip in half.

"No," she whispered, and my heart twisted in another direction. A worse kind of breaking loomed. She stared up at me. "I can't."

"Perhaps you're right," I whispered. Maybe she was, after all, just as bound as I was.

She leaned toward me, her eyes tightening with what looked like concern. "What time will I see you tomorrow?"

I took a deep breath, trying to settle myself, to shake off the sense of doom. I forced myself to speak in a lighter tone. "That depends... it's a Saturday, don't you want to sleep in?"

"No," she shot back immediately.

It made me want to smile. "The same time as usual, then. Will Charlie be there?"

She grinned. "No, he's fishing tomorrow." This obviously pleased her as much as her attitude about it angered me. Why was she determined to put herself so wholly at my mercy—at the mercy of the worst part of me?

"And if you don't come home?" I asked through my teeth. "What will he think?"

Her face was smooth. "I have no idea. He knows I've been meaning to do laundry. Maybe he'll think I fell in the washer."

I glared at her—I did not find her joke humorous in the slightest. She scowled back for a moment, and then her face relaxed.

She changed the subject. "What are you hunting tonight?"

It was so strange. On the one hand, she didn't seem to take the danger seriously at all. On the other, she was so calm in accepting the ugliest facets of my life.

"Whatever we find in the park. We aren't going far."

"Why are you going with Alice?"

Alice was listening intently now.

I frowned. "Alice is the most... supportive." There were other words I'd like to say for Alice's benefit, but they would only confuse Bella.

"And the others?" Bella nearly whispered, her voice shifting from curious to anxious. "What are they?" She would be horrified if she knew how easily they could all hear that whisper.

There were also many ways to answer this question. I chose the least frightening. "Incredulous, for the most part." They were definitely that.

Her eyes darted to the back corner of the cafeteria, where my family sat. Alice had warned them, and they were all looking elsewhere.

"They don't like me," she guessed.

"That's not it," I quickly countered.

Ha! Rosalie thought.

"They don't understand why I can't leave you alone," I continued, trying to ignore Rose.

Well, that's true enough.

Bella made a face. "Neither do I, for that matter."

I shook my head, thinking of her ridiculous assumption before—that I didn't care for her as much as she cared for me. I thought I'd explained this.

"I told you—you don't see yourself clearly at all. You're not like anyone I've ever known. You fascinate me."

She looked doubtful. Maybe I needed to be more specific.

I smiled at her. Despite everything on my mind, it was important for her to understand this. "Having the advantages I do . . ." I brushed two of my fingers casually across my forehead. "I have a better than average grasp of human nature. People are predictable. But you . . . you never do what I expect. You always take me by surprise."

She glanced away from me, and there was something unsatisfied about her expression. This specific detail had obviously not convinced her.

"That part is easy enough to explain," I continued quickly, waiting for her eyes to return to me. "But there's more. . . ." So much more. "And it's not so easy to put into words—"

Goggle at me, *will you, you bat-faced little nuisance?*

Bella's face went white. She looked frozen, as though she couldn't look away from the back corner of the room.

I turned quickly and shot Rosalie a threatening glare, my lips pulling away from my teeth. I hissed quietly at her.

She flashed a glance at me from the corner of her eye, then angled her head away from us both. I looked back to Bella just as she turned to stare at me.

She started it, Rosalie thought sullenly.

Bella's eyes were huge.

"I'm sorry about that," I murmured quickly. "She's just worried." It irritated me to have to defend Rosalie's behavior, but I couldn't think of another way to explain. And at the heart of Rosalie's hostility, this *was* the true issue. "You see... it's dangerous for more than just me if, after spending so much time with you so publicly..."

I couldn't finish. Filled with horror and shame, I stared down at my hands—the hands of a monster.

"If?" she prompted.

How could I not answer her now?

"If this ends... badly."

My head fell into my palms. I didn't want to see her eyes as understanding dawned, as she realized what I was saying. For all this time, I'd been trying to earn her trust. And now I'd had to tell her exactly how much I didn't deserve it.

It was right to have her know. This would be the moment when she would walk away. And that was good. My first, instinctive rejection of Alice's panic was wearing off. I couldn't honestly promise Bella that I was no danger to her.

"And you have to leave now?"

I looked up at her slowly.

Her face was calm—there was a hint of sorrow in the pucker mark between her brows, but no fear at all. The perfect trust I'd seen when she'd jumped into my car in Port Angeles was evident again in her eyes. Though I didn't deserve it, she still trusted me.

"Yes," I told her.

My answer made her frown. She should have been only relieved to see me go, but instead, she was sad.

I wished I could smooth away the little *v* between her eyebrows with my fingertip. I wanted her to smile again.

I forced myself to grin at her. "It's probably for the best. We still have fifteen minutes of that wretched movie left to endure in Biology—I don't think I could take any more."

I guessed that this was true—that I would not have been able to endure. That I would have made more mistakes.

She smiled back, and it was obvious that she understood at least part of what I meant.

Then she jumped slightly in her seat, startled.

I heard Alice step up behind me. I was not surprised. I'd seen this part before.

"Alice," I greeted her.

Her excited smile was reflected in Bella's eyes.

"Edward," she responded, copying my tone.

I followed my script.

"Alice, Bella," I said, introducing them as concisely as possible. I kept my eyes on Bella and gestured halfheartedly with one hand. "Bella, Alice."

"Hello, Bella. It's nice to *finally* meet you."

The emphasis was subtle, but annoying. I shot her a quick glare.

"Hi, Alice," Bella answered, her voice unsure.

I won't push my luck, Alice promised. "Are you ready?" she asked me aloud.

As if she didn't know my answer. "Nearly. I'll meet you at the car."

I'll get out of your way now. Thanks.

Bella stared after Alice, a small frown curving her lips downward. When Alice disappeared through the doors, she turned slowly to face me.

"Should I say 'Have fun,' or is that the wrong sentiment?" she asked.

I smiled at her. "No, 'Have fun' works as well as anything."

"Have fun, then," she said, a little forlorn.

"I'll try." But that wasn't true. I would only be missing her while I was away. "And you try to be safe, please." It didn't matter how often I had to say goodbye, the same panic returned whenever I thought of her unprotected.

"Safe in Forks," she mumbled. "What a challenge."

"For you it *is* a challenge," I pointed out. "Promise?"

She sighed, but her smile was good-humored. "I promise to try to be safe," she said. "I'll do the laundry tonight—that ought to be fraught with peril."

I didn't enjoy the reminder of the earlier part of our conversation. "Don't fall in."

She tried to keep her face serious, and failed. "I'll do my best."

It was so hard to leave. I made myself stand. She rose to her feet, too.

"I'll see you tomorrow," she sighed.

"It seems like a long time to you, doesn't it?" Strange what a long time it seemed to me, too.

She nodded, dejected.

"I'll be there in the morning," I promised.

Alice was right about this much—I wasn't finished making mistakes. I couldn't stop myself again as I leaned across the table and brushed my fingers along her cheekbone. Before I could do any more harm, I turned and left her there.

Alice was waiting in the car.

"Alice—"

First things first. We have an errand to run, don't we?

Pictures of Bella's house flashed through her mind. An empty set of hooks—designed to hold keys—on the kitchen wall. Me in Bella's room, scanning her dresser top and desk. Alice literally following her nose through the front room. Alice again, in a small laundry room, grinning, with a key in her hand.

I drove quickly to Bella's. I would have been able to find the key myself—the smell of metal was easy enough to trace, particularly metal painted with the oils from her fingers—but Alice's way was definitely faster.

The images refined. Alice would go in alone, I saw, through the front door. She decided a dozen different places to look for an extra house key, then located it when she resolved to check under the eaves over the front door.

When we arrived at the house, it took Alice only seconds to follow the course she'd already set for herself. After locking the front door's handle but leaving the deadbolt unlatched as she'd found it, Alice climbed into Bella's truck. The engine grumbled to life with the volume of a thunderclap. There was no one home to notice it now.

The trip back to school was slower, hampered by the maximum speed the old Chevy was able to produce. I wondered how Bella could stand it, but then she seemed to prefer driving slowly. Alice parked in the space my Volvo had left open, and shut the noisy engine off.

I looked at the rusty behemoth, imagining Bella in it. It had survived Tyler's van with barely a scratch, but obviously there were no airbags or crumple zones. I felt my eyebrows pull together.

Alice climbed into my passenger seat.

Here, she thought. She held out a piece of stationery and a pen.

I took them from her. "I'll concede that you're useful."

You couldn't survive without me.

I wrote a brief note, then darted out to leave it on the driver's seat of Bella's truck. I knew there was no real power to the action, but hopefully it would remind her of her promise. It did make me feel just a little bit less anxious.

15. PROBABILITY

"Now, Alice," I began as I shut my door.

She sighed. *I'm sorry. I wish I didn't have to—*

"It's not *real*," I interrupted, accelerating away from the parking lot. I didn't have to think about the road. I knew it too well. "It's just an old vision. Before everything. Before I knew I loved her."

In her head, it was there again, that worst of all visions—the agonizing potential that had tortured me for so many weeks, the future Alice had seen the day I'd pushed Bella out of the way of the van.

Bella's body in my arms, twisted and white and lifeless...a ragged, blue-edged gash across her broken neck...her blood red on my lips and blazing crimson in my eyes.

The vision in Alice's memory brought a furious snarl ripping up my throat—an involuntary response to the pain that lashed through me.

Alice froze, her eyes anxious.

It's the same place, Alice had realized today in the cafeteria, her thoughts tinged with a horror I hadn't understood at first.

I'd never looked beyond the ghastly central image—I could barely stand to see that much. But Alice had been examining her visions for decades longer than I. She knew how to remove her feelings from the equation, how to be impartial, how to look at the picture without flinching away from it.

Alice had been able to absorb details...like the scenery.

The gruesome tableau was set in the same meadow where I planned to take Bella tomorrow.

"It *can't* still be valid. You didn't *see* it again, you just remembered it."

Alice shook her head slowly.

It's not just a memory, Edward. I see it now.

"We'll go somewhere else."

In her head, backgrounds to her vision spun like whirling kaleidoscopes, changing from bright to dark and back. The foreground remained the same. I cringed away from the pictures, trying to push them from my mental eye, wishing I could blind it.

"I'll cancel," I said through my teeth. "She's forgiven my broken promises before."

The vision shimmered, wavered, and then returned to solidity, with sharp, clear edges.

Her blood is so strong to you, Edward. As you get closer to her...

"I'll go back to keeping my distance."

"I don't think that will work. It didn't before."

"I'll leave."

She flinched at the agony in my voice, and the picture in her head shivered again. The seasons changed, but the central figures remained.

"It's still there, Edward."

"How can that *be*?" I snarled.

"Because if you leave, you will come back," she said, her voice implacable.

"No," I said. "I can stay away. I know I can."

"You can't," she said calmly. "Maybe...if it was just your own pain..."

Her mind raced through a flipbook of futures. Bella's face from a thousand different angles, always tinted gray, sunless.

She was thinner, unfamiliar hollows beneath her cheekbones, deep circles under her eyes, her expression empty. One could call it lifeless—but it would only be a metaphor. Not like the other visions.

"What's wrong? Why is she like that?"

"Because you've left. She's not…doing well."

I hated it when Alice spoke like that, in her strange present-future tense, which made it sound like the tragedy was happening right now.

"Better than other options," I said.

"Do you really think you could leave her like that? Do you think you wouldn't come back to check? Do you think when you saw her that way, you would be able to keep from speaking?"

As she asked her questions, I saw the answers in her head. Myself in the shadows, watching. Creeping back to Bella's room. Seeing her suffer through a nightmare, curled into a ball, her arms tight around her chest, gasping for air even in her sleep. Alice curled in on herself, too, wrapping her arms tensely around her knees in sympathy.

Of course Alice was right. I felt an echo of the emotions that I would feel then, in this version of the future, and I knew I would come back—just to check. And then, when I saw this…I would wake her. I would not be able to watch her suffer.

The futures realigned into the same inevitable vision, only delayed a bit.

"I should never have come back," I whispered.

What if I'd never learned to love her? What if I hadn't known what I was missing?

Alice was shaking her head.

There were things I saw, while you were away….

I waited for her to show me, but she was focusing very hard on just looking at my face now. Trying *not* to show me.

"What things? What did you see?"

Her eyes were pained. *They weren't pleasant things. At some point—if you hadn't come back when you did, if you'd never loved her—you would have come back for her anyway. To... hunt her.*

Still no pictures, but I didn't need them to understand. I reeled away from her, nearly losing control of the car. I stomped on the brake, and pulled off the road. The tires tore into the ferns and threw patches of moss onto the pavement.

The thought had been there, in the very beginning, when the monster was nearly unbridled. That there was no guarantee that I wouldn't eventually follow her, wherever she might go.

"Give me something that will work!" I exploded. Alice cringed away from the volume. "Tell me another path! Show me how to stay away—where to go!"

In her thoughts, suddenly another vision replaced the first. A gasp of relief choked through my lips when the horror was removed. But this vision was not much better.

Alice and Bella, arms around each other, both marble white and diamond hard.

One too many pomegranate seeds, and she was bound to the underworld with me. No way back. Springtime, sunlight, family, future, soul, all stolen from her.

It's sixty-forty...ish. Maybe even sixty-five-thirty-five. There's still a good chance you won't kill her. Her tone was one of encouragement.

"She's dead, either way," I whispered. "I'll stop her heart."

"That's not exactly what I meant. I'm telling you that she has futures beyond the meadow...but first she has to go through the meadow—the metaphorical meadow—if you catch my meaning."

Her thoughts...it was difficult to describe...*widened* out as if she was thinking everything at the same time—and I could see a tangle of threads, each thread a long line of frozen images, each thread a future told in snapshots, all of them snared together in a messy knot.

"I don't understand."

All her paths are leading to one point—all her paths are knotted together. Whether that point is in the meadow, or somewhere else, she's tied to that moment of decision. Your decision, her decision.... Some of the threads continue on the other side. Some...

"Do not." My voice faltered through my tight throat.

You can't avoid it, Edward. You're going to have to face it. Knowing it could easily go either way, you still have to face it.

"How do I save her? Tell me!"

"I don't know. You'll have to find the answer yourself, in the knot. I can't see exactly what form it will take, but there will be a moment, I think—a test, a trial. I can see that, but I can't help you with it. Only the two of you can choose in that moment."

My teeth ground together.

You know that I love you, so listen to me now. Putting this off won't change anything. Take her to your meadow, Edward, and—for me, and especially for you—bring her back again.

I let my head fall into my hands. I felt sick—like a damaged human, a victim of disease.

"How about some good news?" Alice asked gently.

I glared up at her. She smiled a small smile.

Seriously.

"Tell me, then."

"I've seen a third way, Edward," she said. "If you can get through the crisis, there's a new path out there."

"A new path?" I echoed blankly.

"It's sketchy. But look."

Another picture in her head. Not as sharp as the others. A trio in the cramped front room of Bella's house. I was on the aged sofa, Bella beside me, my arm casually slung around her shoulders. Alice sat on the floor beside Bella, leaning against her leg in a familiar fashion. Alice and I were exactly the same as we always were, but this was a version of Bella I'd never seen before. Her skin was still soft and translucent, pink across the cheeks, healthy. Her eyes were still warm and brown and human. But she was different. I analyzed the changes, and realized what I was seeing.

Bella was not a girl, but a woman. Her legs looked a little longer, as if she'd grown an inch or two, and her body had rounded subtly, giving a new curvature to her slender frame. Her hair was sable-dark, as if she'd spent little time in the sun during the intervening years. Not many years, maybe three or four. But she was still human.

Joy and pain washed through me. She was still human; she was aging. This was the desperate, unlikely future that was the only one I could live with. The future that did not cheat her of either life or afterlife. The future that would take her away from me someday, as inevitably as day turned to night.

"It's still not very probable, but I thought you'd like to know it was there. If you two get through the crisis, this is out there."

"Thank you, Alice," I whispered.

I put the car into drive, and pulled onto the road again, cutting off a minivan chugging along under the limit. I accelerated automatically, barely registering the process.

Of course, this is all you, she thought. She was still picturing the unlikely trio on the sofa. *This doesn't take her wishes into account.*

"What do you mean? Her wishes?"

"Did it never occur to you that Bella might not be willing to lose you? That one short mortal life might not be long enough for her?"

"That's insanity. No one would choose—"

"No need to argue about it now. Crisis first."

"Thanks, Alice," I said again, caustically this time.

She trilled a laugh. It was a nervous sound, birdlike. She was every bit as on edge as I was, almost as horrified by the tragic possibilities.

"I know you love her, too," I muttered.

It's not the same.

"No, it isn't."

After all, Alice had Jasper. She had the center of her universe safely at her side—even more indestructible than most. And his soul was not on her conscience. She had brought Jasper nothing but happiness and peace.

I love you. You can do this.

I wanted to believe her, but I knew when her words were built on sure foundations, and when they were no more than ordinary hope.

I drove in silence to the edge of the national park and found an inconspicuous place to leave the car. Alice didn't move when the car stopped. She could see that I would need a moment.

I closed my eyes and tried not to hear her, not to hear anything, to really focus my thoughts toward a decision. A resolution. I pressed my fingertips hard against my temples.

Alice said I would have to make a choice. I wanted to scream out loud that I'd already decided, that there was no decision, but even though it felt as though my whole being yearned for nothing but Bella's safety, I knew the monster was still alive.

How did I kill it? Silence it forever?

Oh, he was quiet now. Hiding. Saving his strength for the fight that was coming.

For a few moments, I thought seriously about killing myself. It was the only way I knew to be sure that the monster didn't survive.

But how? Carlisle had exhausted most of the possibilities in the beginning of his new life, and had never come close to ending his own story, despite his very real determination to do so. I would have no success acting alone.

Any of my family would be capable of doing it for me, but I knew that none of them would, no matter how I begged. Even Rosalie, who I'm sure would claim to be angry enough to do it, who might bluster and threaten the next time I saw her, would not. Because even though she sometimes hated me, she always loved me. And I knew if I could trade places with any of them, I would feel and act exactly the same way. I would not be able to harm any of my family, no matter how much pain they were in, no matter how much they wanted out.

There were others.... But Carlisle's friends wouldn't help me. They would never betray him so. I could think of one place I might go with the power to end the monster very quickly... but doing that would put Bella in danger. Though I'd not been the one to tell her the truth about myself, she knew things she was forbidden to know. It was nothing that would ever bring her the wrong kind of attention, unless I did something stupid, like go to Italy.

It was too bad the Quileute treaty was toothless these days. Three generations ago, all I would have had to do was walk to La Push. A useless idea now.

So those ways of killing the monster weren't possible.

Alice seemed so sure that I had to go forward, to meet this head-on. But how could that be the right thing to do, when the possibility that I would kill Bella existed?

I flinched. The idea was so painful, I couldn't imagine how the monster could get past my aversion to overcome me. He didn't give anything away, just silently bided his time.

I sighed. Was there any choice *but* to face this head-on? Did it count as courage if one was compelled? I was sure it did not.

All I could do, it seemed, was cling to my decision with both hands, with all my strength. I would be stronger than my monster. I would not hurt Bella. I would do the most right thing that was left to me. I would be who she needed me to be.

And then suddenly, as I thought those words, it didn't feel so impossible. Of course I could do that. I could be the Edward that Bella wanted, that she needed. I could grasp hold of that one sketchy future I could live with, and then will it into being. For Bella. Of course I could do that, if it was for her.

It felt stronger, this decision. Clearer. I opened my eyes and looked at Alice.

"Ah. That looks better," she said. In her head, the tangle of threads was still a hopelessly confusing maze to me, but she saw more in it than I did. "Seventy-thirty. Whatever you're thinking, keep thinking it."

Perhaps just accepting the immediate future was the key. Facing it. Not underestimating my own evil. Bracing for it. Preparing.

I could do the most basic preparation now. This was why we were here.

Alice saw my action before I took it, and she was out her door and running before I had opened my own. I felt a shallow sensation of humor and almost smiled. She could never outrun me; she always tried to cheat.

And then I was running, too.

This way, Alice thought when I'd nearly caught up. Her mind was ranging ahead, looking for quarry. But while I caught the scent of several nearby options, clearly they weren't what she wanted. She disregarded everything she saw.

I wasn't exactly sure what she was searching so minutely for, but I followed her unhesitatingly. She ignored a few more flocks of deer, leading me deeper into the forest, angling south. I saw her searching ahead, seeing us in different corners of the park—all of them familiar. She drifted east, starting to curve north again. What was she looking for?

And then her thoughts settled on a slinking movement in the brush, glimpses of a tawny hide.

"Thanks, Alice, but—"

Shh! I'm hunting.

I rolled my eyes, but continued following her. She was trying to do something nice for me. There was no way for her to know how little it all mattered. I'd been force-feeding myself so much lately I doubted I would notice the difference between a lion and a rabbit.

It didn't take us long to find her vision, now that she was focused on it. Once the movements of the animal were audible, Alice slowed to let me take the lead.

"I really shouldn't, the park's lion population—"

Alice's mental tone was exasperated. *Live a little.*

There never was much point in fighting with Alice. I shrugged and passed her. I'd caught the scent now. It was easy to shift into another mode—just let the blood pull me forward as I stalked my prey.

It was relaxing to stop thinking for a few minutes. Just to be another predator—the apex predator. I heard Alice head east, searching for her own meal.

The lion hadn't noticed me yet. He, too, was heading east on his own search, looking for something to hunt. Some other animal's day would end better, thanks to me.

I was on him in a second. Unlike Emmett, I saw no point in giving the beast a chance to fight back. It would make no difference, and wasn't it more humane to do it quickly? I snapped the lion's neck and then quickly drained the warm body. I wasn't that thirsty to begin with, so there wasn't any real relief tied to the action. Force-feeding again.

When I was done, I followed Alice's scent north. She'd found a sleeping doe, bedded down in a nest of brambles. Alice's hunting style was more like mine than Emmett's. It didn't look like the creature had even woken up.

"Thank you," I told her, to be courteous.

You're welcome. There's a bigger herd back to the west.

She got to her feet and led the way again. I bit back my sigh.

We were both done after one more. I was too full again, my insides feeling uncomfortably liquefied. I was surprised that she was ready to quit, though.

"I don't mind continuing," I told her, wondering if she'd seen that I would sit the next round out and was being polite.

"I'm going out tomorrow with Jasper," she told me.

"Didn't he just—"

"I've recently decided that more preparations are necessary," she said, smiling. *A new possibility.*

In her mind, I saw our home. Carlisle and Esme waiting expectantly in the front room. The door opening, myself walking through, and next to me, holding my hand…

Alice laughed, and I tried to bring my face back under my control.

"How?" I asked. "*When?*"

"Soon." *Possibly Sunday…*

"*This* Sunday?"

Yes, the one that comes after tomorrow.

Bella was perfect in the vision—human and healthy, smiling at my parents. She wore the blue blouse that made her skin glow.

As for how, I'm not entirely sure. This is just an outlying chance, but I wanted Jasper prepared.

Jasper at the foot of the stairs now, nodding politely to Bella, his eyes light gold.

"This is…through the knot?"

One of the threads.

It spun out again in her mind, the long ropes of possibilities. So many converging on tomorrow…not enough emerging on the other side.

"Where am I at?"

She pursed her lips. *Seventy-five-twenty-five?* She thought it like a question, and I could see she was being generous.

C'mon, she thought as she saw me hunch in on myself. *You'd take that bet. I did.*

Automatically, my lips pulled back over my teeth.

"Please!" she said. "Like I was going to pass up such an opportunity. This isn't just about Bella. I'm relatively confident that she'll be fine. This is about teaching Rosalie and Jasper some respect."

"You're not omniscient."

"I'm close enough."

I could not match her joking mood. "If you were omniscient, you'd be able to tell me what to do."

You'll figure it out, Edward. I know you will.

If only I could know that, too.

No one but my mother and father were home when we returned. Emmett had no doubt warned the others to make themselves scarce. It didn't matter to me one way or another. I didn't have the energy to care about their stupid game. Alice, too, ran off in search of Jasper. I was grateful for the thinning of the mental conversations. It helped me a little as I tried to concentrate.

Carlisle was waiting by the foot of the stairs, and his thoughts were hard to block, filled with all the same questions to which I'd just begged Alice for answers. I didn't want to admit to him all the weaknesses that kept me from running away before any more damage was done. I didn't want Carlisle to know the horror that would have come to pass if I hadn't come back to Forks when I did, the depths to which my monster would have sunk.

I gave him one tight nod in acknowledgment as I passed him. He knew what it meant—that I was aware of all his fears, and that I had no good answer. With a sigh, he nodded back. He followed up the stairs more slowly, and I heard him join Esme in her study. They didn't speak. I tried to ignore what she thought as she analyzed his expression: her alarm, her pain.

Carlisle, of all the others, even Alice, understood best how it was for me, the never-ending chatter and babble and commotion that was the inside of my head; he'd lived with me longest. So, without a word, he now led Esme to the large window we often used as an exit. Within seconds, they were far enough away that I could hear nothing. Silence at last. The only commotion in my head now was of my own making.

At first I moved slowly, at barely more than human speed, as I showered, cleaning the residue of the forest from my skin and hair. As before, in the car, I felt damaged, impaired, as if my strength had been drained away. All in my head, of course. It would be nothing but a miracle, a gift, if I could somehow truly lose my strength. If I could be weak, harmless, a danger to no one.

I'd almost forgotten my earlier fear—such a conceited fear—that Bella would find me repulsive when I revealed my true self in the sunlight. I was disgusted at myself for wasting even a moment over that selfish concern. But as I looked for fresh clothes, I had to think of it again. Not because it mattered whether she was sickened by me, but because I had a promise to keep.

I rarely gave what I wore a first thought, let alone a second. Alice stocked my closet with a wide variety of items that all seemed to go together. The main point of clothing was to help us blend in—to embrace the current time period's fashion, to downplay our pallor, and to cover as much of our skin as possible without looking shockingly out of season. Alice pushed the limits within those constraints, offended by the idea of trying to make us look unnoticeable. She chose her own clothing and dressed the rest of us as a form of artistic expression. Our skin was covered, its pallid hue was never put in contrast with deeper tones, and we certainly were up to the minute with current style. But *blend* we did not. It seemed a harmless indulgence, like the cars we drove.

Alice's forward-thinking taste aside, all my clothes were, if nothing else, designed for maximum coverage. If I were going to fulfill the spirit of my promise to Bella, I would need more than my hands exposed. The smaller my exposure, the easier it would be for her to compartmentalize my disease. She *needed* to see me for what I was.

At that moment I remembered a shirt, stuck in the back recesses of my closet, that I'd never worn.

The shirt was an anomaly. Usually, Alice wouldn't get us anything that she couldn't *see* us wearing. Typically, she was quite strict in following the letter of the law. I recalled the afternoon, two years ago, when I'd first seen the shirt hanging with a new lot of Alice's acquisitions, tacked on at the very back, as if she knew it was all wrong.

"What's this for?" I asked her.

She'd shrugged. *I don't know. It looked nice on the model.*

There hadn't been anything hidden in her thoughts. She seemed as confused as I was by the impulsive purchase. And yet, she hadn't let me throw the shirt away, either.

You never know, she'd insisted. *You might want it someday.*

I pulled the shirt out now, and felt a strange wave of awe. A chill, almost, if I were capable of feeling such a thing. Her uncanny premonitions reached so far, stretched their tentacles so deep into the future, that even she didn't understand all the actions she took. Somehow she'd sensed, years before Bella had chosen to come to Forks, that at some point I would be facing this most bizarre trial.

Perhaps she *was* omniscient after all.

I slipped into the white cotton shirt, unnerved by the look of my bare arms in the mirror inside the door. I buttoned it, sighed, then unbuttoned it again. Exposing my skin was the whole point. But I didn't have to be so conspicuous right from the start. I grabbed a pale beige sweater and pulled it over the top. I was much more comfortable that way, just the collar of the white shirt showing above the crew neckline, covered up as was normal. Maybe I would leave the sweater on. Maybe full disclosure was the wrong path.

I wasn't moving as slowly anymore. It was almost comical, with all the dire fears and resolutions in my head, that the more familiar fear, the one that had recently dictated almost all my movements, should still be able to control me so easily.

I hadn't seen Bella for hours. Was she safe now?

Strange that I should even be able to worry about the millions of dangers that weren't *me*. None of them were close to as deadly. And yet, and yet, and yet... what if?

Though I'd always planned to spend the night with Bella's scent, more important tonight than any night before, now I was in a hurry to be there.

I was early and, of course, everything was fine. Bella was still doing laundry—I could hear the thumping and sloshing of the unbalanced washing machine and smell the scent of softener sheets blowing hot from the dryer's exhaust. Part of me wanted to smile as I thought of her teasing at lunch, but the superficial humor was too weak to overcome my ongoing panic. I could hear Charlie watching a sports recap in the front room. His quiet thoughts seemed mellow, sleepy. I was sure that Bella hadn't changed her mind and told him of her real plans for tomorrow.

Despite everything, the easy, simple flow of the Swans' uneventful evening was calming. I perched in my usual tree and let it lull me.

I found myself feeling jealous of Bella's father. His was a simple life. Nothing serious weighed on his conscience. Tomorrow was just a normal day, with familiar, pleasant hobbies to look forward to.

But the next day...

It wasn't in his power to guarantee what that next day would be for him. Was it in mine?

I was surprised to hear the sound of a hair dryer from the shared bathroom. Bella didn't usually bother. Her hair was, as far as I had seen in my nights of protective—if inexcusable—surveillance, wet as she slept, drying over the course of the night. I wondered why the change. The only explanation I could think of was that she wanted her hair to look nice. And as the person she planned to see tomorrow was me, that meant she must have wanted it to look nice for me.

Maybe I was wrong. But if I was right...how exasperating! How endearing! Her life had never been in deeper peril, but she still cared that I, the very menace threatening her life, liked her appearance.

It took longer than usual, even after the extra time with the dryer, for the lights to go out in her room, and I could hear some quiet commotion inside before that happened. Curious, always too curious, it felt like hours before I could be sure I'd waited long enough for her to be sleeping.

Once inside, I could see I hadn't needed to wait quite so long. She slept more serenely than usual tonight, her hair fanned smoothly across the pillow over her head, her arms relaxed at her sides. Deeply under, she did not so much as murmur.

Her room immediately revealed the source of the tumult I'd heard. Piles of clothes were thrown over every surface, even a few across the foot of her bed, under her bare feet. I acknowledged again the pleasure and the pain of knowing that she wanted to be attractive for me.

I compared the feelings, the ache and the soaring, to my life before Bella. I'd been so jaded, so world-weary, as if I'd experienced every emotion there was to be felt. What a fool. I'd barely sipped at the cup life had to offer. Only now was I aware of all I'd missed, and how much more I had to learn. So much suffering ahead, more than the joy, certainly. But the joy was so sweet and so strong that I would never forgive myself for missing a second of it.

I thought of the emptiness of a life without Bella, and it brought to mind one night I'd not thought of for a very long time.

It was December 1919. More than a year had passed since Carlisle had transformed me. My eyes had cooled from brilliant red to a mellow amber, though the stress of keeping them so was constant.

Carlisle had kept me as isolated as possible while I worked through those unruly first months. After almost a year, I felt quite sure that the madness had passed, and Carlisle accepted my self-evaluation without question. He prepared to introduce me into human society.

At first it was only an evening here or there: As well-fed as possible, we would walk along a small town's main street after the sun was safely below the horizon. It surprised me then, how we could blend in at all. The human faces were so completely different from ours—their dull, pitted skin, their poorly molded features, so rounded and lumpy, the mottled colors of their imperfect flesh. The clouded, rheumy eyes must be nearly blind, I thought, if they could really believe we belonged to their world. It was several years before I grew accustomed to human faces.

I was so focused on controlling my instinct to kill during these excursions that I barely registered as language the cacophony of thought that assaulted me; it was just noise. As my ability to ignore my thirst grew stronger, so the thoughts in the crowd became clearer, harder to dismiss, the danger of the first challenge supplanted by the irritation of the second.

I passed these early tests, if not with ease, then at least with perfect results. The next challenge was to live among them for a week. Carlisle chose the busy harbor in Saint John, New Brunswick, booking us rooms in a small clapboard inn near the West Side docks. Besides our ancient landlord, all the neighbors we encountered were sailors and dockhands.

This was an arduous challenge. I was entirely surrounded. The scent of human blood was ever present. I could smell the touch of human hands on the fabrics in our room, catch the scent of human sweat wafting through our windows. It tainted every breath I took.

But though I was young, I was also obstinate and determined to succeed. I knew that Carlisle thought very highly of my rapid progress, and pleasing him had become my chief motivation. Even in my relative quarantine up to this point, I'd heard enough of human thought to know that my mentor was unique in this world. He was worthy of my idolization.

I knew his plan for escape, should the challenge prove too much for me, though he meant to hide it from me. It was nearly impossible for him to keep a secret. Despite the sense of being encompassed by human blood on every side, there existed a quick retreat through the frigid waters of the harbor. We were but a few streets from the gray, opaque depths. If temptation were close to triumph, he would urge me to run.

But Carlisle believed I was able—too gifted, too strong, too *intelligent* to fall victim to my baser desires. He must have seen how I responded to his internal praises. It made me arrogant, I think, but it also shaped me into the man I saw in his head, so determined was I to earn the approval he'd already given.

Carlisle was shrewd like that.

He was also very kind.

It was my second Christmas holiday as an immortal, though it was the first year I appreciated the change of seasons—the year before, I'd been too racked with the newborn frenzy to be aware of much else. I knew that Carlisle worried privately about what I would miss. All the family and friends I'd known in my human years, all the traditions that had brightened the gloomy weather. He needn't have worried. The wreaths and the candles, the music and the gatherings... none of it seemed to apply to me. I looked at it from what seemed an impossible distance.

He sent me out one evening about midway through our week, to take a stroll alone for the first time. I took my assignment very seriously and did all I could to appear as human as possible, bundling myself into thick layers of clothes, pretending I felt the cold. Once outside, I kept my body rigid against every temptation, my movements slow and deliberate. I passed a few men headed home from the icy docks. No one addressed me, but I did not go out of my way to avoid contact. I thought of my future life, when I would be as controlled and at ease as Carlisle, and imagined a million strolls like this one. Carlisle had put his life on hold to deal with me, but I was determined that I would soon be an asset to him rather than a burden.

I was quite proud of myself as I returned to our room, shaking the snow off my wool cap. Carlisle would be anxious for my report, and I was keen to give it to him. It had not been so difficult after all, going out among them with only my own will for protection, and I pretended nonchalance as I strolled through the door, only belatedly noticing the strong scent of resin.

I'd been preparing to amaze Carlisle with the ease of my success, but he was waiting to surprise me.

The beds were carefully stacked in the corner, the wobbly desk shoved behind the door to make room for a fir tree tall enough to brush the ceiling with its highest branch. The needles were wet, dustings of snow still visible in places, so quickly had he melted the candle stubs to the ends of the branches. They were all aglow, reflecting warm and yellow against Carlisle's smooth cheek. He smiled widely.

Merry Christmas, Edward.

I realized with a bit of embarrassment that my great accomplishment, my solo expedition, had been merely a ruse. And then I was glad again to think that Carlisle trusted my control so much that he'd been willing to send me off on a sham trial in order to surprise me this way.

"Thank you, Carlisle," I responded quickly. "And a merry Christmas to you." Truthfully, I wasn't sure how I felt about the gesture. It seemed...somehow juvenile—as if my human life were just a larval stage that I had left far behind, along with all its trappings, and now I was expected to return to inching along in the mud despite the existence of my wings. I felt too old for this display, but at the same time, touched that Carlisle would try to give me this, a momentary return to my former joys.

"I've got popcorn," he told me. "I thought you might like to join in the trimming?"

In his mind, I saw what this meant to him. I heard, not for the first time, the depth of the guilt he felt for having drawn me into this life. He would give me whatever little pieces of human pleasure he thought possible. And I would not be so spoiled as to deny him his own pleasure in this.

"Of course," I agreed. "I imagine it will be quick work this year."

He laughed and went to coax the embers in the hearth to life.

It was not difficult to relax into his vision of a family holiday, albeit a very small and unusual family. Though I found my role easy to perform, the sense lingered of not belonging to this world I was playing at. I wondered if I would settle over time into the life Carlisle had created, or if I would always feel like an alien creature. Was I more of a true vampire than he was? Too much a creature of blood to embrace his more human sensibilities?

My questions were answered with time. I was still more a newborn than I realized in those days, and everything got easier as I aged. The sense of alienation faded, and I found I did belong in Carlisle's world.

However, in that particular season, my concerns left me more vulnerable than I should have been to the thoughts of a stranger.

The next night we met with friends—my very first social encounter.

It was after midnight. We'd left the town and ventured into the hills to the north, searching for an area far enough from humankind to be safe for my hunt. I kept a tight rein on myself then, working to check the eager senses that yearned to be set free, to lead me through the night to something that would satiate my thirst. We must be sure we were far enough away from the populace. Once I'd set those powers loose, I would not be strong enough to turn away from the scent of human blood.

This should be safe, Carlisle approved, and he slowed to let me lead the hunt. Perhaps we would find some wolves, also out hunting in the thick snow. More likely in this weather, we'd have to dig the animals from their dens.

I let my senses range free—it was a distinct relief to do so, like relaxing a long-constricted muscle. At first, all I could smell was the clean snow and the bare branches of the deciduous trees. I registered the relief of smelling no humans at all, no desire, no pain. We ran silently through the thick forest.

And then I caught a new scent, both familiar and strange. It was sweet and clear and purer than the fresh snow. There was a brightness to the fragrance that was only linked to two scents that I knew—Carlisle's and my own. But it was otherwise unfamiliar.

I jerked to a halt. Carlisle caught the scent and froze beside me. For the tiniest part of a second, I listened to his anxiety. And then it turned to recognition.

Ah, Siobhan, he thought, immediately calm. *I didn't know she was on this side of the world.*

I looked at him questioningly, not sure if it was right to speak aloud. I felt apprehensive, despite his ease. The unfamiliar put me on my guard.

Old friends, he assured me. *I suppose it's time for you to meet more of our kind. Let's find them.*

He seemed serene, but I detected a hushed concern behind the thoughts he composed into words for me. I wondered for the first time why we'd never come in contact with another vampire thus far. From Carlisle's lessons, I knew we were not that rare. He must have kept me from the others deliberately. But why? He did not fear any physical danger now. What else would motivate him?

The scent was quite fresh. I could distinguish two different trails. I looked at him questioningly.

Siobhan and Maggie. I wonder where Liam is? That's their coven, the three of them. They usually travel together.

Coven. I knew the word, but had always thought of it in relation to the larger militarized groups that had dominated Carlisle's history lessons. The Volturi coven, and before them, the Romanians and the Egyptians. But if this Siobhan could have a coven of three, did the word then apply to us also? Were Carlisle and I a coven? That didn't seem to fit us. It was too... cold. Perhaps my understanding of the word was imperfect.

It took us a few hours to catch up with our quarry, for they were running, too. The trail took us deeper and deeper into the snowy wasteland, which was fortunate. Had we come too close to human habitation, Carlisle would have asked me to wait behind. Using my sense of smell to track was not much different from using it to hunt, and I knew I would be overwhelmed should I cross a human trail.

When we were close enough that I could just make out the sound of their running feet ahead of us—they were taking no pains to be noiseless, and obviously not concerned about being followed—Carlisle called loudly, "Siobhan!"

The movement ahead ceased for a brief moment, and then they were bounding back toward us, an assertiveness to the sound that had me tensing in spite of Carlisle's confidence. He halted and I stopped close to his side. I'd never known him to be wrong, but still I found myself crouching almost automatically.

Easy, Edward. It's a difficult thing at first, meeting an equal predator. But there is no reason for concern here. I trust her.

"Of course," I whispered, and I straightened beside him, though I could not keep my posture from rigid tautness.

Perhaps this was why he had kept his other acquaintances from me. Maybe this strange instinct to defend was too strong when one was already overwhelmed with newborn passion. I tightened my hold on my locked muscles. I would not disappoint him now.

"Is that you, Carlisle?" a voice rang out, like the clear, deep tone of a church bell.

At first only one vampire emerged from the snow-dusted trees. She was the largest woman I had ever seen—taller than either Carlisle or me, with broader shoulders and thicker limbs. However, there was nothing masculine about her. She was profoundly female in shape—aggressively, forcefully female. It was clear she'd had no intention of passing for a human tonight—she wore only a simple, sleeveless linen shift with an intricately designed silver chain as a belt.

It had been in another lifetime that I had last noticed a woman *this* way, and I found I was hard pressed to know where to put my eyes. I centered them on her face, which, like her body, was intensely female. Her lips were full and curved, her deep crimson eyes enormous and fringed by lashes thicker than the needles on the pine boughs. Her glossy black hair was piled into a generous roll on top of her head, with two thin wooden rods carelessly stabbed through to hold it in place.

I found it a strange relief to look on another face so like Carlisle's—perfect, smooth, lacking the fleshy lumpiness of human faces. The symmetry was soothing.

A half second later, the other vampire appeared, leaning out from behind the larger female's side. This one was less remarkable—just a small girl, not much more than a child. Where the tall female seemed to have an excess of everything, this girl was the picture of *lack*. She looked all bones beneath her plain, dark dress, her wary eyes too big for her face, though it, like her companion's, was comfortingly flawless. Only the girl's hair existed in abundance—a wild thatch of bright red curls that appeared to be knotted beyond the possibility of recovery.

The larger female leaped forward toward Carlisle, and it took all my self-control not to jump between them to stop her. I realized in that instant, observing the musculature of her substantial limbs, that I would only be able to *try*. It was a humbling thought. Perhaps Carlisle had been protecting my ego, too, by keeping me isolated.

She embraced him, enveloping him in her bare arms. Her bright teeth were exposed, but only in what looked to be a friendly smile. Carlisle clasped his arms around her waist and laughed.

"Hello, Siobhan. It's been too long."

Siobhan released him but kept her hands on his shoulders.

"Where have you been hiding, Carlisle? I was beginning to worry something untoward had happened to you." Her voice was nearly as low as his, a vibrant alto, with the lilt of the Irish dockworkers transformed into something magical.

Carlisle's thoughts turned to me, a hundred lightning flashes of our last year. At the same time, Siobhan's eyes darted swiftly to my face and away.

"It's been a busy time," Carlisle said, but I was more focused on Siobhan's thoughts.

Practically a newborn...but his eyes. Strange, but not the same strange as Carlisle's. Amber rather than gold. He's quite pretty. I wonder where Carlisle found him.

Siobhan took a step back. "I'm being rude. I've never met your companion."

"Allow me to introduce you. Siobhan, this is Edward, my son. Edward, this is, as I'm sure you've inferred, my friend of many years, Siobhan. And this is her Maggie."

The little girl cocked her head to the side, but not in acknowledgment. The thin lines of her eyebrows pushed together as if she was concentrating very hard on some puzzle.

Son? Siobhan thought, at first thrown by the word. *Ah, so he's chosen to* create *his companion after all this time. Interesting. I wonder why now? There must be something special about the boy.*

What he says is true, Maggie thought simultaneously. *But there's something missing. Something Carlisle isn't speaking.* She nodded once, as if to herself, and then glanced at Siobhan, who was still examining me.

"Edward, how delightful to meet you," Siobhan said. She offered me her hand, her gaze lingering on my irises, as if trying to quantify their exact shade.

I knew only the human response for this kind of meeting. I took her hand and brushed my lips against the back of it, noting the glassy smoothness of her skin against mine.

"A pleasure," I responded.

How charming. She let her hand drop, smiling widely at me. *So pretty. I wonder what his gift might be, and why it appealed to Carlisle?*

I was taken aback by her thought—only comprehending, when she used the word *gift*, exactly what she'd meant before, when she'd presumed there must be something *special* about me—but I'd had enough practice by now to hide my reaction from her interested eyes.

Of course she was right. I did have a gift. But... Carlisle had been honestly surprised when he'd understood what I could do. I knew, thanks to my gift, that he was not pretending. There was no lie, no evasion in his thoughts when he'd answered my own *whys*. He was very lonely. My mother had pleaded for my life. My face had unconsciously promised some virtue that I wasn't entirely sure I embodied.

I was still mulling over both the rightness and the wrongness of her assumptions as she turned back to Carlisle. One final thought about me lingered as she moved.

Poor boy. I suppose Carlisle has imposed his odd habits on the lad. That's why his eyes are so strange. How tragic—to be deprived of the greatest joy of this life.

At the time, this conclusion did not trouble me as much as her other speculation. Later—their conversation lasted through the night and trapped us away from our rented rooms until the sun had set—when we were alone again, I spoke to him about it. Carlisle told me Siobhan's history, her fascination with the Volturi, her curiosity about the world of mystic vampire talents, and finally her discovery of a strange child who seemed to know more than was humanly possible. Siobhan had changed Maggie not because of any need for companionship or personal concern for the girl, who might, under other circumstances, have been dinner, but because she was eager to collect a talent for her own coven. It was a different way of viewing the world, a less human way than Carlisle had managed to preserve. He'd withheld the information about my own talent from Siobhan (this explained Maggie's strange response to my introduction; she knew Carlisle was holding something back by virtue of her own gift), not certain how Siobhan would have reacted to his having acquired access to such a rare and powerful gift without even a search. Because it was no more than a strange coincidence that I should have turned out to be talented. My gift to read minds was part of me, so Carlisle did not wish it away any more than he would have wanted to change the color of my hair or the timbre of my voice. However, he never saw that gift as a commodity for his use or advantage.

I thought about these revelations every so often, less and less as time went on. I grew more comfortable in the human world, and Carlisle returned to his previous work as a surgeon. I studied medicine, among many other subjects, while he was away, but always from books, never in the hospital. Only a few years later, Carlisle found Esme and we returned to a more reclusive life while she acclimated. It was a busy time, full of new knowledge and new friends, so it was several more years before Siobhan's pitying words began to trouble me.

Poor boy.... How tragic—to be deprived of the greatest joy of this life.

Unlike her other conjecture—so easy to disprove when I had the transparent honesty of Carlisle's thoughts to read—this idea began to fester. It was that phrase, *the greatest joy of this life*, that eventually led to my separation from Carlisle and Esme. In the pursuit of that promised joy, I took human life over and over again, thinking that, in the arrogant application of my *gift*, I could do more good than harm.

The first time I tasted human blood, my body was overwhelmed. It felt totally filled and totally *well*. More alive than before. Even though the blood was not of the greatest quality—my first prey's body was saturated with bitter-tasting drugs—it made my usual fare seem like ditch water. And yet...my mind remained slightly removed from my body's gratification. I couldn't keep from seeing the ugliness. I couldn't forget what Carlisle must think of my choice.

I assumed those qualms would fade. I found very bad men who had kept their bodies clean, if not their hands, and savored the better quality. Mentally, I tabulated the number of lives I might be saving with my judge, jury, and executioner operation. Even if I was just saving one per kill, just the next victim on the list, wasn't that better than if I'd let these human predators continue?

It was years before I gave up. I was never sure then why blood wasn't the existence-crowning ecstasy that Siobhan had believed it to be, why I continued to miss Carlisle and Esme more than I enjoyed my freedom, why the weight of each kill seemed to accumulate until I was crippled under their combined load. Over the years after my return to Carlisle and Esme, as I struggled to relearn all the discipline I'd abandoned, I came to the conclusion that Siobhan might not know anything greater than the call of blood, but I had been born to something better.

And now, the words that had once haunted me, once driven me, came back with surprising force.

The greatest joy of this life.

I had no doubts. I now knew the meaning of the phrase. The greatest joy of *my* life was this fragile, brave, warm, insightful girl sleeping so peacefully nearby. Bella. The very greatest joy that life had to offer me, and the greatest pain when she was lost.

My phone vibrated silently in my shirt pocket. I whipped it out, saw the number, and held it to my ear.

"I see that you can't speak," Alice said quietly, "but I thought you would want to know. It's eighty-twenty now. Whatever you're doing, keep doing it." She hung up.

Of course I couldn't trust the confidence in her voice when I didn't have her thoughts to read, and she knew that. She could lie to me over the phone. But I still felt encouraged.

What I was doing was basking, drowning, wallowing in my love for Bella. I didn't think it would be difficult to keep doing that.

16. THE KNOT

BELLA SLEPT SO SOUNDLY THROUGH THE NIGHT THAT IT was unnerving.

For what seemed a very long time now, from the first moment I'd caught her scent, I'd been powerless to keep my own state of mind from careening wildly from one extreme to the other every minute of the day. Tonight was worse than usual—the burden of the hazard immediately ahead had pushed me to a peak of mental stress beyond anything I'd known in a hundred years.

And Bella slept on, limbs relaxed, forehead smooth, lips turned up at the corners, her breath flowing softly in and out as evenly as a metronome. In all my nights with her, she'd never been so at peace. What did it mean?

I could only think that it meant she did not understand. Despite all the warnings I'd given her, she still didn't believe the truth. She trusted me too much. She was wrong to do so.

She didn't stir when her father peeked into her room. It was still early; the sun had not yet risen. I held my place, certain I was invisible in my shadowed corner. Her father's shrouded thoughts were tinged with regret, with guilt. Nothing too serious, I thought, simply an acknowledgment that he was leaving her alone again. For a moment he wavered, but a sense of obligation—plans, companions, promised rides—pulled him away. That was my best guess.

Charlie made a great deal of noise gathering his fishing things from the coat closet under the stairs. Bella had no reaction to the commotion. Her lids never so much as fluttered.

Once Charlie was gone, it was my turn to exit, though I was loath to leave the serenity of her room. Despite everything, her peaceful sleep had calmed my spirits. I took one final lungful of fire, and then held it inside my chest, cradling the pain close until it could be replenished.

The tumult resumed as soon as she was awake; whatever calm she had found in her dreams seemed to have vanished in the light. The sound of her movements was hurried, and a few times she tweaked the curtains, looking for me, I thought. It made me impatient to be with her again, but we had agreed on a time and I didn't want to prematurely interrupt her preparations. Mine were made, but felt incomplete. Could I ever be truly ready for a day such as this?

I wished I could feel the joy of it—an entire day by her side, answers to every question I could ask, her warmth surrounding me. At the same time, I wished I could turn my back on her house this moment and run in the opposite direction—that I could be strong enough to run to the far side of the world and stay there, never to endanger her again. But I remembered Alice's vision of Bella's bleak, shadowed face and knew that I could never be that strong.

I'd worked myself into a fine dark mood by the time I dropped from the shadows of the tree and crossed her front lawn. I tried to erase the evidence of my state of mind from my face, but I couldn't seem to remember how to shape my muscles the right way.

I knocked quietly, knowing she was listening, then heard her feet stumble down the last few stairs to the hall. She ran to the door and fought with the bolt for a long moment, finally yanking the door open so forcefully that it smacked into the wall with a bang.

She looked into my eyes and was abruptly still, the peace of the previous night evident in her smile.

My mood, too, lightened. I drew in a breath, replacing the stale burn with fresh pain, but the pain was so much less than the joy of being with her.

An errant curiosity drew my eyes to her clothes. Which outfit had she decided on? I remembered the ensemble at once—now that I thought about it, this sweater had been laid in the most prominent position, draped over her obsolete computer, with a white button-down underneath and blue jeans just to the side. Light tan, white collar, medium blue denim...I didn't have to look at myself to know the shades and styles were nearly identical.

I chuckled once. Something in common again.

"Good morning."

"What's wrong?" she responded.

There were a thousand answers to that question and I was taken aback for an instant, but then I saw her glance down at herself and inferred it was to search for the reason behind my laugh.

"We match," I explained.

I laughed again as she took this in, examining my clothes and then her own, with a surprised look on her face. Suddenly, the surprise shifted to a frown. Why? I couldn't think of a reason to find the coincidence anything more or less than mildly amusing. Was there some deeper reason she'd chosen these clothes, some reason that made her angry when I laughed? How could I ask that without sounding strange? I could only be sure that her reason for choosing thusly had not been the same as mine.

I shuddered internally at the thought of the purpose behind my wardrobe and what it portended. But I shouldn't shy away from this. I shouldn't want to hide myself from her. She deserved to know everything.

Her smile returned as she walked with me to her truck—suddenly smug. I wasn't going to back out of the promise I'd made, but I didn't particularly like it. I knew it wasn't rational. She drove herself around in this antique monstrosity daily and nothing bad ever happened to her. Of course, the bad things seemed to wait until I was there to be their horrified witness. My expression must have led her to believe I was upset about the arrangement.

"We made a deal," she gloated, leaning across the seat to unlock the passenger door.

I could only wish my concerns were that trivial.

The decrepit engine coughed its way to life. The metal frame vibrated so violently I worried something would shake loose.

"Where to?" she half shouted over the cacophony. She wrenched the gearshift into reverse and looked back over her shoulder.

"Put your seat belt on," I insisted. "I'm nervous already."

She threw a dark look at me, but snapped her buckle into place, and then sighed.

"Where to?" she said again.

"Take the one-oh-one north."

She kept her eyes on the road as she drove slowly through town. I wondered if she would accelerate when we were on the main road, but she continued at three miles per hour below the posted speed limit. The sun was still low in the eastern horizon, shrouded in thin layers of cloud. But according to Alice, it would be sunny by midday. I wondered if—at this rate—we would be safely in the woods before the sunlight could touch me.

"Were you planning to make it out of Forks before nightfall?" I asked, knowing she would object to the defamation of her truck. She reacted as expected.

"This truck is old enough to be your car's grandfather," she snapped. "Have some respect." But she goaded the engine slightly faster. Two miles above the speed limit now.

I felt a little relieved when we were finally free of downtown Forks. Soon there was more forest than civilization outside the window. The engine droned on like a jackhammer biting into granite. Her eyes never strayed from the road for a second. I wanted to say something, to ask her what she was thinking about, but I didn't want to distract her. There was something almost fierce about her concentration.

"Turn right on the one-ten," I told her.

She nodded to herself, then slowed down to a crawl to take the turn.

"Now we drive till the pavement ends."

"And what's there?" she asked. "At the pavement's end?"

An empty forest. A total lack of witnesses. A monster. "A trail."

Her voice was higher, tighter, when she responded, still staring only at the road. "We're hiking?"

The concern in her tone worried me. I hadn't considered... The distance was very short, and the way was not difficult, not so different from the trail behind her house.

"Is that a problem?" Was there somewhere else to take her? I hadn't made any backup plans.

"No," she said quickly, but her voice was still a little strained.

"Don't worry," I assured her. "It's only five miles or so, and we're in no hurry." Truly—suddenly feeling a wave of panic as I realized how short the distance was indeed—I would love nothing more than a delay.

The furrow was back. After a few empty seconds, she started to chew on her lower lip.

"What are you thinking?"

Did she want to turn around? Had she changed her mind about all of it? Did she wish she'd never answered the door this morning?

"Just wondering where we're going," she replied. Her tone aimed for casual, but missed it by a few inches.

"It's a place I like to go when the weather is nice." I glanced through the window and she did, too. The clouds were no more than a thin veil now. They would burn off soon.

What did she think she would see when the sun touched my

skin? What mental image had she conjured to explain today's field trip to herself?

"Charlie said it would be warm today."

I thought of her father, pictured him beside the river, enjoying the pleasant day. He didn't know he was at a crossroads, a possible life-destroying nightmare waiting, so close, to engulf his entire world.

"And did you tell Charlie what you were up to?" I asked the question without hope.

She smiled, eyes straight ahead. "Nope."

I wished she didn't sound so happy about it. Still, I knew there was one witness, one voice to speak for Bella if she didn't come home.

"But Jessica thinks we're going to Seattle together?"

"No," she said, complacent. "I told her you canceled on me—which is true."

What? I hadn't heard this. It must have happened while I was hunting with Alice. Bella had covered my tracks for me as if she *wanted* me to get away with her murder.

"No one knows you're with me?"

She flinched slightly at my tone, but then her chin came up and she forced a smile. "That depends. I assume you told Alice?"

I had to take a deep breath to keep my voice even. "That's very helpful, Bella."

Her smile disappeared, but she gave no other indication that she'd heard me.

"Are you so depressed by Forks that it's made you suicidal?"

"You said it might cause trouble for you," she said quietly, all humor gone. "Us being together publicly."

I remembered the exchange perfectly, and wondered how she had gotten it so backward. I hadn't told her that so she would try to make herself *more* vulnerable to me. I'd told her so she would run away from me.

"So you're worried about the trouble it might cause *me*," I asked through my teeth, trying to place the words in exactly the right order so that it would be impossible for her not to hear the inherent ridiculousness of her position. "If *you* don't come *home*?"

Eyes on the road, she nodded once.

"How can you not *see* how wrong I am?" I hissed, too angry to slow the words down into something comprehensible for her. Telling her never worked. I would have to show her.

She seemed nervous, but in a new way, her eyes *almost* shifting to look at me, yet never quite breaking away from the road. Frightened by my anger, though not in the way she should be. Just worried that she'd made me unhappy. I didn't have to read her mind to anticipate the established pattern.

As usual, I wasn't truly angry with her—only myself. Yes, her responses toward me were always backward. But that was because, in another way, they were right. She was always too kind. She gave me credit I didn't deserve, worried over my feelings as if they mattered. Her very goodness was what put her in this danger. Her virtue, my vice, the two opposites binding us together.

We'd reached the end of the paved road. Bella pulled the truck onto the loamy shoulder and killed the engine. The sudden quiet was almost shocking after the long auditory assault. She disengaged her seat belt and slid quickly from the truck without looking at me. With her back to me, she pulled her sweater over her head. It took her a few seconds' struggle, and then she tied the sleeves around her waist. I was surprised to see that her shirt mirrored my own in more than color; it too left her arms bare to the shoulder. This was more of her than I was used to seeing, but despite the fascination that immediately sparked, what I felt most was concern. Anything that interrupted my concentration was a danger.

I sighed. I didn't want to go through with this. There were many serious reasons, life and death reasons, but in this moment, my greatest dread was the expression on her face, the revulsion in her eyes, when she finally *saw* me.

I would face it head-on. Pretend to be brave, to be bigger than this selfish fear, even if it was no more than a charade.

I slipped my own sweater off, feeling glaringly conspicuous. I'd never uncovered so much of my skin around anyone but my family.

Jaw clenched, I slid out of the truck—leaving the sweater so I wouldn't be tempted—and shut the door. I stared into the forest. Maybe if I got off the road and into the trees, I wouldn't feel so exposed.

I felt her eyes on me, but I was too cowardly to turn. I looked over my shoulder instead.

"This way." The words came out clipped, too fast. I had to get my anxiety under control. I started to walk slowly forward.

"The trail?" Her voice was an octave higher than usual. I glanced at her again—she looked nervous as she walked around the front end of the truck to meet me. There were so many things that might be frightening her, I couldn't be sure which it was.

I tried to sound like a normal person. Light, funny. Maybe I could ease her apprehension, if not my own. "I said there was a trail at the end of the road, not that we were taking it."

"No trail?" She said the word *trail* as if she were referring to the last life vest on a sinking ship.

I squared my shoulders, formed my lips into a false smile, and turned to face her.

"I won't let you get lost," I promised.

It was worse than I'd been braced for. Her mouth actually fell open, like a character in the kind of sitcom that had a laugh track. She did a quick double take, her eyes running up and down my bared skin.

And this was nothing. Just pale skin. Well, extremely pale skin, bent in a slightly inhuman way over the angularity of my inhuman musculature. If this was her response to no more than my skin in the shade...

Her face fell. It was as if my former despondency had transferred to her, had landed with the weight of all my hundred years. Perhaps this was all that was needed. Maybe she'd seen enough.

"Do you want to go home?"

If she wanted to leave me, if she wanted to walk away now, I would let her go. I would watch her disappear, and endure it. I wasn't quite sure how, but I would find a way.

Her eyes flashed with some unfathomable reaction, and she said, "No!" so quickly, it was almost a retort. She hurried to my side, coming so close that I would only have had to lean a few inches to brush my arm against hers.

What did it mean?

"What's wrong?" I asked. There was still pain in her eyes, pain that made no sense combined with her actions. Did she want to leave me or not?

Her voice was low and nearly inflectionless as she answered. "I'm not a good hiker. You'll have to be very patient."

I didn't believe her entirely, but it was a kind lie. Obviously she was concerned about the lack of a conventional trail to follow, but that was hardly enough to create the grief in her expression. I leaned closer and smiled as gently as I could, trying to coax a smile in return. I hated the shadow of misery lingering around the edges of her lips, her eyes.

"I can be patient," I assured her, lightening my tone. "If I make a great effort."

She half smiled at my words, but one side of her mouth refused to turn up.

"I'll take you home," I promised. Perhaps she felt she had no choice but to face this trial by fire, that she owed it to me in some way. She owed me nothing. She was free to walk away whenever she wished.

I was taken aback by her response. Rather than accept the out I was offering with relief, she quite distinctly scowled at me. When she spoke, her tone was caustic.

"If you want me to hack five miles through the jungle before sundown, you'd better start leading the way."

I stared at her, dumbfounded, waiting for more—for something that would make it clear how I'd offended her—but she just lifted her chin and narrowed her eyes as if in challenge.

Not knowing what else to do, I held my arm out to usher her forward, lifting a protruding branch higher with my other hand. She stomped underneath it, then swatted a smaller limb out of her way.

It *was* easier in the forest. Or maybe I had just needed a moment to process her first reaction. I led the way, holding the foliage to clear her path. Mostly she kept her eyes down, not as if she were avoiding looking at me, but as if she didn't trust the ground. I saw her glare at a few roots as she stepped over them and made the connection then—surely a clumsy person would be nervous about the uneven terrain. However, that still didn't explain her earlier gloom or her following anger.

Many things were easier in the forest than I expected them to be. Here we were, totally alone, no witnesses, and yet it didn't feel dangerous. Even the few times that we reached an obstacle—a fallen log across the way, an outcropping of rock too high to step over—and I instinctively reached out to help her, it was no more difficult to touch her than it had been at school. *Not difficult* was hardly the correct description. It was thrilling, pleasurable, just as it had been before. When I lifted her gently, I heard her heart drum in double time. I imagined my heart would sound just the same if it could also beat.

It probably felt safe, or safe enough, because I knew this wasn't the place. Alice had never seen me killing Bella in the middle of the forest. If only I didn't have to hold Alice's vision inside my head.... Of course, *not* knowing that possible future, not preparing for it, might have been the very ignorance that would lead to Bella's death. It was all so circular and impossible.

Not for the first time in my life, I wished that I could make my brain slow down. Force it to move at human speed, if only just for a day, an hour, so that I wouldn't have time to obsess over and *over* again about the same solutionless problems.

"Which was your favorite birthday?" I asked her. I badly needed some distraction.

Her mouth screwed up into something that was halfway between a wry smile and a scowl.

"What?" I asked. "Is it not my day to ask questions?"

She laughed and her hand fluttered as though she was waving away that concern. "It's fine. I just don't know the answer. I'm not a big fan of birthdays."

"That's...unusual." I couldn't think of another teenager I'd met who thought the same way.

"It's a lot of pressure," she said, shrugging. "Presents and stuff. What if you don't like them? You've got to get your game face on right away so you don't hurt anyone's feelings. And people *look* at you a lot."

"Your mother isn't an intuitive gift giver?" I guessed.

Her answering smile was cryptic. I could tell she would say nothing negative about her mother, though she'd obviously been scarred.

We walked for a half mile in silence. I was hoping she would volunteer more, or ask a question that would tell me where her thoughts were, but she kept her eyes on the forest floor, concentrating. I tried again.

"Who was your favorite teacher in elementary school?"

"Mrs. Hepmanik," she responded without a pause. "Second grade. She let me read in class pretty much whenever I wanted."

I grinned at her. "A paragon."

"Who was your favorite grade school teacher?"

"I don't remember," I reminded her.

She frowned. "Right. Sorry, I didn't think—"

"No need to apologize."

It took me another quarter mile to think of a question she couldn't turn around on me too easily.

"Dogs or cats?"

Her head tilted to one side. "I'm not really sure....I think maybe cats? Cuddly, but independent, right?"

"Have you never had a dog?"

"I've never had either. Mom says she's allergic."

Her response was oddly skeptical.

"You don't believe her?"

She paused again, not wanting to be disloyal. "Well," she said slowly, "I caught her petting a lot of other people's dogs."

"I wonder why...?" I mused.

Bella laughed. It was a carefree sound, totally lacking any kind of bitterness.

"It took me forever to talk her into letting me have a fish. I finally figured out that she was worried about being stuck at home. I've told you how she loved to take off every weekend we could—go visit some little town or minor historical monument she'd never seen before. I showed her those time-release food tablets that can feed the fish for over a week, and she relented. Renée just can't stand an anchor. I mean, she already had me, right? One huge life-altering anchor was enough. She wasn't going to volunteer for more."

I kept my face very smooth. This insight of hers—which I didn't doubt, she'd always seen through me so easily—put a darker spin on my interpretation of her past. Was Bella's need to be a caretaker based not on her mother's helplessness, but on a feeling of needing to earn her place? It made me angry to think that Bella might ever have felt unwanted, or that she needed to prove her worth. I had the oddest desire to wait on her hand and foot in some socially acceptable way, to show Bella that her merely existing was more than enough.

She didn't notice me trying to control my reaction. With another laugh, she continued. "It was probably for the best that we never tried anything bigger than a goldfish. I wasn't very good at pet ownership. I thought maybe I'd been overfeeding the first one, so I really cut back on the second, but that was a mistake. And the third one"—she looked up at me, baffled—"I honestly don't know what his problem was. He kept jumping out of the bowl. Eventually, I didn't find him soon enough."

She frowned. "Three in a row—I guess that makes me a serial killer."

It was impossible not to laugh, but she didn't seem offended. She laughed with me.

As our amusement subsided, the light changed. Alice's promised sunshine had arrived above the thick canopy, and immediately I felt jittery and anxious again.

I knew that this emotion—*stage fright* was the closest term I could come up with—was truly ridiculous. So what if Bella found me repulsive? If she rejected me in disgust? That was fine, better than fine. That was literally the smallest, tiniest sort of misery that could hurt me today. Was vanity, the fragility of ego, truly that strong a force? I'd never believed it had that kind of power over me, and I didn't think so now. Obsessing over this reveal kept me from obsessing over other things. Like the rejection that would follow the disgust. Bella walking away from me, and knowing that I had to let her go. Would she be so frightened by me that she'd refuse to let me lead her back to the truck? Surely I would have to at least get her safely to the road. Then she could drive away alone.

Though my whole frame felt like it might crumple with the pain of that image, there was something much worse—the looming test Alice had seen. Failing that test...I couldn't imagine. How would I live through that? How would I find a way to *stop* living?

We were so close.

Bella noticed the change in light as we passed through a thinner patch of forest. She frowned teasingly. "Are we there yet?"

I pretended to be equally lighthearted. "Nearly. Do you see the brightness ahead?"

She narrowed her eyes at the forest before us, the concentration line forming between her brows. "Um, should I?"

"Maybe it's a bit too soon for your eyes," I allowed.

A shrug. "Time to visit the optometrist."

The silence seemed heavier as we progressed. I could tell when Bella spotted the brightness of the meadow. She smiled almost unconsciously and her stride lengthened. She wasn't watching the ground anymore; her eyes were locked on the filtered glow of sunshine. Her eagerness only made my reluctance heavier. More time. Just another hour or two . . . Could we stop here? Would she forgive me if I balked?

But I knew there was no point in delay. Alice had seen that it would come to this, sooner or later. Avoidance would never make it easier.

Bella led the way now, no hesitation as she pushed through the hedge of ferns and into the meadow.

I wished I could see her face. I could imagine how lovely the place would be on a day like this. I could smell the wildflowers, sweeter in the warmth, and hear the low burble of the stream on the far side. The insects hummed, and far away, birds trilled and crooned. There were no birds nearby now—my presence was enough to frighten all the larger life from this place.

She walked almost reverently into the golden light. It gilded her hair and made her fair skin glow. Her fingers trailed over the taller flowers, and I was reminded again of Persephone. Springtime personified.

I could have watched her for a very long time, perhaps forever, but it was too much to hope that the beauty of the place could make her forget the monster in the shadows for long. She turned, eyes wide with amazement, a wondering smile on her lips, and looked back at me. Expectant. When I didn't move, she began walking slowly in my direction. She lifted one arm, offering her hand in encouragement.

I wanted to be human so badly in that moment that it nearly crippled me.

But I was not human, and the time had come for perfect discipline. I held my palm up, a warning. She understood, but was not afraid. Her arm dropped and she stayed where she was. Waiting. Curious.

I took a deep breath of the forest air, consciously registering her scorching scent for the first time in hours.

Even trusting Alice's visions as much as I did, I wasn't sure how there could be any more to this story. It would have to end now, wouldn't it? Bella would see me, and be all the things she should have been from the beginning: terrified, disgusted, appalled, repelled...and done with me.

It felt as though I would never do anything more difficult than this, but I forced my foot to lift and shifted my weight forward.

I would face this head-on.

With all that...I couldn't bear the first reaction on her face. She would be kind, but it would be impossible for her to disguise that initial instant of shock and revulsion. So I would give her a moment to compose herself.

I closed my eyes as I stepped into the sunlight.

17. CONFESSIONS

I FELT THE SUN, WARM AGAINST MY SKIN, AND I WAS GLAD I couldn't see that, either. I didn't want to look at myself now. For the longest half second I'd ever lived through, everything was silent. And then Bella screamed.

"Edward!"

My eyes flashed open, and I fully expected to see her running away from all I had just revealed myself to be.

But she was running right at me in a collision course, her mouth open in distress. Her hands were half-extended toward me, and she tripped and stumbled her way through the long grass. Her expression wasn't frightened, but it was desperate. I didn't understand what she was doing.

I couldn't let her crash into me, whatever she was intending. I needed her to keep her distance. I raised my hand again, palm forward.

She faltered, then wobbled in place for a moment, exuding anxiety.

As I stared into her eyes, saw my reflection there, I thought perhaps I understood. Mirrored in her eyes, what I resembled most was a man on fire. Though I'd debunked her myths, she must have held on to them subconsciously.

Because she was worried. Frightened *for* the monster rather than *of* it.

She took a step toward me, and then hesitated when I moved a half step back.

"Does that hurt you?" she whispered.

Yes, I'd been right. She wasn't afraid for herself, not even now.

"No," I whispered back.

She stepped another foot closer, careful now. I let my hand fall.

She still wanted to be closer to me.

Her expression shifted as she approached. Her head cocked to the side, and her eyes first narrowed, then grew huge. Even with this much space between us, I could see the effects of the light refracting off my skin shining prism-like against her own. She moved another step and then another, keeping the same distance away as she slowly circled around me. I stayed completely motionless, feeling her eyes touch my skin as she moved out of my sight. Her breath came more quickly than usual, her heart pumped faster.

She reappeared on my right, and now there was a tiny smile beginning to form around the edges of her lips as she completed her circle and faced me again.

How could she smile?

She walked closer, stopping when she was only ten inches away. Her hand was raised, curled close to her chest, as if she wanted to reach out and touch me but was afraid to. The sunlight shattered off my arm and whirled against her face.

"Edward," she breathed. There was wonder in her voice.

"Are you frightened now?" I asked quietly.

It was as if my question was totally unexpected, as if it shocked her. "*No.*"

I stared into her eyes, unable to stop myself from fruitlessly trying—again—to hear her.

She reached toward me, very slowly, watching my face. I thought perhaps she was waiting for me to tell her to stop. I didn't. Her warm fingers grazed the back of my wrist. She stared intently at the light that danced from my skin to hers.

"What are you thinking?" I whispered. In this moment, the constant mystery was once again acutely painful.

She shook her head slightly, and seemed to struggle for the words. "I am..." She stared up into my eyes. "I didn't know...." She took a deep breath. "I've never seen anything more beautiful—never imagined something so beautiful could exist."

I stared back at her in shock.

My skin was blazing with the most flagrant symptom of my disease. In the sun, I was less human than at any other time. And she thought I was... beautiful.

My hand lifted automatically, turning to take hers, but I forced myself to make it drop, not to touch her.

"It's very strange, though," I said. Surely she could understand that this was part of the horror.

"Amazing," she corrected.

"You aren't repulsed by my flagrant lack of humanity?"

Though I was fairly sure now what her answer would be, it was still astonishing to me.

She half smiled. "Not repulsed."

"You should be."

Her smile widened. "I'm feeling like humanity is pretty overrated."

Carefully, I pulled my arm out from underneath her warm fingertips, hiding it behind my back. She valued humanity so lightly. She didn't realize the depths of what its loss would mean.

Bella took another half step forward, her body so close that its warmth became more pronounced, more present than the sun's. She lifted her face toward mine, and the light gilded her throat, the play of shadows emphasizing the coursing of her blood through the artery just behind the corner of her jaw.

My body reacted instinctively—venom welling, muscles coiling, thoughts scattering.

How quickly it surfaced! We'd been in this arena of visions mere seconds.

I stopped breathing and took a long step away from her, raising my hand again in warning.

She didn't try to follow. "I'm...sorry," she whispered, the sound of the words lilting up, turning them into a question. She didn't know what she was apologizing for.

I carefully loosed my lungs, and took a controlled breath. Her scent was no more painful than usual—not overwhelming, the way I was half-afraid I would suddenly find it.

"I need some time," I explained.

"Okay." Still a whisper.

I moved around her, slow deliberate steps, and walked to the center of the meadow. I sat down in a patch of low grass, and locked my muscles in place, as I had done before. I breathed carefully in and out, listening as her hesitant footsteps crossed the same distance, tasting her fragrance as she sat down next to me.

"Is this all right?" she asked, uncertain.

I nodded. "Just...let me concentrate."

Her eyes were huge with confusion, with concern. I didn't want to explain. I closed my own.

Not in cowardice, I told myself. Or not *just* in cowardice. I did need to concentrate.

I focused on her scent, on the sound of the blood gushing through the chambers of her heart. Only my lungs were allowed motion. Every other part of me I imprisoned into rigid immobility.

Bella's heart, I reminded myself as my involuntary systems reacted to the stimuli. Bella's life.

I was always so careful to *not* think about her blood—the scent I couldn't avoid, but the fluid, the movement, the pulse, the hot liquidity of it—these were things I could not dwell on. But now I let it fill my mind, invade my system, attack my controls. The gushing and throbbing of it, the pounding and sloshing. The surge through the biggest arteries, the ripple through the smallest vein. The heat of it, heat that washed in waves across my exposed skin despite the distance between us. The taste of it burning on my tongue and aching in my throat.

I held myself captive, and observed. A small part of my brain was able to stay detached, to think through the onslaught. With that small bit of rationality, I examined my every reaction minutely. I calculated the amount of strength needed to curb each response, and weighed the strength I possessed against that tally. It was a near calculation, but I believed that my will was stronger than my bestial nature. Slightly.

Was this Alice's knot? It didn't feel...complete.

All the while, Bella sat almost as still as I was, thinking her private thoughts. Could she imagine any part of the turmoil inside my mind? How did she explain this strange, silent standoff to herself? Whatever she thought of it, her body was calm.

Time seemed to slow with her pulse. The sound of the birds in distant trees turned sleepy. The cascade of the little stream grew somehow more languid. My body relaxed, and even my mouth stopped watering eventually.

Two thousand three hundred sixty-four of her heartbeats later, I felt more in control than I had in many days. Facing things was the key, as Alice had predicted. Was I ready? How could I be sure? How would I ever be sure?

And how did I break this long hush I'd imposed? It was starting to feel awkward to me; it must have felt so to her for a while.

I unlocked my pose and lay back in the grass, one hand casually behind my head. Feigning the physical sign of emotion was old habit. Perhaps if I portrayed relaxation, she would believe it.

She only sighed quietly.

I waited to see if she would speak, but she sat silent as before, thinking whatever it was she might be thinking, alone in this remote place with a monster who reflected the sun like a million prisms. I could feel her eyes on my skin, but I didn't imagine her revolted anymore. The imaginary weight of her gaze—now that I knew it was admiring, that she found me beautiful regardless of everything—brought back that electric current I'd felt with her in the dark, an imitation of life running through my veins.

I let myself get lost in the rhythms of her body, let the sound and the warmth and the smell comingle, and I found that I could still master my inhuman desires, even while the phantom current moved under my skin.

This took most of my attention, though. And inevitably, this quiet waiting period would end. She would have so many questions—much more pointed now, I imagined. I owed her a thousand different explanations. Could I handle everything at once?

I decided to try to juggle a few more tasks while still tuning in to the flow and ebb of her blood. I would see if the distraction was too much.

First, I gathered information. I triangulated the exact location of the birds I could hear, and then by their calls identified each one's genus and species. I analyzed the irregular splash that revealed life in the stream, and after equating the water displaced with the size of the fish, deduced the most likely variety. Categorized the nearby insects—unlike the more developed species, insects ignored my kind as they would a stone—by the speed of their wing movements and the elevation of their flight, or the tiny clicking sounds of their legs against the soil.

As I continued to classify, I added calculation. If there were currently 4,913 insects in the area of the meadow, which was roughly 11,035 square feet, how many insects on average would exist in the 1,400 square miles of the Olympic National Park? What if insect populations dropped 1 percent for each 10 feet of elevation? I brought up in my head a topographic map of the park and started computing the numbers.

Concurrently, I thought through the songs I'd heard most rarely in my century of life—nothing common that I'd heard played more than once. Tunes I'd heard walking past the open door of a bar, peculiar family lullabies lisped by children in their cradles as I ran by in the night, discarded attempts by the music students writing their theater projects in the buildings adjacent to my college classroom. I mouthed through the verses quickly, noting all the reasons each was doomed to failure.

Her blood still pulsed, her heat still warmed, and I still burned. But I could keep my hold on myself. My grip did not loosen. I was in control. Just enough.

"Did you say something?" she whispered.

"Just…singing to myself," I admitted. I didn't know how to explain what I was doing more clearly, and she didn't pursue the question further.

I could feel that the silence was coming to an end, and this did not frighten me. I was growing almost comfortable with the situation, feeling strong and in control. Perhaps I was through the knot after all. Perhaps we were safe on the other side and all of Alice's hopeful visions were now on their way to becoming real.

When the change in her breathing telegraphed a new direction to her thoughts, I was intrigued rather than worried. I expected a question, but instead I heard the grass shift around her as she leaned toward me, and the sound of the pulse in her hand moved closer.

One soft, warm fingertip traced slowly across the back of my hand. It was a very gentle touch, but the response in my skin was electric. A different kind of burning than that in my throat, and even more distracting. My calculations and audio recall stuttered and stalled, and she had all my attention, even as her heart throbbed wetly just a foot from my ear.

I opened my eyes, eager to see her expression and guess at her thoughts. I was not disappointed. Her eyes were bright with wonder again, the corners of her lips turned up. She met my gaze and her smile grew more pronounced. I echoed it.

"I don't scare you?" I hadn't scared her away. She wanted to be here, with me.

Her tone was teasing when she answered. "No more than usual."

She leaned closer, and laid all of her hand against my forearm, slowly stroking down toward my wrist. Her skin felt fever-hot against mine, and though a tremor quivered through her fingers, there was no fear in that touch. My eyelids slipped closed again as I tried to contain my reaction. The electric current felt like an earthquake rocking through my core.

"Do you mind?" she asked, and her hand paused in its progress.

"No," I responded quickly. And then, because I wanted her to know some little bit of my experience, I continued, "You can't imagine how that feels." I couldn't have imagined it before this moment. It was beyond any pleasure I'd ever felt.

Her fingers traced back up to the inside of my elbow, outlining patterns there. She shifted her weight and her other hand reached for mine. I felt her tug lightly and realized she wished to turn my hand over. As soon as I complied, though, both her hands froze and she gasped quietly.

I glanced up, swiftly realizing my mistake—I'd moved like a vampire rather than a human.

"Sorry," I muttered. But, as our eyes met, I could already tell I'd done no real harm. She'd recovered from the surprise without the smile ever leaving her face. "It's too easy to be myself with you," I explained, and then I let my eyelids close again, so I could focus everything on the feel of her skin against mine.

I felt the pressure as she started to try to lift my hand. I moved my hand in concert with her motion, knowing that it would take quite a bit of effort for her to heft even just my hand without my help. I was a little heavier than I looked.

She held my hand close to her face. Warm breath seared against my palm. I helped her angle my hand this way and that as the pressure of her fingers indicated. I opened my eyes to see her staring intently, rainbow sparks dancing across her face as the light moved back and forth across my skin. The furrow was there again between her eyes. What question troubled her now?

"Tell me what you're thinking." I said the words gently, but could she hear that I was begging? "It's still so strange for me, not knowing."

Her mouth pursed just a little, and her left eyebrow rose a fraction of an inch. "You know, the rest of us feel that way all the time."

The rest of us. The vast family of humanity that did not include me. Her people, her kind.

"It's a hard life." The words did not sound like the joke I meant them to be. "But you didn't tell me."

She answered slowly. "I *was* wishing I could know what you were thinking. . . ."

There was obviously more. "And?"

Her voice was low; a human would have had a hard time hearing her. "I was wishing I could believe that you were real. And I was wishing that I wasn't afraid."

A flash of pain stabbed through me. I'd been wrong. I had frightened her after all. Of course I had.

"I don't want you to be afraid." It was an apology and a lament.

I was surprised when she grinned almost impishly. "Well, that's not exactly the fear I meant, though that's certainly something to think about."

How was she joking now? What could she mean? I sat up halfway, too eager for answers to pretend nonchalance any longer.

"What are you afraid of, then?"

I realized how close our faces were. Her lips, closer than they had ever been to mine. No longer smiling, parted. She inhaled through her nose and her eyelids half closed. She stretched closer as if to catch more of my scent, her chin angling up half an inch, her neck arching forward, her jugular exposed.

And I reacted.

Venom flooded my mouth, my free hand moved of its own volition to seize her, my jaws wrenched open as she leaned in to meet me.

I threw myself away from her. The madness hadn't reached my legs and they launched me all the way back to the far edge of the meadow. I moved so quickly I didn't have time to gently release my hand from hers; I'd yanked it away. My first thought as I landed crouched in the shadows of the trees was her hands, and relief washed over me when I saw they were still attached to her wrists.

Relief followed by disgust. Loathing. Revulsion. All the emotions I'd feared to see in her eyes today multiplied by a hundred years and the sure knowledge that I deserved them and more. Monster, nightmare, destroyer of lives, mutilator of dreams—hers and mine both.

If I were something better, if I were somehow stronger, instead of a brutal near pass at death, that moment could have been our first kiss.

Had I just failed the test then? Was there no longer hope?

Her eyes were glassy; the whites showed all around her dark irises. I watched as she blinked and they refocused, fastening on my new position. We stared at each other for a long moment.

Her lower lip trembled once, and then she opened her mouth. I waited, tensed, for the recrimination. For her to scream at me, to tell me never to come near her again.

"I'm...sorry...Edward," she whispered almost silently.

Of course.

I had to take a deep breath before I could respond.

I calibrated the volume of my voice to be just loud enough for her to hear, trying to keep my tone gentle. "Give me a moment."

She sat back a few inches. Her eyes were still mostly whites.

I took another breath. I could still taste her from here. It fueled the constant burn, but no more than that. I felt...the way I normally did around her. There was no hint in my mind or body now, no sense that the monster was lurking so near to the surface. That I could snap so easily. It made me want to shriek and tear trees out by their roots. If I couldn't feel the edge, couldn't see the trigger, how could I ever protect her from myself?

I could imagine Alice's encouragement. I *had* protected Bella. Nothing *had* happened. But though Alice might have seen that much, watching when my break was still the future and not the past, she couldn't know how it had felt. To lose control of myself, to be weaker than my worst impulse. Not to be able to stop.

But you did stop. That's what she would say. She couldn't know how *not enough* that was.

Bella never looked away from me. Her heart was racing twice as fast as normal. Too fast. It couldn't be healthy. I wanted to take her hand and tell her everything was fine, she was fine, she was safe, there was nothing to worry about—but these would be such obvious lies.

I still felt...normal—what normal had become in these last months, at least. In control. Just exactly the same as before, when my confidence had nearly killed her.

I walked back slowly, wondering if I should keep my distance. But it didn't seem right to shout my apology across the meadow at her. I didn't trust myself to be as close to her as before. I stopped a few paces away, at a conversational distance, and sat on the ground.

I tried to put everything I felt into the words. *"I am so very sorry."*

Bella blinked and then her eyes were too wide again; her heart hammered too fast. Her expression was stuck in place. The words didn't seem to mean anything to her, to register in any way.

In what I immediately knew was a bad idea, I fell back on my usual pattern of trying to keep things casual. I was desperate to remove the frozen shock from her face.

"Would you understand what I meant if I said I was only human?"

A second too late, she nodded—just once. She tried to smile at my tasteless attempt to make light of the situation, but that effort just marred her expression further. She looked pained, and then, finally, afraid.

I'd seen fear on her face before, but I'd always been quickly reassured. Every time I'd half hoped that she'd realized I wasn't worth the immense risk, she'd disproved my assumption. The fear in her eyes had never been fear of *me*.

Until now.

The scent of her fear saturated the air, tangy and metallic.

This was exactly what I'd been waiting for. What I'd always told myself I wanted. For her to turn away. For her to save herself and leave me burning and alone.

Her heart hammered on, and I wanted to laugh and cry. I was getting what I wanted.

And all because she'd leaned in just one inch too close. She'd gotten near enough to smell my scent, and she'd found it pleasant, just as she found my face attractive and all of my other snares compelling. Everything about me made her want to move closer to me, just exactly as it was designed to.

"I'm the world's best predator, aren't I?" I made no attempt to hide the bitterness in my voice now. "Everything about me invites you in—my voice, my face, even my *smell*." It was all so much *overkill*. What was the point of my charms and lures? I was no rooted flytrap, waiting for prey to land inside my mouth. Why couldn't I have been as repulsive on the outside as I was on the inside? "As if I need any of that!"

Now I felt out of control, but not in the same way. All my love and yearning and hope were crumbling to dust, a thousand centuries of grief stretched out in front of me, and *I didn't want to pretend anymore*. If I could have no happiness because I was a monster, then let me be that monster.

I was on my feet, racing like her heart, in two tight circles around the edge of the clearing, wondering if she could even see what I was showing her.

I jerked to a stop where I'd stood before. This was why I didn't need a pretty voice.

"As if you could outrun me." I laughed at the thought, the grotesque comedy of the image in my head. The sound of my laugh bounced in harsh echoes off the trees.

And after the chase, there would be the capture.

The lowest branch of the ancient spruce beside me was in easy reach. I ripped the limb from the body without any effort at all. The wood shrieked and protested, the bark and splinters exploded from the site of the injury. I weighed the bough for a moment in my hand. Roughly eight hundred sixty three pounds. Not enough to win in a fight with the hemlock across the clearing to my right, but enough to do some damage.

I flicked the branch at the hemlock tree, aiming for a knot about thirty feet from the ground. My projectile hit dead center, the thickest end of the bough smashing with a booming *crunch* and disintegrating into shards of shattered wood that rained down on the ferns below with a faint hissing. A fissure split through the center of the knot and snaked its way a few feet in either direction. The hemlock tree trembled once, the shock radiating through the roots and into the ground. I wondered if I'd killed it. I'd have to wait a few months to know. Hopefully it would recover; the meadow was perfect as it was.

So little effort on my part. I'd not needed to use more than a tiny fraction of my available strength. And still, so much violence. So much harm.

In two strides I was standing over her, just an arm's length way.

"As if you could fight me off."

The bitterness disappeared from my voice. My little tantrum had cost me no energy, but it had drained some of my ire.

Throughout it all, she'd never moved. She remained paralyzed now, her eyes frozen open. We stared at each other for what seemed like a long time. I was still so angry at myself, but there was no fire left in it. It all seemed pointless. I was what I was.

She moved first. Just a little bit. Her hands had fallen limp in her lap after I'd wrenched away from her, but now one of them twitched open. Her fingers stretched up slightly in my direction. It was probably an unconscious movement, but it was eerily similar to when she'd pleaded "Come back" in her sleep and reached for *something*. I'd wished then that she could be dreaming of me.

That was the night before Port Angeles, the night before I learned that she already knew what I was. If I'd been aware of what Jacob Black had told her, I never would have believed she could dream of me except in a nightmare. But none of it had mattered to her.

There was still terror in her eyes. Of course there was. But there seemed to be a plea in them, too. Was there any chance she wanted me to come back to her now? Even if she did, should I?

Her pain, my greatest weakness—as Alice had shown me it would be. I hated to see her frightened. It broke me to know how much I deserved that fear, but more than either of those burdens, I could not *bear* to see her grief. It stripped me of my ability to make anything close to a good decision.

"Don't be afraid," I begged in a whisper. "I promise—" No, that had become too casual a word. "I *swear* not to hurt you. Don't be afraid."

I moved closer to her slowly, making no movement that she would not have time to anticipate. I sat gradually, in deliberate stages, so that I was once again where we'd begun. I slouched down a bit so that my face was level with hers.

The pace of her heart eased. Her lids relaxed back into their usual place. It was as if my proximity calmed her.

"Please forgive me," I pleaded. "I can control myself. You caught me off guard, but I'm on my best behavior now." What a pathetic apology. Still, it brought a hint of a smile to the corner of her lips. And like a fool, I fell back into my immature efforts to be amusing. "I'm not thirsty today, honestly."

I actually winked at her. One would think I was thirteen instead of a hundred and four.

But she laughed. A little out of breath, a little wobbly, but still a real laugh, with real mirth and relief. Her eyes warmed, her shoulders loosened, and her hands opened again.

It felt so *right* to gently place my hand back inside hers. It shouldn't, but it did.

"Are you all right?"

She stared at our hands, then glanced up to meet my gaze for a moment, and finally looked down again. She started to trace the lines across my palm with the tip of her finger, just as she had been doing before my frenzy. Her eyes returned to mine and a smile slowly spread across her face till the little dimple appeared in her chin. There was no judgment and no regret in that smile.

I smiled back, feeling as though I could only just now appreciate the beauty of this place. The sun and the flowers and the gilded air, they were suddenly there for me, joyous and merciful. I felt the gift of *her* mercy, and my stone heart swelled with gratitude.

The relief, the confusion of joy and guilt, suddenly reminded me of the day I'd come home, so many decades ago.

I hadn't been ready then, either. I'd planned to wait. I wanted my eyes to be golden again before Carlisle saw me. But they were still a strange orange, an amber that tended more toward red. I was having difficulty adapting to my former diet. It had never been so hard before. I was afraid that if I didn't have Carlisle's help, I wouldn't be able to keep going. That I would fall back into my old ways.

It worried me, having that evidence so clear in my eyes. I wondered what was the worst reception I could expect? Would he just send me away? Would he find it difficult to look at me, to see what a disappointment I had become? Was there a penance he would demand? I would do it, whatever he asked. Would my efforts to improve move him at all, or would he just see my failure?

It was simple enough to find them; they hadn't moved far from the place I'd left them. Maybe to make it easier for me to return?

Their house was the only one in this high, wild spot. The winter sun was glinting off the windows as I approached from below, so I couldn't tell if anyone was home. Rather than take the shorter route through the trees, I paced toward them through an empty field, blanketed in snow, where—even bundled up against the sun's glare—I would be easy to spot. I moved slowly. I didn't want to run. It might alarm them.

It was Esme who saw me first.

"Edward!" I heard her cry, though I was still a mile out.

In less than a second I saw her figure dart through a side door, racing through the rocks surrounding the mountain ledge and stirring up a thick cloud of snow crystals behind her.

Edward! He's come home!

It was not the mindset I'd been expecting. But then, she hadn't seen my eyes clearly.

Edward? Can it be?

My father was following close behind her now, catching up with his longer stride.

There was nothing but a desperate hope in his thoughts. No judgment. Not yet.

"Edward!" Esme shouted with an unmistakable ring of joy in her voice.

And then she was upon me, her arms wrapped tight around my neck, her lips kissing my cheek over and over again. *Please don't go away again.*

Only a second later, Carlisle's arms encircled us both.

Thank you, he thought, his mind fervent with sincerity. *Thank you for coming back to us.*

"Carlisle...Esme...I'm so sorry. I'm so—"

"Shush, now," Esme whispered, tucking her head against my neck and breathing in my scent. *My boy.*

I looked up into Carlisle's face, leaving my eyes open wide. Hiding nothing.

You're here. Carlisle stared back at my face with only happiness in his mind. Though he had to know what the color of my eyes meant, there was no off note to his delight. *There's nothing to apologize for.*

Slowly, hardly able to trust that it could be so simple, I raised my arms and returned my family's embrace.

I felt that same undeserved acceptance now, and I could barely believe that all of it—my bad behavior, both voluntary and involuntary—was suddenly behind us. But her forgiveness seemed to wash the darkness away.

"So where were we, before I behaved so rudely?" I remembered where *I* had been. Just inches from her parted lips. Enraptured by the mystery of her mind.

She blinked twice. "I honestly can't remember."

That was understandable. I breathed in fire and blew it back out, wishing it would do some actual damage to me.

"I think we were talking about why you were afraid, besides the obvious reason." The obvious fear had probably driven the other out of her mind completely.

But she smiled and looked down at my hand again. "Oh, right."

Nothing more.

"Well?" I prompted.

Rather than meet my gaze, she started tracing patterns across my palm. I tried to read their sequences, hoping for a picture or even letters—E-D-W-A-R-D-P-L-E-A-S-E-G-O-A-W-A-Y—but I could find no meaning in them. Just more mysteries. Another question she would never answer. I didn't deserve answers.

I sighed. "How easily frustrated I am."

She looked up then, her eyes probing mine. We stared at each other for a few seconds, and I was surprised at the intensity of her gaze. I felt that she was reading me more successfully than I was ever able to read her.

"I was afraid," she began, and I realized gratefully that she was answering my question after all. "Because . . . for, well, obvious reasons, I can't *stay* with you." Her eyes dropped again as she said the word *stay*. I understood her clearly, for once. I could hear that when she said *stay*, she didn't mean for this moment in the sunshine, for the afternoon or the week. She meant it the way I wanted to say it to her. *Stay always. Stay forever.* "And I'm afraid that I'd like to stay with you, much more than I should."

I thought of all that would entail if, after all, I forced her to do exactly as she described. If I made her stay forever. Every sacrifice she would bear, every loss she would mourn, every stinging regret, every aching, tearless stare.

"Yes." It was hard to agree with her, even with all that pain fresh in my imagination. I wanted it so much. "That is something to be afraid of, indeed. Wanting to be with me." Selfish me. "That's really not in your best interest."

She scowled at my hand as if she didn't like my acknowledgment any more than I did.

This was a dangerous path to even hint at. Hades and his pomegranate. How many toxic seeds had I already infected her with? Enough that Alice had seen her pale and grieving in my absence. Though it felt as though I, also, had been corrupted. Hooked. Addicted with no hope of recovery. I couldn't fully form the picture in my head. *Leaving her.* How would I survive? Alice had shown me Bella's anguish in my absence, but what would she see of me in that version of the future, if she looked? I couldn't believe I would be anything more than a broken shadow, useless, crumpled, empty.

I spoke the thought aloud, but mostly to myself. "I should have left long ago. I should leave now. But I don't know if I *can*."

She still stared at our hands, but her cheeks warmed. "I don't want you to leave," she mumbled.

She *wanted* me to stay with her. I tried to fight the happiness, the surrender it pulled me toward. Was the choice even mine, or was it hers alone now? Would I stay until she told me to go? Her words seemed to echo in the faint breeze. *I don't want you to leave.*

"Which is exactly why I should." Surely the more time we were together, the harder it would grow to be apart. "But don't worry. I'm essentially a selfish creature. I crave your company too much to do what I should."

"I'm glad." She said the words simply, as if this was an obvious thing. As if every girl would be pleased that her favorite monster was too selfish to put her before himself.

My temper flared, anger pointed only at myself. With rigid control, I removed my hand from hers.

"Don't be! It's not only your company I crave! Never forget

that. Never forget I am more dangerous to you than I am to anyone else."

She looked at me quizzically. There was no fear anywhere in her eyes now. Her head cocked slightly to the left.

"I don't think I understand exactly what you mean—by that last part anyway," she said, her tone analytical. It reminded me of our conversation in the cafeteria, when she had asked about hunting. She sounded as if she were gathering data for a report—one she was vitally interested in, but still, no more than an academic inquiry.

I couldn't help but smile at her expression. My anger vanished as quickly as it had come. Why waste time with ire when there were so many more pleasant emotions available?

"How do I explain?" I murmured. Naturally she had no idea what I was talking about. I had not been terribly specific when it came to my reaction to her scent. Of course I hadn't; it was an ugly thing, something I was deeply ashamed of. Not to mention the overt horror of the subject. How to explain, indeed. "And without frightening you again . . . hmmmm."

Her fingers uncurled, stretching toward my own. And I couldn't resist. I placed my hand gently back inside hers. The willingness of her touch, the eager way she wrapped her fingers tightly around mine, helped to calm my nerves. I knew I was about to tell her everything—I could feel the truth churning inside me, ready to erupt. But I had no idea how she would process it, even as generous as she always was toward me. I savored this moment of her acceptance, knowing it could end abruptly.

I sighed. "That's amazingly pleasant, the warmth."

She smiled and looked down at our hands, too, fascination in her eyes.

There was no help for it. I was going to have to be obscenely graphic. Dancing around the facts would only confuse her, and she needed to know this. I took a deep breath.

"You know how everyone enjoys different flavors? Some people love chocolate ice cream, others prefer strawberry?"

Ugh. It sounded worse out loud than I would have thought for such a weak beginning. Bella nodded in what looked like polite agreement, but otherwise her expression was smooth. Perhaps it would take a minute to sink in.

"Sorry about the food analogy," I apologized. "I couldn't think of another way to explain."

She grinned—a smile with real humor and affinity; the dimple sprang into existence. Her grin made me feel as though we were in this ludicrous situation together, not as opponents but as partners, working side by side to find a solution. I couldn't think of anything I would wish for more—besides, of course, the impossible. That I could be human, too. I grinned back at her, but I knew my smile was neither as genuine nor as guiltless as hers.

Her hands tightened around mine, prompting me to continue.

I spoke the words slowly, trying to use the best analogy possible, knowing even as I did that I was failing. "You see, every person smells different, has a different essence. If you locked an alcoholic in a room full of stale beer, he'd gladly drink it. But he could resist, if he wished to...if he were a *recovering* alcoholic. Now let's say you placed in that room a glass of hundred-year-old brandy, the rarest, finest cognac—and filled the room with its warm aroma—how do you think he would fare then?"

Was I painting too sympathetic a picture of myself? Describing a tragic victim rather than a true villain?

She stared into my eyes, and while I automatically tried to hear her internal reaction, I got the feeling that she was trying to read mine as well.

I thought through my words and wondered whether the analogy was *strong* enough.

"Maybe that's not the right comparison." I mused. "Maybe it would be too easy to turn down the brandy. Perhaps I should have made our alcoholic a heroin addict instead."

She smiled, not as widely as before, but with a cheeky twist to her pursed lips. "So what you're saying is, I'm your brand of heroin?"

I almost laughed with surprise. She was doing what I was always trying to do—make a joke, lighten the mood, deescalate—only she was successful.

"Yes, you are exactly my brand of heroin."

It was surely a horrific admission, and yet, somehow, I felt relief. It was all her doing, her support and understanding. It made my head spin that she could somehow forgive *all* of this. How?

But she was back to researcher mode.

"Does that happen often?" she asked, her head tilting curiously to one side.

Even with my unique ability to hear thought, it was hard to make exact comparisons. I didn't truly feel the sensations of the person I listened to; I only knew their thoughts about those feelings.

How I interpreted thirst wasn't even exactly the way the rest of my family did. To me, the thirst was a fire burning. Jasper described it as a burning, too, but to him it was like acid rather than flame, chemical and saturating. Rosalie thought of it as profound dryness, a screaming lack rather than an outside force. Emmett tended to evaluate his thirst in the same way; I supposed that was natural, as Rosalie had been the first and most frequent influence in his second life.

So I knew of the times the others had had difficulty resisting, and when they had not been able to resist, but I couldn't know exactly how potent their temptation had been. I could make an educated guess, however, based on their standard level of control. It was an imperfect technique, but I thought it should answer her curiosity.

This was more horror. I couldn't look her in the eye while I answered. I stared at the sun instead as it slipped closer to the edge of the trees. Every second gone hurt me more than they ever had—seconds I could never have with her again. I wished we didn't need to spend these precious seconds on something so distasteful.

"I spoke to my brothers about it.... To Jasper, every one of you is much the same. He's the most recent to join our family. It's a struggle for him to abstain at all. He hasn't had time to grow sensitive to the differences in smell, in flavor—" I flinched, realizing too late where my rambling had taken me. "Sorry," I added quickly.

She gave an exasperated little *huff.* "I don't *mind.* Please don't worry about offending me, or frightening me, or whichever. That's the way you think. I can understand, or I can try to at least. Just explain however you can."

I tried to settle myself. I needed to accept that through some miracle, Bella was able to know the darkest things about me and not be terror-stricken. Able not to hate me for it. If she was strong enough to hear this, I needed to be strong enough to speak the words. I looked back at the sun, feeling the deadline in its slow descent.

"So...," I began again slowly, "Jasper wasn't sure if he'd ever come across someone who was as...appealing as you are to me. Which makes me think not. Emmett has been on the wagon longer, so to speak, and he understood what I meant. He says twice, for him, once stronger than the other."

I finally met her gaze. Her eyes were narrowed just slightly, her focus intent. "And for you?" she asked.

That was an easy answer, with no guesswork needed. "Never."

She seemed to consider that word for a long moment. I wished I knew what it meant to her. Then her face relaxed a bit.

"What did Emmett do?" she asked in a conversational tone.

As if this were just some storybook fairy tale I was sharing with her, as if good always won the day and—though the road might get dark at points—nothing truly evil or permanently cruel was allowed to happen.

How could I tell her about these two innocent victims? Humans with hopes and fears, people with families and friends who loved them, imperfect beings who deserved the chance to improve, to try. A man and a woman with names now inscribed on simple headstones in obscure graveyards.

Would she think better or worse of us if she knew that Carlisle had required our attendance at their funerals? Not just these two, but every victim of our mistakes and lapses. Were we a tiny bit less damned because we had listened to those who knew them best describe their shortened lives? Because we bore witness to the tears and cries of pain? The monetary aid we'd anonymously provided to make sure there was no unnecessary physical suffering seemed crass in retrospect. Such a weak recompense.

She gave up waiting for an answer. "I guess I know."

Her expression was mournful now. Did she condemn Emmett while she gave me so much mercy? His crimes, though much greater than two, were less in total than mine. It pained me that she would think badly of him. Was this—the specificity of two victims—the offense she would balk at?

"Even the strongest of us fall off the wagon, don't we?" I asked weakly.

Could this be forgiven, too?

Perhaps not.

She winced, flinching away from me. No more than an inch, but it felt like a yard. Her lips pulled into a frown.

"What are you asking? My permission?" The hard edge in her voice sounded like sarcasm.

So here was her limit. I'd thought she'd been extraordinarily kind and merciful, too forgiving, in truth. But actually, she'd simply underestimated my depravity. She must have thought that, for all my warnings, I'd only ever been tempted. That I'd always made the better choice, as I had in Port Angeles, driving away from bloodshed.

I'd told her that same night how, despite our best efforts, my family made mistakes. Had she not realized that I'd been confessing to murder? No wonder she accepted things so easily; she thought I was always strong, that I only had near misses on my conscience. Well, it wasn't her fault. I'd never explicitly admitted to killing anyone. I'd never given her the body count.

Her expression softened while I spiraled. I tried to think of how to say goodbye in such a way that she would know how much I loved her, but not feel threatened by that love.

"I mean," she explained suddenly, no edge in her tone, "is there no hope, then?"

In a fraction of a second I replayed our last exchange in my head, and realized how I'd misinterpreted her reaction. When I had begged pardon for past sins, she'd thought I was excusing a future, but imminent, crime. That I meant to—

"No, no!" I had to fight to slow my words down to human speed—I was in such a hurry to have her hear them. "Of course there's hope! I mean, of course I won't—"

Kill you. I couldn't finish the sentence. Those words were agony to me, imagining her gone. My eyes bored into hers, trying to communicate everything I couldn't say. "It's different for us," I promised. "Emmett…these were strangers he happened across. It was a long time ago, and he wasn't as… practiced, as careful, as he is now."

She sifted through my words, heard the parts I hadn't said.

"So if we'd met…" She paused, searching for the right scenario. "Oh, in a dark alley or something…?"

Ah, here was a bitter truth.

"It took everything I had not to jump up in the middle of that class full of children and—"

Kill you. My eyes fell from hers. So much shame.

Still, I couldn't leave her any flattering illusions about me.

"When you walked past me," I admitted, "I could have ruined everything Carlisle has built for us, right then and there. If I hadn't been denying my thirst for the last, well, too many years, I wouldn't have been able to stop myself."

I could see the classroom so clearly in my mind. Perfect recall was more a curse than a gift. Did I need to remember with such precision every second of that hour? The fear that had dilated her eyes, the reflection of my monstrous countenance in them? The way her scent had destroyed every good thing about me?

Her expression was far away. Maybe she was remembering, too.

"You must have thought I was possessed."

She didn't deny it.

"I couldn't understand why," she said in a fragile voice. "How you could hate me so quickly..."

She'd intuited the truth in that moment. She'd understood correctly that I *had* hated her. Almost as much as I'd desired her.

"To me, it was like you were some kind of demon, summoned straight from my own personal hell to ruin me." It was painful to relive the emotion of it, to remember seeing her as *prey*. "The fragrance coming off your skin...I thought it would make me deranged that first day. In that one hour, I thought of a hundred different ways to lure you from the room with me, to get you alone. And I fought them each back, thinking of my family, what I could do to them. I had to run out, to get away before I could speak the words that would make you follow.... You would have come."

What must it be like for her to know this? How did she align the opposing facts? Me, would-be murderer, and me, would-be lover? What did she think of my confidence, my certainty that she would have followed the murderer?

Her chin lifted a centimeter. "Without a doubt," she agreed.

Our hands were still carefully intertwined. Hers were nearly as still as mine, aside from the blood pulsing through them. I wondered if she felt the same fear that I did—the fear that they might have to come apart, and she wouldn't be able to find the courage and forgiveness necessary to bring them together again.

It was a little easier to confess when I wasn't looking into her eyes.

"And then," I continued, "as I tried to rearrange my schedule in a pointless attempt to avoid you, you were there—in that close, warm little room, the scent was maddening. I so very nearly took you then. There was only one other frail human there—so easily dealt with."

I felt the shiver move down her arms to her hands. With every new attempt to explain, I found myself using more and more distressing words. They were the right words, the truthful words, and they were also so ugly.

There was no stopping them now, though, and she sat silent and nearly motionless as they gushed out of me, more confessions mixed up in explanations. I told her about my unsuccessful attempt to run away, and the arrogance that brought me back; how that arrogance had shaped our interactions, and how the frustration of her hidden thoughts had tormented me; how her scent had never stopped being both torture and temptation. My family wove in and out of the story and I wondered whether she could see how they influenced my actions at every turn. I told her how saving her from Tyler's van had changed my perspective, had forced me to see that she was more to me than just a risk and an irritant.

"In the hospital?" she prompted when my words ran out. She studied my face with compassion, with eager, nonjudgmental desire for the next chapter. I was no longer shocked by her benevolence, but it would always be miraculous to me.

I explained my misgivings, not for saving her, but for exposing myself and consequently my family, so that she would understand my harshness that day in the empty corridor. This led naturally into my family's varied reactions, and I wondered what she thought of the fact that some of them had wanted to silence her in the most permanent way possible. She didn't shiver now, or betray any fear. How strange it must be for her, to learn the whole story, the dark now woven through the light she'd known.

I told her how I'd tried to feign total indifference to her after that, to protect us all, and how unsuccessful I'd been.

I wondered privately, not for the first time, where I would be now if I had not acted so instinctively that day in the school parking lot. If—as I'd just grotesquely described to her—I had stood by and let her die in a car accident, then revealed myself to the human witnesses in the most monstrous way possible. My family would have had to flee Forks immediately. I imagined their reactions to that version of events would have been… mostly the opposite. Rosalie and Jasper would not have been angry. A trifle smug, perhaps, but understanding. Carlisle would have been deeply disappointed, but still forgiving. Would Alice have mourned the friend she'd never gotten to meet? Only Esme and Emmett would have reacted in a manner nearly identical to their first reactions: Esme with concern for my well-being, Emmett with a shrug.

I knew that I would have had some small inkling of the disaster that had befallen me. Even that early, after just a few words exchanged, my fascination with her was strong. But could I have guessed the vastness of the tragedy? I thought not. I would have ached, certainly, and then gone about my empty half life never realizing how very much I had lost. Never knowing actual happiness.

It would have been easier to lose her then, I knew. Just as I would never have known joy, I wouldn't have suffered the depths of pain I now knew to exist.

I contemplated her kind, sweet face, so dear to me now, so much the center of my world. The only thing I wanted to look at for the rest of time.

She gazed back, the same wonder in her eyes.

"And for all that," I concluded my long confession, "I'd have fared better if I had exposed us all at that first moment, than if now, here—with no witnesses and nothing to stop me—I were to hurt you."

Her eyes widened, not in fear or surprise. Fascination.

"Why?" she asked.

This explanation would be as difficult as any of the others, with many words I hated to say, but there were also words I very much wanted to speak to her.

"Isabella…Bella." It was a pleasure just to say her name. It felt like a kind of avowal. *This is the name to which I belong.*

I carefully loosed one hand and stroked her soft hair, warm

from the sun. The joy of the simple touch, the knowledge that I was free to reach out to her this way, was overwhelming. I grasped her hands again.

"I couldn't live with myself if I ever hurt you. You don't know how it's tortured me." I hated to look away from her sympathetic expression, but it was too hard to see her *other* face, the one from Alice's vision, in the same frame. "The thought of you, still, white, cold... to never see you blush scarlet again, to never see that flash of intuition in your eyes when you see through my pretenses... it would be unendurable." That word did nothing to convey the anguish behind the thought. But I was through the ugly part now, and I could say the things I'd wanted to tell her for so long. I met her eyes again, rejoicing in this confession.

"You are the most important thing to me now. The most important thing to me ever."

Just as the word *unendurable* was not enough, so were these words weak echoes of the feelings they tried to describe. I hoped she could see in my eyes exactly how inadequate they were. She was always better at knowing my mind than I was at reading hers.

She held my exultant gaze for just a moment, pink creeping into her cheeks, but then her eyes fell to our hands. I thrilled to the beauty of her complexion, seeing only the loveliness and nothing else.

"You already know how I feel, of course," she said, her voice not much louder than a whisper. "I'm here... which, roughly translated, means I would rather die than stay away from you."

I wouldn't have thought it possible to feel such euphoria and such regret at the same time. She wanted *me*—bliss. She was risking her very life for me—unacceptable.

She scowled, her eyes still lowered. "I'm an idiot."

I laughed at her conclusion. From a certain angle, she had a point. Any species that ran so headlong into the arms of its most dangerous predator wouldn't survive long. It was a good thing she was an outlier.

"You are an idiot," I teased gently. And I would never stop being grateful for it.

Bella glanced up with a puckish grin, and we both laughed together. It was such a relief to laugh after my grueling revelations that my laugh shifted from humor to sheer joy. I was sure she felt the same. We were utterly in sync for one perfect moment.

Though it was impossible, we belonged together. Everything was wrong with this picture—a killer and an innocent leaning close, each basking in the presence of the other, totally at peace. It was as if we'd somehow ascended to a better world, where such impossibilities could exist.

I was suddenly reminded of a painting I'd seen many years ago.

Whenever we canvassed the countryside for likely towns in which to settle, Carlisle would frequently make side trips to duck into old parish churches. He seemed unable to stop himself. Something about the simple wooden structures, usually dark for lack of good windows, the floorboards and pew backs all worn smooth and smelling of layer upon layer of human touches, brought him a reflective kind of calm. Thoughts of his father and his childhood were brought to the fore, but the violent end seemed far away in those moments. He remembered only pleasant things.

On one such diversion, we found an old Quaker meetinghouse around thirty miles north of Philadelphia. It was a small building, no bigger than a farmhouse, with a stone exterior and a very Spartan arrangement inside. So plain were the knotty floors and straight-backed pews that I was almost shocked to see an adornment on the far wall. Carlisle's interest was piqued as well, and we both examined it.

It was quite a small painting, no more than fifteen inches square. I guessed that it was older than the stone church that housed it. The artist was clearly untrained, his style amateurish. And yet, there was something in the simple, poorly wrought image that managed to convey an emotion. There was a warm vulnerability to the animals depicted, an aching kind of tenderness. I was strangely moved by this kinder universe the artist had envisioned.

A better world, Carlisle had thought to himself.

The sort of world where this present moment could exist, I thought now, and felt that aching tenderness again.

"And so the lion fell in love with the lamb...," I whispered.

Her eyes were so open and accessible for one second, and then she flushed again and looked down. She steadied her breath for a moment, and her impish smile returned.

"What a stupid lamb," she teased, stretching out the joke.

"What a sick, masochistic lion," I countered.

I wasn't sure that was a true statement, though. In one light, yes, I was deliberately causing myself unnecessary pain and enjoying it, the textbook definition of masochism. But the pain was the price...and the reward was so much more than the pain. Really, the price was negligible. I would pay it ten times over.

"Why...?" she murmured, hesitant.

I smiled at her, eager to know her mind. "Yes?"

A hint of the forehead crease began to form. "Tell me why you ran from me before."

Her words hit me physically, lodging in the pit of my stomach. I couldn't understand why she would want to rehash a moment so loathsome.

"You know why."

She shook her head, and her brows pulled down. "No, I mean, *exactly* what did I do wrong?" She spoke intently, serious now. "I'll have to be on my guard, you see, so I better start learning what I shouldn't do. This, for example"—she stroked her fingertips slowly up the back of my hand to my wrist, leaving a trail of painless fire—"seems to be all right."

How like her to take the responsibility on herself.

"You didn't do anything wrong, Bella. It was my fault."

Her chin lifted. It would have implied stubbornness if her eyes were not so pleading.

"But I want to help, if I can, to not make this harder for you."

My first instinct was to continue insisting that this was my problem and not something for her to worry about. Yet I knew that she was simply trying to understand me, with all my strange and monstrous quirks. She would be happier if I just answered her question as clearly as possible.

How to explain bloodlust, though? So shameful.

"Well... it was just how close you were. Most humans instinctively shy away from us, are repelled by our alienness.... I wasn't expecting you to come so close. And the smell of your throat—"

I broke off, hoping I had not disgusted her.

Her mouth was pursed as if fighting off a smile.

"Okay, then, no throat exposure." She made a show of tucking her chin against her right collarbone.

It was clearly her intention to ease my anxiety, and it worked. I had to laugh at her expression.

"No, really," I reassured her. "It was more the surprise than anything else."

I lifted my hand again and rested it lightly against her neck, feeling the incredible softness of her skin there, the warm give of it. My thumb grazed her jawline. The electric pulse that only she could awaken started to thrum through my body.

"You see," I whispered. "Perfectly fine."

Her pulse began to race as well. I could feel it under my hand and hear her galloping heart. Pink flooded her face from her chin to her hairline. The sound and sight of her response, rather than awakening my thirst again, seemed only to speed the rush of my more human reactions. I couldn't remember ever feeling this alive; I doubted I ever had, even when I'd *been* alive.

"The blush on your cheeks is lovely," I murmured.

I gently extracted my left hand from hers, and arranged it so that I was cradling her face between my palms. Her pupils dilated and her heartbeat increased.

I wanted so much to kiss her then. Her soft, curving lips, ever so slightly parted, mesmerized me and drew me forward. But, though these new human emotions now seemed so much stronger than anything else, I didn't fully trust myself. I knew I needed one more test. I thought I'd passed through Alice's knot, but still felt something was lacking. I realized now what more I had to do.

One thing I'd always avoided, never let my mind explore.

"Be very still," I warned her. Her breath hitched.

Slowly, I leaned close, watching her expression for any hint that this was unwelcome to her. I found none.

Finally, I let my head dip forward, and turned it to lean my cheek against the base of her throat. The heat of her warm-blooded life pulsed through her fragile skin and into the cold stone of my body. That pulse leaped beneath my touch. I kept my breathing steady as a machine, in and out, controlled. I waited, judging every minuscule happening inside my body. Perhaps I waited longer than necessary, but it was a very pleasant place to linger.

When I felt sure that no trap waited for me here, I proceeded.

Cautiously I readjusted, using slow, steady movements so that nothing would surprise or frighten her. As my hands drifted from her jaw to the points of her shoulders, she shivered, and for a moment I lost my careful hold on my breathing. I recovered, settling myself again, and then moved my head so that my ear was directly over her heart.

The sound of it, loud before, seemed to surround me in stereo now. The earth beneath me didn't seem quite as steady, as if it rocked faintly to the beat of her heart.

The sigh escaped against my will. *"Ah."*

I wished I could stay like this forever, immersed in the sound of her heart and warmed by her skin. It was time for the final test, though, and I wanted it behind me.

For the first time, as I breathed in the sear of her scent, I let myself imagine it. Rather than blocking my thoughts, cutting them off and forcing them deep down, out of my conscious mind, I allowed them to range unfettered. They did not go willingly, not now. But I forced myself to go where I had always avoided.

I imagined tasting her . . . draining her.

I'd had enough experience to know what the relief would feel like, if I were to utterly quench my most bestial need. Her blood had so much more pull for me than any other human's I'd encountered—I could only assume that the relief and pleasure would be that much more intense.

Her blood would soothe my aching throat, erasing all the months of fire. It would feel as if I had never burned for her; the alleviation of pain would be total.

The sweetness of her blood on my tongue was harder to imagine. I knew I had never experienced any blood so perfectly matched to my desire, but I was sure it would satisfy every craving I had ever known.

For the first time in three quarters of a century—the span I had survived without human blood—I would be totally sated. My body would feel strong and whole. It would be many weeks before I thirsted again.

I played the sequence of events through to the end, surprised, even as I let these taboo imaginings loose, at how little they appealed to me now. Even withholding the inevitable sequel—the return of the thirst, the emptiness of the world without her—I felt no desire to act on my imaginings.

I also saw very clearly in that moment that there was no separate monster and never had been one. Eager to disconnect my mind from my desires, I had—as was my habit—personified that hated part of myself to distance it from the parts that I considered *me*. Just as I had created the harpy to give myself someone to fight. It was a coping mechanism, and not a very good one. Better to see myself as the whole, bad and good, and work with the reality of it.

My breathing continued steadily, the bite of her scent a

welcome counterpoint to the glut of other physical sensations that overwhelmed me as I held her.

I thought I understood a little better what had happened to me before, in the violent reaction that had terrified us both. I had been so convinced that I *might* be overwhelmed, that when I actually *was* overwhelmed, it was almost a self-fulfilling prophecy. My anxiety, the agonizing visions I'd obsessed over, plus the months of self-doubt that had shaken my former confidence all combined to weaken the determination that I now knew was *absolutely* up to the job of protecting Bella.

Even Alice's nightmare vision was suddenly less vibrant, the colors leaching away. Its power to shake me was ebbing, because, and this was obvious now, *that future was entirely impossible.* Bella and I would leave this place hand in hand, and my life would finally begin.

We were through the knot.

I had no doubt that Alice saw this, too, and that she was rejoicing.

Though I was exceptionally comfortable in my current position, I was also eager for the rest of my life to unfold.

I leaned away from her, letting my hands trace along the length of her arms as they dropped to my side, full of simple happiness to just see her face again.

She looked at me curiously, unaware of the momentous occurrences inside my head.

"It won't be so hard again," I promised, though I realized as I spoke that my words probably made little sense to her.

"Was that very hard for you?" she asked with sympathetic eyes.

Her concern warmed me to the core.

"Not nearly as bad as I imagined it would be. And you?"

She gave me one disbelieving glance. "No, it wasn't bad... for me."

She made it look so easy, being embraced by a vampire. But it must take more courage than she let on. "You know what I mean."

She smiled a wide, warm, lopsidedly dimpled grin. It was clear that if it *did* take any effort to bear my nearness, she would never admit to it.

Giddy. That was the only word I could think of to describe the high I was experiencing. It wasn't a word I often thought of in relation to myself. Every thought in my head wanted to spill out through my lips. I wanted to hear every thought in hers. That, at least, was nothing new. Everything else was new. Everything had changed.

I reached for her hand—without first exhaustively debating the act in my mind—simply because I wanted to feel it against my skin. I felt free to be spontaneous for the first time. These new impulses were completely unrelated to the old.

"Here." I placed her palm against my cheek. "Do you feel how warm it is?"

Her reaction to this first instinctive act of mine was more than I'd expected. Her fingers trembled against my cheekbone. Her eyes grew round and the smile slipped away. Her heartbeat and her breathing accelerated.

Before I could regret the deed, she leaned closer and whispered, "Don't move."

A thrill shivered through me.

Her request was easily accomplished. I froze myself into the absolute stillness that humans were incapable of duplicating. I didn't know what she intended—acclimating herself to my *lack* of a circulatory system seemed unlikely—but was eager to find out. I closed my eyes. I wasn't sure whether I did this to free her from the self-consciousness of my scrutiny, or because I wanted no distractions from this moment.

Her hand began to move very slowly. First she stroked my cheek. Her fingertips grazed across my closed eyelids, and then brushed a half circle beneath them. Where her skin met mine, it left a trail of tingling heat. She traced the length of my nose and then, with the trembling in her fingers more pronounced now, the shape of my lips.

My frozen form melted. I let my mouth fall slightly open, so that I could breathe in the nearness of her.

One finger caressed my bottom lip again, and then her hand fell away. I felt the air cool between us as she leaned back.

I opened my eyes and met her gaze. Her face was flushed, her heart still raced. I felt a phantom echo of the pace inside my own body, though no blood pushed it.

I *wanted*... so many things. Things I had not felt any need for in my entire immortal life before I met her. Things I was sure I had not wanted before I was immortal, either. And I felt that some of them, things I'd always thought impossible, might, in fact, be very possible.

But while I felt comfortable with her now as far as my thirst was concerned, I was still too strong. So much stronger than she was, every limb of my body unyielding as steel. I must always think of her fragility. It would take time to learn exactly how to move around her.

She stared at me, waiting, wondering what I thought of *her* touches.

"I wish... I wish you could feel the... complexity," I fumbled to explain. "The confusion I feel. That you could understand."

A tendril of her hair, caught in the breeze, danced in the sun, catching the light with a reddish shine. I reached out to feel the texture of that errant lock between my fingers. And then, because it was so close, I couldn't resist stroking her face. Her cheek felt like velvet left out in the sun.

Her head tilted into my hand, but her eyes remained intent on my face.

"Tell me," she breathed.

I couldn't imagine where to even begin. "I... don't think I can. I've told you, on the one hand, the hunger, the thirst, that"—I gave her an apologetic half smile—"deplorable creature I am, I feel for you. And I think you can understand that, to an extent. Though as you are not addicted to any illegal substances, you probably can't empathize completely.... But..."

My fingers seemed to search out her lips of their own accord. I brushed them lightly. Finally. They were softer than I'd imagined. Warmer.

"There are other hungers," I continued. "Hungers I don't even understand, that are foreign to me."

She gave me that slightly skeptical look again. "I may understand *that* better than you think."

"I'm not used to feeling so human," I admitted. "Is it always like this?" The wild current singing through my system, the magnetic pull drawing me forward, the feeling that there might never be a closeness that would be close enough.

"For me?" She paused, considering. "No, never. Never before this."

I took both her hands between mine.

"I don't know how to be close to you," I cautioned her. "I don't know if I can."

Where to set the limits to keep her safe? How to keep selfish desire from pushing those limits unwisely?

She shifted closer to me. I held myself still and careful while she rested the side of her face against the bare skin of my chest—I'd never been more grateful for Alice's influence on my wardrobe than in this second.

Her eyes slid closed. She sighed contentedly. "This is enough."

The invitation was not something I could resist. I knew I was capable of getting this much right. With meticulous care, I wrapped my arms lightly around her, truly holding her in my embrace for the first time. I pressed my lips against the crown of her head, breathing in her warm scent. A first kiss, though a stealthy one—unrequited.

She chuckled once. "You're better at this than you give yourself credit for."

"I have human instincts," I murmured into her hair. "They may be buried deep, but they're there."

The passing of time was meaningless while I cradled her, my lips against her hair. Her heart moved languorously now, her breath was slow and even against my skin. I only noticed the change when the shadow of the trees fell over us. Without the reflection off my skin, the meadow seemed suddenly darker, evening rather than afternoon.

Bella heaved a deep sigh. Not contented this time, but regretful.

"You have to go," I guessed.

"I thought you couldn't read my mind."

I grinned and then pressed one last hidden kiss to the top of her head. "It's getting clearer."

We'd been a long time here, though now it seemed like mere seconds. She would have human needs she was neglecting. I thought of the long, slow trek to get to the meadow, and I had an idea.

I pulled away—reluctant to end our embrace no matter what came next—and placed my hands lightly on her shoulders.

"Can I show you something?" I asked.

"Show me what?" she asked, a hint of suspicion in her voice. I realized my tone was more than a little enthusiastic.

"I'll show you how *I* travel in the forest," I explained.

Her lips pursed, doubtful, and the crease between her brows appeared, deeper than before, even when I'd nearly attacked her. It surprised me a little; she was usually so curious and fearless.

"Don't worry," I reassured her. "You'll be very safe, and we'll get to your truck much faster."

I grinned encouragingly at her.

She considered for a minute, and then whispered, "Will you turn into a bat?"

I couldn't suppress my laughter. I didn't really want to. I couldn't remember ever feeling so free to be myself. Of course, that wasn't exactly true; I was always free and open when it was just me and my family. However, I never felt like *this* with my family—ecstatic, wild, every cell of my body alive in a new, electric way. Being with Bella intensified all sensation.

"Like I haven't heard that one before," I teased once I could speak again.

She grinned. "Right. I'm sure you get that all the time."

I was on my feet in an instant, holding out one hand to her. She eyed it doubtfully.

"Come on, little coward," I coaxed. "Climb on my back."

She stared at me for a moment, hesitating. I wasn't sure whether she was wary of this idea of mine, or just wasn't sure exactly how to approach me. We were very new to this physical closeness, and there was still plenty of shyness between us.

Deciding that the latter was the problem, I made it easy for her. I lifted her from the ground and gently arranged her limbs around me as if for a piggyback ride. Her pulse quickened and her breath caught, but once she was in place, her arms and legs constricted around me. I felt enveloped in the warmth of her body.

"I'm a bit heavier than your average backpack." She sounded worried—that I might not be able to bear her weight?

"Hah," I snorted.

It struck me how easy it was, not to carry her insignificant weight, but to have her literally wrapped around me. My thirst was so wholly overshadowed by my happiness that it barely caused me any conscious pain.

I took her hand from where it was gripped around my neck, and held her palm to my nose. I inhaled as deeply as I could. Yes, there the pain was. Real, but unimpressive. What was a little fire to all this light?

"Easier all the time," I breathed.

I took off at a relaxed lope, choosing the smoothest route back to our starting point. It would cost me a few extra seconds to go the long way, but we would still get to her truck in minutes rather than hours. It was better than to jostle her with a more vertical path.

Another new, joyous experience. I'd always loved to run—for nearly a hundred years, it had been my purest physical happiness.

But now, sharing this with her, no distance between us bodily or psychically, I realized how much more pleasure there could be in simply running than I'd ever imagined. I wondered if it thrilled her as much as it did me.

One qualm nagged at me. I'd been in a hurry to get her home as soon as that seemed to be her wish. However...surely we should have concluded that most momentous interlude with a proper finale, a sort of seal on our new understanding? A benediction. But I'd been too hasty to realize it was missing until we were already in motion.

It wasn't too late. My system was electrified again as I thought of it: a true kiss. Once I'd assumed it impossible. Once I'd mourned that this impossibility seemed to hurt her as well as me. Now I was sure it was both possible...and fast approaching. The electricity ricocheted around the inside of my stomach and I wondered why humans had thought to name such a wild sensation *butterflies*.

I slowed to a smooth stop just a few paces from where she'd parked.

"Exhilarating, isn't it?" I asked, eager for her reaction.

She didn't respond, and her limbs retained their taut grip around my waist and neck. A few quiet seconds passed with no answer. What was wrong?

"Bella?"

Her breath came in a gasp, and I realized that she'd been holding it. I should have noticed that.

"I think I need to lie down," she said faintly.

"Oh." I was in dire need of practice with *human*. I hadn't even thought of the possibility of motion sickness. "I'm sorry."

I waited for her to release her hold, but she didn't relax one locked muscle.

"I think I need help," she whispered.

With slow, gentle movements I freed first her legs, then her arms, and pulled her around so that I was holding her cradled against my chest.

The state of her complexion alarmed me at first, but I had seen this same chalky green before. I'd held her in my arms that day, too, yet what a wholly different affair it was now.

I knelt down and set her on a soft patch of ferns.

"How do you feel?"

"Dizzy... I think."

"Put your head between your knees," I advised.

She complied automatically, as if this was a practiced response.

I sat beside her. Listening to her measured breathing, I found that I was more anxious than the situation merited. I knew this was nothing serious, just a bit of queasiness, and yet... seeing her pale and ill bothered me more than was reasonable.

A few moments later, she lifted her head experimentally. She was still pale, but not as green. A faint sheen of sweat covered her brow.

"I guess that wasn't the best idea," I muttered, feeling like an ass.

She smiled a wan smile. "No, it was very interesting," she lied.

"Hah," I huffed sourly. "You're as white as a ghost—no, you're as white as *me*."

She took a slow breath. "I think I should have closed my eyes." As she said the words, her lids followed suit.

"Remember that next time." Her color was improving, and my tension eased in direct correlation with the pink infusing her cheeks.

"Next time?" She groaned theatrically.

I laughed at her sham scowl.

"Show-off," she muttered. Her lower lip jutted out, rounded and full. It looked incredibly soft. I imagined how it would give, bringing us even closer.

I rolled to my knees, facing her. I felt nervous, and restless, and impatient, and unsure. The yearning to be closer to her reminded me of the thirst that used to control me. This, too, was demanding, impossible to ignore.

Her breath was hot against my face. I leaned closer.

"Open your eyes, Bella."

She complied slowly, looking up at me through her dense lashes for a moment before lifting her chin so that our faces were aligned.

"I was thinking, while I was running..." My voice trailed off; this was not the most romantic beginning.

Her eyes narrowed. "About not hitting the trees, I hope."

I chuckled as she tried to hold back a grin. "Silly Bella. Running is second nature to me. It's not something I have to think about."

"Show-off," she repeated, with more emphasis this time.

We were off topic. It was surprising this was even possible, close as our faces were. I smiled and redirected.

"No, I was thinking there was something I wanted to try."

I put my hands lightly on either side of her face, leaving her plenty of room to move away if this was unwelcome.

Her breath caught, and she automatically angled her head closer to mine.

I used an eighth of a second to recalibrate, testing every system in my body to be completely positive that nothing would take me off guard. My thirst was well under control, sublimated to the very bottom of my physical needs. I regulated the pressure in my hands, in my arms, the way my torso curved toward her, so that my touch would be lighter against her skin than the breeze. Though I was sure the precaution was unnecessary, I held my breath. There was no such thing as too careful, after all.

Her eyelids slid shut.

I closed the tiny distance between us, and pressed my lips softly against hers.

Though I'd thought I was prepared, I was not entirely ready for the combustion.

What strange alchemy was this, that the touch of lips should be so much more than the touch of fingers? It made no logical sense that simple contact between this specific area of skin should be so much more powerful than anything I'd yet experienced. It felt as if a new sun was bursting into being where our mouths met, and my whole body was filled to a shatter point with the brilliant light of it.

I only had a fraction of a second to grapple with the potency of this kiss before the alchemy impacted Bella.

She gasped in reaction, her lips parting against mine, the fever of her breath burning my skin. Her arms wound around my neck, her fingers twisted into my hair. She used that leverage to crush her lips more tightly to mine. Her lips felt warmer than before, as fresh blood flowed into them. They opened wider, an invitation. . . .

An invitation it would not be safe for me to accept.

Gingerly, with the lightest force possible, I eased her face away from mine, leaving my fingertips in place against her skin to keep her at that distance. Apart from that small shift, I held myself motionless and tried, if not to ignore the temptation, at least to separate myself from it. I noted the unpleasant return of a few predatory reactions—an excess of venom in my mouth, a tightening in my core—but these were superficial responses. While perhaps it would be unfair to say that rationality was in total control, at least it was not a *feeding* passion that made that statement untrue. A much more agreeable passion held me in its thrall. Its nature, however, did not eliminate the need to moderate it.

Bella's expression was both overwhelmed and apologetic.

"Oops," she said.

I couldn't help but think what her innocent actions might have precipitated just a few hours ago.

"That's an understatement," I agreed.

She was unaware of the progress I'd made today, but she had always acted as if I were in perfect control of myself, even when it wasn't true. It was a relief to finally feel as if I deserved some of that trust.

She tried to move back, but my hands were locked around her face. "Should I . . . ?"

"No," I assured her. "It's tolerable. Wait for a moment, please."

I wanted to be very careful that nothing was escaping me. Already, my muscles had relaxed and the influx of venom dissipated. The urge to wrap my arms around her and continue the alchemy of kissing was a harder impulse to deny, but I used my decades of practicing self-control to make the right choice.

"There," I said when I was totally calm.

She was fighting another smile. "Tolerable?" she asked.

I laughed. "I'm stronger than I thought." I would have never believed how in control I was able to be now. This was very rapid progress indeed. "It's nice to know."

"I wish I could say the same. I'm sorry."

"You *are* only human, after all."

She rolled her eyes at my weak joke. "Thanks so much."

The light that had filled my body during our kiss lingered. I felt so much happiness, I wasn't sure how to contain it all. The overwhelming joy and general bemusement made me worry I wasn't being responsible enough. I should take her home. It wasn't so hard to think of ending this afternoon's utopia, because we would leave together.

I stood and offered her my hand. This time she took it quickly, and I pulled her to her feet. She wobbled there, looking unsteady.

"Are you still faint from the run?" I asked. "Or was it my kissing expertise?" I laughed out loud.

She wrapped her free hand around my wrist to steady herself. "I can't be sure," she teased. "I'm still woozy. I think it's some of both, though." Her body swayed closer to mine. It seemed intentional rather than vertiginous.

"Maybe you should let me drive."

All disequilibrium seemed to vanish. Her shoulders squared. "Are you insane?"

If she were driving, I would need her to keep both hands on the wheel and I could do nothing to distract her. If I were driving, however, there would be much more leeway.

"I can drive better than you on your best day. You have much slower reflexes." I smiled so that she would know I was teasing. Mostly.

She didn't argue with the facts. "I'm sure that's true, but I don't think my nerves, or my truck, could take it."

I tried to do the dazzling thing she'd accused me of before. I still wasn't exactly sure what qualified. "Some trust, please, Bella?"

It didn't work, perhaps because she was looking down. She patted her jeans pocket, then pulled out her key and wrapped her fingers into a fist around it. She looked up again, and shook her head.

"Nope," she told me. "Not a chance."

She started toward the road, stepping around me. Whether she was actually still dizzy or just moved clumsily, I didn't know. But she staggered on the second step and I caught her before she could fall. I pulled her against my chest.

"Bella," I breathed. All the jocularity vanished from her eyes, and she leaned into me, her face tilted up toward mine. Kissing her immediately seemed like both a fantastic and a terrible idea. I forced myself to err on the side of caution.

"I've already expended a great deal of personal effort at this point to keep you alive," I reminded her in a playful tone. "I'm not about to let you behind the wheel of a vehicle when you can't even walk straight. Besides, friends don't let friends drive drunk," I concluded, quoting the Ad Council slogan. It was a dated reference for her; she'd been only three when the campaign was launched.

"Drunk?" she protested.

I grinned a crooked smile at her. "You're intoxicated by my very presence."

She sighed, accepting defeat. "I can't argue with that." Holding her fist up, she let the key drop from her hand and fall into mine.

"Take it easy," she cautioned. "My truck is a senior citizen."

"Very sensible."

Her lips pursed into a frown. "And are you not affected at all? By my presence?"

Affected? She'd utterly transformed every part of me. I barely recognized myself.

For the first time in a hundred years, I was *grateful* to be what I was. Every aspect of being a vampire—all but the danger to her—was suddenly acceptable to me, because it was what had let me live long enough to find Bella.

The decades I had endured would not have been so difficult had I known what was waiting for me, that my existence was advancing toward something better than I could have imagined. It had not been years of killing time, as I had thought; it had been years of progress. Refining, preparing, mastering myself so that I could have *this* now.

I wasn't entirely sure of this new self yet; the violent ecstasy suffusing my every cell seemed unsustainable in the long term. Still, I never wanted to go back to the old me. That Edward seemed unfinished now, incomplete. As though half of him was missing.

It would have been impossible for him to do this—I leaned down and pressed my lips to the corner of her jaw, just above her pulsing artery. I let my lips brush softly along her jawline to her chin, and then kissed my way back to her ear, feeling the velvet give of her warm skin under the faint pressure. I returned slowly to her chin, so close to her lips. She shivered in my arms, reminding me that what was unprecedented warmth for me was icy winter to her. I loosed my hold.

"Regardless," I whispered in her ear. "I have better reflexes."

18. MIND OVER MATTER

INSISTING UPON DRIVING HAD BEEN A VERY GOOD IDEA. There were all those things, of course, that would be out of the question if she needed to concentrate her human senses on the road—hand-holding, eye-gazing, general joy-radiating. But more than this, the feeling of being filled to the point of bursting with pure light hadn't dimmed at all. I knew how overwhelming it was for me; I wasn't sure how much it would compromise a human system. Much safer to let my inhuman system tend to the road.

The clouds were shifting as the sun set. Every now and then a lance of fading red sunlight would strike my face. I could imagine the terror I would have felt only yesterday to have been exposed in this way. Now it made me want to laugh. I felt filled with laughter, as if the light within me needed that escape.

Curious, I switched on her radio. I was surprised that it was tuned to nothing but static. Then, considering the volume of the engine, I deduced that she didn't bother much with driving music. I twisted the knob until I found a semi-audible station. It was playing Johnny Ace, and I smiled. "Pledging My Love." How apt.

I began to sing along, feeling a little cheesy, but also enjoying the chance to say these words to her. *Always and forever, I'll love only you.*

She never took her eyes off my face, smiling in what I could now accurately construe as wonder.

"You like fifties music?" she asked when the song ended.

"Music in the fifties was good. Much better than the sixties, or the seventies, ugh!" Though there were certainly excellent outliers, the artists that were played most often on the limited radio options then were not my favorites. I'd never warmed up to disco. "The eighties were bearable."

She pressed her lips together for a moment, her eyes tensing as if something worried her. Quietly, she asked, "Are you ever going to tell me how old you are?"

Ah, she was afraid to distress me. I smiled at her easily. "Does it matter much?"

She seemed relieved by my light response. "No, but I still wonder.... There's nothing like an unsolved mystery to keep you up at night."

And then it was my turn to worry. "I wonder if it will upset you."

She hadn't been disgusted by my inhumanity, but would she have a different reaction to the years between us? In many very real ways, I was still seventeen. Would she see it that way?

What had she imagined already? Millennia behind me, gothic castles and Transylvanian accents? Well, none of that was impossible. Carlisle knew those types.

"Try me," she challenged.

I looked into her eyes, searching their depths for the answers. I sighed. Shouldn't I have developed some courage after the events behind us? But here I was again, terrified to frighten her. Of course, there was no way forward but total honesty.

"I was born in Chicago in 1901," I admitted. I turned my face toward the road ahead so she wouldn't feel scrutinized as she did the mental math, but I couldn't help stealing a look from the corner of my eye. She was artificially composed, and I realized that she was carefully modulating her reactions. She didn't want to appear frightened any more than I wanted to scare her.

The more we came to know each other, the more we seemed to mirror each other's feelings. Harmonizing.

"Carlisle found me in a hospital in the summer of 1918," I continued. "I was seventeen, and dying of the Spanish influenza."

At this her control slipped, and she gasped in shock, her eyes huge.

"I don't remember it well," I assured her. "It was a very long time ago, and human memories fade."

She did not look entirely comforted, but she nodded. She said nothing, waiting for more.

I had just mentally committed to total honesty, but I realized now that there would have to be limits. There were things she should know... but also details that would not be wise to share. Maybe Alice was right. Maybe, if Bella was feeling anything close to the way I was feeling now, she would think it imperative to prolong this feeling. To *stay* with me, as she'd said in the meadow. I knew it would be no simple thing for me to deny Bella anything she wanted. I chose my words with care.

"I do remember how it felt, when Carlisle... *saved* me. It's not an easy thing, not something you could forget."

"Your parents?" she asked in a timid voice, and I relaxed, glad she'd chosen not to fixate on that last part.

"They had already died from the disease. I was alone." These weren't hard words to say. This part of my history almost felt more like a story I'd been told than actual memories. "That was why he chose me. In all the chaos of the epidemic, no one would ever realize I was gone."

"How did he... save you?"

So much for avoiding the difficult questions. I thought about what was most important to keep from her.

My words danced around the edges of her question. "It was difficult. Not many of us have the restraint necessary to accomplish it. But Carlisle has always been the most humane, the most compassionate of us.... I don't think you could find his equal throughout all of history." I considered my father for a moment, and wondered if my words were adequate praise. Then I continued with the rest of what I thought it safe for her to know. "For me, it was merely very, very painful."

While the other memories that might have brought pain—the loss of my mother in particular—were confused and faded, the memory of *this* pain was exceptionally clear. I flinched slightly. If there ever came a time that Bella *did* ask again, with full knowledge of what it meant to stay with me, this memory would be all the aid I needed to say no. I recoiled from the idea of her facing such pain.

She absorbed my answer, lips pursed and eyes narrowed in thought. I wanted to know her reaction, but I knew that if I asked, I would face more pointed questions. I continued my history, hoping to distract her.

"He acted from loneliness. That's usually the reason behind the choice. I was the first in Carlisle's family, though he found Esme soon after. She fell from a cliff. They brought her straight to the hospital morgue, though somehow, her heart was still beating."

"So you must be dying, then, to become..."

Not distracted enough. Still trying to discern the mechanism. I hurried to redirect.

"No, that's just Carlisle. He would never do that to someone who had another choice. It is easier he says, though, if the blood is weak."

I shifted my gaze to the road again. I shouldn't have added that. I wondered if I was dancing closer to the answers she sought because part of me wanted her to know, wanted her to find a way to stay with me. I had to be better at controlling my tongue. To keep the selfish part of myself bridled.

"And Emmett and Rosalie?"

I smiled at her. She probably realized I was being evasive, and yet she was willing to let it go to make me comfortable.

"Carlisle brought Rosalie to our family next. I didn't realize till much later that he was hoping she would be to me what Esme was to him—he was careful with his thoughts around me."

I remembered my disgust when he'd finally slipped. Rosalie had not been a welcome addition in the beginning—in truth, life had been more complicated for all of us ever since her inclusion—and learning that Carlisle had envisioned an even closer relationship for her and me was horrifying. The extent of my aversion would be impolite to share. Ungentlemanly.

"But she was never more than a sister." That was probably the kindest way to sum up that chapter. "It was only two years later that she found Emmett. She was hunting—we were in Appalachia at the time—and found a bear about to finish him off. She carried him back to Carlisle, more than a hundred miles, afraid she wouldn't be able to . . . do it herself."

We'd been outside Knoxville then—not an ideal place for us, weather-wise. We had to stay inside most days. It wasn't a long-term situation, though—Carlisle was researching some pathology studies at the University of Tennessee's medical school. A few weeks, a few months . . . it wasn't really a difficult ask. We had access to several libraries, and the nightlife in New Orleans wasn't inconveniently far, not for creatures as swift as we. However, Rosalie, out of her newborn stage but not yet comfortable with very close proximity to humans, refused to entertain herself. Instead, she moped and whined, finding fault with every suggestion for amusement or self-improvement. To be fair, perhaps she did not whine so much out loud. Esme was not as irritated as I was.

Rosalie preferred to hunt by herself, and though I really should have watched after her, it was a relief to us both that I didn't object very strenuously. She knew how to be careful. We all were practiced at restraining our senses until we were in unpopulated areas. And though I was reluctant to attribute any virtue to this unwelcome interloper, even I had to admit that she was incredibly gifted at self-control. Mostly due to stubbornness and, in my opinion, a desire to best me.

So when the sound of Rosalie's footsteps, thudding faster and heavier than usual, broke the predawn calm of that Knoxville summer, her familiar scent preceded by the strong aroma of human blood and her thoughts wild and incoherent, my initial expectation was *not* that she had made a mistake.

In the first year of Rosalie's second life, before she had disappeared on her several missions of revenge, her thoughts had given her away clearly and thoroughly. I knew what she was planning, and I'd informed Carlisle. The first time, he counseled her gently, urging her to let go of her past life, certain that if she did she would forget, and then her pain could lessen. Revenge could not bring back anything she had lost. But when his guidance met only the implacability of her fury, he gave her advice on how best to be discreet about her forays. Neither of us could argue that she didn't deserve vengeance. And we both couldn't help but believe that the world would be a better place without the rapists and murderers who had ended her life.

I'd believed she'd gotten them all. Her thoughts had long since calmed, no longer obsessed with the desire to break and tear, maim and mutilate.

But as the smell of blood flooded the house like a tsunami, I immediately assumed that she'd discovered another accomplice to her death. Though I did not think very highly of her in general, my faith in her ability to do no harm was strong.

All my expectations were turned upside down as she cried out in panic, calling for Carlisle's help. And then, beneath the shrill sound of her distress, I caught the sound of one very feeble heartbeat.

I raced from my room, finding her in the front parlor before she'd even finished her cry. Carlisle was already there. Rosalie, hair unusually disordered, her favorite dress stained with blood so heavily that the skirt's hem was dyed deep crimson, carried in her arms a giant of a human man. He was barely conscious, eyes wandering the room out of sync with each other. His skin had been torn again and again by evenly spaced slashes, some of his bones clearly broken beneath.

"Save him!" Rosalie almost screamed at Carlisle. "Please!"

Please please please, her thoughts begged.

I saw what the words cost her. When she inhaled to replace the air she'd used, she flinched against the power of the fresh blood so close to her mouth. She held the man farther from herself, turning her face away.

Carlisle understood her anguish. He swiftly removed the man from her arms and laid him on the parlor rug with gentle hands. The man was too far gone even to groan.

I watched, shocked by the strange tableau, automatically holding my breath. I should have already left the house. I could hear Esme's thoughts, quickly retreating. Once she'd caught the scent of blood, she'd known to flee, though she was just as confused as I.

It's too late, Carlisle realized, examining the man. He was loath to disappoint Rosalie; though she was clearly unhappy in this second life he'd given her, she rarely asked for anything from him. Certainly never with this level of agony. *He must be family*, Carlisle thought. *How can I bear to hurt her again?*

The big man—not that much older than I was, now that I really looked at his face—closed his eyes. His shallow breathing stuttered.

"What are you waiting for?" Rosalie shrieked. *He's dying! He's dying!*

"Rosalie, I..." Carlisle held out his bloodied hands helplessly.

Then an image surfaced in her mind, and I understood exactly what she was asking for.

"She doesn't mean for you to heal him," I translated quickly. "She means for you to *save* him."

Rosalie's eyes flashed to me, a look of intense gratitude altering her features in a way I'd never seen before. For one instant, I remembered how very beautiful she was.

We didn't have long to wait for Carlisle's decision.

Oh! Carlisle thought. And then I saw exactly how much he would do for Rosalie, how much he felt he owed her. There was barely any deliberation.

He was already kneeling beside the broken figure as he shooed us away. "It's not safe for you to stay," he said, his face inclining toward the man's throat.

I grabbed Rosalie's bloodied arm as I rushed to the door. She didn't resist. We both escaped the house, not pausing till we'd reached the nearby Tennessee River and immersed ourselves.

There, lying in the cool mud at the river's edge, Rosalie letting the blood sluice from her dress and her skin, we had our first real conversation.

She didn't speak often, just showed me in her mind how she'd found the man, a total stranger, about to die, and how something in his face had made that future intolerable to her. She didn't have words for why. She didn't have words for *how*—how she'd managed to complete her harrowing journey without killing him herself. I saw her run for miles, faster than she'd ever moved before, aching to satisfy her thirst the entire way. While she relived it all, her mind was unguarded and vulnerable. She was trying to understand, too, almost as confused as I was.

I wasn't looking for yet another addition to my family. I'd never been particularly concerned about what Rosalie wanted or needed. But suddenly, seeing this all through her eyes, I could only root for her happiness. For the first time, we were on the same side.

We couldn't return for a while, though Rosalie was anxious in the extreme to know what was happening. I assured her that Carlisle would have come for us if he'd been unsuccessful. So for now we would just have to wait till it was safe.

Those hours changed us both. When Carlisle finally came to call us home, we returned as brother and sister.

The pause as I remembered how I'd come to love my sister was not very long. Bella was still waiting for the rest of the story. I thought of where I'd left off: Rosalie, dripping with blood, holding her face as far away from Emmett as she could. Her posture in the image reminded me of a more recent memory: me struggling to carry a lightheaded Bella to the nurse's office. It was an interesting juxtaposition.

"I'm only beginning to guess how difficult that journey was for her," I concluded. Our fingers were knotted together. I lifted our hands and, with the back of mine, stroked her cheek.

The last bit of red light in the sky faded to deep purple.

"But she made it," Bella said after a short silence, eager for me to continue.

"Yes. She saw something in his face that made her strong enough." Amazing that she'd been right. Astonishing that they'd matched up perfectly, like two halves of a whole. Fate or astronomical good luck? I'd never been able to decide. "And they've been together ever since. Sometimes they live separately from us, as a married couple." And oh, how I appreciated those times. I loved Emmett and Rosalie separately, but Emmett and Rosalie alone together, heard only by my inescapable mental reach, were a grueling ordeal. "But the younger we pretend to be, the longer we can stay in any given place. Forks seemed perfect, so we all enrolled in high school." I laughed. "I suppose we'll have to go to their wedding in a few years, *again*."

Rosalie loved to get married. The chance to do it over and over was probably her favorite thing about immortality.

"Alice and Jasper?" Bella asked.

"Alice and Jasper are two very rare creatures. They both developed a conscience, as we refer to it, with no outside guidance. Jasper belonged to another... family." I avoided the correct word, controlling a shiver as I thought of his beginnings. "A *very* different kind of family. He became depressed, and he wandered on his own. Alice found him. Like me, she has certain gifts above and beyond the norm for our kind."

This surprised Bella enough to break through her calm façade. "Really? But you said you were the only one who could hear people's thoughts."

"That's true. She knows other things. She *sees* things—things that might happen, things that are coming." Things that now would never happen. I was past the worst of it. Though still... it bothered me how hazy the new vision had been, the one I could live with. The other—Alice and Bella both white and cold—had been so much clearer. That didn't matter. It couldn't. I'd subdued one impossible future and I would triumph over this one, too.

"But it's very subjective," I continued, hearing the harder edge in my voice. "The future isn't set in stone. Things change."

I glanced at her cream and apricot skin, almost to reassure myself that she was as she should be, and then looked away when she caught my gaze. I could never be certain how much she was reading in my eyes.

"What kinds of things does she see?" Bella wanted to know.

I gave her the safe answers, the proven prophecies.

"She saw Jasper and knew that he was looking for her before he knew it himself." Their union had been a magical thing. Whenever Jasper thought of it, the entire household relaxed into dreamy contentment, so powerful were his communal emotions. "She saw Carlisle and our family, and they came together to find us."

I'd missed that first introduction, when Alice and Jasper had presented themselves to an extremely wary Carlisle, a frightened Esme, and a hostile Rosalie. It was Jasper's warlike appearance that had them all so apprehensive, but Alice knew exactly what to say to ease their anxiety. Of course she knew exactly what to say. She'd envisioned every possible version of that momentous meeting, and then chosen the best. It was no accident that Emmett and I had been away. She'd preferred the smoother scene without the family's primary defenders in residence.

It was hard to believe how firmly entrenched they were by the time Emmett and I arrived, just a few days later. We were both shocked, and Emmett was ready for battle the second he laid eyes on Jasper. But Alice ran forward to throw her arms around me before a word could be spoken.

I wasn't frightened by what might have been construed as an attack. Her thoughts were so sure of me, so full of *love* for me, I thought I'd had the first memory loss of my second life. Because this tiny immortal knew me perfectly, better than anyone else in my current or former family. Who was she?

Oh, Edward! At last! My brother! We're finally together!

And then, with her arms tight around my waist—and my own arms hesitantly coming to rest around her shoulders—she thought swiftly through her life from her first memory to that very moment, and then forward in time through the highlights of our next few years together. It felt very strange to realize in that instant that now I knew her, too.

"This is Alice, Emmett," I told him, still embracing my new sister. Emmett's aggressive pose changed to one of confusion. "She's part of our family. And that's Jasper. You're going to love him."

There were so many stories about Alice, so many miracles and phenomena, paradoxes and enigmas, I could have spent the rest of the week just telling Bella the bullet-point version. Instead, I gave her a few of the simpler, more mechanical details.

"She's most sensitive to nonhumans. She always sees, for example, when another group of our kind is coming near. And any threat they may pose." Alice had become one of the family's defenders, too.

"Are there a lot of... your kind?" Bella asked, sounding a little shaken by the idea.

"No, not many," I assured her. "But most won't settle in any one place. Only those like us, who've given up hunting you people"—I raised an eyebrow at her and squeezed her hand—"can live together with humans for any length of time. We've only found one other family like ours, in a small village in Alaska. We lived together for a time, but there were so many of us that we became too noticeable." Also Tanya, the matriarch of that clan, was persistent to the point of harassment. "Those of us who live... differently tend to band together."

"And the others?"

We'd reached her home. It was empty, no lights in any

windows. I parked in her usual spot and turned the engine off. The sudden quiet felt very intimate, there in the dark.

"Nomads, for the most part," I answered. "We've all lived that way at times. It gets tedious, like anything else. But we run across the others now and then, because most of us prefer the North."

"Why is that?"

I grinned and nudged her gently with my elbow. "Did you have your eyes open this afternoon? Do you think I could walk down the street in the sunlight without causing traffic accidents? There's a reason why we chose the Olympic Peninsula, one of the most sunless places in the world. It's nice to be able to go outside in the day. You wouldn't believe how tired you can get of nighttime in eighty-odd years."

"So that's where the legends came from," she said, nodding to herself.

"Probably."

There was actually a precise source behind the legends, but that wasn't something I wanted to get into. The Volturi were very far away and very much absorbed in their mission to police the vampire world. They would never affect Bella's life beyond the lore they'd concocted to protect immortals' privacy.

"And Alice came from another family, like Jasper?" she asked.

"No, and that *is* a mystery. Alice doesn't remember her human life at all."

I'd seen that first memory. Bright morning sunlight, a light mist hanging in the air. Tangled grass surrounding her, broad oak trees shading the hollow where she woke. Besides that, a blankness, no sense of identity or purpose. She'd looked at her pale skin, shimmering in the sun, and not known who or what she was. And then the first vision had taken her.

A man's face, fierce but also broken, scarred but beautiful. Deep red eyes and a mane of golden hair. With this face came a profound conviction of belonging. And then she saw him speaking a name.

Alice.

Her name, she realized.

The visions told her who she was, or shaped her into who she would become. These were the only help she would get.

"And she doesn't know who created her," I told Bella. "She awoke alone. Whoever made her walked away, and none of us understand why, or how, he could. If she hadn't had that other sense, if she hadn't seen Jasper and Carlisle and known that she would someday become one of us, she probably would have turned into a total savage."

Bella pondered this in silence. I was sure it was difficult for her to comprehend. It had taken my family a while to adjust, as well. I wondered what her next question would be.

And then her stomach gurgled, and I realized that we'd been together all day and she'd eaten nothing in that time. Ah, I needed to keep better focused on her human needs!

"I'm sorry, I'm keeping you from dinner."

"I'm fine, really," she said too quickly.

"I've never spent much time around anyone who eats food," I apologized. "I forget." It was a poor excuse.

Her expression was totally open as she responded, vulnerable. "I want to stay with you."

Again, the word *stay* seemed to carry so much more weight than it usually did.

"Can't I come in?" I asked gently.

She blinked twice, clearly thrown by the idea. "Would you like to?"

"Yes, if it's all right."

I wondered if she thought I had to have an explicit invitation in order to come inside. The thought made me smile, and then frown as I felt a spasm of guilt. I would need to come clean with her. Again. But how to broach such a shameful admission?

I stewed on that while I got out and opened the passenger door for her.

"Very human," she commended.

"It's definitely resurfacing."

We walked together at human speed across her shadowed, silent yard as if this were a normal thing. She flickered glances at me as we walked, smiling to herself. I reached up and pulled the house key from its hiding place as we passed, then opened the door for her. She hesitated, looking down the dark hallway.

"The door was unlocked?" she asked.

"No, I used the key from under the eave."

I replaced the key in question while she moved to turn on the porch lamp. When she turned back, yellow light made harsh shadows across her face as she raised both eyebrows at me. I could see she meant the look to be stern, but the corners of her lips were puckered as though she was fighting a smile.

"I was curious about you," I confessed.

"You spied on me?"

It didn't seem to be a joking matter, but she sounded as if she were about to laugh.

I should have confessed all then, but I went along with her teasing tone. "What else is there to do at night?"

It was the wrong choice, a cowardly choice. She heard only a joke, not an admission. Strange again to realize how, even with the huge potential nightmares resolved, there continued to be much to fear. Of course, this issue was nothing but my own fault, my own extremely poor behavior.

She shook her head slightly, then gestured for me to enter. I moved past her down the hall, switching on lights as I went so she wouldn't have to stumble in the dark. I took a seat at her small kitchen table and looked around, examining the angles that were invisible from outside the window. The room was tidy and warm, bright with gaudy yellow paint that was somehow endearing in its failed attempt to mimic sunshine. Everything smelled like Bella, which should have been quite painful, but I found that I enjoyed it in a strange way. Masochistic, indeed.

She stared at me with a hard to read expression. A little confusion, I guessed, a little bit of wonder. As though she wasn't sure I was real. I smiled and pointed her toward the refrigerator. She whirled in that direction with an answering grin. I hoped she had some food easily accessible. Perhaps I should have taken her to dinner? But it felt wrong to think of subjecting ourselves to a crowd of strangers. Our new understanding was still too unique, too raw. Any obstacle that would force silence would be unendurable. I wanted her to myself.

It only took her a minute to find an acceptable option. She cut out a square of casserole and heated it in the microwave. I could smell oregano, onions, garlic, and tomato sauce. Something Italian. She stared intently at the plate while it revolved.

Perhaps I would learn to cook food. Not being able to appreciate flavors the same way a human did would definitely be a hurdle, but there seemed to be quite a bit of math to the process, and I was sure I could teach myself to recognize the correct smells.

Because, suddenly, I felt sure that this was just the first of our quiet evenings in, rather than a singular event. We would have years of this. She and I together, just enjoying each other's company. So many hours...the light inside me seemed to stretch and grow, and I thought again that I might shatter.

"How often?" Bella asked without looking at me.

My thoughts were so caught up in this tremendous image of the future that I didn't follow her at once. "Hmmm?"

She still didn't turn. "How often did you come here?"

Oh, right. Time to have courage. Time to be honest, no matter the consequences. Though after the day I'd had, I felt fairly sure that she would eventually forgive me. I hoped.

"I come here almost every night."

She spun to look at me with startled eyes. "Why?"

Honesty.

"You're interesting when you sleep. You talk."

"No!" she gasped. Blood washed into her cheeks and didn't stop there, coloring even her forehead. The room grew infinitesimally warmer as her blush heated the air around her. She leaned against the counter behind her, gripping it so hard that her knuckles turned white. Shock was the only emotion I could see in her expression, but I was sure others would come soon.

"Are you very angry with me?"

"That depends!" she blurted out breathlessly.

That depends? I wondered what could possibly mitigate my crime. What could make it less or more horrible? I was disgusted by the thought that she was reserving judgment until she knew exactly how offside my lurking had been. Did she imagine that I was as depraved as any peeping tom? That I'd leered at her from the shadows, hoping for her to expose herself? If my stomach could turn, it would have.

Would she believe me if I tried to explain my torment at being separated from her? Could anyone believe the kinds of catastrophes I'd imagined, thinking she might not be safe? They had all been so far-fetched. And yet, if I were separated from her now, I knew the same impossible dangers would begin to plague me again.

Long seconds passed, the microwave shrilled out its announcement that its work was done, but Bella didn't speak again.

"On?" I prompted.

Bella groaned the words. "What you heard!"

I felt a rush of relief that she did not believe me capable of a viler kind of surveillance. Her only worry was embarrassment at what I might have heard her say? Well, on that matter I could comfort her. *She* had nothing to be ashamed of. I jumped up and rushed to take her hands. Part of me thrilled to the fact that I could do this so easily.

"Don't be upset!" I pleaded. Her eyes were downcast. I leaned in so that our faces would be on the same level, and waited until she met my gaze.

"You miss your mother. You worry about her. And when it rains," I murmured, "the sound makes you restless. You used to talk about home a lot, but it's less often now. Once you said, 'It's too *green.*'"

I laughed quietly, trying to coax a smile from her. Surely she could see there was no need for mortification.

"Anything else?" she demanded, raising one eyebrow. The way she half turned her face away, her eyes moving down and then darting back up again, helped me realize what she was worried about.

"You did say my name," I admitted.

She inhaled and then blew out a long sigh. "A lot?"

"How much do you mean by 'a lot,' exactly?"

Her eyes dropped to the floor. "Oh no!"

I reached out and wrapped my arms carefully around her shoulders. She leaned into my chest, still hiding her face.

Did she think I had ever been anything but overjoyed to hear my name on her lips? It was one of my favorite sounds, along with the sound of her breath, the sound of her heart....

I whispered my response into her ear. "Don't be self-conscious. If I could dream at all, it would be about you. And I'm not ashamed of it."

How I had once wished to be able to dream of her! How I'd ached for that. And now, reality was better than dreams. I wouldn't want to miss one second of it for any kind of unconsciousness.

Her body relaxed. A happy sound, almost a hum or a purr, sighed out of her.

Could this really be it? Was I to have no punishment at all for my outrageous behavior? This felt more like a reward. I knew I owed her a deeper penance.

I became aware of another sound beyond her heart thrumming in my arms. A car was drawing closer and the thoughts of the driver were very quiet. Tired after a full day. Looking forward to the promise of food and comfort that the warm lights in the windows offered. But I couldn't be perfectly sure that was what he was thinking.

I didn't want to move from where I was. I pressed my cheek against Bella's hair and waited until she also heard her father's car. Her body stiffened.

"Should your father know I'm here?"

She hesitated. "I'm not sure...."

I brushed my lips quickly against her hair and then released her with a sigh.

"Another time, then..."

I ducked out of the room and darted up the stairs into the darkness of the tiny hall between bedrooms. I'd been here once before, finding a blanket for Bella.

"Edward!" she called in a stage whisper from the kitchen.

I laughed just loud enough for her to know that I was close.

Her father stomped up to the front door, scraping each of his boots twice against the mat. He shoved his key into the lock, and then grunted when the handle turned with the key, already unlatched.

"Bella?" he called as he swung the door open. His thoughts registered the smell of the food in the microwave, and his stomach grumbled.

I realized that Bella, also, had *still* not eaten. I supposed it was a good thing her father had interrupted us. I would starve her at this rate.

But some small part of me was just a little...wistful. When I'd asked if she wanted her father to know I was here, that we were together, I'd hoped that the answer would be different. Of course, she had so much to consider before introducing me to him. Or she might never want him to know she had someone like me in love with her, and that was perfectly fair. More than fair.

And truly, it would have been inconvenient to meet her father officially in my current state of dress. Or *un*dress. I supposed I should be grateful for her reticence.

"In here," Bella called to her father. I heard his soft grunt of acknowledgment as he locked the door, and then his boots stomping toward the kitchen.

"Can you get me some of that?" Charlie asked. "I'm bushed."

It was easy to understand the sounds of Bella moving around the kitchen while Charlie settled himself, even without a more convenient set of thoughts to watch through. Chewing—Bella was finally eating something. The refrigerator opening and closing. The microwave whirring. Liquid—too thick for water, I would guess milk—poured into glasses. A dish set gently on the wooden table. Chair legs scraping against the floor as Bella sat down.

"Thanks," Charlie said, and then they both were chewing for a long moment.

Bella broke the companionable silence. "How was your day?" Her inflections sounded off, as if her mind was elsewhere. I smiled.

"Good, the fish were biting...how about you? Did you get everything done that you wanted to?"

"Not really—it was too nice out to stay indoors." Her casual answer wasn't as relaxed as his. She wasn't a natural at hiding things from her father.

"It was a nice day," he agreed, sounding oblivious to the edge in her voice.

A chair moved again.

"In a hurry?" Charlie asked.

Bella swallowed loudly. "Yeah, I'm tired. I'm going to bed early." Her footsteps moved to the sink and the water began to run.

"You look kinda keyed up," Charlie continued. Not so oblivious as I'd thought. I wouldn't miss these things if his thoughts weren't so hard to get to. I tried to make sense of them. Bella's eyes flashing to the hall. The suddenly brighter color in her cheeks. This seemed to be all he was aware of. Then a sudden confusion of images, nebulous and without context. A 1971 mustard-yellow Impala. The Forks High School gym, decorated with crepe paper. A porch swing and a girl with bright green barrettes in her pale hair. Two red vinyl seats at a shiny chrome bar in a tacky diner. A girl with long, dark curls, walking along a beach under the moon.

"Do I?" Bella asked with put-on innocence. Water ran in the

sink, and I could hear the sound of bristles against melamine.

Charlie was still thinking about the moon. "It's Saturday," he announced randomly.

Bella didn't seem to know how to respond. I wasn't sure where he was going with this, either.

Finally, he continued. "No plans tonight?"

I thought I understood the images now. Saturday nights from his youth? Maybe.

"No, Dad, I just want to get some sleep." She sounded anything but tired.

Charlie sniffed once. "None of the boys in town your type, eh?"

Was he worried that she wasn't having a normal teen experience? That she was missing out? For a second I felt a deep twinge of doubt. Should I be worried about the same? What I was keeping her from?

But then the sureness and sense of *right* from the meadow washed over me. We belonged together.

"No, none of the boys have caught my eye yet." Bella's tone was slightly patronizing.

"I thought maybe that Mike Newton…you said he was friendly."

I hadn't expected *that*. A sharp blade of anger twisted in my chest. Not anger, I recognized. Jealousy. I wasn't sure if I'd ever disliked anyone quite so much as that pointless, insignificant boy.

"He's *just* a friend, Dad."

I couldn't tell if Charlie was upset by her answer or relieved by it. Perhaps a mixture of both.

"Well, you're too good for them all, anyway," he said. "Wait till you get to college to start looking."

"Sounds like a good idea to me," Bella agreed quickly. She turned the corner and started up the stairs. Her footsteps were slow—probably to emphasize her assertion that she was sleepy—and I had plenty of time to beat her to her room. Just in case

Charlie followed. It would hardly be in line with her wishes for him to find me here, half-dressed, eavesdropping.

" 'Night, honey," Charlie called after her.

"See you in the morning, Dad," she responded in a voice that tried to sound tired but failed badly.

It felt wrong to sit in the rocking chair as usual, invisible in the dark corner. It had been a hiding place when I hadn't wanted her to know I was here. When I was being deceitful.

I lay across her bed, the most obvious place in the room, where there could be no hint of trying to disguise my presence.

I knew that her scent would engulf me here. The smell of detergent was fresh enough to suggest she'd washed the sheets recently, but it didn't overpower her own fragrance. Overwhelming as it was, it was also painfully pleasant to be surrounded in such a sharp way by the evidence of her existence.

As soon as she entered the room, Bella stopped dragging her feet. She slammed the door shut behind her, then ran on her tiptoes to the window. Right past me without a glance. She shoved the window open and leaned outside, staring into the night.

"Edward?" she stage-whispered.

I suppose my resting place was not that obvious after all. I laughed quietly at my failed attempt to be aboveboard, then answered her.

"Yes?"

She spun so fast that she nearly lost her balance. With one hand, she gripped the window ledge for stability. Her other hand clutched at her throat.

"Oh," she choked out. Almost in slow motion, she slid down the wall behind her until she was sitting on the wooden floor.

Once again, it seemed as though everything I did was wrong. At least this time it was funny rather than terrifying.

"I'm sorry."

She nodded. "Just give me a minute to restart my heart." In reality, her heart was thrumming from the shock I'd just given her.

I sat up, all my movements deliberate and slow. Moving like a human. She watched, her eyes riveted to each motion, a smile starting to form at the corners of her lips.

Noticing her lips made me feel that she was much too far away. I leaned toward her and picked her up carefully, my hands wrapped around the tops of her arms, then set her down beside me, only an inch of space between us. Much better.

I placed my hand on top of hers, welcoming the smolder of her skin with something like relief. "Why don't you sit with me?"

She grinned.

"How's the heart?" I asked, though it was beating so strongly I could feel the subtle vibrations dancing through the air around her.

"You tell me," she countered. "I'm sure you hear it better than I do."

Accurate. I laughed softly while her smile grew wider.

The pleasant weather wasn't quite over yet; the clouds parted and a silvery sheen of moonlight touched her skin, making her look like something entirely celestial. I wondered how I looked to her. Her eyes seemed filled with wonder, much as mine must be.

Below us, the front door opened and closed. There were no other thoughts near the house besides Charlie's muffled narrative. I wondered where he was going. Not far...There was a creak of metal, a muted clank. Something almost like a schematic flashed through his head.

Ah. Her truck. It surprised me a little that Charlie was going to this extreme to curb whatever he thought Bella was up to.

I was about to mention Charlie's odd behavior when her expression suddenly changed. Her eyes slid to the bedroom door and then back to me.

"Can I have a minute to be human?" she asked.

"Certainly," I responded at once, amused by her phrasing.

Abruptly, her brows lowered and she frowned at me. "Stay," she ordered in a stern tone.

It was the easiest demand anyone had ever made of me. Nothing I could imagine would compel me to leave this room now.

I made my voice serious to match hers. "Yes, ma'am." I straightened up and conspicuously locked all my muscles into place. She smiled, pleased.

It took her a minute to gather her things, and then she left the room. She made no attempt to hide the sound of the door closing. Another door banged more loudly. The bathroom. I supposed part of this was convincing Charlie she wasn't up to anything nefarious. It was unlikely that he could imagine what exactly she *was* up to. But it was a wasted effort. Charlie came back inside just a moment later. The sound of the shower running upstairs did seem to confuse him, I thought.

While I waited for Bella, I finally took the opportunity to examine her small media collection beside the bed. There weren't many surprises, after all my interrogations. I found just one hardback in her library, too new to be in paperback yet. It was her copy of *Tooth and Claw*, the one of her favorites that I'd never read. I'd not yet taken time to catch up on this lack—I'd been too busy following Bella around like a demented bodyguard. I opened the novel now and began.

I was aware as I read that Bella was taking longer than usual. As ever, the constant anxiety that she would at last see something in me to avoid quickly reared its head. I tried to ignore it. There could be a million reasons why Bella dawdled. I focused on the book instead. I could see why it was one of her favorites—it was both strange and charming. Of course, any story of triumphant love would fit my humor today.

The bathroom door opened. I replaced the book—noting the page number, 166, so I could return to it later—and assumed my statue-like pose from before. But I was disappointed; rather than return, she shuffled down the stairs. Her steps came to a stop on the bottom tread.

“ ’Night, Dad,” she called out.

Charlie’s thoughts felt slightly scrambled, but I couldn’t make out anything else.

“ ’Night, Bella,” he mumbled back.

And then she was dashing back up the stairs, skipping steps in apparent haste. She flung the door open—her eyes were searching the darkness for me before she was inside—and then shut it firmly behind herself. When she found me exactly as she expected, a wide grin spread across her face.

I broke my perfect stillness to return it.

She hesitated for a second—her eyes flashing down to her well-worn pajamas—and then crossed her arms in an almost apologetic posture.

I thought perhaps I understood the earlier delay. Not a fear of monsters, rather a more common fear. Shyness. I could easily imagine how, away from the sun and magic of the meadow, she might feel unsure. I was on unfamiliar ground as well.

I fell back on old habits, trying to tease her out of her insecurity. I appraised her new ensemble with a smile and commented, “Nice.”

She frowned, but her shoulders relaxed.

“No,” I insisted. “It looks good on you.”

Perhaps too casual a descriptor. With her wet hair looping in long seaweed tangles around her shoulders, and her face glowing in the moonlight, she looked more than good. The English language needed a word that meant something halfway between a goddess and a naiad.

“Thanks,” she murmured, and then she came to sit beside me, just as close as before. This time she sat cross-legged. Her knee touched my leg, a bright point of heat.

I gestured to the door, and then the room beneath us, where her father’s thoughts were still in a snarl.

“What was all that for?” I asked.

She smiled a tiny, smug smile. “Charlie thinks I’m sneaking out.”

"Ah." I wondered how much my read of the evening with her father matched her own. "Why?"

She opened her eyes extra wide, feigning innocence. "Apparently, I look a little overexcited."

Playing along with her joke, I placed my hand beneath her chin and gently lifted her face toward the moonlight as if to better examine it. However, touching her face put all jokes far out of my head.

"You look very warm, actually," I murmured and, without stopping to think of every possible consequence, I leaned in and pressed my cheek against hers. My eyes closed of their own volition.

I breathed in her scent. Her skin blazed exquisitely against mine.

Her voice was husky when she spoke. "It seems to be…" She lost her voice for a moment, then cleared her throat and continued. "Much easier for you now. To be close to me."

"Does it seem that way to you?"

I thought about this assumption as I let my nose skim along the edge of her jaw. The physical pain in my throat had never eased in the slightest, though it did nothing to take away from the pleasure of touching her. While parts of my mind were lost in the miracle of the moment, other parts had never stopped calibrating the actions of every muscle, monitoring every bodily reaction. It took up quite a bit of my mental capacity, in fact, but then, an immortal mind had a great deal of space to spare. This did not damage the moment, either.

I lifted her curtain of damp hair and then pressed my lips lightly against the impossibly soft skin just beneath her ear.

She took a shaky breath. "Much, much easier."

"Hmm," was my only comment. I was very much involved in the exploration of her moonlit throat.

"So I was wondering," she began, but then fell silent when my fingers traced the fragile line of her collarbone. She took another unsteady breath.

"Yes?" I encouraged, my fingertips dipping into the hollow above the bone.

Her voice was higher and trembling as she asked, "Why is that, do you think?"

I chuckled. "Mind over matter."

She leaned away from me and I froze, on guard at once. Had I crossed a line? Been inappropriate? She stared back at me, seeming just as surprised as I was. I waited for her to say something, but she just gazed at me with ocean-deep eyes. All the while, her heart fluttered so quickly that it sounded like she'd just run a marathon. Or was very frightened.

"Did I do something wrong?" I asked.

"No—the opposite." Her lips curled into a smile. "You're driving me crazy."

A little shocked, I could only ask, "Really?"

Her heart was still thrumming away...not in fear, but in *desire.* Knowing this now sent the electric pulse in my own body into overdrive.

My answering smile was probably too wide.

Her grin grew to match mine. "Would you like a round of applause?"

Did she think I was so sure of myself? Could she not guess how entirely out of my wheelhouse all this was? There were many things I excelled at, most of them due to my extra-human abilities. I knew when I could be confident. This was not any of those times.

"I'm just...pleasantly surprised. In the last hundred years or so"—I paused and almost laughed at her somewhat smug reaction before I continued; she loved my honesty—"I never imagined anything like this." Nothing close. "I didn't believe I would ever find someone I wanted to be with in another way than my brothers and sisters." Perhaps romance always seemed a slightly foolish thing to everyone until one actually fell into it. "And then to find, even though it's all new to me, that I'm good at it—at being with you...."

Words rarely failed me, but this was an emotion I'd never experienced, that I had no name for.

"You're good at everything," she said, her tone implying that this was so obvious she shouldn't have had to say it out loud.

I shrugged in mock acceptance, and then laughed quietly with her, mostly with joy and wonder.

Her laugh faded, and a hint of the worry line appeared between her brows. "But how can it be so easy now? This afternoon..."

Though we were more in sync than we'd ever been, I had to remember that her afternoon in the meadow and my afternoon in the meadow had been quite different experiences. How could she begin to understand the kinds of changes I'd gone through in those hours we'd been together in the sun? Despite the new intimacy, I knew I would never explain to her exactly how I'd gotten to this place. She would never know what I had allowed myself to imagine.

I sighed, choosing my words. I wanted her to understand as much as I could share. "It's not *easy.*" It would never be easy. It would always be painful. None of that mattered. *Possible* was all I would ever ask for. "But this afternoon, I was still... undecided." Was that the best word to describe my sudden fit of violence? I couldn't think of another. "I am sorry about that. It was unforgivable for me to behave so."

Her smile became benevolent. "Not unforgivable."

"Thank you," I murmured before returning to the task of explaining. "You see...I wasn't sure if I was strong enough, and..." I took one of her hands and held it against my skin, smoldering embers against ice. It was an instinctive gesture, and I was surprised to find that it did somehow make it easier to speak. "While there was still that possibility that I might be"—I inhaled her scent from the most fragrant point inside her wrist, reveling in the fiery pain—"overcome...I was susceptible. Until I made up my mind that I *was* strong enough, that there was no possibility at all that I would...that I ever could..."

My sentence trailed off, unfinished, as I finally met her gaze. I took both her hands in mine.

"So there's no possibility now." I couldn't tell if she meant it as a statement or a question. If it was a question, she seemed very sure of the answer. And I wanted to sing with joy that she was *right.*

"Mind over matter," I said again.

"Wow, that was easy." She was laughing again.

I laughed, too, effortlessly falling into her exuberant mood.

"Easy for *you*!" I teased. I freed one of my hands to touch the tip of her nose with my index finger.

Abruptly, the jocularity felt off, somehow abrasive. All my anxieties swirled through my head like a whirlpool. My humor vanished and I found myself choking out another warning.

"I'm trying. If it gets to be too much, I'm fairly sure I'll be able to leave."

The frown that crossed her face featured an unexpected note of outrage.

But I wasn't finished cautioning. "And it will be harder tomorrow. I've had the scent of you in my head all day, and I've grown amazingly desensitized. If I'm away from you for any length of time, I'll have to start over again. Not quite from scratch, though, I think."

She leaned toward my chest, then swayed back again, as if she were catching herself. It reminded me of how she'd tucked her chin before. *No throat exposure.*

"Don't go away, then."

I took a steadying breath—a steadying, burning breath—and forced myself to stop panicking. Could she understand that the invitation in her words spoke to my greatest desire?

I smiled at her, wishing I could display a similar kindness on my face. It came so easily to her.

"That suits me. Bring on the shackles—I'm your prisoner."

I wrapped my hands around her delicate wrists as I spoke, laughing at the image in my mind. They could bind me in iron, or steel, or some stronger alloy yet to be discovered, and none of that would hold me the way one look from this fragile human girl could.

"You seem more optimistic than usual. I haven't seen you like this before," she noted.

Optimistic...an astute observation. My cynical old self seemed an entirely a different person.

I leaned closer to her, her wrists still locked in my hands. "Isn't it supposed to be like this? The glory of first love, and all that. It's incredible, isn't it, the difference between reading about something, seeing it in the pictures, and experiencing it?"

She nodded, thoughtful. "Very different. More...*forceful* than I'd imagined."

I contemplated the first time I'd really experienced the difference between first- and secondhand emotion. "For example: the emotion of jealousy," I said. "I've read about it a hundred thousand times, seen actors portray it in a thousand different plays and movies. I believed I understood that one pretty clearly. But it shocked me....Do you remember the day that Mike asked you to the dance?"

"The day you started talking to me again." She said this like a correction, as if I were prioritizing the wrong part of the memory.

But I was lost in what had happened just before that, reliving with perfect recall the first time I'd ever felt that specific passion.

"I was surprised," I mused, "by the flare of resentment, almost fury, that I felt—I didn't recognize what it was at first. I was even more aggravated than usual that I couldn't know what you were thinking, why you refused him. Was it simply for your friend's sake? Was there someone else? I knew I had no right to care either way. I *tried* not to care...." My mood shifted as the story followed its path. I laughed once. "And then the line started forming."

As I had expected, her answering scowl only made me want to laugh again.

"I waited, unreasonably anxious to hear what you would say to them, to watch your expressions. I couldn't deny the relief I felt, watching the annoyance on your face. But I couldn't be sure.... That was the first night I came here."

A slow flush began in her cheeks, but she leaned closer, intense rather than embarrassed. The atmosphere transformed once more, and I found myself mid-confession for the hundredth time today. I whispered more softly now.

"I wrestled all night while watching you sleep...with the chasm between what I knew was *right*, moral, ethical, and what I *wanted*. I knew that if I continued to ignore you as I should, or if I left for a few years, till you were gone, that someday you would say yes to Mike, or someone like him. It made me angry."

Angry, miserable, as if life were draining of all color and purpose.

In what seemed an unconscious movement, she shook her head, denying this vision of her future.

"And then, as you were sleeping, you said my name."

Looking back, it seemed as though those brief seconds were the turning point, the divide. Though I had doubted myself a million times in the interim, once I'd heard her call to me, I'd never had another choice.

"You spoke so clearly," I continued, my voice just a breath. "At first I thought you'd woken. But you rolled over restlessly and mumbled my name once more, and sighed. The feeling that coursed through me then was unnerving, staggering. And I knew I couldn't ignore you any longer."

Her heart beat more quickly.

"But jealousy...it's a strange thing. So much more powerful than I would have thought. And irrational! Just now, when Charlie asked you about that vile Mike Newton—"

I didn't finish, remembering that I should probably not reveal exactly how strong my feelings about the hapless boy had become.

"I should have known you'd be listening," she muttered.

It wasn't really an option to *not* hear anything that happened so close. "Of course."

"*That* made you feel jealous, though, really?" Her tone changed from annoyance to disbelief.

"I'm new at this," I reminded her. "You're resurrecting the human in me, and everything feels stronger because it's fresh."

Unexpectedly, a smug little smile puckered her lips. "But honestly, for *that* to bother you, after I have to hear that Rosalie—Rosalie, the incarnation of pure beauty, *Rosalie*—was meant for you. Emmett or no Emmett, how can I compete with that?"

She said the words as though she was playing her trump card. As if jealousy were rational enough to weigh out the physical attractiveness of the third parties, and then be felt in direct proportion.

"There's no competition," I promised her.

Gently and slowly, I used her imprisoned wrists to pull her closer to me, until her head rested just under my chin. Her cheek seared against my skin.

"I *know* there's no competition. That's the problem," she grumbled.

"Of course Rosalie *is* beautiful in her way...." It wasn't as if I could deny Rosalie's exquisiteness, but it was an unnatural, heightened thing—sometimes more disturbing than attracting. "But even if she wasn't like a sister to me, even if Emmett didn't belong with her, she could never have one tenth, no, one hundredth of the attraction you hold for me. For almost ninety years I've walked among my kind, and yours...all the time thinking I was complete in myself, not realizing what I was seeking. And not finding anything...because you weren't alive yet."

I felt her breath against my skin as she whispered her response. "It hardly seems fair. I haven't had to wait at all. Why should I get off so easily?"

No one had ever had more sympathy for the devil. Still, I wondered that she could count her own sacrifices so lightly.

"You're right. I should make this harder for you, definitely." I gathered both of her wrists into my left hand so that my right was free, then brushed lightly down the length of her dripping hair. Its texture, slippery like this, wasn't so far from the sea-weed I'd imagined before. I twisted a strand between my fingers as I listed her forfeitures. "You only have to risk your life every second you spend with me, that's surely not much. You only have to turn your back on nature, on humanity... what's that worth?"

"Very little," she breathed into my skin. "I don't feel deprived of anything."

Perhaps it was not surprising that Rosalie's face flickered behind my eyelids. In the last seven decades, she had taught me a thousand different aspects of humanity to mourn.

"Not yet."

Something in my voice had her tugging against my hold, pulling back from my chest as she tried to see my face. I was about to free her when something outside our intense moment intruded.

Doubt. Awkwardness. Worry. The words were no clearer than usual, and there wasn't much time for conjecture.

"What—?" she began, but before she could voice her question, I was on the move. She caught herself against the mattress as I darted to the dark corner where I habitually spent my nights.

"Lie down," I whispered just loud enough for her to hear the urgency in my voice. I was surprised that she hadn't noticed Charlie's footsteps coming up the stairs. To be fair, it sounded like he was trying to be furtive.

She reacted immediately, diving under her quilt and curling into a ball. Charlie's hand was already turning the knob. As the door cracked open, Bella took a deep breath and then slowly exhaled. The motion was overdone, slightly theatrical.

Huh, was the only reaction I could read from Charlie. As Bella performed her next sleeping breath, Charlie eased the door closed. I waited until his own bedroom door was closed and I'd heard the creak of mattress springs before I returned to Bella.

She must have been waiting for the all clear, still curled in a rigid ball, still amplifying her slow and even breathing. If Charlie had really watched her for a few seconds, he probably would have known she was pretending. Bella wasn't particularly good at deception.

Following these strange new instincts—they'd yet to lead me astray—I lowered myself onto the bed beside her and then slid under her quilt and put my arm around her.

"You are a terrible actress," I said conversationally, as if it were a perfectly routine thing for me to lie with her this way. "I'd say that career path is out for you."

Her heart drummed loudly again, but her voice was as casual as mine. "Darn it."

She nestled herself against me, closer than before, then lay still and sighed with contentment. I wondered if she would fall asleep like this, in my arms. It seemed unlikely, given the pace of her heart, but she didn't speak again.

Unbidden, the notes of her song came into my head. I started to hum along almost automatically. The music seemed to belong here, in the place where it had been inspired. Bella didn't comment, but her body tensed, as if she were listening carefully.

I paused to ask, "Should I sing you to sleep?"

I was surprised when she laughed quietly. "Right, like I could sleep with you here!"

"You do it all the time."

Her tone hardened. "But I didn't *know* you were here."

I was glad that she still seemed upset by my transgressions. I knew I deserved some kind of punishment, that she should hold me accountable. However, she didn't move away from me. I couldn't imagine a punishment that would carry any weight while she allowed me to hold her.

"So if you don't want to sleep . . . ?" I asked. Was this like food? Was I selfishly keeping her from something vital? But how could I leave when she wanted me to stay?

"If I don't want to sleep . . . ?" she echoed.

"What do you want to do then?" Would she tell me if she was exhausted? Or would she pretend she was fine?

It took her a long moment to answer. "I'm not sure," she said at last, and I couldn't help but wonder what options she had run through in her deliberations. I'd been very forward in joining her like this, but it felt oddly natural. Did it feel that way to her? Or just presumptuous? Did it make her, like me, imagine more? Is that what she'd thought through for so long?

"Tell me when you decide." I would make no suggestions. I would let her lead.

Easier said than done. In her silence, I found myself leaning closer to her, letting my face brush along the length of her jaw, breathing in both her scent and her warmth. The fire was such a part of me now that it was easy to notice other things. I'd always thought of her scent with fear and desire. But there were so many layers to its beauty that I hadn't been able to appreciate before.

"I thought you were desensitized," she murmured.

I returned to my earlier metaphor to explain. "Just because I'm resisting the wine doesn't mean I can't appreciate the bouquet. You have a very floral smell, like lavender...or freesia." I laughed once. "It's mouthwatering."

She swallowed loudly, then spoke with an assumed nonchalance. "Yeah, it's an off day when I don't get *somebody* telling me how edible I smell."

I laughed again, and then sighed. I would always regret this part of my response to her, but it wasn't such a weighty thing anymore. One small thorn, so irrelevant in the face of the rose's beauty.

"I've decided what I want to do," she announced.

I waited eagerly.

"I want to hear more about you."

Well, not as interesting for me, but she could have whatever she wanted. "Ask me anything."

"Why do you do it?" she breathed, quieter than before. "I still don't understand how you can work so hard to resist what you . . . *are*. Please don't misunderstand, of course I'm glad that you do. I just don't see why you would bother in the first place."

I was glad she asked this. It was important. I tried to find the best way to explain, but my words faltered in a few places. "That's a good question, and you are not the first one to ask it. The others—the majority of our kind who are quite content with our lot—they, too, wonder at how we live. But you see, just because we've been . . . dealt a certain hand . . . it doesn't mean that we can't choose to rise above—to conquer the boundaries of a destiny that none of us wanted. To try to retain whatever essential humanity we can."

Was that clear? Would she understand what I meant?

She didn't comment, and she didn't move.

"Did you fall asleep?" I whispered so quietly that it couldn't possibly wake her if that were the case.

"No," she said quickly. And added nothing more.

It was frustrating and hilarious how much nothing had changed despite everything changing. I would always be driven frantic by her silent thoughts.

"Is that all you were curious about?" I encouraged.

"Not quite." I couldn't see her face, but I knew she was smiling.

"What else do you want to know?"

"Why can you read minds—why only you?" she demanded. "And Alice, seeing the future . . . why does that happen?"

I wished I had a better answer. I shrugged and admitted, "We don't really know. Carlisle has a theory—he believes that we all bring something of our strongest human traits with us into the next life, where they are intensified, like our minds, and our senses. He thinks that I must have already been very sensitive to the thoughts of those around me. And that Alice had some precognition, wherever she was."

"What did he bring into the next life, and the others?"

This was an easier answer; I'd considered it many times before. "Carlisle brought his compassion. Esme brought her ability to love passionately. Emmett brought his strength, Rosalie..." Well, Rose had brought her beauty. But that seemed a less than tactful answer in light of our earlier discussion. If Bella's jealousy was even a tiny bit as painful as my own, I didn't want her to have a reason to feel it again. "Her...tenacity. Or you could call it pigheadedness." Surely this was true as well. I laughed quietly, imagining how she must have been as a human girl. "Jasper is very interesting. He was quite charismatic in his first life, able to influence those around him to see things his way. Now he is able to manipulate the emotions of those around him—calm down a room of angry people, for example, or excite a lethargic crowd, conversely. It's a very subtle gift."

She was quiet again. I wasn't surprised; it was a lot to process.

"So where did it all start?" she asked at last. "I mean, Carlisle changed you, and then someone must have changed him, and so on...."

Another answer that was only conjecture. "Well, where did you come from? Evolution? Creation? Couldn't we have evolved in the same way as other species, predator and prey? Or..." Though I didn't always agree with Carlisle's unshakable faith, his answers were just as likely as any others. Sometimes, perhaps because his mind was so firm, they felt *most* likely. "If you don't believe that all this world could have just happened on its own, which is hard for me to accept myself, is it so hard to believe that the same force that created the delicate angelfish with the shark, the baby seal and the killer whale, could create both our kinds together?"

"Let me get this straight." She was trying to sound as serious as before, but I could hear the joke coming. "I'm the baby seal, right?"

"Right," I agreed, and then laughed. I closed my eyes and pressed my lips to the top of her head.

She twitched, shifted her weight. Was she uncomfortable? I prepared to free her, but she settled again, snug against my chest. Her breath seemed just slightly deeper than before. Her heart had relaxed into a steady rhythm.

"Are you ready to sleep?" I murmured. "Or do you have any more questions?"

"Only a million or two."

"We have tomorrow, and the next day, and the next. . . ." It had been a powerful thought in the kitchen, the idea of many more evenings spent in her company. It was more powerful now, curled up together in the dark. If she wished it, there was actually very little time we needed to be separated. Less time apart than together. Did she feel the shattering joy, too?

"Are you sure you won't vanish in the morning? You are mythical, after all." She asked her question with no humor at all. It sounded like a serious concern.

"I won't leave you," I promised. It felt like a vow, a covenant. I hoped she could hear that.

"One more, then, tonight . . ."

I waited for her question, but she didn't continue. I was mystified when her heart started to move jaggedly again. The air around me heated with the pulse of her blood.

"What is it?"

"No, forget it," she said quickly. "I changed my mind."

"Bella, you can ask me anything."

She said nothing. I couldn't imagine anything she would be frightened to ask at this point. Her heart sped again, and I groaned aloud. "I keep thinking it will get less frustrating, not hearing your thoughts. But it just gets worse and *worse*."

"I'm glad you can't read my thoughts," she countered at once. "It's bad enough that you eavesdrop on my sleep-talking."

Strange that this would be her one objection to my stalking, but I was too eager for her missing question, the one that made her heart race, to worry about that now.

"Please?" I pleaded.

Her hair brushed back and forth across my chest as she shook her head.

"If you don't tell me, I'll just assume it's something much worse than it is." I waited, but that bluff didn't move her. In truth, I had no ideas, either trivial or dark. I tried begging again. "Please?"

"Well..." She hesitated, but at least she was talking. Or not. Silence fell again.

"Yes?" I prompted.

"You said...that Rosalie and Emmett will get married soon...." She trailed off, leaving me baffled again at her train of thought. Did she want an invitation?

"Is that...marriage...the same as it is for humans?"

Even as quickly as my brain worked, it took me a second to follow. It should have been more obvious. I needed to keep firmly in mind that nine times out of ten—in my experience with her, at least—whenever her heart started to race, it had nothing to do with fear. It was usually attraction. And should this train of thought be in any way shocking when I had just recently *climbed into her bed* with her?

I laughed at my own obtuseness. "Is *that* what you're getting at?"

My question sounded light, but I could not help responding to the subject at hand. The electricity rioted through my body, and I had to resist the urge to reposition myself so that my lips could find hers. That wasn't the right answer. It couldn't be. Because there was an obvious second question following the first.

"Yes, I suppose it is much the same," I answered. "I told you, most of those human desires are there, just hidden behind more powerful desires."

"Oh."

She didn't continue. Maybe I was wrong.

"Was there a purpose behind your curiosity?"

She sighed. "Well, I did wonder...about you and me... someday...."

No, not wrong. The sudden grief felt like a weight pressing against my chest. How I wished I had a different answer to give her.

"I don't think that... *that*..."—I avoided the word *sex* because she did—"would be possible for us."

"Because it would be too hard for you?" she whispered. "If I were that... close?"

It was hard not to imagine.... I refocused.

"That's certainly a problem," I said slowly. "But that's not what I was thinking of. It's just that you are so soft, so *fragile*. I have to mind my actions every moment that we're together so that I don't hurt you. I could kill you quite easily, Bella, simply by accident." I reached up carefully to lay my hand against her cheek. "If I was too hasty... if for one second I wasn't paying enough attention, I could reach out, meaning to touch your face, and crush your skull by mistake. You don't realize how incredibly *breakable* you are. I can never, never afford to lose any kind of control when I'm with you."

Admitting to this obstacle seemed less shameful than confessing my thirst. After all, my strength was simply part of what I was. Well, my thirst was, too, but the intensity of it around her was unnatural. That aspect of myself felt indefensible, disgraceful. Even now that it was under control, I was mortified it existed.

She thought over my answer for a long time. Perhaps my wording was more frightening than I'd intended. But how would she understand if I edited the truth too much?

"Are you scared?" I asked.

Another pause.

"No," she said slowly. "I'm fine."

We were silent for another pensive moment. I wasn't thrilled with where my thoughts went in her silence. Even though she'd told me so much about her own past that didn't align... even though she'd introduced the topic with such bashfulness... I couldn't help but wonder. And I knew well enough by now that if I ignored my intrusive curiosity, it would only begin to fester.

I tried to sound indifferent. "I'm curious now, though.... Have *you* ever...?"

"Of course not," she answered at once, not angrily, but incredulously. "I told you I've never felt like this about anyone before, not even close."

Did she think I hadn't been paying attention?

"I know," I assured her. "It's just that I know other people's thoughts. I know love and lust don't always keep the same company."

"They do for me. Now, anyway, that they exist for me at all."

Her use of the plural was a kind of acknowledgment. I knew that she loved me. The fact that we both also *lusted* was definitely going to complicate matters.

I decided to answer her next question before she could ask it. "That's nice. We have that one thing in common, at least."

She sighed, but it sounded like a pleased sigh.

"Your human instincts...," she asked slowly. "Well, do you find me attractive, in *that* way, at all?"

I laughed out loud at that. Was there any way in which I did *not* want her? Mind and soul and body, *body* no less than either of the others. I smoothed her hair against her neck.

"I may not be a human, but I am a man."

She yawned, and I suppressed another laugh. "I've answered your questions, now you should sleep."

"I'm not sure if I can."

"Do you want me to leave?" I suggested, though I was extremely loath to do so.

"No!" In her outrage, her answer was much louder than the whispers we'd been using all night. No harm done; Charlie's snores didn't even stutter.

I laughed again, then pulled myself closer to her. With my lips against her ear, I began humming her song again, so quietly it was little more than a breath.

I could feel the difference when she crossed over into unconsciousness. All the alertness escaped her muscles, until they were loose and languid. Her breathing slowed and her hands curled together against her chest, almost as if in prayer.

I felt no desire to move. Ever again, in fact. I knew eventually she would begin to toss, and I would have to get out of her way so as not to wake her, but for now, nothing could be more perfect. I was still unused to this joy, and it didn't really feel like something a person *could* get used to. I would embrace it for as long as that was possible, and know that no matter what happened in the future, just having this one paradisiacal day was worth any pain that might follow.

"Edward," Bella whispered in her sleep. "Edward...I love you."

19. HOME

I WONDERED IF I WOULD EVER SPEND A NIGHT HAPPIER than this one. I doubted it.

As she slept, Bella told me again and again that she loved me. More than the words themselves, the sound of perfect bliss in her tone was all I could ever want. I made her truly happy. Did that not excuse everything else?

Eventually, in the very early morning, she settled into deeper sleep. I knew she wouldn't speak again. After finishing her book—one of my favorites now, too—I'd thought mostly about the day ahead, about Alice's vision of Bella visiting my family. Though I'd seen it clearly in Alice's head, it was hard to believe. Would Bella want that? Did I?

I considered Alice's fairly well-developed friendship with Bella, of which Bella was completely ignorant. Now that I felt assured about the future I was pursuing—and the likelihood of it happening—it *did* feel a little cruel to keep Alice away from her. What would Bella think of Emmett? I wasn't one hundred percent sure that he would behave himself. He would find it hilarious to say something off-putting or frightening. Maybe, if I promised him something he wanted...A wrestling match? A football game? There had to be a price he'd accept. I'd already seen how Jasper would keep his distance, but had Alice thought to tell him that, or was her vision contingent on my action? Of course, Bella had met Carlisle, but it would be something different now. I found that the idea of Bella spending time with Carlisle was appealing to me. He was the very best of us. It could only make her think more highly of us all to know him better. And then, Esme would be ecstatic to meet Bella. The thought of Esme's pleasure almost had my mind made up.

There was just the one obstacle, really.

Rosalie.

I realized there was prep work I absolutely had to accomplish before I could even think of bringing Bella home. And that meant leaving her.

I gazed at her now, deep in her dreams. I'd moved to the floor beside her bed when she'd begun her nightly gyrations. I leaned against the edge of the mattress, one hand outstretched, a lock of her hair wrapped around my finger. I sighed and untangled myself. It had to be done. She would never know I'd left. But *I* would miss *her* for even this short interlude.

I hurried home, hoping to conclude my tasks in the briefest time possible.

Alice had done her part, as usual. Most of the things I wanted to accomplish were just details. Alice knew which were most vital, and sure enough, Rosalie was waiting on the front porch, perched on the top step of the stairs, as I ran up to the house.

Alice had not told her much. Rosalie's face was a little confused when I first spotted her, as if she had no idea what she was waiting for. As soon as she caught sight of me, her confusion turned to a scowl.

Oh, what now!

"Rose, please," I called to her. "Can we talk?"

I should have realized Alice was just helping you.

"And herself, a little."

Rosalie stood up, brushing her jeans off.

"Please, Rose?"

Fine! Fine. Say what you have to say.

I swept my arm out as an invitation. "Come for a walk with me?"

She pursed her lips but nodded. I led the way around the house, to the edge of the night-black river. At first we were silent as we paced north along the bank. There was no sound but the gush of the water.

It was by design I'd chosen this path. I hoped it would remind her of the day I'd been thinking of earlier, the day she'd brought Emmett home. The first time we'd found common ground.

"Can we get on with this?" she complained.

Though she sounded only irritated, I could hear more in her head. She was nervous. Still afraid that I was angry about her bet? A little ashamed of that, I thought.

"I want to ask you a favor," I told her. "It won't be easy for you, I know."

This was not the direction she'd been expecting. My gentle tone only made her angrier, though.

You want me to be nice to the human, she guessed.

"Yes. You don't have to like her, if you'd rather not. But she's part of my life, and that makes her part of your life, too. I know you didn't ask for this, and you don't want it."

No, I do not, she agreed.

"You didn't ask my permission to bring Emmett home," I reminded her.

She sniffed derisively. *That's different.*

"More permanent, certainly."

Rosalie stopped walking, and I paused with her. She stared at me, surprised and suspicious.

What do you mean by that? Aren't you talking about permanence?

Her thoughts were so caught up with these questions, it took me by surprise when she spoke to a different subject.

"Did you feel *harmed* when I chose Emmett? Did that injure you in any way?"

"Of course not. You chose very well."

She sniffed again, unimpressed with my flattery.

"Could you give me the chance to prove that I have, too?"

Rosalie spun away from me, striding north again, breaking a path now through the untamed forest.

I can't look at her. When I look at her, I can't see her as a person. I just see a waste.

Against my intentions, I felt my anger flare. I bit back a growl, and tried to compose myself. Rosalie glanced over her shoulder and saw the change in my expression. She paused again, swinging around to face me. Her features softened.

I am *sorry. I don't mean that to sound so cruel. I just can't… I can't watch her do this.* "She's got a chance for *everything*, Edward," Rosalie whispered, her whole body rigid with intensity. "A whole life of possibilities ahead of her, and she's going to waste it *all*. Everything I lost. I can't *bear* to watch it."

I stared back at her, shaken.

I'd been annoyed by Rosalie's strange jealousy, which indeed had roots in my preference for Bella. That part was all so petty. But this was something different, so much deeper. I felt that I understood her now for the first time since I'd saved Bella's life.

I reached out carefully to place my hand on her arm, expecting she would shake it off. But she just stood very still.

"I'm not going to let that happen," I promised, matching her intensity.

She examined my face for a long moment. Then she pictured Bella in her mind. It wasn't the perfect representation of Alice's visions, more of a caricature, really. But it was clear what she meant. Bella's skin was white, her eyes bright red. The image was flavored with heavy disgust.

This is not your goal?

I shook my head, just as disgusted. "No. No, I want her to have *everything*. I won't take anything away from her, Rose. Do you understand? I won't hurt her that way."

She was unsettled now, too. *But…how do you see that… working?*

I shrugged, feigning a nonchalance I didn't feel. "How long until she grows bored with a seventeen-year-old? Do you think I can keep her interested until she's twenty-three? Maybe twenty-five? Eventually... she'll move on." I tried to control my face, to hide what the words cost me, but she saw through me.

This is a dangerous game you're playing, Edward.

"I'll find a way to survive. After she goes..." I flinched, my hand falling to my side.

"That's not what I meant," she said. *Look, you're not up to my personal standards, but there's not a human man alive who can compare with you, and you know it.*

I shook my head. "Someday she'll want more than I can give her." There was so much I couldn't give her. "You would have wanted more, wouldn't you? If you were in her position, and Emmett in mine?"

Rosalie took my question seriously, thinking it through. She imagined Emmett just as he was now, his easy smile, his hands held out to her. She saw herself human again, still lovely but less remarkable, reaching back to him. Then she imagined her human self turning away from him. Neither image seemed to satisfy her.

But I know what I lost, she thought, her tone subdued. *I don't think she'll see it that way.* "I'm going to sound like an octogenarian now," she continued aloud, the faintest hint of levity suddenly in her voice. "But... you know kids these days." She smiled weakly. "All about the here and now, no thought for five years into the future, let alone fifty. What will you do when she asks you to change her?"

"I'll tell her why it's wrong. I'll tell her everything she'll lose."

And when she begs*?*

I hesitated, thinking of Alice's vision of a grieving Bella, her hollow cheeks, her body curled in on itself in agony. What if my presence, and not my absence, were the reason she felt that way? I imagined her full of Rosalie's bitterness.

"I'll refuse."

Rose heard the iron in my tone, and I could see that she finally understood my resolve. She nodded to herself.

I still think it's too dangerous. I'm not sure you're that strong.

She turned around and started walking slowly back toward the house. I kept pace with her.

"Your life isn't what you wanted," I began quietly. "But in the last seventy years or so, would you say you've had at least five years of pure happiness?"

Flashes of the best parts of her life, all of them revolving around Emmett, moved through her head, though I could see that, obstinate as ever, she didn't want to agree with me.

I smiled halfheartedly. "Ten years, even?"

She wouldn't answer me.

"Let me have my five years, Rosalie," I whispered. "I know it can't last. Let me be happy while happiness is possible. Be part of that happiness. Be my sister, and if you can't love my choice the way I love yours, can you at least pretend to tolerate her?"

My words, gentle and quiet, seemed to hit her like bricks. Her shoulders were suddenly stiff, brittle.

I'm not sure what I can do. Seeing everything I want... out of my reach... It's too painful.

It would be painful for her, I knew that. But I also knew that her regret and sorrow wouldn't equal even a fraction of the anguish that was waiting for me. Rosalie's life would go back to what it was now. Emmett would be there throughout to comfort her. But I... I would lose everything.

"Will you try?" I demanded, my voice sterner than before.

Her walk slowed for a few seconds, and her eyes were on her feet. Finally, her shoulders slumped and she nodded. *I can try.*

"There's a chance... Alice saw Bella coming to the house in the morning."

Her eyes flashed up, angry again. *I need more time than that.*

I held my hands up, placating. "Take the time you need."

It made me sad, and tired, to see that her eyes were suspicious again. Maybe she wasn't strong enough. She seemed to feel the judgment in my gaze. She looked away, then suddenly ran for the house. I let her go.

My other errands did not take so long, nor were they as difficult. Jasper agreed easily to my request. My mother was glowing with happy anticipation. What I'd wanted from Emmett no longer applied; it was clear he'd be with Rosalie, and she'd be somewhere far from here.

Well, it was a start. At least I'd gotten Rose to promise to try.

I even took a second to put on fresh clothes. Though the sleeveless shirt Alice had given me long ago had not brought about any of the miseries I'd feared—and *had* brought some pleasures I hadn't anticipated—I still found it strangely distasteful. I was more comfortable in my usual clothes.

I passed Alice on my way out, leaning up against the pillar at the edge of the porch steps, near where Rosalie had waited before. Her grin was smug. *Everything looks perfect for Bella's visit. Just as I'd envisioned.*

I wanted to point out that what she saw now was still just a vision, changeable as the first, but why bother?

"You're not taking Bella's desires into account," I reminded her.

She rolled her eyes. *When has Bella ever said no to you?*

It was an interesting point.

"Alice, I—"

She interrupted, already knowing my question.

See for yourself.

She pictured the intertwined ribbons of Bella's future. Some were solid, some insubstantial, some disappearing into mist. They were more ordered now, no longer snarled into the messy knot. It was a relief that the most nightmarish of futures was entirely missing. But there, in the sturdiest thread, Bella of the bloodred eyes and diamond skin still held the most prominent place. The vision I was looking for was only part of the more nebulous lines, ribbons at the periphery. Bella at twenty, Bella at twenty-five. Flimsy-seeming visions, blurred around the edges.

Alice wrapped her arms tight around her legs. She didn't need to read thoughts or the future to read the frustration in my eyes.

"That's never going to happen."

When have you ever said no to Bella?

I scowled at her on my way down the steps, and then I was running.

Only moments later I was in Bella's room. I put Alice out of my mind and let the calm of her quiet slumber wash over me. It looked as if she hadn't moved at all. And yet, my being away—even briefly—had changed things. I felt...unsure again. Rather than sitting beside her bed as I had before, I found myself back in the old rocking chair. I didn't want to be presumptuous.

Charlie rose not too long after I'd returned, before the first hints of dawn had even begun to light the sky. I felt confident, due to his usual patterns and also his murky but cheerful thoughts, that he was going fishing again. Sure enough, after a quick peek into Bella's room that found her more convincingly asleep than she'd been the night before, he tiptoed downstairs and started rummaging through his fishing gear under the stairs. He left the house just as the clouds outside took on a faint, gray luminosity. Again, I heard the rusty creaking of Bella's truck's hood. I flitted to the window to watch.

Charlie propped the hood on the strut and then replaced the battery cables that he'd left dangling to the sides. It wasn't a particularly difficult problem to solve, but maybe he'd assumed that Bella wouldn't even attempt to fix her truck in the dark. I wondered where he'd imagined she'd want to go.

After a brief moment of loading rods and tackle into the back of his police cruiser, Charlie drove away. I returned to my former place and waited for Bella to wake.

More than an hour later, when the sun was fully up behind the thick blanket of clouds, Bella finally stirred. She threw one of her arms across her face, as if to block the light, then groaned quietly and rolled onto her side, pulling the pillow on top of her head.

Abruptly, she gasped, "Oh!" and lurched dizzily up into a

sitting position. Her eyes struggled to focus, and it was obvious she was searching for something.

I'd never seen her like this, first thing in the morning. I wondered if her hair always looked this way, or if I'd been responsible for the extraordinary mussing.

"Your hair looks like a haystack, but I like it," I informed her, and her eyes snapped to my position. Relief saturated her expression.

"Edward! You stayed!" Awkward from lying still for so long, she struggled to get to her feet, and then bounded across the room directly toward me, flinging herself into my arms. Suddenly my worries about presumption felt a little silly.

I caught her easily, steadying her on my lap. She seemed shocked by her own impulsiveness, and I laughed at her apologetic expression.

"Of course," I told her.

Her heart thudded, sounding confused. She'd given it very little time to adjust from sleep to sprint. I rubbed her shoulders, hoping to calm it.

She let her head fall against my shoulder.

"I was sure it was a dream," she whispered.

"You're not that creative," I teased her. I couldn't remember dreaming myself, but from what I'd heard in other human brains, I rather thought it was not a very coherent or detailed thing.

Suddenly, Bella bolted upright. I dropped my hands out of the way as she scrambled to her feet.

"Charlie!" she choked.

"He left an hour ago—after reattaching your battery cables, I might add. I have to admit I was disappointed. Is that really all it would take to stop you, if you were determined to go?"

She rocked indecisively from her toes to her heels, her eyes flicking from my face to the door and then back again. A few seconds passed while she seemed to struggle with some decision.

"You're not usually this confused in the morning," I said, though it wasn't actually something I would know. I never saw her until she'd had plenty of time to wake up. But I hoped that—as she usually did when I assumed something—she would contradict me, and then explain whatever dilemma faced her. I held out my arms to let her know she was welcome—so extremely welcome—to return to me if she wished.

She swayed toward me again, and then frowned. "I need another human minute."

Of course. I was sure I would get better at this.

"I'll wait," I promised her. She'd asked me to stay, and until she told me to go, I would be waiting for her.

This time there was no long delay. I could hear Bella banging cabinets and slamming doors. She was in a rush today. I heard the brush tearing through her hair and it made me wince.

It was only a few moments until she rejoined me. Two high spots of color marked her cheeks, and her eyes were bright and eager. Still, she moved more carefully as she approached me this time, and paused, unsure, when her knees were an inch from mine. She seemed unconscious of the fact that she was warily wringing her hands.

I could only guess she was shy again, that she felt the same unease after being separated that I had felt returning to her room this morning. And—as I was sure was true for me as well—there was absolutely no need for it.

I gathered her carefully into my arms. She curled up willingly against my chest, her legs draped over mine.

"Welcome back," I murmured.

She sighed, contented. Her fingers traced down my right arm, slow and searching, and then back up again while I rocked lazily back and forth, moving to the rhythm of her breathing.

Her fingertips wandered across my shoulder, then paused at my collar. She leaned back, staring up at my face with a dismayed expression.

"You *left*?"

I grinned. "I could hardly leave in the clothes I came in—what would the neighbors think?"

Bella's dissatisfaction only intensified. I didn't want to explain the errands I'd had to run, so I said the one thing I was absolutely sure would distract her.

"You were very deeply asleep—I didn't miss anything. The talking came earlier."

As anticipated, Bella groaned.

"What did you hear?" she demanded.

It was impossible to hold on to my jocular mood. It felt as though my insides were melting into liquid joy as I told her the truth. "You said you loved me."

Her eyes dropped, and she pressed her face against my shoulder, hiding.

"You knew that already," she whispered. The heat of her breath saturated the cotton of my shirt.

"It was nice to hear, just the same," I murmured into her hair.

"I love you."

The words hadn't lost their ability to thrill me. On the contrary, they were more overpowering now. It meant much to have her choose to say them, knowing I was listening.

I wanted even stronger words, words that could accurately describe what she had become to me. There was nothing left inside me that wasn't entirely about her. I remembered our first conversation, remembered thinking then that I did not truly have a life. That was no longer the case.

"You are my life now," I whispered.

Though the sky was still full of thick clouds, the sun buried deep behind them, the room somehow filled with golden light. The air turned clearer, purer than the normal atmosphere. We rocked slowly, my arms around her, savoring the perfection.

As I'd thought so often in the past twenty-four hours, I knew I would be totally satisfied with every part of the universe if I never had to move again. The way her body was melted against mine, I thought she must feel the same.

Ah, but I had responsibilities. I needed to keep my unruly joy in check and be practical.

I held her just a little tighter for one second, then forced my arms to relax.

"Breakfast time?" I suggested.

Bella hesitated, perhaps as averse as I was to allowing any space to come between us. Then she twisted her torso away from me, leaning back so I could see her face.

Her eyes were round with terror. Her mouth fell open and her hands flew up to protect her throat.

I was so horrified by her obvious distress that I couldn't process what was happening. My senses flailed out wildly around us like tentacles, looking for whatever danger threatened.

And then, before I could dive out the window with her in my arms and run for safety, her expression relaxed into a sly smile. I finally understood the connection between my words and her reaction, the joke she was making.

She giggled. "Kidding! And you said I couldn't act."

It took me half a second to compose myself. Relief made me feel weak, but the shock also left me agitated. "That wasn't funny."

"It was very funny," she insisted, "and you know it."

I couldn't help but smile at her. I supposed if vampire jokes were going to become a thing with us, I could bear it. For her sake.

"Shall I rephrase? Breakfast time for the human."

She smiled blithely. "Oh, okay."

While I was willing to accept a future of bad jokes, I wasn't entirely ready to let her off the hook for this one.

I moved with extreme care, but I didn't move slowly. I hoped she would be as shocked as I'd been—though definitely not as frightened—as I folded her over my shoulder and darted from the room.

"Hey!" she complained, her voice bouncing with my movement, and I slowed slightly on the way down the stairs.

"Whoa," she gasped as I turned her upright and set her down gently on a kitchen chair.

She looked up at me and smiled, clearly not shaken in the least. "What's for breakfast?"

I frowned. I'd not had time to figure out the human food thing. Well, I knew the basics of what it should look like at least, so I could probably improvise....

"Er..." I hesitated. "I'm not sure. What would you like?" Hopefully something straightforward.

Bella laughed at my confusion and stood up, stretching her arms over her head. "That's all right," she assured me. "I fend for myself pretty well." She raised one eyebrow and added—with an arch smile—"Watch me hunt."

It was enlightening and alluring to watch her in her element. I hadn't seen her this confident and at ease before. It was clear she could have located everything she was looking for while wearing a blindfold. First a bowl, and then—stretching up on her toes—a box of off-brand Cheerios from a high shelf. Spinning to tug open the fridge while also pulling a spoon from a drawer she then nudged shut with her hip. It was only after she'd assembled everything on the table that she hesitated.

"Can I...get you anything?"

I rolled my eyes. "Just eat, Bella."

She took one bite of the inedible-looking slush and chewed quickly, glancing up at me. After she'd swallowed, she asked, "What's on the agenda for today?"

"Hmmm..." I'd meant to work up to this, but I would be lying to her now if I said I had no ideas. "What would you say to meeting my family?"

Her face blanched. Well, if her answer was no, that was that. I wondered how Alice had gotten it wrong.

"Are you afraid now?" My question sounded almost as if I wanted her to say yes. I supposed I had been waiting for *something* that would be too much.

The answer was obvious in her eyes, but she said, "Yes," in a low, tremulous voice, which I hadn't expected. She never admitted when she was afraid. Or, at least, she never admitted when she was afraid of *me*.

"Don't worry, I'll protect you," I said, smiling halfheartedly. I wasn't trying to convince her. There were a million other things we could do together today that wouldn't make her feel as though her life was on the line. But I wanted her to know that I would always put myself between her and any danger, meteor or monster.

She shook her head. "I'm not afraid of *them*. I'm afraid they won't…like me. Won't they be, well, surprised that you would bring someone"—she frowned—"like *me* home to meet them? Do they know that I know about them?"

A sudden pulse of unexpected anger rocked me. Maybe it was because she was right, about Rosalie at least. I hated that Bella referred to herself this way, as though there were something wrong with her, and not the other way around.

"Oh, they already know everything," I said, and the anger was clear in my voice. I tried to smile, but I could tell it didn't soften my tone. "They'd taken bets yesterday, you know, on whether I'd bring you back, though why anyone would bet against Alice, I can't imagine." I realized I was prejudicing her against them, but it was fair she should know. I tried to rein in my ire. "At any rate, we don't have secrets in the family. It's not really feasible, what with my mind reading and Alice seeing the future and all that."

She smiled weakly. "And Jasper making you feel all warm and fuzzy about spilling your guts, don't forget that."

"You paid attention."

"I've been known to do that every now and then." She frowned as if concentrating, and then nodded. Almost as if she were accepting the invitation.

"So did Alice see me coming?"

Bella spoke in her matter-of-fact voice, as though our topic was quite mundane. *I* was surprised, though, because it sounded very much like she was agreeing to go to meet my family. As if Alice's vision meant there wasn't another choice.

Her total acceptance of Alice's word as law touched my rawest nerve. I hated the possibility that even now, I might be ruining Bella's life.

"Something like that," I admitted, and turned my face as if I were looking out the windows into the backyard. I didn't want her to see how upset I was. I could feel her eyes on me, and doubted I was fooling her.

Forcing myself to fix the mood I'd created, I looked back to her and smiled as naturally as I could. "Is that any good?" I asked, gesturing to her cereal. "Honestly, it doesn't look very appetizing."

"Well, it's no irritable grizzly...." She trailed off when she processed my reaction, then focused on her food, eating quickly now.

She was thinking hard about something, too, staring into a middle distance as she chewed, but I doubted our thoughts were in sync at this moment.

I gazed out the windows again, letting her eat in peace. I looked at the small yard, remembering the sunny day I'd watched her there. Remembering the darkness of the clouds overtaking her. It was too easy to slip back into that despair, to second-guess all my good intentions and see them as nothing but selfishness.

I turned back to her in turmoil, only to find her watching me with fearless eyes. She trusted me, as she always had. I took a deep breath.

I would live up to her trust. I knew I could. When she looked at me that way, there was nothing I couldn't do.

Well, so Alice would be proven right in this one minor, simple prophecy. That was no surprise. I wondered how much of Bella's acceptance was just to please me? Probably the larger portion. There was something closely related that I very much wanted, but I worried that Bella would again agree just for my sake. Well, I could at least share my opinion, and see how she reacted.

"And you should introduce me to your father, too, I think," I said casually.

She was taken aback. "He already knows you."

"As your boyfriend, I mean."

Her eyes narrowed. "Why?"

"Isn't that customary?" I sounded at ease, but her resistance rattled me.

"I don't know," she admitted. Her voice was quieter—less sure—when she continued. "That's not necessary, you know. I don't expect you to... I mean, you don't have to pretend for me."

Did she think this was an unwelcome chore I was undertaking for her sake alone? "I'm not pretending," I promised.

She looked down at her breakfast, stirring the remnants of her cereal listlessly.

Perhaps it was better to just get to the *no*.

"Are you going to tell Charlie I'm your boyfriend or not?"

Still looking down, she asked softly, "Is that what you are?"

This was not the rejection I had feared. Clearly, I was misunderstanding something. Was it because I wasn't human that she didn't think Charlie should know about me? Or was it something else?

"It's a loose interpretation of the word *boy*, I'll admit."

"I was under the impression that you were something more, actually," she whispered, face still lowered as if she were talking to the table.

Her expression reminded me again of that charged conversation at lunch, how she'd thought our feelings were unequal, that mine were lesser. I couldn't understand how asking to meet her father had led her to this train of thought. Unless... was it the impermanence of the word *boyfriend*? It was a very human, *fleeting* sort of concept. Truly, the word didn't encompass even the smallest fraction of what I wanted to be to her, but it was the word Charlie would understand.

"Well, I don't know if we need to give him all the gory details," I answered softly. I reached out with one finger to raise her face so that I could see her eyes. "But he will need some explanation for why I'm around here so much. I don't want Chief Swan getting a restraining order put on me."

"Will you be?" she asked anxiously, ignoring my mild joke. "Will you really be here?"

"As long as you want me." Until she asked me to leave, I was hers.

She almost glared at me, so intense was her gaze. "I'll always want you. Forever."

I heard Alice's certainty again: *When have you ever said no to Bella?*

I heard Rosalie's questions: *What will you do when she asks you to change her? And when she begs?*

Rosalie was right about one thing, though. When Bella said the word *forever*, it didn't mean the same thing to her as it meant to me. For her, it meant merely a very long time. It meant she couldn't see the end yet. How could anyone who had lived only seventeen years comprehend what fifty years meant, let alone eternity? She was human, not a frozen immortal. Within just a few years, she would reinvent herself many times over. Her priorities would shift as her world grew wider. The things she wanted now wouldn't be the things she wanted then.

I walked slowly to her side, knowing my time was running out. I traced her face with my fingertips.

She stared back at me, trying to understand. "Does that make you sad?" she asked.

I didn't know how to answer her. I just watched her face, feeling as if I could see it changing infinitesimally with each passing beat of her heart.

She never looked away. I wondered what she saw in my face. If she thought at all about how it would never change.

The feeling of sand slipping through the neck of an hourglass only intensified. I sighed. There wasn't time to waste.

I glanced at her nearly empty bowl. "Are you finished?"

She stood up. "Yes."

"Get dressed—I'll wait here."

Without a word, she complied.

I needed that minute alone. I wasn't sure why I was lost in so many ominous thoughts. I needed to get myself in hand. I had to grasp every second of happiness I was allowed, all the more because those seconds were numbered. I knew I had a great capacity for ruining even the best moments with my wretched doubts and endless overthinking. What a waste, if I were only to have a few years, to spend any of them wallowing.

Through the ceiling, I listened to the sound of Bella wrestling with her wardrobe. There was not as much commotion as two nights ago, when she was preparing for our trip to the meadow, but it was close. I hoped she wasn't too stressed about how she would appear to my family. Alice and Esme already loved her unconditionally. The others wouldn't notice her clothes—they would only see a human girl brave enough to visit a house full of vampires. Even Jasper would have to be impressed by that.

I'd pulled myself together by the time she ran back down the stairs. Just focus on the day ahead. Focus on the next twelve hours at Bella's side. Surely that was enough to keep me smiling.

"Okay, I'm decent," she called as she took the stairs two at a time. I caught her as she nearly collided with me. She looked up with a wide grin, and all my lingering doubts crumbled away.

As I'd known she would be, she was wearing the blue blouse she'd worn in Port Angeles. My favorite, I supposed. She looked so pretty. And I liked the way she'd pulled her hair back. There was no way for her to hide behind it now.

Impulsively, I wrapped my arms around her and held her close. I breathed in her fragrance, and smiled.

"Wrong again," I teased. "You are utterly *in*decent. No one should look so tempting, it's not fair."

She pushed against my hold and I loosened my arms. She leaned back just far enough to read my face.

"Tempting how?" she asked, cautious. "I can change. . . ."

Last night, she'd asked me if I was attracted to her as a woman. Though I felt it was so obvious as to be ridiculous, maybe, somehow, she still didn't understand.

"You are so absurd." I laughed, and then kissed her forehead, letting the feel of her skin against my lips wash like a wave of electricity down the length of my body. "Shall I explain how you are tempting me?"

Slowly, my fingers followed the length of her spine, discovering the curve at the small of her back, then resting atop the slope of her hip. Though I'd meant to tease her, I was soon lost in the moment as well. My lips brushed against her temple, and I heard my breath speeding to match her heart. Her fingers trembled against my chest.

I only had to incline my head, and then her lips, so soft and warm, were just a hair's breadth away from my own. Carefully, wary of the power of the alchemy, I touched my lips to hers.

While my whole body again overflowed with light and electricity, I waited for her reaction, ready to disengage if things got out of hand. She was more careful this time, holding herself nearly motionless. Even her trembling had stilled.

Moving with what caution I could muster in the face of what I was feeling, I pressed my lips more firmly against hers, savoring their soft yield. I was not as much in control of myself as I should have been. I let my lips fall open, wanting to feel her breath in my mouth.

Just at that moment, her legs seemed to give out, and she slid through my arms toward the floor.

I caught her at once, holding her upright. I held up her head with my left hand; it rocked, loose on her neck. Her eyes were closed and her lips white.

"Bella?" I shouted, panicking.

She gasped in a loud breath and her eyelids fluttered. I realized that I hadn't heard the sound of her breathing in a while—longer than was right.

Another ragged breath and her feet struggled to find the floor.

"You...," she sighed with her eyes still half-closed, "made... me... faint."

She had actually *stopped breathing* to kiss me. Probably in a misguided attempt to make things less difficult for me.

"What am I going to do with you?" I half growled. "Yesterday I kiss you, and you attack me! Today you pass out on me!"

She giggled, choking on her own laughter as her lungs tried to pull in the necessary oxygen. I was still supporting most of her weight.

"So much for being good at everything," I muttered.

"That's the problem. You're too good." She took a deep breath. "Far, far too good."

"Do you feel sick?" At least her lips had not gone green. A delicate shade of pink was creeping into them as I watched.

"No," she answered, her voice stronger. "That wasn't the same kind of fainting at all. I don't know what happened.... I think I forgot to breathe."

I'd noticed.

"I can't take you anywhere like this," I grumbled.

She took another breath, and then straightened in my arms. She blinked fast five times, and lifted her chin into its most stubborn position.

"I'm fine." Her voice was stronger, I had to concede. And the color had already come back into her face. "Your family is going to think I'm insane anyway, what's the difference?"

I examined her carefully. Her breathing had evened out. Her heart sounded stronger than it had a moment ago. She seemed to be supporting her own weight without difficulty. The roses in her cheeks were getting brighter with every passing second, set off by the vivid blue of her blouse.

"I'm very partial to that color with your skin," I told her. That made her blush even more intensely.

"Look," she said, interrupting my scrutiny. "I'm trying really hard not to think about what I'm about to do, so can we go already?"

Her voice was back to normal strength as well.

"And you're worried, not because you're headed to meet a houseful of vampires, but because you think those vampires won't approve of you, correct?"

She grinned. "That's right."

I shook my head. "You're incredible."

Her smile widened. She took my hand and pulled me to the door.

I decided it was better to pretend that the driving arrangements were already settled than to ask her about them. I let her lead the way to her truck, and then deftly opened the passenger door for her. She didn't object in any way; she didn't even glare at me. I felt this was a promising sign.

While I drove, she sat up alertly and stared out her window, watching the houses race past us. I could see that she was nervous, but I also guessed that she was curious. Once it was clear we were not going to stop at any given house, she lost all interest in it and looked to the next. I wondered how she pictured my home.

As we left the town behind us, she seemed to get more apprehensive. She glanced at me a few times, as if she wanted to ask a question, but when she caught me looking at her, she turned back to the window quickly, her ponytail whipping out behind her. Her toes started tapping against the floor of the truck cab, though I hadn't put the radio on.

When I turned onto the drive, she sat up straighter, and then her knee was bouncing in time with her toes. Her fingers pressed so tightly against the window frame that their tips turned white.

As the drive wound on and on, she started to frown. And truly, it did look like we were headed somewhere just as remote and uninhabited as the meadow. The stress mark appeared between her brows.

I reached out and brushed her shoulder, and she gave me a strained smile before turning to the window again.

Finally, the drive broke through the last fringe of the forest and onto the lawn. Still in the shade of the big cedars, it didn't feel like an abrupt change.

It was odd to look at the familiar house and try to imagine how it would appear to new eyes. Esme had excellent taste, so I knew the house was objectively beautiful. But would Bella see a structure that was trapped in time, that belonged to another era, yet was clearly new and strong? As if we'd traveled backward in time to find it, rather than it aging forward to us?

"Wow," she breathed.

I cut the engine and the following silence strengthened the impression that we could be in another part of history.

"You like it?" I asked.

She glanced at me from the corner of her eye, then looked back to the house. "It…has a certain charm."

I laughed and tweaked her ponytail, then slid out of the car. Less than a second passed, and I was holding her door open for her.

"Ready?"

"Not even a little bit." She laughed, breathless. "Let's go."

She ran a hand over her hair, searching for tangles.

"You look lovely," I assured her, and took her hand.

Her palm was moist, and not as warm as usual. I rubbed the back of her hand with my thumb, trying to communicate without words that she was perfectly safe, and everything would be fine.

She started to slow as we walked up the porch steps, and her hand was trembling.

Hesitating would only prolong her unease. I opened the door, already knowing exactly what was on the other side.

My parents were just where their thoughts had placed them in my mind's eye, and just as Alice had envisioned them. They stood back half a dozen paces from the door, giving Bella some breathing space. Esme was as nervous as Bella seemed to be, though for her, that meant perfect stillness rather than Bella's agitation. Carlisle's hand rested on the small of her back in a comforting fashion. He was used to interacting with humans casually, but Esme was shy. It was rare that she ventured out alone to mix with the mortal world. A true homebody, she was quite happy to let the rest of us bring the world back to her as needed.

Bella's eyes darted around the room, taking it in. She was slightly behind me, as if using my body as a shield. I couldn't help but feel relaxed inside my home, though I knew it was the opposite for her. I squeezed her hand.

Carlisle smiled warmly at Bella, and Esme quickly followed suit.

"Carlisle, Esme, this is Bella." I wondered whether Bella heard the note of pride in my voice as I introduced her.

Carlisle moved forward with deliberate slowness. He held out his hand, a little tentative.

"You're very welcome, Bella."

Perhaps because she already knew Carlisle, Bella seemed suddenly more comfortable. Looking confident, she stepped forward to meet his advance—while not untangling her fingers from mine—and shook his offered hand without even a wince at the chill. Of course, she was surely used to that by now.

"It's nice to see you again, Dr. Cullen," she said, sounding like she really meant it.

Such a brave girl, Esme thought. *Oh, she's darling.*

"Please, call me Carlisle."

Bella beamed. "Carlisle," she repeated.

Esme joined Carlisle then, moving in the same slow, careful way. She placed one hand on Carlisle's arm, and extended the other. Bella took it without hesitation, smiling at my mother.

"It's *very* nice to know you," Esme said, affection radiating from her smile.

"Thank you," Bella said. "I'm glad to meet you, too."

Though the words were conventional enough on both sides, they both spoke with such earnestness that the exchange carried a deeper significance.

I adore her, Edward! Thank you for bringing her to see me!

I could only smile at Esme's enthusiasm.

"Where are Alice and Jasper?" I asked, but it was more of a prompt. I could hear them waiting at the top of the stairs, Alice timing her perfect entrance.

My question seemed to be what she was waiting for. "Hey, Edward!" she called as she darted into view. Then she ran—really ran, not in a human way—down the steps and hurtled to a stop just inches from Bella. Carlisle, Esme, and I all froze in surprise, but Bella didn't so much as flinch, even when Alice sprang forward to kiss her cheek.

I shot her a warning look, but Alice wasn't paying any attention to me. She was living halfway between this moment and a thousand future moments, exulting in finally getting to begin her friendship. Her feelings were very sweet, but I couldn't enjoy them. More than half of her yet-to-be memories featured the white, lifeless Bella, so flawless and so cold.

Alice was oblivious to my reaction, focused on Bella.

"You do smell nice," she commented. "I never noticed before."

Bella blushed and all three of them looked away.

I tried to think of a way to ease the awkwardness, but then, like magic, there was no awkwardness. I was perfectly comfortable, and I could feel Bella's tension melt out of her body.

Jasper followed Alice down the stairs, not racing but not moving cautiously like Carlisle and Esme, either. There was no need for him to put on a show. Everything he did seemed natural and right.

In truth, he was laying it on a little thick.

I gave him a sardonic look, and he grinned at me, then stopped by the newel post, leaving what might have felt like an odd distance between himself and the rest of us, but of course it couldn't feel odd if he didn't want it to.

"Hello, Bella."

"Hello, Jasper." She smiled easily, then looked at Esme and Carlisle. "It's nice to meet you all—you have a very beautiful home."

"Thank you," Esme answered. "We're so glad that you came."

She's perfect.

Bella glanced at the stairs again, expectant. But I knew there would not be any more introductions this morning.

Esme understood the look as well.

I'm sorry. She wasn't ready. Emmett's trying to calm her down.

Should I make excuses for Rosalie? Before I could decide what to say, Carlisle caught my attention.

Edward.

I looked at him automatically. His intensity contrasted with the easy mood Jasper had created.

Alice saw some visitors. Strangers. At the rate they're moving, they'll find us tomorrow night. I thought you should know immediately.

I nodded once, my lips pressing into a thin line. What miserable timing. Well, I supposed the silver lining was that I was now free to explain to Bella why I was kidnapping her. She would understand. Charlie wouldn't. I'd have to figure out the safest, least disruptive plan. Or rather, *we* would. She would certainly have opinions.

I looked to Alice for a visual clarification, but she was thinking about the weather.

"Do you play?" Esme asked, and I glanced over to see that Bella was eyeing my piano.

Bella shook her head. "Not at all. But it's so beautiful. Is it yours?"

Esme laughed. "No. Edward didn't tell you he was musical?"

Bella gave me the strangest look, as if this news was irritating. I wondered why. Did she have a yet undiscovered prejudice against pianists?

"No," she answered Esme. "I should have known, I guess."

What does she mean, Edward? Esme wondered, as if I would know the answer. Luckily, her expression was confused enough to compel Bella to explain.

"Edward can do everything," Bella clarified. "Right?"

Carlisle repressed his amusement, but Jasper laughed out loud. Alice was watching the conversation that would happen twenty seconds from now; this was old news to her.

Esme gave me her best disapproving-mother look. "I hope you haven't been showing off—it's rude."

"Just a bit," I admitted, laughing, too.

He looks so happy, Esme thought. *I've never seen him this way. Thank goodness he found her at last.*

"He's been too modest, actually," Bella disagreed. Her eyes flickered to the piano again.

"Well, play for her," Esme encouraged.

I shot my mother a betrayed look. "You just said showing off was rude."

Esme was holding back a laugh of her own. "There are exceptions to every rule."

If she's not totally hooked yet, that should do it.

I stared back, deadpan.

"I'd like to hear you play," Bella volunteered.

"It's settled then." Esme put her hand on my shoulder and nudged me toward the piano.

Fine, if that's what they wanted. I kept Bella's hand so she would have to join me. This was her idea, after all.

I'd never been self-conscious about my music before—there was never anybody but family or close friends around to hear me, and besides Esme, most of them barely seemed to notice I was playing. So this was a new feeling. Maybe if Esme hadn't mentioned showing off before, it wouldn't have felt so forced.

I sat on the bench off-center, pulling Bella down to sit beside me. She smiled at me eagerly. I stared back at her, frowning, hoping she recognized that I was only doing this because she'd asked.

I chose Esme's song—it was a joyful song, a triumphant song, suited to the day's mood.

As I began, I watched Bella's reaction from the corner of my eye. I didn't need to look at the keys, but I didn't want to make her feel scrutinized.

After just the first few measures, her mouth fell open.

Jasper laughed again; this time Alice joined him. Bella

stiffened, but didn't turn. Her eyes narrowed, her gaze never leaving my fingers, chasing them as they moved across the keys.

I heard Alice skip to the stairs at the same time that Carlisle thought, *Well, that's probably enough of us for now. We don't want to overwhelm her.*

Esme was disappointed, but she followed Alice upstairs. They would all pretend that this was just a normal day, that it was nothing momentous to have a human inside our house. One by one, they flitted away to the tasks they would have been pursuing if I hadn't brought the mortal home.

Bella was still entirely focused on the motion of my hands, but I thought she was not…as eager as before? Her brows were pressing down over her eyes. I didn't understand her expression.

I tried to cheer her, turning my head to catch her attention and winking once. That usually made her smile.

"Do you like it?" I asked.

Her head tilted to the side and then something seemed to occur to her. Her eyes grew huge again.

"*You* wrote this?" she said, her tone strangely accusatory.

I nodded and added, "It's Esme's favorite," like an apology, though I wasn't sure what I was trying to excuse.

Bella stared at me, strangely forlorn. Her eyes closed, and her head rocked slowly from side to side.

"What's wrong?" I implored.

She opened her eyes and finally smiled, but it wasn't a happy smile.

"I'm feeling extremely insignificant," she admitted.

I was stunned for a moment. I supposed Esme's earlier words about showing off were the crux of the matter. Her idea that my music would win over whichever corners of Bella's heart remained ambivalent was obviously misguided.

How to explain that all these things I could do, things that came with such ridiculous ease because of what I was, were entirely meaningless? They didn't make me special or superior. How to show her that everything I was had never been enough to make me worthy of her? That she was the lofty goal I'd been trying to reach for so long?

I could only think of one way. I created a simple bridge and shifted into a new song. She watched my expression now, expecting me to respond. I waited until I was through the main structure of the melody, hoping she would recognize it.

"You inspired this one," I murmured.

Could she feel how this music came from the very core of my being? And that my core, along with everything else I was, centered wholly on her?

For a few moments, I let the notes of the song fill in the spaces that my words never quite could. The melody expanded as I played, drifting away from its former minor key, reaching now for a happier resolution.

I thought I should allay her earlier fears. "They like you, you know. Esme especially." Bella had probably been able to see that herself.

She twisted to peek over her shoulder. "Where did they go?"

"Very subtly giving us some privacy, I suppose."

"*They* like me," she groaned. "But Rosalie and Emmett..."

I shook my head impatiently. "Don't worry about Rosalie. She'll come around."

She pursed her lips, unconvinced. "Emmett?"

"Well, he thinks *I'm* a lunatic, it's true." I laughed once. "But he doesn't have a problem with you. He's trying to reason with Rosalie."

The corners of her lips pulled down. "What is it that upsets her?"

I took a breath and exhaled slowly—stalling. I wanted to say only the most necessary parts, and say them in the least upsetting way.

"Rosalie struggles the most with...with what we are," I explained. "It's hard for her to have someone on the outside know the truth. And she's a little jealous."

"*Rosalie* is jealous of *me*?" She looked as though she wasn't sure whether I was joking.

I shrugged. "You're human. She wishes that she were, too."

"Oh!" That revelation stunned her for a moment. But then the frown returned. "Even Jasper, though..."

The sense that everything was perfectly natural and easy had faded as soon as Jasper had stopped concentrating on us. I imagined she was remembering his introduction without that influence, and seeing for the first time the strangeness of the wide space he had left between them.

"That's really my fault. I told you he was the most recent to try our way of life. I warned him to keep his distance."

I'd said the words lightly, but after a second, Bella shivered.

"Esme and Carlisle?" she asked quickly, as if eager for a new subject.

"Are happy to see me happy. Actually, Esme wouldn't care if you had a third eye and webbed feet. All this time she's been worried about me, afraid that there was something missing from my essential makeup, that I was too young when Carlisle changed me.... She's ecstatic. Every time I touch you, she just about chokes with satisfaction."

She pursed her lips. "Alice seems very...enthusiastic."

I tried to keep my composure, but I heard the edge of ice in my answer. "Alice has her own way of looking at things."

Her aspect had been tense for most of our exchange, but suddenly she was grinning. "And you're not going to explain that, are you?"

Of course she'd noticed all my strange reactions to any mention of Alice; I'd not been very subtle. At least she was smiling now, pleased to catch me out. I was sure she had no idea *why* I was irritated with Alice. Just letting me know that *she* knew that I was keeping something from her seemed to be enough for her now. I didn't respond, but I didn't think she was expecting me to.

"So what was Carlisle telling you before?" she asked.

I frowned. "You noticed that, did you?" Well, I knew I needed to tell her this.

"Of course."

I thought of that little shudder when I'd explained about Jasper....I hated to alarm her again, but she *should* be frightened.

"He wanted to tell me some news," I admitted. "He didn't know if it was something I would share with you."

She sat up straighter, alert. "Will you?"

"I have to, because I'm going to be a little...overbearingly protective over the next few days—or weeks—and I wouldn't want you to think I'm naturally a tyrant."

My trivializing did not put her at ease.

"What's wrong?" she demanded.

"Nothing's wrong, exactly. Alice just sees some visitors coming soon. They know we're here, and they're curious."

She repeated my word in a whisper. "Visitors?"

"Yes...well, they aren't like us, of course—in their hunting habits, I mean. They probably won't come into town at all, but I'm certainly not going to let you out of my sight till they're gone."

She shuddered so hard I could feel the motion in the bench beneath us.

"Finally, a rational response!" I muttered. I thought of all the horrifying things she'd accepted about me without a tremor. Only *other* vampires were scary, apparently. "I was beginning to think you had no sense of self-preservation at all."

She ignored that, and started to watch my hands moving over the keys again. After a few seconds, she took a deep breath and slowly exhaled. Had she processed another waking nightmare so easily?

It seemed so. She examined the room now, her head turning slowly as she scrutinized my home. I could imagine what she was thinking.

"Not what you expected, is it?" I guessed.

She was still cataloguing with her eyes. "No."

I wondered what had surprised her most: the light colors, the vast openness of the space, the wall of windows? It was all very carefully designed—by Esme—*not* to feel like some kind of fortress or asylum.

I could hazard what a normal human would have predicted. "No coffins, no piled skulls in the corners; I don't even think we have cobwebs... what a disappointment this must be for you."

She didn't react to my joke. "It's so light... so open."

"It's the one place we never have to hide."

While I'd been focused on her, the song I was playing had strayed back to its roots. I found myself in the middle of the bleakest moment—the moment when the obvious truth was unavoidable: Bella was perfect as she was. Any interference from my world was a tragedy.

It was too late to save the song. I let it end as it had before, with that heartbreak.

Sometimes it was so easy to believe that Bella and I were right together. In the moment, when impulsivity led, and everything came so naturally... I could believe. But whenever I looked at it logically, without allowing emotion to trump reason, it was clear that I could only hurt her.

"Thank you," she whispered.

Her eyes were swimming in tears. While I watched, she quickly wiped her fingers across her lower lids, rubbing the moisture away.

This was the second time I'd seen Bella cry. The first time, I'd hurt her. Not intentionally, but still, by implying we could never be together, I'd caused her pain.

Now she cried because the music I'd created for her had touched her. Tears caused by pleasure. I wondered how much of this unspoken language she had understood.

One tear still glistened in the corner of her left eye, shining in the brightness of the room. A tiny, clear piece of her, an ephemeral diamond. Acting on some strange instinct, I reached out to catch it with my fingertip. Round on my skin, it sparkled as my hand moved. I swiftly touched my finger to my tongue, tasting her tear, absorbing this minute particle of her.

Carlisle had spent many years attempting to understand our immortal anatomy; it was a difficult task, based mostly on assumption and observation. Vampire cadavers were not available for study.

His best interpretation of our life systems was that our internal workings must be microscopically porous. Though we could swallow anything, only blood was accepted by our bodies. That blood was absorbed into our muscles and provided fuel. When the fuel was depleted, our thirst intensified to encourage us to replenish our supply. Nothing besides blood seemed to move through us at all.

I swallowed Bella's tear. Perhaps it would never leave my body. After she left me, after all the lonely years had passed, maybe I would always have this piece of her inside me.

She stared at me curiously, but I had no sane way to explain. Instead, I returned to her earlier curiosity.

"Do you want to see the rest of the house?" I offered.

"No coffins?" she double-checked.

I laughed and stood, pulling her up from the piano bench. "No coffins."

I led her upstairs to the second floor; she'd seen most of the first, all but the unused kitchen and the dining room were visible from the front door. As we climbed, her interest was evident. She studied everything—the railing, the pale wood floors, the picture-frame paneling that lined the hallway at the top. It was like she was preparing for an exam. I named the owner of each room we passed, and she nodded after each designation, ready for the quiz.

I was about to round the corner and follow the next flight of stairs up, but Bella stopped suddenly. I looked to see what she was staring at so bemusedly. Ah.

"You can laugh," I said. "It *is* sort of ironic."

She didn't laugh. She stretched out her hand as if she wished to touch the thick oak cross that hung there, dark and somber against the lighter wood behind it, but her fingertips didn't make contact.

"It must be very old," Bella murmured.

I shrugged. "Early sixteen thirties, more or less."

She stared up at me, her head tilted to one side. "Why do you keep this here?"

"Nostalgia. It belonged to Carlisle's father."

"He collected antiques?" she suggested, sounding as if she already knew her guess was wrong.

"No," I answered. "He carved this himself. It hung on the wall above the pulpit in the vicarage where he preached."

Bella looked up at the cross, her stare intense. She didn't move for so long that I started to get anxious again.

"Are you all right?" I murmured.

"How old is Carlisle?" she shot back.

I sighed, trying to quell the old panic. Would this story be the one that would be too much? I scrutinized every minute muscle twitch in her face as I explained.

"He just celebrated his three hundred and sixty-second birthday." Or close enough. Carlisle had chosen a day for Esme's sake, but it was only his best guess. "Carlisle was born in London, in the sixteen forties, he believes. Time wasn't marked as accurately then, for the common people anyway. It was just before Cromwell's rule, though. He was the only son of an Anglican pastor. His mother died giving birth to him. His father was an intolerant man. As the Protestants came into power, he was enthusiastic in his persecution of Roman Catholics and other religions. He also believed very strongly in the reality of evil. He led hunts for witches, werewolves...and vampires."

She'd been keeping up a good charade for the most part, almost as if she were dissociating from the facts. But when I spoke the word *vampires*, her shoulders stiffened and she held her breath for an extra second.

"They burned a lot of innocent people. Of course the real creatures that he sought were not so easy to catch." This still haunted Carlisle—the innocents his father had murdered. And even more, those murders Carlisle had been unwillingly involved in. I was glad for his sake that the memories were blurred and always fading more.

I knew the stories of Carlisle's human years as well as I knew my own. As I described his ill-fated discovery of an ancient London coven, I wondered if this would sound real to her at all. This was irrelevant history, set in a country she'd never seen, separated from her own existence by so many years that she had no context for it.

She seemed spellbound, though, as I described the attack that had infected Carlisle and killed his associates, carefully leaving out the details I'd rather she didn't dwell on. When the vampire, driven by thirst, had wheeled around and fallen on his pursuers, he'd only slashed Carlisle twice with his venom-covered teeth: once across the palm of his outstretched hand, and once through his bicep. It had been a melee, the vampire struggling to quickly subdue four men before the rest of the mob got too close. After the fact, Carlisle had theorized that the vampire was hoping to drain them all, but he chose self-preservation over a more bounteous meal, grabbing the men he could carry and running. It was not self-preservation from the mob, of course; those fifty men with their crude weapons were no more dangerous to him than a kaleidoscope of butterflies. However, the Volturi were less than a thousand miles away. Their laws had been established for a millennium by this point, and their demand that every immortal exercise discretion for the benefit of all was universally accepted. The story of a vampire sighting in London, attested to by fifty witnesses with drained corpses as proof, would not have gone over well in Volterra.

The nature of Carlisle's wounds was unfortunate. The gash in his hand was far from any major vessels, the slash in his arm had missed both the brachial artery and the basilic vein. This meant a much slower spread of the venom, and a longer transition period. As the conversion from mortal to immortal was the most painful thing any of us had ever experienced, an extended version was not ideal, to say the least.

I'd known the pain of that same extended version. Carlisle had been...unsure when he decided to change me into his first companion. He'd spent a great deal of time with other, more experienced vampires—the Volturi included—and he knew that a better placed bite would result in a quicker conversion. However, he'd never found another vampire *like* himself. All the others were obsessed with blood and power. No one else craved a kinder, more familial life as he did. He wondered whether his slow conversion and the weak entry points of his infection had been somehow responsible for the difference. So when creating his first son, he chose to imitate his own wounds. He'd always felt bad about that, especially as he later found that the method of conversion actually had no bearing on the personality and desires of the new immortal.

He hadn't had time to experiment when he found Esme. She was much closer to death than I had been. To save her, it had been imperative to get as much venom into her system as close to her heart as possible. All in all, a much more frenzied effort than it had been with me—and yet Esme was the gentlest of us all.

And Carlisle the strongest. I now told Bella what I could about his extraordinarily disciplined conversion. I found myself editing things that perhaps I shouldn't have, but I didn't want to dwell on Carlisle's excruciating pain. Maybe, given her obvious curiosity about the process, it would have been a good thing to describe; perhaps it would have deterred her from wanting to know more.

"It was over then," I explained, "and he realized what he had become."

All the while, lost in my own thoughts as I told the familiar tale, I'd been observing her reactions. For the most part, she kept the same expression fixed on her face; I think she meant it to look like attentive interest, totally devoid of any unnecessary emotional recoils. However, she held herself too stiffly for her ploy to be believable. Her curiosity was real, but I wanted to know what she really thought, not what she wanted me to think she thought.

"How are you feeling?" I asked.

"I'm fine," she answered automatically. But her mask slipped a little bit. Still, all I could read on her face was a desire to know more. So this story hadn't been enough to frighten her away.

"I expect you have a few more questions for me."

She grinned, totally self-possessed, seemingly fearless. "A few."

I smiled back. "Come on, then, I'll show you."

20. CARLISLE

We walked back along the hall to Carlisle's office. I paused at the door, waiting for his invitation.

"Come in," Carlisle said.

I led her inside and watched her animatedly examine this new room. It was darker than the rest of the house; the deep mahogany wood reminded him of his earliest home. Her eyes ran across the rows and rows of books. I knew her well enough to see that the sight of so many books in one room was something of a dream to her.

Carlisle marked the page in the one he was reading and then stood to welcome us.

"What can I do for you?" he asked.

Of course, he'd heard all our conversation in the hall, and he knew we were here for the next installment. He wasn't bothered by my sharing his story; he didn't seem surprised that I would tell her everything.

"I wanted to show Bella some of our history. Well, your history, actually."

"We didn't mean to disturb you," Bella said quietly.

"Not at all," Carlisle assured her. "Where are you going to start?"

"The Waggoner," I said.

I put one hand on her shoulder and turned her gently to face the wall behind us. I heard her heartbeat react to my touch, and then Carlisle's almost silent laugh at her reaction.

Interesting, he thought.

I watched Bella's eyes widen as she took in the gallery wall of Carlisle's office. I could imagine the way it might disorient a person seeing it for the first time. There were seventy-three works, in all sizes, mediums, and colors, crammed together like a wall-sized puzzle with only rectangular pieces. Her gaze couldn't find anywhere to settle.

I took her hand and led her to the beginning. Carlisle followed. As on the page of a book, the story began at the far left. It was not a showy piece, monochromatic and maplike. In fact, it *was* part of a map, hand-painted by an amateur cartographer, one of the very few originals that had survived the centuries.

Her brows furrowed.

"London in the sixteen fifties," I explained.

"The London of my youth," Carlisle added from a few feet behind us. Bella flinched, surprised by his closeness. Of course she wouldn't have heard his movements. I squeezed her hand, trying to reassure her. This house was a strange place for her to be, but nothing here would hurt her.

"Will *you* tell the story?" I asked him, and Bella turned to see what he would say.

I'm sorry, I wish I could.

He smiled at Bella and spoke aloud to her. "I would, but I'm actually running a bit late. The hospital called this morning—Dr. Snow is taking a sick day. Besides"—he looked to me—"you know the stories as well as I do."

Carlisle smiled warmly at Bella as he exited. Once he had gone, she turned back to examine the small painting again.

"What happened then?" she asked after a moment. "When he realized what had happened to him?"

Automatically, I looked to a larger painting, one column over and one row down. It wasn't a cheerful image: a gloomy, deserted landscape, a sky thick with oppressive clouds, colors that seemed to suggest the sun would never return. Carlisle had seen this piece through the window of a minor castle in Scotland. It so perfectly reminded him of his life at its darkest point that he'd wanted to keep it, though the old memory was painful. To him, the existence of this devastated landscape meant that someone else had once understood.

"When he knew what he had become, he rebelled against it. He tried to destroy himself. But that's not easily done."

"How?" she gasped.

I kept my eyes on the evocative emptiness of the painting as I described Carlisle's suicide attempts.

"He jumped from great heights. He tried to drown himself in the ocean...but he was young to the new life, and very strong. It is amazing that he was able to resist...feeding"—I glanced quickly at her but she was staring at the painting—"while he was still so new. The instinct is more powerful then, it takes over everything. But he was so repelled by himself that he had the strength to try to kill himself with starvation."

"Is that possible?" she whispered.

"No, there are very few ways we can be killed."

She opened her mouth to ask the most obvious follow-up, but I spoke quickly to distract her.

"So he grew very hungry, and eventually weak. He strayed as far as he could from the human populace, recognizing that his willpower was weakening, too. For months he wandered by night, seeking the loneliest places, loathing himself...."

I described the night he found another way to live, the compromise of animal blood, and his recovery to a rational creature. Then leaving for the continent—

"He *swam* to France?" she interrupted, disbelieving.

"People swim the Channel all the time, Bella," I pointed out.

"That's true, I guess. It just sounded funny in that context. Go on."

"Swimming is easy for us—"

"Everything is easy for *you*," she complained.

I smiled at her, waiting to be sure she was done.

She frowned. "I won't interrupt again, I promise."

My smile widened, knowing what her reaction would be to the next bit.

"Because, technically, we don't need to breathe."

"You—"

I laughed and put one finger against her lips. "No, no, you promised. Do you want to hear the story or not?"

Her lips moved against my touch. "You can't spring something like that on me, and then expect me not to say anything."

I let my hand fall to rest against the side of her neck.

"You don't have to *breathe*?"

I shrugged. "No, it's not necessary. Just a habit."

"How long can you go . . . without *breathing*?"

"Indefinitely, I suppose; I don't know." The longest I'd ever gone was a few days, all of it underwater. "It gets a bit uncomfortable—being without a sense of smell."

"A bit uncomfortable," she repeated in a fragile voice, barely over a whisper.

Her eyebrows were drawn together, her eyes narrowed, her shoulders rigid. The exchange, which had been funny to me a moment before, was abruptly humorless.

We were so different. Though we'd once belonged to the same species, we shared only a few superficial traits now. She must finally feel the weight of the distortion, the distance between us. I lifted my hand from her skin and dropped it to my side. My alien touch would only make that gap more obvious.

I stared at her troubled expression, waiting to see if this would be one truth too many. After a few long seconds, the stress in her features eased. Her eyes focused on my face, and a different kind of unease marked hers.

She reached up with no hesitation to press her fingers against my cheek. "What is it?"

Concern for me again. So apparently this wasn't the *too much* I'd been fearing.

"I keep waiting for it to happen."

She was confused. "For what to happen?"

I took a deep breath. "I know that at some point, something I tell you or something you see is going to be too much. And then you'll run away from me, screaming as you go." I tried to smile at her, but I didn't do a very good job. "I won't stop you. I want this to happen, because I want you to be safe. And yet, I want to be with you. The two desires are impossible to reconcile...."

She squared her shoulders, her chin jutted out. "I'm not running anywhere," she promised.

I had to smile at her brave façade. "We'll see."

"So, go on," she insisted, scowling a little at my doubtful response. "Carlisle was swimming to France."

I measured her mood for one more second, then turned back to the gallery. This time I pointed her toward the most ostentatious of all the paintings, the brightest, the most garish. It was meant to be a portrayal of the final judgment, but half the thrashing figures seemed to be involved in some kind of orgy, the other half in a violent, bloody combat. Only the judges, suspended above the pandemonium on marble balustrades, were serene.

This one had been a gift. It wasn't something Carlisle would have ever picked out for himself. But when the Volturi had pressed upon him the souvenir of their time together, it wasn't as if he could have said no.

He had some affection for the gaudy piece—and for the distant vampire overlords depicted in it—so he kept it with his other favorites. They had been very kind to him in many ways, after all. And Esme liked the small portrait of Carlisle hidden in the midst of the mayhem.

While I explained Carlisle's first few years in Europe, Bella stared at the painting, trying to make sense of all the figures and swirling colors. I found my voice becoming less casual. It was hard to think of Carlisle's quest to subdue his nature, to become a blessing to mankind rather than a parasite, without feeling again all the awe his journey deserved.

I'd always envied Carlisle's perfect control but, at the same time, believed it was impossible for me to duplicate. I realized now that I'd chosen the lazy way, the path of least resistance, admiring him greatly, but never putting in the effort to become more *like* him. This crash course in restraint that Bella was teaching me might have been less fraught if I'd worked harder to improve in the last seven decades.

Bella was staring at me now. I tapped the relevant scene in front of us to refocus her attention on the story.

"He was studying in Italy when he discovered the others there. They were much more civilized and educated than the wraiths of the London sewers."

She concentrated on the tableau I indicated, and then laughed suddenly, a little shocked. She'd recognized Carlisle despite the robe-like costume he was painted in.

"Solimena was greatly inspired by Carlisle's friends. He often painted them as gods. Aro, Marcus, Caius." I gestured to each as I said their names. "Nighttime patrons of the arts."

Her finger hesitated just above the canvas. "What happened to them?"

"They're still there. As they have been for who knows how many millennia. Carlisle stayed with them only for a short time, just a few decades. He greatly admired their civility, their refinement, but they persisted in trying to cure his aversion to 'his natural food source,' as they called it. They tried to persuade him, and he tried to persuade them, to no avail. At that point, Carlisle decided to try the New World. He dreamed of finding others like himself. He was very lonely, you see."

I touched only lightly on the following decades, as Carlisle struggled with his isolation and finally began to consider a course of action. The story turned more personal, and also more repetitive. She'd heard some of this before: Carlisle finding me on my deathbed and making the decision that had changed my destiny. And now, that decision was affecting Bella's destiny, too.

"And so we've come full circle," I concluded.

"Have you always stayed with Carlisle, then?" she asked.

With unerring instinct, she'd found the one question I least wanted to answer.

"Almost always," I answered.

I placed my hand on her waist to guide her out of Carlisle's office, wishing I could also guide her away from this train of thought. But I knew she was not going to let that stand. Sure enough...

"Almost?"

I sighed, unwilling. But honesty must take precedence over shame. "Well," I confessed, "I had a typical bout of rebellious adolescence—about ten years after I was born, created, whatever you want to call it. I wasn't sold on his life of abstinence, and I resented him for curbing my appetite. So I went off on my own for a time."

"Really?" Her intonation was not what I expected. Rather than being disgusted, she sounded eager to hear more. This didn't match her reaction in the meadow, when she'd seemed so surprised that I was guilty of murder, as though that truth had never occurred to her. Perhaps she'd grown used to the idea.

We started up the stairs. Now she seemed indifferent to her surroundings; she only watched me.

"That doesn't repulse you?" I asked.

She considered that for half a second. "No."

I found her answer upsetting. "Why not?" I nearly demanded.

"I guess... it sounds reasonable?" Her explanation ended on a higher pitch, like a question.

Reasonable. I laughed, the sound too harsh.

But instead of telling her all the ways it was neither reasonable nor forgivable, I found myself giving a defense.

"From the time of my new birth, I had the advantage of knowing what everyone around me was thinking, both human and nonhuman alike. That's why it took me ten years to defy

Carlisle. I could read his perfect sincerity, understand exactly why he lived the way he did."

I wondered if I would ever have gone astray if I had not met Siobhan and others like her. If I hadn't been aware that every other creature like myself—we'd not yet stumbled across Tanya and her sisters—thought the way Carlisle lived was ludicrous. If I had only known Carlisle, and never discovered another code of conduct, I think I would have stayed. It made me ashamed that I'd let myself be influenced by others who were never Carlisle's equals. But I'd envied their freedom. And I'd thought I would be able to live above the moral abyss they all sank to. Because I was *special*. I shook my head at the arrogance.

"It took me only a few years to return to Carlisle and recommit to his vision. I thought I would be exempt from the depression that accompanies a conscience. Because I knew the thoughts of my prey, I could pass over the innocent and pursue only the evil. If I followed a murderer down a dark alley where he stalked a young girl—if I saved her, then surely I wasn't so terrible."

There were a great many humans I'd saved this way, and yet, it never seemed to balance out the tally. So many faces flashed through my memories, the guilty I'd executed and the innocents I'd saved.

One face lingered, both guilty and innocent.

September 1930. It had been a very bad year. Everywhere, the humans struggled to survive bank failures, droughts, and dust storms. Displaced farmers and their families flooded cities that had no room for them. At the time, I wondered whether the pervasive despair and dread in the minds around me were a contributing factor to the melancholy that was beginning to plague me, but I think even then I knew that my personal depression was wholly due to my own choices.

I was passing through Milwaukee, as I'd passed through Chicago, Philadelphia, Detroit, Columbus, Indianapolis, Minneapolis, Montreal, Toronto, city after city, and then returned, over and over again, truly nomadic for the first time in my life. I never strayed farther south—I knew better than to hunt near that hotbed of newborn nightmare armies—nor farther east, as I was also avoiding Carlisle, less for self-preservation and more out of shame in that case. I never stayed more than a few days in any one place, never interacted with the humans I wasn't hunting. After more than four years, it had become a simple thing to locate the minds I sought. I knew where I was likely to find them, and when they were usually active. It was disturbing how easy it was to pinpoint my ideal victims; there were so many of them.

Perhaps that was part of the melancholy, too.

The minds I hunted were usually hardened to all human pity—and most other emotions besides greed and desire. There was a coldness and a focus that stood out from the normal, less dangerous minds around them. Of course, it had taken most of them some time to reach this point, where they saw themselves as predators first, and anything else second. So there was always a line of victims I had been too late to save. I could only save the next one.

Scanning for such minds, I was able to tune out everything more human for the most part. But that evening in Milwaukee, as I moved quietly through the darkness—strolling when there were witnesses, running when there were not—a different kind of mind caught my attention.

He was a young man, poor, living in the slums on the outskirts of the industrial district. He was in a state of mental anguish that intruded upon my awareness, though anguish was not an uncommon emotion in those days. But unlike the others who feared hunger, eviction, cold, sickness—want in so many forms—this man feared himself.

I can't. I can't. I can't do this. I can't. I can't. It was like a mantra in his head, repeating endlessly. It never resolved into anything stronger, never became *I won't*. He thought the negatives, but meanwhile he was planning.

The man hadn't done anything...yet. He had only dreamed of

what he wanted. He had only watched the girl in the tenement up the alley, never spoken to her.

I was a bit flummoxed. I had never condemned anyone to death whose hands were clean. But it seemed likely this man would not have clean hands for long. And the girl in his mind was just a young child.

Unsure, I decided to wait. Perhaps he would overcome the temptation.

I doubted it. My recent study of the basest of human natures had left little room for optimism.

Down the alley where he lived, where the buildings leaned precariously together, there was a narrow house with a recently collapsed roof. No one could get to the second floor safely, so that was where I hid, motionless, while I listened through the next several days. Examining the thoughts of the people crowded into the sagging buildings, it didn't take me long to find the child's thin face in a different, healthier set of thoughts. I found the room where she lived with her mother and two older brothers and watched her through the day. This was easy; she was only five or six and so didn't wander far. Her mother called her back when she rambled out of sight; Betty was her name.

The man watched, too, when he wasn't scouring the streets for day labor. But he kept his distance from her in the daytime. It was at night that he paused outside the window, hiding in the shadows while a single candle burned in her family's room. He marked at what time the candle was blown out. He noted the location of the child's bed—just a newspaper-stuffed cushion under the open window. It was getting cool at night, but the smells in the over-crowded house were unpleasant. Everyone kept their windows open.

I can't do this. I can't. I can't. His mantra continued, but he began to prepare. A piece of rope he found in a gutter. Some rags he plucked off a clothesline during his nighttime surveil-lance that would work as a gag. Ironically, he chose the same dilapidated house where I hid to store his collection. There was a cave-like space under the collapsed stairs. This was where he would bring the child.

Still I waited, unwilling to punish before I was positive of the crime.

The hardest part, the part he struggled with, was that he knew he would have to kill her afterward. This was distasteful, and he didn't like to consider the *how* of it. But this qualm, too, was overcome. It took another week.

By this time, I was quite thirsty, and bored with the repetition in his mind. However, I knew I could not justify my own murders unless I was acting within the rules I'd created for myself. Punish only the guilty, only those who would grievously harm others if they were spared.

I was oddly disappointed the night he came for his ropes and gags. Against reason, I'd hoped he would stay guiltless.

I followed him to the open window where the child slept. He didn't hear me behind him, would not have seen me in the shadows if he had turned. The chanting in his head was over. He *could*, he had realized. He could do this.

I waited until he reached through the window, until his fingers brushed her arm, looking for a good hold....

I grabbed him by the neck and leaped to the roof three stories up, where we landed with a low thud.

Of course he was terrified by the ice-cold fingers wrapped around his throat, bewildered by the sudden flight through the air, confused as to what was happening. But when I spun him to face me, somehow he understood. He didn't see a man when he looked at me. He saw my empty black eyes, my death-pale skin, and he saw *judgment*. Though he didn't come close to guessing what I actually was, he was absolutely correct about what was happening.

He realized that I had saved the child from him, and he was relieved. Not hardened like the others, not cold and sure.

I didn't, he thought as I lunged. The words were not a defense. He was glad he had been stopped.

He had been my only technically innocent victim, the one who had not lived to become the monster. Ending his progression toward evil had been the right thing, the only thing to do.

As I considered them all, every one of those I'd executed, I didn't regret any of their deaths individually. The world was a better place for each one of their absences. But somehow this didn't matter.

And in the end, blood was just blood. It quenched my thirst for a few days or weeks, and that was all. Though there was physical pleasure, it was too marred by the pain of my mind. Stubborn as I was, I could not avoid the truth. I was happier without human blood.

The total sum of death became too much for me. It was only a few months later that I gave up on my selfish crusade, gave up trying to find something meaningful in the slaughter.

"But as time went on," I continued, wondering how much she'd intuited that I hadn't said, "I began to see the monster in my eyes. I couldn't escape the debt of so much human life taken, no matter how justified. And I went back to Carlisle and Esme. They welcomed me back like the prodigal. It was more than I deserved." I remembered their arms around me, remembered the joy in their minds when I returned.

The way she looked at me now was also more than I deserved. I supposed my defense had worked, no matter how weak it sounded to me. But Bella must have been used to making excuses for me by now. I couldn't imagine how else she could bear to be around me.

We'd reached the last door along the hallway.

"My room," I informed her as I held it open.

I expected her reaction. The close scrutiny returned. She analyzed the view of the river, the abundance of shelving for my music, the stereo, the lack of traditional furniture, her eyes skipping from one detail to the next. I wondered if it was as interesting to her as her room had been to me.

Her eyes lingered on the wall treatments.

"Good acoustics?"

I laughed and nodded, then turned on the sound system. Even as low as the volume was, the speakers hidden in the walls and ceiling made it sound like we were in a concert hall with the performers. She smiled, then wandered over to the closest shelf of CDs.

It felt surreal to see her in the center of a space that was almost always an isolated retreat. We'd spent most of our time together in the human world—school, town, her home—and it had always made me feel the interloper, the one who didn't belong. Less than a week ago, I couldn't have believed she would ever be so relaxed and comfortable in the middle of my world. She was no interloper; she belonged perfectly. It was as if the room had never been complete till now.

And she was here under no pretext. I'd told no lies, revealed every one of my sins. She knew it all, and still wanted to be in this room, alone with me.

"How do you have these organized?" she wondered, trying to make sense of my collection.

My mind was so caught up in the pleasure of having her here, it took me a second to respond.

"Ummm, by year, and then by personal preference within that frame."

Bella could hear the abstraction in my voice. She glanced up at me, trying to understand why I was staring at her so intently.

"What?" she asked, her hand straying self-consciously to her hair.

"I was prepared to feel...relieved. Having you know about everything, not needing to keep secrets from you. But I didn't expect to feel more than that. I *like* it. It makes me...happy."

We smiled together.

"I'm glad," she said.

It was easy to see she was telling nothing but the truth. There were no shadows in her eyes. It brought her as much pleasure to be in my world as being in hers brought me.

A flicker of unease twisted my expression. I thought of pomegranate seeds for the first time in a while. It felt right to have her here, but was that just my selfishness blinding me? Nothing had scared her away from me, but that didn't mean that she *shouldn't* be frightened. She'd always been too brave for her own good.

Bella watched my face change. "You're still waiting for the running and the screaming, aren't you?"

Close enough. I nodded.

"I hate to burst your bubble," she said, her voice blasé, "but you're really not as scary as you think you are. I don't find you scary at all, actually."

It was a well-performed lie, especially considering her usual lack of success with deception, but I knew she made the joke mostly to keep me from feeling dejected or worried. Though I sometimes regretted the depth of her leniency toward me, it did shift my mood. It was a funny joke, and I couldn't resist playing along.

I smiled, showing too much of my teeth. "You *really* shouldn't have said that."

She'd asked to see me hunt, after all.

I coiled into a parody of my actual hunting stance, a loose, playful version. Exposing even more of my teeth, I growled softly; it was almost a purr.

She started to back away, though there was no real fear on her face. At least, no fear of physical harm. She did look a little afraid that she was about to become the butt of her own joke.

She swallowed loudly. "You wouldn't."

I sprang.

She wasn't able to see much of the action; I moved at immortal speed.

Launching myself across the room, I scooped her up into my arms as I flew by. I shaped myself into a sort of defensive armor around her, so that when we collided with the sofa, she felt none of the impact.

By design, I'd landed on my back. I held her against my chest, still curled within my arms. She seemed a little disoriented, as though she wasn't sure which way was up. She struggled to sit, but I wasn't finished making my point.

She tried to glare at me, but her eyes were too wide to make the expression effective.

"You were saying?" I asked, my voice a playful snarl.

She tried to catch her breath. "That you are . . . a very, very . . . terrifying monster."

I grinned at her. "Much better."

Alice and Jasper were bounding up the stairs. I could hear Alice's eagerness to offer an invitation. She was also very curious about the sounds of a struggle emanating from my room. She hadn't been watching me, so now she only saw what she would find when they arrived; the way we'd gotten so disarranged was already in the past.

Bella was still trying to free herself.

"Um, can I get up now?"

I laughed at her continued breathlessness. Despite her overconfidence, I'd still been able to truly startle her.

"Can we come in?" Alice asked from the hallway, aloud for Bella's sake.

I sat up, now holding Bella on my lap. There was no need to pretend here, though I assumed a more respectful distance would be necessary in front of Charlie.

Alice was already walking into the room as I answered, "Go ahead."

While Jasper hesitated in the doorway, she settled herself in the middle of my rug, a wide grin on her face. "It sounded like you were having Bella for lunch, and we came to see if you would share," she teased.

Bella braced herself, her eyes flying to my face for reassurance. I smiled and pulled her tighter against my chest.

"Sorry, I don't believe I have enough to spare."

Jasper followed her into the room, unable to help himself. The emotions inside were nearly intoxicating to him. In this moment,

I knew Bella's feelings were just the same as mine, for there was no counterbalance to the atmosphere of bliss that Jasper was getting high on now.

"Actually," he said, changing the subject. I could see that he wanted to control what he was feeling, to regulate it. The ambience was overwhelming. "Alice says there's going to be a real storm tonight, and Emmett wants to play ball. Are you game?"

I paused, looking to Alice.

Lightning fast, she ran through a few hundred images from that possible future. Rosalie was absent, but Emmett wouldn't miss a game. Sometimes his team won, sometimes mine did. Bella was there watching, her face delighted by the otherworldly display.

"Of course you should bring Bella," she encouraged, knowing me well enough to understand my hesitation.

Oh. Jasper was caught off guard. Internally, he readjusted his idea of what was to come. He would not be able to relax, as he'd planned. But experiencing the emotions Bella and I made each other feel...that was a trade he could accept.

"Do you want to go?" I asked Bella.

"Sure," she answered quickly. And then after a tiny pause, "Um, where are we going?"

"We have to wait for thunder to play ball," I explained. "You'll see why."

Her concern was more obvious now. "Will I need an umbrella?"

I laughed that this was her worry, and Alice and Jasper joined in.

"Will she?" Jasper asked Alice.

Another flash of images, this time tracking the course of the storm.

"No. The storm will hit over town. It should be dry enough in the clearing."

"Good, then," Jasper said. He found that he was excited by the idea of spending more time with Bella and me. His enthusiasm spread out from his body, infecting the rest of us. Bella's expression changed from cautious to eager.

Cool, Alice thought, glad that her plan was now certain. She wanted recreational time with Bella, too. *I'll leave you to sort out the details.*

"Let's go see if Carlisle will come," she said, bouncing up from the floor.

Jasper poked her in the ribs. "Like you don't already know."

She was out the door in the same breath. Jasper followed more slowly, savoring each second near us. He paused to shut the door behind himself, an excuse to linger that much longer.

"What will we be playing?" Bella asked as soon as the door was closed.

"*You* will be watching. We will be playing baseball."

She looked at me skeptically. "Vampires like baseball?"

I answered her with put-on gravitas. "It's the American pastime."

21. THE GAME

THE TIME ALWAYS WENT SO QUICKLY. SOON BELLA WOULD need to eat another meal, and currently there was no food at all in my house; I planned to rectify that in the near future. Time to return to the human world. As long as we were together, it was not a burden but a joy.

So a meal, a little while to soak up her nearness, and then I'd have to leave her. I expected she would want to talk to Charlie alone before my introduction. But as soon as I turned onto her street, it was clear that my expectations for the afternoon were thwarted.

A 1987 Ford Tempo that had seen better days was parked in Charlie's usual spot. And under the meager protection of the porch roof, a boy stood behind a man in wheelchair.

Bella beat him home, the old man thought. *That's unfortunate.*

Hey, it's Bella! The boy's thoughts were much more enthusiastic.

I could think of only one reason that Billy Black would be unhappy to see Bella arrive before her father. And that reason involved a broken treaty. I would have confirmation soon enough; Billy hadn't seen me yet.

"Has he forgotten who the treaty actually protects?" I hissed.

Bella glanced up at me, confused, though I doubted I'd spoken slowly enough for my words to be intelligible.

Jacob saw me in the driver's seat just a second before Billy did. *Him again. So she must be dating him.* His enthusiasm vanished.

NO! Billy's thought was a shout, and then a mental groan. *No.*

I heard his half-articulated fears—should he tell his son to run? Was it already too late?—and then his guilt.

How did it know?

I saw that I was right, that this visit was no innocent social call.

Parking the truck against the curb, I locked eyes with the frightened man.

"This is crossing the line." I enunciated clearly this time. I hoped he could read my lips.

Bella understood immediately. "He came to warn Charlie?" She sounded horrified by the idea.

I nodded, not breaking away from Billy's stare. After a second more, he looked down.

"Let me deal with this," Bella suggested.

As much as I would have loved to get out of the truck and stalk up to the helpless duo—to lean over them, intimidating, close enough that all the little signs of what I was would feel like they were screaming at the old man, to bare my teeth and snarl a warning in a voice that would sound anything but human, to watch his hair stand on end and hear his heart splutter with panic—I knew it was a bad idea. For one thing, Carlisle wouldn't like it. For another, though the boy was well aware of the legends, he would never believe them. Unless I got in their faces and flaunted my less human side.

"That's probably best," I agreed. "Be careful, though. The child has no idea."

Annoyance flashed suddenly across her face. I was confused until she spoke.

"Jacob is not that much younger than I am."

It was the word *child* that had offended her.

"Oh, I know," I teased.

Bella sighed and reached for the door handle, no happier about separating than I was.

"Get them inside so I can leave. I'll be back around dusk," I promised.

"Do you want my truck?"

"I could *walk* home faster than this truck moves."

She smiled for a second, and then her face fell. "You don't have to leave," she murmured.

"Actually, I do." I glanced at Billy Black. He was staring again, but he looked away quickly when he met my gaze. "After you get rid of them . . ." I felt a smile spreading across my face, a little too wide. "You still have to prepare Charlie to meet your new boyfriend."

"Thanks a lot," she moaned.

But while she clearly worried about Charlie's reaction, I could see that she would go through with this. She would give me a label in her human world, something to let me belong there.

My smile softened. "I'll be back soon."

I appraised the humans on the porch one more time. Jacob Black was embarrassed, thinking caustic thoughts about his father for dragging him out to spy on Bella and her boyfriend. Billy Black was still suffused with fear, expecting me to suddenly begin butchering everyone in sight. It was insulting.

In that frame of mind, I leaned over to kiss Bella goodbye. Just to mess with the old man, I pressed my lips to her throat rather than her lips.

The agonized shouting in his head was nearly drowned out by the sound of Bella's heart racing, and I wished the irritating humans would disappear.

But her eyes were on Billy now, appraising his distress.

"*Soon*," she commanded. After one short, forlorn look, she opened the door and climbed out.

I sat very still as she jogged through the light rain to the door.

"Hey, Billy. Hi, Jacob," she said with forced enthusiasm. "Charlie's gone for the day—I hope you haven't been waiting long."

"Not long," the man said quietly. He kept glancing at me and then away again. He held up a brown paper bag. "I just wanted to bring this up."

"Thanks. Why don't you come in for a minute and dry off?"

She acted like she was unaware of his piercing stare, unlocking the door and then gesturing for them to enter, a smile glued to her face. She waited till they were inside the house to follow.

"Here, let me take that," she said to Billy while she turned to shut the door behind her. Her eyes locked with mine for one instant, and then the door was closed.

I quickly moved from Bella's truck to my usual tree before they could reach any windows that had a view of this side of the yard. I wasn't going to leave until the Blacks did. If things were going to get tense with the tribe again, I needed to know exactly how far Billy was willing to go today.

"Fishing again? Down at the usual spot? Maybe I'll run by and see him." *Even more urgent now. I didn't know it had gotten so bad. Poor Bella, she doesn't realize—*

"No," Bella protested sharply at the same time my teeth snapped together. "He was headed someplace new... but I have no idea where."

Even through the walls, I could hear that her tone was seriously off. Billy also noticed.

What's this? She doesn't want me to see Charlie. She couldn't know why I need to warn him.

I could see Bella's expression as he analyzed it; her eyes flashed, her chin lifted stubbornly. It reminded him of one of his daughters, the one who never visited.

I need to talk to her alone.

"Jake," he said slowly, "why don't you go get that new picture of Rebecca out of the car? I'll leave that for Charlie, too."

"Where is it?"

Jacob's pure, clear thoughts were all gloomy now, replaying the kiss in the truck. It affected him in a much different way than it did his father. He knew she was too old to think of him the way he wished she would, but it depressed him to see the proof. He sniffed once and then winced, distracted.

Something's gone rancid in here, he thought, and I wondered if he was reacting to his father's gift in the paper bag; I'd smelled nothing amiss this morning.

"I think I saw it in the trunk," Billy lied smoothly. "You may have to dig for it."

Neither Billy nor Bella spoke again until Jacob exited the front door, his shoulders slumped and his face down. He trudged to the car, ignoring the rain, and—with a sigh—started to sift through a pile of old clothes and forgotten junk. He was still rehashing the kiss, trying to decide how into it Bella was.

Billy and Bella were facing off in the hallway.

How do I start…?

Before he could say anything, Bella turned and walked away toward the kitchen. He watched her retreating figure for a second, and then followed.

The refrigerator door creaked, then rustling ensued.

Billy watched as she slammed the fridge and whirled around to face him. He noted the defensive set of her mouth.

Bella spoke first, her voice unfriendly. She'd obviously decided there was no point in acting oblivious. "Charlie won't be back for a long time."

She must be keeping that thing a secret for her own reasons. She needs to know, too. Maybe I can say enough to warn her without actually breaking the treaty.

"Thanks again for the fish fry." Bella's words were clearly a dismissal, but Billy didn't think she looked surprised when he held his ground. She sighed and folded her arms across her chest.

"Bella," Billy said, his voice no longer casual. It was deeper now, graver.

She held as perfectly still as it was possible for a human to stand and waited for him to continue.

"Bella," he repeated. "Charlie is one of my best friends."

"Yes."

He said the words very slowly. "I noticed you've been spending time with one of the Cullens."

"Yes," she said again, barely veiling her hostility now.

He didn't respond to her tone. "Maybe it's none of my business, but I don't think that is such a good idea."

"You're right," she retorted. "It *is* none of your business."

So angry.

His voice turned ponderous again as he considered his wording carefully. "You probably don't know this, but the Cullen family has an unpleasant reputation on the reservation."

Very careful. He stayed just barely on the right side of the line.

"Actually, I did know that." Bella's words flew hot and fast, in direct contrast to his. "But that reputation couldn't be deserved, could it? Because the Cullens never set foot on the reservation, do they?"

This pulled him up short. *She knows! She knows? How? And how could she . . . ? She couldn't. She can't know the whole truth.* The revulsion that colored his thoughts made my teeth grind again.

"That's true," he finally conceded. "You seem . . . well informed about the Cullens. More informed than I expected."

"Maybe even better informed than you are?"

What could they have told her that would make her so defensive of them? Not the truth. Some romantic fairy tale, no doubt. Well, obviously she won't be convinced by anything I have to say.

"Maybe." He was annoyed to have to agree with her. "Is Charlie as well informed?"

He watched her expression get more evasive. "Charlie likes the Cullens a lot."

Charlie doesn't know anything.

"It's not my business," Billy said. "But it may be Charlie's."

Bella's gaze dissected his expression for a long moment.

The girl looks like a lawyer.

"Though it would be my business, again, whether or not I think that it's Charlie's business, right?" she asked. It didn't really sound like a question.

Again, they locked eyes.

Finally, Billy sighed.

Charlie wouldn't believe me anyway. I can't alienate him again. I need to be able to keep watch on this situation.

"Yes, I guess that's your business, too."

Bella sighed and her posture relaxed. "Thanks, Billy," she said, her voice softer now.

"Just think about what you're doing, Bella," Billy urged.

Her answer was too quick. "Okay."

Another thought caught my attention. I'd paid little notice to Jacob's fruitless search, too focused on Billy and Bella's standoff. But now he realized—

Oh man, I'm a moron. He wanted me out of the way.

Full of dismay over how his father might be embarrassing him, and with a measure of guilty fear that Bella might have told on him about the treaty breaking, Jacob slammed the trunk and loped toward the front door.

Billy heard the trunk and knew his time was up. He made his final plea.

"What I meant to say was . . . don't do what you're doing."

Bella didn't answer, but her expression was gentler now. Billy had a faint moment of hope that she was listening to him.

Jacob banged the front door open. Billy glanced over his shoulder, so I couldn't see Bella's reaction.

"There's no picture anywhere in that car," Jacob grumbled loudly.

"Hmm. I guess I left it at home," Billy said.

"Great," his son retorted with heavy sarcasm.

"Well, Bella, tell Charlie . . ." Billy waited for a beat before continuing. "That we stopped by, I mean."

"I will," she replied, voice sour again.

Jacob was surprised. "Are we leaving already?"

"Charlie's gonna be out late," Billy explained, already wheeling himself toward the door.

What was even the point of coming up? Jacob complained internally. *Old man is getting senile.* "Oh. Well, I guess I'll see you later, then, Bella."

"Sure," Bella said.

"Take care," Billy added in a warning voice.

Bella didn't answer.

Jacob helped his father over the threshold and down the one step of the porch. Bella followed them to the door. She glanced toward the empty truck, then waved once toward Jacob and shut the door while Jacob was still loading his father into the car.

Though I would have liked to join Bella and talk over what had just happened, I knew my job wasn't done yet. I heard her stamping up the stairs as I dropped from the tree and cut through the woods behind her house.

It was much more difficult to follow the Blacks in the daytime while on foot. I couldn't very well pace them along the highway. I ducked in and out of the thicker knots of forest, listening for the thoughts of anyone close enough to see me. I beat them to the La Push turnoff, and chanced a full-tilt sprint across the rainy highway while the only visible car was headed in the other direction. Once I was on the west side of the road, there was plenty of cover. I waited for the old Ford to appear, then ran parallel to them through the dark trees.

The two weren't talking. I wondered if I had missed any earlier recriminations from Jacob. The boy's head was busy replaying the kiss again, and he was concluding morosely that Bella had been *very* into it.

Billy's mind was caught up in a memory. I was surprised that I remembered this, too. From a different angle.

It was over two and a half years ago. My family had been in Denali at the time, just a short courtesy visit on our way from one semipermanent home to the next. Groundwork for the move back to Washington had included one unique chore. Carlisle already had his job lined up and Esme had bought her fixer-upper sight unseen. My siblings' and my fake transcripts had been transferred to Forks High School. But the last step of preparation was the most important—while also the most atypical. Though we'd moved back to former homes in the past—after an appropriate amount of time had elapsed—we'd never had to give warning of our arrival before.

Carlisle had started with the internet. He'd found an amateur genealogist named Alma Young working out of the Makah Reservation. Pretending to be another family history enthusiast, he'd asked about any descendants of Ephraim Black who might still live in the area. Mrs. Young had been excited to give Carlisle the good news: Ephraim's grandson and great-grandchildren all lived in La Push, just down the coast. Of course she didn't mind giving Carlisle the phone number. She was sure Billy Black would be thrilled to hear from his very distant cousin.

I'd been in the house when Carlisle had made the next call, so of course I'd heard everything Carlisle had said. Billy was remembering his side of it now.

It had been such an ordinary day. The twins were out with friends, so it was just Billy and Jacob at home. Billy was teaching the boy how to whittle a sea lion out of madrona wood when the phone rang. He'd wheeled himself to the kitchen, leaving the child so focused on his work that he barely noticed his father leaving.

Billy had assumed it was Harry, or maybe Charlie. He'd answered with a cheerful "Hello!"

"Hello. Is this Billy Black?"

He didn't recognize the voice on the other end of the line, but there was something sharp and clear about it that put his back up for some reason.

"Yes, this is Billy. Who's asking?"

"My name is Carlisle Cullen," the soft yet piercing voice told Billy, and it felt like the floor was falling out from under him. For a wild second, he'd thought he was having a nightmare.

This name and this keen-edged voice were part of a legend, a horror story. Though he'd been warned and prepared, it had all been such a very long time ago. Billy had never actually believed that one day he'd have to live in the same world as that horror story.

"Does my name mean anything to you?" the voice asked, and Billy noticed how young it sounded. Not hundreds of years old, as it should.

Billy had struggled to find his own voice. "Yes," he finally rasped.

He thought he heard a faint sigh.

"That's good," the monster replied. "It makes it easier for us to fulfill our duty."

Billy's mind went numb as he realized what the monster was saying. Duty. He was speaking of the treaty. Billy struggled to remember the secret accords he'd so carefully memorized. If the monster said he had a duty to discharge, then that could only mean one thing.

All the blood drained from Billy's face and the walls seemed to tilt around him, though he knew he was sitting safe and stable in his wheelchair.

"You're coming back," he choked out.

"Yes," the monster agreed. "I know this must be... unpleasant for you to hear. But I assure you that your tribe is in no danger, nor are any of the people in Forks. We have not changed our ways."

Billy couldn't think of anything to say. He'd been locked into this treaty since before his birth. He wanted to object, to threaten... but treaty or no, there was nothing he could do.

"We'll be living outside Forks." The monster rattled off a set of numbers, and it took Billy a moment to realize they were coordinates, lines of longitude and latitude. He scrambled for something to write with, and came up with a black Sharpie but no paper.

"Again," he demanded hoarsely.

The numbers came more slowly this time, and Billy scrawled them down his arm.

"I'm not sure how well you know the agreement—"

"I know it," Billy interrupted. The blood drinkers got a five-mile radius around the location of their lair that was off limits for any member of the tribe. It was a small space compared to the land that belonged to the tribe, but in this moment it seemed like much too much.

How would they convince any of the children to obey this rule? He thought of his own headstrong daughters and his happy-go-lucky son. None of them believed any of the stories. And yet if they ever made an innocent mistake…they'd be fair game.

"Of course," the monster said politely. "We know it very well, too. You have nothing to worry about. I'm sorry for any distress this causes you, but we will not impact your people in any way."

Billy just listened, numb again.

"Our current plan is to live in Forks for about a decade."

Billy's heart stopped. Ten years.

"My children will be attending the local high school. I don't know if any of your tribe's children come up to the school—"

"No," Billy whispered.

"Well, if anyone wishes to, I can assure you it will not be unsafe."

The faces of the children of Forks flashed through Billy's mind. Was there nothing he could do to protect them?

"Let me give you my number. We'd be happy to have a more cordial—"

"No," Billy said, stronger this time.

"Of course. Whatever makes you most comfortable."

And then a panicked thought intruded. The monster had spoken of his *children….*

"How many?" Billy asked. His voice sounded like he was being strangled.

"Pardon me?"

"How many of you are there?"

For the first time, the smooth, confident voice hesitated. "Two more found our family many years ago. There are seven of us now."

Very slowly and deliberately, Billy hung up the phone.

And then I had to stop running. I'd not quite reached the treaty line, but this particular memory made me loath to cut it too close. I turned north and headed homeward.

So nothing very helpful from Billy's thoughts. I felt reasonably sure that he would follow the same pattern: return to his safe zone and contact his cronies. They would hash through the new information—which was pretty meager—and come to the same conclusion. There was nothing they could do. The treaty was their only protection.

I imagined that Billy's longstanding friendship with Charlie would be the point of contention. Billy would fight very hard to be allowed to warn Charlie in a more detailed fashion. A cold one had chosen his only daughter as…a victim, a target, a meal; I could guess how Billy would choose to describe our relationship.

Surely the others, more impartial than Billy, would insist on his silence.

Regardless, Billy's earlier attempt to alert Charlie to the danger of Carlisle working at the hospital hadn't gone well. Adding in a heavy helping of the fantastical would certainly not help. Billy had already recognized that himself.

I was nearly home. I would give Carlisle the update and my analysis of the situation. There really wasn't much else to do. I was positive his reaction would be the same. Much like the Quileutes, we had no option besides following the treaty to the letter.

I darted across the freeway again when there were no cars passing. As soon as I was on the drive, I heard the sound of a familiar engine coming from the garage. I stopped dead in the middle of the single lane and waited.

Rosalie's red BMW rounded the curve and screeched to a stop.

I waved halfheartedly.

You know I'd hit you if it wouldn't mess my car up.

I nodded.

Rosalie revved her engine once, then sighed.

"You heard about the game, I guess."

Just let me go, Edward. I could see in her mind that she had no destination in mind. She only wanted to be away from here. *Emmett will stay. That's enough, isn't it?*

"Please?"

She closed her eyes and inhaled deeply. *I don't understand why this is so important to you.*

"*You* are important to me, Rose," I said simply.

Everyone will have more fun without me.

I shrugged. She might be right.

I won't be nice.

I smiled. "I don't require *nice*. I only asked for toleration."

She hesitated.

"It won't be that bad," I promised. "Maybe you'll win the game soundly, make me look bad."

One corner of her mouth quirked up as she fought a smile. *I get Emmett and Jasper.*

She always picked the obvious muscle.

"Deal."

She took another deep breath, instantly regretting our agreement. She tried to imagine being in the same place as Bella and...struggled.

"Nothing is going to happen tonight, Rose. She's not making any decisions. She's just going to watch us play a game, that's all. Think of it as an experiment."

In that...it might blow up?

I gave her a tired look. She rolled her eyes.

"If it doesn't work, we'll regroup and come up with another solution."

Rosalie had a plethora of other solutions, most of them profane, but she was ready to surrender. She would try...but I could see that she would not work very hard at being civil. It was a start.

I suppose I should change, then. With that, she threw her car into reverse and gunned it back toward the house, climbing from zero to sixty before she was fully out of view. I took the shorter route straight through the forest.

Inside, Emmett was watching four different baseball games at the same time on the big screen. His head was turned away, though, listening to the sound of Rosalie's car squealing into the garage.

I gestured to the TV. "Nothing you'll find there will help you win tonight."

You talked Rose into playing?

I nodded once, and a huge grin split his face.

I owe you one.

I pursed my lips. "Really?"

He was intrigued that I clearly wanted something. *Sure, what do you want?*

"Your best behavior around Bella?"

Rose flitted through the room and up the stairs, pointedly ignoring us both.

Emmett thought about my request. *What exactly does that entail?*

"Not terrifying her on purpose."

He shrugged. "Seems fair."

"Excellent."

I'm just glad you're back. The last months had dragged unusually for Emmett, first with my moods and then with my absence.

I almost apologized, but I knew he wasn't upset with me now. Emmett lived for the present.

"Where are Alice and Jasper?"

Emmett was watching the games again. *Hunting. Jasper wants to be ready. Funny thing—seemed like he was excited for tonight, more than I would have expected.*

"Funny," I agreed, though I had a little more insight into why.

Edward, dear, I can hear you dripping on my floors. Please change into something dry and mop that up.

"Sorry, Esme!"

I dressed for Charlie this time, pulling out one of the more impressive rain jackets that I rarely wore. I wanted to look like a person who was taking the weather seriously, concerned about avoiding the cold and the wet. It was the little details that set humans at ease.

Automatically, I tucked my bottlecap into the pocket of my new jeans.

While I was mopping, I thought about the short journey to the baseball clearing tonight, and realized that—after yesterday—Bella might not be too keen on running with me to our destination. I knew there would have to be *some* running, but the shorter the distance the better, I assumed.

"Can I borrow your Jeep?" I asked Emmett.

Nice jacket. He chuckled. *Do try to stay dry and cozy.*

I waited with an overdone expression of patience.

"Sure," he agreed. "But now you owe me one."

"I'm delighted to be in your debt."

I darted back upstairs to the sound of his laughter.

It was a quick conference with Carlisle—like me, he could see no course of action besides continuing on as we were. And then I was hurrying back to Bella.

Emmett's Jeep was in many ways the most conspicuous of our cars just by sheer size. But there weren't many people out in the downpour, and the rain would make it hard for anyone to see who was driving. People would assume the massive vehicle was from out of town.

I wasn't sure how much time Bella would need, so I turned up the street a block from hers to make sure she was ready for me.

Before I was even to the end of the street, I could tell Charlie's thoughts were in a dither. She must have begun. I caught a glimpse of Emmett's face in his head. What was that about?

I pulled over by a patch of forest between homes and let the engine idle.

I was close enough now to make out their spoken voices. The nearby houses were not silent, but those other voices, both mental and physical, were easily ignored. I was so attuned to the sound of Bella's voice by now that I could have picked it out over a stadium full of shouting.

"It's Edward, Dad," she was saying.

"Is he?" her father demanded. I tried to make sense of what they were saying about me.

"Sort of, I guess," she admitted.

"You said last night that you weren't interested in any of the boys in town," he remonstrated.

"Well, Edward doesn't live in town, Dad.... And anyways, it's kind of at an early stage, you know? Don't embarrass me with all the boyfriend talk, okay?"

I was able to put together the thread of the conversation then. I tried to understand from Charlie's emotions how perturbed he was by her revelation, but he seemed extra stoic tonight.

"When is he coming over?"

"He'll be here in a few minutes." Bella sounded more agitated about this than her father.

"Where is he taking you?"

Bella groaned theatrically. "I hope you're getting the Spanish Inquisition out of your system now. We're going to play baseball with his family."

There was a second of silence, and then Charlie started laughing. "*You're* playing baseball?"

From Charlie's tone, it was evident that—despite her stepfather's occupation—Bella wasn't a huge fan of the sport.

"Well, I'll probably watch most of the time."

"You must really like this guy." He sounded more suspicious now. From the flashbacks running through his head, I thought he must be trying to piece together how long this relationship had been going on. He felt newly justified in his suspicions of the night before.

I revved the engine and made a quick U-turn. She'd finished her prep work, and I was anxious to be with her again.

I parked behind her truck and darted up to the doorway. Charlie was saying, "You baby me too much."

I pressed the doorbell, and then flipped my hood up. I was good at passing for human, but it felt a lot more important right now than it usually did.

I heard Charlie's footsteps coming toward the door, closely followed by Bella's. Charlie's mind seemed to be vacillating between anxiety and humor. I thought he was still enjoying the idea of Bella willingly being involved in a baseball game; I was almost positive I had it right.

Charlie opened the door, his eyes focused at about my shoulder height; he'd been expecting someone shorter. He readjusted, and then staggered half a step back.

I'd experienced the reaction often enough in the past that I didn't need clearer thoughts to understand. Like any normal human, suddenly standing just a foot away from a vampire would send adrenaline racing through his veins. Fear would twist in his stomach for just a fraction of a second, and then his rational mind would take over. His brain would force him to ignore all the little discrepancies that marked me as other. His eyes would refocus and he would see nothing more than a teenage boy.

I watched him come to that conclusion, that I was just a normal boy. I knew he would be wondering what his body's strange reaction had been about.

Abruptly an image of Carlisle flitted through his head, and I thought he must be comparing our faces. We really didn't look much alike, but the similarities in our coloring were enough for most people. Maybe it wasn't enough for Charlie. He was definitely dissatisfied about something.

Bella was watching nervously over Charlie's shoulder.

"Come on in, Edward." He stepped back and gestured for me to follow. Bella had to dance out of his way.

"Thanks, Chief Swan."

He sort of smiled, almost unwillingly. "Go ahead and call me Charlie. Here, I'll take your jacket."

I shrugged it off quickly. "Thanks, sir."

Charlie gestured to the small living room alcove. "Have a seat there, Edward."

Bella made a face, clearly wanting to be on our way.

I chose the armchair. It seemed a little forward to take the sofa, where Bella would have to sit next to me—or Charlie would. Probably better to keep the family together for an official first date.

Bella didn't like my choice. I winked at her while Charlie was settling himself.

"So I hear you're getting my girl to watch baseball," Charlie said. Amusement was winning in his expression.

"Yes, sir, that's the plan."

He chuckled aloud now. "Well, more power to you, I guess."

I politely laughed along.

Bella jumped to her feet. "Okay, enough humor at my expense. Let's go." Hurrying back to the hall, she shoved her arms into her own jacket. Charlie and I followed. I grabbed my jacket on the way and slipped it on.

"Not too late, Bell," Charlie cautioned.

"Don't worry, Charlie, I'll have her home early," I said.

He eyed me keenly for a second. "You take care of my girl, all right?"

Bella performed another dramatic groan.

It felt more satisfying than I would have thought to say the words "She'll be safe with me, I promise, sir" and be confident that they were true.

Bella walked out.

Charlie and I laughed together again, though this time it was more genuine on my part. I smiled at Charlie and waved as I followed Bella outside.

I didn't get very far. Bella had frozen on the small porch, staring at Emmett's Jeep. Charlie crowded behind me, looking to see what had slowed Bella's determination to escape.

He whistled in surprise. "Wear your seat belts," he said gruffly.

Her father's voice galvanized her. She dashed out into the pouring rain. I kept my speed human but used my considerably longer legs to get to the passenger side first and open the door for her. She hesitated for a moment, eyeing the seat, then the ground, then the seat again. She took a deep breath and bent her legs as though about to jump. Charlie couldn't see much of us through the Jeep's windows, so I lifted her into the seat. She gasped in surprise.

I walked around to my door, waving to Charlie again. He waved back perfunctorily.

Inside the car, Bella was struggling with the seat belt. Holding a buckle in each hand, she looked up at me and said, "What's all this?"

"It's an off-roading harness."

She frowned. "Uh-oh."

After a second of searching, she found a tongue, but it wouldn't fit into either of the two buckles she tried it with. I chuckled once at her baffled expression, then snapped all her attachments into place. Her heart drummed louder than the rain when my hands brushed across the skin of her throat. I let my fingers trail across her collarbones once before I settled into my seat and started the engine.

As we pulled away from the house she said, sounding a little alarmed, "This is a . . . um . . . *big* Jeep you have."

"It's Emmett's. I didn't think you'd want to run the whole way," I admitted.

"Where do you keep this thing?"

"We remodeled one of the outbuildings into a garage."

She eyed the empty harness behind my back. "Aren't you going to put on your seat belt?"

I just looked at her.

She frowned and started to roll her eyes, but the expression got stuck midroll.

"Run the *whole* way?" Her voice rose to a higher octave than usual. "As in, we're still going to run part of the way?"

"You're not going to run," I reminded her.

She moaned. "*I'm* going to be sick."

"Keep your eyes closed, you'll be fine."

Her front teeth bit deep into her lower lip.

I wanted to reassure her—she would be safe with me. I leaned over to kiss the top of her head. And then I flinched.

The rain in her hair affected her scent in a way I hadn't expected. The burn in my throat, which had seemed so stable, seized me in a sudden flare. A groan of pain escaped my lips before I could block it.

I straightened up at once, putting space between us. She was staring at me, confused. I tried to explain.

"You smell so good in the rain."

Her expression was wary as she asked, "In a good way, or in a bad way?"

I sighed. "Both, always both."

The rain pelted the windshield like hail, sharp and loud, sounding more solid than a liquid. I turned onto the off-road track that would take us as deep into the forest as the Jeep could go. It would cut a few miles off the run.

Bella stared out the window seemingly lost in thought. I wondered whether my answer had upset her. But then I noticed how tightly she was bracing herself against the window frame, her other hand gripped around the edge of her seat. I slowed down, taking the ruts and the rocks as smoothly as I could.

It seemed as though every method of travel besides her lethargic dinosaur of a truck was unpleasant to her. Maybe this bumpy ride would make her less loath to travel the most convenient way.

The track died in a small open space surrounded by close-packed fir trees—there was just enough room to turn a vehicle around in order to head back down the mountain. I shut off the engine, and suddenly it was nearly silent. We'd run through the storm; it was just misting now.

"Sorry, Bella," I apologized. "We have to go on foot from here."

"You know what? I'll just wait here."

She sounded breathless again. I tried to read her face to see how serious she was. I couldn't tell if she was really that frightened, or being stubborn.

"What happened to all your courage?" I demanded. "You were extraordinary this morning."

The corners of her lips twisted up into a very small smile. "I haven't forgotten the last time yet."

I dashed around the car to her side, wondering about that smile. Was she teasing me a little?

I opened the door for her, but she didn't move. The harness must still be an impediment. I worked quickly to free her.

"I'll get those," she protested. But it was already done before she could add, "You go on ahead."

I considered her expression for a moment. She looked a little nervous, but not terrified. I didn't want her to give up on traveling with me. For one thing, it was the simplest way of getting around. But more than that... before Bella, running had been my favorite thing. I wanted to share it with her.

But first I had to convince her to give it another try.

Maybe I would attempt a more dynamic form of *dazzling*.

I thought through all our past interactions. In the early days, I'd often misinterpreted her reactions to me, but now I saw things through a new filter. I knew that if I looked into her eyes with a certain intensity, she would often lose her train of thought. And then when I kissed her, she forgot all kinds of things—common sense, self-preservation, and even life-sustaining activities like breathing.

"Hmmm..." I considered how to proceed. "It seems I'm going to have to tamper with your memory."

I lifted her out of the Jeep and set her gently on her feet. She stared at me, a little nervous, a little excited.

She raised her eyebrows. "Tamper with my memory?"

"Something like that."

In the past, I'd had the strongest effect on her when I'd been searching most intensely to hear her secret thoughts. Amused by the futility, I tried again. I stared deeply into her clear, dark eyes. My own narrowed and I struggled fiercely through the silence. Of course there was nothing to hear.

She blinked four times fast, her nervous expression shifting to one that was more... stunned.

I felt I was on the right path.

Leaning closer, I placed my hands against the hardtop, one on either side of her head. She took a half step back, pressing herself against the door. Did she need more space? Her chin angled up, her face set at the perfect incline for me to kiss her. Probably not, then. I moved a few inches closer. Her eyes closed halfway, her lips parted.

"Now, what exactly are you worrying about?" I murmured.

She blinked fast again, and took a gasping breath—I wasn't at all sure what I was supposed to be doing about her frequent breathing lapses. Did I need to remind her at intervals?

"Well..." She swallowed, then sucked in another ragged breath. "Um, hitting a tree. And dying. And then getting sick."

I grinned at her order of events, then forced my face back into its former expression of intensity. Slowly I leaned down and pressed my lips into the small indentation between her collarbones. Her breath caught and her heart fluttered.

My lips moved against the skin of her throat. "Are you still worried now?"

It took her a moment to find her voice. "Yes?" She whispered the word, unsure. "About hitting trees... and getting sick?"

Slowly I tilted my face up, tracing the length of her throat with my nose and lips. I breathed my next question into the hollow just under the edge of her jaw. Her eyes slid all the way closed.

"And now?"

She was breathing in quick pants. "Trees?" she gasped. "Motion sickness?"

I brushed my lips up the side of her face, then softly kissed first one eyelid, then the next.

"Bella, you don't really think I would hit a tree, do you?" My tone was gently chiding. After all, she was the one who thought I was good at everything. Perhaps if I made the question about her faith in me.

"No," she breathed. "But *I* might."

Slow and deliberate, I kissed my way across her cheek, pausing right at the edge of her mouth. "Would I let a tree hurt you?"

My upper lip touched her lower lip with the slightest pressure imaginable.

"No," she sighed. It was a soft sound, almost a coo.

Now my lips moved lightly against hers as I whispered, "You see, there's nothing to be afraid of, is there?"

"No," she agreed with a shuddering sigh.

And then, though I'd only been intending to overwhelm *her*, I found myself wholly overcome.

It didn't feel like my mind was in control. My body was as much in command as it was when I hunted—impulse and appetite overthrowing reason. Only now my desire was not for the old needs I'd had time to master. These were new passions, and I hadn't yet learned how to govern them.

My mouth crushed too roughly against hers, my hands strained her face closer to my own. I wanted to feel her skin against every part of me. I wanted to hold her so close that we could never be separated.

This new fire—a fire without pain, that ravaged only my ability to think—raged even hotter when her arms wrapped tightly around my neck and her body bowed into mine. Her heat and her pulse were fused against my own form from chest to thigh. I was drowning in sensation.

Her lips opened against mine, with mine, and it seemed every part of me could think of nothing but deepening that kiss.

Ironically, it was my basest instinct that saved her.

Her warm breath surged into my mouth, and my involuntary reflexes reacted—venom flowed, muscles clenched. It was enough of a shock to bring me back to myself.

I reeled away from her, feeling her hands slide down my neck and chest.

Horror flooded my mind.

How close had I just come to harming her? To *killing* her?

I could see it as clearly as I could see her startled face in front of me now—a world without her. I'd considered this fate so many times that I didn't have to imagine now the vastness of that empty world, the agony of it. I knew it wasn't a world I could endure.

Or... a world in which she was miserable. If she, in total innocence, had touched her tongue to one of the razor-sharp edges of my teeth...

"Damn it, Bella!" I gasped, barely hearing the words that twisted out of me. "You'll be the death of me, I swear you will." I shuddered, sickened by myself.

Killing her would surely kill me, too. Her life was my only life—my fragile, finite life.

She braced her hands against her knees, trying to catch her breath.

"You're indestructible," she mumbled.

She was close to right about my physical durability, so different from her own; she didn't know how soundly my existence was knotted to hers. And she didn't know how close she'd just been to vanishing.

"I might have believed that before I met you," I groaned and took a deep breath. It didn't feel safe to be alone with her. "Now let's get out of here before I do something really stupid."

I reached for her and she seemed to understand the need to hurry. She didn't object as I lifted her onto my back. She wrapped her arms and legs fast around me, and I had to struggle for a second again to keep my mind in control of my body.

"Don't forget to close your eyes," I warned her.

Her face pressed tight against my shoulder.

The run wasn't long, but it was long enough for me to get myself in order. It seemed I couldn't trust anything when it came to my instincts; just because I was confident about my self-control in one way didn't mean I could take any other control for granted. I would have to take a step back and draw a careful line to protect her. I would have to limit physical contact to some form that didn't affect her ability to breathe or mine to think. It was pathetic that the second concern should be more important than the first.

She never moved during the short journey. I heard her breath coming evenly, and her heartbeat seemed stable, if slightly elevated. She held still even when I came to a stop.

I reached behind me to stroke her hair. "It's over, Bella."

She loosened her arms first, taking a deep breath, and then relaxed her taut legs. Suddenly, the warmth of her body vanished.

"Oh!" she huffed.

I spun around to find her splayed awkwardly on the ground like a child's doll tossed to the floor. The shock in her eyes was rapidly turning to indignation, as if she had no idea how she'd gotten there, but knew someone was surely to blame.

I'm not sure why it was so funny. Perhaps I was just overwrought. Maybe it was the powerful relief I was beginning to feel now that the close call was once again behind me. Or I just needed the release.

For whatever reason, I started laughing and couldn't immediately stop.

Bella rolled her eyes at my reaction, sighed, and stood up. She tried to wipe the mud off her jacket with such a long-suffering expression that I could only laugh harder.

She glared at me once, then marched forward.

I choked back my humor and darted after to catch her lightly by the waist, trying to force my voice to sound composed as I asked, "Where are you going, Bella?"

She wouldn't look at me. "To watch a baseball game," she answered. "You don't seem to be interested in playing anymore, but I'm sure the others will have fun without you."

"You're going the wrong way," I informed her.

She inhaled once through her nose, tilted her chin to an even more stubborn angle, then spun 180 degrees and stomped off in the opposite direction. I caught her again. This was not the correct way, either.

"Don't be mad," I pleaded. "I couldn't help myself. You should have seen your face." Another laugh escaped; I tried to swallow the one that followed.

She finally looked up, meeting my gaze with anger sparking in her eyes. "Oh, you're the only one who's allowed to get mad?"

I remembered how little she liked double standards.

"I wasn't mad at you," I assured her.

Her voice nearly dripped acid as she quoted me. " 'Bella, you'll be the death of me.' "

My humor turned black but didn't totally disappear. I'd spoken more truth in that moment of wild emotion than I'd meant to. "That was simply a statement of fact."

She twisted in my hold, trying to pull away. I put one hand against her cheek so she couldn't hide her face from me.

Before I could say more, she insisted, "You were mad!"

"Yes," I agreed.

"But you just said—"

"That I wasn't mad at *you*." Nothing seemed funny now. She'd taken the blame on herself. "Can't you see that, Bella? Don't you understand?"

She frowned, confused and frustrated. "See what?"

"I'm never angry with you," I explained. "How could I be? Brave, trusting...*warm* as you are." Forgiving, kind, sympathetic, sincere, *good*...essential, crucial, life-giving...I could have gone on for a while, but she interrupted.

"Then why...?" she whispered.

I assumed her unfinished thought was something along the lines of *Why did you snap at me so cruelly?*

I took her face between both my hands, trying to communicate with my eyes as much as with my words, trying to put more force into each one.

"I infuriate myself," I told her. "The way I can't seem to keep from putting you in danger. My very existence puts you at risk. Sometimes...I truly hate myself. I should be stronger, I should be able to—"

I was surprised when her fingers touched my lips, blocking the rest of what I wanted to say.

"Don't," she murmured.

The confusion had disappeared from her face, leaving only kindness behind.

I lifted her hand from my mouth and pressed it to my cheek.

"I love you," I told her. "It's a poor excuse for what I'm doing, but it's still true."

She stared at me with such warmth, such...adoration. There seemed to be only one answer to such a look.

It would have to be a restrained answer. There could be no more impulsiveness.

"Now, please try to behave yourself," I murmured, speaking more to myself than to her.

Gently, I pressed my lips against hers for one brief second.

She was very still, holding even her breath. I straightened up quickly, waiting for her to breathe again.

She sighed.

"You promised Chief Swan that you would have me home early, remember? We'd better get going."

Helping me again. I wished my weakness didn't force her to have to be so strong.

"Yes, ma'am."

I freed her, taking one of her hands to lead her forward on the correct course. We only had ten yards to go before we passed the edge of the wood and entered the huge, open field my family simply called *the clearing*. The trees had been scraped away by a glacier long ago, and now just a thin layer of soil covered the bedrock beneath. Wild grass and bracken were the only things that flourished here now. It was a convenient play place for us.

Carlisle was setting up the diamond while Alice and Jasper practiced some new tricks she wanted to perfect: If Jasper decided in advance to run a certain direction, Alice could see this decision and throw to his new position before he'd telegraphed the move. It didn't give them much of an advantage, but as closely matched as we all were, anything had the potential to make them more competitive.

Esme was waiting for Bella and me, with Emmett and Rosalie sitting close beside her. When we stepped into view, I saw Rosalie yank her hand out of Esme's before she turned her back to us and walked away.

Well, she hadn't promised nice. I knew it was a large enough concession for her to simply be here.

Utterly ridiculous. Esme didn't agree with me. She'd been trying to cajole Rose out of her mood all afternoon without much effect, and she was exasperated.

It'll be all right once we start, Emmett was thinking. Like me, he was just relieved Rose had come.

Esme and Emmett moved forward to welcome us. I gave Emmett a cautioning look, and he grinned at me. *Don't worry, I promised.*

He eyed Bella with interest. It was one thing to be around humans while visiting in their world, but something else entirely to have one visit ours. It was exciting. And a human who was, to his mind, more or less one of us now. He had only positive experiences with adding to the family. He was eager to include Bella as well.

I might have enjoyed his enthusiasm, but underneath his fascination with something new, I could see that he didn't doubt Alice's version of things.

I would be patient. They would all come to understand over time.

"Was that you we heard, Edward?" Esme asked. She made her voice louder than was necessary so Bella wouldn't be left out.

"It sounded like a bear choking," Emmett added.

Bella smiled shyly. "That was him."

Emmett grinned at her, pleased with her gameness to play along.

"Bella was being unintentionally funny," I explained.

Alice was rocketing toward us. I supposed it shouldn't worry me that she was being so *herself*. She could see better than I could guess what would frighten Bella and what would not.

She skipped to a stop just an arm's length away.

"It's time," Alice intoned solemnly, working the oracle vibe for Bella's benefit. Thunder shattered the stillness right on cue. I shook my head.

"Eerie, isn't it?" Emmett murmured to Bella, winking when she looked surprised that he was addressing her. She grinned at him, only a little hesitant.

He glanced at me. *I* like *her*.

"Let's go!" Alice urged, reaching for Emmett's hand. She knew exactly how long we could get away with playing unrestrained, and she didn't want to waste any time. Emmett was no less eager to get started. Together, they raced toward Carlisle.

Can I have a moment with her? I'd like her to be comfortable with me, Esme entreated. I could see how much it meant to her, for Bella to see her as a person and a friend, not something to be feared. I nodded, then turned to Bella.

"Are you ready for some ball?" I grinned, easily inferring from Charlie's comments that this evening was an anomaly for her. Well, hopefully we could keep her entertained.

"Go team?"

I laughed at her put-on enthusiasm, and then gave Esme her desired space, chasing after Emmett and Alice.

I listened to Esme chatting with Bella as I joined the others. She didn't have any information she wanted to impart or extract—she just wanted to interact with Bella—but I was riveted regardless. I divided my attention between that conversation and the one around me.

"Edward and I already picked teams," Rosalie said. "Jasper and Emmett are with me."

Alice was unsurprised. Emmett liked the odds. Jasper was less enthused; he preferred to work with Alice rather than against her. Carlisle was, like me, pleased at Rosalie's engagement with the game.

Esme was complaining about our poor sportsmanship, obviously preparing Bella for the worst.

Carlisle pulled out a quarter. "Call it, Rose."

"She chose the teams," I objected.

Carlisle looked at me and then pointedly at Alice, who had already seen that the coin would fall heads up.

"Rose," he said again, and flipped the quarter into the air.

"Heads."

I sighed, and she grinned. Carlisle caught the coin neatly and flipped it onto his forearm.

"Heads," he confirmed.

"We'll bat," Rosalie said.

Carlisle nodded, and he, Alice, and I moved to take our fielding positions.

Esme was telling Bella about her first son now, and I was surprised at the intimate direction their conversation had taken. This was Esme's rawest wound, but she was gentle and composed as she spoke. I wondered why she'd decided to share that.

Or perhaps Esme hadn't decided at all. There was something about the way Bella listened.... Hadn't I been eager to spill every dark secret I'd ever had? Hadn't young Jacob Black betrayed an ancient treaty simply to amuse her? She must have this effect on everyone.

I moved into deep left field. I could still hear Bella's voice clearly.

"You don't mind, then? That I'm...all wrong for him?" Bella asked.

Poor child, Esme thought. *This must be so overwhelming for her.*

"No," she told Bella, and I could hear that this was true. All Esme wanted was my happiness. "You're what he wants. It will work out, somehow."

But, like Emmett, she could only see one way. I was glad I was far enough out that Bella couldn't read my face clearly.

Alice waited until Esme was in the umpire's position, Bella at her side, before she stepped onto the makeshift mound.

"All right, batter up," Esme called.

Alice hurled out the first pitch. Emmett, too eager, took a massive swing that whistled so closely by the ball that the air pressure disrupted the straight line of the pitch. Jasper snagged the ball out of the air, then whipped it back to Alice.

"Was that a strike?" I heard Bella whisper to Esme.

"If they don't hit it, it's a strike," Esme responded.

Alice fired another pitch across the plate. Emmett had recalibrated. I was running before I heard the detonation as the bat and the ball collided.

Alice had already seen where the ball was headed, and that I was fast enough. It took a bit of the fun out of the game—honestly, Rose should have known better than to let Alice and me play on the same team—but I was intending to win tonight.

I raced back with the ball, hearing Esme call Emmett out right as I made it back to the edge of the clearing.

"Emmett hits the hardest, but Edward runs the fastest," Esme was explaining to Bella.

I grinned at them, happy to see that Bella looked entertained. Her eyes were wide, but so was her smile.

Emmett took Jasper's place behind home plate while Jasper took the bat, though it was Rosalie's turn to catch. That was irritating; surely standing within a ten-foot radius of Bella was not that enormous a burden. I was starting to wish I hadn't pushed to get her here.

Jasper wasn't planning to see how fast I could run; he knew he couldn't hit as far as Emmett. Instead, he caught Alice's pitch off the end of the bat, driving the ball close enough to Carlisle that it was obvious he would need to be the one to chase it. Carlisle dashed right to scoop it up, then raced Jasper to first base. It was very close, but Jasper's left foot connected with the base just before Carlisle connected with him.

"Safe," Esme declared.

Bella was leaning up on her tiptoes, her hands covering her ears with the *v* visible between her brows, but she relaxed as soon as Carlisle and Jasper were on their feet again. She glanced toward me, and her smile came back.

I could feel the palpable tension as Rosalie took her turn at bat. Though Bella was out of her line of sight while she faced Alice on the mound, Rosalie's shoulders seemed to curl inward, away from Bella. Her stance was stiff and her expression rigid with distaste.

I glared at her critically, and she curled her lip at me.

You wanted me here.

Rose was distracted enough that Alice's first pitch sailed past her into Emmett's hand. She frowned more deeply and tried to concentrate.

Alice launched the ball toward Rose again; this time Rose got a piece of it, whacking it past third. I ran in, but Alice already had it. Instead of throwing Rose out, for which there was time, Alice whirled and bolted toward home. Jasper was already halfway between third and home. He put his shoulder down as though he was planning to knock Alice off the plate the way he had Carlisle, but Alice didn't wait for him to charge her. She executed a clever half-spin, half-slide maneuver, gliding past him and then tagging him from behind. Esme called him out, but Rosalie had made use of the distraction to get to second.

I could guess their next play before Emmett traded spots with Jasper again. Emmett would hit a long sacrifice fly to get Rosalie home. Alice had seen the same, but it looked like they would succeed. I moved back to the tree line, but if I ran to the spot Alice saw the ball heading to before Emmett actually hit it, Esme would penalize us for cheating. I coiled my muscles, ready to race—not the ball, but Alice's vision.

Emmett hit this one high rather than long, knowing gravity was slower than I was. It worked, and I ground my teeth as Rosalie touched home plate.

Bella, however, was delighted. She clapped her hands with a huge smile, impressed by the play. Rosalie didn't acknowledge Bella's spontaneous applause—she wouldn't even look at her, instead rolling her eyes at me—but I was surprised to hear that she was ever so slightly...softened. I supposed it wasn't that remarkable; I knew how much Rosalie craved admiration.

Maybe I should tell her some of the complimentary things Bella had said about her beauty...but she might not believe me. If she would look at Bella now, she would see Bella's obvious marveling. That would probably soothe Rose even more, but she refused to look.

Still, it made me more hopeful. A little time and a lot of compliments...we could win Rose over together.

Emmett, too, was enjoying Bella's excited amazement. He already liked her more than I'd expected, and he found this game more fun with an animated audience. And just as Rose loved admiration, Emmett loved fun.

Carlisle, Alice, and I ran in while Rosalie's team took the field. Bella greeted me with huge eyes and a wide smile.

"What do you think?" I asked.

She laughed. "One thing's for sure, I'll never be able to sit through dull old Major League Baseball again."

"And it sounds like you did so much of that before."

Then she pursed her lips. "I am a little disappointed."

She hadn't looked disappointed. "Why?"

"Well, it would be nice if I could find just one thing you didn't do better than everyone else on the planet."

Ugh.

Rosalie wasn't the only one who groaned at that, but she was loudest.

How long will the goo goo eyes take? Rosalie demanded. *The storm won't last forever.*

"I'm up," I said to Bella. I retrieved the bat from where Emmett had tossed it, and walked to the plate.

Carlisle crouched behind me. Alice showed me the direction of Jasper's pitch.

I bunted.

"Coward," Emmett growled as he chased down the ball, which was bouncing unpredictably. Rose was waiting for me on second, but I made it in plenty of time. She scowled at me and I grinned back.

Carlisle stepped up to the plate and leaned into his stance. I could hear his intention, and Alice's prediction that he would be successful. I set myself, every muscle ready to surge. Jasper threw a fast curveball—Carlisle angled his bat perfectly.

I wished I could warn Bella to cover her ears again.

The sound it made when Carlisle connected was not something that could be convincingly explained away as thunder. It was lucky that humans were so unsuspicious, that they didn't *want* to believe in anything unnatural.

I was running full out, listening through the echoing boom to the sound of Rosalie racing through the forest. If she moved fast enough—but no, Alice could see the ball landing on the ground.

I hit home plate before the ball was halfway to its eventual destination. Carlisle was just rounding first. Bella blinked fast when I came to a stop a few feet from her, as if she hadn't been fully able to follow my run.

"Jasper!" Rosalie called from somewhere still deep in the

forest. Carlisle flew past third. The sound of the ball zooming in our direction whistled through the trees. Jasper darted to the plate, but Carlisle slid under him just before the ball smacked into Jasper's palm.

Esme called, "Safe."

"Beautiful," Alice congratulated us, holding her hand up for a high five. We both obliged her.

We could all hear Rosalie's teeth grinding.

I went to stand beside Bella, lacing my fingers loosely through hers. She smiled up at me, her cheeks and nose pink from the cold, but her eyes glowing with excitement.

Alice was thinking of a hundred different ways to tip the ball as she picked up the bat, but she couldn't see a way past Jasper and Emmett. Emmett was hovering close to third, knowing that Alice didn't have the muscle to outstrip Rosalie's fielding.

Jasper pitched a fastball, and Alice drove it toward right field. He raced the ball to first, grabbed it, and tagged the base before Alice could get there.

"Out."

I squeezed Bella's fingers once, then went to take my turn again.

This time I tried to get one past Rosalie, but Jasper tossed out a slow pitch, robbing me of the momentum I needed. I grounded the ball, but only made it to first before Rosalie blocked me.

Carlisle smashed the ball straight down against the rocky ground, hoping it would pop up high enough that I would have a chance to get around the bases, but Jasper leaped up and got it back in play too quickly. Emmett had me cornered on third.

Alice ran through the possibilities as she approached the plate, but the outlook wasn't encouraging. She did her best, though, driving the ball as hard as she could down the right foul line. Jasper didn't take the bait, not even trying to tag her out before he fired the ball back to Emmett, who stood like a brick wall in front of home plate. I didn't have a lot of choices. There was no way to make it past him, but if our entire team got stranded on the bases—according to our family rules—that meant an automatic end to the inning.

I charged Emmett, who looked thrilled by my choice, but before I could even try to dance around him to the plate, Rosalie was already complaining.

"Esme—he's trying to force an out." This was also against the family rules.

Of course, Emmett tagged me, there just wasn't any way around him.

"Cheater," Rose hissed.

Esme gave me a reproving look. "Rose is right. Take the field."

I shrugged, and headed to the outfield.

Rose's team did better this time. Both she and Jasper got around off one of Emmett's big hits, though I was pretty sure she'd cheated. The path of the ball shifted in flight, almost as if something smaller had knocked it off course, but I was too deep in the trees to see where that projectile had come from. I had time to throw Emmett out, at least. Rosalie's next long fly was too low; Alice was able to jump for it. Jasper got on base again, but I stopped Emmett's line drive before it reached the forest, and Carlisle and I caught Jasper between us on his way to third.

As the game progressed, I watched for signs that Bella was getting bored. But every time I looked, she seemed completely engrossed. This was something new to her, at least. I knew we didn't look much like humans playing baseball. I monitored her expression, waiting for the novelty to wear off. We had hours left in the storm, and Emmett and Jasper wouldn't want to miss any of it. If Bella were weary, or too cold, though, I would excuse myself. I winced internally, thinking of how well that would go over with Rosalie. Ah, well, she would survive.

Manners wore thin as the score fluctuated, and I wondered what Bella would think of us, Esme's warning notwithstanding. But when Rosalie shouted that I was a "pathetic, cheating tool" (because I'd known exactly which tree to scale in order to catch her fly ball) and later a "leprous swine" (tagging her out at third),

Bella just laughed along with Esme. Rosalie wasn't the only one hurling insults as we played, but this time Carlisle wasn't the only person who *wasn't*. I was on my best behavior, though I could see this irritated Rosalie more than if I'd matched her trash talking.

So it was a win-win.

We were in the eleventh inning—our innings never lasted more than a few minutes; we wouldn't stop at any particular number, we'd just end when the storm did—and Carlisle was batting first. Alice could see another big hit coming, and I wished that one of us were on base. Sure enough, Emmett—taking his turn on the mound—couldn't resist trying to throw a fast strike past Carlisle, and thus gave him all the power he needed to crush the ball so hard it sailed far past where Rosalie had any hope of stopping it. The sound reverberated off the mountains, more like an explosion than thunder.

While that sound was still echoing around us, another sound caught my attention.

"Oh!" The sound huffed out of Alice as though someone had punched her.

The images were pouring through her head in a torrent. An avalanche of new futures swirled unintelligibly, seemingly disconnected from each other. Some were blinding bright and some so dark there was nothing to see. A thousand different backgrounds, most of them unfamiliar.

Nothing was left of the future she'd been perfectly confident in before this moment. Whatever had changed was big enough that it left no part of our destiny untouched. Alice and I both felt a shiver of panic.

She focused. Working quickly, she traced the new visions back to their beginnings. The churning images funneled into a narrow moment very close to the present, almost immediate.

Three strangers' faces. Three vampires she saw running toward us.

I darted to Bella, considering racing away with her immediately. But there were near futures of us alone, outnumbered....

"Alice?" Esme asked.

Jasper rocketed to Alice's side almost faster than I'd moved to Bella's.

"I didn't see," Alice whispered. "I couldn't tell."

She was comparing visions now. The older ones where, tomorrow night, the three strangers would approach the house. It was a future I was prepared for; Bella and I were far away in that version.

Something had changed their plans. She moved forward, just a few minutes, into this new timeline. A friendly meeting was a possibility, introductions, a request. Alice realized what had happened. But I was fixated on the fact that Bella was there in this vision, quietly in the background.

We were all in a tight circle at this point, Alice at our center.

Carlisle leaned close, putting one hand on her arm. "What is it, Alice?"

Alice shook her head quickly, as though trying to force the pictures in her head to line up in a way that made sense. "They were traveling much quicker than I thought. I can see I had the perspective wrong before."

"What changed?" Jasper had been with Alice for so long that he understood better than anyone besides me how her talent worked.

"They heard us playing," Alice told us; the strangers would reveal this information in the friendly version of events. "And it changed their path."

Everyone stared at Bella.

"How soon?" Carlisle demanded, turning toward me.

It was not an easy distance for me to hear across. It helped that on a late, stormy night like this, the mountains around us were mostly empty of humans. It helped more that there were no other vampires in the area. Vampire minds were slightly more resonant; I could hear them from a greater distance, pinpoint them more easily. So I was able to locate them—aided by the landmarks I'd seen in Alice's vision—but I could only catch the most dominant thoughts.

"Less than five minutes," I told him. "They're running—they want to play."

His eyes flashed to Bella again. *You have to get her away from here*. "Can you make it?"

Alice focused on one strand of possibility for me. Trying to escape, Bella on my back.

Bella didn't slow me down very much—it wasn't the burden of her weight but the need to move carefully so as not to hurt her that impeded me—but I wouldn't be quite fast enough. This strand tied into the other future I'd seen: us surrounded, outnumbered...

The strangers were not so enthusiastic about baseball as to be careless. Alice saw that they would come at the clearing from three different angles, surveilling, before regrouping to present a united front. If any of them heard me running, they would come to investigate.

I shook my head. "No, not carrying—"

Carlisle's thoughts roiled in alarm.

"Besides," I hissed, "the last thing we need is for them to catch the scent and start hunting."

"How many?" Emmett demanded.

"Three," Alice growled.

Emmett snorted. The sound was so at odds with the tension that I could only stare at him blankly.

"Three?" he scoffed. "Let them come."

Carlisle was considering options, but I could already see there was only one. Emmett was right: There were enough of us that the strangers would have to be suicidal to start a fight.

"Let's just continue the game," Carlisle agreed, though I didn't need to read minds to hear how unhappy he was with this decision. "Alice said they were simply curious."

Alice started combing through all the possibilities for an encounter here in the clearing, the images more solid now that a decision had been made. It looked like the vast majority were peaceable, though they all began with tension. There were a few outliers on the spectrum of outcomes where something ignited a standoff, but those were less clear. Alice couldn't see what would trigger the conflict—some decision yet to be made. She didn't see any stable version that would result in physical combat here.

But there was so much she couldn't interpret yet. I saw the blinding sunlight again, and neither of us could understand *where* she was seeing.

I knew Carlisle's decision was the only decision, but I felt sick to my core. How could I have allowed this to happen?

"Edward," Esme whispered. *Are they thirsty? Are they hunting now?*

Thirst wasn't in their thoughts, and in Alice's vision, every second more clear, their eyes were a satiated red.

I shook my head at her.

That's something, at least. She was nearly as horrified as I was. Her thoughts were, like mine, snarled up in the idea of Bella's being in danger. Though Esme was no fighter, I could hear how fierce this made her feel. She would defend Bella as if she were her own child.

"You catch, Esme," I directed. "I'll call it now."

Esme took my place quickly, but her focus was locked on Bella's position.

No one was eager to stray deep into the field. They hovered close, ears all trained toward the forest. Alice, like Esme, had no intention of moving away from Bella. Her protective thoughts were not exactly like Esme's—not as maternal—but I could see that she, too, would shield Bella at any cost.

Despite the sick feeling consuming me, I could feel a rush of gratitude for their commitment.

"Take your hair down," I murmured to Bella.

It wasn't much of a disguise, but the most obviously human thing—besides her scent and her heartbeat—was her skin. The more of it we could hide...

She immediately pulled the band from her ponytail and shook

her hair out, letting it fall around her face. It was clear she understood the need to hide.

"The others are coming now," she stated. Her voice was quiet, but even.

"Yes," I said. "Stay very still, keep quiet, and don't move from my side, please."

I placed a few locks of her hair in a better position to camouflage her face.

"That won't help," Alice murmured. "I could smell her across the field."

"I know," I snapped.

"What did Esme ask you?" Bella whispered.

I thought about lying. She must already be terrified. But I told her the truth. "Whether they were thirsty."

Her heart thudded out of rhythm, then picked up faster than before.

I was vaguely aware of the others pretending to continue the game, but my mind was so focused on what was coming that I saw nothing of their façade.

Alice watched her visions solidify. I saw how they would split up, which routes they would take, and where they would reassemble before confronting us. I was relieved to see that none of them would cross Bella's earlier trail before entering the clearing. Perhaps that was why Alice's vision of the cordial if cautious meeting held firm. Of course, there were hundreds of possibilities once they were here. I saw myself defending Bella many times, the others always standing with me—well, Rosalie taking Emmett's flank; it looked like she had little interest in protecting anyone besides him. There were a few fragile future threads where it came to a fight, but they were as insubstantial as steam. I couldn't get a good view of the outcome.

I could hear their minds approaching, still distant, but clearer. It was obvious that none of them had any hostility toward us, though the one trailing the pack—the redheaded female Alice had seen—was skittish with anxiety. She was prepared to run for it if she felt any hint that we were aggressive. The two males were just excited about the possibility of some recreation. They seemed to be comfortable with approaching a group of strangers, and I assumed they were nomads familiar with how things worked here in the North.

They were splitting up now, doing their due diligence before exposing themselves.

If Bella hadn't been here, if she'd rejected the idea of spending her evening watching us play...well, I probably would have been with her. And Carlisle would have called me to let me know the strangers had arrived early. I would have been anxious, of course. But I would have known I'd done nothing wrong.

Because I should have foreseen this possibility. The noise of playing vampires was a very specific sound. If I'd taken the time to think through all the conceivable contingencies, if I'd not accepted Alice's vision of the strangers coming tomorrow as gospel—set my watch to it, so to speak—if I'd been circumspect rather than enthusiastic...

I tried to imagine how I would have felt if this encounter had taken place six months ago, before I'd ever seen Bella's face. I thought I would have been...unperturbed. Once I'd seen these visitors' minds, I would have been confident that there was nothing to worry about. Probably, I would even have been excited about the novelty of newcomers and the variation they would add to the pattern of our usual game.

Now I could feel nothing but dread, panic...and guilt.

"I'm sorry, Bella," I breathed just loud enough for her to hear. The strangers were too close for me to risk speaking at a greater volume. "It was stupid, irresponsible, to expose you like this. I'm so sorry."

She just stared at me, whites showing all around her irises. I wondered if she kept silent because of my warning, or if she just had nothing to say to me.

The strangers reunited at the southwest corner of the clearing. Their movements were audible now. I shifted my position so that my body would hide hers and began tapping my foot quietly to the rhythm of her heartbeat, hoping to disguise it as long as I could by creating a plausible source for the sound.

Carlisle turned to face the whisper of their approaching feet, and the others followed his lead. We would not give away any of our advantages, but would pretend to have no more than our extensive vampire senses to guide us.

Frozen, motionless as if we were hewn from the rock around us, we waited.

22. THE HUNT

By the time the strangers entered the clearing, their faces were already so well known to me that it felt as though I were recognizing them rather than seeing them for the first time.

The smaller, ill-favored male started in the lead, but he quickly fell back in a practiced maneuver.

He was focused on our numbers, singling out the threats. He assumed we were two or possibly three friendly covens, meeting for the game. He was very aware of Emmett, hulking beside Carlisle. And then me, obviously agitated; it was strange for a vampire to twitch in anxiety. None of them knew what to make of my cadenced tapping.

For the smallest part of a second, I struggled with the feeling that something was missing in his tally, but there was too much for me to concentrate on to have time to track down that impression.

The male in the lead was tall and handsomer than average, even for a vampire. His thoughts were very confident. His coven meant no mischief here; though, naturally, this large grouping of covens was surprised to be approached by strangers, he was sure we would work it out quickly. He, too, reacted to Emmett's size and my tension, but was then distracted by Rosalie.

I wonder if she's mated? Hmm, they do seem to be even in numbers.

His eyes skipped over the rest of us, then settled on Rose again.

The female with the vivid red hair was tenser than any of us, her body nearly vibrating with anxiety. She had a hard time keeping her intense glare off Emmett.

There're too many. Laurent is a fool.

She'd already catalogued a thousand different routes for escape. Currently, she felt her best chance was to sprint due north to the Salish Sea, where we couldn't follow her scent. I wondered that she wouldn't opt for the much nearer Pacific coast, but I couldn't see her reasons if she didn't think of them.

I found myself hoping the jittery female would break for cover and the others follow, but Alice didn't see that.

The redhead was watching the plainer male, waiting for him to run first. Her eyes danced to Emmett again, and she moved reluctantly as she followed the others closer.

The two males seemed unable to keep their eyes off Emmett for long, either. I found myself appraising my brother. He seemed even bigger than usual tonight, and there was something unnerving about his taut stillness.

Still the leader, Laurent, was sure of his plan. If our covens could get along with each other, then we could get along with his. Everyone would calm down and then we could all play. And he would get to know the glowing blonde....

He smiled in a friendly way, slowing his approach and then stopping as he got within a few yards of Carlisle. His gaze flickered to Rosalie, to Emmett, to me, then back to Carlisle.

"We thought we heard a game," he said. He had a faint French accent, but his internal voice came to him in English. "I'm Laurent, these are Victoria and James."

They didn't appear to have much in common, this urbane traveler from the continent and his two more feral followers. The female was irritated by his introduction; she was almost consumed by the need to escape. The other male, James, was a little amused at Laurent's confidence. He was enjoying the unpredictable nature of this encounter and was keen to see how we would respond.

Vic hasn't split yet, he was thinking. *So it probably won't come to anything.*

Carlisle smiled at Laurent, his friendly, open face momentarily disarming even the frightened Victoria. For one second, they all focused entirely on him instead of Emmett.

"I'm Carlisle," he introduced himself. "This is my family, Emmett and Jasper; Rosalie, Esme, and Alice; Edward and Bella." He gestured vaguely in our direction as he spoke, not drawing attention to me individually or Bella behind me. Laurent and James were reacting to the information that we were not separate tribes, but I wasn't entirely paying attention.

In the second that Carlisle said Jasper's name, I realized what I'd been missing.

Jasper—lacerated with scars on every visible portion of his skin, tall and lean and fierce as any stalking lion, eyes brutal with remembered kills—should have been at the forefront of their assessments. His warlike aspect should, even now, be coloring this negotiation.

I glanced at him from the corner of my eye, and found myself...so incredibly bored. It seemed as if there could be nothing less interesting in the world than this nondescript vampire standing docilely to one side of our grouping.

Nondescript? Docile? *Jasper?*

Jasper was concentrating so hard that, had he been human, his body would have been dripping with sweat.

I'd never seen him do this before, or even guessed that it was possible. Was this something he'd developed during his years in the South? Camouflage?

He was concurrently smoothing the tension surrounding the newcomers and making anyone looking in his direction feel singularly uninterested. Nothing could be duller than examining this nothing male at the back of the group, so unimportant....

And not just him…He was covering Alice, Esme, and Bella in the same haze of tediousness.

This was why none of them had realized yet. Not because of Bella's disheveled hair or my ridiculous tapping. They couldn't cut through the sense of overwhelming mundaneness to look at her closely. She was just one among many, not worth examining.

Jasper was really extending himself to protect the vulnerable members of our family. I could hear his total concentration. He wouldn't be able to hold it if things got physical, but for now he had Bella encased in a more clever protection than I could have imagined.

Gratitude swamped me again.

I blinked hard and refocused on the strangers. They were affected by Carlisle's charm, though they did not forget Emmett's intimidating size or my intensity.

I tried to absorb the soothing calm that Jasper was exuding, but while I could see its effect on the others, I couldn't access it. I realized that Jasper was presenting what he wanted, and that included me on edge, a threat, a distraction.

Well, I could certainly lean into that role.

"Do you have room for a few more players?" Laurent was asking, just as amicable as Carlisle.

"Actually, we were just finishing up," Carlisle responded, his tone oozing warmth. "But we'd certainly be interested another time. Are you planning to stay in the area for long?"

"We're headed north, in fact, but we were curious to see who was in the neighborhood. We haven't run into any company in a long time."

"No, this region is usually empty except for us and the occasional visitor, like yourselves."

Carlisle's easy friendliness, along with Jasper's influence, was winning them over. Even the edgy redhead was beginning to calm. Her thoughts tested this sense of safety, analyzing it in a way that was strange to me. I wondered whether she was aware of Jasper's performance, but she didn't seem suspicious. It was more like she questioned her own gut feeling.

James was a little disappointed that a game did not seem to be imminent. And also...that the confrontation had eased. He missed the excitement of the unknown.

Laurent was absorbing Carlisle's poise and confidence. He wanted to know more about us. He wondered what subterfuge we used to disguise our eyes, and why.

"What's your hunting range?" Laurent asked. This was a normal thing, an expected question among nomads, but I worried that it would alarm Bella. Whatever she felt, she was motionless and silent as a human could be behind me. The rhythm of her heart, and thus my drumming foot, didn't change.

"The Olympic Range here, up and down the Coast Ranges on occasion," Carlisle told him, not lying, but also not disabusing Laurent of his assumption. "We keep a permanent residence nearby. There's another permanent settlement like ours up near Denali."

This surprised all of them. Laurent was merely confused, but anything unexpected seemed to turn to fear in the mind of the panicky female; for her, all the effects of Jasper's efforts vanished in an instant. James, however, was intrigued. Here was something new and different. Not only was our coven immense, we were apparently not even nomadic. Perhaps this detour wasn't entirely wasted.

"Permanent?" Laurent asked, bewildered. "How do you manage that?"

James was pleased that Laurent had spoken, so his curiosity could be assuaged without any effort on his part. In a way, his reluctance to draw attention to himself reminded me of Jasper's much more effective camouflage. I wondered why James would want to play it safe this way. It didn't seem to line up with his desire for diversion.

Or did he, like Jasper, have something to hide?

"Why don't you come back to our home with us and we

can talk comfortably?" Carlisle proposed. "It's a rather long story."

Victoria twitched, and I could see that she was holding herself in place by will alone. She guessed what Laurent's answer would be, and, oh, how she wanted to run. James gave her an encouraging look, but it didn't alleviate her stress. Still, she would follow his lead.

Could it be this easy? It would be simple to split up if they accepted the invitation, with Carlisle and Emmett safely leading the strangers away. Thanks to Jasper, they might never realize what we were hiding from them.

I looked into Alice's view of the future—a little more difficult at the moment, as I had to ignore Jasper's potent veil of tedium, which tried, with energy, to convince me that there must be *something* more interesting to do.

Alice was focused on the closest possible futures. It surprised me that they all ended in a standoff now. A few of the possible fights were clearer than before.

So it would *not* be that easy.

In Laurent's mind, I heard nothing but interest and the coming assent; James was in agreement. Victoria looked for a trap, rigid with dread.

None of them had any intention to cause trouble or even examine our numbers more closely. What would change their minds?

I could think of only one factor that was so sure, so unaffected by any decision or whim.

The weather.

I braced myself, knowing there was nothing I could do. Jasper's eyes flickered to me. He felt my new anguish.

"That sounds very interesting, and welcome," Laurent was saying. "We've been on the hunt all the way down from Ontario, and we haven't had the chance to clean up in a while."

Victoria shuddered, trying to subtly catch James's attention, but he ignored her.

"Please don't take offense, but we'd appreciate it if you'd

refrain from hunting in this immediate area," Carlisle cautioned them. "We have to stay inconspicuous, you understand."

Carlisle's voice was perfectly assured. I envied him his hopefulness.

"Of course," Laurent agreed. "We certainly won't encroach on your territory. We just ate outside of Seattle, anyway."

Laurent laughed, and Bella's heartbeat stuttered for the first time. The movement of my foot faltered quickly, trying to disguise the variation. None of the strangers seemed to notice.

"We'll show you the way if you'd like to run with us," Carlisle offered, and only Alice and I knew that it was too late for his plan to succeed. It was so close now—her visions were racing to collide with the present. "Emmett and Alice, you can go with Edward and Bella to get the Jeep."

It happened exactly as he said Bella's name.

Just a gentle breeze, a mild flutter from a new direction, an aberration caused by the tail end of the storm swirling westward. So mild. So inescapable.

Bella's scent, fresh and immediate, wafted directly into the strangers' faces.

All of them were affected, but while Laurent and Victoria were predominantly confused by the delicious smell coming out of nowhere, James shifted instantaneously into hunting mode. Jasper's camouflage wasn't strong enough to deter that kind of focus.

There was no point in pretending any longer. As if he were reading my thoughts, Jasper pulled his concealment back in that second, leaving only himself and Alice still hidden. I realized it was better that he do this, that it would only alert these nomads to his extra talents if he tried to keep Bella obscured now. Yet I still felt a weak prick of betrayal.

But that was only the smallest part of my awareness. Most of my faculties were overwhelmed with fury.

James thrust forward into a crouch. His mind was empty of thought besides the hunt, intent on immediate gratification.

I gave him something else to think about.

I crouched in front of Bella, ready to launch myself into the hunter before he could get any closer to her, all my abilities concentrated on his thoughts. I roared a warning at him, knowing only self-preservation had any hope of distracting him at this point.

My rage was strong enough that I half wanted him to ignore my threat.

The pinpoint focus of his eyes widened out, away from Bella, as he appraised me. A strange flicker of surprise wove through his mind. He was almost...*incredulous* that I had moved to block him. I could only guess that he was used to acting unopposed. He hesitated, wavering between prudence and desire. It would be foolish to ignore the others—this was not a contest between just the two of us. But he could barely resist my challenge. He wasn't sure he wanted to resist.

"What's this?" Laurent cried. I didn't waste any attention for his reaction.

I saw the ploy in James's thoughts before he moved. I was in place to block his new angle before the movement was finished. His eyes narrowed, and he adjusted his evaluation of the danger I posed.

Faster than I thought. Too fast?

He was suspicious of me now. Of all of us. Why hadn't he noticed the girl before? She was so obvious, her apricot skin soft and matte in contrast with the shine of the rest.

"She's with us," I heard Carlisle warn in a new voice, friendliness gone.

James flashed a glance at him and was aware again of Emmett looming, massive and eager, beside Carlisle.

I was surprised at his frustration. James didn't want to be careful. He was anxious for a fight. However—still poised to strike—he spared part of his focus to tune in for some movement from Victoria, but she was frozen with fear.

My own attention was compromised as Laurent finally reacted.

"You brought a snack?" he asked, disbelieving.

Like James, he moved a step closer to Bella, though his move was more instinctual than aggressive.

That didn't matter to me. I twisted slightly, my eyes never leaving the greater threat, and snarled my rage in Laurent's direction, baring my teeth at him. Unlike James, Laurent immediately retreated.

James shifted again, testing my concentration. I was in place to answer his maneuver before the motion was complete. His lips pulled back over his teeth.

"I said she's with us," Carlisle repeated, his voice closer to a growl than I'd ever heard it before.

"But she's *human*," Laurent pointed out. There was still no aggression in his mind. He was only baffled and frightened. He couldn't make sense of this situation, but he realized that James's ill-considered offensive might get them all killed. He glanced toward Victoria, checking her reaction much as James had. As if she were some kind of weathervane.

Emmett was the one to respond to Laurent. I didn't know if it was Jasper who made it feel as though the ground shook as he took one step closer to the conflict, or if it was just Emmett being Emmett.

"Yes," he rumbled, his tone absent of all emotion and inflection. The steel of his voice seemed to cut straight through the center of the confrontation, evoking a sudden chill in the air.

I was pretty sure that was Jasper's work, but I didn't split my concentration to be sure.

It was effective. The hunter straightened out of his crouch.

I read his reactions minutely, holding my defensive position against the possibility of a trick. I expected anger, frustration. I'd seen before that he was arrogant, not used to being obstructed. Having to concede to a larger force than his own would surely infuriate him.

But instead, a sudden excitement jolted through his thoughts. Though his eyes never entirely left Bella or me, he was cataloguing in his peripheral vision the threats facing him. Not with fear or annoyance, but with a strange, wild pleasure. His eyes still skipped over Jasper and Alice, seeing them only as numbers in a census. Emmett's threatening mass seemed abruptly exhilarating to him.

"It appears we have a lot to learn about each other," Laurent observed in a mollifying tone.

And then James's inexplicable elation gave way to planning. To strategy. To memories of past victories. And for the first time, I realized—with dread and panic—that he was no mere hunter.

"Indeed," Carlisle agreed, his voice hard.

I desperately wanted to know what Alice was seeing now, but I couldn't afford to miss any detail in my adversary's thoughts.

I listened as he remembered cornering target after target, as he relived the lengths of his more exhaustive pursuits, as he catalogued the opposition he'd overcome to get to his prey. None of the previous challenges were greater than what he was looking at now. Eight—no, seven, he corrected. A coven of seven—certainly with some talents among them—and one helpless human girl who smelled better than any meal he'd had in the last century.

Thrilling.

He couldn't start here, with so many protecting her.

Wait until they separate. Use the time for reconnaissance.

"But we'd like to accept your invitation," Laurent was saying to Carlisle. James was only superficially aware of the conversation; he was absorbed in his planning.

Until Laurent added, "And, of course, we will not harm the human girl. We won't hunt in your range, as I said."

This broke through both James's new exhilaration and his vigilant focus. He turned away from me to stare at Laurent with amazement, but Laurent was facing Carlisle, and he didn't see as the shock turned to loathing.

You dare speak for me?

The heat of his reaction made it clear that the coven would

not stay intact. I heard James's resolution to use Laurent as long as he was convenient, but he would rather kill him than leave him behind when that usefulness was over. It appeared that his desire to destroy Laurent was based entirely on this one comment; I couldn't find another source of resentment. James was easily provoked, I decided, and unforgiving. Perhaps I could use that.

James had no thought of Victoria choosing Laurent. I wondered whether they were a mated pair, but his thoughts didn't give away any special feeling for her. They must have been together longer than the alliance with Laurent. They were the original coven, and he the interloper. It fit with how easily James contemplated disposing of the newcomer.

"We'll show you the way," Carlisle said, less like an offer and more like a command. "Jasper, Rosalie, Esme?"

Jasper didn't like this—separating from Alice, especially when things were going poorly. But he couldn't argue with Carlisle now. We needed to present a united front, and he didn't want to draw attention to himself. Carlisle had no idea of the cover Jasper was generating. Jasper resigned himself to keeping up the concealment as long as necessary; if a fight was coming, he intended it to be an ambush.

He looked at Alice, who nodded at him. She was confident she wasn't in danger. He accepted that but was still unhappy. She darted to Bella's side.

Without needing to discuss, Jasper, Esme, and Rose moved together to obstruct James's view of Bella as they joined Carlisle.

James was not perturbed. His desire to attack had vanished. He was plotting now.

Emmett retreated last, his eyes on James as he moved backward into position beside me.

Carlisle gestured for Laurent and his coven to lead the way out of the clearing. Laurent complied quickly, with Victoria right behind. Her mind was still full of escape routes.

James hesitated for a fraction of a second, and his eyes

returned to us. I knew Bella was invisible behind Emmett, but he wasn't looking for her this time. He stared directly into my eyes and smiled.

Something caught his attention—Alice, uncloaked as Jasper moved away from her. There was a flicker of surprise as he took in her face for the first time, perhaps wondering why he hadn't thought to appraise her before, but that surprise did not resolve into words before he turned and dashed after the others. Carlisle and Jasper ran close on his heels, Rose and Esme following.

I had to work to keep my voice from coming out as a snarl or a shriek. "Let's go, Bella."

She seemed paralyzed. Her wide eyes were so blank that I wondered whether she even understood what I was saying. But I didn't have time to soothe her, or treat her if she were in shock. Right now the only priority was escape.

I took her elbow and pulled her in the opposite direction from where the others had just disappeared. After one staggering step, she found her footing and half ran to keep up with me. Emmett and Alice moved behind us, hiding her, just in case.

I was positive James would not follow Laurent back to our house. When he found an opportunity, he would break off and circle back to catch Bella's trail. I couldn't know how long it would take him to find that opportunity, but I had to act as if he were already watching. If he were, it would be better to let him think that we would move at Bella's speed. I doubted he would be surprised for long when her scent became suddenly tenuous in the trees, but if we could obscure how we were traveling, he would have to pause to reassess.

His thoughts were too far away for me to pinpoint him now, though I had a sense of where the larger group was. I couldn't be positive he was still with them. If he ran up the side of one of these peaks, he'd have a good view of our movements. Still, I chafed at our velocity—or lack thereof.

Emmett and Alice didn't comment on our pace. They were both aware that we might have an audience, though Alice couldn't see clearly what James was doing. His path wasn't going to cross ours here, nor in the near future. She'd only seen the strangers in the clearing in the first place because they had decided to interact with us. It wasn't easy for her to see outsiders unless they were with a member of her family. James would be mostly invisible until he decided to accost one of us.

It seemed hours till we reached the edge of the clearing, but I knew it was really just minutes. As soon as we were deep enough into the trees to be invisible to any watcher, I lifted Bella and settled her against my back. She understood, not too far gone into shock, then. She wrapped her legs tightly around my waist and locked her arms around my neck. Her face was tucked down against my shoulder blade again.

I thought it would feel better, safer, when I was running, when we were racing away from the danger at an acceptable speed, but the momentum did nothing to dissolve the solid block of panic that seemed to weigh me down. I knew this was an illusion—I was flying through the trees as fast as I could go without hurting her—but I couldn't shake the feeling that I was making no progress at all.

Even when the Jeep appeared, and in less than a second I had Bella in the backseat, it felt like I was lagging behind.

"Strap her in," I hissed to Emmett. He'd chosen the back with Bella, recognizing that he would be her bodyguard as long as I needed to drive. He was willing, even eager.

For once, Emmett's disposition toward humor was quelled—a mercy, as I would not have been able to bear it now. His temper was roused, and his thoughts were all directed toward violence.

Alice sat by me, and without my asking, she was sprinting through all the futures we could face now. Mostly there was a dark road ahead of us, flying away under the tires, with no clear destination in mind. But there were other futures going in the wrong direction, back in Forks, inside Bella's home and our own, though I couldn't imagine what would turn me around.

We lurched and careened across the rough road as fast as I

dared go without chancing flipping the Jeep, but it continued to feel like I was losing a race.

While Alice kept searching—there was the blistering sunlight again, why would we choose that kind of location when it would trap us indoors?—I focused on the road. Finally we were back to the highway, and I wished fervently we were in another car, any other—mine, Rose's, Carlisle's. The Jeep wasn't modified for racing. But there was nothing for it.

I was vaguely aware of the sound of my own voice, snarling out half-articulated obscenities, but it felt distant from me, as though not under my control.

That was the only sound besides the roar of the engine, the tires moving against the wet road, Bella's uneven breathing in the back, and her thudding heart.

Alice was seeing a hotel room now, but it could be anywhere. The curtains were closed.

"Where are we going?"

Bella's question sounded like it was coming from a distance, too. My thoughts were too wound up inside Alice's visions or frozen with dread for me to compose an answer. It was almost as if the question didn't apply to me.

Her voice had quavered, little more than a whisper. But now it turned hard.

"Dammit, Edward! Where are you taking me?"

I pulled away from the confusing swirl of Alice's futures so that I could be present. Bella must be terrified.

"We have to get you away from here—far away—now," I explained.

I would have thought the idea of being *far away* would be a welcome one, but she was suddenly shouting, her hands fighting with the harness as she tried to loose herself.

"Turn around! You have to take me home!"

How did I explain to her that she'd lost her home for now, that the loathsome hunter had stolen more than that from her tonight?

The priority for the moment, though, was keeping her from throwing herself out of the Jeep.

Emmett was already wondering if he should restrain her. I spoke his name, low and hard, so he would know that I wanted him to do this. He caught her wrists carefully in his huge hands and immobilized them.

"No! Edward! No," she howled at me. "You can't do this!"

I didn't know what she thought I was doing. Did she think I had a choice? The sound of her anger, her desperation, made it hard to concentrate. It felt like I was the one hurting her, rather than the danger of the tracker.

"I have to, Bella," I hissed. "Now please be quiet." I needed to see what Alice was seeing.

"I won't!" she shouted at me. "You have to take me back—Charlie will call the FBI! They'll be all over your family—Carlisle and Esme! They'll have to leave, to hide forever!"

This was what she was worried about? I supposed it shouldn't surprise me that she was going to pieces over the wrong menace.

"Calm down, Bella. We've been there before." So we had to start over. It seemed a meaningless thing at the moment.

"Not over me, you don't!" she shrieked. "You're not ruining everything *over me*!"

She thrashed against Emmett's hold. The only part of her that was still was her trapped hands. Emmett stared at her, confused.

What am I supposed to do?

Before I could tell Bella why she had it wrong or tell Emmett that he was doing fine, Alice decided to join me in the present.

"Edward, pull over."

The calmness in her voice irritated me. She was thinking about what Bella was saying, though—*clearly*—none of those concerns meant anything. Alice should have known better. Bella didn't grasp what had happened. How could she? She had no context for any of this.

I gunned the engine automatically, suddenly realizing that

Alice didn't have all the context, either. For all her prescience, there were things she couldn't see.

"Edward." Alice was still calm, her tone so reasonable. "Let's just talk this through."

"You don't understand," I exploded. "He's a tracker, Alice, did you *see* that? He's a tracker!"

Emmett reacted more powerfully to the word than Alice did. Because of course she *had* seen that—the moment I'd decided to shout it at her.

We'd not had a great deal of exposure to trackers, aside from stories. The most powerful of them were far away, serving in Italy. Carlisle knew one, but as he was the furthest thing from sociable, none of us had ever met Alistair. Emmett and Alice only knew trackers as those with a talent for finding things, finding people. They didn't understand the concept in the more dynamic sense. James didn't just have a talent for finding people. Tracking was everything to him.

"Pull over, Edward," Alice said, as if I hadn't spoken.

I glowered at her while urging the engine faster.

That's not how tonight goes, she thought with perfect assurance. "Do it, Edward."

"Listen to me, Alice," I seethed, wishing I could put everything I knew directly into her head for once instead of the other way around. She didn't get it. "I saw his mind. Tracking is his passion, his obsession—and he wants her, Alice—*her*, specifically. He begins the hunt tonight."

She was unmoved by my outburst. "He doesn't know where—"

I cut her off, impatient with her refusal to *see*. "How long do you think it will take him to cross her scent in town? His plan was already set before the words were out of Laurent's mouth."

Bella gasped, and then she was shrieking again. "Charlie! You can't leave him there! You can't leave him!"

"She's right," Alice said. Still too calm.

My foot eased off the accelerator without my giving it that

order. Obviously, I couldn't have Charlie in danger, either. But how could I be in two places at once?

"Let's just look at our options for a minute," Alice coaxed.

I was shocked by the image suddenly in her head. I'd not seen her tracing this future—I would have interrupted, and violently, if I had—but she somehow had it all laid out. Complete.

Alice saw one version of the future in which the tracker lost interest and abandoned the chase.

It's meaningless to him without the prize, she explained.

It looked just like the old vision, but I could tell it was new. Freshly generated. Bella, her eyes blazing a red so bright it nearly glowed, her features as sharp as though they had been chiseled from diamond, her skin whiter than ice.

Sure enough, the tracker disappeared from this version of destiny.

And Bella's brilliant eyes stared at me coldly...accusingly.

I wrenched the Jeep onto the shoulder and braked hard. We jerked to a stop.

"There are no *options*," I snarled at Alice.

"I'm not leaving Charlie!" Bella yelled at me.

"We have to take her back," Emmett interjected.

"No."

Emmett looked at me in the rearview mirror. "He's no match for us, Edward. He won't be able to touch her."

"He'll wait." He enjoyed the waiting.

Emmett smiled without amusement. "I can wait, too."

I wanted to rip my hair out in frustration. "You didn't *see*—you don't understand! Once he commits to a hunt, he's unshakable. We'd have to kill him."

Emmett looked at me like I was being slow.

Of course we have to kill him, he thought, but his spoken words were milder. He was being uncharacteristically sensitive, aware of the fragile human he was confining. "That's an option."

"And the female," I reminded him. "She's with him." This

didn't affect Emmett at all, so I added, "If it turns into a fight, the leader will go with them, too," though I doubted that.

"There are enough of us."

Did he count Rose and Esme in his tally? Of course not. He thought he could do it alone, as if they would stand and face him directly, without subterfuge.

"There's another option," Alice repeated.

It's coming anyway. Why not embrace it and make her safe now?

The fury that gripped me felt dangerous, as though I might actually hurt Alice now, despite loving her. I tried to contain it, letting it vent only in words.

"*There is no other option!*" I roared, inches from her face.

Alice didn't flinch.

Don't be stupid about this. There are too many futures, too many twists and turns that I can't unravel. It's too far-reaching. You're right that he won't give up.... Unless he has no motivation to continue.

In Alice's head, I could see decades of James hunting Bella while I tried to hide her. A thousand different traps and ruses. Clearly, he'd be harder to kill than Emmett imagined.

Well, I had no problem being vigilant for decades. I wouldn't trade her life for an easier future.

A small, shaky voice interrupted us.

"Does anyone want to hear my plan?"

"No," I snapped, still glaring at Alice. She scowled back.

"Listen," Bella continued. "You take me back—"

"*No.*"

"You take me back," she insisted, her voice stronger and angrier now. "I tell my dad I want to go home to Phoenix. I pack my bags. We wait till this tracker is watching, and then we run. He'll follow us and leave Charlie alone. Charlie won't call the FBI on your family. Then you can take me any damned place you want."

So she wasn't thinking entirely irrationally, offering herself as a sacrifice in exchange for Charlie's life or our protection. She had a plan.

"It's not a bad idea, really," Emmett mused. He had little faith in the tracker's abilities; he'd rather leave a trail to follow than have no idea from what direction the enemy would appear. He also thought it would be quicker this way, and despite his words before, Emmett really wasn't much for patience.

Alice considered, watching how Bella's resolve shifted her futures. She could see that, if nothing else, the tracker would be there for the performance.

"It might work," she allowed. New visions were crowding fast upon the old. We'd split up, three different directions, leaving only the trail we wanted to leave. She saw Emmett and Carlisle hunting in the forest. Sometimes Rosalie was there, too, sometimes it was Emmett and Jasper, but no grouping held stable.

"And we simply can't leave her father unprotected. You know that," Alice added, still watching the play of the images. This part she was sure of. We would go back and give the tracker something to focus on besides Charlie.

But in these very clear visions, the tracker was too close to Bella. The thought strained my already raw nerves.

"It's too dangerous," I muttered. "I don't want him within a hundred miles of her."

"Edward, he's not getting through us." Emmett was frustrated by what he saw as my trying to prevent a fight. He didn't feel any of the stakes.

Alice worked through the immediate outcomes of this decision—a decision *she* was making now, seeing that I was frozen with uncertainty. There was no version that ended in a fight at Charlie's house. The tracker would only wait and observe.

"I don't see him attacking," she confirmed. "He'll try to wait for us to leave her alone."

"It won't take long for him to realize that's not going to happen."

"I *demand* that you take me home," Bella ordered, working to make her voice sound more assertive.

I tried to think through the haze of panic, desperation, and guilt. Did it make sense to set our own trap rather than to wait for the tracker to set his? That *sounded* right, but when I tried to imagine allowing Bella to be in closer proximity to him, essentially making her bait, I couldn't force the picture into my mind.

"Please," she whispered, and there was pain in her voice.

I thought of the tracker finding Charlie at home alone. I knew *this* must be in the forefront of Bella's mind. I could only imagine how panicked and desperate it would make her. None of my family was vulnerable that way. Bella was my only vulnerability.

We had to lead the tracker away from Charlie. That much was obvious. This was the only part of her plan that actually mattered. But if it didn't work the first time, if the tracker didn't see our performance, I wouldn't push our luck. We'd come up with another version. Emmett could babysit Charlie as long as necessary. I knew he'd be happy to take on the tracker alone. I was also sure, given Jasper's enhancements in the clearing, that the tracker would never willingly put himself within Emmett's reach.

"You're leaving tonight, whether the tracker sees or not," I told Bella, feeling too defeated to look up. "You tell Charlie that you can't stand another minute in Forks. Tell him whatever story works. Pack the first things your hands touch, and then get in your truck. I don't care what he says to you. You have fifteen minutes." I looked in the mirror, meeting her gaze. Her expression was stoic now. "Do you hear me? Fifteen minutes from the time you cross the doorstep."

I revved the engine, then executed a tight U-turn, in a different kind of hurry now. I wanted to get the *bait* part over with as quickly as possible.

"Emmett?" she asked.

I could see in Emmett's mind that she was looking at her fettered hands.

"Oh, sorry," Emmett muttered, freeing her.

He waited for me to object, then relaxed when I didn't.

Now that the decision was made, I focused on Alice's visions again. There weren't very many options, maybe thirty solid versions. In most of them, the tracker would show up at Charlie's house about two minutes after we did, keeping a safe distance. In a few, he came after we were gone. But even in those, he ignored Charlie and followed our trail.

After that, the possibilities narrowed further. We would go home. The tracker would stay even farther back, not wanting to risk a confrontation. The redhead would be waiting for him there. My family would split up. In no version did Laurent help James and Victoria. So we would only have to split into three groups.

The one thing I didn't understand was how the makeup of those three groups kept shifting. It didn't make sense.

Regardless, the next part was very clear.

"This is how it's going to happen," I explained to Emmett. "When we get to the house, if the tracker is not there, I will walk her to the door. Then she has fifteen minutes." I met Bella's eyes in the mirror again. "Emmett, you take the outside of the house. Alice, you get the truck. I'll be inside as long as she is. After she's out, you two can take the Jeep home and tell Carlisle."

"No way," Emmett objected. "I'm with you." *You owe me one, remember?*

It shouldn't surprise me he would want that. This was probably why the future groupings were confused.

"Think it through, Emmett. I don't know how long I'll be gone."

"Until we know how far this is going to go, I'm with you."

There was no wavering in his mind. Maybe it was for the best. I let it go.

In Alice's head, it was Carlisle and Jasper hunting in the forest now.

"If the tracker *is* there," I continued, "we keep driving."

"We're going to make it there before him," Alice insisted.

It was ninety-nine percent certain, but I wasn't taking any chances with some outlier version that was less clear than the others.

"What are we going to do with the Jeep?" Alice asked.

"You're driving it home."

"No, I'm not," she said with absolute certainty.

The vision of how we would divide shifted around again.

I growled a string of archaic curses in her direction.

Bella interrupted in a low voice. "We can't all fit in my truck."

As if we were going to make our escape in that geriatric sloth. I said nothing, though, knowing how sensitive she was about her truck. I didn't have the energy for a pointless argument.

When I didn't respond, she whispered, "I think you should let me go alone."

I'd missed her meaning again. Naturally, she'd think it was her job to sacrifice herself so that Charlie could have a redundant number of bodyguards.

"Bella, please just do this my way, just this once," I begged, though it didn't sound like pleading when the words came through my clenched teeth.

"Listen, Charlie's not an imbecile. If you're not in town tomorrow, he's going to get suspicious."

There were so many layers of meaning I missed entirely with her. Was this the real reason for her willingness to endanger herself, creating a believable alibi for me?

"That's irrelevant," I said in a tone that was intended to sound final. "We'll make sure he's safe, and that's all that matters."

"Then what about this tracker?" she countered. "He saw the way you acted tonight. He's going to think you're with me, wherever you are."

All three of us froze, surprised by this direction. Even Alice. She'd been paying attention to other futures than this conversation.

Emmett embraced the logic immediately. "Edward, listen to her. I think she's right."

"Yes, she is," Alice agreed.

She could see that Bella was right: whichever grouping I was part of was the group the tracker would choose to follow. It would undermine the plan and make an offensive all but impossible. Worst of all, it would make her bait again, and this time there were too many futures to be sure she'd be safe.

But what was the other option? *Leave* Bella?

"I can't do that."

Bella spoke up again, her voice as calm as if her first pronouncement had already been accepted. "Emmett should stay, too. He definitely got an eyeful of Emmett."

"What?" Emmett demanded, stung.

But Alice knew what he was really objecting to. "You'll get a better crack at him if you stay."

The divisions, fluctuating so wildly before, seemed to be settling. She saw me with Emmett and Carlisle, first fleeing through the forest, and then changing course in order to hunt.

Where was Bella in this future?

I stared at Alice. "You think I should let her go alone?"

I saw the answer in her visions before she could say it out loud. A standard room in a mediocre hotel, Bella curled into a tight ball as she slept, Alice and Jasper frozen sentinels in the other room.

"Of course not. Jasper and I will take her."

"I can't do that." But my voice was hollow now. I couldn't see another way. If the tracker was going to choose me as the mark, then I *should* be far away from Bella. I would have to control the panic, the anguish, and be a hunter. I tried to quash the small amount of pleasure in the idea of destroying the vampire who'd ignited this nightmare. Bella's safety was the only factor.

Bella was not done with her suggestions.

"Hang out here for a week," she said quietly. I glanced at her again in the mirror. How little she understood about what had been started tonight. "A few days?" she offered, seeming to think I was objecting to her timeline. I could only pray this would end in a week.

"Let Charlie see you haven't kidnapped me," she continued, "and lead this James on a wild-goose chase. Make sure he's completely off my trail. Then come and meet me. Take a roundabout route, of course, and then Jasper and Alice can go home."

I looked through Alice's reaction to this plan, and felt the first relief of the night when I saw that this was possible. There were futures where I would find Bella with Alice and Jasper. The particular destiny I traced resolved into going underground in the long term. The tracker had evaded me. But there were many other threads weaving and unweaving in her mind. In some of them, I found Bella to take her home. Again, the brilliant sunlight intruded, disorienting me. Where were we?

"Meet you where?" I asked. Bella's decisions were the ones driving the future. She must already know this answer.

Her voice was certain. "Phoenix."

But I'd seen the next act in Alice's head. I'd heard the cover story Bella would give Charlie, and I knew what the tracker would hear.

"No. He'll hear that's where you're going," I reminded her.

"And you'll make it look like that's a ruse, *obviously*." She drew out the last word, sounding annoyed. "He'll know that we'll know that he's listening. He'll never believe I'm actually going where I say I am going."

"She's diabolical," Emmett chuckled.

I was not so convinced. "And if that doesn't work?"

"There are several million people in Phoenix," Bella said, her tone still irritated. I wondered if it was fear that was sapping her patience. I knew it had exhausted mine.

"It's not that hard to find a phone book," I growled.

She rolled her eyes. "I won't go *home*."

"Oh?"

"I'm quite old enough to get my own place."

Alice decided to interrupt our pointless bickering. "Edward, we'll be with her."

"What are *you* going to do in *Phoenix*?"

"Stay indoors."

Emmett didn't have access to Alice's visions, but the picture in his head was close to what I knew was coming. Emmett and I in the forest, hot on the tracker's trail. "I kind of like it," he said.

"Shut up, Emmett."

"Look, if we try to take him down while she's still around, there's a much better chance that someone will get hurt—she'll get hurt, or you will, trying to protect her. Now, if we get him alone..." The picture in his head morphed as he imagined the tracker cornered now, himself closing in.

If we could manage it, if we could deal with the tracker quickly, then this would be the right choice. Why was it so painful to make?

I would feel better if there was any evidence that Bella was concerned about her own safety at all. That she understood everything she was risking. That it wasn't just her own life on the line.

Maybe that was the key. She never worried about herself... but she always worried about me. If I made this about my distress rather than her actual mortal peril, perhaps she would be more cautious.

My control was weak. I spoke in barely more than a whisper, worried that I might scream otherwise. "Bella."

She met my eyes in the mirror. Hers were defensive rather than afraid.

"If you let anything happen to yourself—anything at all—I'm holding you personally responsible," I said softly. "Do you understand that?"

Her lips trembled. Had she finally realized the danger? She swallowed loudly and muttered, "Yes."

Close enough.

Alice's mind was in a million places, many of them a sunny

freeway viewed through dark-tinted glass. Bella always sat in the backseat, Alice's arm around her, staring blankly ahead. Jasper watched from the driver's seat. I thought of my brother, trapped in a small vehicle with Bella's scent for so many hours.

"Can Jasper handle this?" I demanded.

"Give him some credit, Edward," Alice chided. "He's been doing very, very well, all things considered."

But her mind flashed through a dozen future scenes, just in case. Jasper didn't lose focus in a single one.

I appraised Alice. The tiny exterior made her look fragile, but I knew she was a fierce opponent. The tracker or anyone else would underestimate her. That should count for something. Still, I felt uneasy picturing her having to physically protect Bella.

"Can *you* handle this?" I muttered.

Her eyes narrowed in outrage—put on; she'd seen the question coming.

I could take you blindfolded.

She snarled at me, long and loud, a disturbingly ferocious sound that echoed against the Jeep's glass and pushed Bella's heart into a sprint.

For half a second, I couldn't help but smile at Alice's ridiculous display, and then all humor vanished again. How had it come to this? How would I let myself be separated from Bella, no matter how lethal her guardians?

Another unpleasant thought flickered through my brain. Bella and Alice alone, embarking on their foreseen friendship. Would Alice tell Bella *her* solution to this nightmare?

I nodded once, a sharp jerk, to let her know that I'd accepted her role as Bella's protector. "But keep your opinions to yourself," I warned.

23. GOODBYES

THAT WAS THE LAST THING ANYONE SAID AS WE RACED back to Forks. Of course the way would seem much shorter when I was terrified of arriving. All too soon we were pulling up to Bella's home, the lights shining from every window, both upstairs and down. The sounds of a college basketball game drifted from the front room. I strained to hear anything not human in the vicinity, but the tracker didn't seem to have arrived yet. And Alice still could see no future in which this stop turned into an attack.

Maybe we should just stay. Let Bella return to her normal life while the rest of us became perpetual sentries. I could count on Emmett, Alice, Carlisle, Esme—and I was fairly certain Jasper, as well—to join me in such a vigil. The tracker would find it impossible to get to her with so many eyes—and minds—watching. Was unified strength the safer option than dividing into thirds?

But as I considered this, Alice saw how the tracker would wait, how he would adapt. How he would, after the boredom set in, begin a war of attrition. Bella's friends disappearing in the night. Favorite teachers. Charlie's coworkers. Random humans who had no connection to her. The numbers would add up to the point where the resulting scrutiny would force us to disappear, regardless. And I could guess how Bella would feel about all those innocents paying with their lives for her continued safety.

So the original plan would have to be enough.

It was hard to process the strange physical sensation that accompanied this realization. I knew that an actual pit had not opened in the center of my torso, but the impression was unnervingly realistic. I wondered if it was some long-forgotten human response that I'd never felt in my immortal life because I'd never had a reason to panic quite like this.

We needed to move. Though I knew the point was to give the tracker something to follow, I still wanted to have Bella long gone before he could arrive.

"He's not here," I told Emmett. Alice already knew. "Let's go."

Alice and I slid silently from the Jeep, minds ranging through distance and time. Alice saw the tracker showing up while we were still inside. The sound of my teeth grinding seemed extra loud.

"Don't worry, Bella," Emmett was saying—in a voice I found much too upbeat—while he loosed her from the harness. "We'll take care of things here quickly."

"Alice," I hissed.

She darted to the truck, then dropped to the ground and slid under the running boards. In a fraction of a second, she'd pulled herself against the undercarriage, totally invisible, even to a vampire.

"Emmett."

He was already moving, scaling the tree in the front yard. His weight bent the pine noticeably, but he moved on quickly to the next tree over. He would keep moving while we were inside. This was a lot more obvious than Alice's hidden spot, but he'd see anything coming and would be a solid deterrent, if nothing else.

Bella waited for me to open her door. She looked frozen in place with terror, the only movement the slow crawl of tears down her cheeks. She came to life when I reached for her, letting me help her gently from the car. I was surprised by how difficult it was to touch her now, knowing that I was going to leave her.

The heat of her skin burned in a new, painful way. Ignoring this unfamiliar ache, I wrapped my arm around her, hoping my body would shield her, and hurried her to the house.

"Fifteen minutes," I reminded her. It was too much time. I longed to be far away from this targeted place.

"I can do this," she replied in a stronger voice than I expected. There was steel in the set of her jaw.

As we gained the porch, she pulled back against my forward progress. I stopped automatically, though my muscles screamed at the delay.

Her dark eyes were intense as she stared into mine. She reached up to press her palms against either side of my face.

"I love you," she said, her voice a whisper that strained like a scream. "I will always love you, no matter what happens now."

The pit in my stomach yawned open as if it would rip me in half. "Nothing is going to happen to you, Bella," I snarled.

"Just follow the plan, okay?" she insisted. "Keep Charlie safe for me. He's not going to like me very much after this, and I want to have the chance to apologize later."

I didn't know what she meant. My brain was too chaotic with panic to try to decipher her obscure thought processes now.

"Get inside, Bella," I urged. "We have to hurry."

"One more thing—don't listen to another word I say tonight!"

Before I could make any progress in understanding either cryptic request, Bella pushed up onto her toes and crushed her lips against mine with what might be bruising force—for her. More force than I would have ever dared to use with her myself.

Red washed across her cheeks and forehead as she spun away from me. Her tears, which had slowed for our brief and incomprehensible conversation, were flowing freely. I couldn't fathom why she was raising one leg until she kicked violently against the front door—it flew open.

"Go *away*, Edward!" she screeched at top volume. Even over the sound of the TV, there was no way Charlie would miss a word.

She slammed the door shut in my face.

"Bella?" Charlie called out, alarmed.

"Leave me alone!" she shrieked back. I heard her footsteps pound up the stairs, and another slamming door.

Obviously her frozen silence in the Jeep had not been terrified petrification, but rather preparation. She had a script. My role was to be invisible and silent, I guessed.

Charlie ran up the stairs after her, his footsteps lurching and unsteady. I imagined he was only halfway awake.

I scaled the side of the house, waiting beside her window to see if Charlie would follow her into the room. I couldn't see Bella at first, which caused me a spasm of fresh panic, but then she was climbing to her feet beside her bed holding a duffel bag and some kind of small knitted sack.

Charlie's fist hammered against her door. The doorknob rattled—she'd taken the time to lock it—and then the hammering started up again.

"Bella, are you okay? What's going on?"

I slid the window open and ducked inside while Bella yelled, "I'm going home!" in response.

"Did he hurt you?" Charlie demanded through the door, and I winced while I ran to the dresser to help her pack. Charlie wasn't wrong.

Despite that, Bella screamed, "NO!" She joined me at the dresser, seeming to expect to find me there. She held open the duffel bag and I tossed clothes into it, trying to get a variety of items. It wouldn't help her blend in if she only had t-shirts.

The keys to her truck were on the dresser top. I pocketed them.

"Did he break up with you?" Charlie asked in a moderated tone. This question didn't sting.

But Bella's answer was a surprise.

"No!" she yelled again, though I thought maybe this—a breakup—was the easiest excuse. I wondered where the script would lead.

Charlie battered against the door again, the rhythm impatient. "What happened, Bella?"

She yanked futilely on the zipper of the now full duffel bag.

"I broke up with *him*!" she shouted.

I moved her fingers out of the way and fastened the zipper, then weighed the bag in my hand. Was it too heavy for her? She reached for it, impatient, and I put the strap carefully over her shoulder.

I rested my forehead against hers for one precious second.

"I'll be in the truck." My whisper did nothing to hide the desperation in my voice. "Go!"

I urged her toward the door, then dove back out the window so I would be in place when she exited.

Emmett was on the ground, waiting for me. He jerked his chin toward the east.

I cast my mind in that direction, and sure enough, the tracker was little more than half a mile out.

The big one is playing watchman tonight. Patience.

So he'd seen Emmett in the trees, but he couldn't see either of us now. Would he assume I was here, or would he be watching for an ambush? I wished we had Jasper with us now. If we could come at him from three sides…

Edward, Alice cautioned from her hiding place. She thought of the possibilities spinning off from my train of thought. The tracker was slippery. We would leave Bella vulnerable.

"What happened? I thought you liked him," Charlie was demanding. He was back downstairs now.

I made a firm decision about what would happen next.

On it, Alice responded. She slithered out from under the truck and ducked into the Jeep. Once she had it in neutral, she pushed it silently out of the driveway, one hand on the doorframe, the other reaching up as high as she could to move the steering wheel with two fingers. I didn't want the sudden roar of the Jeep's engine to distract Charlie from Bella's performance. It was better if he thought I was already gone.

Emmett watched Alice for half a second, then raised his eyebrows at me. *Do I help her?*

I shook my head. *Charlie*, I mouthed back at him. *Follow on foot.*

He nodded, then leaped up into the tree, where he would be visible again. It would make the tracker keep his distance. He didn't retreat, however, even when he caught sight of Emmett; he was fascinated with the scene playing out and confident he could outrun any sudden pursuit. It made me want to prove him wrong. But I couldn't risk falling into a trap with Bella so near.

"I *do* like him," Bella was explaining, her words muffled and breaking. She was crying freely now, and I knew that she wasn't a good enough actress to fake these tears. The pain in her voice was palpable. The chasm in my stomach twisted in answering agony. She shouldn't have to do this. She was paying for my mistake. My foolishness.

"That's the problem," she railed. "I can't *do* this anymore! I can't put down any more roots here! I don't want to end up trapped in this *stupid*, boring town like Mom! I'm not going to make the same dumb mistake she did. I *hate* it—I can't stay here another minute!"

Charlie's mental response was deeper, more searing than I would have expected.

Bella's weighed-down footsteps moved toward the front door. I climbed silently into the cab of her truck and shoved the key into place, then ducked down. Emmett was close to the front door of the house now, in the shadows. Still, the distance from the door to the truck seemed long. I concentrated on the tracker. He hadn't moved, listening intently to the drama unfolding inside the house.

What would he hear? This much: Bella preparing to escape, to run. Not planning to return in the near future.

He would know that Emmett had seen him. He would have to assume that Bella knew he could hear. Or would he?

"Bells, you can't leave now," Charlie said quietly, urgently. "It's nighttime."

“I’ll sleep in the truck if I get tired.”

Charlie imagined his daughter unconscious in the dark cab of the truck, on the side of a freeway in the middle of nowhere, while all around her, dark, amorphous shapes crept closer and closer. It wasn’t an entirely coherent nightmare, but my own panic, savage and irrational, echoed his own.

“Just wait another week,” he begged. “Renée will be back by then.”

Bella’s footsteps stuttered to a halt. There was a low sound—her shoe squeaking as she turned around to face him?

“What?”

I slid back out of the truck, and hesitated in the middle of the front yard. What would I do if his words confused her, delayed her? Did she realize the tracker was near?

“She called while you were out.” Charlie was tripping over his words, rushing to get them out. “Things aren’t going so well in Florida, and if Phil doesn’t get signed by the end of the week, they’re going back to Arizona. The assistant coach of the Sidewinders said they might have a spot for another shortstop.”

Charlie and I both waited, not breathing, for her response.

“I have a key,” she muttered, and her footsteps were now at the door. The knob started to turn. I darted back to the truck.

Her words sounded like a weak excuse. The tracker would have to assume this was a story for Charlie and the opposite of the truth.

The door didn’t open.

“Just let me go, Charlie,” Bella said. I could tell she meant the words to sound angry, but the pain in her voice overwhelmed any other emotion.

The door swung open at last. Bella shoved through, Charlie right behind her, his hand outstretched. She seemed aware of that hand, cringing away from it.

I crouched against the floorboards, mostly invisible. I couldn’t help peeking out the window. Without turning to look at her father, Bella growled, "It didn't work out, okay?" She jumped off the porch, but Charlie was motionless now. "I really, really *hate* Forks!"

The words seemed simple enough, but crushing anguish speared Charlie through where he stood. His mind swirled, almost like vertigo. In his thoughts was another face, so much like Bella's and also tearstained. But this woman's eyes were pale blue.

It seemed Bella had scripted these words with care. Charlie stood, stunned and splintering, as Bella ran awkwardly across the small lawn, the heavy duffel compromising her balance.

"I'll call you tomorrow!" she yelled back toward Charlie while she heaved the bulky bag into the bed of the truck.

He hadn't recovered enough to respond.

I could no longer doubt that Bella understood the gravity of the situation. I knew she would never cause anyone this kind of pain, especially not her father, if there were any other way at all.

I'd put her in this hellish position.

Bella ran around the front of the truck. The quick, fearful glances she threw over her shoulder now were not for Charlie. She yanked the truck door open and jumped into the driver's seat. She reached to turn the key as if knowing it would be waiting for her in the ignition. The engine's roar shattered the silence of the night. This would be easy enough for the tracker to follow.

I reached out to brush the back of her hand, wishing I could comfort her, but knowing nothing could make this better.

As soon as she'd reversed out of the driveway, she dropped her right hand from the wheel so that I could hold it. The truck chugged down the street at its maximum speed. Charlie didn't leave his post at the door, but the street curved and we were quickly out of view. I moved into the passenger seat.

"Pull over," I suggested.

She blinked hard against the tears that streamed down her face and then splashed off the rain jacket she still wore. She passed Alice, without seeming to notice the Jeep on the side of the road. I wondered whether she could see at all.

Alice, still pushing the Jeep so the noisy engine wouldn't alert Charlie, easily kept up with us.

"I can drive," Bella insisted, but her words broke and dragged. She sounded exhausted.

She barely registered surprise when I pulled her gently over my lap and eased into the driver's position. I kept her close beside me. She drooped there, wilting.

"You wouldn't be able to find the house," I said as my excuse, but she didn't seem to be waiting for a reason. She didn't care.

We were far enough from the house now (though I could still hear Charlie's frozen thoughts, motionless in the doorway) that Alice jumped up into the Jeep and started the engine. When the headlights came on behind us, Bella stiffened and twisted to stare out the back window, heart thudding.

"It's just Alice." I took her left hand now and squeezed it.

"The tracker?" she whispered.

He's following now. Alice could hear Bella's whisper easily over the grind of the engine. *Emmett's waiting till he's clear of the house.*

"He heard the end of your performance," I told her.

"Charlie?" Her voice strained raw.

Alice kept me updated. *The tracker's past the house. I don't see him going back. Em's catching up.*

"The tracker followed us," I assured Bella. "He's running behind us now."

This did not comfort her. Her breath caught and then she whispered, "Can we outrun him?"

"No," I admitted. Not in this ridiculous truck.

Bella turned to watch out the window, though I was sure the Jeep's headlights would blind her to everything else. Alice was watching all the futures related to Charlie that she could perceive. A human she'd never met was not the easiest subject for her. But it didn't look as if the hunter or his apprehensive companion had any plans to return.

Emmett was running in the road close behind us now. I was

surprised at his intentions. I would have expected he'd be itching to catch the tracker in pursuit, to bring this ordeal to a quick and violent end. Instead, his thoughts were focused on Bella. His few moments as bodyguard seemed to have affected him deeply. Her safety was his current priority.

Bella brought out everyone's protective side.

Emmett was imagining the tracker watching; only Alice and I knew he was carefully keeping his distance, just following the sound of the truck through the darkness. He wouldn't put himself in closer range tonight. Still, Emmett wanted to make it clear that the tracker would have to go directly through him to get to Bella. He made a running leap that propelled him over the Jeep and into the bed of the truck. I fought with the steering as the truck reacted.

Bella shrieked, her voice rasping with the effort.

I covered her mouth, muffling the sound so she could hear me. "It's Emmett," I said.

She inhaled through her nose, slumping again. I freed her mouth and pulled her tight against my side. It felt as if every muscle in her body were trembling.

"It's okay, Bella. You're going to be safe," I murmured. It didn't feel like she'd even heard me speak. The tremors continued. Her breath came quick and shallow.

I tried to distract her. Speaking in my normal voice, as though there were no danger or terror, I said, "I didn't realize you were still so bored with small-town life. It seemed like you were adjusting fairly well—especially recently. Maybe I was just flattering myself that I was making life more interesting for you."

Perhaps it was not the most sensitive observation, considering how her escape had upset her, but it did pull her from her abstraction. She fidgeted, sitting up a little straighter.

"I wasn't being nice," she whispered, ignoring my frivolous words and going straight to the painful part. She stared down as if ashamed to meet my gaze. "That was the same thing my mom said when she left him. You could say I was hitting below the belt."

I'd assumed it was something like that, given the image in Charlie's head.

"Don't worry, he'll forgive you," I promised.

She looked up at me earnestly, desperate to believe what I was saying. I tried to smile at her, but I couldn't force my face to obey.

I tried again. "Bella, it's going to be all right."

She shuddered. "But it won't be all right when I'm not with you." Her words were barely more than a breath.

My arm flexed around her convulsively while the hole in my stomach stretched wider. Because she was right. Everything would be wrong when she wasn't with me. I didn't quite know how I would function.

I forced my face smooth and made my voice as light as I could. "We'll be together again in a few days." As I said the words, I willed them to be true. They still felt like a lie. Alice saw so many different futures.... "Don't forget," I added, "this was your idea."

She sniffed. "It was the best idea. Of course it was mine."

I attempted to smile again, then gave up.

"Why did this happen? Why me?" She whispered the questions flatly, as though they were rhetorical.

I answered anyway, my voice sharp-edged. "It's my fault. I was a fool to expose you like that."

She stared up at me, surprised. "That's not what I meant."

What other reason could there be? Whose fault but my own?

"I was there," she continued. "Big deal. It didn't bother the other two. Why did this James decide to kill *me*?" She sniffled again. "There're people all over the place, why me?"

It was a fair question, an astute question. And there were more answers than one. She deserved a full explanation.

"I got a good look at his mind tonight. I'm not sure if there's anything I could have done to avoid this, once he saw you. It *is* partially your fault." My voice twisted and I hoped she could hear the black humor in it, the irony. "If you didn't smell so appallingly luscious, he might not have bothered. But when I defended you..." I remembered his incredulity, his indignation even, that I would stand in his way. The arrogance, the ire. "Well, that made it a lot worse. He's not used to being thwarted, no matter how insignificant the object. He thinks of himself as a hunter and nothing else. His existence is consumed with tracking, and a challenge is all he asks of life. Suddenly we've presented him with a beautiful challenge—a large clan of strong fighters all bent on protecting the one vulnerable element. You wouldn't believe how euphoric he is now. It's his favorite game, and we've just made it his most exciting game ever."

No matter how I analyzed it, there was no way around this. Once I'd taken her to the clearing, this was the only outcome. If I hadn't opposed him, perhaps it wouldn't have triggered his love of the game.

"But if I had stood by," I muttered, mostly to myself, "he would have killed you right then."

"I thought...," she whispered, "I didn't smell the same to the others." She hesitated. "As I do to you."

"You don't." What she was to me, simply physically, was something more intense than I'd ever seen in any other immortal's mind. "But that doesn't mean that you aren't still a temptation to every one of them. If you *had* appealed to the tracker, or any of them, the same way you appeal to me, it would have meant a fight right there."

Her body shuddered against mine.

It would have been easier, though, I realized now, if it had come to a fight. I felt certain the frightened redhead would have run, and I doubted that Laurent would have stood with the tracker when it was an obviously losing prospect. Even if they'd all joined in, they could never have survived. Especially with Jasper launching a surprise attack from the midst of his smokescreen while all eyes were riveted on Emmett. I'd seen enough of his memories to believe that Jasper could probably have handled all three. Not that Emmett would have let him.

And if we were a normal coven (though we could never be considered normal at our size), we probably would have attacked just for the insult.

But we weren't normal, we were civilized. We tried to live to a higher standard. A gentler, more peaceable standard. Because of our father.

Because of Carlisle, tonight we had hesitated. We had chosen the more humane route, because that was our habit, our way of life.

Did that make us…weaker?

I flinched at the thought, but then immediately decided that our choice was still the right one, even if it did make us weak. I could feel that. It resonated deeply in my mind, my being…or my soul, if such a thing existed. Whatever it was that drove this corporeal form.

It didn't matter now. Alice might give us some power over the future, but the past was as lost for us as it was for anyone else. We had *not* attacked, and now we had the more complicated version still ahead. The coming fight could not be avoided.

"I don't think I have any choice but to kill him now," I murmured. "Carlisle won't like it."

But he would understand, I was sure. We'd given this tracker the option to walk away. He wasn't going to take us up on the offer. There was only kill or be killed now.

"How can you kill a vampire?" Bella's voice was a whisper. I could still hear the sound of suppressed tears in it.

I should have anticipated the question.

She stared up at me with a different kind of fear than before, almost as though she was concerned the task would fall to her. Of course, I could never be sure with Bella.

I made no attempt to soften the realities. "The only way to be sure is to tear him to shreds, and then burn the pieces."

"And the other two will fight with him?"

"The woman will." If she could control her terror, that is. "I'm not sure about Laurent. They don't have a very strong bond—he's only with them for convenience. He was embarrassed by James in the meadow." Not to mention that James had made plans to kill Laurent. Perhaps I'd tip him off; that was sure to shift alliances.

"But James and the woman—they'll try to kill you?" she whispered, her voice distorted by pain.

And then I understood. Of course she was panicking about the wrong thing as usual.

"Bella, don't you *dare* waste time worrying about me," I hissed. "Your only concern is keeping yourself safe and—please, please—*trying* not to be reckless."

She ignored that. "Is he still following?"

"Yes. He won't attack the house, though. Not tonight."

Not while we were together. Was our splitting up exactly what the tracker wanted? But I remembered what Alice saw happening if we tried to guard Bella here. I had no love for Mike Newton, but neither he nor anyone else in Forks was an acceptable sacrifice.

I turned off onto the drive, dully noting that there was no sense of relief in reaching my home. There was no space out of harm's way while the tracker lived.

Emmett was still riled. I wished I could tell him the tracker's location to ease his agitation, but I couldn't risk being overheard. The tracker had guessed that we had extra abilities—it would only help him if we gave clues as to what they were.

I noticed his thoughts drifting to the edges of my hearing just as Alice chimed in.

He meets the female now, on the other side of the river. They split up again and watch. She takes the mountainside; he takes the trees.

The extra distance didn't make me feel any better.

Emmett's overzealous bodyguard mindset was operating at full steam by this point. As we rolled up to the house, he leaped from the truck bed and paced to the passenger side. He wrenched the door open and reached for Bella.

"Gently," I reminded him almost silently.

I know.

I could have stopped him. This wasn't necessary. But then, was any precaution too much at this point? If I'd been more cautious, we wouldn't be in this predicament.

It did feel safer in a strange way to see Emmett, massive and indestructible, cradling Bella in his colossal arms—she was barely visible behind them. He ducked through the front door before a second had passed. Alice and I were at his sides instantly.

The rest of my family was gathered in the living room, all on their feet, and in the middle of their circle, Laurent.

His thoughts were frightened, apologetic. The fear was only heightened when Emmett set Bella carefully on her feet beside me and took a deliberate step forward, a bass growl building in his chest. Laurent took a quick half step back.

Carlisle gave Emmett a warning look, and he settled back on his heels. Esme stood close to Carlisle's side, her eyes flashing from my face to Bella's and then back again. Rosalie was also staring at Bella, *glaring* at Bella, but I ignored her as best I could. I had more important things to deal with.

I waited until Laurent's eyes flickered to me.

"He's tracking us," I told him, prompting the thoughts I wanted to hear.

Of course he's tracking the human. And he'll find her. "I was afraid of that," he said aloud.

I need to get out of the way, his thoughts continued. *James can't think I've chosen another side. The last thing I need is him looking for me afterward.* Laurent suppressed a shudder. *Perhaps I could tell him I'm just gathering info. His face, though, when he divided from us in the woods... Better to disappear while he's caught up in this hunt.*

My teeth were grinding again. Laurent eyed me nervously.

He knew James well enough to understand the rupture he'd caused in the clearing. Though I felt no desire to do him favors, I knew he'd be grateful enough when James was dead.

"Come, my love," I heard Alice whisper in Jasper's ear. I hadn't noticed him especially as we came in; he was still camouflaging himself. Jasper didn't question Alice now, even in his thoughts. The two of them darted up the stairs hand in hand. Laurent didn't bother to watch them leave, so effective was Jasper's effort. I saw that Alice would write down the necessary information so Laurent could not overhear. It wouldn't take her long to pack what they would need.

"What will he do?" Carlisle demanded of Laurent, though I could have answered as well.

"I'm sorry," Laurent said with every sign of sincerity. *Sorry I ever met those demons. I should have known better than to play with fire. Damned boredom made me foolish.* "I was afraid, when your boy there defended her, that it would set him off." *Of course it would. He ensured James would never quit till they were both dead. It's as if these strangers live in some other world. Or think they do. The real world is about to intrude on that fantasy.*

"Can you stop him?" Carlisle pressed.

Ha! "Nothing stops James when he gets started."

"We'll stop him," Emmett growled.

Laurent eyed Emmett almost hopefully. *If only it were possible. It would certainly make my life easier.*

"You can't bring him down," Laurent warned. He seemed sure he was doing us a great favor by giving us this information. "I've never seen anything like him in my three hundred years. He's absolutely lethal. That's why I joined his coven."

A few scattered memories of his adventures with James and Victoria ran through his head, though Victoria was always a background figure, on the fringes. James had kept Laurent's life interesting, at least, but the sadism of these rampages had begun to bother Laurent in the last few years. By that point, there hadn't been a safe way to disengage himself.

He wished he could feel optimistic now, but he'd seen James triumph over impressive odds. His eyes turned to Bella, and all he saw was a human girl, one of billions, nothing to distinguish her from any of the others.

He didn't think the words before he spoke them aloud. "Are you sure it's worth it?"

The roar that ripped through my teeth was as loud as a detonation. Laurent immediately slid into a submissive posture, while Carlisle held his hand up.

Control, Edward. This one is not our enemy.

I worked to calm my fury. Carlisle was right, though Laurent was certainly not our friend, either.

"I'm afraid you're going to have to make a choice," Carlisle said.

There aren't many choices left to me, Laurent thought. *I can only make myself scarce and hope James doesn't think I'm worth the trouble.* His mind ranged back over the slightly less fraught conversation they'd been having before our arrival and fastened on one piece of information. *I've clearly burned my bridges with this company, but perhaps I could surround myself with other friends. Talented friends.*

"I'm intrigued by the life you've created here." He felt he was choosing his words very diplomatically, trying to make eye contact with each of us. My access to his inner monologue rather ruined the effect for me. "But I won't get in the middle of this. I bear none of you any enmity, but I won't go up against James. I think I will head north—to that clan in Denali." He imagined five strangers like Carlisle, slow to attack, but with great numbers and talents among them. Perhaps that would give James pause.

A feeling of gratitude had Laurent turning to warn Carlisle again. "Don't underestimate James. He's got a brilliant mind and unparalleled senses. He's every bit as comfortable in the human world as you seem to be, and he won't come at you head-on." A few of James's convoluted ploys ran through his memory.

The tracker had patience...and a sense of humor. A dark one.

"I'm sorry for what's been unleashed here," Laurent continued. "Truly sorry."

He inclined his head, submissive again, but his eyes darted to Bella and away, his thoughts mystified by the risk we were taking for her sake. *They don't understand about James,* he decided. *They don't believe me. I wonder how many of them he'll leave alive.*

Laurent thought us weak. He saw our apparent domesticity as a deficiency. I'd worried the same thing earlier, but not now. *Weak* was not the impression I planned to leave with James. But let Laurent believe James would win. He could hide in terror for the next century and I would not mourn his discomfort.

"Go in peace," Carlisle said, both offer and command.

Laurent's eyes swept through the room, appreciating a kind of life he'd left behind long ago. Though this was not a palace, and he'd lived in several, there was an atmosphere of permanence and sanctuary here that he'd not felt in centuries.

He nodded once at Carlisle, and for a brief moment, I felt a strange kind of yearning from the dark-haired vampire toward my father. A sense of respect and a desire to belong. But he quashed the emotion before it could take root, and then he was racing out the door, with no intention of slowing until he was safely in the ocean, his scent untraceable.

Esme dashed across the living room to start the steel shutters rolling down the huge windows that comprised the back wall of the house.

"How close?" Carlisle asked me.

Laurent was almost outside my range and not slowing. He had no desire to run into James on his way out. He'd hear nothing we said. I reached for James. Alice's vision had given me the direction. It was far enough that he, too, would not be able to hear our plans.

"About three miles out past the river. The tracker is circling around to meet up with the female."

He would join her on higher ground, where he could watch in which direction we ran.

"What's the plan?" Carlisle asked.

Though I knew the tracker couldn't hear, and the shutters were still groaning, I kept my voice low. "We'll lead him off, and then Jasper and Alice will run her south."

"And then?"

I knew what he was asking. I looked straight into his eyes as I answered. "As soon as Bella is clear, we hunt him."

Though Carlisle knew this was coming, he still felt a flare of pain. "I guess there's no other choice."

Carlisle had been scrupulously protecting life for three centuries. He'd always been able to find common ground with other vampires. This would not be easy for him, but he was no stranger to difficulty.

We needed to hurry, not to give the tracker any more time than necessary before we gave him a trail to chase. But there were practicalities we needed to address before we could run.

I caught Rose's eye. "Get her upstairs and trade clothes."

Confusing the scent was the obvious first step. I'd take something of Bella's with me, too, and create a trail that would goad the tracker forward.

Rosalie knew this, but her eyes flashed with disbelief.

Don't you see what she's done to us? She's ruined everything! And you want me to protect *her?*

She spit the rest of her answer aloud, resolved that Bella would hear it, too. "Why should I? What is she to me? Except a menace—a danger you've chosen to inflict on all of us!"

Bella jerked as if Rosalie had slapped her.

"Rose...," Emmett murmured, putting one hand on her shoulder. She shook it off. Emmett's eyes cut to me, half expecting me to spring at her.

But none of this mattered. Rose's spoiled temper tantrums had always been irritating, but this petty flare-up was ill timed, and time was something I didn't have enough of.

If she'd decided to cease being my sister tonight, that was her choice and I accepted it.

"Esme?" I knew what her response would be.

"Of course!"

Esme understood the time limits. She lifted Bella carefully into her arms, much as Emmett had, though the effect was very different, and flew up the stairs with her.

"What are we doing?" I heard Bella ask from Esme's office.

I left Esme to it, and focused on my part. The tracker and his wild partner had moved outside my range. They couldn't hear us, but I was sure they could see us. They would see our vehicles leave. And they would follow.

What do we need? Carlisle asked.

"The satellite phones. The larger sports bag. Are the tanks full?"

I'll do it. Emmett sprinted out the front door toward the garage. We always kept several gas drums ready for emergencies.

"The Jeep, the Mercedes, and her truck, too," I whispered after him.

Got it.

We're splitting into three? Carlisle was also wary of dividing our force.

"Alice sees it's the best way."

He accepted that.

He'll get hurt. He doesn't think. He just rushes in. This is all her fault!

Rosalie was assailing me with a torrent of grievances. I found it easy to tune her out. Easy to pretend she wasn't even there.

What's my part? Carlisle wanted to know.

I hesitated. "Alice saw you with Emmett and me. But we can't leave Esme alone to watch Charlie. . . ."

Carlisle turned to Rosalie with a stern expression. "Rosalie. Will you do your part for our family?"

"For *Bella*?" She sneered the name.

"Yes," Carlisle responded. "For our family, as I said."

Rosalie glared at him resentfully, but I could hear her

pondering the options. If she protracted this fit, turned her back on all of us, then Carlisle would certainly stay here with Esme rather than be on the front line, keeping Emmett from dangerous excesses. Rosalie saw only the danger to Emmett. But part of her was growing nervous about my visible detachment.

She finally rolled her eyes. "Of course I won't let Esme go alone. *I* actually care about this family."

"Thank you," Carlisle responded—with more warmth than I would have bothered with—and then dashed out of the room.

Emmett was just coming through the front door with the large bag we kept some of our sports toys in slung over his shoulder. The bag was big enough to fit a small person. Bulky with equipment, it looked like there might already be someone inside it.

Alice appeared at the top of the stairs, just in time to meet Bella and Esme as they emerged from Esme's office. Together, they lifted Bella by the elbows and rushed her down the stairs. Jasper followed. He was clearly on edge, tightly wound, his eyes roaming restlessly across the windows at the front of the house. I tried to use his savage appearance to calm myself. Jasper was more lethal than the thousands of vampires who'd tried to destroy him. Today he'd exhibited new skills I'd never imagined, and I was sure he had other tricks up his sleeve. The tracker had no idea what he was up against. Bella would be safer with Jasper standing guard than anyone. And with Alice beside him, the tracker couldn't take them by surprise. I tried to believe that.

Carlisle was already back with the phones. He gave Esme one, and then brushed her cheek. She looked up at him with total confidence. She was sure we were doing the right thing, and because of that, we would be successful. I wished I had her faith.

She handed me a wad of fabric. Socks. Bella's scent was fresh and strong. I shoved them in my pocket.

Alice took the other phone from Carlisle.

"Esme and Rosalie will be taking your truck, Bella," Carlisle told her, as if asking permission. It was so like him.

Bella nodded.

"Alice, Jasper—take the Mercedes. You'll need the dark tint in the South."

Jasper nodded. Alice already knew this.

"We're taking the Jeep. Alice, will they take the bait?"

Alice concentrated, her hands clenched into fists. It wasn't a simple process, looking for maneuvers that never actually came in contact with any of us, but she was tuning in to these new enemies. She'd get better with time. Hopefully we wouldn't need that. Hopefully we would end this tomorrow.

I saw the tracker flying through the treetops, focused on the fleeing Jeep. The redhead keeping her distance, following the sound of Bella's truck as it chugged north a few minutes later. There were only the smallest of variations.

By the time she relaxed her vigil, we were both positive.

"He'll track you. The woman will follow the truck. We should be able to leave after that."

Carlisle nodded. "Let's go."

I thought I was ready. The passing seconds were already pounding in my head like drumbeats. But I wasn't.

Bella seemed so forlorn at Esme's side, her eyes bewildered, as if she couldn't process how everything had changed so quickly. Only an hour ago, we were perfectly happy. And now she was hunted, left to vampires she barely knew for her protection. She'd never looked so vulnerable as she did standing there, alone in a room full of inhuman strangers.

Could a dead heart break?

I was at her side, my arms tight around her, pulling her off the ground. Her warmth in my arms was quicksand and I *wanted* to drown in it, to never pull free. I kissed her just once, worried that the plans would all crumble into chaos if I couldn't make myself step away from her. Part of me didn't care if every human life in Forks and La Push and Seattle were sacrificed to keep her by my side.

I had to be stronger than that. I would end this. I would make her safe again.

It felt as though all the cells in my body were dying off one by one as I set her back on her feet. My fingers lingered against her face, and then stung as I forced them free.

Stronger than this, I reminded myself. I had to shut down all this agony so I could do my job. Destroy the danger.

I turned away from her.

I'd thought I'd known what burning felt like.

Carlisle and Emmett fell into step beside me. I took the bag from Emmett. I knew what the tracker expected—that I would be too weak to let her out of my sight. I cradled the bag as though it contained something infinitely more precious than footballs and hockey sticks as I rushed down the front steps flanked by my brother and my father.

Emmett climbed into the backseat of the Jeep and I placed the bag upright beside him, then quickly slammed the door, trying to look stealthy about it. I was in the driver's seat in a flash, Carlisle already beside me, and then we were jolting up the drive at a pace that would have horrified Bella if she'd actually been there with us.

I couldn't think like that. I had to trust Alice and Jasper and keep my head focused on my part.

The tracker was still too far away for me to hear him. But I knew he was watching, following. I'd seen it in Alice's head.

Turning north onto the freeway, I accelerated. The Jeep was a lot faster than the truck, but it wasn't fast enough to get any headway, even at the maximum speed I could chance without risking the engine. But I didn't want to outrun the tracker now. He would only see that I was pushing the Jeep hard, as though escape were truly the motive. I hoped he wouldn't realize I'd chosen the Jeep for just this purpose. He didn't know what else I had in my garage.

For just a flicker, he was close enough to hear.

...take a ferry? It's a long way around otherwise. I could cut through....

"Make the call," I said, barely moving my lips, though I knew he was too far behind us to see my face.

Carlisle didn't bring the phone to his ear; he kept it by his thigh, out of sight, as he dialed one-handed. We all heard the quiet click as Esme picked up. She said nothing.

"Clear," Carlisle whispered. He disconnected.

And I was disconnected, too. I had no way to see what she was doing now. No chance to hear her voice. I shoved the despair away from me before I could start wallowing.

I had a job to do.

24. AMBUSH

THE TRACKER CHOSE TO RUN BEHIND US, UNWILLING TO guess at our route. Every now and then I would catch the edge of his thoughts, but never more than a few words, or a view of the Jeep. He followed on higher ground, in the mountains, unconcerned when it took him miles from the road. He could still see us.

I didn't want to think about where Bella was now, what she might be doing and saying. It would be too distracting. But there were a few things left undone.

I whispered instructions to Carlisle and he typed messages to Alice's phone. It probably wasn't necessary, but it made me feel better.

"Bella needs to eat at least three times every twenty-four-hour period. And hydration is important. She should have water on hand. Ideally eight hours of sleep."

Carlisle, still keeping the phone low, texted as quickly as I could speak.

"And..." I hesitated. "Tell Alice not to talk about our conversation before in the Jeep. If Bella has questions, deflect them. Tell her I'm very serious about this."

Carlisle looked at me curiously, but typed my message.

I imagined Alice on the other end, rolling her eyes.

She only texted back the letter *y* in acknowledgment. I took that to mean that Bella was still awake, and Alice intended to keep my instructions to herself. She must see an unpleasant reckoning if she ignored me.

Emmett was mostly thinking about what he would do when he had the tracker in his grasp. His imaginings were pleasant to watch.

When we had to refuel, I used one of the large gas cans Emmett had loaded into the backseat. In my pocket, Bella's socks would leave the faintest trace of her scent in the air. I moved in a blurred rush, as if my only goal was to race away again, and I was pleased when the tracker came closer to watch. For a moment, he was no more than a mile away. I wanted to take advantage, to flip this flight into an ambush, but it was too soon. We were still too near the water.

I didn't try to be evasive about our route, driving in the straightest line the curving freeways allowed toward my destination. I hoped the tracker would interpret this the way I wanted him to—that I had a destination in mind, somewhere defensible, somewhere I felt safe. He knew little about us, but he knew this much: We had more physical assets available to us than the average nomad. Also, we were many. Perhaps he would imagine even more allies waiting in the forests to the north.

And I *had* considered running toward Tanya's family. I was sure they would help. Kate, particularly, would be an excellent addition to our hunting team. But they were also too close to the water. The tracker might take one look at the five of them and break for the ocean. All he'd need to do to disappear was submerge. It was impossible to track someone underwater. And he could come out anywhere—five miles down the beach, or in Japan. We'd never be able to follow. We'd have to regroup and start over.

I was headed toward the national parks near Calgary, more than six hundred miles from the nearest open water.

Once we turned on the tracker, he would know that he'd been

led astray, and Bella wasn't with us. He would run, and we would chase. I felt confident I could outrun him, but I needed a course with enough length. Six hundred miles gave me some padding.

I wanted to finish this quickly.

We drove through the night, only decreasing our speed occasionally when I heard a speed trap waiting ahead. I wondered what the tracker made of that. He'd already guessed I had extra abilities. This was surely giving away more than I wanted to, but the other option was too slow. Let him see this—my giving up information about my advantages—as another sign that we were intent on some specific destination. A safe house? That would have to make him curious.

I wished I could hear the theories in his head, but he kept back just far enough for me to see only the sporadic glimpse. He must have formed a theory about my talents, and he probably wasn't far off.

The tracker ran on, tireless, and from the little I could hear, enjoying himself immensely.

His enjoyment irritated me, but it was a good thing. As long as he was content with what he was currently doing, it gave me time to get to my chosen arena for our ambush.

As the time passed, though, I got nervous. The sun was closer to the western horizon than the eastern. We'd done nothing interesting but stop to refuel a few times—always leaving hints of Bella's scent. But would this long run bore him? Would he be willing to follow for potentially days and days, through the northern territories and into the Arctic Circle if we kept going? Could he abandon his chase before he was absolutely sure Bella wasn't in the Jeep?

"Ask Alice if she sees the hunter quitting before we're set."

Carlisle complied quickly.

A few minutes later, the letter *n*.

That settled my nerves.

The sun moved slowly closer to the western mountains as we neared my target. I wanted to get him close enough for me to hear him. I needed to do something to interest him.

We were on a small freeway that led to Calgary. We could have continued to Edmonton, waited for full dark, but I was getting more and more anxious. I wanted to stop running away and start hunting.

I turned off onto a small side road that led into the southernmost end of Banff National Park. The road did curve around eventually back to Calgary, but it wasn't the fastest way to get anywhere. It represented a new behavior we hadn't exhibited up to this point. That would have to pique his interest.

Carlisle and Emmett knew what the change meant. Both were suddenly tense. Emmett was more than just tense—he was thrilled, eager to get to the fight.

This side road took us quickly away from the barren, early spring farmlands that lined the road to Calgary. We'd started climbing immediately, and now we were surrounded by trees again. It looked quite similar to home, but drier. I couldn't hear another mind anywhere nearby. The sun was on the other side of the mountain we were climbing.

"Emmett," I breathed. "I'll buy you a new Jeep."

He chuckled once. *No worries.*

We could pretend to stop for gas again—it was nearly time—but this change of pace would have the tracker on edge. We'd have to move fast.

"On my word," I told them, waiting for the first touch of the tracker's mind.

Emmett's hand was on the door handle.

This road was much rougher than the last. I hit a rut that had the Jeep jolting out of our lane. As I worked to control the vehicle, suddenly the tracker's voice was there.

...must have a place close...

"*Go*," I snarled.

We all three threw ourselves out of the speeding Jeep.

I landed on the balls of my feet, and I was sprinting toward the sound of the tracker's thoughts before the others had got their balance.

Oh ho, a trap after all!

The tracker did not sound either upset or frightened by the sudden reversal in roles. He was still having fun.

I pushed myself, blurring through the trees we'd just driven past. I could hear Carlisle and Emmett behind me, Emmett charging through the underbrush like a rhinoceros. His louder attack might cover some of the sounds of my own. Maybe the tracker would think I was farther back than I actually was.

It was a great relief to run, to move under my own propulsion, after the long drive stuck inside the Jeep. It was a relief not to have to rely on road, but just to take the shortest route toward my target.

The tracker was fast, too. It didn't take long before I was glad I'd given myself six hundred miles to catch him.

He curved west toward the far-distant Pacific as we climbed higher into the eastern edge of the Rockies.

Carlisle and Emmett were falling farther behind. Was that the tracker's hope? Separate us and take us out one at a time? I was on my guard, waiting for another sudden turnabout. I welcomed the idea of his attack. Part of me was full of fury, another part was just anxious to finish this.

I couldn't hear his mind—he was slightly out of range—but I could follow his scent easily enough.

His path turned northward.

He ran and I ran. Minutes passed, then hours.

We veered northeast.

I wondered whether he had a plan or was just running aimlessly to throw me off.

I could barely hear Emmett's charge through the forest. They had to be several miles back now. But I thought I could hear something ahead. The tracker moved quietly, but not silently. I was gaining on him.

And then the noise of his progress was gone completely.

Had he stopped? Was he waiting to attack?

I ran faster, eager to spring his trap.

And then I heard a faraway splash at the same time I crested a snow-dusted ridge that broke off in a steep cliff.

Far below, a deep glacial lake, long and narrow, almost like a river.

Water. Of course.

I wanted to dive after him, but I knew that would give him the advantage. There were miles of bank where he could emerge. I would have to be methodical, which would take time. He had no such impediments.

The slow way was to run the perimeter of the lake, looking for traces of him. I'd have to be careful not to miss his exit. He wouldn't walk up onto the bank and start running again. He'd try to leap out, to put some distance between the water's edge and his scent.

The slightly faster way was to split the distance with Emmett and Carlisle; we could cut the perimeter into thirds.

But there was also the *fastest* way.

Emmett and Carlisle were getting closer. I ran back to Carlisle, my hand stretched out in front of me. It only took him a second to understand what he wanted. He tossed me the phone. I turned again and ran with them, texting Alice.

Tell me which one of us finds the trail.

We reached the overlook of the long lake.

"Emmett," I breathed almost silently. "You decide to take the south bank from this point and then follow it around to the east. Carlisle, decide to run the north along this bank. I'll take the far side."

I pictured it, committed to it, diving into the dark blue water, shooting across to the opposite shore, then running north to meet up with Carlisle at the far tip of the lake.

The phone vibrated silently.

Em, she texted. *Southern tip.*

I showed them her text, and then handed the phone back to Carlisle. He had a waterproof bag to protect it. I dove, and heard Emmett push off behind me. I held myself straight as a knife, determined to cut into the water with as little sound as possible.

The water was very clear, and just a few degrees warmer than freezing. I swam several yards below the surface, invisible in the night. I could make out the sound of Emmett behind me, but he was nearly silent. I couldn't hear Carlisle at all.

I slipped out of the lake at its southernmost point. The only sounds behind me were the drops of water falling off Emmett and hitting the stony bank.

I took the right, and Emmett the left.

There was a ripple as Carlisle emerged. I glanced back. The phone was in his hand again, and he was motioning to Emmett. I'd chosen the right way. Sure enough, only a few yards farther and I caught the hint of the tracker's scent. It was above us—he'd leaped into the branches of a tall lodgepole pine. I scaled the tree and found his trail leading off through the branches of the surrounding trees.

And then I was on the chase again.

I fumed as I flew through the branches. We'd lost enough time with the lake that he was many miles ahead now.

He was doubling back the way we'd come. Would south be his choice? Back to Forks to find Bella's trail? It was a solid seven-hour trek, if run straight. Would he want to give me that long a chance to catch up to him?

But as the endless night wore on, he changed direction a dozen times. He moved predominantly west, easing his way toward the Pacific, I imagined. And he kept finding ways to build his lead, to slow us.

Once it was a wide cliff. We each decided the directions we would search at the base, but Alice just kept texting *n n n n n*. Her view of the tracker was so limited, she could only see how we reacted to his trail. It took too long for me to see the damage in the cliff face where he'd broken his fall halfway down and then scaled sideways across the stone.

Another time he found a river. Again, we exhaustively imagined the routes we'd go searching. He stayed in the water for a very long way. We lost nearly fifteen minutes before Alice saw that Carlisle would find the tracker's trail thirty-six miles southwest.

It was maddening. We ran and swam and swung through the forest as fast as we were able, but he just toyed with us, constantly building his lead. He was very practiced and, I was sure, quite confident in his success. The advantage was entirely his now. We'd keep lagging behind, and eventually he'd be able to lose us completely.

The thousands of miles between Bella and me kept me always anxious. This plan, leading him away, was turning out to be no more than a minor delay in his real search.

But what else could we do? We had to keep chasing after him and hope we could somehow catch him out. This was supposed to be our big chance to stop him without endangering Bella. We were doing a pathetic job.

He confused the trail again in another miles-long glacial lake. There were dozens just like this, all raking north to south through the Canadian valleys as if a giant hand had gouged its fingers down the center of the continent. The tracker took advantage of them often, and each time we had to imagine and decide, then wait for Alice's *C* or *Em* or *Ed*, a *y* or an *n*. We got faster at the mental part, but every pause put him farther ahead.

The sun rose, but the clouds were thick today and the tracker didn't slow. I wondered what he would have done if the sun was shining. We were on the west side of the mountains now, and running into human towns again. Probably he would have just quickly slaughtered any witnesses if he'd had to.

I was certain he was heading for the ocean and a clean getaway. We were much closer to Vancouver now than to Calgary. He didn't seem interested in moving south, back to Forks. There was a slight northern trend.

Honestly, he didn't need any more stratagems. He had enough of a lead to just race flat out to the coast with no chance of us catching up.

But then the trail led into yet another lake. I was ninety percent sure that he was toying with us simply for his own entertainment. He could have escaped, but it was more fun to make us jump through his hoops.

I could only hope that his arrogance would somehow backfire, that he'd make a bad choice that would put him within our reach, but I doubted it. He was too good at this game.

And we kept following. Giving up didn't feel like a valid option.

Midmorning, Esme texted. *Can you talk?*

Is there any chance he'll hear me? Carlisle wanted to know.

"If only," I sighed.

Carlisle called Esme and they spoke while we ran. She had no real news, she was mostly worried about us. The redhead was still in the area, but she wouldn't come within five miles of Esme or Rosalie. Rosalie had done some scouting, and it appeared the redhead had gone to the high school in the night, and through most of the public buildings in town. She'd hadn't gone north toward our house again, and she'd only gone as far south as the municipal airstrip, but she seemed to be hiding herself to the east, maybe keeping close to Seattle for a bigger hunting ground. She'd tried Charlie's house one time, but not until he'd left for work. Esme had never been more than a few yards from Charlie throughout, which was impressive, since he had no idea she was there.

There was nothing more, no clues. She and Carlisle exchanged pained *I love you*s, and then we were back to the mind-numbing chase. The tracker was headed north again, enjoying himself too much to take the easy escape.

It was midafternoon when we came to another lake, crescent-shaped and not as large as the others he'd used to slow us. Without having to discuss it, we each decided to follow our usual search routes. Quickly, Alice responded *Em*. Backtracking to the south, then.

Once we had his scent again, it led us through a small town

tucked into a mountain pass. It was big enough for a light flow of traffic on the narrow streets. We had to slow down—and I hated that, even though I knew it didn't matter. We were too far behind for our speed to make any difference. But it soothed me to think that he'd probably had to move at human speed, too. I wondered why he would bother. Maybe he was thirsty. I was sure he knew he had time to stop for a bite.

We darted from building to building, trusting my senses to let us know if anyone was watching, running when we could. We were obviously not dressed warmly enough for the weather here—and if anyone looked closely, we were also soaking wet—and I tried to weave us around human vantage points to avoid catching any attention.

We made it to the outskirts of town without discovering any fresh corpses, so he must not have been looking to quench his thirst. What was he seeking, then?

To the south now.

We followed his trail to a large, rough shed in the middle of an open field, thick with thorny brambles that were still winter bare. The wide doors to the shed were propped open. The inside of the shed was mostly empty, just stacks of mechanical and automotive clutter lining the walls. The scent led into the shed and was more set into the ground here, as if he'd lingered for a moment. I could only think of one reason, and I searched for the scent of blood. Nothing. All I could smell was exhaust... gasoline....

I felt sick as I realized what I hadn't seen at first. With a low oath, I darted out of the shed and vaulted over the tall brambles. Emmett and Carlisle followed, back on high alert after the stupefying hours of failure.

And there, on the other side, was a long line of flattened dirt, rolled as smooth as possible, about two hundred feet wide, stretching at least a mile to the west.

It was private airstrip.

I cursed again.

I'd been too focused on the water escape. There was an air escape, too.

The plane would be tiny and slow, not much faster than a car. No more than one hundred forty miles an hour, if it was in good condition. The slipshod little hangar made me think it probably wasn't. He'd have to stop for gas frequently if he intended to go far.

But he could go in any direction at all, and we had no way to follow.

I looked at Carlisle, and his eyes were just as disappointed and hopeless as mine.

Will he go back to Forks to try to pick up her trail?

I frowned. "It would make sense, but it seems a little obvious. Not quite his style."

Where else can we go?

I sighed.

Should I?

I nodded. "Make the call."

He pressed the redial button. It only rang once.

"Alice?"

"Carlisle," I heard her breathe.

I leaned closer, anxious, though I could already hear.

"Are you totally secure?" he asked.

"Yes."

"We lost him about a hundred seventy miles northeast of Vancouver. He took a small plane. We have no idea where he's headed."

"I just saw him," she said urgently, and also totally unsurprised by our failure. "He's headed to a room somewhere, no clues to the location, but it was unusual. Mirrors covering the walls, a gold band around the middle of the room, like a chair rail, mostly empty but for one corner with an old AV set up. There was another room, too, a dark room, but all I could see was that he was watching VHS tapes. I have no idea what that means. But whatever made him get in that plane...it was leading him to those rooms."

It wasn't enough information to help. The tracker could be planning to enjoy some downtime, for all we knew. Maybe he wanted to make us wait, make us stew. Ratchet up our anxiety. It seemed in line with his personality. I pictured him in an empty house somewhere random, watching old movies while we crawled out of our skins awaiting his return. This was exactly what we'd wanted to avoid.

The good news was that Alice was seeing him independently of us now. I could only hope that with continued familiarity, she would get a better line on him. I wondered whether there was any significance to the rooms she described that would tie back to us. Maybe it meant that we would eventually hunt him down to one of those places. If Alice got a better view of the surroundings, it was a possibility. That was a comforting thought.

I held my hand out for the phone, and Carlisle handed it over.

"Can I speak to Bella, please?"

"Yes." She turned her head away from the receiver. "Bella?"

I could hear Bella's feet thudding as she ran awkwardly across the room, and if I hadn't been so demoralized, I would have smiled.

"Hello?" she asked breathlessly.

"Bella." Relief saturated my voice. The brief separation had already taken a toll.

"Oh, Edward," she sighed. "I was so worried!"

Of course. "Bella, I told you not to worry about anything but yourself."

"Where are you?"

"We're outside of Vancouver. Bella, I'm sorry—we lost him." I didn't want to tell her how he'd toyed with us. It would make her nervous that he'd gotten the upper hand so easily. It made *me* nervous. "He seems suspicious of us—he's careful to stay just far enough away that I can't hear what he's thinking. But he's gone now—it looks like he got in a plane. We think he's heading back to Forks to start over." Well, we had no other theories, anyway.

"I know. Alice saw that he got away," she said with perfect composure.

"You don't have to worry, though," I assured her, though she didn't sound worried. "He won't find anything to lead him to you. You just have to stay there and wait till we find him again."

"I'll be fine. Is Esme with Charlie?"

"Yes—the female has been in town. She went to the house, but while Charlie was at work. She hasn't gone near him, so don't be afraid. He's safe with Esme and Rosalie watching."

"What is she doing?"

"Probably trying to pick up the trail. She's been all through the town during the night. Rosalie traced her through the airport...." The airstrip to the south of town. Maybe we weren't wrong about his intentions after all. I continued before Bella could notice my distraction. "All the roads around town, the school...she's digging, Bella, but there's nothing to find."

"And you're *sure* Charlie's safe?" she demanded.

"Yes, Esme won't let him out of her sight. And we'll be there soon." We were definitely headed there now. "If the tracker gets anywhere near Forks, we'll have him."

I started to move, loping south. Carlisle and Emmett followed suit.

"I miss you," she whispered.

"I know, Bella. Believe me, I know." I couldn't believe how diminished I felt apart from her. "It's like you've taken half my self away with you."

"Come and get it, then," she suggested.

"Soon, as soon as I possibly can. I *will* make you safe first," I vowed.

"I love you," she breathed.

"Could you believe that, despite everything I've put you through, I love you, too?"

"Yes, I can, actually." It sounded like she was smiling as she spoke.

"I'll come for you soon."

"I'll be waiting," she promised.

It hurt to end the call, to disconnect from her again. But I was in a hurry now. I passed the phone back to Carlisle without looking, and then pushed my lope into a sprint. Depending on how difficult it was for the tracker to locate fuel, we might actually be able to beat him back to Forks, if that was where he was going.

Carlisle and Emmett worked to keep up.

We were back in Forks in three and a half hours, taking the fastest route straight through the Salish Sea. We went directly to Charlie's house, where Esme and Rosalie were on watch, Esme in the back of the house, and Rosalie in the tree in the front yard. Emmett went quickly to join her while Carlisle and I went to Esme.

Now that I was here to appreciate them, Rosalie was thinking bitter thoughts about how selfishly I was putting everyone's lives in danger. I paid no attention to her.

Bella's house was ominously quiet, though there were several lights on downstairs. I realized what was missing—the sound of a game from the TV in the living room. I found Charlie's mind in its usual spot, sitting on the sofa, facing the dark TV. His thoughts were totally silent, as though he had gone numb. I winced, glad Bella didn't have to see this.

It took only a few seconds of discussion, and then we scattered. Carlisle stayed with Esme, and I felt much better that he was there with her. Emmett and Rosalie did a sweep through the center of town and then searched the area around the airstrip, looking for an abandoned prop plane.

I ran east, following the redhead's trail. I wouldn't mind cornering her. But her scent only led into the Puget Sound. She wasn't taking any chances.

I swept the familiar Olympic Park on my way back to Charlie's, just to see if the redhead had gone anywhere interesting, but she seemed to have made a beeline for the Sound. She wasn't the type to risk a confrontation.

Back at Bella's house, I took over watch while Esme and Carlisle scouted north to see if the redhead had emerged from the water near Port Angeles and was trying to come at Charlie from another angle. I doubted it, but we had nothing better to do. If the tracker wasn't coming back to Forks—which seemed evident at this point—and the redhead had gone to meet him, then we would have to regroup and come up with a new plan. I hoped someone else had an idea, because my head was a blank.

It was nearly two-thirty in the morning when my phone buzzed quietly. I accepted the call without looking, expecting a report from Carlisle.

Alice's voice erupted from the phone, trilling with speed.

"He's coming here, he's coming to Phoenix, if he's not already here—I saw the second room again, and Bella recognized the sketch, it's her mother's house, Edward—he's coming after Renée. He can't know we're here, but I don't like Bella so close to him. He's too slippery, and I can't see him well enough. We've got to get her out of here, but somebody's got to find Renée—he's going to spread us too thin, Edward!"

I felt dizzy, dazed, though I knew it was an illusion. There was nothing wrong with my mind or my body. But the tracker had gone around me again, circling, always in my blind spot. Whether by design or by luck, he was about to be in the same place as Bella while I was fifteen hundred miles away from her.

"How long till he's there?" I hissed. "Can you nail it down?"

"Not perfectly, but I know it's soon. No more than a few hours."

Was he flying straight there? Had he been leading us farther away from her on purpose?

"None of you have gone near Renée's house?"

"No. We've not set foot anywhere outside this hotel. We're nowhere close to the house."

It was too far to make running an efficient option. We'd have to fly. And a big plane was the fastest way.

"The first flight to Phoenix leaves Seattle at six-forty," Alice told me, a step ahead. "You'll need to cover up. It's ludicrously sunny here."

"We'll leave Esme and Rosalie here again. The redhead won't come near them. Get Bella ready. We'll keep the same groups. Emmett, Carlisle, and I will take her somewhere far away, somewhere random, till we can figure out the next step. You find her mother."

"We'll be there when you land."

Alice hung up.

I started running, dialing Carlisle as I sprinted for Seattle. They'd have to catch up to me.

25. RACE

Even when the plane's wheels touched the tarmac, my impatience refused to ebb. I reminded myself that Bella was surely less than a mile distant now and it wouldn't be many minutes more before I could see her face again, but that only made the urge stronger to rip the emergency door off its hinges and sprint to the building rather than wait through the interminable taxiing. Carlisle could feel my agitation in my absolute stillness, and he nudged my elbow lightly to remind me to move.

Though our row's window shade was down, there was an excess of direct sunlight in the plane. My arms were folded so that my hands were hidden, and I'd let the hood of my airport-shop hoodie fall forward to keep my face in shadow. We probably looked ridiculous to the other passengers—especially Emmett, bulging out of a sweatshirt that was several sizes too small—or as though we thought we were some kind of celebrities hiding behind our hoods and dark glasses. More probably northern bumpkins who had no frame of reference for spring temperatures in the Southwest. I caught one man thinking that we'd all remove the sweatshirts before we made it down the length of the jetway.

The plane in the air had felt unbearably slow; this taxiing might kill me.

Just a little more restraint, I promised myself. She'd be there at the end of this. I'd take her away from here, and we'd hide together while we figured this out. The thought soothed me a tiny amount.

In reality, it took very little time for the plane to find its assigned gate, open and ready. There were a million possible delays that hadn't gotten in our way. I should have been grateful.

We were even fortunate enough to end up at a gate on the north side of the airport, tucked into the late-morning shadow of the larger terminal. That would make it easier for us to move fast.

Carlisle's fingers rested lightly on my elbow while the crew took its time going through checks. Outside the plane, I could hear the mechanical Jetway maneuvering into place, and the knock against the hull when that was achieved. The crew ignored the sound, the two forward-cabin stewards staring together at a passenger list.

He nudged me again, and I pretended to breathe.

Finally, the steward approached the door and worked to heave it out of the way. I desperately wanted to help him, but Carlisle's fingertips on my arm kept me focused.

With a hiss, the door opened, and warm outside air mixed with the stale cabin air. Stupidly, I searched for some trace of Bella's scent, though I knew I was still too far. She'd be deep inside the air-conditioned terminal, past the security post, and her pathway there would follow a route from some distant parking garage. Patience.

The seat belt light turned off with a tinny ding, then all three of us were moving. We eased around the humans and were at the door so quickly that the steward took a surprised step back. It moved him out of our way, and we took advantage of that.

Carlisle tugged the back of my sweatshirt, and I reluctantly let him pass me. It would only make a few seconds' difference if he set the pace, and certainly he would be more circumspect than I. No matter what the tracker did, we had to adhere to the rules.

I'd memorized the layout of this terminal in the onboard pamphlet, and we'd been loosed into the branch closest to the exit. More good luck. Of course I couldn't hear Bella's mind, but I should be able to find Alice and Jasper. They'd be with the other families waiting to greet passengers, just up ahead to the right.

I'd started to edge ahead of Carlisle again, anxious to finally see Bella.

Alice's and Jasper's minds would stand out from the humans' like spotlights surrounded by campfires. I'd be able to hear them any—

The chaos and agony of Alice's mind hit me then, like a sudden vortex erupting out of a calm sea, sucking me under.

I staggered to a stop, paralyzed. I didn't hear what Carlisle said, barely felt his attempts to pull me forward. I was vaguely aware of *his* awareness of the human security officer eyeing us suspiciously.

"No, I've got your phone right here," Emmett was saying too loudly, providing an excuse.

He grabbed me under one elbow and started to move me forward. I scrambled to find my footing while he half carried me, but I couldn't quite feel the floor under me. The bodies around me seemed translucent. All I could really see was Alice's memories.

Bella, pale and withdrawn, twitching with nerves. Bella, desperate-eyed, walking away with Jasper.

A memory of a vision: Jasper rushing back to Alice, agitated.

She didn't wait for him to come to her. She followed his scent to where he waited outside a women's restroom, face clouded with concern.

Alice following Bella's scent now, finding the second exit, darting at a speed that was a little too conspicuous. The hallways full of people, the crowded elevator, the sliding doors to the outside. A curb teeming with taxis and shuttles.

The end of the trail.

Bella had vanished.

Emmett propelled me into the giant, atrium-like space where Alice and Jasper waited tensely in the shadow of a massive pillar. The sun slanted down at us through a glass ceiling, and Emmett's hand on my neck forced me to bow my head, to keep my face in shadow.

Alice could see Bella a few seconds from now, in a taxi, speeding along a freeway through brilliant sunlight. Bella's eyes were closed.

And in just a few minutes more: a mirrored room, fluorescent tubes bright overhead, long pine boards across the floor.

The tracker, waiting.

Then blood. So much blood.

"Why didn't you go after her?" I hissed.

The two of us weren't enough. She died.

I had to force myself to keep moving through the pain that wanted to freeze me into place again.

"What's happened, Alice?" I heard Carlisle ask.

The five of us were already moving in an intimidating formation toward the garage where they'd parked. Thankfully, the glass ceiling had given way to simpler architecture, and we were out of danger from the sun. We moved faster than any of the human groups, even the late ones running past us for their connections, but I chafed at the speed. We were too slow. Why pretend now? What did it matter?

Stay with us, Edward, Alice cautioned. *You're going to need us all.*

In her mind: blood.

To answer Carlisle's question, she shoved a piece of paper into his hand. It was folded into thirds. Carlisle glanced at it and recoiled.

I saw it all in his head.

Bella's handwriting. An explanation. A hostage. An apology. A plea.

He passed the note to me—I crumpled it in my hand, shoved it into my pocket.

"Her mother?" I growled softly.

"I haven't seen her. She won't be in the room. He may have already..."

Alice didn't finish.

She remembered Bella's mother's voice on the phone, the panic in it.

Bella had gone to the other room to calm her mother. And then the vision had overtaken Alice. She hadn't put the timing together. She hadn't seen.

Alice was spiraling in guilt. I hissed, low and hard.

"There's not time for that, Alice."

Carlisle was almost inaudibly muttering the pertinent information to Emmett, who had become impatient. I could hear his horror as he understood, his sense of failure. It was nothing compared to mine.

I could not let myself feel this now. Alice saw the tightest of windows. It was maybe impossible. It was absolutely impossible that we could catch up to Bella before her blood started flowing. Part of me knew what this meant, that there would be a gap of time between the tracker's finding her and her death. A wide gap. I couldn't allow myself to understand.

I had to be fast enough.

"Do we know where we're going?"

Alice showed me a map in her head. I felt her relief that she'd gotten the most vital information in time. After the first vision, but before the call from Bella's mother, Bella had given her the crossroads near the place the tracker had chosen to wait. It was just under twenty miles, with freeway almost all the way. It would only take minutes.

Bella didn't have that long.

We were through the baggage claim area and into the elevator bay. Several groups with carts loaded with suitcases were waiting for the next set of doors to open. We moved in synchronization to the stairwell. It was empty. We flew upward and were in the garage in less than a second. Jasper started for where they'd left the car, but Alice caught his arm.

"Whatever car we take, the police are going to be searching for its owners."

The brilliant freeway gleamed in her mind, blurring with speed. Blue and red lights spinning, a roadblock, some kind of accident—it wasn't totally clear yet.

They all froze, not sure what this meant.

There was no time.

I moved too fast down the line of cars while the others recovered and followed at a more judicious pace. There weren't many people in the garage, none who could see me plainly.

I heard Alice instructing Carlisle to retrieve his bag from the trunk of the Mercedes. Carlisle kept a medical kit in every car he drove in case of emergencies. I didn't let myself think about that.

There wasn't time to find the perfect option. Most of the cars here were bulky SUVs or practical sedans, but there were a few options a little faster than the others. I was hesitating between a new Ford Mustang and a Nissan 350Z, hoping Alice would see which would serve better, when the hint of an unexpected scent caught my attention.

As soon as I smelled the nitrous, Alice saw what I was looking for.

I darted to the far end of the garage, right up to the edge of the intruding sunlight, where someone had parked their souped-up WRX STI far away from the elevators in hopes that no one would park next to it and ding the paint.

The paint job was hideous—violently orange bubbles the size of my head rising from what appeared to be deep purple lava. I'd never seen a car so conspicuous in a hundred years.

But it was obviously well maintained, somebody's baby. Nothing was stock, everything designed for racing, from the splitter to the huge aftermarket spoiler. The windows were tinted so dark I doubted they were legal, even here in this land of sun.

Alice's vision of the road ahead was much clearer now.

She was already beside me, some other car's broken-off antenna in hand. She'd flattened it between her fingers and shaped a small hook at the end. She popped the lock before Jasper, Emmett, and Carlisle, black leather satchel in hand, caught up to us.

Ducking into the driver's seat, I wrenched off the casing on the steering column and twisted the ignition wires together. Next to the gearshift was a second stick, this one topped with two red buttons labeled "Go Go 1" and "Go Go 2"—I appreciated the owner's commitment to upgrades, if not his sense of humor. I could only hope the nitrous canisters were full. The gas tank was at three quarters, plenty more than I needed. The others climbed into the car, Carlisle in the passenger seat and the rest in the back, and the engine was thrumming eagerly as we reversed into the aisle. No one blocked my way. We tore down the length of the enormous garage toward the exit. I clicked on the heating button on the dash. It would take a moment for the nitrous to heat from gas to liquid.

"Alice, give me thirty seconds ahead."

Yes.

The descent was a tight corkscrew that spiraled down four floors. Midway, I ran up against the back of an Escalade on its way out, as Alice had seen I would. The way was so narrow I had no option but to ride its tail and try to startle the other driver with one long honk. Alice saw that wouldn't work, but I couldn't resist.

We spun out of the last curve into a wide, sunlit payment bay. Two of the six lanes were empty, and the Escalade headed for the closest. I was already to the last kiosk.

A thin red-and-white-striped arm stretched across the lane. Before I could even really consider ramming through it, Alice was shouting at me in her head.

If the police start chasing us now, we don't make it!

My hands clenched the neon orange steering wheel too hard. I forced my fingers to relax while I pulled up to the automated window. Carlisle grabbed the ticket, stuck behind the visor in an obvious way, and held it out to me.

Alice snagged it. She could see I was as likely to put my fist through the card reader as I was to wait patiently for the machine to work. I drove another two feet forward so Jasper could roll down his window and pay with one of the no-name cards we used to stay anonymous.

He'd pulled his dark sleeve to his fingertips. There was the barest glimmer as he reached out the window to shove the ticket into the slot.

I concentrated on the striped arm. It was the checkered flag. As soon as it lifted, the race was on.

The card reader made a whirring sound. Jasper punched a button.

The arm popped up and I hit the accelerator.

I knew the road. Alice had seen the length of it and everything in our way. It was the middle of the day and the traffic wasn't terrible. I could see the holes in the pattern.

It took me twelve seconds to shift through the gears until I was in sixth. I didn't plan to shift down again.

The first section of the freeway was mostly empty, but a merge loomed ahead. Not enough time to make full use of a NOS canister. I veered to the far left to get around the influx.

I could say this for Arizona: The sun might be ridiculous, but the freeways were exceptional. Six wide, smooth lanes, with shoulders ample enough on either side that it was as good as eight. I used the left shoulder now to streak by two pickups who thought they belonged in the fast lane.

Everything was flat and sun-blasted around the highway, wide open with no place to hide from the light, the sky an enormous pale blue dome that seemed almost white in the glaring heat. The whole valley was bared to the sun like food in a broiler. A few twiglike trees scarcely clinging to life were the only features breaking up the dull expanses of gravel. I couldn't see the beauty Bella saw here. I didn't have time to try.

My speed was up to one twenty. I could probably get another thirty out of the STI, but I didn't want to push her too hard yet.

There was no way to know if the engine had been tuned to stage two or three; it would be touchy, unstable. I could only watch the oil pressure and temperature and listen carefully to how hard the engine was working.

The huge, arcing overpass that would carry us to the north-bound freeway was approaching, and it was only one lane. With a very wide right shoulder.

I skidded back across the six lanes to make the exit. A few cars swerved in surprise, but they were all a distance behind me by the time they reacted.

Alice saw that the shoulder was not quite wide enough.

"Em, Jazz, I'm going to lose the side mirrors," I growled. "Give me a view."

They both twisted in their seats to stare at the road to the left, right, and behind. The view in their minds gave me a much better range than the mirrors anyway.

I flew alongside the slower traffic, unable to keep my speed over a hundred. I gritted my teeth and held tight to the wheel as I scraped by the wide van that was riding the right lane line. With a screech of metal, my left mirror ripped off against the van's side, and my right mirror exploded against the concrete barrier.

Bella was running across a white-hot sidewalk, stumbling. Or she would be soon.

"Just the road, Alice," I spit through my teeth.

Sorry. I'm trying.

Her panic bled through her thoughts. Bella was running into a parking lot. Or would be soon.

"Stop!"

She closed her eyes and tried to see nothing but the pavement ahead.

I knew these images had the power to render me useless. I forced them out of my mind.

It wasn't as hard to do as I expected.

Everything was the road. I could see it in three hundred sixty degrees and thirty seconds into the future. As I merged onto the northbound freeway, drifting across the lanes to the left shoulder again, up to one thirty now, it felt like our minds were bound together into one perfectly focused organism, greater than the sum of its parts. I saw the patterns in the traffic ahead, shifting and congealing, and I could see the right way through every snarl.

We flew through the shade of two separate overpasses so quickly that the flash of darkness felt like strobing.

One forty-five.

Fifteen seconds ahead of me, the perfect bubble of space opened. I swerved into the center lane and flipped the clear safety cover off the bright red "Go Go 1" button.

The timing was perfect. The exact instant I was clear, I punched the button, the NOS spray hit, and the car shot forward as if fired from a cannon.

One fifty-five.

One seventy.

Bella was opening a glass door into a dark, empty room. Or would be soon.

Alice refocused, also surprised at the ease of doing so. Her thoughts flickered to Jasper, and I understood.

As a man of peace, Jasper struggled. But as a man of war, he was more than I'd ever imagined.

We were all sharing his battle focus now, something he'd used to keep his newborns on track back in his war years. It worked perfectly in this vastly different situation, blending us into one hyperfunctional machine. I embraced it, letting my mind spear-point our charge.

The hit of nitrous was already waning.

One fifty.

I searched for the next opportunity.

They're setting up the first roadblock, Alice noted. Neither of us was concerned. They were building it too close to intercept us. We'd be past it before they could pull it together.

And the second. She showed me the spot on the map in her

head. Far enough ahead that it would be a problem, even with another window opening in just four seconds.

I considered my options while Alice showed me the consequences. The time was too short—we had no choice but to switch cars.

Abstracted, I flipped up the safety and depressed "Go Go 2." The STI kicked forward obediently.

One seventy.

One eighty.

Alice showed me the specific vehicles available ahead and I sifted through our choices.

The Corvette would be cramped, and our combined weight would be more of a factor than it was with this street racer. I mentally drew a line through a few other vehicles. And then Alice saw it—a glossy black BMW S1000 RR. Top speed one ninety.

Edward, it's impossible.

The image of myself astride the sleek black motorcycle was so appealing that for a second I ignored her.

Edward, you're going to need every one of us.

Suddenly her thoughts were full of mayhem and blood, human and inhuman screaming, the sound of shredding metal. Carlisle was at the center, his hands dyed glistening red.

Jasper kept me from steering off the road. His grip on my emotions was so strong in that second that it felt like a fist clenched tight around my throat.

Together we forced my mind back to the lanes in front of me. It was the shortest part of the journey we'd have left; the car didn't matter so much. Alice flipped through sedans, minivans, and SUVs.

There it was. A brand-new Porsche Cayenne Turbo, too new for plates yet—top speed one eighty-six—already adorned with a stick-figure family on the back window. Two daughters and three dogs.

A family would slow us. Alice used my decision to take this

car and looked ahead into what that meant. Luckily there was only the driver inside. A thirty-something female with a dark brown ponytail.

Alice couldn't see Bella on the sidewalk anymore. That part was past now. As was the parking lot. Bella was inside with the tracker.

I let Jasper keep me focused.

"We're changing cars under the next overpass," I warned them.

Alice assigned our roles in a trilling voice, the words flowing faster than the speed of a hummingbird's wings.

Carlisle dug through his bag.

Emmett flexed unconsciously.

I overtook the white SUV, hating the necessity of slowing down to pace it. Every second I lost, Bella would pay for in pain. Against all my instincts, I shifted down to fourth gear.

The BMW motorcycle sped out of reach. I repressed a sigh.

The overpass was half a mile ahead. The shadow that it threw was only fifty-three feet long; the sun was almost directly above us now.

I started to crowd the Cayenne toward the left. She changed lanes. I followed quickly, then straddled the lane lines so that I was halfway into hers. She started to slow and so did I.

Alice helped me time it. I pulled slightly ahead of the Cayenne and then steered left again, forcing my way into her lane while decelerating sharply. The driver slammed on the brakes.

Just behind us, the Corvette I'd considered before swerved into another lane, laying on the horn as he passed. The whole traffic amoeba lurched to the right as one to avoid us.

We came to a full stop in the last ten feet of shade.

All of us exited simultaneously. Curious faces flew by us at seventy miles per hour.

The driver of the Cayenne was climbing out of her car, too, her face in a scowl and her ponytail swinging with rage. Carlisle darted forward to meet her. She had one second to react to the fact that the most handsome man she'd ever seen was responsible for running her off the road, and then she was collapsing into him. She probably hadn't even had time to feel the prick of the needle.

Carlisle carefully laid her unconscious body on the raised concrete shelf beside the shoulder. I took the driver's seat. Jasper and Alice were already in the back. Alice had the door open for Emmett. He was crouched beside the STI, his eyes on Alice, waiting for her command. Alice watched the traffic racing toward us for the moment of least damage.

"Now," she cried.

Emmett flipped the gaudy STI into the oncoming traffic.

It rolled into the second and third lanes from the right. A prolonged series of crunches began as car after car slammed on the brakes and then slammed into the car in front of them anyway. Airbags popped loudly from the dashboards. Alice saw injuries, but no fatalities. The police, already racing after us, were only seconds away.

The sounds faded. Carlisle and Emmett were in their seats and I was racing forward again, desperate to make up for the seconds we'd lost here.

The tracker loomed over Bella. His fingers stroked her cheek. It was only seconds away.

One sixty-five.

On the other side of the divided highway, four patrol cars screamed in the other direction, headed for our accident. They paid no attention to the soccer mom SUV speeding north.

Only two more exits.

One eighty.

I couldn't feel any strain in the SUV, but I knew the danger now lay not in engine failure—it would take a lot to compromise this German-built tank—but in the integrity of the tires. They weren't manufactured for this kind of speed. I couldn't risk blowing any of them, but it was physically painful to ease my foot back from the gas pedal.

One sixty.

Our exit was racing toward us. I whipped around a semi and swerved to the right.

Alice showed me the setup. An intersection spanned the length of the overpass. At the top of this exit, a streetlight was just turning yellow. In one second, the west side of the intersection would get a green arrow and two lanes of vehicles would cross the middle of the road.

Silently urging the tires to hold themselves together, I mashed down the accelerator.

One seventy.

We shot up the exit on the narrow left shoulder, passing within inches of the cars stopped for the light.

I careened left under the now-red light, the back of the SUV drifting out to the right as I narrowly made the turn, almost touching the concrete barrier on the north side of the overpass.

The cars headed to the on-ramp were already halfway across the intersection. There was nothing to do but hold my course steady.

I bolted past the Lexus leading the charge with not an inch to spare.

Cactus Road wasn't as helpful as the freeway—only two lanes with dozens of residential roads and even some driveways opening onto it. Four lights between us and the mirrored room. Alice saw we would hit two of them on red.

A speed limit sign—forty miles an hour—flew by.

One twenty.

The road gave me one small advantage: A suicide lane edged by bright yellow lines ran right down the middle of almost its entire length.

Bella was crawling across the pine floorboards. The tracker raised his foot.

Alice refocused but my mind veered. For a tenth of a second, I was back in my Volvo in Forks, thinking of ways to kill myself.

Emmett would never... but maybe Jasper. He alone could feel

what I felt. Maybe he would *want* to end my life, just to escape that pain. But probably he would run away instead. He wouldn't want to hurt Alice. So that left the longer trip to Italy.

Jasper reached forward to touch his fingertips to the back of my neck. It felt like novocaine washing over my anguish.

I tore down the center lane uninterrupted for a mile, veering back into the legal lanes to fly under the first green light. The next intersection rushed toward me. The suicide lane transitioned to a left turn lane, with three cars already lined up and waiting. The right turn lane was mostly empty. I was able to avoid the motorcycle in it by popping up onto the sidewalk for a second, fighting to keep the SUV from rolling.

I glanced at the speedometer: eighty. Unacceptable.

I darted through the light cross traffic—fortunately a few drivers had seen me coming and lurched to a stop halfway into the intersection—and reclaimed the suicide lane.

One hundred.

The coming intersection was bigger than the last, wider and twice as congested.

"Alice, give me every possibility!"

In her head, the vehicles on the road froze. She spun them counterclockwise and then back again. I saw them stretching first vertically and then horizontally. The pattern was tight, but there were tiny holes. I memorized them.

One twenty.

If we clipped another car at this speed, both cars would be destroyed. We'd have no choice but to race out into the blinding sunlight and bolt for Bella's location. People would see... something. None of the others were as fast as I was. I didn't know what the story would be—aliens or demons or secret government weapons—but I did know there would be a story. And then what? How would I save Bella when the immortal authorities came, asking questions? I could not involve the Volturi, not unless I was too late.

But Bella was *screaming*.

Jasper ramped up my novocaine dosage. Numbness soaked through my skin and into my brain.

I jammed my foot against the gas pedal and swerved into the oncoming lanes of traffic.

There was just enough space to weave between the other cars. They were all moving so slowly compared to me that it felt like dodging around standing objects.

One thirty.

I snaked my way through the frozen intersection, crossing to the right side of the road as soon as it was clear.

"Nice," Emmett hissed.

One forty.

The final light would be green.

But Alice had different ideas.

"Turn left here," she said, showing me a narrow residential road behind the commercial area where the dance studio was located. The street was lined with towering eucalyptus trees, quivering leaves more silver than green. The spotty shade was almost enough for us to move through undetected. No one was outside. It was too hot.

"Slow down now."

"There's not enough—"

If he hears us, she dies!

Unwillingly, I moved my foot to the brake pedal and started slowing. The angle for the turn was sharp enough that I would have rolled the SUV if I hadn't. I took the turn at only sixty.

Slower.

My jaw locked in place as I braked down to forty.

"Jasper," Alice hissed at top speed, her words nearly silent despite her fervor. "You cut around the building and come through the front. The rest of us go through the back. Carlisle, get ready."

Blood all over the shattered mirrors, pooling on the wooden floors.

I pulled the Cayenne into the shade of one of the soaring trees and parked with only the slightest sound of tires against loose stones on the pavement. An eight-foot block wall demarcated the border between residential and commercial. The opposite side of the road was edged with close-packed, stuccoed houses, all with their shades down to keep the interiors cool.

Moving in perfect synchronicity thanks to Jasper, we darted from the car, leaving every door slightly open so there would be no unnecessary noise. Traffic churned both north and west of the commercial building; surely it would cover any sounds we might make.

Maybe a quarter of a second had passed. We surged over the wall, leaping far enough to avoid the bed of gravel at its base and landing almost silently on pavement. There was a small alley behind the building. A dumpster, a stack of plastic crates, and the emergency exit.

I didn't hesitate. I could already see what was behind that door. Or what would be behind the door one second from now. I angled my body so there would be no mistakes, no tiny window the tracker could slip through, and then launched myself at the door.

26. BLOOD

Through the door.

It shattered around me, flying off the wall in pieces.

The roar that exploded from my core was entirely instinctual. The tracker's head jerked up, and then he dove for the crimson shape on the floor below him. I saw one pale hand stretched out in futile self-defense.

The obstacle of the door had not slowed my momentum. I flew into the tracker mid-lunge, throwing him away from his target, smashing him into the floor with enough force to crater the wooden planks.

I rolled, pulling him over me, and then kicked him to the center of the room. Where Emmett was waiting.

For the entire quarter of a second that I was grappling with the tracker, I was barely aware of him as a living creature. He was just an object in my way. I knew that at some point in the near future, I would be jealous of Emmett and Jasper. I would wish for the chance to claw and slash and sever. But that was all meaningless now. I spun.

As I had known she would be, Bella was crumpled against the wall, framed by splintered mirrors. Everything was red.

All the terror and pain I'd been subduing since I'd first heard

Alice's dread in the airport crashed into me in an unstoppable tidal wave.

Her eyes were closed. Her pale hand had fallen limp beside her. Her heartbeat was weak, faltering.

I didn't decide to move, I was just there beside her, kneeling in her blood. Fire burned through my chest and my head, but I couldn't separate out the different kinds of pain. I was afraid to touch her. She was broken in so many places. I could make it worse.

I heard my own voice, rambling the same words over and over again. Her name. *No. Please.* Again and again like a record skipping. But I wasn't in control of the sound.

I heard myself screaming Carlisle's name, but he was already there, kneeling in the blood on her other side.

The words pouring from my mouth weren't words anymore, just mangled, heaving sounds. Sobs.

Carlisle's hands traced from her scalp to her ankle and then back again so quickly, they blurred. He pressed both hands to her head, seeking ruptures. He pushed two fingers tight against a spot three inches behind her right ear. I couldn't see what he was doing; her hair was saturated with crimson.

A weak cry broke through her lips. Her face spasmed with pain.

"Bella!" I begged.

Carlisle's calm voice was the antithesis to my raw screaming. "She's lost some blood, but the head wound isn't deep. Watch out for her leg, it's broken."

A howl of pure rage ripped through the room, and for a second I thought Emmett and Jasper were in trouble. I touched their minds—they were already gathering up the broken pieces—and realized that the sound had come from me.

"Some ribs, too, I think," Carlisle added, still preternaturally calm.

His thoughts were practical, impassive. He knew I would be listening. But he was also encouraged by his examination. We were in time. The damage was not critical.

I caught the *if*s in his assessment, though. If he could get the bleeding under control. If a rib didn't puncture her lung. If the internal damage was no more than it seemed. If, if, if. His years of trying to keep human bodies alive gave him a plethora of insights into things that could go wrong.

Her blood had soaked through my jeans. It covered my arms. I was painted in it.

Bella moaned in pain.

"Bella, you're going to be fine." My words were pleading, begging. "Can you hear me, Bella? I love you."

Another moan, but no—she was trying to speak.

"Edward," she gasped.

"Yes, I'm here."

She whispered, "It *hurts*."

"I know, Bella, I know."

The jealousy surfaced then, like a fist punching through the center of my chest. I wanted so badly to break the tracker, to rip him into long, slow strips. So much pain and so much blood and I'd never be able to make him answer for it. It wasn't enough that he was dying, that he would burn. It would never be enough.

"Can't you do anything?" I snarled at Carlisle.

"My bag, please," he called coolly to Alice.

Alice made a tiny choking sound.

I couldn't force my eyes away from Bella's bruised, blood-spattered face. Under the gore, her skin was paler than I'd ever seen it. Her eyelids didn't so much as flutter.

But I reached out to Alice's mind and saw the complication.

I'd yet to truly register the lake of blood I was kneeling in. I knew, somewhere inside, my body was probably reacting to it. But wherever that reaction was, it was so deep below the pain that it hadn't surfaced yet.

Alice loved Bella, but she was not physically prepared for this. She hesitated, teeth clenched, trying to swallow back the venom.

Emmett and Jasper, too, were struggling. They'd pulled the shattered pieces of the tracker—and I could only vehemently hope that those pieces were still somehow able to process pain—out of the room. Emmett was watching Jasper closely for a break. Emmett himself was in admirable control. His concern for Bella was deeper than his usual carefree frame of mind allowed for.

"Hold your breath, Alice," Carlisle said. "It will help."

She nodded and stopped breathing as she darted forward and then back, leaving Carlisle's satchel next to his leg. She'd moved so carefully that she didn't even get blood on her shoes. She retreated to the destroyed emergency exit, gasping for fresh air.

Through the open door drifted the faint sounds of sirens, looking for the car that had raced so recklessly through the city streets. I doubted they would find the stolen car parked in the shade on a quiet side street, but I didn't really care if they did.

"Alice?" Bella gasped.

"She's here." I babbled the words. "She knew where to find you."

Bella whimpered. "My hand *hurts*."

I was surprised by her specificity. There was so much damage.

"I know, Bella. Carlisle will give you something. It will stop."

Carlisle was suturing the tears in her scalp so quickly his movements were blurring again. No bleed could escape his eyes. He was able to repair the larger vessels with tiny stitches that another surgeon would not be able to duplicate under perfect conditions even with mechanical assistance. I wished he would take a break and get some painkillers into her system, but I could hear under his controlled calm that there was more damage to her head than he liked. She'd lost so much blood. . . .

With a sudden jolt, Bella twitched half upright. Carlisle caught her head in his left hand to steady it in his iron grip. Her eyes flew open—the whites bloodred with broken vessels—and she shrieked with more strength than I would have guessed she had left.

"My hand is *burning*!"

"Bella?" I cried. Idiotically, for an instant I could think only of the fire raging though my own body. Was I hurting her?

Her eyes fluttered, blinded by blood and blood-soaked hair.

"The fire!" she screamed, her back arching despite a groaning in her ribs. "Someone stop the *fire*!"

The sound of her agony stupefied me. I knew that I understood the truth of what she was saying, but panic scrambled all the meanings in my head. It felt like someone else was forcing my head to turn away from her face, forcing my eyes to focus on the crimson-stippled hand she was thrusting away from herself, the fingers seizing, twisting to the torture.

A short, shallow slice was torn through the skin across the heel of her hand. It was nothing to her other injuries. Already the blood was slowing. . . .

I knew what I was seeing, but I couldn't form the right words.

All I could gasp out was, "Carlisle! Her hand!"

He glanced up unwillingly from his work, his fingers pausing for the first time. And then the shock hit him, too.

His voice was hollow. "He bit her."

There were the words: *He bit her.* The tracker had bitten Bella. The fire was venom.

In slow motion, I saw it replay in my memory. I ripped through the door. The tracker lunged. Bella's hand shot out in front of her. I slammed into him, forcing him away. But his teeth were exposed, his neck extended. . . . I'd been a millisecond too slow.

Carlisle's hands were still motionless. *Fix her*, I wanted to scream at him, but I knew, as he did, that his efforts were worthless now. Everything broken inside her would knit together on its own. Every shattered bone, every gash, every tiny leaking tear beneath her skin, all would be whole soon.

Her heart would stop and never beat again.

Bella screamed and writhed in misery.

Edward.

Alice had returned, finding some new resolve that let her crouch beside Carlisle now, red seeping into her shoes. Lightly, she brushed the hair from Bella's blood-spotted eyes.

You can't let it happen this way. She was thinking of Carlisle.

Carlisle was also remembering. The teeth marks on his own palm, and the long, protracted suffering of his change.

Then he thought of me.

A phantom burn raced along my hand, my arm. I remembered, too.

"Edward, you have to do it," Alice insisted.

I could make this easier, faster for Bella. She didn't have to suffer as long as I had.

She would still suffer. The pain would be unimaginable. The fire would torture her for days. Just...not as many days.

And at the end of it—

"No!" I howled, but I knew my protest was useless.

Alice's vision was so strong now it seemed inevitable. Like history, not future. Bella, stone white, her eyes glowing a hundred times brighter than the slaughter scene surrounding us now.

My own memory intruded, shoving another image into juxtaposition with Alice's vision: Rosalie. Resentful, regretful. Always mourning what she'd lost. Never resigned to what had been done to her. She'd had no choice, and she'd never forgiven us.

Could I bear to have Bella stare at me with the same regrets for the next thousand years?

Yes! the most selfish part of me insisted. Better that than to have her disappear now, to slip away from me.

But *was* it better? If she could grasp every ramification and every loss, would *she* choose this way?

Did *I* even fully understand the cost? Was I aware of everything I'd traded in exchange for my immortality? Had the tracker just met the same black wall of nothingness that I was destined for someday? Or would there be eternal flames for the both of us?

"Alice," Bella groaned, her eyes sliding closed. Was she recognizing Alice's return, or was she just giving up on my help? I was doing nothing but falling apart.

Bella started screaming again, a long unbroken wail of agony.

Edward! Alice shouted at me. Her impatience with my

hesitation was reaching a frenzy, but she didn't trust herself enough to act.

Alice saw that I was drowning. She saw my futures spinning out into a thousand different kinds of despair. On the outer edges, she even saw me doing the one unimaginable thing I hadn't yet consciously considered. The thing I was *sure* I was too weak for. Until I saw it in her mind, I didn't realize that version even existed inside my head.

Now I could see it.

Killing Bella.

Was it the right thing? To stop her pain? To give her, in her total and perfect innocence, a chance at a different destiny than the inevitable one I knew I was facing? A different kind of afterlife than the cold, bloodthirsty one she was burning toward now?

The pain was too much, and I couldn't trust my thoughts, spinning out of control because *Bella was screaming*.

I turned my eyes and mind to Carlisle, hoping for some assurance, some absolution, but I met something entirely different.

In his mind, a coiled desert viper, sand-colored scales sliding across each other with a dry, rasping sound.

The image was so unexpected that I froze again with shock.

"There may be a chance," Carlisle said.

There was just a glimmer of hope in his head. He saw what Bella's suffering was doing to me now; he, too, feared what forcing her into this life would do to both her and me in the future. And yet, the sliver of hope…

"What?" I begged him. What was the chance?

Carlisle started stitching her scalp again. He had enough faith in this idea that he thought it might be necessary to finish repairing her wounds.

"See if you can suck the venom back out," he said, calm again. "The wound is fairly clean."

Every muscle in my body locked down.

"Will that work?" Alice demanded. She looked ahead to

answer her own question. Nothing was clear. No decision had been made. My decision was not made.

Carlisle didn't look up from his work. "I don't know. But we have to hurry."

I knew how the venom would spread. She'd felt the first burn just a moment ago. It would climb slowly up her wrist, into her arm. Then faster and faster.

There was no time for this.

But! I wanted to scream. *But I'm a vampire!*

I would taste the blood and I would frenzy. Especially *her* blood. Only the burning she was feeling now was stronger than the flames in my throat, my chest. If I gave in even a tiny bit to that need…

"Carlisle, I…" My voice faltered in shame. Did he even realize what he was suggesting? "I don't know if I can do that."

Carlisle's fingers moved the suture needle so quickly it was all but invisible. He'd moved to the back of her head, on the left now. There were so many wounds.

His voice was even but heavy. "It's your decision, Edward, either way."

Life or death or half life, my decision. But was life even in my power? I'd never been that strong.

"I can't help you," he apologized. "I have to get this bleeding stopped here if you're going to be taking blood from her hand."

Bella thrashed as a new wave of pain rocked her, jerking her twisted leg.

"Edward!" she screamed.

Her blood-filled eyes snapped open, and this time they focused sharply, boring into my own. Imploring, beseeching.

Bella was burning.

"Alice!" Carlisle snapped. "Get me something to brace her leg!"

Alice darted out of my peripheral vision, and I could hear her ripping boards up from the floor and snapping them into usable sizes.

"Edward!" Carlisle's voice had lost its control. Pain bled through. Pain for me, pain for Bella. "You must do it *now*, or it will be too late."

Bella's eyes begged, desperate for relief.

Bella was burning, and I was exactly the wrong person to save her. Absolutely and literally the worst person in the entire universe for this task.

But I was the only one here to do it.

You have to do this, I ordered myself. *There is no other way. You cannot fail.*

I grasped her twisting hand, smoothing her clenched fingers and holding them still. I stopped breathing and bent to press my mouth to her hand.

The skin on the edges of the wound was already cooler than the rest of her hand. Changing. Hardening.

I sealed my lips around the small gash, closed my eyes, and then began.

It was only a trickle of blood—the venom had already begun healing the wound. Just a few drops to start with. Barely enough to wet my tongue.

It hit me like an explosion. A bomb detonating inside my body and mind. The first time I'd caught Bella's scent, I thought I'd be undone. That was a paper cut. This was a decapitation. My brain was severed from my body.

But it wasn't pain. Bella's blood was the opposite of pain. It erased every burn I'd ever suffered. And it was so much more than just the absence of pain. It was satisfaction, it was *bliss*. I felt suffused with a strange kind of joy—a joy of the body alone. I was healed and alive, every nerve ending thrumming with contentment.

As I pulled from the wound, it reversed the effects of the venom. The blood started to flow steadily, coating my tongue, my throat. The sharp, icy taste of the venom was a weak counterpoint. It did nothing to interfere with the power of her blood.

Rapture. Elation.

My body knew well that there was more to be had, close at hand. *More*, my body hummed, *more*.

But my body couldn't move. I'd forced it motionless and I kept it so. I could hardly think to know why, but I refused to release my hold.

I had to think. I had to stop *feeling* and think.

There was something outside the bliss.

Pain, there was pain that the pleasure couldn't reach. Pain that was both outside and inside my mind.

The pain was high-pitched and dissonant. It swelled into a crescendo.

Bella was screaming.

I reached out mentally for something to hold on to, and found a life ring waiting.

Yes, Edward. You can *do this. See? You are going to save her.*

Alice showed me a thousand glimpses of the future. Bella smiling, Bella laughing, Bella reaching for my hand, Bella holding her arms open for me, Bella staring into my eyes with fascination, Bella walking next to me at school, Bella sitting beside me in her truck, Bella sleeping in my arms, Bella pressing her hand against my cheek, Bella holding my face and pressing her lips carefully against mine. A thousand different scenes with Bella, healthy and whole, alive and happy, and with me.

The bliss, the physical joy, dimmed.

The taste of venom was strong. It was still too soon.

I will show you when, Alice promised.

But I felt myself careening past the place where I *could* stop. I was losing myself. I was going to kill her, my body thrilling with joy the entire time.

Bella's screaming quieted, loosening my connection to the pain I needed to feel. She whimpered a few times, and then sighed.

I was going to kill her.

"Edward?" she whispered.

"He's right here, Bella," Alice soothed.

Right here killing you.

I was barely aware of anything else. Sound faded, the light seemed dim behind my lids, there was nothing else really, just the blood. Even Alice's thoughts, nearly screaming at me, felt muted and far away.

It's time, Alice told me. *Now, Edward.*

Through my near-total absorption, I could taste that. The icy sting was gone. A new chemical flavor took its place, however, and some piece of me realized that Carlisle had been working fast.

Stop, Edward! Now!

But Alice could see I was lost. I could hear her wondering frantically if she could pull me off Bella, or if that fight would just injure Bella more.

"Stay, Edward," Bella sighed, peaceful now. "Stay with me...."

Her quiet voice slid into my head, somehow stronger than Alice's panic, louder than all the chaos inside and around me. The sound of her confidence was a key turning; it seemed to reconnect my brain to my body. It made me whole again.

And I simply let her hand fall away from my lips. I raised my head and looked at her face. Still spattered with blood, still ashy, eyes closed, but calm now. Her pain was eased.

"I will," I promised her through bloodstained lips.

Her mouth twitched into a frail smile.

"Is it all out?" Carlisle asked. He worried he'd been too quick with the painkiller, that it might be covering the venom burn.

But Alice had seen it would be fine.

"Her blood tastes clean." The sound of my voice was rough, grating. "I can taste the morphine."

"Bella?" Carlisle asked in a low, clear voice.

"Mmmmm?" was her response.

"Is the fire gone?"

"Yes," she breathed, a little clearer now. "Thank you, Edward."

"I love you."

She sighed, eyes still closed. "I know."

The chuckle that bubbled up from my chest surprised me. I had her blood on my tongue. It was probably tinting the edges of my irises red even now. It was drying into my clothes and dyeing my skin. But she could still make me laugh.

"Bella?" Carlisle asked again.

"What?" Her tone was testy now. She looked half-asleep and impatient to find the other half.

"Where is your mother?"

Her eyes flickered for a second, and then she exhaled. "In Florida. He *tricked* me, Edward. He watched our *videos*."

Though she was nearly unconscious from trauma and morphine, it was clear she was deeply offended by this invasion of privacy. I smiled.

"Alice?" Bella struggled to open her eyes, and then quit, but her words were as urgent as she could make them in her condition. "Alice, the video—he knew you, Alice, he knew where you came from. . . . I smell gasoline?"

Emmett and Jasper were back from siphoning the accelerant we needed. The sirens still wailed in the distance, but from another direction now. They weren't going to find us.

With a somber expression, Alice flitted across the ravaged floor to the media center by the door. She picked up the small handheld video recorder that was still running. She switched it off.

In the instant she decided to retrieve the camera, hundreds of future fragments flashed through her mind—images of this room, of Bella, of the tracker, of the blood. It was everything she would see when she played back the recording, too fast and disordered for either of us to absorb much. Her eyes flashed to mine.

We'll deal with this later. We have a hundred things to do now to make sense of this nightmare.

I could tell she was purposely directing her thoughts away from the camera as she ran through the rather involved chores we now must accomplish, but I didn't push. Later.

"It's time to move her," Carlisle said. The smell of the gasoline

Emmett and Jasper were applying to the walls was becoming overwhelming.

"No," Bella murmured. "I want to sleep."

"You can sleep, sweetheart," I crooned in her ear. "I'll carry you."

Her leg was wrapped tightly inside Alice's floorboard splint, and Carlisle had found time to tape her ribs. Moving more carefully than I ever had before, I lifted her from the blood-soaked floor, trying to support every part of her.

"Sleep now, Bella," I whispered.

27. CHORES

"Do we have time to—" Alice began.

"No," Carlisle interrupted. "Bella needs blood immediately."

Alice sighed. If we went to the hospital first, things got more complicated.

Carlisle sat beside me in the backseat of the Cayenne, fingers pressed lightly against Bella's carotid artery, one hand supporting her head. Her splinted leg stretched out across Emmett's thighs on the other side of me. He wasn't breathing. He stared out the window, trying not to think about the blood drying all over Bella, Carlisle, and me. Trying not to think about what I had just done. The impossibility of it. The strength he knew he didn't have.

Instead he mulled over his dissatisfaction with the fight. Because, *honestly*. He'd *had* the tracker. Totally contained, though the tracker fought and squirmed and thrashed to avoid Emmett's crushing arms. There was no chance any of this struggle could have helped him, and Emmett was already breaking him when Jasper lunged into the blood-drenched room.

Jasper, mangled and ferocious, eyes sharp and empty at the same time, looking like some forgotten god or incarnation of war, projecting an aura of pure violence. And the tracker had stopped trying. In that fraction of a second when he saw Jasper (for the first time, but Emmett didn't know that), he'd surrendered to his fate. No matter that his fate was sealed once Emmett had gotten his hands on him, *this* was what demoralized him.

It was driving Emmett crazy.

Someday soon I would have to describe to Emmett what he'd looked like in the clearing and why. I doubted anything else would soothe the sting.

Jasper was in the driver's seat, his window cracked to the hot, dry outside air, though like Emmett, he wasn't breathing. Alice sat beside him, directing everything—the turns, the lanes to travel in, the highest speed he could go without attracting unwanted attention. She had him at sixty-seven miles per hour now. I would have pushed that, but Alice was confident that she would get us to the hospital faster than I could. Dodging patrol cars would only slow us down and complicate *everything.*

Although Alice was monitoring every facet of this drive, her mind was in a dozen different places, finding ways through the necessary errands in front of her, working through the consequences of every choice available.

A few things she was sure of.

Now she pulled out her phone and called the airline—one she already knew would have the right flight—and booked one ticket for the two-forty to Seattle. It would be tight, but she could see Emmett on the plane.

She saw the day ahead as clearly as if it were happening, and I saw it all, too.

First, Jasper would drop Carlisle, Bella, and me at St. Joseph's. There were closer hospitals, but Carlisle insisted. He knew a surgeon there who would vouch for him, and it was a nationally recognized level-one trauma center. His urgency, and Bella's ashen complexion—though her heart continued steady and strong—made it difficult for me to do much besides silently panic and curse our circumspect speed.

"She'll be fine," Alice growled quietly at me when she saw I was about to complain again. She shoved a picture into my head of Bella sitting up in a hospital bed, smiling, though she was all over bruises.

I caught her slight deception, though. "And *when* exactly is this?"

A day or two, okay? Three tops. It's fine. Relax.

My panic skyrocketed as I processed that. Three days?

Carlisle didn't have to read thoughts to understand my expression.

"She just needs time, Edward," Carlisle assured me. "Her body needs rest to recover, and so does her mind. She's going to be okay."

I tried to accept that, but felt myself spiraling again. I focused on Alice. Her methodical planning was better than my useless agitation.

The hospital, she saw, would be tricky. We were in a stolen car that was linked to another stolen car and a twenty-seven-car pileup on the 101. There were multiple cameras around the emergency entrance. If we could just stop to switch to a better vehicle, something close enough to the rental Alice would acquire later... It was only a matter of fifteen minutes or so, just a short detour and she knew exactly where to look—

I growled, and she sniffed once without looking at me.

It never gets less annoying, Emmett grumbled internally.

So no car exchange. Alice accepted this and moved on. We'd have to park out of range of the cameras, which would make us more conspicuous. Why not pull right under the metal overhang with our unconscious patient? Why carry her farther than necessary? At least there would be shade for Carlisle and me to run in, otherwise we would have to brave the cameras and Alice would have to find her way into whatever security stronghold was used to store the recordings. And she simply didn't have time for that. She had to check into a hotel and create a scene of violent injury stat. Because it was supposed to have happened *before* we arrived at the hospital.

So that was obviously urgent. But first she needed blood.

The blood should be quick. When I burst through the emergency room doors looking like someone had thrown a bucket of crimson paint at me, and with a motionless body in my arms, it was going to cause something of a stir. Every able-bodied staff member within a hundred yards of the emergency entrance would be running to meet us within seconds. It would be simple enough for Alice to slide in behind Carlisle and walk purposefully past the front desk. No one would question her, she could see that. A pair of blue booties available in a box attached to the wall would cover the stains on her shoes, and then it was simply a matter of darting into the emergency wing's blood storage room through a closing door.

"Em, give me your hoodie."

Careful not to jostle Bella's leg, Emmett yanked the sweatshirt over his head and tossed it to Alice. It was remarkably clean, especially compared to Carlisle's and my clothes.

Emmett wanted to ask what she needed it for, but he didn't dare to open his mouth and possibly taste or smell his surroundings.

Alice shrugged into the enormous sweatshirt. It pooled around her tiny body, and yet, somehow, there was an air of the avant-garde about it. Alice could pull off anything.

Alice saw herself in the blood bank again, filling the sweatshirt's ample pockets.

"What's Bella's blood type?" she asked Carlisle.

"O positive," Carlisle responded.

So some good had come from Bella's accident with Tyler's van. At least we knew this.

Alice was probably being overthorough. Would anyone bother to type the blood she would leave at the scene of the "accident"? Perhaps, if it looked too much like a crime scene.... No harm in her being meticulous, I supposed.

"Leave enough for Bella," I cautioned.

She twisted in her seat so that I could see her roll her eyes, then turned back and kept planning.

Jasper and Emmett would be in the stolen car, engine running. It would only take her two and a half minutes to get in and out.

She would choose a hotel near the hospital to make the timing less conspicuous. As she decided this, she saw the hotel she wanted just a few blocks south. It wasn't someplace she would ever actually *stay*, of course, but it would do for a grisly tableau.

It felt like watching in real time as she ran through the check-in.

Alice strides into the modest lobby of the hotel. On her, the maroon-dyed shoes and the long hoodie tied around her waist look like a fashion statement. The woman at the desk is alone. She looks up, not very interested at first, but then she processes Alice's stunning face. She stares with awe, barely noticing that Alice's hands are free.

But Alice is dissatisfied.

The vision rewinds. Alice is back in the hospital, exiting the blood bank with her pockets full of four cold, quietly sloshing bags. She makes the shortest detour, ducking into a curtained-off treatment area. A woman sleeps, her vitals beeping on the monitors behind her. There is a sack with the women's belongings, and beside it a blue duffel bag. Alice takes the bag and returns to the hallway. The detour adds only two seconds to her trip.

Alice is back in the hotel lobby. She wears no sweatshirt, and the duffel bag is slung over her shoulder. The woman behind the counter does her double take. There is nothing wrong with the picture now. Alice asks for two rooms, double occupancy for one, single for the other. She puts her driver's license—not a fake—on the counter with a credit card in her own name. She chatters about her companions, her father and her brother, who have gone to find covered parking for the car. The woman starts typing on her computer. Alice glances at her wrist; it's bare.

The vision pauses.

"Jasper, I need your watch."

He held out his arm, and she took the bespoke Breguet—a gift from her—off his wrist. He didn't bother to wonder why; he was too used to this. The watch hung loose against her hand. She wore it like a bangle bracelet, and it looked perfect. She could start a trend.

The vision resumes.

Alice looks at the watch dangling in such a chic way from her wrist.

"It's only ten-fifty," she says to the woman. "Your clock there is fast."

The woman nods absently, typing the time Alice has just fed her into the reservation.

Alice grows a little too still, waiting for the woman to finish. It takes much longer than it should, but there's nothing to do but wait.

Finally the woman hands her two sets of key cards, and writes down the numbers. They both start with a one: 106 and 108.

The vision rewinds.

Alice walks into the lobby. The woman behind the counter does her double take. Alice asks for two rooms, double occupancy for one, single for the other. *Second floor, please, if that's not too much trouble.* She puts her cards on the counter. She chatters about her companions. The woman starts typing in her computer. Alice corrects the time. Alice waits.

The woman hands her two sets of key cards. She writes down the numbers 209 and 211. Alice smiles at her and takes the keys. Alice moves at human speed until she is in the stairwell.

Alice ducks into both rooms, dropping the duffel bag in the first, and turns lights on, closes curtains, puts out the "do not disturb" signs. Blood bags in hand, she flits down the empty hallway to another stairwell. No one sees her. She pauses at the landing in the middle of the flight. At the base of the stairs is an exit to the outside. The door is flanked by a floor-to-ceiling pane of glass. There is no one near the exit on the outside.

Alice dials her phone.

"Sound the horn for three seconds."

An obnoxiously loud klaxon rises from the parking lot, covering the sound of the heavy traffic on the freeway (a different freeway, one we did not all but shut down).

Alice hurls herself down the stairs, curling like a bowling ball. She smashes through the dead center of the tall window. The glass lands on the sidewalk and gravel, some of it flying all the way to the pavement of the parking lot. It creates a pattern like a sunburst, glittering in the white shine from above. Alice retreats to the shadow of the door, and—one by one—rips the blood bags open using the broken glass fragments in the window frame, leaving blood on the edges. She flings the contents of one bag so it sprays out in a fan like the glass. The next two she pours onto the edge of the sidewalk, letting it pool up and soak into the concrete and run onto the pavement.

The horn goes silent.

Alice dials again. "Pick me up."

The Cayenne appears almost immediately. Alice dashes through the sunlight to duck into the back, the last bag of blood clutched in her hand.

And then I was back in the present with her. Alice was satisfied with how that section would play out. She turned her attention to the next parts. None of it as much fun, but all still vital.

"*Fun,*" I scoffed. She ignored me.

Back to the airport. She chooses a white Suburban from the rental counter. It doesn't look that much like the Cayenne, but it's large and white and any witness with a story that doesn't match will be written off. She doesn't see any such witness, but she's being meticulous.

Alice drives the Cayenne. She's having an easier time with the scent than Jasper and Emmett; even though Bella is no longer in danger from them, the smell burns them when they breathe. They follow at a distance in the Suburban. She finds a car wash called Deluxe Detail. She pays with cash, and warns the boy at the counter—who is staring, mesmerized, at her face—that her niece threw up a bunch of tomato juice in the backseat. She points to her shoes. The besotted boy promises that the car will be spotless when they're finished. (No one will question this story. The technician, fearing the scent of vomit will make him ill, will breathe only through his mouth.) She gives the name Mary. She thinks about washing her shoes off in the bathroom but sees that it won't help very much.

She will wait an hour for the car to be finished. She calls the hotel after the first fifteen minutes have passed, ducking out the back door and standing in the shade where the sounds of vacuums and sprayers keep anyone from overhearing her words.

She apologizes to the same woman at the front desk, her voice frantic. A visiting friend, a *horrible* accident in the back stairwell. The window...the *blood*...(Alice is barely coherent). Yes, she's at the hospital with the friend now. But the *window*! The *glass*! Someone else could get *hurt*. Please, it should be cordoned off until maintenance can clean it up. She has to go—they're going to let her in to see her friend. Thank you. *So* sorry.

Alice sees that the woman at the desk will not call the police. She will call management. They will direct the woman to get everything cleaned up before someone else is hurt. That will be the story when the legal papers are served: They cleaned up the evidence for safety's sake. They will wait in miserable suspense for the lawsuit that never comes. It will be more than a year before they start to believe their amazing luck.

The detailing done, Alice examines the backseat. There's no visible evidence. She tips the technician. Alice gets into the Cayenne and takes a deep breath in through her nose. Well, the car won't pass a luminol test, but she sees that it won't get one.

Jasper and Emmett follow her to a mall in downtown Scottsdale. She parks the Cayenne on the third floor of a huge parking garage. It will be four days before the security guard reports the abandoned vehicle.

Alice and Jasper go shopping while Emmett waits in the rental car. She buys a pair of tennis shoes in a busy Gap. No one looks down at her feet. She pays cash.

She buys Emmett a T-shirt-thin hoodie that actually fits him. She buys six large bags of clothes in her size, Carlisle's size, Emmett's size, and my own. She uses a different ID and credit card than she used at the hotel. Jasper acts as a Sherpa for her.

Finally, she buys four suitcases that don't match. She and Jasper wheel them to the rental car, where she pulls tags and fills them all with brand-new clothes.

She throws her bloody shoes in a dumpster on their way out.

There are no rewinds or replays. Everything goes perfectly smoothly.

Jasper and Alice drop Emmett off at the airport. He takes one of the carry-on suitcases; he looks less conspicuous than he did for the morning flight.

They find Carlisle's Mercedes where they left it in the parking garage. Jasper kisses Alice and starts the long drive home.

Once the boys are gone, Alice empties the last unit of blood onto the backseat and floor of the rental car. She takes it to a do-it-yourself car wash outside a gas station. She doesn't do nearly as good a job cleaning up as the detailers. She'll get fined when she returns the car.

It will be raining when Emmett lands in Seattle, only a half hour till sunset. A taxi will take him to the ferry. It will be easy for him to slip into the Puget Sound, ditching the suitcase in the water, and then—swimming and running—it will be just thirty minutes until he gets to the house. He'll take Bella's truck and immediately head back to Phoenix.

Alice frowned in the present and shook her head. This plan would take too long. The truck was incredibly slow.

We were just four minutes from the hospital now. Bella was still breathing slowly and evenly in my arms, and we were all still covered in blood. Emmett and Jasper were both still holding their breath. I blinked and tried to reorient myself. When Alice's visions were detailed like this, it was easy to lose track of what was happening in the moment. She was better at acclimatizing back and forth than I was.

Alice opened her phone again and dialed a number. She was swimming in Emmett's sweatshirt, Jasper's watch dangling from her wrist.

"Rose?"

In the tight, quiet space, we could all hear Rosalie's panicked voice. "What's happening? Emmett—"

"Emmett's *fine*. I need—"

"Where's the tracker?"

"The tracker is out of the picture."

Rosalie gasped audibly.

"I need you to rent a flatbed tow truck," Alice instructed. "Or buy one, whatever's faster—something with some kick. Load Bella's truck and meet Emmett in Seattle. His flight lands at five-thirty."

"Emmett's coming home? What happened? Why am I towing that ridiculous truck?"

For a brief moment, I wondered why Alice was sending Emmett home at all. Why not let Rosalie just bring the truck here? It was the obvious solution. And then I realized that Alice couldn't *see* Rosalie helping us in that way, and I felt an ice-cold wave of bitterness at the reminder. Rosalie had made her choice.

Emmett wanted to reach for the phone, to calm Rose, but he was still unable to open his mouth.

It was amazing how well both he and Jasper were doing. I thought the extra stimulation of the fight was probably still affecting them, helping them ignore the blood.

"Don't worry about it," Alice said curtly. "I'm just cleaning up the loose ends. Emmett will give you all the details. Let Esme know it's over, but we'll be detained for a bit. She should stay near Bella's father in case the redhead—"

Rosalie's voice went flat. "She's coming for Charlie?"

"No, I don't see that," Alice assured her. "But better safe, right? Carlisle will call her as soon as he can. Hurry up, Rose, you've got a deadline."

"You're such a brat."

Alice disconnected the phone.

Well, Emmett will get to keep the clothes, at least. I'm glad. They're going to look amazing on him.

Emmett was pleased with the call. Happy to know he would be with Rose in just hours, and she would get his side of the story. No reason at all to mention the ridiculous thing with Jasper. If Alice didn't see any problems with the redhead, then Rose could make the ride back to Phoenix with him. Or maybe she wouldn't want to.... He looked down at Bella's wan face, her fractured leg. A deep swell of fraternal affection and concern washed over him.

She's such a good kid. Rose is going to have to get over this, he thought to himself. *Pronto.*

Alice's brow was furrowed. She thought through her chores and looked at the consequences of all the hundreds of choices she had made. She saw herself at the hospital, bringing us clothes from our suitcases so we could get out of our bloody things. Had she caught everything? Had any details slipped her mind?

Everything was fine. Or it would be.

"Well done, Alice," I whispered approvingly.

She smiled.

Jasper pulled up to the emergency room, keeping his distance from the camera on this side of the entrance, looking for our shade.

I adjusted my grip on Bella and prepared to go through it all again for the first time.

28. THREE CONVERSATIONS

Dr. Sadarangani, Carlisle's friend, did make things smoother. Carlisle had him paged while they were still bringing a gurney for Bella. It only took minutes for Dr. Sadarangani to get Bella started on her first transfusion. Once she was receiving blood, Carlisle relaxed. He was fairly sure that everything else was in order.

It was not so easy for me to be calm. Of course I trusted Carlisle, and Dr. Sadarangani seemed competent. I could read their honest judgment of her status. I heard the wonder of Dr. Sadarangani and the doctors on his team when they inspected the perfect suturing of Bella's wounds, the impeccable setting of her leg in the field. I heard Dr. Sadarangani behind closed doors, regaling his coworkers with tales of Dr. Cullen's exploits in the inner-city hospital in Baltimore where they'd worked together fourteen years ago. I heard the surprise he voiced at Carlisle's unchanged appearance, and his silent suspicions that—despite Carlisle's claims that the cool, humid air of the Pacific Northwest was a natural fountain of youth—Carlisle had been experimenting in plastics. He was sanguine enough about Bella's case to beg Carlisle to look in on a few of his as yet undiagnosed patients, declaring to his interns that they would never see a better diagnostician than Dr. Cullen. And Carlisle was confident enough in her condition that he agreed to go help others.

But this wasn't life or death for either of them the way it was for me. That was *my* life on the gurney. My life, pale and unresponsive, covered in tubes and tape and plaster. I kept myself together as best I could.

As the attending physician, Dr. Sadarangani had made the first call to Charlie, which was painful to listen to. Carlisle quickly took over for him and explained the fictional version of what he and I were doing here as succinctly as possible, assured Charlie that everything was going well, and promised to call soon with more information. I could hear the panic in Charlie's voice and was sure that he was no more persuaded than I.

It didn't take very long before Bella was presumed in stable condition and placed in a recovery room. Alice hadn't even returned from her errands.

The new blood pulsing through Bella's body altered her scent in a way I should have anticipated, but it took me by surprise. While I was aware of a significant lessening of my thirst-pain, I didn't enjoy the change. This strange blood seemed an interloper, alien. It wasn't part of her and I resented the intrusion, irrational as that was. Her scent would begin to return in just twenty-four hours, before she'd even woken up. But she would not entirely replace that which was lost for many weeks. Regardless, this brief distortion was too strong a reminder that, at some point in the future, the scent that had compelled me for so long would be lost to me forever.

Everything had been done that could be done. Now there was nothing left but the waiting.

During the interminable lull, there were few things that could hold my attention. I updated Esme. Alice returned, but left quickly when she saw that I would rather be alone. I stared through the east-facing window at a busy road and a few modest skyscrapers. I listened to the steady beat of her heart to stay sane.

A few conversations, however, had some significance for me.

Carlisle waited until he was in Bella's room with me to call Charlie again. He knew I would want to listen.

"Hello, Charlie."

"Carlisle? What's happening?"

"She's had a transfusion and an MRI. Things look very good so far. It doesn't appear there are any internal injuries we missed."

"Can I talk to her?"

"They're keeping her sedated for a while. It's perfectly normal. She would be in too much pain if she were awake." I winced while Carlisle continued. "She needs to heal for a few days."

"Are you *sure* everything is okay?"

"I promise you, Charlie. I will tell you the moment there is something to worry about. She really is going to be fine. She'll be on crutches for a while, but other than that, she'll be back to normal."

"Thank you, Carlisle. I'm so glad you were there."

"So am I."

"I know this must be putting you out—"

"Don't even mention it, Charlie. I'm only too happy to stay with Bella till she's ready to come home."

"I'll admit, that does make me feel a lot better. Will... will Edward be staying, too? I mean, with school and everything..."

"He's already spoken with his teachers," Carlisle said, though actually Alice was the one who would set everything up, "and they're letting him work remotely. He's keeping track of Bella's homework, too, though I'm sure the teachers will cut her a break." Carlisle pitched his voice a bit lower. "He's gutted about all this, you know."

"I'm not sure I understand. He—Edward talked you into going to all the way to Phoenix?"

"Yes. He was extremely concerned when Bella left. He felt responsible. He thought he had to put it right."

"What even *happened*?" Charlie asked, sounding bewildered. "One minute everything is normal and then Bella is shrieking about liking your boy, and that being a problem, and then she's running out in the middle of the night? Did you get anything coherent out of yours?"

"Yes, we had time to discuss everything on the way here. I guess Edward told Bella how much he cares for her. He said at first she seemed happy, but then something clearly started to bother her. She got upset and wanted to go home. When they got there, she told him to go away."

"Yeah, I was there for that."

"Edward still doesn't understand what it was all about. They didn't have a chance to talk before..."

Charlie sighed. "That part I get. It's some complicated stuff with her mother. She was overreacting just a little, I think."

"I'm sure she had her reasons."

Charlie harrumphed uncomfortably. "But what do you think about all this, Carlisle? I mean, they're just teenagers. Isn't this a little...intense?"

Carlisle's answering laugh was breezy. "Don't you remember being seventeen?"

"Not really, no."

Carlisle laughed again. "Do you remember the first time you fell in love?"

Charlie was quiet for a minute. "Yeah, I do. Hard stuff to forget."

"It is indeed." Carlisle sighed. "I'm so sorry, Charlie. If we hadn't come here, she wouldn't have even been in that stairwell in the first place."

"Now, now, don't start with *that*, Carlisle. If you weren't there, she could have fallen through a window anywhere. And she wouldn't have been so lucky if you weren't close by."

"I'm just happy she's safe."

"It's killing me not to be there."

"I'd happily arrange a flight—"

"No, that's not the problem." Charlie sighed. "You know we don't get a lot of serious crime up here, but that nasty assault case from last summer is finally going to trial and if I'm not here to testify, it would only help the defense."

"Of course, Charlie. There's no need for you to worry. Do your job, put the bad guy away, and I'll make sure Bella is back to you in good condition, very soon."

"I wouldn't be able to stay in my right mind if you weren't there. So thank you again. I'm sending Renée out. That will probably make Bella happier anyway."

"That's a wonderful idea. I'm delighted to get the chance to meet Bella's mother."

"I'm warning you now, she'll make a fuss."

"That's certainly her prerogative as a mother."

"Thank you again, Carlisle. Thank you for taking care of my girl."

"Of course, Charlie."

Carlisle only sat with me a few moments after he disconnected. It was always difficult for him to sit still inside a hospital full of suffering humans. It should have made me feel better that he had no concerns about leaving Bella. It didn't.

The next significant thing to happen was the arrival of Bella's mother. It was nearly midnight when Alice let me know that Renée would be in Bella's room in fifteen minutes.

I tried to clean myself up a little in the attached bathroom. Alice had brought us the new clothes, so I wasn't looking macabre, at least. Fortunately, by the time I'd thought to check, my eyes were back to normal, a dark ocher. Not that a small ring of red would have been so noticeable with everything else that was going on; I just didn't want to see it myself.

Done with that, I went back to brooding. I wondered if Bella's mother would hold me more responsible than her father had. If either of them had known the real story…

My wallowing was abruptly interrupted by something unexpected. Something I'd never heard before, which was rare indeed: a voice so clear and strong that for a second I thought someone had come in the room without my noticing.

My daughter. Please, someone. Where do I go? My baby…

My next thought was that someone was shouting or screaming in the hospital lobby downstairs—as that seemed to be the location of the voice, now that I was concentrating—but no one had noticed a ruckus.

However, they had all noticed something else.

A woman, maybe thirty, maybe older. Pretty, but visibly distraught. Her distress was eye-catching, conspicuous, though she stood quietly in an out of the way corner, seeming unsure. Several orderlies and two nurses with places to be paused to see what she needed.

It was obviously Bella's mother. I'd seen her in Charlie's mind, and she bore a striking resemblance to her daughter. I'd thought Charlie's memory was of Renée as a younger woman, but it could also have been more current. She hadn't aged much. I guessed that she and Bella would often be mistaken for sisters.

"I'm looking for my daughter. She came in this afternoon. She was in an accident. She fell through a window…."

Renée's physical voice was perfectly normal, similar to but a little higher pitched than Bella's own. Her mental voice, however, was piercing.

It was fascinating to watch how the other minds responded. No one seemed to notice the ringing mental broadcast, yet everyone was compelled to help her. Somehow, they were picking up on her need, and unable to ignore it. I listened, mesmerized by the interplay between her mind and theirs. An orderly and a nurse led her through the halls, towing her small bag for her, anxious to help.

I remembered my earlier speculations about Bella's mother—my curiosity to understand what kind of mind had combined with Charlie's to create someone as distinct and unusual as Bella.

Renée was the opposite of Charlie. I wondered whether that was somehow what had brought them together in the beginning.

With her redundant number of guides, it didn't take Renée long to find Bella's room. She picked up another escort on her way: Bella's assigned RN, who was immediately drawn to Renée's urgency.

For a moment, I imagined Renée as a vampire. Would her thoughts shout audibly at everyone, inescapable? I couldn't imagine that she would be very popular. I was surprised to find myself smiling at the thought—well and truly distracted.

Renée hurried into the room, dropping her bag at the door, the RN close beside her. At first Renée didn't notice me leaning against the window, her eyes only for her daughter. Bella lay unmoving, the bruises just starting to bloom across her face. Her head was wrapped in gauze—though Carlisle had managed to keep them from shaving her hair—and there were tubes and monitors hooked to her everywhere. Her broken leg was casted from toes to thigh, and elevated on a contoured foam support.

Bella, oh baby, look at you. Oh no.

Another similarity to Bella—Renée's blood was sweet. Not in the same way as Bella's. Renée's was *too* sweet, almost cloying. It was an interesting, if not entirely appealing, fragrance. I'd never noticed anything unusual about Charlie's scent, but combined with Renée's it had made for something potent.

"She's sedated," the RN said quickly as Renée approached the bed, hands outstretched. "She'll be out for a bit, but you'll be able to talk to her in a few days."

"Can I touch her?" It was a whisper and a shout.

"Sure, you can pat her arm right there if you like, just be gentle."

Renée stood by her daughter and rested two fingers lightly against Bella's forearm. Tears started to cascade down Renée's cheeks, and the RN put a motherly arm around her. It was hard for me to hold my place. I wanted to comfort her, too.

I'm so sorry, baby. I'm so, so sorry.

"There, there, honey. She's gonna be fine, all right? That pretty doctor stitched her up as neat as I've ever seen. You don't need to cry, hon. Why don't you come sit over here and relax? It was a long flight, I bet. You came in from Georgia?"

Renée sniffed. "Florida."

"You must be exhausted. Your daughter's not going anywhere and she's not doing any tricks, either. Why don't you try to get some sleep, hon?"

Renée let herself be led toward the blue vinyl recliner in the corner of the room.

"Do you need anything? We've got some toiletries at the counter if you want to freshen up," the nurse offered. She was a grandmotherly type, with long gray hair rolled into a bun on top of her head. Her nametag said "Gloria." I'd met her earlier and not noticed her much, but I found myself feeling fondly toward her now. Was that for her kindness, or was I reacting to Renée's appreciation? What a strange thing it was, being near someone who projected—apparently totally unconsciously—her thoughts this way. I supposed it was a little like Jasper, though rough and unsophisticated in comparison. And it wasn't emotional projection, it was definitely her thoughts. Only I was aware I was hearing them.

This gave new dimension to what Bella's life with her mother must have been. No wonder she had been so protective, so nurturing. No wonder she'd given up her childhood to take care of this woman.

"I've got my things." Renée nodded tiredly to the small suitcase in the doorway.

I was feeling a bit like an elephant in the room. Neither of them had noticed me yet, though I was quite obvious. The lights were dimmed for nighttime, but still bright enough for the nurses to do their work.

I decided to announce my presence.

"Let me get that for you."

I moved quickly to place her bag on a small counter convenient to the recliner.

Like Charlie's, Renée's first reaction was a sudden spike of fear and adrenaline. She shook that off quickly, assuming she was just overtired and my unexpected movement had startled her.

I'm so jumpy. But who could this be? Um, hmm. Is this the pretty doctor? He looks too young.

"Oh, hey there, son," Gloria said, a little disapproving. She'd had time to grow used to both Carlisle and me. "I thought you'd gone home."

"My father asked me to keep an eye on Bella while he's helping Dr. Sadarangani. He left me some specific things he wanted watched." I'd used the same excuse several times today. I'd said it with confidence, and the nurses had let their objections slide.

"Are they still at it? They're going to fall asleep standing up."

Of course, Dr. Sadarangani had long ago headed home. But he'd introduced Carlisle to the hematologist on the night shift, and Carlisle was off consulting on some of the more difficult cases.

Bella's mother was broadcasting her confusion. Gloria jumped in to make the introductions.

"This is Dr. Cullen's son. Dr. Cullen is the one who saved your daughter's life."

"You're Edward," Renée realized.

This *is the boyfriend? Oh boy. Bella doesn't stand a chance.*

"I only have the one recliner, honey," Gloria said, "and I think Mrs. Dwyer needs it more than you."

"Of course. I slept earlier. I'm perfectly comfortable standing."

"It's very late...."

I want to talk to him.

"It's fine," Renée said out loud. "I'd like to hear about the accident, if it's okay. We'll be *very* quiet."

I wanted to laugh at that.

"Of course. I'll just do my rounds and check in later on. Try to get some rest, hon."

I smiled as warmly as I could at the woman, and she softened a little.

Poor kid. He's really worried. Won't hurt anything if he stays, especially with the mom here.

I walked over to Renée and held my hand out. She shook it

weakly without standing, exhausted. She recoiled slightly from the chill; an echo of her earlier adrenaline rush washed through her.

"Oh, sorry, the AC is freezing in here. I'm Edward Cullen. I'm very glad to meet you, Mrs. Dwyer, I just wish it was under better circumstances."

He sounds very mature. The room resonated with her approval.

"Call me Renée," she said automatically. "I…I'm sorry, I'm not really myself."

My, but he's handsome.

"Of course you're not. You should rest, as the nurse said."

"No," Renée objected quietly—in her physical voice, at least. "Do you mind talking with me for just a minute?"

"Of course not," I answered. "I'm sure you have a thousand questions."

I picked up the molded plastic chair from beside Bella's bed and moved it closer to Renée.

"She didn't tell me about you," Renée announced. Her thoughts rang with hurt.

"I…I'm sorry. We haven't been…dating for very long."

Renée nodded, and then sighed. "I think it's my fault. Things have been stressful with Phil's schedule and, well, I haven't been the best listener."

"I'm sure she would have told you soon." And then, in the face of her self-doubt, I lied. "I didn't tell my parents for a bit, either. I think neither of us wanted to jinx things by speaking too soon. It's a little silly."

Renée smiled. *That's sweet.* "It's not silly."

I smiled back.

What a heartbreaking smile. Oh, I hope he's not playing with her.

I found myself stumbling to reassure her. "I'm so sorry about what happened. I feel horribly responsible and I'd do anything to make it right. If I could trade places with her, I'd do it." Nothing but the truth there.

She reached out to pat my arm. I was glad the sleeve was thick enough to conceal my skin's temperature. "It's not your fault, Edward."

I wished she were right.

"Charlie told me some of the story, but he was pretty confused," she said.

"I think we all were. Bella, too." I thought of that night, so innocent to begin with, all pleasure and happiness. How quickly everything had gone awry. I felt as though I was still trying to catch up.

"That's my fault," Renée said, suddenly miserable. "I think I messed my girl up. For her to run away because she cares about you—that's all on me."

"No, don't think that." I knew how much it had hurt Bella to say those things to Charlie. I could imagine what she would feel to know her mother was taking this on herself. "Bella's a very strong-willed person. She does what *she* wants. Anyway, she probably just needed some sun."

Renée smiled a tiny bit at that. "Maybe."

"Did you want to hear about the accident?"

"No, I just said that to the nurse. Bella fell down some stairs, it's not that unusual." It was amazing how easily both of her parents accepted the story. "The window was unfortunate."

"Very."

"I just wanted to get to know you a little. Bella wouldn't be acting this way if her feelings were mild. She's never cared seriously about anyone before. I'm not sure she knows what to do."

I smiled at her again. "She and I both."

Sure, handsome, she thought doubtfully. *He's very smooth.*

"Be gentle with my baby," she ordered, more forceful. "She feels things very deeply."

"I promise you I will never do anything to hurt her." I said the words, and I meant them in the strongest way—I would give anything to keep Bella happy and safe—but I wasn't sure they were true. Because what would hurt Bella the most? I couldn't escape the truest answer.

Pomegranate seeds and my underworld. Hadn't I just witnessed a brutal example of how badly my world could go wrong for her? And she was lying here broken because of it.

Surely, keeping her with me would be the greatest hurt possible.

Hmm, he thinks he means it. Well, people get broken hearts, and then they recover. It's part of life. But then she thought of Charlie's face and was uneasy. *I can't think, I'm so tired. It will all make sense in the morning.*

"You should sleep. It's very late in Florida." I could hear how distorted with pain my voice had become, but she didn't know my voice that well.

She nodded, eyes drooping. "Wake me if she needs anything?"

"Yes, I will."

She nestled into her uncomfortable chair and was quickly unconscious.

I moved my chair back to Bella's side. It was strange to see her so still in sleep. I wished more than anything that she would start mumbling something from her dreams. I wondered whether I was there with her, in the dark. I didn't know if it was right to hope that I was.

While I listened to mother and daughter breathe, I thought about Alice for the first time since she'd left me here alone. It was unlike her to give me this much space, no matter how desperate my mental state. I realized I'd been expecting her to check on Bella and me for some time now. And I could only guess one reason why she had avoided me instead.

I'd had plenty of time to process the events of the day, but I *hadn't*. I'd just stared at Bella and wished fruitlessly that I'd been more, that I'd been better. That I'd found the right thing and stuck to it before this nightmare could have touched her.

Now I realized there was something more I had to do. I knew

it would be painful, but also that it would not be painful *enough*. I deserved worse. I didn't want to leave Bella, but this wasn't the place. I would call Alice. I wasn't sure where she had gone to hide from me.

I stepped out into the hall—much to the interest of two nurses, who had wondered whether I would ever leave the room—and before I could reach for my phone I heard Alice's thoughts coming up the stairs. I walked out to meet her just inside the stairwell doors.

She was carrying something in her hands, something small and black and wrapped in thin cords, and she held it as though she wished she could crush her hands together to destroy it. Part of me was surprised she hadn't.

I've had this argument with you over three hundred times, but I could never convince you.

"No, you can't. I need to see this."

Agree to disagree. But here. She shoved the camera toward me, and I could see she was happy to be rid of it. I took it unwillingly. It felt dark and wrong in my hand. *Go somewhere you can be alone.*

I nodded. It was good advice.

I'll keep an eye on Bella. It's not necessary, but I know it will make you feel better.

"Thank you."

Alice darted out of the stairwell.

I wandered the halls, which were quiet this late, but not unoccupied. I thought of ducking into a vacant patient room, but that didn't feel secluded enough. I made my way to the lobby and exited to the grounds. This felt more alone, but I could still see the odd security officer making rounds. As long as I walked with purpose, they didn't mind me, but if I were to linger, I was sure they would come question me.

I searched for a bubble of empty space, and was relieved to find an area devoid of human thoughts just across the large circular drive.

It seemed ironic that the deserted building was the campus chapel, lit and unlocked, despite the hour. I knew the place would have comforted Carlisle, but I was fairly sure nothing could help me now.

From the inside, I couldn't find a way to lock the door, so I went to the very front of the room, as far from that door as possible. There were wooden folding chairs instead of pews. I pulled one against the wall, in the shadow of the organ.

Alice had left me with headphones. I put them in my ears.

Closing my eyes, I took a deep breath. Once I saw this, I would have it in my head forever. There would never be a release from it. That seemed fair. Bella had lived it. I would only have to watch.

I opened my eyes and powered the camera on. The replay screen was just two inches across. I didn't know whether to be grateful for that, or if I deserved to see it on a much larger scale.

The video began on a close-up of the tracker's face. James—the name was too benign for what he was. He smiled at me, and I knew that this was what he wanted—to smile at *me*. This was all for me. What followed would be a conversation between the two of us. One-sided, but for all that would happen, Bella would never be the object. I was.

"Hello," he said in a pleasant tone. "Welcome to the show. I hope you enjoy what I've prepared for you. I'm sorry that it's a little rushed, a little thrown together. Who would have guessed it would only take me a few days to win? Before the curtain goes up, so to speak, I'd like to remind you that this is really your own fault. If you'd stayed out of my way, it would have been quick. This is more fun, though, isn't it? Again, enjoy!"

The video cut to black, and then a new "scene" began. I recognized the angle of the camera. It was in place on top of the TV, pointed across the long wall of mirrors. The tracker was just leaning away. His speed, as he darted to the far-right side of the shot, was almost invisible to the camera—only a disjointed flicker was recorded. He settled himself there by the emergency exit, freezing in place with one hand extended. In that hand, a black rectangle. A remote control. His head was cocked slightly to the side, listening. He heard something too low for the recording, and smiled directly at the camera. At me.

Then I could hear her, too. Running, stumbling feet. Strained breathing. A door opened, and then a pause.

The tracker lifted his remote and pressed a button.

Louder than anything else so far, coming through the speakers right under the camera, Bella's mother's voice cried out in panic.

"Bella? Bella?"

In the other room, the footsteps were running again.

"Bella, you scared me!" Renée said.

Bella burst into the room, panicked and searching.

"Don't you ever do that to me again," Renée continued with a laugh.

Bella spun to the sound of her mother's voice, turned to face me now, her eyes focusing just below the camera. I watched as the realization hit. She hadn't entirely processed the trick yet, but I could see the relief beginning. Her mother wasn't in danger.

The sound from the speakers went silent. Bella moved reluctantly. She didn't want to see, but she knew he was there. She stiffened when her eyes found him, waiting motionlessly. I could only see the side of her face, but I could see him clearly as he smiled at her.

He approached, and I had to loosen my fingers. It was too soon to crush the recorder. He passed her, continued to the TV to set the remote down. As he did so, he looked into the camera and winked at me. Then he turned to face her. The way he turned his body put his back to me, but I had a perfect view of Bella. The camera was angled so that I couldn't see him in the mirrors. That must have been a mistake on his part. I imagined he wanted me to see his performance.

"Sorry about that, Bella, but isn't it better that your mother didn't really have to be involved in all this?"

Bella looked at him with a strange, almost relaxed expression. "Yes."

"You don't sound angry that I tricked you."

"I'm not." Truth radiated in her tone.

The tracker hesitated for one second. "How odd. You really mean it." His head cocked to the side, but I could only guess at his expression. "I will give your strange coven this much, you humans can be quite interesting. I guess I can see the draw of observing you. It's amazing—some of you seem to have no sense of your own self-interest at all."

He leaned toward her as though he was expecting an answer, but she stayed silent. Her eyes were opaque, giving nothing away.

"I suppose you're going to tell me that your boyfriend will avenge you?" he asked, his voice taunting. The taunt was not for her.

"No, I don't think so," Bella replied quietly. "At least, I asked him not to."

"And what was his reply to that?"

"I don't know. I left him a letter."

Please, please don't come after him, she'd written in that letter. *I love you. Forgive me.*

Her manner was almost casual. This seemed to bother the tracker, because his voice was sharper now, his tone twisting into something ominous.

"How romantic." The sarcasm was palpable. "A last letter. And do you think he will honor it?"

Her eyes were still impossible to read, but her face was calm as she said, "I hope so."

Please, this is the only thing I can ask you now, she'd written. *For me.*

"Hmmm. Well, our hopes differ, then." His voice turned sour. Bella's composure was disrupting the scene he had planned. "You see, this was all just a little too easy, too quick. To be quite honest, I'm disappointed. I expected a much greater challenge. And, after all, I only needed a little luck."

Bella's expression was patient now, like a parent who knows that her toddler's story is going to be long and rambling but is determined to humor him anyway.

The tracker's voice grew harder in response. "When Victoria couldn't get to your father, I had her find out more about you. There was no sense in running all over the planet chasing you down when I could comfortably wait for you in a place of my choosing...."

The tracker kept going, working to keep his words slow and smug, but I could feel the undercurrent of his frustration. He started talking faster. Bella didn't react. She waited, patient and polite. It was obvious this rattled him.

I'd thought little about how the tracker had found Bella—there hadn't been time for anything besides action—but this all made sense. None of it surprised me. I winced a little when I realized our flight to Phoenix had been the trigger for his last move. But it was only one of a thousand mistakes on my conscience.

He was wrapping up his monologue—I wondered whether he thought I would be impressed?—and I tried to brace myself for what would follow.

"Very easy, you know," he concluded. "Not really up to my standards. So, you see, I'm hoping you're wrong about your boyfriend. Edward, isn't it?" It was a silly thing, to pretend he'd forgotten my name. He couldn't forget it any more than I would ever forget his.

Bella didn't answer him. She was looking a little confused now. As though she didn't understand the point. She didn't realize the show wasn't for her.

"Would you mind, very much, if I left a little letter of my own for your Edward?"

The tracker walked backward until he was out of the frame. The picture suddenly zoomed tight on only Bella's face.

Her expression was perfectly clear to me. She was starting to realize. She'd known he was going to kill her. She had never considered that he would torture her first. Panic touched her eyes for the first time since she'd discovered her mother was safe.

My own fear and horror grew with hers. How would I survive this? I didn't know. But she had, so I must.

When the tracker was sure I'd had time to absorb her dawning fear, he widened the frame again, turning the angle slightly so that I could now see his reflection in the mirror over Bella's shoulder.

"I'm sorry, but I just don't think he'll be able to resist hunting me after he watches this." He was satisfied again with his production. Bella's terror was the drama he'd been waiting for, expecting. "And I wouldn't want him to miss anything. It was all for him, of course. You're simply a human, who unfortunately was in the wrong place, at the wrong time, and indisputably running with the wrong crowd, I might add."

He stepped into frame again, moving closer to her. His smile was twisted in the mirrors. "Before we begin..."

Bella's lips were white.

"I would just like to rub it in, just a little bit." His eyes met mine in the mirror. "The answer was there all along, and I was so afraid Edward would see that and ruin my fun. It happened once, oh, ages ago. The one and only time my prey escaped me."

Alice had shown me the way to make the tracker lose interest. He didn't realize that I'd rejected the idea. He would never have understood why.

He began another monologue, and though I recognized that his need to gloat was the reason Bella had survived long enough for us to get there, I was still grinding my teeth in frustration until he said the words *little friend*, and I realized this was something more. This was what Bella had tried to tell us. *Alice, the video—he knew you, Alice, he knew where you came from.*

"...She didn't even seem to notice the pain, poor little creature," the tracker was explaining. "She'd been stuck in that black hole of a cell for so long. A hundred years earlier and she would have been burned at the stake for her visions. In the nineteen twenties, it was the asylum and the shock treatments. When she opened her eyes, strong with her fresh youth, it was like she'd never seen the sun before. The old vampire made her a strong new vampire, and there was no reason for me to touch her then. I destroyed the old one in vengeance."

"Alice," Bella breathed. The revelation didn't bring any color back into her face. Her lips were ever so faintly green now. Would she pass out? I found myself hoping there would be a break, a moment of escape, even though I knew it couldn't last.

There was a lot to think about here, and at some point I would want to know what Alice felt, but not now. Not now.

"Yes, your little friend. I *was* surprised to see her in the clearing." He made eye contact with me again. "So I guess her coven ought to be able to derive some comfort from this experience. I get you, but they get her. The one victim who escaped me, quite an honor, actually.

"And she did smell so delicious. I still regret that I never got to taste...She smelled even better than you do. Sorry—I don't mean to be offensive. You have a very nice smell. Floral, somehow..."

He walked closer and closer until he was looming over her, then reached out with one hand, and I nearly crushed the camera again. He didn't hurt her yet, he just played with a strand of her hair, drawing out her dread. Milking it.

I slid out of the chair, to the ground, and put the camera on the floor beside me. I clenched my fists tightly together. It was good I had done this. Next the tracker reached out to softly stroke her cheek, and I wondered if I would break my hands.

"No, I don't understand," the tracker concluded. "Well, I suppose we should get on with it." He looked at me again, the hint of a smile on his lips. He wanted me to see that he was eager, that he was going to enjoy this. "And then I can call your friends and tell them where to find you, and my little message."

Bella started to tremble. Her face was so ashen I was surprised she was still on her feet. The tracker started to circle her, smiling at me in the mirror. He crouched, his eyes shifted to her face, and that smile turned into an exhibition of teeth.

Terrified, she broke for the back door. I guessed this is what he wanted, that he'd been trying to goad her into action. His bared teeth shifted into a pleased smile as he leaped in front of her and, with a dismissive backhand, hurled her toward the wall of mirrors.

She was airborne for one fleeting, endless pause, and then with a metallic clang, a crunch of bone, and the shattering of glass, she slammed into the brass ballet barre and the mirror behind it. The barre burst free of its brackets and crashed to the boards below. Her body followed, completely limp as she slid to the floor, splinters of glass catching the light like glitter around her. I hoped again that she was unconscious. But then I saw her eyes.

Stunned, helpless, petrified.

My hands ached with the crushing pressure of my grip, but I couldn't relax them.

The tracker sauntered toward her, his eyes focused in the mirror on the lens of the camera, staring at me.

"That's a very nice effect," he pointed out to me, hoping I wasn't taking any of his planning for granted. "I thought this room would be visually dramatic for my little film. That's why I picked this place to meet you. It's perfect, isn't it?"

I didn't know if Bella was aware of his shift in attention, or if she was just acting on instinct alone, but she twisted painfully to put her hands on the floor and began crawling for the entrance.

The tracker laughed quietly at her pathetic attempt, and then he was standing over her.

Alice had shown me this. I wished I could look away. But I couldn't, and the tracker's foot came down hard against her calf. I heard both snaps as her tibia and her fibula gave way.

Her whole body jerked, and then her scream filled the small room, ricocheting off the glass and the polished wood. It felt like a drill boring into my ears through the headphones. Her face strained with the agony, and tiny blood vessels burst inside her eyes.

"Would you like to rethink your last request?" he asked Bella, all his focus on her now. He pointed one toe and pressed it with delicate care into the nexus of the break.

Bella screamed again, the sound scraping and tearing out of her throat.

"Wouldn't you rather have Edward try to find me?" the tracker prompted like a director on the edge of the stage.

The tracker was going to torture her until she begged me to hunt him. She must know that I would understand that her answer was coerced. Surely she would give him what he wanted quickly.

"Tell him what he wants to hear," I whispered uselessly to her.

"No!" she rasped hoarsely. For the first time she stared into the camera's lens, her bloody eyes pleading, speaking directly to me. "No, Edward, don't—"

He kicked her in her upturned face.

I'd already seen the mark of this blow developing across the left side of her face. There were two tiny fissures in her cheekbone. He'd been careful, knowing if he kicked her with even a fraction of his strength, it would kill her, and he wasn't done yet. It was just a tap, really.

She flew through the air again.

I saw his mistake immediately, watching her trajectory.

The glass was already broken, the buckled edges pointing outward like ragged silver teeth. Her head hit nearly the same spot as before, but this time the glass teeth ripped into her scalp as gravity pulled her down to the floor. The sound of her skin giving way was impossible to miss.

He turned to watch, and in the mirror I saw his expression tighten when he realized what he'd done.

Blood was already seeping through her hair, trickling in crimson threads down the sides of her face, rolling down her neck and pooling in the hollows above her collarbones. Just watching this called fire into my throat, and the memory of the taste of that blood.

The blood found the floor, dripping in loud splats as it started to puddle around her elbows.

There was so much blood, flowing so quickly. It was overwhelming. I watched, shocked that she'd survived this. The tracker watched, too, all his planning and all his conceit fading. His face turned feral, inhuman. Some small part of him wanted to fight his thirst—I could see that in his eyes—but he wasn't conditioned for control. He could barely remember his audience or his show.

A hunting snarl ripped from between his teeth. Instinctively, she raised one hand to protect herself. Her eyes were already closed, life bleeding from her face.

An explosive crunch, a roar. The tracker lunged. A pale shape flashed so quickly through the shot that it was impossible to make it out. The tracker vanished from the scene. I saw the crimson mark of his teeth across Bella's palm, and then her hand fell, lifeless, into the lake of blood with a quiet splash.

I watched, entirely numb, as my image on the screen sobbed and Carlisle's worked to save her. My eyes were pulled to the bottom right corner of the shot, where every now and then, some piece of the tracker would flash through the picture. Emmett's elbow, the back of Jasper's head. It was impossible to create any sense of the fight from these little glimpses. Someday, I would have Emmett or Jasper remember it for me. I doubted it would soothe any of the rage I felt. Even if I *had* been the one to rip the tracker apart and burn him, it wouldn't have been enough. Nothing could make this right again.

Eventually, Alice walked toward the lens. A spasm of agony crossed her features, and I knew she was seeing a vision of the recording, and also, I was sure, a vision of me watching it now. She picked up the camera, and the screen went dark.

I reached slowly for the camera and then, just as slowly, methodically crushed it into a pile of metal and plastic dust.

When that was done, I pulled from my shirt pocket the little bottle cap I'd been carrying around with me for weeks. My token of Bella—my talisman, my silly but reassuring physical link to her.

It flashed dully in my hand for a moment, and then I pulverized it between my thumb and index finger and let the fragments of steel fall onto the remains of the camera.

I didn't deserve any link, any claim to her at all.

I sat for a long time in the empty chapel. At one point, music started playing quietly through the speakers, but no one entered and there was no sign that anyone had noticed me here. I guessed the music was on an automatic timer. It was the adagio sostenuto from Rachmaninoff's second piano concerto.

I listened, numb and cold, trying to remind myself that Bella was going to be all right. That I could get up now and return to her side. That Alice had seen that her eyes would open again in only thirty-six more hours. A day and a night and a day.

None of that seemed relevant now. Because it was my fault, everything she had suffered.

I stared out the high windows across from me, watching the black of night slowly give way to a pale gray sky.

And then I did something I hadn't done in a century.

Curled there in a ball on the floor, motionless with agony... I prayed.

I didn't pray to my God. I'd always instinctively known that there was no deity for my kind. It made no sense for immortals to have a god; we had taken ourselves out of any god's power. We created our lives, and the only power strong enough to take them away again was another like us. Earthquakes couldn't crush us, floods couldn't drown us, fires were too slow to catch us. Sulfur and brimstone were irrelevant. We were the gods of our own alternate universe. Inside the mortal world but over it, never slaves to its laws, only our own.

There was no God that I belonged to. No one for me to supplicate. Carlisle had different ideas, and maybe, just maybe, an exception could be made for someone like him. But I wasn't like him. I was stained like all the rest of our kind.

Instead, I prayed to *her* God. Because if there was some higher, benevolent power in her universe, then surely, *surely*, he or she or it would have to be concerned about this bravest and kindest daughter. If not, there was really no purpose to any such entity. I had to believe she mattered to that distant God, if one existed at all.

So I prayed to her God for the strength I would need. I knew I wasn't strong enough in myself—the power would have to come from the outside. With perfect clarity, I recalled Alice's visions of Bella abandoned—her bleak, shadowed, empty, hollow face. Her pain and her nightmares. I'd never been able to imagine my resolve *not* breaking, *not* caving to the knowledge of her grief. I couldn't imagine it now. But I would have to do it. I had to learn the strength.

I prayed to her God with all the anguish of my damned, lost soul that he—or she, or it—would help me protect Bella from myself.

29. INEVITABILITY

ALICE HAD SEEN THE MOMENT WHEN BELLA WOULD finally open her eyes. There were practical reasons why I needed to have some time alone with her before she spoke to anyone else; Bella knew nothing of our cover actions. Of course, Alice or Carlisle could have handled this, and Bella was bright enough to feign amnesia until she could get her story straight, but Alice knew I needed more than just to clear up the narrative.

Over the hours of waiting, Alice had introduced herself to Renée, and then proceeded to charm her until they were now close confidantes, in Renée's head, at least. It was Alice who convinced Renée to go have lunch at the perfect time.

This was just after one o'clock in the afternoon. I'd had the blinds closed against the morning sun, but I'd be able to crack them soon. The sun was on the other side of the hospital now.

Once Renée was gone, I pulled my chair close to Bella's bed, resting my elbows on the edge of the mattress next to her shoulder. I didn't know if she would have felt the time passing, or if her mind would still be back in that accursed room of mirrors. She would need reassurance, and I knew her well enough to be sure that my face would comfort her. For good or ill, I put her at ease.

She started to fidget right on schedule. She'd moved before, but this was a more concentrated effort. Her forehead creased when her efforts caused her pain, and the little stress *v* appeared between her brows. As I had so often wanted to do, I brushed softly across that *v* with my index finger, trying to erase it. It faded slightly, and her eyes started to flutter. The beeping of her heart rate monitor accelerated slightly.

Her eyes opened, then closed. She tried again, squinting against the brightness of the overhead lights. She looked away, toward the window, while her eyes adjusted. Her heart was beating faster now. Hands struggling with the monitor lines, she reached for the tubing under her nose, obviously meaning to remove it. I caught her hand.

"No you don't," I said quietly.

As soon as she heard my voice, her heart started to slow.

"Edward?" She couldn't turn her head as far as she wanted. I leaned closer. Our eyes met, and hers, still dotted with red, started filling with tears. "Oh, Edward, I'm so sorry."

It hurt in a very specific and piercing kind of way when she apologized to me.

"Shhh," I insisted. "Everything's all right now."

"What happened?" she asked, her forehead wrinkling as though she was trying to solve a riddle.

I'd had my answer planned. I'd thought through the gentlest way to explain. Instead, my own fears and remorse came flooding through my lips.

"I was almost too late. I could have been too late."

She stared at me for a long moment, and I watched as the memories returned. She winced, and her breathing accelerated. "I was so stupid, Edward. I thought he had my mom."

"He tricked us all."

Urgency had her brows pulling together. "I need to call Charlie and my mom."

"Alice called them." She'd taken over for Carlisle, and now she chatted with Charlie several times a day. Like Renée, he was entirely bewitched. I knew Alice had been planning the post-wakeup call. She was excited it would happen today. "Renée is here—well, here in the hospital. She's getting something to eat right now."

Bella shifted her weight as if she was about to lurch out of bed. "She's here?"

I caught her shoulder and held her in place. She blinked a few times, looking around herself, dizzy.

"She'll be back soon," I assured her. "And you need to stay still."

This didn't calm her the way I'd intended. Her eyes were panicked. "But what did you tell her? Why did you tell her I'm here?"

I smiled slightly. "You fell down two flights of stairs and through a window."

Given the way both her parents had accepted our story—not just that it was possible, but that it was somehow to be expected—I felt justified in adding, "You have to admit, it could happen."

She sighed, but she seemed calmer now that she knew the alibi. She stared down at her sheet-covered body for a few seconds.

"How bad am I?" she asked.

I listed off the larger injuries. "You have a broken leg, four broken ribs, some cracks in your skull, bruises covering every inch of your skin, and you've lost a lot of blood. They gave you a few transfusions. I didn't like it—it made you smell all wrong for a while."

She smiled, and then winced. "That must have been a nice change for you."

"No, I like how *you* smell."

She looked carefully into my eyes then, searching. After a long moment of this, she asked, "How did you do it?"

I didn't know why this subject was so unpleasant. I *had* succeeded. I knew Emmett, Jasper, and Alice were awestruck by my accomplishment. But I couldn't see it the same way. It had been too close. I remembered with such unbearable clarity how badly my body had wanted to stay in that bliss forever.

I couldn't meet her gaze any longer. I looked down at her hand, taking it carefully into mine. The wires spilled out on either side.

"I'm not sure," I whispered.

She didn't speak, and I could feel her eyes on me, waiting for a better answer. I sighed.

My words were barely louder than a breath. "It was impossible...to stop. Impossible. But I did."

I tried to smile at her then, to meet her gaze. "I *must* love you."

"Don't I taste as good as I smell?" She grinned at her joke, then flinched, feeling the damage to her cheekbone.

I didn't try to play along with her lighthearted tone. Obviously, she shouldn't be smiling.

"Even better," I answered honestly, if a little bitterly. "Better than I'd imagined."

"I'm sorry."

I rolled my eyes. "Of all the things to apologize for."

She examined my expression, and seemed unsatisfied by what she found. "What *should* I apologize for?"

Nothing, I wanted to say, but I could see she was in an apologetic mood, so I gave her something to reflect on. "For very nearly taking yourself away from me forever."

She nodded absently, accepting that. "I'm sorry."

I stroked the back of her hand, wondering if she could feel my touch through all the dressings. "I know why you did it. It was still irrational, of course. You should have waited for me, you should have told me."

This made no sense to her. "You wouldn't have let me go."

"No," I said through my teeth. "I wouldn't."

Her eyes were far away for a moment, and her heart sped. A shudder rocked through her, and then she hissed at the pain that caused.

"Bella, what's wrong?"

She whimpered. "What happened to James?"

Well, I could set her at ease about this much. "After I pulled him off you, Emmett and Jasper took care of him."

She frowned, winced, then smoothed her expression. "I didn't see Emmett and Jasper there."

"They had to leave the room... there was a lot of blood." A river of it. For a second, it felt as though I were still stained with it.

"But you stayed," she breathed.

"Yes, I stayed."

"And Alice, and Carlisle..." Her voice was full of wonder.

I smiled just a little. "They love you, too, you know."

Her expression was abruptly anxious again. "Did Alice see the tape?"

"Yes."

It was a subject we were currently avoiding. I knew she was doing her own research, and she knew I wasn't ready to discuss it with her yet.

"She was always in the dark," Bella said urgently. "That's why she didn't remember."

It was so very Bella that all her concern would be focused on someone else, even in this moment.

"I know. She understands now."

I wasn't sure what my face was doing, but it concerned Bella. She tried to reach up, to touch my cheek, but stopped when the IV pulled at her hand.

"Ugh," she groaned.

Had she dislodged the IV? Her motion hadn't been that rough, but it wasn't as if I could examine it closely.

"What is it?" I demanded.

"Needles," she said. She was staring up at the ceiling now, concentrating as if there were something more riveting than basic acoustic tiles above her. She took a deep breath, and I was stunned to see some pale green edging her lips.

"Afraid of a needle," I grumbled. "Oh, a sadistic vampire,

intent on torturing her to death, sure, no problem, she runs off to meet him. An *IV*, on the other hand..."

She rolled her eyes. The green was already fading.

Then her eyes cut to me and she asked in a troubled tone, "Why are *you* here?"

I'd thought...but that didn't matter. "Do you want me to leave?"

Maybe what I needed to do would be easier than I'd thought. Pain stabbed through the general region of my obsolete heart.

"No!" she protested; it was almost a shout. She deliberately moderated her volume back to a near whisper. "*No*, I meant, why does my *mother* think you're here? I need to have my story straight before she gets back."

"Oh."

Of course it wouldn't be that easy. So many times I'd thought she was done with me, but she never was.

"I came to Phoenix to talk some sense into you," I explained, using the same sincere and guileless voice I used when I needed the nurses to believe that I was supposed to stay in this room. "To convince you to come back to Forks. You agreed to see me, and you drove out to the hotel where I was staying with Carlisle and Alice." I opened my eyes wide, made them extra innocent. "Of course I was here with parental supervision....But you tripped on the stairs on the way to my room and...well, you know the rest. You don't need to remember any details, though; you have a good excuse to be a little muddled about the finer points."

She considered this for a second. "There are a few flaws with that story. Like no broken windows."

I couldn't help grinning. "Not really. Alice had a little bit too much fun fabricating evidence. It's all been taken care of very convincingly—you could probably sue the hotel if you wanted to."

This idea obviously scandalized her.

I stroked her unbruised cheek softly. "You have nothing to worry about. Your only job now is to heal."

And then her heart started racing. I looked for signs of pain, I thought through my words for something upsetting, but then I noticed the dilation of her pupils and realized. She was responding to my touch.

Her eyes focused on the machine beeping out her heart's excesses, and narrowed. "That's going to be embarrassing."

I laughed quietly at her expression. A light blush was coloring her good cheek.

"Hmm, I wonder. . . ."

I was already only inches from her face. Slowly, I erased that distance. Her heart raced faster. When I kissed her, my lips barely brushing against hers, that rhythm stuttered. Her heart literally skipped a beat.

I jerked away from her, anxious until her heart resumed a healthy cadence.

"It seems that I'm going to have to be even more careful with you than usual."

She frowned, winced, then said, "I was not finished kissing you. Don't make me come over there."

I smiled at the threat, then gently kissed her again, quitting as soon as her heart started acting up. It was a very short kiss.

She looked about to complain, but this experiment had to be put on hold regardless.

I scooted my chair a foot from her bed. "I think I hear your mother."

Renée was climbing the stairs now, on her way to get some quarters from her bag, worrying about the junk food she'd been consuming over the past few days. She wished she had time for a gym visit, but for now the stairs would have to do.

Bella's face contorted. I assumed it was pain. I leaned close again, desperate for something to do.

"Don't leave me," Bella said, a sob close to the surface of her voice. Her eyes were tight with fear.

I didn't want to think about this reaction.

In my head, Alice's vision tormented me. Bella, curled in on herself in agony, gasping for air....

I gathered myself for a moment, then tried to answer casually. "I won't. I'll...take a nap."

I grinned at her and then dashed to the turquoise easy chair and reclined it all the way back. After all, Renée had told me to use it whenever I needed a break. I closed my eyes.

"Don't forget to breathe," she whispered. I remembered her playing asleep for her father's benefit, and fought a smile. I took an exaggerated breath.

Renée was walking by the nurses' station now.

"Any change?" she asked the nurse's assistant on duty, a solid younger woman named Bea. It was clear from Renée's absent-minded tone that she expected a negative response. She kept walking.

"Actually, there's been some fluctuation on her monitors. I was about to go in."

Oh no, I shouldn't have left.

Renée was taking longer strides now, worried. "I'll check on her and let you know...."

The aide, rising out of her chair, sat back down again, bowing to Renée's desires.

Bella twitched and the bed squeaked. It was obvious how much her mother's distress upset her.

Renée opened the door quietly. Of course she wanted Bella to wake up, but it still felt rude to be noisy.

"Mom!" Bella whispered joyously.

I couldn't see Renée's expression while pretending to sleep, but her thoughts were overwhelmed. I heard her footsteps falter. And then she noticed my sleeping form.

"He never leaves, does he?" she mumbled quietly, and shouted mentally—I'd gotten used to the volume, though; it wasn't as startling as it used to be. But she was a little appeased. She'd begun to wonder if I *ever* slept.

"Mom, I'm so glad to see you!" Bella enthused.

Renée was startled for a second by Bella's bloodstained eyes. Her own started to well with tears at this fresh proof of Bella's suffering.

I peeked through my lids to watch Renée gingerly embrace her daughter. The tears had overflowed onto Renée's cheeks.

"Bella, I was so upset!"

"I'm sorry, Mom. But everything's fine now, it's okay."

It was uncomfortable to listen to Bella, in her condition, soothe her healthy mother, but I supposed this had always been their relationship. Perhaps the way Renée's unique mind interacted with others had made her into a something of a narcissist. It would be hard to avoid, when everyone catered to your unspoken needs.

"I'm just glad to finally see your eyes open." Though she winced internally again at their gruesome condition.

There was a moment of silence, and then Bella asked doubtfully, "How long have they been closed?"

I realized this was something we'd not yet discussed.

"It's Friday, hon," Renée told her. "You've been out for a while."

Bella was shocked. "Friday?"

"They had to keep you sedated for a while, honey—you've got a lot of injuries."

"I *know*," Bella agreed with emphasis. I wondered how much pain she was in now.

"You're lucky Dr. Cullen was there. He's such a nice man.... Very young, though. And he looks more like a model than a doctor...."

"You met Carlisle?"

"And Edward's sister Alice. She's a lovely girl."

"She is!"

Renée's piercing thoughts turned to me again. "You didn't tell me you had such good friends in Forks."

Very, very good friends.

Suddenly, Bella moaned.

My eyes opened of their own accord. They didn't give me away; Renée's gaze was trained on Bella, too.

"What hurts?" she demanded.

"It's fine," Bella assured Renée, though I could tell the assurance was for me, too. Our eyes locked for a second before I closed mine again. "I just have to remember not to move."

Renée fluttered uselessly over her daughter's inert form. When Bella spoke again, her voice was bright. "Where's Phil?"

Renée was totally distracted, which I thought was rather the point.

I haven't told her the good news. Oh, she'll be so happy.

"Florida—oh, Bella! You'll never guess! Just when we were about to leave, the best news!"

"Phil got signed?" Bella asked. I could hear the smile in her voice, sure of the answer.

"Yes! How did you guess? The Suns, can you believe it?"

"That's great, Mom," Bella said, but there was a little blankness in her tone that told me she had no idea who the Suns were.

"And you'll like Jacksonville so much." Renée was nearly bursting with enthusiasm. Her thoughts shouted along with her words, and I was sure those thoughts would work on Bella the way they worked on everyone else. She began to gush about the weather, the ocean, the adorable yellow house with the white trim, never doubting that Bella would be just as thrilled as she was.

I knew every aspect of Renée's plan for Bella's future. Renée had mentally enthused about her happy news a hundred times while we waited for Bella to wake. In many ways, her plan was exactly the answer I'd been looking for.

"Wait, Mom!" Bella said, confused. I imagined Renée's enthusiasm smothering her like a heavy down comforter. "What are you talking about? I'm not going to Florida. I live in Forks."

"But you don't have to anymore, silly." Renée laughed. "Phil will be able to be around so much more now.... We've talked about it a lot, and what I'm going to do is trade off on the away games, half the time with you, half the time with him."

Renée waited for Bella's delight to dawn.

"Mom," Bella said slowly, "I *want* to live in Forks. I'm already settled in at school, and I have a couple of girlfriends. . . ."

Renée's eyes shifted to glare at me again.

"And Charlie needs me," Bella continued. "He's just all alone up there, and he can't cook *at all*."

"You want to stay in Forks?" Renée asked as though the words made no sense in that order. "Why?"

That boy is the real reason.

"I told you—school, Charlie—ouch!"

Again, I had to look. Renée hovered over Bella, her hands reaching out hesitantly, not sure where to touch. She ended up putting one hand on Bella's forehead.

"Bella, honey, you hate Forks." Renée sounded concerned that Bella had forgotten.

Bella's voice took on a defensive edge. "It's not so bad."

Renée decided to cut to the heart of it.

"Is it this boy?" she whispered. It was more an accusation than a question.

Bella hesitated, then admitted, "He's part of it. . . . So, have you had a chance to talk with Edward?"

"Yes, and I want to talk to you about that."

"What about?" Bella responded innocently.

"I think that boy is in love with you," Renée whispered.

"I think so, too."

Is Bella in love? How much have I missed? How could she not tell me? What am I supposed to do?

"And . . . how do you feel about him?"

Bella sighed, and then her tone was nonchalant. "I'm pretty crazy about him."

"Well, he *seems* very nice, and my goodness, he's incredibly good-looking, but you're so young, Bella. . . ."

And you're too much like Charlie. It's too soon.

"I know that, Mom," Bella agreed easily. "Don't worry about it. It's just a crush."

"That's right," Renée said.

Good. So she's not getting all intense and Charlie-ish about this. Oh, is that the time? I'm late.

Bella picked up on Renée's sudden distraction. "Do you need to go?"

"Phil's supposed to call in a little while. . . . I didn't know you were going to wake up. . . ."

The phone is probably ringing at the house right now. I should have found the number here.

"No problem, Mom." Bella couldn't entirely hide her relief. "I won't be alone."

"I'll be back soon. I've been sleeping here, you know," Renée added, flaunting her Good Mother behavior.

"Oh, Mom, you don't have to do that!" Bella was upset by the idea of her mother sacrificing for her. That wasn't the direction their relationship went. "You can sleep at home—I'll never notice."

"I was too nervous," Renée admitted, self-aware enough to sound sheepish after her brag. "There's been some crime in the neighborhood, and I don't like being there alone."

"Crime?" Bella was instantly on high alert.

"Someone broke into that dance studio around the corner from the house and burned it to the ground—there's nothing left at all! And they left a stolen car right out front. Do you remember when you used to dance there, honey?"

We weren't the only ones who had stolen cars. The tracker's had actually been parked around the south side of the dance studio. We hadn't known to clean up his crimes as well as our own. And it was helpful to our alibis, as that car had been boosted a day before we'd arrived in Phoenix.

"I remember," Bella said with a quaver in her voice.

I had a difficult time holding my position. Renée, too, was moved.

"I can stay, baby, if you need me."

"No, Mom, I'll be fine. Edward will be with me."

Of course he will. Oh well, I really have to do some laundry and I should probably clean out the fridge. That milk is months old.

"I'll be back tonight."

"I love you, Mom."

"I love you, too, Bella. Try to be more careful when you walk, honey, I don't want to lose you."

I worked to control the grin that burst through my façade.

Bea came in to make her rounds, weaving around Renée in a practiced way to get to Bella's monitors.

Renée kissed Bella on the forehead, patted her hand, and then made her getaway, eager to tell Phil the news that Bella was better.

"Are you feeling anxious, honey?" Bea inquired. "Your heart rate got a little high there."

"I'm fine," Bella assured her.

"I'll tell your RN that you're awake. She'll be in to see you in a minute."

Before the door was closed behind Bea, I was at Bella's side.

Her eyebrows were raised high, either worried or impressed. "You stole a car?"

I knew she meant the car in the parking lot, but she wasn't wrong. Except that it was two cars. "It was a good car, very fast," I told her.

"How was your nap?" she asked.

All the playfulness of our interaction faded. "Interesting."

The change in mood confused her. "What?"

I stared at the tall mound that was her mangled leg, not sure what she would see in my eyes. "I'm surprised," I said slowly. "I thought Florida...and your mother...well, I thought that's what you would want."

"But you'd be stuck inside all day in Florida," she pointed out, not following. "You'd only be able to come out at night, just like a real vampire."

The way she phrased it made me want to smile, but I also wanted very much *not* to smile.

"I would stay in Forks, Bella. Or somewhere like it. Someplace where I couldn't hurt you anymore."

She stared at me with a blank expression, as though I'd answered her in Latin. I waited for her to process my meaning. Then her heart started to beat faster and her breathing shifted into hyperventilation. She flinched with every breath, her expanding lungs pushing against her broken ribs.

An echo of the grieving future Bella flashed across her face.

It was hard to watch. I wanted to say something to ease her pain, her *terror*, but this was supposed to be the right thing. It did not feel right, but I couldn't trust my own selfish emotions.

Gloria walked into the room, just in for her afternoon shift. She appraised Bella with an expert eye.

I'd say she's about at a six. It's good to see her poor eyes open, though.

"Time for more pain meds, sweetheart?" she asked kindly, tapping the IV feed.

"No, no," Bella objected, breathless. "I don't need anything."

"No need to be brave, honey. It's better if you don't get too stressed out; you need to rest."

Gloria waited for Bella to change her mind. Bella carefully shook her head, her expression a mixture of pain and defiance.

Gloria sighed. "Okay. Hit the call button when you're ready."

She glanced at me, not sure how she felt about my constant vigil, and then looked at Bella's monitors once more before leaving.

Bella's eyes were still wild. I put my hands on either side of her face, barely touching the broken left cheek. "Shh, Bella, calm down."

"Don't leave me," she begged, her voice breaking.

And this was why I was not strong enough by myself. How could I cause her more agony? She lay here now in taped-together pieces, struggling with pain, and her one plea was that I stay.

"I won't," I told her, while I mentally qualified my answer. *Not until you're whole again. Not until you're ready. Not until*

I find the strength. "Now relax before I call the nurse back to sedate you."

It was as though she could hear my mental caveats. Before—before the hunt and the horror—I'd promised her many times that I would stay. I'd always meant it, and she'd always believed. But now she saw through me. The rhythm of her heart wouldn't settle.

I stroked my fingers along her whole cheek. "Bella, I'm not going anywhere. I'll be right here as long as you need me."

"Do you swear you won't leave me?" she whispered. Her hand twitched toward her ribs. They must be aching.

She was too fragile for this now. I should have known, and waited. Even if Renée had just offered her the perfect option for a vampire-free life.

I took her face in my hands again, let the consuming love I felt for her fill my eyes, and lied with all the experience of a hundred years of daily deception.

"I swear."

The tension in her limbs relaxed. Her eyes did not release mine, but after a few seconds her heart eased into its normal rhythm.

"Better?"

Her eyes were wary, her voice unsure when she answered. "Yes?"

She must have sensed that I was still holding something back.

I needed her to believe me, just long enough to let her safely heal. I couldn't be responsible for complicating her recovery.

So I tried to act as I would if I were hiding nothing. As if I were exasperated by her agitated response. I made an annoyed face and muttered the words, "Overreacting just a little bit, don't you think?"

I said them too fast; she probably couldn't understand.

"Why did you say that?" she whispered, a tremor in her voice. "Are you tired of having to save me all the time? Do you *want* me to go away?"

I wanted to laugh for a hundred years at the idea of me tiring of her. Or cry for a thousand.

But the time would come, I was sure now, when I would have to convince her otherwise. So I tempered my response, made it lukewarm, moderate.

"No, I don't want to be without you, Bella, of course not. Be rational. And I have no problem with saving you, either—if it weren't for the fact that I was the one putting you in danger… that I'm the reason that you're here."

The truth had found its way into the end of my speech.

Bella scowled at me. "Yes, you are the reason—the reason I'm here *alive*."

I couldn't hold on to the lukewarm. I whispered to hide the pain. "Barely. Covered in gauze and plaster and hardly able to move."

"I wasn't referring to my most recent near-death experience," she snapped at me. "I was thinking of the others—you can take your pick. If it weren't for you, I would be rotting away in the Forks cemetery."

I recoiled from the image, but then returned to my point, not letting her sidetrack my remorse.

"That's not the worst part, though. Not seeing you there on the floor…crumpled and broken." I fought to regain control over my voice. "Not thinking I was too late. Not even hearing you scream in pain—all those unbearable memories that I'll carry with me for the rest of eternity. No, the very worst was feeling…knowing that I couldn't stop. Believing that I was going to kill you myself."

She frowned. "But you didn't."

"I could have. So easily."

Again, her heart started to pound.

"Promise me," she hissed.

"What?"

She was glaring at me now. "You know what."

Bella had heard the direction of my words. She could hear me talking myself up to the strength I needed. I had to remember that she read my mind a thousand times better than I could read hers. I had to put my need to confess aside. The most important thing now was her recovery.

I tried to only say true things so she wouldn't see through me as easily as before. "I don't seem to be strong enough to stay away from you, so I suppose that you'll get your way... whether it kills you or not."

"Good." But I could hear she was not convinced. "You told me how you stopped.... Now I want to know why."

"Why?" I echoed blankly.

"*Why* you did it. Why didn't you just let the venom spread? By now I would be just like you."

I'd never explained this to her. I'd danced around her questions with such care. I knew that she hadn't uncovered *this* truth in any internet research. I saw red for a moment, and in the center of that red, Alice's face.

"I'll be the first to admit that I have no experience with relationships." Bella's words flowed quickly—worried about what she'd given away and trying to distract me. "But it just seems logical... a man and woman have to be somewhat equal... as in, one of them can't always be swooping in and saving the other one. They have to save each other *equally*."

There was truth to what she was saying, but she was missing the central point. I could never be her equal. There was no way back for me. And that was the only equality that left her unscathed.

I crossed my arms on the edge of her mattress and let my chin rest on them. It was time to calm the fervor of this discussion.

"You *have* saved me," I told her calmly. This was true.

"I can't always be Lois Lane," she warned me. "I want to be Superman, too."

I kept my voice soft, soothing, but I had to avert my eyes. "You don't know what you're asking."

"I think I do."

"Bella, you *don't* know," I murmured, my voice still gentle. "I've had almost ninety years to think about this, and I'm still not sure."

"Do you wish that Carlisle hadn't saved you?"

"No, I don't wish that." I never would have met her if he hadn't. "But my life was over. I wasn't giving anything up." Except a soul.

"You *are* my life. You're the only thing it would hurt me to lose."

She was describing my side of our relationship exactly.

And what will you do when she begs? the memory of Rosalie whispered in my head.

"I can't do it, Bella. I won't do that to you."

"Why not?" Her voice was rough, louder with anger. "Don't tell me it's too hard! After today, or I guess it was a few days ago...anyway, after *that*, it should be nothing."

I struggled to hold on to my calm.

"And the pain?" I reminded her. I didn't want to think about it. I hoped she didn't want to, either.

Her face went white. It was hard to watch. She struggled with the memory for a long moment, and then her chin came up.

"That's my problem. I can handle it."

"It's possible to take bravery to the point where it becomes insanity," I murmured.

"It's not an issue. Three days. Big deal."

Alice! It was probably good I had no idea where she was right now. I realized this was on purpose. She was going to avoid me until I'd calmed down, I was sure. I wanted to call her, to tell her what I thought of this cowardly evasion, but I would bet she wouldn't answer.

I refocused. If Bella wanted to continue this discussion, I was going to continue to point out the things she hadn't considered.

"Charlie?" I said succinctly. "Renée?"

This was harder for her to make light of. Long minutes passed while she worked to find an answer. Once she opened her mouth, and then closed it again. She never looked away, but the defiance in her eyes slowly turned to defeat.

Finally she lied. It was obvious, like it usually was.

"Look, that's not an issue either. Renée has always made the choices that work for her—she'd want me to do the same. And Charlie's resilient, he's used to being on his own. I can't take care of them forever. I have my own life to live."

"Exactly," I said, my voice heavy. "And I won't end it for you."

"If you're waiting for me to be on my deathbed, I've got news for you! I was just there!"

I waited till I was sure my voice would be even. "You're going to recover."

She took a deep breath, winced, and then spoke slowly in a low voice. "No, I'm not."

Did she think I was lying about her condition? "Of course you are," I said earnestly. "You may have a scar or two...."

"You're wrong. I'm going to die."

I couldn't maintain my composure. I heard the stress in my voice. "Really, Bella. You'll be out of here in a few days. Two weeks at most."

She stared back at me dejectedly. "I may not die now... but I'm going to die sometime. Every minute of the day, I get closer. And I'm going to get *old*."

Anxiety shifted to despair as I grasped her meaning. Did she think this was something I had not considered? That I'd somehow missed this glaring fact, that I'd not noticed the tiny changes in her face, highlighted by my rigid sameness? That, lacking Alice's gift, I couldn't see the obvious future?

My face fell into my hands. "That's how it's supposed to happen. How it should happen. How it would have happened if I didn't exist—and *I shouldn't exist*."

Bella snorted.

I looked up, startled by the shift in her mood.

"That's stupid," she said. "That's like going to someone who's just won the lottery, taking their money, and saying, 'Look, let's just go back to how things should be. It's better that way.' And I'm not buying it."

"I'm hardly a lottery prize," I growled.

"That's right. You're much better."

I rolled my eyes, but then tried to regain a portion of composure. This wasn't good for her, as her monitors could attest.

"Bella, we're not having this discussion anymore. I refuse to damn you to an eternity of night and that's the end of it."

I realized as soon as my words were out how dismissive they sounded. I knew how she would respond before her eyes narrowed.

"If you think that's the end, then you don't know me very well. You're not the only vampire I know," she reminded me.

Again, I saw red. "Alice wouldn't dare."

"Alice already saw it, didn't she?" Bella said, confident, though it appeared Alice had kept *some* things to herself. "That's why the things she says upset you. She knows I'm going to be like you . . . someday."

"She's wrong." I was confident, now, too. I'd circumvented Alice before. "She also saw you dead, but that didn't happen, either."

"You'll never catch *me* betting against Alice."

She stared at me, defiant again. I felt the stern lines of my own face, and worked to relax them. This was a waste of time, and there was so little of that left.

"So where does that leave us?" she asked hesitantly.

I sighed, and then laughed once without much humor. "I believe it's called an *impasse*."

An impasse that led to an inevitability.

Her heavy sigh echoed mine. "Ouch."

I looked at her face, and then the call button.

"How are you feeling?"

"I'm fine," she said unconvincingly.

I smiled at her. "I don't believe you."

Her lip pushed out. "I'm not going back to sleep."

"You need rest. All this arguing isn't good for you." My fault, of course, always my fault.

"So give in," she suggested.

I pressed the button. "Nice try."

"No!" she complained.

"Yes?" Bea's voice sounded tinny through the little speaker.

"I think we're ready for more pain medication," I told her. Bella scowled at me, and then winced.

"I'll send in the nurse."

"I won't take it," Bella threatened.

I looked pointedly at her IV bag. "I don't think they're going to ask you to swallow anything."

Her heart took off again.

"Bella, you're in pain. You need to relax so you can heal. Why are you being so difficult? They're not going to put any more needles in you now."

Her face had lost all its stubbornness; she was only troubled now. "I'm not afraid of the needles. I'm afraid to close my eyes."

I reached out to hold her face, and smiled at her with perfect sincerity. This wasn't difficult. All I wanted—all I would ever want—was to look into her eyes forever. "I told you I'm not going anywhere. Don't be afraid. As long as it makes you happy, I'll be here."

Until you're healthy, until you're ready. Until I find the strength I need.

She smiled despite the pain. "You're talking about forever, you know."

A mortal kind of *forever.*

"Oh, you'll get over it," I teased. "It's just a crush."

She tried to shake her head, but gave up with a wince. "I was shocked when Renée swallowed that one. I know *you* know better."

"That's the beautiful thing about being human," I said quietly. "Things change."

"Don't hold your breath."

I had to laugh at her sour expression. She knew how long I could hold my breath.

Gloria bustled in with syringe already in hand.

He needs to give her some peace and quiet, poor thing.

I moved out of her way before her "Excuse me" was half out of her mouth. I leaned against the wall at the other end of the room, giving Gloria space. I didn't want to irritate her enough that she would try to kick me out again. I wasn't sure where Carlisle was.

Bella stared at me anxiously, worried I was going to walk right out and keep going. I tried to make my expression reassuring. I would be here when she woke up. As long as she needed me.

Gloria injected the painkiller into the port. "Here you go, honey. You'll feel better now."

Bella's "Thanks" was less than grateful.

It took only seconds for Bella's eyelids to close.

"That ought to do it," Gloria murmured.

She gave me a pointed glance, but I stared toward the window, pretending I didn't see. She shut the door quietly behind herself.

I flitted back to Bella, cradling the good side of her face in my hand.

"Stay." The word was slurred.

"I will," I promised her. She was drifting now, and I felt able to speak the truth. "Like I said, as long as it makes you happy... as long as it's what's best for you."

She sighed, only partly conscious. " 'S not the same thing."

"Don't worry about that now, Bella. You can argue with me when you wake up."

The corners of her lips curled into a faint smile. " 'Kay."

I leaned down and kissed her temple, then whispered "I love you" into her ear.

"Me too," she breathed.

I laughed halfheartedly. "I know." That was the problem.

She fought against the sedation, turning her head toward me... searching.

I kissed her bruised lips softly.

"Thanks."

"Anytime."

"Edward?" She could barely shape my name.

"Yes?"

"I'm betting on Alice," she mumbled.

Her face went slack as she sank fully into unconsciousness.

I buried my face in the hollow of her neck and breathed in her searing essence, wishing again, as I had in the beginning, that I could dream with her.

EPILOGUE: AN OCCASION

THEY KEPT HER IN THE HOSPITAL FOR SIX MORE DAYS. I could tell the time seemed interminable to her. She was anxious to get back to normal life, to be free of the doctors who poked and prodded, to have all the needles out of her skin.

For me, the time sped by, despite the constant agony of seeing her in the hospital bed, of knowing she was in pain and there was nothing I could do to alleviate any of it. This time was my secured time; it would be undeniably wrong to leave when she was still broken. I wanted to stretch out every second, even though they hurt. But they raced by me.

I hated the minutes I had to be away from her, while the doctors consulted with Bella and Renée, though it was easy enough to eavesdrop from the stairwell. Perhaps it was better sometimes; I couldn't always control my face.

That first day after she awoke, for example, when Dr. Sadarangani enthused over the X-rays, pleased at how clean the breaks were, how neatly they would heal, all I could see in that moment was the tracker's foot descending onto her leg. All I could hear was the crisp snap of her bones. It was good that no one could see my face then.

She saw that her mother was restless—uneasy about a long-term substitute job at a Jacksonville primary school that would be given away if she wasn't available soon—but still determined to be with Bella while she was in Phoenix. It wasn't particularly hard for Bella to convince Renée she was just fine and that Renée should go back to Florida. Her mother left two days before we did.

Bella was on the phone with Charlie often, especially after Renée left, and now that the danger was past, now that he'd had time to consider all the angles, he was beginning to be angry. Not at Bella, of course not. His anger was pointed in the right direction. After all, none of this would have happened if not for me. His burgeoning friendship with Alice confused the issue for him, but I was sure what I would read in his quiet brain upon my return.

I tried to avoid more serious conversations with Bella. It was easier than I expected. We were rarely alone—even after Renée left, a constant influx of nurses and doctors took her place—and Bella was often drowsy from the medications. She seemed content enough that I was near. She didn't beg me again for guarantees. But at times I felt sure I saw the doubt in her eyes. I wished I could erase that doubt, that I could mean my promises, but it was better not to speak than to lie again.

And then, so quickly, we were arranging transport home.

Charlie's plan was that Bella would fly home with Carlisle while Alice and I drove the truck back to Washington. Carlisle fielded that call; we needed no discussion for him to know my opinion on the subject. He convinced Charlie that Alice and I had missed too much school already, and Charlie was unable to argue with him. We would fly home together. Carlisle would ship the truck home. He promised Charlie this was easy to arrange and not at all expensive.

How different it was, returning to the same airport where my worst nightmare had begun. We flew out after dark, so the glass ceilings above were no longer a danger. I wondered what Bella saw when she looked at these wide halls—did she think of the pain and terror of the last time she was here, too? No longer racing, we moved slowly, Alice pushing Bella in her wheelchair so that I could walk beside her, holding her hand. As I had expected, Bella didn't like needing the chair, nor the curious glances thrown her way. Now and then she scowled at her thick, white cast as if she wanted to tear it off with her bare hands, but she never complained aloud.

She slept on the flight, and quietly murmured my name in her dreams. It would have been so easy to ignore the past and allow myself to relive our one perfect day, to stay in a time when the sound of my name on her lips didn't burn with guilt and omens. But the looming separation was too sharp to allow for fantasy.

Charlie met us at SeaTac, though it was after eleven and the drive back to Forks would take him nearly four hours. Both Carlisle and Alice had tried to talk him out of it, but I understood. And, though his thoughts were just as clouded as before, it was still obvious that I was right. He'd come to put the blame in the right place.

Not that he harbored any dark suspicions that I'd shoved her down the stairs myself, but rather he felt that Bella would never have acted so impulsively if I hadn't goaded her to it. Though he had a mistaken idea of what had driven Bella to Arizona, he wasn't wrong about the central assumption. It was ultimately my fault.

It should have been a long drive behind Charlie's police car, dutifully going exactly the speed limit, but the time was still moving too quickly. Even being temporarily separated from her did nothing to slow down those hours.

We all settled into the new routine with minimal delays. Alice took over as nurse and lady-in-waiting, and Charlie could not adequately express his gratitude. Bella, too, though embarrassed that she needed someone to help her with her most basic and intimate needs, was glad that someone was Alice. It was as if during those few days in Phoenix, Alice's vision of Bella as her best friend had come fully to fruition. They were so at ease with each other—already flush with a plethora of inside jokes and confidences—as if they'd been companions for many years rather than just weeks. Charlie occasionally watched in confusion, wondering why Bella had never revealed their close connection, but he was too thankful for Alice, as well as charmed by her, to aggressively pursue answers. He was just happy with this, the best possible version of having a grievously injured daughter to care for. Alice was at the Swan house nearly as often as I was, though much more visible to Charlie during her time there.

Bella had been conflicted about school.

"On the one hand," she'd told me, "I just want things back to normal. And I don't want to get more behind." It was very early the second morning after our return—she'd been sleeping so much in the day that her schedule was reversed. "On the other, the thought of everyone looking at me while I'm in *that* thing..." She glared menacingly toward the innocent wheelchair folded beside the bed.

"If I could carry you at school, I would, but..."

She sighed. "That probably wouldn't help with the staring."

"Probably not. However, while you have never appreciated the fact that I am actually frightening, I promise you I can do something about any staring."

"How?"

"I'll show you."

"Now I'm curious. So back to school ASAP."

"Whatever you want."

I flinched internally as soon as the words were out. I'd been careful not to say anything that would bring up our conversation in the hospital for rehashing, but she let my comment pass this time.

In fact, she seemed just as unwilling as I was to talk about the future. I thought this was probably why having things "back to normal" seemed appealing to her. Perhaps she hoped we could forget this episode as though it had merely been one bad chapter, rather than the foreshadowing to the only possible conclusion.

It was easy to make good on that unimportant promise. On

her first day back, as I wheeled her from class to class, all I had to do was make eye contact with anyone who seemed too interested. A slight narrowing of my eyes, a tiny curl of my upper lip, and any gawkers were quickly persuaded to focus elsewhere.

Bella was unconvinced. "I'm not sure you're doing anything really. I'm just not very exciting. I shouldn't have worried."

As quickly as Carlisle would allow, she traded in her plaster cast for a walking cast and a pair of crutches. I preferred the chair. It was hard to watch her struggle with the crutches, to be unable to help, but she seemed relieved to be moving under her own power again. After a few days, she grew less awkward.

The story circulating through the school was wrong on all counts. Bella's disastrous fall through the hotel window was common knowledge, first spread by Charlie's deputies around the community. But Charlie had been more taciturn about *why* Bella was in Phoenix. So Jessica Stanley had filled in the gaps—Bella and I had gone to Phoenix together for me to meet her mother. Jessica insinuated this was because our relationship was becoming very serious. Everyone accepted her version; most had already forgotten where the tale had originated.

Jessica was left to her own invention for this gossip, as Bella rarely spent much time with her out of class. It was no different than when I'd stopped the van in the very beginning—Bella knew how to be tight-lipped when she wanted to be. And now she sat at our table, with Alice, Jasper, and me. Even with Emmett and Rosalie absent—they pretended to eat outside now, hiding in the car if sunlight threatened—none of the humans braved our presence to join Bella. I didn't like that she was becoming alienated from her former friends, especially Angela, but I assumed that eventually things would go back to how they'd been before I'd intruded on her life.

After we were gone.

Though the time never really slowed, the routine started to feel normal, and I had to keep my guard up. Sometimes I would slip; she would smile up at me and I would be inundated by that sense of rightness, the feeling that the two of us were designed to be together. It was hard to remember that this feeling, so pure and strong, was a lie. Hard to remember, until she twisted her torso too sharply and winced at her healing ribs, or put her foot down too hard and gasped, or moved her wrist just so and the pale, shiny new scar across the heel of her hand caught the light.

Bella healed and time passed. I clung to each second.

Alice had a new scheme that would disrupt the routine, to her mind in a pleasant way. Knowing Bella would object, at first I resisted. But then the more I considered, the more I saw things from a different perspective.

Not Alice's perspective. Alice's motivations were probably at least seventy percent selfish; she loved a makeover. My own I judged to be around ten percent. Yes, this was a memory that I wanted to have. I'd admitted that to myself. However, my main motive was to modify one specific chapter in Bella's future. It was for her sake that I went along with Alice's bizarre plan.

I had a vision—not like Alice, not a true prophecy. It was just a probable scenario. This vision created an intense kind of ache throughout my entire body; it was half agony and half pleasure.

I envisioned Bella twenty years from now, maturing gracefully into middle age. Like her mother, she would hold on to the image of youth longer than most, but when the lines came, they would not mar her beauty. I imagined her somewhere sunny in a pretty but simple house that was, unless she changed her ways significantly, filled with clutter. Adding to the clutter would be children, two or three. Maybe one boy with Charlie's curly hair and smile, and a girl who, like Bella, took after her mother.

I did not try to picture their father, or think about how his face might be reflected in her children; that was all agony.

One day when they were young adolescents, younger than Bella was now, perhaps prompted by a teenage rom-com on TV (though Alice had told me that the consumption of media would change quite a bit in the next decade; she was waiting for certain companies to form so she could invest in them), one of the children would ask Bella what *her* high school prom was like.

Bella would smile and say, "I wasn't really into dances. I didn't go to prom." And the children would be dissatisfied. Their mother never had any good stories about her teenage years. Hadn't she ever done *anything* interesting?

Bella would have no funny, lighthearted stories, just a dearth of normal experience, just secrecy and danger and tales so fantastical she might one day wonder whether they had ever been more than her imagination.

Or... Bella could laugh when her child asked, and her eyes would suddenly seem far away.

"It was crazy," she would say. "I didn't really want to go, you know I'm no dancer. But my lunatic best friend kidnapped me for a makeover and my boyfriend took me over my protests. It wasn't so bad in the end. I'm glad I went. At the very least to see the decorations—they were like a budget version of the movie *Carrie*. No, you can't watch *Carrie*. Not yet."

So it was for that moment in Bella's future that I'd allowed Alice to go through with her pushy and somewhat intrusive plan. More than allowed it, I'd aided and abetted.

And this was how I found myself in a tuxedo—chosen by Alice, naturally; at least I hadn't had to do any of the shopping—a spray of freesia in my hands, waiting at the base of the stairs for Alice's big reveal.

I'd seen it all in her head, but she didn't care. She wanted every trite scene from the dramatic pageant that was a human prom.

Alice had given Charlie a heads-up that Bella would be out late, making it clear that she, Alice, would be an integral part of the evening from start to finish. Charlie never objected to anything involving Alice. He often objected to things that involved me, though usually only in his own mind.

I listened as Alice helped Bella hobble toward the stairs, Alice's arm around Bella's waist, Bella's arm over Alice's shoulder, leaning on her heavily. Bella had become fairly adept with her crutch but Alice had taken it away from her for tonight. I wasn't sure how much of that was for the aesthetic, and how much was to keep Bella from trying to escape. Then, a few steps from the edge of the stairs, Alice squirmed out of Bella's hold and urged her to continue alone.

"What?" Bella protested. "I can't walk in *this*."

"It's just a few steps. You'll manage. I don't look right, I'll mess up the picture."

"What *picture*?" Bella's voice rose half an octave. "There better not be anyone taking pictures of me!"

"No one's taking any pictures. I just meant the *mental picture*. Calm down."

"Mental picture? Who's going to see?"

"Just Edward."

Well, that worked. Alice noted that Bella's eyes lit up at the mention of my name, and that she moved with an eagerness absent through the entirety of the hair and makeup session. Alice was a little miffed about that.

Bella moved slowly and awkwardly into view, eyes searching for me.

I'd seen the dress in Alice's head, but not like this. The thin chiffon was ruched and ruffled to provide a semblance of modesty, but it still clung to her skin in a very distracting way. The design exposed her alabaster shoulders, then fell graceful and sheer down her arms to fold in at her wrists. The body of the dress was gathered in an asymmetrical line that gave her shape subtle hourglass contours.

Of course it was deep blue in color; Alice had noticed my preference.

On one foot, Bella wore a blue satin shoe with a stiletto heel and long ribbons wrapped up her leg to hold it in place. On the other foot, her dingy walking cast. I was a little surprised Alice hadn't painted that blue to match.

I stared at Bella while she stared, wide-eyed, at me.

"Wow," she said.

"Indeed," I agreed, appraising her gown in an obvious way.

She glanced down and blushed. Then she shrugged her shoulders as if to say, *Well, this is me in a dress.*

I knew Alice liked the idea of Bella descending the stairway grandly, but she'd already realized that was just a fantasy. I darted up the stairs to meet her. After securing the flowers into her hair—Alice had left one spot free from cascading curls for just this purpose—I lifted Bella into my arms. She was used to this by now. I carried her a lot of places when no one human was there to see.

It was faster, of course, but it was also simply a relief to hold her close. To feel that she was safe and protected for this moment.

"Have fun," Alice called, darting back to her room. She was in her own dress before I'd finished carrying Bella down the stairs. I could hear Rosalie and the others waiting for her—some patiently, some not so much—in the garage. Alice paused to draw on a few stripes of theatrical eyeliner.

I brought Bella to the Volvo and settled her carefully into the passenger seat, making sure all her chiffon and ribbons were tucked out of the way of the door. I was surprised by her silence. Now, and before. She'd complained to Alice about being made up, but she'd never voiced any objections to the dance.

I got into the driver's seat and we headed down the driveway.

"At what point exactly are you going to tell me what's going on?" she asked, putting more annoyance in her voice than there was in her expression.

I examined her face, looking for the joke. Aside from the put-on crabby attitude, she seemed in earnest. I couldn't quite believe she was so oblivious.

"I'm shocked that you haven't figured it out yet," I answered with a grin, playing along. Because she had to be teasing.

She drew in a sudden breath, and I looked for the reason. She was just staring at me.

"I did mention that you looked very nice, didn't I?" she asked.

I thought her earlier *wow* had probably conveyed that.

"Yes."

She frowned again, returning to her petulance. "I'm not coming over anymore if Alice is going to treat me like Guinea Pig Barbie when I do."

Before I could either defend or condemn Alice, my phone rang in my pocket. I pulled it out quickly, wondering whether Alice had more instructions for me, but it was Charlie.

As a general rule, Bella's father didn't call me. So it was with some trepidation that I answered. "Hello, Charlie?"

"Charlie?" Bella whispered, anxious, too.

Charlie cleared his throat, and I could feel his awkwardness through the line.

"Uh, hey, Edward. I'm sorry to disturb your, um, evening, but I wasn't quite sure. . . . See, Tyler Crowley just showed up here in a tux and he seems to think *he's* taking Bella to prom?"

"You're kidding!" I laughed.

It was rare that someone other than Bella took me by surprise.

I hadn't noticed Tyler thinking anything about this stunt while at school, but then, I'd been so caught up in embracing every second I had with Bella, there were probably many inconsequential things I'd missed.

"What is it?" Bella hissed.

"I'm out to sea on this one," Charlie continued, uncomfortable.

"Why don't you let me talk to him?" I offered.

I could hear the relief in Charlie's voice when he answered. "Can do." Then he spoke away from the phone. "Here, Tyler, it's for you."

Bella was staring at my face, worried about what was happening between her father and me. She didn't notice the bright red car that suddenly swerved around us. I ignored Rosalie's pleasure at passing me—I always ignored Rosalie now—and concentrated on the call.

The boy's voice broke as he said, "Yeah?"

"Hello, Tyler, this is Edward Cullen." My tone was perfectly polite, though it took a little work to keep it that way. As entertained as I'd been just a moment ago, a sudden flare of territorial feelings now swamped me. It was an immature reaction, but I couldn't deny I felt it.

Bella sucked in a sharp breath. I glanced at her out of the corner of my eye and then looked back to the road. If she had—somehow—been in earnest before, she was no longer in the dark.

"I'm sorry if there's been some kind of miscommunication, but Bella is unavailable tonight," I said to Tyler.

"Oh," he responded.

The jealous, protective instinct persisted and my response was stronger than it should have been.

"To be perfectly honest, she'll be unavailable every night, as far as anyone besides myself is concerned. No offense. And I'm sorry about your evening."

Though I knew the words were wrong to say, I couldn't help smiling at the thought of how Tyler was receiving them. And what he would feel when I saw him at school on Monday. I hung up the call and turned to assess Bella's reaction.

Bella's face was bright red and her expression was furious.

"Was that last part a bit too much?" I worried. "I didn't mean to offend you."

It had been a very domineering kind of thing to say, and while I was fairly positive that Bella had no interest in Tyler, it wasn't really my place to make that decision for her.

What I'd said was wrong in other ways, too, but not in a way that I thought would upset her.

Though she'd never demanded another promise from me since the hospital, there was always the undercurrent of her doubt. I'd been forced to find a way to balance her need for assurance against my inability to deceive her.

I was taking our relationship one day at a time, one hour at a time. I didn't look into the future. It was enough that I could feel it coming. When I promised her forever now, I meant as far as I could see. And I wasn't looking.

"You're taking me to *the prom*!" she shouted.

She really hadn't known. I didn't know what to do with that. What else could we be doing in formal attire in Forks tonight?

And now there were actual tears brimming in her eyes and she had one hand clenched around the door handle as though she wanted to throw herself from the car rather than face the horror of a high school dance.

Unobtrusively, I locked the doors.

I didn't know what to say; I hadn't imagined that she could misunderstand. So I said probably the stupidest thing possible under the circumstances.

"Don't be difficult, Bella."

She stared out the window like she was still thinking of jumping.

"Why are you doing this to me?" she moaned.

I pointed at my tuxedo. "Honestly, Bella, what did you think we were doing?"

She scrubbed at the tears falling down her cheeks, her face horrified. She looked like I'd just told her I'd murdered all her friends and she was next.

"This is completely ridiculous," I pointed out. "Why are you crying?"

"Because I'm *mad*!" she shouted.

I considered turning around. The dance was meaningless, really, and I hated to upset her like this. But I thought of that faraway conversation in her future and held my ground.

"Bella," I said softly.

She met my gaze and seemed to lose her grip on her fury. I still had the power to dazzle her, if nothing else.

"What?" she asked, totally distracted.

"Humor me?" I pleaded.

She stared at me for a second longer, with what looked more like adoration than ire, and then shook her head in surrender.

"Fine, I'll go quietly," she said, resigned to her fate. "But you'll see. I'm way overdue for more bad luck. I'll probably break my other leg. Look at this shoe! It's a death trap!"

She pointed her toes in my direction.

The contrast between the thick satin ribbons laced up her narrow calf, ballet-style, and her ivory skin was beautiful in a way that transcended fashion. In this place of endless winter wardrobes, it was fascinating to see parts of her I'd never seen before. This was where my ten percent of selfishness came into play.

"Hmm," I breathed. "Remind me to thank Alice for that tonight."

"Alice is going to be there?"

From her tone, this was more comforting than my presence.

I knew I needed to give her full disclosure. "With Jasper, and Emmett... and Rosalie."

The worried *v* formed between her eyebrows.

Emmett had tried, they all had—everyone except me. I'd not spoken to Rosalie since the night she'd refused to help save Bella's life. Now she was living up to her reputation for supernatural stubbornness. She was never openly hostile toward Bella during the rare times they were in the same room together, unless aggressively ignoring someone's existence equaled hostility.

Bella shook her head again, obviously deciding not to think about Rosalie.

"Is Charlie in on this?"

"Of course," I said, leaving out that the entire town of Forks and probably most of the county was in on the secret of prom being held tonight. They'd even put up top secret posters and banners all over the school. Then I laughed. "Apparently, Tyler wasn't, though."

Her teeth audibly clenched, but I guessed this angry reaction was more about Tyler than it was about me.

We pulled into the school parking lot, and this time Bella noticed Rosalie's car, parked front and center. She eyed it nervously while I parked a lane over, then got out and walked to her side at human speed. I opened her door and held out my hand.

Her arms were folded across her chest. She pursed her lips. It had clearly occurred to her that, with human witnesses around, I couldn't just throw her over my shoulder and force her into that terrifying place of horror and dread, our high school cafeteria.

I sighed heavily, but she didn't move.

"When someone wants to kill you, you're as brave as a lion," I complained. "And then when someone mentions dancing..." I shook my head in disappointment.

But she looked genuinely frightened of the word *dancing*.

"Bella, I won't let anything hurt you," I promised. "Not even yourself. I won't let go of you once, I promise."

She considered that, and it did seem to calm some of her terror.

"There, now," I coaxed, "it won't be so bad."

I leaned into the car and put my arm around her waist. Her throat was at my lips, her fragrance as strong as a forest fire, but more delicate than the flowers in her hair. She didn't resist as I drew her from the car.

Wanting to make it clear that I was serious about my promise, I kept my arm wrapped tightly around her as I half carried her toward the school. It was frustrating not to be able to just lift her.

Soon enough we were at the cafeteria. They had the doors propped open wide. All the tables had been removed from the long room. The overhead lights were all off, replaced with miles of borrowed Christmas tree lights that were stapled to the walls in an uneven scallop pattern. It was quite dim, but not enough to disguise the outdated décor. The crepe paper garlands appeared to have been used before, faded and creased as they were. The balloon arches were new, though.

Bella giggled.

I smiled with her.

"This looks like a horror movie waiting to happen," she observed.

"Well, there are *more* than enough vampires present," I agreed.

I continued to move her to the ticket line, but her attention was on the dance floor now.

My siblings were showing off.

It was a kind of release, I supposed. We were always very… contained. We couldn't escape some notice, our inhuman faces assured that, but we did everything possible to give no one another reason to stare.

Tonight Rosalie, Emmett, Jasper, and Alice were really dancing. They melded a hundred styles from other decades into new creations that could belong to any time at all. Of course they were graceful beyond human ability. Bella wasn't the only one staring.

Some brave humans also danced, but they kept their distance from the showboating vampires.

"Do you want me to bolt the doors so you can massacre the unsuspecting townsfolk?" she whispered. The idea of a mass murder sounded more appealing to her than the reality of prom.

"And where do you fit into that scheme?" I wondered.

"Oh, I'm with the vampires, of course."

I had to smile. "Anything to get out of dancing."

"Anything."

She turned to watch my siblings again while I bought two tickets. As soon as that was accomplished, I started moving toward the dance floor. Better to get the part she feared most out of the way. She wouldn't be able to relax until it was over.

She limped slower than before, resisting.

"I've got all night," I reminded her.

"Edward," she whispered, horror in her voice. She looked up at me with panic-stricken eyes. "I *honestly* can't dance!"

Did she think I was going to abandon her in the middle of the floor, and then stand back to watch, expecting a solo performance?

"Don't worry, silly," I said gently. "I *can*."

I lifted her arms and placed them around my neck. I put my hands around her waist and lifted her a few inches from the floor. Pulling her body against mine, I lowered her so that her satin-clad toes and her plaster-clad toes rested on top of my shoes.

She grinned.

Holding almost all of her weight in my hands, I spun us into the middle of the floor, where my siblings held court. I didn't try to keep up with them, I just held her close and whirled in a loose waltz to the music.

Her arms tightened around my neck, pulling us even closer.

"I feel like I'm five years old," she laughed.

I caught her up so her feet were a foot in the air and whispered, "You don't look five," into her ear.

She laughed again as I set her feet down on my toes. Her eyes sparkled with the glimmer of the Christmas lights.

The song changed. I shifted the tempo of our waltz. The music was slower now, dreamier. Her body was melted to mine. I wished I could freeze us here, stop time forever and stay in this dance.

"Okay," she murmured. "This isn't half-bad."

These were close to the words I'd hoped she would say to her children. It was encouraging that it hadn't taken twenty years for her to come to this conclusion.

Nope, I'm not going to do it. I'll give the money back. Ugh, this is so embarrassing. Why does my *dad have to be the insane one? Why couldn't it be Quil's?*

The clear thoughts hesitating in the doorway were very familiar. Even in his angst and self-consciousness, his mind radiated a kind of purity. He was more honest with himself than most.

"What is it?" Bella had noticed my sudden abstraction.

I wasn't ready to answer. I felt a depth of rage that closed my throat. So the Quileutes were going to keep pushing, straining against the treaty *they'd* made, the treaty that did nothing but protect *them*. It was as if they couldn't be happy until we did kill someone. They wanted us to be monsters.

Bella twisted in my arms to see what I was looking at.

Jacob Black walked hesitantly through the door, blinking as his eyes adjusted to the low light. It didn't take him long to see what he was looking for.

Dang, she is here. I can't believe I'm doing this. I can't believe my dad thinks that guy is an actual vampire. *This is so completely stupid.*

He didn't hesitate, though, despite his embarrassment. Ignoring the ticket stand, the boy marched like a soldier through the ring of dancers toward us. Even in my anger, I had to admire his straightforward courage.

Should've worn some garlic, I guess. He snorted.

I didn't realize I'd snarled audibly till Bella hissed, "Behave!"

"He wants to chat with you." There was no way to avoid it. Like the first dance, better to get it out of the way. I shouldn't let myself get angry. Did it really matter if that group of toothless old men broke the treaty? It wouldn't change much, even if they paid for a billboard on the 101 that read: *The local doctor and his children are VAMPIRES. You have been warned.* No one would believe. Even his son didn't believe.

I held still as Jacob approached. He mostly looked at Bella, his expression comical in its reluctance.

"Hey, Bella, I was hoping you would be here." It was obvious this was the exact opposite of what he'd been hoping.

Bella's voice was warm when she answered. I was sure she could see his distress, too, and being Bella, she would want to ease it. "Hi, Jacob. What's up?"

He smiled at her, then looked at me. He didn't have to look up to do it. The boy had grown several inches since the last time I'd seen him. He didn't look as much a child as he had then.

"Can I cut in?" he asked. His tone was respectful; he didn't want to overstep.

I knew my anger was pointless, and it certainly wasn't directed at this blameless boy, but I couldn't quite keep it in check. Rather than let either of them hear it in my voice, I just set Bella gently on her feet and stepped away.

"Thanks," Jacob said in the cheery tone that seemed to be his default.

I nodded, inspected Bella's face once to make sure she was comfortable with this, and then walked away.

Huh, Jacob was thinking. *That is an* awful *perfume Bella's wearing.*

Strange. Bella wore no scent besides the flowers in her hair. But perhaps another couple had strayed closer, now that I had moved away.

"Wow, Jake, how tall are you now?" I heard her say.

"Six-two." This was a point of pride.

She looks totally fine aside from the cast. Billy's blowing things out of proportion, as usual.

When I reached the north wall of the cafeteria, I turned around and leaned back against it. Lauren Mallory and her date were circling stiffly just behind Jacob's back. I wondered if she was the one who smelled bad.

Jacob and Bella weren't exactly dancing. He had his hands at her waist, and her hands were resting lightly on his shoulders. She swayed a little to the music, but seemed nervous to try to move her feet at all. Jacob shuffled in place.

"So, how did you end up here tonight?" There was no real curiosity in her voice. She'd already figured out what this intrusion meant.

Jacob was eager to place the blame where it belonged. "Can you believe my dad paid me twenty bucks to come to your prom?"

"Yes, I can," she said, her voice still kind, though it must have been annoying to have a near stranger trying to supervise her life.

She's being so nice about this. She's the nicest girl I know.

"Well, I hope you're enjoying yourself, at least," Bella continued. "Seen anything you like?" She nodded playfully to a line of girls standing along the wall to my left.

"Yeah," Jacob said, "but she's taken."

This information was not a surprise to me—I'd been witness multiple times to his crush on Bella. His blunt honesty, however, was unexpected. Bella didn't know how to respond. After one glance at his face to see if he was joking—he wasn't—she looked down at her unmoving feet.

Probably shouldn't have said that, but what the hell. Nothing to lose.

"You look really pretty, by the way," he added.

Bella frowned. "Um, thanks." She changed the subject, bringing it around to the one he most wanted to avoid, the one that would send him on his way. "So why did Billy pay you to come here?"

Jacob shifted his weight from foot to foot, uncomfortable. "He said it was a 'safe' place to talk to you. I swear the old man is losing his mind."

She's going to think I'm crazy, too.

Bella laughed with him, but the sound was forced.

"Anyway," Jacob continued, grinning to ease the tension. "He said that if I told you something, he would get me that master cylinder I need."

Bella smiled in earnest now. "Tell me, then. I want you to get your car finished."

Jacob sighed, moved by her smile. *I wish he* was *a vampire. That might make some room for me.*

"Don't get mad, okay?" *She's already been nicer than I had any reason to expect.*

"There's no way I'll be mad at you, Jacob," Bella promised. "I won't even be mad at Billy. Just say what you have to."

"Well—this is so stupid, I'm sorry, Bella." He took a deep breath. "He wants you to break up with your boyfriend. He asked me to tell you 'please.'"

Jacob shook his head, hoping to distance himself from the obnoxious message.

Bella's smile was full of compassion. "He's still superstitious, eh?"

"Yeah. He was...kind of over the top when you got hurt down in Phoenix. He didn't believe..." *That they didn't do it. He thought they sucked your blood or something crazy like that.*

Her voice went flat for the first time. "I fell."

"I know that," Jacob said quickly.

"He thinks Edward had something to do with me getting hurt?" Sharp now.

They were both perfectly still, as if there were no music.

Jacob looked away from her glare.

Now I've pissed her off for real. Should have told Billy to mind his business or leave me out of it.

Bella's mien softened, reacting to his upset. "Look, Jacob," she said, kind again. Jacob responded to the change, meeting her gaze. "I know Billy probably won't believe this, but just so *you* know...Edward really did save my life. If it weren't for Edward and his father, I'd be dead." Her sincerity was impossible to doubt.

"I know," Jacob agreed quickly. He didn't want to think about Bella dying. A swell of gratitude started to build inside his mind. He wouldn't listen the next time his father said something disparaging about Carlisle.

She smiled up at him.

It was strange how much older he seemed tonight. They looked like peers now, maybe just because of his new height. As awkward as her injured leg made their dance-adjacent movement, she seemed more comfortable with him than with many of her other human friends. Perhaps his very pure, open mind had that effect on people.

A strange thought crossed my mind, half imagination, half fear.

Would that pretty, cluttered little house be in La Push?

I shook the idea away. It was just irrational jealousy. Jealousy was such a human emotion, powerful but senseless—based on nothing more than watching her pretend to dance with a friend. I would not let the future trouble me.

"Hey, I'm sorry you had to come do this, Jacob," Bella was saying. "At any rate, you get your parts, right?"

"Yeah," he muttered.

Would he know if I lied? I can't say the rest. It's enough.

Bella read his expression. "There's more?" she asked, incredulous.

"Forget it," he mumbled, looking away. "I'll get a job and save the money myself."

She waited for him to meet her gaze. "Just spit it out, Jacob."

"It's so bad."

I shouldn't have come. This is my own fault for agreeing to this.

"I don't care," she insisted. "Tell me."

"Okay... but, *geez*, this sounds bad." Jacob inhaled deeply. "He said to tell you, no, to *warn* you, that—and this is his plural, not mine..." Jacob lifted his right hand and with two fingers made quotations marks in the air. " 'We'll be watching.' "

He watched for her reaction, ready to bolt.

Bella broke into a peal of laughter, as if he'd just told the funniest joke she'd ever heard. She couldn't stop. Her words came between chuckles. "Sorry you had to do this, Jake."

He was overwhelmed with relief. *She's right. It's hilarious.*

"I don't mind *that* much." *She looks so pretty. I never would have seen her in this dress if I hadn't come. Worth it right there, even with the gross perfume.* "So, should I tell him you said to butt the hell out?"

She sighed. "No. Tell him I said thanks. I know he means well."

The song ended, and Bella let her arms drop. My cue.

Jacob kept his hands on her waist, unsure if she could stand without help. "Do you want to dance again? Or can I help you get somewhere?"

"That's all right, Jacob. I'll take it from here."

Jacob recoiled from my voice, so unexpectedly close. He took a step back, a sharp frisson of fear shooting up his spine.

"Hey, I didn't see you there," he mumbled. *Can't believe I'm letting Billy get in my head this way.* "I guess I'll see you around, Bella."

"Yeah, I'll see you later," she said with enough enthusiasm that he recovered his composure. He waved, then muttered, "Sorry," one more time before he headed for the door.

I pulled Bella into my arms, sliding my feet under hers again. I waited for the warmth of her body to erase the coldness that enveloped mine. I wouldn't think about the future. Just this night, this minute.

She nestled her cheek against my chest, humming with contentment.

"Feeling better?" she murmured.

Of course she would read my mood.

"Not really," I sighed.

"Don't be mad at Billy. He just worries about me for Charlie's sake. It's nothing personal," she assured me.

"I'm not mad at Billy. But his son is irritating me."

It was too much truth. Though the boy didn't really irritate me; a mind that expansive would always be a welcome respite from the average human's. It was what he represented that hurt me. Someone good and kind and *human*.

I needed to force myself into the right frame of mind.

She leaned away, staring up at me with curiosity and a little bit of concern. "Why?"

I mentally shook off my funk and answered her playfully. "First of all, he made me break my promise."

She didn't remember.

I forced a smile. "I promised I wouldn't let go of you tonight."

"Oh. Well, I forgive you," she said easily.

"Thanks." I frowned in what I hoped was a joking way. "But there's something else."

She waited for me to explain.

"He called you *pretty*." My voice made the word into something unpleasant. "That's practically an insult, the way you look right now. You're much more than beautiful."

She relaxed now and laughed, worry for her friend evaporating. "You might be a little biased."

I smiled better this time. "I don't think that's it. Besides, I have excellent eyesight."

She stared at the twinkle lights spinning around us. Her heartbeat was slower than the tempo of the song playing, so I moved to that rhythm instead. A hundred voices, spoken and thought, swirled past us, but I didn't really hear them. The sound of her heart was the only sound that mattered.

"So," she said when the song shifted again. "Are you going to explain the reason for all of this?"

When I didn't follow, she looked pointedly at the crepe paper garlands.

I thought about what I could tell her. Not the vision; she would have too many objections. And that was so far into the future, a future that I was trying very hard not to think about. But maybe I could tell her a little of the thought behind it. Though this wasn't something we could discuss with an audience.

I changed the direction of our dance, spinning her toward the back exit. We circled past a few of her friends. Jessica waved, unhappily comparing Bella's dress to her own, and Bella smiled back. None of her human classmates seemed totally happy with their night besides Angela and Ben, staring blissfully into each other's eyes. That made me smile, too.

I pushed the door open with my back, still dancing. There was no one outside, though the night was very mild. The clouds to the west still held a fading bit of gold from the setting sun.

As no one could see us, I felt free to swing her up into my arms. I carried her away from the cafeteria, into the shadows of the madrone trees, where it was nearly midnight dark. I sat on the same bench where I'd watched her that sunny morning so many weeks ago, but kept her cradled close against my chest. In the east, a pale moon was shining through lace-thin clouds. It was an odd moment, the sky balanced perfectly between evening and full night.

She was still waiting for her explanation. "The point?" she asked quietly.

"Twilight again," I mused. "Another ending. No matter how perfect the day is, it always has to end."

These days mattered so much, and ended so quickly.

She tensed. "Some things don't have to end."

There was nothing I could say to that. She was right, but I knew she wasn't thinking of the same permanent things I was. Things like pain. Pain didn't have to end.

I sighed, and then answered her question. "I brought you to the prom because I don't want you to miss anything. I don't want my presence to take anything away from you, if I can help it. I want you to be *human*. I want your life to continue as it would have if I'd died in nineteen-eighteen like I should have."

She shuddered and then shook her head violently twice, as though trying to dislodge my words. But when she spoke, her voice was teasing. "In what strange parallel dimension would I *ever* have gone to prom of my own free will? If you weren't a thousand times stronger than me, I would never have let you get away with this."

I smiled. "It wasn't so bad, you said so yourself."

Her eyes were clear and miles deep. "That's because I was with you."

I looked at the moon again. I could feel her gaze on my face. There was no time to worry about the future now. The present was much more pleasant. I thought of the very recent past, and her strange disorientation tonight. What had taken the place of the obvious answer in her mind?

I smiled down at her. "Will you tell me something?"

"Don't I always?"

"Just promise you'll tell me," I insisted.

"Fine," she agreed, unwilling.

"You seemed honestly surprised when you figured out that I was taking you here."

"I *was*," she interrupted.

"Exactly," I said. "But you must have had some other theory.... I'm curious—what did you *think* I was dressing you up for?"

This seemed like an easy question, playful and in the moment. Nothing that could lead me into the future again.

But she hesitated, more serious than I expected. "I don't want to tell you."

"You promised."

She frowned. "I know."

I almost smiled when the old curiosity and impatience flared. Some things never changed. "What's the problem?"

"I think it will make you mad," she said solemnly. "Or sad."

I couldn't align her grave expression with my somewhat silly question. I was afraid of her answer now, afraid it would restart the pain I tried so hard to avoid, but I knew I could never bear to leave my curiosity unanswered.

"I still want to know. Please?"

She sighed. Her eyes traced across the silver clouds.

"Well," she said after a long moment. "I assumed it was some kind of... occasion. But I didn't think it would be some trite human thing... prom!" She made a scoffing noise.

I took a short moment to control my reaction.

"Human?" I asked.

She looked down at her beautiful dress, tugging absently on a chiffon ruffle. I knew what was coming. I let her find the words she wanted.

"Okay," she finally said. Her stare was a challenge now. "So I was hoping that you might have changed your mind... that you were going to change *me*, after all."

I had so many years to feel this pain. I wished she weren't forcing me to feel it now. Not while she was still in my arms. Not while she was in the lovely dress, the moonlight glinting off her pale shoulders, shadows like pools of night held in the curve of her collarbones.

I chose to ignore the pain and focus on just the surface of her answer.

I touched my lapel. "You thought that would be a black-tie occasion, did you?"

She frowned, embarrassed. "I don't know how these things work. To me, at least, it seems more rational than prom does."

I tried to smile, but that just irritated her.

"It's not funny," she said.

"No, you're right, it's not. I'd rather treat it like a joke, though, than believe you're serious."

"But I am serious."

"I know," I sighed.

It was a strange kind of pain. There was no temptation in it at all. Though what she wanted was my perfect future, an erasure of decades of agony, it didn't appeal to me. I could never pay for my own happiness with the loss of hers.

When I'd poured out my heart to her distant God, I'd begged for strength. This much he'd given me: I felt no desire at all to see Bella immortal. My only want, my only need, was to have her life untouched by darkness, and that need consumed me.

I knew the future loomed, but I didn't know exactly how long I had. I was committed to staying until she was totally healed, so I had a few more weeks until she was back on two feet, at least. Part of me wondered if it wouldn't be right to wait until she outgrew me, as I'd originally planned. Wouldn't that mean the least pain for her? It would be so easy to fall into that version. But I wasn't sure if I had that long. The future felt like it was pressing closer. I didn't know what the sign would be, but I knew I would recognize it when it came.

I'd tried so hard to avoid this conversation, but I could see it would make her happier to have it now. I swallowed all my pain and grief and forced myself back into this moment. I would be with her while I could be.

"And you're really that willing?" I asked.

She bit her lip and nodded.

"So ready for this to be the end," I sighed, stroking my finger down the side of her face. "For this to be the twilight of your life, though your life has barely started. You're ready to give up everything."

"It's not the end, it's the beginning," she whispered.

"I'm not worth it."

I already knew she didn't count her human losses. And she had definitely never considered eternal losses. No one was worth that.

"Do you remember when you told me that I didn't see myself very clearly?" she asked. "You obviously have the same blindness."

"I know what I am."

She rolled her eyes, annoyed with my refusal to agree with anything.

I found it suddenly easy to smile. She was so eager, so impatient to trade anything to be with me. It was impossible not to be moved by such a love.

I decided we could use a little playfulness.

"You're ready now, then?" I asked, raising one eyebrow.

"Um. Yes?" She swallowed, nervous.

I leaned closer to her, keeping my movement unhurried. My lips finally touched the skin of her throat.

She swallowed again.

"Right now?" I whispered.

She shivered. Then her body tensed, her hands clenched into fists, and her heart started hammering faster than the faraway music from the dance.

"Yes," she whispered.

My game had failed. I laughed at myself and straightened up. "You can't really believe that I would give in so easily."

She relaxed. Her heart slowed. "A girl can dream," she said.

"Is that what you dream about? Being a monster?"

"Not exactly." She didn't like the word I'd used. Her voice dropped lower. "Mostly I dream about being with you forever."

There was pain in her voice, doubt. Did she think I didn't want her the same way? I wished I could ease her mind, but I couldn't.

I traced the shape of her lips and breathed her name. "Bella." I hoped she could hear the devotion in my voice. "I *will* stay with you." *As long as I can, as long as it's allowed, as long as it doesn't hurt you. Until the sign comes, until it's impossible for me to ignore.* "Isn't that enough?"

She smiled, but she was unappeased. "Enough for now."

Bella didn't realize *now* was all we had. My breath came out as a groan.

Her fingertips brushed along the edge of my jaw. "Look," she said. "I love you more than everything else in the world combined. Isn't that enough?"

And then I could smile a genuine smile. "Yes, it is enough," I promised. "Enough for forever."

This time I spoke of the *real* forever. My eternal forever.

As the night finally overcame the end of the day, I leaned forward again and kissed the warm skin of her throat.

Acknowledgments

This book has been my nemesis for so many years that it's hard to remember everyone who helped me along the way, but here are the heavy lifters:

My three amazing children, Gabriel, Seth, and Eli (now all grown men!), who behaved themselves so admirably over the last fifteen years that I was able to invest all the time I would have spent worrying about the bad choices they *didn't* make into worrying about the bad choices my fictional people *did* make.

My super-capable husband, who handles most of the math-related and technological aspects of my life.

My mother, Candy, who quietly refused to ever accept that I had given up on this book.

My business partner, Meghan Hibbett, who keeps Fickle Fish Productions on track while I abandon the physical world for long periods of time. Also my best friend, Meghan Hibbett, who is my primary outlet when I need to scream and cry and rage over misbehaving characters.

My agent, Jodi Reamer, who let me take my time with this one but was prepared to jump into action the second I was ready.

My film agent, Kassie Evashevski, whose calm good sense keeps me off ledges.

All the great people at Little, Brown Books for Young Readers, who have given me such extraordinary support—especially Megan Tingley, who has been with me for all seventeen years (!) of my writing career, and Asya Muchnick, who is the kindest and most insightful of editors.

Roger Hagadone, the photographer who has shot our stunning, memorable covers. I can't imagine what the feel of the saga would be without your artistry.

The gorgeous ladies of the Method Agency, Nikki and Bekah, who are always cheerful about the weird things I ask them to do.

So many gifted creators who've made incredible Twilight Saga websites and fanart.

So many authors who have created incredible worlds for me to escape into.

So many musicians who have unknowingly been the soundtrack in my head.

And finally, the readers who were so patiently eager for this book. I never would have finished without your support. You belong on this page. Please, write your name on the line below and give yourself a high five.

____